THE
BURNING
GOD

THE
BURNING
GOD

R. F. KUANG

HARPER
Voyager

Harper*Voyager*
An imprint of HarperCollins*Publishers* Ltd
1 London Bridge Street
London SE1 9GF

www.harpercollins.co.uk

First published by HarperCollins*Publishers* 2020
1

A catalogue record for this book is available from the British Library

ISBN: 978-0-00-833914-2 (HB)
ISBN: 978-0-00-833915-9 (TPB)

Designed by Paula Russell Szafranski

Set in Sabon LT Std

Printed and bound in the UK by CPI Group (UK) Ltd, Croydon CR0 4YY

MIX
Paper from
responsible sources
FSC
www.fsc.org   **FSC™ C007454**

To my dear readers,

who stayed with this series until the end,

and came prepared with a bucket for their tears

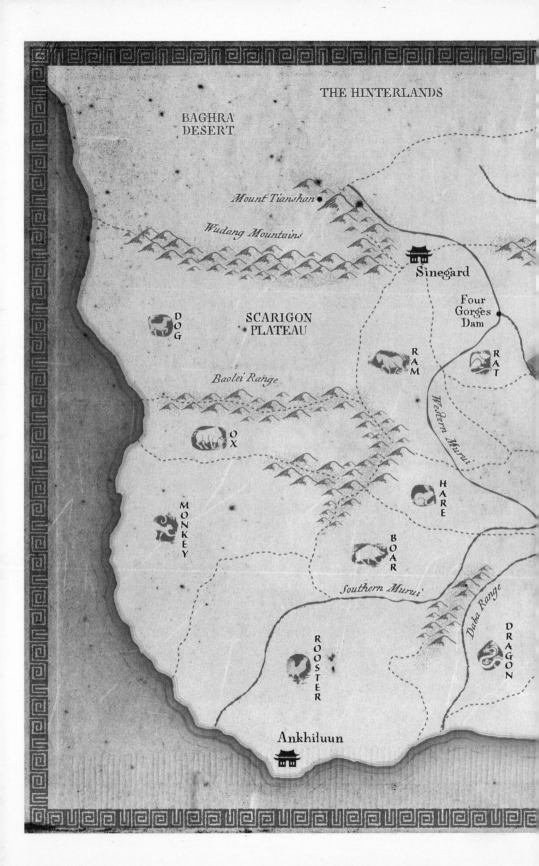

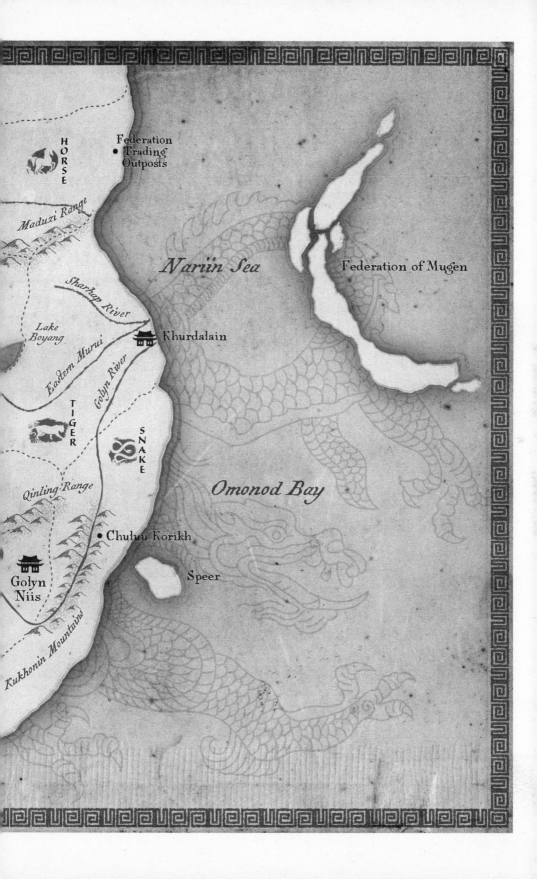

PROLOGUE

"We shouldn't be doing this," Daji said.

The campfire burned an unnatural shade of purple, sparking and hissing reproachfully as if it could sense her guilt. Tendrils of flame reached out like grasping hands that transformed into flickering faces that, months later, still made Daji's stomach twist with shame. She looked away.

But the dead were seared into the backs of her eyelids, their mouths still open in shock at her betrayal. Their whispers echoed in her mind, the same way they echoed every night in her dreams.

Murderer, they said. *Ingrate. Whore.*

Fear squeezed her chest. "Riga, I don't think—"

"Too late for second guesses now, sweetheart." Across the fire, Riga was binding a struggling deer with his usual brutal, callous efficiency. He'd already arranged three serrated knives, all looted from the corpses of Ketreyid archers, in a perfect triangle around the fire. Daji hadn't touched hers. She'd been too scared— the glinting metal looked poisonous, resentful. "We're far past the point of no return, don't you think?"

The deer arched its neck, straining to break free. Riga grasped its antlers with one hand and slammed its head to the ground.

The flames jumped higher; the whispers intensified. Daji flinched. "This feels wrong."

Riga snorted. "When did you become such a coward?"

"I'm just worried. Tseveri said—"

"Who cares what she said?" Riga sounded brittle, defensive. Daji knew he, too, was ashamed. She could tell some small part of him wished they'd never started down this path. But he could never admit that. If he did, he'd break.

Riga, pinning the deer's neck down with one knee, jerked twine around its front legs. The deer's mouth opened as if to scream, but the only sound it could make was a hoarse, eerie rasp. "Tseveri's always been full of shit. Prophecy, my ass—don't believe that babble. She was just saying whatever the Sorqan Sira wanted us to hear."

"She said this would kill us," Daji said.

"That's not precisely what she said."

"It's close enough."

"Oh, Daji." Riga tightened the last knot with a cruel yank, examined his handiwork for a moment, then moved to sit down beside her. His hand massaged her back in slow circles. He meant to be comforting. It felt like a trap. "Do you think I'd ever let anything happen to you?"

Daji struggled to keep her breathing even.

Do what he says, she reminded herself. That was the deal she'd made with Ziya. *Keep your head down and obey, or Riga will find some way to get rid of you.* She should be glad for this ritual. It was protection—the ultimate guarantee that Riga could not kill her without killing himself, a shield for her and Ziya both.

But still she was so afraid. What if this was worse than death?

She found her voice. "There has to be some other way—"

"There isn't," Riga snapped. "We won't last much longer like this. This war's gotten too big. Our enemies have grown too many." He gestured with his knife toward the forest. "And if Ziya keeps acting like that, he won't last another day."

He won't last because you've pushed him, Daji wanted to snap back. But she held her tongue for fear of stoking his temper. His cruelty.

You don't have another choice. She'd realized long ago that she needed to make herself absolutely necessary to Riga if she wanted to stay safe. Indispensable, anchored and chained to his very life.

"Come on, Ziya." Riga cupped his hands around his mouth and called out. "Let's get this over with."

The trees were silent.

Riga raised his voice. "*Ziya.* I know you're out there."

Maybe he ran, Daji thought. *Clever bastard.*

She wondered what Riga might do if Ziya really did try to escape. He'd chase him, of course, and likely catch him—Riga had always been the strongest and fastest of them all. The punishment would be terrible. But Daji might fend Riga off for a few minutes, buy Ziya some time, and even if that cost her her life at least one of them would be spared.

But seconds later Ziya came wandering through the forest, stumbling as if drunk. His eyes had that bemused, wild look that Daji had recently grown accustomed to seeing on his face. She knew it meant danger. Her hand crept toward her knife.

Riga stood and approached Ziya like a keeper might a tiger, hands spread cautiously out before him. "How are you?"

"How am I?" Ziya tilted his head. "Whatever do you mean?"

Daji saw Riga's throat pulse.

"Can you come sit down?" Riga asked.

Ziya shook his head, snickering.

"This isn't funny," Riga snarled. "Come here, Ziya."

"Ziya?" Ziya's eyes tipped to the sky. "Who's that?"

Riga reached for his sword. Daji raised her knife. They'd prepared for this, all three of them, with Ziya's consent. They had to strike just before he opened the gate—

Ziya's face split into a horrible grin. "Kidding."

Riga relaxed. "Fuck you."

Daji exhaled and tried to slow her frantically beating heart.

Ziya sat down cross-legged in front of the fire. His eyes flickered toward the bound deer with a cursory interest. "It's acting very tame, isn't it?"

He picked his own knife up from the ground and dangled it before the deer. Fire glinted off the serrated edge. The deer lay still, indifferent. It might have been dead save for its resigned, labored breathing.

"Daji shoved a wad of opium down its mouth," Riga said.

"Ah." Ziya winked at her. "Clever girl."

Daji wished the drug had taken effect earlier. She wished Riga had given it time. But that would require empathy—a trait he most certainly did not possess.

"Look alive, Daji." Riga brandished his knife at her. "Let's not drag this out."

Daji sat frozen in place. For a brief moment she considered running. Her knees trembled.

No. There's no way out. If she didn't do this for herself, she at least had to do it for Ziya.

He liked to fucking joke. He'd never been able to take anything seriously; only he would be amused by the prospect of losing his own mind. But her fear—hers and Riga's—was real. Ziya had been careening on the line between sanity and madness for months, and they didn't know when he'd tip into the void for good. Only this could bring him back.

But oh, how it had cost them.

"Knives up," Riga said.

They obeyed. The deer was tame beneath the blades, eyes open and glassy.

Riga began to speak. Every word of the incantation they'd lied, tortured, and murdered to obtain made the fire rise higher and higher, until flames ten feet high jumped toward the night sky. When Tseveri had spoken these words, they had sounded like music. On Riga's tongue, they sounded like a curse. Daji squeezed her eyes shut, trying to block out the screams in her mind.

Riga finished chanting. Nothing happened.

They sat there for a long time, their confusion mounting, until Ziya's laughter broke the silence.

"What the fuck is wrong with you?" Riga demanded.

"You're saying it wrong," Ziya said.

"The fuck does that mean?"

"It's your accent. This won't work with you butchering the words like that."

"You do it, then." Riga spat something else under his breath. Mugenese words, a slur he'd picked up as a child. *Horse lover.*

"I don't know the words," Ziya said.

"Yes, you do." A malicious edge crept into Riga's voice. "She taught them to you first."

Ziya stiffened.

Don't do it, Daji thought. *Let's kill him and run.*

Ziya began the incantation. His voice turned gradually from a hoarse whisper to a shout, forceful and fluid. This time the words sounded closer to how they'd sounded on Tseveri's tongue. This time they held power.

"Now," Riga whispered, and they raised their knives to slaughter the last necessary innocent.

When it was over, the void flung them back into their material bodies with a shock like icy water. Daji lurched forward, gasping. The earth felt so solid under her legs, the air so sweet. The world became the familiar made strange—solid and beautiful and mystifying. Daji was burning inside, shaking from the sheer power arcing through her body.

She felt more alive than she'd ever been. Now she was three souls instead of one; now she was complete; now she was *more*.

They hadn't fully returned yet from the world of spirit. Their connection hadn't severed. She was still reading into Ziya's and Riga's souls, and their thoughts crashed into her mind so loudly she struggled to separate them from her own.

From Ziya, she felt cold and naked fear combined with a terrible relief. He didn't want this. He'd never wanted any of this. He was so scared of what he might become but also grateful for his deliverance from the alternative. He was grateful to be bound.

From Riga, she felt both giddy delight and a dizzying rush of ambition. He wanted more. He wasn't even paying attention to the panic radiating from Ziya. His thoughts were on greater things. He saw them on a battlefield, at a negotiating table, on three thrones.

To Riga, this had been the last obstacle. Now they were tipping forward into the future he'd always imagined for them.

Daji wanted it, too. She just wasn't sure she'd survive it.

Slowly she opened her eyes. The blood coating her hands looked black in the moonlight. The fire had nearly gone out, yet the smoke threatened to suffocate. Daji almost fell forward into the embers, almost smothered her face in the ash and let it end there.

Strong fingers gripped her shoulder and dragged her back.

"Easy." Riga grinned.

Daji couldn't share in his euphoria.

Years later, when she tortured herself with memories of the three of them at the beginning, before everything had gone so dreadfully wrong, she could never remember how it felt when they were first anchored. Couldn't remember the thrill of power, or the terrifying yet delightful sense of being known. All she remembered was a curdling dread—the certainty that one day, the secrets they'd stolen would be paid for in blood.

And Tseveri. Always in her mind she saw the dead girl's wretched face, and heard so clearly the last warning she'd uttered before Ziya ripped her heart out of her chest.

Here's a prophecy for you, she'd said.

One will die.

One will rule.

And one will sleep for eternity.

PART I

CHAPTER 1

Rin's wrist throbbed.

The air always felt different on the morning of an ambush, as if an electric charge, the crackling residue of a thunderstorm, thrummed through her and every soldier around her. Rin had never felt energy like this when she'd fought for the Republic. In the beginning, Yin Vaisra's troops had been consummate professionals—sullen, grim, there to finish the job and get out. By the end, they'd been fearful. Desperate.

But the soldiers of the Southern Coalition were *angry*, and that force alone had driven them through grueling weeks of basic training, had quickly shaped them into capable killers even though not so long ago many of them had never even touched a sword.

It helped that their fight was personal. Khudla wasn't their town, but this was their province, and everyone in Monkey Province had suffered the same way under Mugenese occupation. Displacement, looting, rape, murder, mass executions. A thousand Golyn Niis–level massacres had played out over the land, and no one had cared, because no one in the Republic or the Empire had ever cared much about the south.

But some in the south had survived to avenge their dead, and those were the men and women who comprised Rin's troops.

As the minutes trickled past, the gathered ranks bristled in anticipation like hunting dogs straining against the leash. And Rin's wrist stung like a conducting rod, a million little jolts of pain shooting through her elbow every second.

"Stop rubbing," Kitay admonished. "You're irritating it."

"It hurts," she said.

"Because you're rubbing it. Leave it alone and it'll heal faster."

Rin ran her fingers over the cracked, bumpy skin that covered the bone of her wrist where it should have extended into a right hand. She clenched her jaw, trying to resist the urge to dig her nails into flesh long rubbed raw.

She'd had the hand amputated the night they made port in Ankhiluun. By then, after two weeks at sea, the appendage had all but rotted into a gangrenous mess. For all of the Black Lily physician's efforts to sterilize the wound, there had remained so many points of exposure in her skin that it was a miracle the infection hadn't spread farther up her arm. The procedure was short. Moag's personal physician had cut away Rin's hand, trimmed down the rotting flesh, and sewed her skin into a neat flap over the exposed bone.

The wound itself healed cleanly enough. But when Rin stopped taking laudanum, the wrist became a torch of unbearable agony. Phantom pains flashed through fingers she no longer had several times an hour. Sometimes they were so bad she slammed her hand at the wall to dull the pricks with a greater pain, only to remember that the hand wasn't there. The pain was imaginary. And she couldn't dull pain that existed purely in her mind.

"You're going to make it bleed," Kitay said.

Rin had, without thinking, begun to scratch again. She cupped her fingers over the stump and squeezed hard, trying to drive out the itching with sheer, numbing pressure. "It's driving me mad. It's not just the itching, it's the fingers. It's like I can still feel them, and they're being pricked with a thousand needles, only I can't do anything about it."

"I think I get it," Kitay said. "I feel it, too, sometimes. Little tremors out of nowhere. Which is strange, if you think about it— I'm the one with fingers, but the pain is coming from you."

Before her surgery, they'd worried that cutting away her rotted right hand might also sever Kitay's. They didn't know the limits of their anchor bond. They knew that death for one meant death for both. They felt each other's pain, and injuries to one manifested in pale, faintly visible scars for the other. But they didn't know what that meant for amputations.

By the time they docked in Ankhiluun, however, Rin's infections were so inflamed that the pain for both of them was unbearable, and Kitay had declared through gritted teeth that if Rin wouldn't cut away the hand, he'd gnaw it off himself.

To their great relief, his own arm remained intact. A ridged white line appeared around his wrist like a bracelet where the incision was made, but his fingers were still functional, if somewhat stiff. Occasionally Rin saw him struggling to hold an ink brush, and he now took much longer to dress in the mornings. But he still had his hand, and though Rin was relieved, she couldn't help but feel a constant, lingering jealousy.

"Can you see it?" She waved her wrist at him. "A little ghost hand?"

"You should put a hook on that," he said.

"I'm not putting a fucking hook on it."

"A blade, then. Then maybe you'd start practicing."

She shot him an irritated look. "I'll get around to it."

"You're never going to get around to it," he said. "Keep acting like this and the first time you pick up a sword will be the last."

"I won't need to—"

"You know you might. Think, Rin, what happens when—"

"Not now," she snapped. "I don't want to talk about this now."

She hated practicing with a sword. She hated fumbling at

things with her left hand that her right hand had once done unconsciously. It made her feel helpless and stupid and inadequate, and she had spent such a long time trying to convince herself that she wasn't powerless anymore. The first time she'd grasped a sword, a week after her surgery, her left arm had shaken with such debilitating weakness that she'd immediately flung the blade to the ground in disgust. She couldn't bear feeling like that again.

"I see the problem," Kitay said. "You're nervous."

"I don't get nervous."

"Bullshit. You're terrified. That's why you're fidgeting. You're scared."

For good fucking reason, Rin thought.

Her throbbing wrist wasn't the problem, just the symptom. She was searching for something, anything to go wrong. Their position could have been compromised. The Mugenese could know they were coming.

Or they might simply lose.

She hadn't dealt with defenses this good before. The Mugenese at Khudla knew Rin's troops were coming; their guard had been up for days. And they were primed to fear nighttime attacks now, even though most ambushing forces wouldn't dare launch such a tricky operation without adequate light. This would be no easy, devastating raid.

But Rin couldn't fail today.

Khudla was a test. She'd been begging the Monkey Warlord for a command position ever since they'd escaped Arlong, only to be told over and over that she couldn't lead entire columns into battle until she had the experience. Today, at last, he'd put her in charge.

Liberating Khudla was her mission, and hers alone. Until now she'd been fighting like a unit of one, a juggernaut of fire that the Southern Coalition threw into battles like a wide-range missile. Now she was leading a brigade of hundreds.

These soldiers fought under her command. That terrified her. What if they died under her command?

"We have this down like clockwork. The guard changes every

thirty minutes," Kitay said. They'd been over this a dozen times before, but he was repeating it to calm her down. "You'll know when the voices change. Get as close as you can before sunset, and then hit during the transition. Do you know the signals?"

She took a deep breath. "Yes."

"Then you've got nothing to worry about."

If only saying it made it so.

The minutes crawled past. Rin watched the sun dipping toward the mountains, dropping reluctantly, as if dragged downward by some creature in the valley below.

After Rin had raised the Phoenix on the Isle of Speer and ended the Third Poppy War, there was no formal surrender by the Federation of Mugen. Emperor Ryohai and his progeny were turned instantly into charcoal statues under mountains of ash. No one in the Mugenese imperial family survived to negotiate for peace.

So there had been no armistice, no treaty. No Mugenese generals provided a map of their troop placements and turned their weapons over to the Nikara leadership. Instead, all remaining Federation soldiers on the mainland became rogue threats—highly skilled roving soldiers without mission or nation. Yin Vaisra, the former Dragon Warlord and newly elected President of the Nikara Republic, could have dealt conclusively with them months ago, but he'd let them roam free to undercut his own allies in a long-term ploy to strengthen his grasp on the crumbling Nikara Empire. Now those scattered platoons had organized into several large independent bands terrorizing the south. For all intents and purposes, the Nikara and the Mugenese remained at war. Even without support from the longbow island, the Mugenese had essentially colonized the south in a matter of months. And Rin had let them, obsessed as she'd been with Vaisra's insurrection while the real war was being fought at home.

She'd failed the south once. She wouldn't do it again.

"Kazuo says the ships are still coming," spoke a voice in Mugini. It was a boy's voice, thin and reedy.

"Kazuo is a fucking idiot," said his companion.

Rin and Kitay crouched hidden behind the tall grass. They'd crept close enough to the Mugenese camp that they could hear patrolmen gossiping idly, their hushed voices traveling far over still night air. Still, Rin's Mugini was rusty from more than a year of disuse, and she had to strain her ears to understand what they were saying.

"This language is like insect chitter," Nezha had once complained, back when they'd been stupid young children crammed into a classroom at Sinegard, when they had yet to realize that the war they were training to fight wasn't hypothetical.

Nezha had hated Mugini lessons, Rin remembered. He hadn't been able to comprehend the language when spoken at its standard rapid clip, so he'd spent class each day mocking it, making his fellow students laugh with gibberish that sounded so much like real sentences.

"*Click click click*," he'd said, and made scuttling noises between his teeth. "Like little bugs."

Like crickets, Rin thought. They'd started calling the Mugenese that in the countryside. Rin didn't know if it was a new slur or an old insult recycled from a time before her birth. She wouldn't have been surprised by the latter. History moved in circles—she'd learned that very well by now.

"Kazuo said that ships have started coming into the ports in Tiger Province," said the first voice she'd heard, the boy's voice. "They're docking in the shadows, ferrying us back handful by handful—"

The second patrolman snorted. "That's bullshit. We'd know by now if they had."

There was a brief silence. Someone stirred in the grass. The patrolmen were lying down, Rin realized. Perhaps they were stargazing. That was stupid of them, wildly irresponsible. But they sounded so very young; they sounded not like soldiers but like children. Did they simply not know any better?

"The moon is different here," the first patrolman said wistfully.

Rin recognized that phrase. She'd learned it at Sinegard—it was an old Mugini expression, some aphorism derived from a myth about a ferryman who loved a woman who lived on a distant star, who built her a bridge between two worlds so that they could finally embrace.

The moon is different here. He meant he wanted to go home.

The Mugenese were always talking about going home. She heard about it every time she eavesdropped on them. They spoke about home like it still existed, like the longbow island was some beautiful paradise where they could easily return if only the ships would come to harbor. They spoke about their mothers, fathers, sisters, and brothers who awaited them on their shores, spared somehow from the scorching pyroclastic flows.

"You'd better get used to this moon," said the second patrolman.

The more they spoke, the younger they sounded. Rin pictured their faces in her head; their voices brought to mind gangly limbs and fuzzy upper lips. They couldn't be older than her—they had to be just over twenty, possibly younger.

She remembered fighting a boy her age during the siege at Khurdalain, what seemed like an eternity ago. Remembered his wide moonlike face and soft hands. Remembered how his eyes bulged when she ran her blade through his stomach.

He must have been so scared. He might have been as scared as she was.

She felt Kitay stiffen beside her.

"They don't want to be here, either." He'd told her this weeks ago. He'd been interrogating some of their Mugenese prisoners, and he'd come away far more sympathetic to them than she was comfortable with. "They're just kids. A quarter of them are younger than we are, and they didn't sign up for this war. Most of them were pulled from their homes and thrown into vicious training camps so that their families wouldn't go to prison or starve. They don't want to kill, they just want to go home."

But their home didn't exist anymore. Those boys had nowhere to escape to. If the gates of reconciliation had ever been open, if there'd ever been the option of repatriating enemy combatants and building slowly toward peace, Rin had slammed them shut long ago.

A wide chasm of guilt, her ever-faithful friend, yawned in the back of her mind.

She pushed it away.

She'd done such a good job of burying her memories; that was the only way she could keep herself sane.

Children can be murderers, she reminded herself. *Little boys can be monsters.*

The lines of war had become far too blurred. Every Mugenese soldier who'd ever put on a uniform was complicit, and Rin didn't have the patience to separate the guilty from the innocent. Speerly justice was absolute. Her retribution was conclusive. She didn't have time to dawdle on what could have been; she had a homeland to liberate.

Her wrist had started to throb again. She exhaled slowly, closed her eyes, and repeated their plan of attack over and over in her mind in an attempt to shake off her nerves.

She traced her fingers across the scars on her stomach. Let them linger on the spot where Altan's handprint was burned into her like a brand. She envisioned those boy patrolmen and transformed them into targets.

I've killed millions of you before, she thought. *This is routine now. This is nothing.*

The sun was a little crimson dot now, the top of it barely visible over the mountaintops. The patrolmen had rotated from their post. The fields, for now, were empty.

"It's time," Kitay murmured.

Rin stood up. They faced each other, hands clasped between them.

"At dawn," she said.

"At dawn," he agreed. He put his hands on her shoulders and kissed her forehead.

This was their standard way of parting, the way they said everything they never spoke out loud. *Fight well. Keep us safe. I love you.*

Every goodbye had to be so much harder for Kitay, who wagered his life on hers every time she set foot on the battlefield.

Rin wished she didn't have that vulnerability. If she could cut out the part of the soul that endangered Kitay—that was endangered by Kitay—then she would.

But the fact that his life was at stake lent an edge to her fighting. It made her sharper, warier, less likely to take risks and more likely to strike hard and fast when she could. She no longer fought from pure rage. She fought to protect him—and that, she had discovered, changed everything.

Kitay gave her one last nod, then disappeared behind the ranks.

"Does he always stay behind?" Officer Shen asked.

Rin liked Officer Shen. A Monkey Province native and veteran of the last two Poppy Wars, Shen Sainang was brusque, efficient, and pragmatic. She despised factional politics, which perhaps explained why she was one of the few officers who had volunteered to follow Rin into her first battle as commander. Rin was grateful for that.

But Shen was too observant. Always asking too many questions.

"Kitay doesn't fight," Rin said.

"Why not?" Shen asked. "He's Sinegard-trained, isn't he?"

Because Kitay was Rin's single link to the heavens. Because Kitay needed to be in a safe and quiet place so that his mind could function as a channel between her and the Phoenix. Because every time Kitay was exposed and vulnerable it doubled Rin's chances of dying.

That was Rin's greatest secret. If the Monkey Warlord knew Kitay was her anchor, he'd know the only way to kill her. And Rin didn't trust him or the Southern Coalition enough to give them that chance.

"He's a Sinegard-trained strategist," Rin said. "Not a foot soldier."

Shen looked unconvinced. "He carries a sword like one."

"Yes, and his mind's more valuable than the sword," Rin said curtly, shutting down the discussion. She nodded toward Khudla. "It's time."

Adrenaline rushed her veins then. Her heartbeat began pounding in her ears, an internal countdown to the slaughter. Across the village perimeter, eight pairs of eyes were trained on Rin—eight squadron leaders, waiting at their vantage points, watching for the flame.

At last, Rin saw a line of Mugenese troops moving down the field. There it was—the patrol switch.

She raised her left hand and gave the signal—a thin stream of fire, burning the air ten feet over her head before it winked away.

The fields moved. Soldiers poured in from the northern and eastern fronts. They flooded out of hiding points in riverbanks, ravines, and forests like ants storming out of an anthill. Rin watched with satisfaction. So what if her columns were thinner than the defense? The Mugenese wouldn't know the first place to look.

She heard a series of signal whistles, clear indications that every squadron had moved successfully into position. Officer Shen's troops took the east. Officer Lin's troops took the north.

Rin stormed the southern quarter alone.

The Mugenese weren't ready. Most had been asleep or preparing to go to sleep. They staggered out of their tents and barracks, rubbing at their eyes. Rin almost laughed at the way their faces morphed into uniform expressions of horror when they saw what had turned the night air so very warm.

She lifted her arms. Wings shot out of her shoulders, glowing ten feet high.

Kitay had once accused her of being too flamboyant, of sacrificing efficiency for attention.

What did it matter? There was no point to subtlety when everyone knew what she was. And Rin wanted this image burned into their eyelids, the last thing they saw before they died—a Speerly and her god.

Men scattered before her like startled hens. One or two had the sense to hurl swords in her direction. Their movements were panicked, their aim poor. Rin advanced, hand splayed outward, fire ensconcing everything she saw.

Then the screaming started, and the ecstasy set in.

Rin had spent so long hating how she felt when she burned, hating her fire and her god. Not anymore. She could admit to herself now that she liked it. She liked letting her basest instincts take over. She reveled in it.

She didn't have to think hard to summon the rage. She only had to remember the corpses at Golyn Niis. The corpses in the research laboratory. Altan burning on the pier, a miserable end to the miserable life they'd given him.

Hate was a funny thing. It gnawed at her insides like poison. It made every muscle in her body tense, made her veins boil so hot she thought her head might split in half, and yet it fueled everything she did. Hate was its own kind of fire and if you had nothing else, it kept you warm.

Once, Rin had wielded fire like a blunt instrument, letting the Phoenix's will control her as if she were the weapon and not the other way around. Once, she'd only known how to act as a gateway for a torrent of divine fire. But such unrestrained explosions were only useful when one intended genocide. Campaigns for liberation demanded precision.

She had spent weeks with Kitay practicing the intricacies of calling the flame. She'd learned to shape it like a sword. To lash it out in tendrils like a whip. She'd learned to mold it into moving, dancing entities—lions, tigers, phoenixes.

She'd learned so many ways to kill with fire. She liked going for the eyes the best. Burning limbs to ash took too long. The human body could sustain a burn for a surprisingly long time, and she wanted her fights over quickly. Really, the entire face presented an excellent target—hair would keep burning, and light head wounds fazed combatants more than other minor wounds could. But if she aimed for the eyes, she could scorch retinas, seal eyelids shut, or blister the surrounding skin, all of which would blind her opponents in seconds.

She saw a flash of movement to her right. Someone was trying to charge her.

The Phoenix cackled. *The audacity.*

Half a second before he reached her, she opened her palm toward his face.

His eyes popped one by one. Viscous fluid dribbled down his cheeks. He opened his mouth to scream, and Rin sent flames pouring down his throat.

This was only grotesque if she saw her opponents as human. But she didn't see humans, because Sinegard and Altan had taught her to compartmentalize and detach. *Learn to look and see not a man but a body. The soul is not there. The body is simply a composite of different targets, and all of them burn so bright.*

"Do you know where the Mugenese come from?" Altan had asked her once. "Do you know what kind of race they are?"

They had been sailing down the Murui toward Khurdalain then. The Third Poppy War had just begun. She'd been fresh out of Sinegard, stupid and naive, a student who was struggling with the fact that she was now a soldier. Altan had just become her commander and she had hung on his every word, so in awe of him she could barely string together a sentence.

She'd realized he was waiting for her to answer, so she'd said the first thing that came to mind. "They're. Um. Related to us?"

"Do you know how?"

She could have repeated any textbook answer to him. Migration induced by droughts or flooding. Exiled aristocracy. Clan warfare dating back to the days of the Red Emperor. No one was really certain. She'd been taught many theories that were all equally plausible. But she'd suspected that Altan wasn't really interested in her answer, so she had shaken her head instead.

She'd guessed right. He'd wanted to tell a story.

"A long time ago the Red Emperor had a pet," he'd said. "It was a beastly thing, some very intelligent ape he'd found in the mountains. One ugly, vicious fucker. Do you know this tale?"

"I don't," she'd whispered. "Tell me."

"The Red Emperor kept it in a cage in his palace," he continued. "Occasionally he brought it out for guests to see. They liked to watch it kill things. They'd release pigs or roosters into its cage to watch it dismember them. I imagine they had great fun. Until one day the beast sprang free of its cage, killed a minister with its bare hands, kidnapped the Red Emperor's daughter, and escaped back to the mountains."

"I didn't know the Red Emperor had a daughter," Rin had said, stupidly. For some reason, she'd found this the most striking detail. History only remembered the princes—the Red Emperor's sons.

"No one does. He would have erased her from the record, after what happened. She became pregnant by the beast but couldn't find any means of expelling the fetus from her womb, not while she was its prisoner, so she gave birth to a little brood of half-men and raised them in the mountains. Years later the Red Emperor sent his generals to chase them out of the Empire, and they fled to the longbow island."

Rin had never heard that iteration of the story, but it made sense. The Nikara did like to compare the Mugenese to monkeys. Half-men, they called them; short and little—even though when she had finally seen a Federation soldier with her own eyes she wouldn't have been able to tell him apart from a Nikara villager.

Altan had paused then, watching her, waiting for her response.

But she'd only had one question, which she hadn't wanted to ask, because she'd known Altan wouldn't have an answer.

If they were beasts, how did they kill us?

Who decided who counted as human? The Nikara thought the Speerlies were beasts, too, and they'd made them warrior slaves for centuries. The enemy was not human—fine. But if they were animals, then they must be inferior. If the Mugenese were inferior, though, then how could they have been the victors? Did that mean that, in this world, one had to be a beast to survive?

Maybe no one was truly a beast. Maybe that was just how murder became possible. You took away someone's humanity, and then you killed them. At Sinegard, Strategy Master Irjah had taught them once that during the heat of battle, they should regard their opponents as objects, abstract and disparate parts and not the sum, because that would make it easier to plunge a blade into a pumping heart. But maybe if you looked at someone as not an object but an animal, you could not only commit the murder without flinching, you could let yourself take some pleasure in it. Then it felt good, the same way kicking down anthills felt good.

"Monkeys raping humans. Half-breed brats. Beastly freaks. Stupid savages." Altan had said the last words with bitter relish, and Rin had thought that perhaps it was because those were the same words so many others used to describe him. "That's where the Mugenese come from."

Rin carved her way through the camp in minutes. The Mugenese presented almost no resistance. The soldiers she'd faced at Sinegard and Khurdalain had been well trained and lethally armed, with lines of glinting swords and an endless supply of chemical weapons they hurled into civilian centers at will. But these soldiers ran instead of fighting, and they died with an ease that astounded her.

This was all too simple, so simple that it made Rin slow down. She wanted to savor this power differential. *Once I was your screaming victim, begging for your mercy. And now you cower before me.*

She shouldn't have slowed.

Because once she slowed, she noticed how unprepared they were. How utterly unlike soldiers they seemed. How young they looked.

The boy before her had a sword, but he wasn't using it. He

didn't even try to fight, only stumbled back with his arms raised, begging for her mercy.

"Please don't," he kept saying.

He might have been the patrolman from before; he spoke in that same reedy, wobbly voice. "*Please.*"

She stayed her hand only because she realized he was speaking Nikara.

She considered him for a moment. *Was* he Nikara? Was he a prisoner of war? He wasn't wearing a Mugenese uniform, he might have been an innocent . . .

"Please," he said again. "Don't—"

His accent sealed his fate. His tones were too clipped. He wasn't Nikara after all, just a clever Mugenese soldier who thought he might fool her into taking mercy.

"Burn," she said.

The boy fell backward. She saw his mouth open, saw his face curdle into a piteous scream just as it blackened and solidified, but she couldn't bring herself to care.

In the end, it was always so easy to kill her heart. It didn't matter that they looked like boys. That they were nothing, nothing like the monsters she had once known. In this war of racial totality, none of that mattered. If they were Mugenese, that meant they were crickets and that meant when she crushed them under her heel, the universe hardly registered their loss.

Once, Altan had made her watch him burn a squirrel alive.

He'd caught it for their breakfast with a simple netted trap. It was still alive when he retrieved it from the trees, wriggling in his grasp. But instead of snapping its neck, he'd decided to teach her a lesson.

"Do you know how exactly fire kills a person?" he'd asked.

She'd shaken her head. She'd watched, entranced, as he conjured fire into his palms.

Altan had such remarkable control over the shape of fire. He was a puppeteer, casually twisting flames into the loveliest shapes:

now a flying bird, now a twisting dragon, now a human figure, flailing inside the cage he made with his fingers until he clamped his palms shut.

She'd been captivated, watching his fingers dance through the air. His question had caught her off guard, and when she spoke, her words were clumsy and stupid. "Through heat? I mean, um . . ."

His lip had curled. "Fire is such an inefficient way to kill. Did you know the moment of death is actually quite painless? The fire eats up all the breathable air around the victim, and they choke to death."

She blinked at him. "You don't want that?"

"Why would you want that? If you want a quick death, you use a sword. Or an arrow." He'd twirled a stream of flame around his fingers. "You don't throw Speerlies into battle unless you want to terrorize. We want our victims to suffer first. We want them to burn, and slowly."

He'd picked up the bound squirrel and wrapped his fingers around its middle. The squirrel couldn't scream, but Rin had imagined the sound, quivering little gasps that corresponded to its twitching limbs.

"Watch the skin," he'd said.

Once the fur burned off, she'd been able to glimpse the pink underneath, bubbling, crackling, hardening to black. "First it boils. Then it starts to slough off. Watch the color. Once you've turned it black, and once that black spreads, there's nothing that can bring them back."

He had held the squirrel out toward her. "Hungry?"

She had glanced down at its little black eyes, bulging and glassy, and her stomach roiled. And she hadn't known what was worse, the way the animal's legs twitched in its death throes, or the fact that the roasted flesh smelled so terribly good.

By the time she'd finished in the southern quarter, the rest of her soldiers had corralled the last Mugenese holdouts into a corner in Khudla's eastern district. They parted to let her through to the front.

"Took you a while," Officer Shen said.

"Got held up," Rin said. "Having too much fun."

"The southern quarter—"

"Finished." Rin rubbed her fingers together, and crackled blood burned black fell to the ground. "Why aren't we attacking?"

"They've taken hostages inside the temple," Shen said.

That was smart. Rin regarded the structure. It was one of the nicer village temples she'd seen in a while, made from stone and not wood. It wouldn't burn easily, and the Mugenese artillery inside had good vantage points from the upper floors.

"They're going to shoot us out," Shen said.

As if to prove her point, a fire rocket shrieked overhead and exploded against the tree ten paces from where they crouched.

"So storm them," Rin said.

"We're afraid they might have gas."

"They would have used it by now."

"They could be waiting for you," Shen pointed out.

That was fair logic. "Then we'll burn it."

"We can't get past the stone—"

"*You* can't get past stone." Rin wiggled her fingers in the air. A fiery dragon danced around her palm. She squinted at the temple, considering. It fell easily within her range; she could extend her flames to a radius of fifty yards. She only needed to sneak a flame through a window. Once past stone, her fire would find plenty of things to burn.

"How many hostages?" Rin asked.

"Does it matter?" Shen asked.

"It does to me."

Shen paused for a long moment, and then nodded. "Maybe five, six. No more than eight."

"Are they important?" Women and children could die without many ramifications. Local leadership likely couldn't.

"Not as far as I can tell. Souji's people are on the other side of town. And he doesn't have family."

Rin mulled over her options one last time.

She could still have her troops storm the temple, but she'd suffer casualties, especially if the Mugenese really did have gas canisters. The Southern Army couldn't afford casualties; their numbers were low enough already.

And her margin of victory mattered. This was her great test. If she came home from this not just victorious but with minimal losses, the Monkey Warlord would give her an army. The decision, then, was clear; she wasn't slinking back with only half her troops.

"Who else knows about the hostages?" she asked Shen.

"Just the men here."

"What about the villagers?"

"We've evacuated everyone we could find," Shen said, which was code for *No one will speak of what you did.*

Rin nodded. "Get your men out of here. At least a hundred paces. I don't want them to inhale any smoke."

Shen looked pale. "General—"

Rin raised her voice. "I wasn't asking."

Shen nodded and broke into a run. The field cleared in seconds. Rin stood alone in the yard, rubbing her fingers against her palm.

Can you feel this, Kitay? Can you tell what I'm doing?

No time for hesitation. She had to do this before the Mugenese ventured out to investigate the silence.

She turned her palm out. Fire roared. She directed the core of the flame toward the locks on the temple doors. She saw the metal warping, twisting into an unbreakable shape.

Then the Mugenese must have caught on, because someone inside started to scream.

Rin increased the heat to a roar loud enough to drown it out, yet somehow it pierced the wall of sound. It was a high squeal of pain. Maybe a woman's, maybe a child's. It almost sounded like a baby. But that didn't mean anything—she knew how shrilly a grown man could scream.

She increased the force of her flame, made it roar so loudly that she couldn't hear herself think. But still the scream penetrated the wall of fire.

She squeezed her eyes shut. She imagined herself falling backward into the Phoenix's warmth, into that distant space where nothing mattered but rage. The thin wail wavered.

Burn, she thought, *shut up and burn.*

CHAPTER 2

"Well done," Kitay said.

She threw her arms around him, pulled him tight against her, and lingered in his embrace for a long while. By now she should have become used to their brief separations, but leaving him behind felt harder and harder every time.

She tried to convince herself that it wasn't solely because Kitay was the one source of her power. That it wasn't just because of her selfish concern that if anything happened to him, she was useless.

No, she also felt responsible for him. *Guilty*, rather. Kitay's mind was stretched like a rope between her and the Phoenix, and between the rage and hatred and shame, he felt *everything*. He kept her safe from madness, and she subjected him to madness in return. Nothing she ever did could repay that debt.

"You're shaking," she said.

"I'm all right," he said. "It's nothing."

"You're lying." Even in the dim light of dawn, Rin could see his legs were trembling. He was far from all right—he could barely stand. They had this same argument after every battle. Every time she came back and saw what she'd done to him, saw his pale, drawn face and knew that to him, it felt like torture. Every time he denied it.

She'd limit her use of flame if only he asked. He never asked.

"I'll be fine," he amended gently. He nodded over her shoulder. "And you're drawing a bit of attention."

Rin turned and saw Khudla's survivors.

This had happened often enough that she knew what to expect.

First they wandered forward in little, tentative clumps. Curious whispering, terrified pointing. Then, when they realized that this new army was not Mugenese but Nikara, not Militia but something new entirely, and that Rin's soldiers were not here to replace their oppressors, they grew braver.

Is she the Speerly? they asked. *Are you the Speerly?*

Are you one of us?

And then the whispers grew louder as the crowd swelled, bodies coalescing around her. They spoke her name, her race, her god. Her legend had already spread to this place; she could hear it rippling through the field.

They reached out to touch her.

Rin's chest constricted. Her breathing quickened; her throat felt blocked.

Kitay's hand tightened around her arm. He didn't have to ask what was wrong; he knew.

"Are you—" he began.

"It's fine," she murmured. "It's fine."

These hands were not the enemy's. She was not in danger. She knew that, but her body didn't. She took a deep breath and composed her face. She had to play the part—had to look like not the scared girl she'd once been or the tired soldier that she was, but the leader they needed.

"You're free," she told them. Her voice quivered with exhaustion; she cleared her throat. "Go."

A hush ran through the crowd when they saw that she spoke

their language—not the abrasive Nikara of the north, but the slow, rolling dialect of the south.

They still regarded her with a kind of awed terror. But she knew this was the kind of fear that turned into love.

Rin raised her voice and spoke, this time without a tremor. "Go tell your families that they've been saved. Tell them the Mugenese can't harm you any longer. And when they ask who broke your shackles, tell them the Southern Coalition is marching across the Empire with the Phoenix at its fore. Tell them we're taking back our home."

As the sun climbed through the sky, Rin commenced Khudla's liberation.

This was supposed to be the fun part. It was supposed to feel good, telling grateful villagers that their erstwhile occupiers were smoldering piles of ash.

But Rin dreaded liberation. Combing through a half-destroyed village to find survivors only meant yet another survey of the extent of Federation cruelty. She'd rather face the battlefield again than confront that suffering. It didn't matter that she'd already seen the worst at Golyn Niis, that she'd witnessed the worst things one could do to a human body dozens of times over. It never got easier.

She'd learned by now that the Mugenese implemented the same three measures every time they occupied a city, three directives so clean and textbook that she could have written a full treatise on how to subdue a population herself.

First, the Mugenese rounded up every Nikara man who resisted their occupation, marched them to the killing fields, and either shot or beheaded them. Beheading was more common; arrows were valuable resources and couldn't always be retrieved intact. They didn't kill all the local men, just those who had threatened to make trouble. They needed laborers.

Second, the Mugenese either repurposed or stripped away the village infrastructure. Anything sturdy they turned into soldiers' barracks, and anything flimsy they tore apart for firewood. When the loose wood was gone, they scoured the homes for furniture, blankets, valuables, and ceramics with which to furnish their barracks. They were very efficient at turning villages into empty shells. Rin often found liberated villagers crowded in pigsties, cramped together knee to knee just to keep warm.

Third, the Mugenese co-opted the local leadership. After all, what did you do when you didn't speak the local language? When you didn't grasp the nuances of regional politics? You didn't supplant the existing leadership structure—that would result in chaos. You grafted yourself onto it. You got the local bullies to do your dirty work for you.

Rin hated the Nikara collaborators. Their crimes, to her, seemed almost worse than those of the Federation. The Mugenese were at least targeting the enemy race—a natural instinct in wartime. But collaborators helped the Mugenese murder, mutilate, and violate their own kind. That was inconceivable. Unforgivable.

Rin and Kitay were always split on how to handle the captured collaborators. Kitay begged for lenience. They were desperate, he argued. They were trying to save their own skins. They might have saved some villagers' skins. *Sometimes compliance saves you pain. Compliance might have saved us at Golyn Niis.*

Bullshit, Rin retorted. Compliance was cowardice. She had no respect for anyone who would rather die than fight. She wanted the collaborators to burn.

But the matter was out of their hands. The villagers invariably settled things themselves. Sometime in the next week, if not in the next day, they would drag the collaborators into the middle of the square, extract their confessions, and then flay, whip, beat, or stone them. Rin never had to intervene. The south delivered its own justice. The catharsis of violence hadn't happened yet in Khudla—it was too early in the morning for a public execution, and the villagers were too starved and exhausted to form a mob— but Rin knew that soon enough, she would hear screaming.

Meanwhile, she had survivors to find. She was looking for

prisoners. The Federation always took captives—political dissidents, soldiers too willful to control but too useful to let die, or hostages they hoped might dissuade their incoming attackers. Sometimes the bodies were freshly dead—either from one last act of vengeance by desperate Mugenese soldiers under siege, or suffocated by smoke from Rin's flames.

More often, however, she found them alive. You couldn't kill hostages if you ever meant to use them.

Kitay led soldiers to search in the eastern edge of the village through the Mugenese-occupied buildings that had escaped the brunt of the destruction. He had a particular talent for finding survivors. He'd once hidden for weeks behind a bricked-up wall at Golyn Niis, cringing and hugging his knees while Federation soldiers dragged Nikara soldiers from their hiding spots and shot them on the streets. He knew how to look for the signs—tarps or stacked debris that seemed out of place, faint footprints in the dust, echoes of shallow breathing in frightened silence.

Rin alone took on the burned wreckage.

She dreaded this task: pulling charred boards aside to find bodies broken and bleeding but still breathing. Too many times they were beyond saving. Half the time she'd caused the destruction herself. Once flames started burning, they were difficult to put out.

Still, she had to try.

"Is anyone here?" she called repeatedly. "Make a noise. Any noise. I'm listening."

She went through every cellar, every abandoned lot and well; shouted out for survivors many times and made sure she listened hard to the echoing silence. It would be a horrible fate to be chained up, slowly starving or suffocating to death because your village had been liberated but the survivors forgot about you. Her eyes watered as she stumbled through a smoky grain cellar. She doubted she'd find anything—already she'd stumbled over two corpses—but she waited a moment before she left. Just in case.

Her patience rewarded her.

"In the back," called a voice.

Rin pulled a flame into her hand, illuminating the far wall of the cellar. She couldn't see anything but empty grain sacks. She stepped closer.

"Who are you?" she demanded.

"Souji." She heard the clink of chains. "Likely the man you're looking for."

She decided she wasn't dealing with an ambush. She knew that flat-tongued, rustic accent. The best Mugenese spies couldn't imitate it; they'd all trained only to speak the curt Sinegardian dialect.

She crossed to the other end of the cellar, stopped, and amplified her torchlight.

Her first goal at Khudla had been liberation. Her second goal was to locate Yang Souji, the famed rebel leader and local hero who had until recently been fending off the Mugenese in southern Monkey Province. The closer she'd marched to Khudla, the more myths and rumors she'd heard about him. Yang Souji had eyes that could see for ten thousand miles. He could speak to animals; he knew when the Mugenese were coming because the birds always warned him. His skin was invulnerable to all kinds of metal—swords, arrowheads, axes, spears.

The man chained to the floor was none of those things. He looked surprisingly young—he couldn't be more than a few years older than she was. A scraggly beard had sprouted over his neck and chin, some indication of how long he'd been chained up, but he sat up straight with his shoulders rolled back, and his eyes shone bright in the firelight.

Despite herself, Rin found him surprisingly handsome.

"So you're the Speerly," he said. "I thought you'd be taller."

"And I thought you'd be older," she said.

"Then we're both a disappointment." He jangled his chains at her. "Took you long enough. Did you really need all night?"

She knelt down and began working at the locks. "Not even a thank-you?"

"You're going to do that one-handed?" he asked skeptically.

She fumbled with the pin. "Look, if you're going to—"

"Give me that." He plucked the pin from her fingers. "Just hold the lock up where I can see it and give me some light—there you go."

As she watched him work at the lock with remarkable dexterity, she couldn't help but feel a flicker of jealousy. It still stung, how the simplest things—picking locks, getting dressed, filling her canteen—had become so damnably difficult overnight.

She'd lost her hand to such a stupid turn of events. If they'd only had a key back then. If they'd just been able to steal a motherfucking *key*.

Her stump itched. She clenched her teeth and willed herself not to scratch it.

Souji undid the lock in less than a minute. He shook his hands free and sighed, cradling his wrists. He bent over toward the chains around his ankles. "That's better. Can you give me some more light?"

She moved the flame closer to the lock, careful not to singe his skin.

She noticed the middle finger on his right hand was missing its top joint. It didn't look like an accident—the middle finger on his left hand was missing a joint as well.

"What's wrong with your hands?" she asked.

"My mother's first two children died in infancy," he explained. "She thought that the gods were stealing them because they were so lovely. So when I entered the world she gnawed the first joint off both my middle fingers." He wiggled his left hand at her. "Made me a bit less attractive."

Rin snorted. "The gods don't want fingers."

"So what do they want?"

"Pain," she said. "Pain, and your sanity."

Souji popped the lock, shook the chains away, and clambered to his feet. "I suppose you would know."

After all likely survivors had been rescued from the wreckage, Rin's troops fell on the battlefield like vultures.

The first time the newly minted soldiers of the Southern Coalition had scavenged for supplies in the wake of a battle, they'd been reluctant to touch the corpses. They'd been superstitious, scared of angering vengeful ghosts of the unburied dead who couldn't return home. Now they raided bodies with hardened disregard, stripping them of anything of value. They looked for weapons, leather, clean linens—Mugenese uniforms were blue, but could be easily dyed—and, prized above all, shoes.

The Southern Coalition's troops suffered terribly from shoddy footwear. They fought in straw sandals, and cotton if they could obtain it, but those cotton shoes were more like slippers, sewn weeks before the battle by wives, mothers, and sisters. Most were fighting in footwear of plaited straw that broke midmarch, fell apart in sticky mud, and offered no protection against the cold.

The Mugenese, however, had sailed over the Nariin Sea wearing leather boots—fine, solid, warm, and waterproof. Rin's soldiers had become very adept at untying the laces, yanking boots off stiffening feet, and tossing them into wheelbarrows to be redistributed later according to size.

While Rin's soldiers combed through the fields, Souji led her toward the former village headman's office, which the Mugenese had repurposed into a headquarters. He provided running commentary on the ruins as they walked, like a disgruntled host apologetic that his home had been found in such a mess.

"It looked loads better than this months ago. Khudla's a nice village—had some lovely historic architecture, until they tore down everything for firewood. And *we* made those barricades," he said somewhat sulkily, pointing to the sandbags around the headquarters. "They just stole them."

For a simple village's defenses, Souji's barricades had been surprisingly well constructed. He'd organized pillboxes the way she would have done it—wooden stakes driven into the ground to provide a lattice framework for layers of sandbags. She'd been taught that method at Sinegard. These defenses, Rin realized, had been built according to Militia guidelines.

"Then how did they get through in the end?" she asked.

Souji blinked at her as if she were an idiot. "They had *gas*."

So Officer Shen was right. Rin stifled a shudder, imagining the impact of the noxious yellow fumes on unsuspecting civilians. "How much?"

"Just one canister," Souji said. "I think they'd been hoarding it, because they didn't use it when they first came. Waited until the third day of fighting, when they had us all barricaded into one place, and then they popped it over the wall. We fell apart pretty quickly after that."

They reached the headquarters. Souji tried the door. It swung open without trouble; no one was left to lock it from the inside.

Food littered the table of the central conference room. Souji picked a wheat bun off its place, tore off a bite, then spat it back out. "Disgusting."

"What, too stale for you?"

"No. It's got too much salt. Gross." Souji tossed the wheat bun back onto the table. "Salt doesn't belong in buns."

Rin's mouth watered. "They have salt?"

She hadn't tasted salt in weeks. Most salt in the Empire was imported from the basins of Dog Province, but those trade networks had completely broken down during Vaisra's civil war. Out in the arid eastern Monkey Province, Rin's army had been subsisting on the blandest rice gruel and boiled vegetables. There were rumored to be a few jars of fermented soy paste hidden in the kitchens at Ruijin, but if they existed, Rin had never seen nor tasted them.

"*We* had salt," Souji corrected. He bent over to examine the contents of a barrel. "Looks like they've eaten through most of it. There's only a handful left."

"Take that back to the public kitchen. We'll treat everyone." Rin leaned over the commander's desk. Documents were strewn all over its surface. Rin found troop numbers, food ration records, and letters written in a scrawled, messy script that she could barely read. Here and there she could make out a few words. *Wife. Home. Emperor.*

She collected them into a neat pile. She and Kitay would pore over them later, see if they bore any meaningful news about the Mugenese. But they were likely months old, like the other correspondence they'd found. Every dead Mugenese general kept letters from the mainland on their desk, as if rereading those Mugini characters could maintain their connection to a motherland they must have known was gone.

"They were reading Sunzi?" Rin picked up the slim text—a Nikara edition, not a translation. "And the *Bodhidharma*? Where'd they get these?"

"Those were mine. Stole them out of the Sinegard library way back in the day." Souji plucked the booklet from her hand. "I take them with me everywhere I go. Those bastards wouldn't have been able to make head or tail of them."

Rin glanced at him, surprised. "You're a Sinegard graduate?"

"Not a graduate. I was there for two years. Then the famine struck, so I went home. Jima didn't let me back in when I returned. But I still needed a paycheck, so I enlisted in the Militia."

So he'd passed the Keju. That was rare for someone from his background—Rin should know. She regarded Souji with a newfound respect. "Why wouldn't they?"

"Because they thought that if I left once, then I'd do it again. That I'd always prioritize my family over my military career. Guess they were right. I would have left the ranks the moment we got wind of the Mugenese invasion."

"And what about now?"

"Whole family's dead." His voice was flat. "Died this past year."

"I'm sorry. Was it the Federation?"

"No. The flood." Souji jerked out a shrug. "We're usually pretty good at seeing floods coming. Not hard to read the weather if you know what you're doing. But not this time. This was man-made."

"The Empress broke the dams," Rin said automatically. Chaghan and Qara felt like such a distant memory that she could speak this lie without struggle. Best that Souji didn't know that the Cike, her old regiment, had deliberately caused the flood that killed his family.

"Broke the dams to stem an enemy that she'd invited in herself." Souji's voice turned bitter. "I know. I'd learned to swim at Sinegard. They hadn't. There's nothing where my village used to be."

Rin felt a stab of guilt. She did her best to ignore it. She shouldn't have to shoulder the blame for that particular atrocity. That flood had been the fault of the twins, an act of environmental warfare to slow the Federation's progress inland.

Who could say if it had worked, or if it had even mattered? What was done was done. The only way to live with your transgressions, Rin had learned, was to lock them away in your mind and leave them in the abyss.

"Why can't you just blow them up?" Souji asked abruptly.

She blinked at him. "What?"

"When you ended the war. When the longbow island went up in smoke. What's stopping you from doing that again in the south?"

"Prudence," she said. "If I burn them, I burn everyone. Fire on that scale doesn't discriminate. A massive genocide on our own territory would—"

"We don't need a massive genocide. Just a little one would do."

"You don't know what you're asking for." She turned away; she didn't want to meet his eyes. "Even the little fires hurt people they shouldn't."

She'd grown tired of this question. That was what everyone wanted to know—why she couldn't simply snap her fingers and incinerate the Mugenese camp like she'd done to their entire island. If she'd finished off a nation once, why couldn't she do it again? Why couldn't she end this whole war in seconds? Wasn't that *so obviously* the next move?

She wished she could do it. There were times when she wanted so badly to send walls of flame roaring across the entire south, clearing out the Mugenese the way one might raze a field of blighted crops, with no regard for the collateral damage.

But every time that desire surged within her, she ran up against the same pulsing black venom that clouded her mind—Su Daji's parting gift, the Seal that cut her off from direct access to the Pantheon.

Maybe it was a blessing that her mind remained blocked by the Seal, that she was forced to use Kitay as a conduit for her power. Kitay kept her sane. Stable. He let her call the fire, but only in targeted, limited bursts.

Without Kitay, Rin was terrified of what she might do.

"If I were you," Souji said, "I would have gotten rid of them all. One single blaze, and the south would be clean. Fuck prudence."

She shot him a wry look. "Then you'd be dead, too."

"Just as well," he said, and sounded like he meant it.

Rin felt as if eternity had passed by the time the sun set. Twenty-four hours ago, she had led troops into battle for the first time. That afternoon, she'd liberated a village. Now her wrist throbbed, her knees shook, and a headache pounded behind her eyes.

She could not silence the memory of that scream in the temple. She needed to silence it.

Back in her tent, she dug a packet of opium out from the bottom of her traveling satchel and pressed a nugget into a pipe.

"Do you have to?" Kitay asked. It wasn't really a question. They'd had this argument a thousand times, and every time arrived at the same lack of resolution. He just felt obligated to express his displeasure. By now they were simply going through the motions.

"It's not your business," she said.

"You need to sleep. You've been up nearly forty-eight hours."

"I'll sleep after this. I can't relax without it."

"It smells awful."

"So go sleep somewhere else."

Silently Kitay stood up and walked out of the tent.

Rin didn't watch him go. She lifted the pipe to her mouth, lit the bowl with her fingers, and breathed in deep. Then she curled over on her side and drew her knees into her chest.

In seconds she saw the Seal—a live, pulsing thing, reeking so strongly of the Vipress's venom that Su Daji might have been standing in the tent right next to her. She used to curse the Seal, used to barrel pointlessly against the immutable barrier of venom that wouldn't leave her mind.

But she'd since found a better use for it.

Rin drifted toward the glistening characters. The Seal tilted toward her, opened, and swallowed her. There was a brief moment of blinding, terrifying darkness, and then she was in a dark room with no doors or windows.

Daji's poison was composed of desire—the things she would kill for, the things she missed so badly she wanted to die.

Altan materialized on cue.

Rin used to be so afraid of him. She'd felt a little thrill of fear every time she'd looked at him, and she'd *liked* it. When he was alive, she'd never known if he was going to caress or throttle her. The first time she'd seen him inside the Seal, he'd nearly convinced her to follow him into oblivion. But now she kept him leashed in her mind, firmly under control, and he spoke only when she wanted him to.

Still the fear remained. She couldn't help it, nor did she want to. She needed someone who could still scare her.

"There you are." He reached a hand out to stroke her cheek. "Did you miss me?"

"Get back," she said. "Sit down."

He held his hands up and obeyed, crossing his legs on the dark floor. "Whatever you say, darling."

She sat down across from him. "I killed dozens of people last night. Probably some of them innocent."

Altan tilted his head to the side. "And how did that make you feel?" His tone was perfectly neutral, without judgment.

Even so, she felt a swell in her chest, a familiar toxic squeeze, like her lungs were eroding under the sheer weight of her guilt. She exhaled, fighting to remain calm. Altan stayed under her control only so long as she was calm. "You would have done it."

"And why would I have done it, kiddo?"

"Because you were ruthless," she said. "You did strategy by the numbers. You would have known you had to do it. You couldn't risk your troops. Soldiers are worth more than civilians, it's just math."

"So there it is." He gave her a patronizing smile. "You did what you needed to. You're a hero. Did you enjoy it?"

She didn't lie. Why would she? Altan was her secret, her conjuration, and no one would ever know what she said here. Not even Kitay.

"Yes."

"Show it to me," Altan said. Hunger was etched across his face. "Show me everything."

She let him see. Relived it all, second by second, in vivid, lurid detail. She showed him the bodies doubling over. The babble of terrified voices pleading for mercy—*No, no, please, no.* The temple transforming into a pillar of flame.

"Good," said Altan. "That's very good. Show me more."

She brought out the memories of ashes, of pristine white bone poking out from charred black piles. She could never burn the bones away entirely, no matter how hard she tried. Some fragment always remained.

She stayed for another minute to let herself feel it—feel all of it, the guilt, the remorse, the horror. She could only feel them in *this* space, where they wouldn't be debilitating, where they wouldn't make her want to crawl across the floor and scratch long streaks of blood into her forearms and thighs.

Then she left the memories alone. Interred here, they wouldn't haunt her again.

She always felt so clean afterward. Like the world was covered in stains and with every enemy she reduced to ash, it became just a little bit more pure.

This was both her absolution and her penance. Once she self-flagellated in her mind, once she replayed the atrocities over and over so much the images lost meaning, then she'd given the dead their due respect. She owed them nothing more.

She opened her eyes. The memory of Altan threatened to resurge in her thoughts, but she forced it back down. He appeared only when she allowed it, only when she wanted to see him.

Once, her memories of Altan had nearly driven her mad. Now his company was one of the only things keeping her sane.

She was finding it easier and easier to cut him off. She'd learned now to divide her mind into clean, convenient compartments. Thoughts could be blocked. Memories suppressed. Life was so much easier when she blockaded off the part of her that agonized over what she'd done. And as long as she kept those parts of her mind separate—the part that felt pain and the part that fought wars—then she would be all right.

"You think they're going to join up?" Kitay asked.

"I'm not sure," Rin said. "They've been a bit surly about everything so far. Ingrates."

They watched, arms crossed, as the men who called themselves the Iron Wolves carried salvageable wreckage out of the village center.

The Iron Wolves were Souji's troops. More of them had survived Khudla's occupation than Rin had feared—their numbers ranked at least five hundred. That was a relief. The Southern Army desperately needed new troops, but suitable recruits were difficult to find in Mugenese-occupied villages. Most young men with any inclination to fight were already buried in the killing fields. The lucky survivors were either too young or too old—or too frightened—to make good soldiers.

But Souji's Iron Wolves were strong, healthy men with plenty of combat experience. Until now, they had been roving protectors of the Monkey Province's backwaters. Many had fled into the forests when Khudla fell. Now they'd returned in hordes. They would make excellent soldiers—but the question was whether they could be convinced to join the Coalition.

Rin wasn't sure. So far the Iron Wolves had been less than grateful to their liberators. In fact the rescue operations had taken a heated turn; Souji's men were terribly territorial and reluctant to take commands that didn't come from Souji himself. They were irked, it seemed, that someone else had swooped in to claim the title of savior. Already Kitay had mediated three quarrels over resource allocation between Iron Wolves and soldiers of the Southern Coalition.

"What's going on there?" Rin asked suddenly.

She pointed. Two of Souji's yellow-banded troops were marching toward their camp, both lugging sacks of rice behind them.

"Ah, fuck." Kitay looked exasperated. "Not this again."

"Hey!" Rin stood up and cupped her hand around her mouth. "You! Stop there."

They kept walking as if they hadn't heard her. She had to run at them, shouting, before they finally stopped.

"Where are you taking that?" she demanded.

They exchanged looks of obvious irritation. The taller one spoke. "Souji told us to bring some rice out to the tents."

"We've set up a communal kitchen." Rin pointed. "You can eat there. That's where all the salvaged food goes. All the scavenging teams were ordered to—"

The shorter one cut her off. "Well, see, we don't take orders from you."

She blinked at him. "I *liberated* this place."

"And that's very kind of you, miss. But we've got this village under control now."

Rin was amazed when, without so much as a final look of disdain, they slung the rice sacks up onto their shoulders and stalked insolently off.

I'll teach you to listen. Her palm sang with heat. She raised her fist, pointed it toward their retreating backs—

"Don't." Kitay caught her by the wrist. "Now isn't the time to start a fight."

"They should be terrified of me," she snarled. "The sheer *nerve*—"

"You can't be mad about stupidity. Just let them go. If we want them on our side, you can't go around burning their balls off."

"What the hell is Souji telling his men?" she hissed. "He knows I'm in command!"

"I doubt he's passed that on."

"They're in for a rude awakening, then."

"And while that's true, you don't have to convince the *soldiers*," Kitay said. "You've got to convince Souji. He's the problem."

"Should have just left him in the cellar," Rin grumbled. "Or we could kill him now."

"Too hard to pull off," Kitay said, unfazed. Rin suggested casual murder on such a regular basis that he'd learned to brush it off. "The timing would be too suspicious. We'd certainly lose his men. You could try to make it look like an accident, but even then it'd be difficult to spin. Souji's not the type to go around tripping off cliffs."

"Then we have to undercut him," Rin said. "Knock him off his pedestal."

But how? She pondered this for a moment. Discrediting him would be too hard. Those men loved Souji. She couldn't sever those bonds overnight.

"That's not necessary," Kitay said. "Don't cut the head off the snake if you can tame it. You've just got to convince him where his interests lie."

"But how?"

He shot her a droll look. "Oh, I think you're good enough at that."

She rubbed her wrist stump into the palm of her good fist. "I'll go have a nice long chat with him then, shall I?"

He sighed. "Be nice."

∞

"To what do I owe the pleasure?" Souji asked. He was crouched over a campfire, digging into a bowl of steaming white rice that smelled much better than the vats of barley porridge in the communal kitchen.

"Get up," Rin said. "We're going for a walk."

"Why?"

"For privacy."

Souji's eyes narrowed. He must have known what was coming, because he gave a nearly imperceptible shake of his head to the closest Iron Wolves. *Leave us*, it said. *I'm fine.*

The men turned and left. Souji stood up. "All right, Princess. I'll walk with you."

Rin wrinkled her nose. "Princess?"

"Sinegard educated? Former Militia elite? That's royalty in my book."

He didn't make it sound like a compliment. Rin chose not to retort; she held her tongue until they'd walked deep into the forest, out of earshot from camp. She might as well let Souji keep his dignity with his men. He'd be less grumpy about taking orders if she did.

She tried a diplomatic opening. "I'm sure you've realized by now we have men and resources that you don't."

"Stop." He held up a hand. "I know what you want. We're not joining any coalitions. Your war isn't my problem."

She scoffed. "You were happy enough about taking our aid yesterday."

"The *Mugenese* are my problem. But don't pretend that this is all about the Federation. Your Southern Coalition is baiting the Republic and you're an idiot if you think I'm getting involved with that."

"Soon enough you won't have a choice. Yin Vaisra—"

Souji rolled his eyes. "Vaisra doesn't care about us."

"He will," she insisted. "You think Vaisra's going to stop after he's conquered the north? I've met the Hesperians, I know their intentions. They won't stop until they've put a church in each of our villages—"

Souji picked at his teeth with the nail of his little finger. "Churches never killed anyone."

"They prop up regime ideologies that do."

"Come on, you're grasping at straws—"

"Am I? You've dealt with them before, have you? No, you'll regret saying that when you're all under Hesperian rule. I've spoken to them. I know how they look at us. None of this—our villages, our people, our freedom—will survive under their intended world order."

"Don't talk to me about survival," Souji snapped. "I've been keeping our people alive for months while you've been playing the hunting dog over at Vaisra's court. What did that get you?"

"I was a fool," Rin said bluntly. "I know that. I was stupid then and I should have seen the signs. But I'm back in the south now, and we can build this army, if you bring your Iron Wolves—"

He cut her off with a laugh. "That's a no, Princess."

"I don't think you understand," she said. "That was an order. Not a request."

He reached out and flicked her on the nose. "And you don't understand: we are not, and never will be, under your command."

Rin blinked, stunned that he would even *dare*.

So this was how things were going to go.

"Oh, Souji." She pulled a flame into her palm. "You don't understand how this works."

She darted toward him just as he reached for his sword. She'd anticipated that. As he swung, she dodged his blade and jammed a foot hard into his left kneecap. He buckled. She swept the other leg out from under him and jumped down onto his chest as he fell, fingers grasping for his neck. She squeezed.

"You don't know who you're dealing with." She leaned down close until her lips brushed his skin, until her breath scorched the side of his face. "I'm not Sinegardian elite. I'm that savage, mud-skinned Speerly bitch that wiped a country off the map. And sometimes when I get a little too angry, I *snap*."

She let just the faintest trickle of fire seep from under her fingers. Souji's eyes bulged. She dug her fingertips farther into his skin.

"You're coming back with me to Ruijin. The Iron Wolves now fight under my command. You'll keep your position as their leader, but you'll make the hierarchy clear to your men. And if you try to mutiny, I'll pick this up where I left off. Understand?"

Souji's throat bobbed. He pawed feebly at her arm.

She tightened her grip. "You're my bitch now, Souji. You do anything I ask without complaint. You'll lick the dirt off my boots if I want. Is that clear?"

He nodded, patting frantically at her wrist.

She didn't budge. Blisters formed and popped under his chin. "I didn't hear an answer."

"Yes," he croaked.

"Yes, what?" She relaxed her grip just enough to let him speak.

"Yes, I'm your bitch. I'll do what you want. Anything. Just—please—"

She released him and let him stand. Little tendrils of smoke wafted out from his neck. Visible beneath his collar was a first-degree burn, a pale red imprint of her skinny fingers.

It would heal quickly, but that scar would never disappear. Souji might cover it with his collar and hide it from his men, but it would be clear as day to him every time he so much as glanced at his reflection.

"Why don't you go put a poultice on that?" she asked. "Wouldn't want it infected."

He backed away from her. "You're insane."

"Everyone vying for this country is insane," she said. "But none of them have skin as dark as ours. I'm the least terrible option you've got."

Souji stared at her for a long time. Rin couldn't read his expression, couldn't tell if his eyes glinted with rage or humiliation. She curled her fist and tensed, ready for another round.

To her surprise, he began to laugh. "All right. You win, you fucking bitch."

"Don't call me a bitch."

"You win, General." He held his hands up in a gesture of mock surrender. "I'll march back with you. Where are we going? Dalian? Heirjiang?"

"I told you," she said. "Ruijin."

He raised a brow. "Why Ruijin?"

"It's built into the mountains. Keeps us safe from almost everything. Why not?"

"I just assumed you'd be somewhere farther south. Near Rooster Province, if your goal is liberation."

"What are you talking about? The occupied areas are clustered at the Monkey border."

"No, they aren't. Most of them are bunched down south in Rooster Province."

"Where, the capital?" Rin frowned. None of this tracked with her intelligence.

"No, somewhere farther down south," Souji said. "A few weeks' march from the ocean. A cluster of tiny villages, you won't know it."

"Tikany," she said automatically.

A little township no one had ever heard of. A dusty, arid place with no riches and no special culture; nothing except a docile population still addicted to opium from the second invasion. A place where Rin had once hoped she would never in her life return.

"Yeah." Souji arched an eyebrow. "That's one of them. Why, do you know the place?"

He said something else after that, but she didn't hear it.

Tikany. The Mugenese were still in Tikany.

We're fools, she thought. *We've been fighting on the wrong front this entire time.*

"Tell your men to pack up," she said. "We head out for Ruijin in two hours."

CHAPTER 3

That evening they began their march back to the base camp of the Southern Coalition. Ruijin lay within the backwoods of the Monkey Province, a poor and calcified land racked by years of banditry, warlord campaigns, famines, and epidemics. It had been the capital of the Monkey Province in antiquity, a lush city famed for its stone shrines built elegantly into the topiary of surrounding bamboo groves. Now it comprised ruins of its former splendor, half eroded by rain and half devoured by the forest.

That made it an excellent place to hide. For centuries, the people of Monkey Province prided themselves on their ability to blend into the mountains during troubled times. They built houses on stilts or up in the trees to keep safe from tigers. They paved winding paths through the dark forest invisible to the untrained eye. In all the stories of old, the Monkeys were stereotyped as backward mountain people—cowards who hid away in trees and caves while the wars of the world passed them by. But those were the same traits that kept them alive.

"Where are we going?" Souji grumbled a week into a continuously uphill hike, during which they'd encountered nothing but endless bumpy paths through hilly forest. "There's nothing up here."

"That's what you think." Rin bent low to check the scores against the base of a poplar tree—a clue that they were still on the right path—and motioned for the column to follow.

The way up the pass was easier than she had remembered it. The sheen had melted off the edges of the ice. She could see plenty of green beneath sheets of snow that hadn't been visible when she'd set out two weeks ago. Against all odds, the Southern Coalition had made it to spring.

Winter in the Monkey Province had been a frigid, arid ordeal for the Southern Coalition. It didn't snow, it hailed. The cold, dry air robbed their breaths from under their noses. The ground turned into a hard, brittle thing. Nothing grew. They'd come so close to starving, and likely would have if an ambushed Mugenese enclave ten miles away hadn't turned out to possess a shocking amount of food stores.

The soldiers hadn't distributed their spoils. Rin couldn't forget the faces of the villagers who'd come out from hiding, thin and exhausted, their relief quickly turning to horror when they realized their liberators were here simply to cart their grain away.

She pushed the memory from her mind. That was a necessary sacrifice. The future of the entire country hinged on the Southern Coalition. What difference did a few lives make?

"Well, this clarifies some things," Souji muttered as he pushed through the undergrowth.

"What are you talking about?"

"You don't hide in the mountains if you're a liberating force."

"No?"

"If you're trying to take back territory, you inhabit the villages you've freed. You expand your base. You set up defenses to make sure the Mugenese don't come back again. But you're just predatory extractors. You'll liberate places, but only for the tribute."

"I didn't hear you complaining when I freed you from that cellar."

"Whatever you say, Princess." Souji's voice took on a judging, mocking tone. "You aren't the salvation of the south. You're just hiding out here until the whole thing blows over."

Several scathing responses leaped to mind. Rin bit them back.

The trouble was that he was right. The Southern Coalition had been too passive, too slow to initiate the wider campaign the rest of the country clearly needed, and she hated it.

The coalition leadership's priority at Ruijin was still sheer survival, which meant ensconcing themselves in the mountains and biding their time while Vaisra's Republic battled for control of the north. But they were barely even surviving. This wouldn't last forever. Ruijin kept them safe for now, for the same reasons it was slowly becoming their tomb.

Not if Rin got her way. Not if they sent every soldier in their army south.

"That's about to change." She jammed her hiking pole into the rocky path and hauled herself up a steep incline. "You'll see."

"You're lost," Souji accused.

"I'm not lost."

She was helplessly lost. She knew they were close, but she had no idea where to go from here. Three months and dozens of expeditions later, Rin still couldn't find the precise entrance to Ruijin. It was a hideout designed to stay invisible. She had to send an intricate flare spiraling high into the air and wait until two sentries emerged from the undergrowth to guide them onto a path that, previously invisible, now seemed obvious. Rin followed along, ignoring Souji's smirk.

Half an hour's hike later, the camp emerged from the trees like an optical illusion; everything was camouflaged so artfully that Rin sometimes thought if she blinked, it might all disappear.

Just past the wall of bamboo stakes surrounding the camp, an excited crowd had gathered around something on the ground.

"What's this about?" Rin asked the closest sentry.

"They finally killed that tiger," he told her.

"Really?"

"Found the corpse this morning. We're going to skin it, but nobody can agree on who gets the pelt."

The tiger had been plaguing the camp since before Rin's troops had left for Khudla. Its growling haunted the soldiers on patrol duty. Dried fish kept disappearing nightly from the food stores. After the tiger dragged an infant out of its tent and left its mauled, half-eaten body by the creek, the Monkey Warlord had ordered a hunting expedition. But the hunters came back empty-handed and exhausted, limbs scratched up by thorns.

"How'd they manage it?" Kitay asked.

"We poisoned a horse," said the sentry. "It was already dying from a peptic ulcer, else we wouldn't have spared the animal. Injected opium and strychnine into the carcass and left it out for the tiger to find. We found the bastard this morning. Stiff as a board."

"You see," Rin told Kitay. "It's a good plan."

"This has nothing to do with your plan."

"Opium kills tigers. Literal and metaphorical."

"It's lost this country two wars," he said. "I don't mean to call you stupid, because I love you, but that plan is so stupid."

"We have the arable land! Moag's happy to buy it up; if we just planted it in a few regions we'd get all the silver we need—"

"And an army full of addicts. Let's not kid ourselves, Rin. Is that what you want?"

Rin opened her mouth to respond, but something over Kitay's shoulder caught her eye.

A tall man stood a little way off from the crowd, arms crossed as he watched her. Waiting. He was Du Zhuden—the right-hand man of the bandit leader Ma Lien. He raised an eyebrow when he saw her glancing his way, and she nodded in response. He jerked his head toward the forest, turned, and disappeared into the trees.

Rin touched Kitay on the arm. "I'll be back."

He'd seen Zhuden, too. He sighed. "You're still going through with this?"

"I don't see any other option."

He was quiet for a moment. "Me neither," he said at last. "But be careful. The monkey's men are watching."

Rin met Zhuden at their usual spot—a crooked rowan tree a mile outside the camp, at the juncture of a small creek burbling just loudly enough to conceal their voices from eavesdroppers.

"You found Yang Souji?" Zhuden's eyes darted warily around as he spoke. The Monkey Warlord had spies everywhere in Ruijin; Rin would not have been surprised if someone had followed her out of camp.

She nodded. "Took a little convincing, but he's here."

"What's he like?"

"Arrogant. Annoying." She grimaced, thinking of Souji's smug, leering grin.

"So he's just like you?"

"Very funny," she drawled. "He's competent, though. Knows the terrain well. Has strong local contacts—he might be better keyed into the intelligence network here than we are. And he comes with five hundred experienced soldiers. They'd die for him."

"Well done," Zhuden said. "We'll just have to make sure they start dying for you."

Rin shot him a grin.

Zhuden wasn't native to Monkey Province. He was a war orphan from Rat Province who had wound up in Ma Lien's band from the usual combination of homelessness, desperation, and a callous willingness to do whatever it took to get ahead. Most importantly, unlike the rest of the southern leadership, he wasn't a mere survivalist.

He, too, thought they were dying slowly in Ruijin. He wanted to expand farther south. And, like Rin, he'd decided on drastic measures to shake things up.

"How's Ma Lien doing?" Rin asked.

"Getting worse," Zhuden said. "Honestly, he might just croak on his own, given time, but we still don't want to risk the off chance that he gets better. You'll want to act soon." He passed her a single vial filled with a viscous piss-yellow fluid. "Careful you don't break that."

She pinched it by the neck and gingerly dropped it into her front pocket. "Did you extract this yourself?"

"Yep. Can't say I enjoyed it."

She patted her pocket. "Thank you."

"Are you going now?" he asked.

"Tonight," she said. "I'm due to meet with Gurubai right now. I'll try one last time to convince him."

They both knew that meeting would come to nothing. She'd been having the same argument with the Monkey Warlord for weeks. She wanted to march out of Ruijin. He wanted to remain in the mountains, and his allies in the leadership of the Southern Coalition agreed. They outnumbered her three votes to one.

Rin was about to flip those numbers.

But not just yet. No need to act in haste; she'd show her hand too early. One thing at a time. She'd give the Monkey Warlord one last chance first, make him think she'd come back cooperative and complacent. She had learned, since her days at Sinegard, to rein in her impulses. The best plans were a secret until their execution. The hidden knife cut the deepest.

"Welcome back," said the Monkey Warlord.

Liu Gurubai had set up his headquarters in one of the few old architectural beauties in Ruijin that still stood, a square stone temple with three walls eaten over by moss. He'd chosen it for security, not comfort. The insides were sparsely furnished, with only a stove dug into the corner wall, two rugs, and a simple council table in the center of the cold, drafty room.

Rin and Kitay sat down across him, resembling two students arriving at their tutor's home for a lesson.

"I brought presents," said Rin.

"Oh, I saw," Gurubai said. "Couldn't help but leave a little mark, could you?"

"I thought they should know who's commanding them."

"Well, I assumed Souji would." Gurubai raised an eyebrow. "Unless you were planning on decapitating him?"

Rin gave him a thin smile and wished fervently she could force a flaming fist down his throat.

When she'd hurtled out of Arlong on a Black Lily ship with her hand a bloody mess, she'd thought that the Monkey Warlord might be different from the series of horrible men she'd hitherto thrown in her lot with. That he'd keep his promises. That he'd treat her not as a weapon but as an ally. That he'd put her in charge.

She'd been so wrong.

She'd underestimated Gurubai. He was brilliant; he'd been the sole survivor of Vaisra's violent purge at Arlong for a reason. He understood power politics in a way she never would, because he'd spent his entire life practicing it. Gurubai understood what made men pledge their support, what won him trust and love. He was used now, after two decades, to calling all the shots. And he did not relinquish power.

"I thought we had agreed," she said lightly, "if the Khudla experiment worked out—"

"Oh, it worked out. You can keep that contingent. Officers Shen and Lin were quite happy with your performance."

"I don't want a single contingent, I want the army."

"Let's not pretend you could handle that."

"I just liberated an entire village with minimal casualties—"

"Your supreme talent for burning things down does not qualify you to be a commander." Gurubai drew out the last syllable of each word as if she wouldn't have understood him otherwise. "You're still learning to manage communication and logistics. Don't rush it, child. Give yourself the space to learn. This isn't Sinegard, where we throw children into war with no preparation. We'll find you something better to do in time."

The condescension in his voice made her fist curl. Her eyes focused on the veins in his neck. They protruded so visibly; it would be so easy to slice them open.

If only. Speerly or no, if she hurt Liu Gurubai, she wouldn't make it out of Ruijin alive.

Kitay kicked her lightly under the table. *Don't.*

She grimaced at him. *I know.*

If Rin was a Speerly outsider and Kitay a Sinegardian elite, then the Monkey Warlord was the true product of the south, a rough-hewn man with shoulders broadened from years of labor, whose gleaming, intelligent eyes were set deep in a face lined like the forest.

Rin had left the south at the first chance she got. The Monkey Warlord had fought and suffered in the south his entire life. He'd watched his grandmother begging for rice in the streets during the Lunar New Year. He'd walked miles to tend water buffalo for a single copper a day. He'd fought in the ragged provincial brigades that rallied to the Trifecta's cause during the Second Poppy War. He hadn't become a warlord through inheritance or sheer ambition; he'd simply moved slowly up through the line of succession as the soldiers around him died. He'd been drafted into an army at thirteen years old for the promise of a single silver coin a month, and he'd stayed in the army for the rest of his life.

His younger brothers had both died fighting the Federation. His clan, once a sprawling village family, had withered away from opium addiction. He'd survived the worst of the past century, and so survival became his greatest skill. He'd become a soldier out of necessity, and that made him a leader whose legitimacy was nigh unquestionable.

Most importantly, he *belonged.* These mountains were part of his blood. Anyone could see it in the tired way he carried his shoulders, the hard glint in his eyes.

Rin may have been a figurehead of power, but Liu Gurubai symbolized the very identity of the south. If she hurt him, Monkey Province would tear her to pieces.

So for now, she compromised.

"I hear there have been developments in the north." She

changed the subject, forcing her tone to stay neutral. "Anything you want to show me?"

"Several updates." If Gurubai was surprised by her sudden acquiescence, he didn't show it. He slid a sheaf of letters across the table. "Your friend wrote back. These arrived yesterday."

Rin snatched up the first page and started poring hungrily down the lines, passing the pages to Kitay once she was done. News from the north always trickled in by little bursts—weeks passed with nothing, and then they received sudden gluts of information. The Southern Coalition had only a handful of spies in the Republic, and most of them were Moag's girls; the few pale-skinned Black Lilies who had been shipped to Arlong with carefully disguised accents to work in teahouses and gambling dens.

Venka had gone north, too. With her pale, pretty face and flawless Sinegardian diction, she blended in perfectly among the aristocrats of the formal capital. At first Rin had been worried she'd be recognized—she was the missing daughter of the former finance minister; she couldn't be more high-profile—but based on Venka's reports, she'd completely transformed with only a wig and several gobs of cosmetics.

No one pays much attention to my face, Venka had written shortly after she arrived. *The dolls of Sinegard, it turns out, are shockingly interchangeable.*

Her report now contained nothing surprising. *Vaisra's still battling it out in the north. Warlords and their successors dropping dead like flies. They can't hold out for long, they're overstretched. Vaisra's turned the siege cities into death zones. It'll all be over soon.*

That wasn't news, only a slow intensification of what they'd known for weeks. Vaisra's Hesperians were ravaging the countryside in their dirigibles, leaving craters and bombed-out hellscapes in their wake.

"Any mention of a southern turn?" Rin asked Gurubai.

"None yet. What you're holding is everything we have."

"Then we're being ignored," she said.

"We're getting *lucky*," Kitay amended. "It's only a matter of time."

The Dragon Warlord Yin Vaisra's great democracy, the one he'd sacked cities and turned the Murui crimson for, had never come into existence. He'd never meant it to. Days after he defeated the Imperial Navy at Arlong, he'd assassinated the Boar Warlord and Rooster Warlord, and then declared himself the sole President of the Nikara Republic.

But he didn't yet have a country to rule. Many former Militia officers, not least of whom included the Empress's former favorite soldier, General Jun Loran, had escaped the purge at Arlong and fled north to Tiger Province. Now the combined forces of the Militia's remnants were almost proving to be a challenge for the Hesperians.

Almost. With each new report that reached Ruijin, the Republic appeared to have extended its reach farther and farther north. That meant Rin was sitting on borrowed time. The Southern Coalition was only one rebellion among many. For the time being Vaisra had his hands tied up with Jun's insurgency, not to mention a country chock-full of bandit gangs that had sprung up in local power vacuums immediately after the war's end. But he wouldn't stay busy for long. Jun couldn't hope to beat Vaisra's forces, not with Hesperian dirigibles at Vaisra's back. Not when thousands of Hesperian soldiers with arquebuses were pumping bullets into Jun's armies.

Rin was grateful that Jun had bought them such a long reprieve. But sooner or later, Vaisra would turn his attention to the south. He'd have to, so long as Rin was alive. A reckoning was inevitable. And when it came, she wanted to be on the offensive.

"You know my feelings on this," she told Gurubai.

"Yes, Runin, I do." He regarded her like an exhausted parent might a troublesome child. "And again, I'm telling you—"

"We're *dying* up here. If we don't take the offensive now, then Nezha will. We need to catch him by surprise, and right now is—"

"I'm not the only one you have to convince. *None* of the Southern Coalition want to overextend themselves. These mountains are their home. And when the wolves come, you protect what's behind your walls."

"It's only home for some of you."

He shrugged. "You're free to leave whenever you like."

He could make that bluff. He knew she had nowhere else to turn.

Her nostrils flared. "We need to at least discuss this, Gurubai—"

"Then we'll discuss it at council." His tone made it very clear that their audience was finished. "You can make your case again to the others, if you're so inclined. Although to be quite honest, it's become a bit repetitive."

"I'm going to keep saying it until someone listens," Rin snapped.

"Whatever you like," Gurubai said. "You do so love to be difficult."

Kitay kicked her beneath the table again just as they stood up to leave.

"I know," Rin muttered. "I *know*."

Some little part of her heart sank as she walked out the door. She wished Gurubai had said yes. She was trying to cooperate. She hated to be the lone contrarian; she *did* want to work with the coalition. This all would have been so much easier if he'd said yes.

But if he wasn't going to budge, then she'd have to force his hand.

Dinner was a rapid affair. Rin and Kitay emptied their bowls in seconds. Not because they were hungry—it was just easier to ignore the mold sprouting on the greens and the tiny maggots squirming around the rice if they wolfed it down without thinking. The fare in the mess halls became worse and worse every time she returned to Ruijin, and the cooks had gone from keeping insects out of the vats to encouraging them on the grounds that the carcasses contained badly needed nutrients. Ant porridge was now a dish Rin ate regularly, though she always had to suppress her gag reflex before she could take the first bite.

The only staple that hadn't started to rot was shanyu root—the starchy white yam that stuck like glue in her throat every time she swallowed. Shanyu tubers, having proved remarkably resistant to frost, grew everywhere on the mountainside. For a time Rin had been quite fond of them; they were filling, easy to steam, and had the slightly sweet taste of fresh-baked bread.

That was months ago. She'd since grown so sick of the taste of raw shanyu, dried shanyu, steamed shanyu, and mashed shanyu that the smell was enough to induce nausea. Still, it was the only fresh food with nutrients she could get her hands on. She forced it down as well.

When she was finished, she stood up and prepared to go pay a visit to the bandit chief Ma Lien.

Kitay moved to follow, but she shook her head. "I can do this alone. You don't need to see this."

He didn't argue the point. She knew he didn't want to come. "Fine. You've got the medicine?"

"In my front pocket."

"And you're *sure* that—"

"Please don't." She cut him off. "We've had this debate a thousand times. Can you think of a better option?"

He sighed. "Just do it quickly. Don't linger."

"Why on earth would I linger?"

"*Rin.*"

"All right." She clapped him on the shoulder and strode toward the forest.

Ma Lien's quarters were built into the cave wall near Ruijin's northern perimeter. It should have been near impossible for Rin to get this close to his private residence without at least three blades at her neck, but in recent days Ma Lien's guards had reevaluated their loyalties. When they saw Rin approach, they nodded silently and let her pass through. None of them would meet her eyes.

Ma Lien's wife and daughter sat outside the cave entrance. They stood up when they saw her, their eyes wide with fear and desperation.

They already know, Rin thought. They'd heard the whispers. Or someone in the ranks—perhaps even Zhuden—had already told them what was about to happen in an effort to save their lives.

"You shouldn't be here," she said.

Ma Lien's wife seized Rin's wrist just as she entered the cave.

"Please," she begged. "Don't."

"Necessity calls." Rin shrugged her hand away. "Don't try to stop me."

"You can spare him, he'll do what you say, you don't have to—"

"He won't," Rin said. "And I do. I hope you've said goodbye."

They knew what would happen next. Ma Lien's men knew. And Rin suspected that, on some level, the Monkey Warlord had to know, too. He might even sanction it. She would, if she were in his position. What did you do when one of your generals kept agitating to fight a war you knew you couldn't win?

You cut your losses.

The cave smelled like sick, a stomach-turning mix of fumes from bitter herbal medicines and the odor of stale vomit. Ma Lien had been suffering from the bloody lung fever since before she'd left for Khudla. The timing was perfect. She'd struck a deal with Zhuden the morning she marched out—if Ma Lien was still ill by the time she returned, and the odds of his recovery seemed slim, then they would seize their chance.

Still, she hadn't expected Ma Lien to disintegrate so quickly. He lay shriveled and desiccated against his sheets. He seemed to have shrunk to half his body weight. Crusted blood lined the edges of his lips. Every time he breathed, an awful rattle echoed through the cave.

Ma Lien was already half-gone. From the looks of it, what Rin was about to do couldn't even properly be called murder. She was only hastening the inevitable.

"Hello, General." She perched herself by the edge of his bed.

His eyes cracked open at the sound of her voice.

She'd been told the illness had taken his vocal cords. *He bleeds when he tries to speak*, Zhuden had said. *And if he gets agitated, he starts choking on it.* She felt a little thrill at the thought. He couldn't mock her, couldn't curse at her, couldn't scream for help. She could taunt him as much as she liked. And all he could do was lie there and listen.

She should have just done the job and left. The smarter, pragmatic part of her was screaming at her to go—it was a risk to stay for so long, to speak where Gurubai's spies might hear her.

But this encounter had been a long time coming. She wanted him to know every reason why he had to die. She wanted to relish this moment. She'd earned this.

She recalled vividly the way he'd shouted her down when she first suggested deploying troops to Rooster Province. He'd called her a savage, sentimental, dirt-skinned, warmongering bitch. He'd railed at Gurubai for letting a little girl into the war council in the first place. He'd suggested she'd be better off dead with the rest of her kind.

He probably didn't remember saying that. Ma Lien was one of those loud, garrulous types. Always tossing insults out like the wind. Always assuming that his bodily strength and the loyalty of his men would insulate him from resentment.

"Do you remember what you said when I first asked for command?" Rin asked.

Spit bubbled by the side of Ma Lien's mouth. She picked a bloodstained bed rag up from the floor and gently rubbed it away.

"You said I was a dumb bitch with no command experience and a genetic lack of rationality." She chuckled. "Your words. You said I was an empty-headed little fool with more power than I knew what to do with. You said I should know my place. You said Speerlies weren't meant to make decisions but to obey."

Ma Lien mouthed something incoherent. She smoothed tendrils of his hair back from his mouth. He was sweating so hard he looked like he'd been drenched in oil. Poor man.

"I didn't come south to be someone's pet again," she said. "You should have understood that about me."

She'd laid her loyalty at the feet of two masters before. Each had betrayed her in turn. She'd trusted first Daji and then Vaisra, and they'd both sold her away without blinking. From now on Rin took charge of her own fate.

She reached into her pocket and pulled out the vial.

Fat yellow scorpions infested the forests around Ruijin. The soldiers had learned to ward them away from the camp by burning lavender and setting traps, but they couldn't wander ten feet into the trees without stumbling upon a nest. And a single nest was all it took to extract a vial's worth of venom.

"I'm not sorry for this," she said. "You shouldn't have gotten in my way."

She tipped the vial toward Ma Lien's mouth. He thrashed, trying to cough the poison out, but she seized his jaw and forced it shut, pinching his nose between her fingers until the liquid seeped down into his throat. After a minute he stopped resisting. She let go.

"You're not going to die immediately," she said. "Scorpion venom paralyzes. Locks up all your muscles."

She dabbed saliva and venom off his chin with the bed rag. "In a while, it'll feel a little hard to breathe. You'll try to call for help, but you'll find your jaw won't move. I'm sure your wife will come in to check on you, but she knows there's nothing she can do. She knows what I'm doing right now. She's probably imagining it all in her head. But maybe she'll love you enough to see you through to the end. Or, if she really loves you, she'll slit your throat."

She stood up. An odd thrill rushed through her head. Her knees shook. She felt giddy, shot through with a bizarre and unexpected energy.

This wasn't her first kill. But this was her first deliberate, premeditated murder. This was the first person she'd killed not out of desperation but with cool, malicious intent.

It felt—

It felt *good*.

She didn't need her pipe to show this to Altan; she heard his laughter as loudly as if he were standing right next to her. She felt divine. She felt like she could leap across mountains if she wanted to. Her hand couldn't stop shaking. The vial dropped from her fingers and shattered against the floor.

Heart pounding, blood pumping with a euphoria that confused her, she left the cave.

"I want to lead two contingents into Rooster Province," Rin said. "Souji says they've clustered there because the flat terrain is easier to navigate. We've been shoring up for a fight on the wrong front. They're not going to push up into the mountains here because they don't need to. They're just going to expand farther south."

The leadership of the Southern Coalition sat assembled around a table in the Monkey Warlord's headquarters. Gurubai, the natural leader, sat at the front. Liu Dai, a former county official and Gurubai's longtime ally, sat on his right. Zhuden was seated to Liu Dai's right as Ma Lien's substitute, but an empty chair remained at the table out of respect. Souji sat in the back left corner, arms crossed, smirking, as if he'd already called this charade for what it was.

"If we strike quickly," Rin continued, "that is, if we take the main nodes before they've gotten the chance to regroup, we could end this whole thing in one drive."

"Just this morning you wanted to turn north to face Vaisra," Gurubai said. "Now you want to drive south. You can't fight a war on two fronts, Rin. Which is it?"

"We've got to go south *just so* we can get the strength to muster a defense against the Hesperians," Rin said. "If we win the south, we get warm bodies. Food stores. Access to river routes, armories, and who knows what else we've been relinquishing to the Mugenese. Our armies will swell by thousands, and we'll have the supply lines to support them. But if we don't clear out the Mugenese first, then we'll be trapped inside the mountains—"

"We're *safe* inside the mountains," Liu Dai interrupted. "No one has invaded Ruijin in centuries, the terrain is too hostile—"

"There's no food here," Rin said. "The wells are drying up. This won't last forever."

"We understand that," Gurubai said. "But you're asking too much of this army. Half these boys only picked up a sword for the first time two months ago. You need to give them time."

"Vaisra won't give them time," Rin snapped. "The moment he's done with Jun, he will bury us."

She'd already lost them. She could tell from their bored, skeptical expressions. She knew this was pointless; this was just another iteration of the same argument they'd rehashed a dozen times now. They were at a stalemate—she had the fire, but they had everything else. And they were seasoned, war-hardened men who, despite everything they publicly proclaimed, couldn't be less happy about sharing power with a girl half their age.

Rin knew that. She was just constitutionally unable to keep silent.

"Rooster Province is finished," Gurubai said. "The Mugenese have overrun the place like ants. Our strategy now should be survival. We can *keep* the Monkey Province. They cannot survive in the mountains. Don't throw this away, Rin."

He spoke like he'd come to this conclusion long ago. A sudden suspicion struck Rin.

"You knew," she said. "You knew they'd taken Rooster Province."

Gurubai exchanged a glance with Liu Dai. "Runin . . ."

"You've known that all along." Her voice rose in pitch. Her cheeks were burning. This wasn't just his standard patronization, this was appalling condescension. *The fucking nerve.* "You knew this entire time and you didn't tell me."

"It wouldn't have made a difference—"

"Did they all know?" She gestured around the room. Little sparks of flame burst forth from her fingers; she couldn't help it. The coalition members cringed back, but that gave her no pleasure. She was far too embarrassed.

What else hadn't they told her?

Gurubai cleared his throat. "Given your impulses, we didn't think it prudent—"

"Fuck you!" she exclaimed. "I'm a member of this council, I've been winning your battles for you, *I deserve to*—"

"The fact remains that you are impulsive and reckless, as evidenced by your repeated demands for command—"

"I deserve full command! That's what I was promised!"

Gurubai sighed. "We are not discussing this again."

"Look." She slammed her hand on the table. "If none of you are willing to make the first move, then just send me. Give me two thousand troops. Just twice the number I took to Khudla. That'll be enough."

"You and I both know why that's not possible."

"But that's our only chance at staying alive—"

"Is it?" Gurubai asked. "Do you really believe that we can't survive in the mountains? Or do you just want your chance to go after Yin Nezha?"

She could have slapped him. But she wasn't stupid enough to take the bait.

"The Yins will not let us live free in this country," she said. She knew how Vaisra operated. He identified his threats—past, current, and potential—and patiently isolated, captured, and destroyed them. He didn't forgive past wrongs. He never failed to wrap up loose ends. And Rin, once his most precious weapon, was now his biggest loose end. "The Republic doesn't want to split territory, they want to wipe us off the map. So pardon me for thinking it might be a good idea to strike first."

"Vaisra is not coming for us." The Monkey Warlord stood up. "He's coming for *you*."

The implication of that sat heavy in the air between them.

The door opened. All hands in the room twitched toward swords. A camp aide stepped in, breathless. "Sir—"

"Not now," snapped the Monkey Warlord.

"No, sir—" The aide swallowed. "Sir, Ma Lien's passed away."

Rin exhaled slowly. There it was.

Gurubai stared at the aide, speechless.

Rin spoke up before anyone else could. "So there's a vacancy."

Liu Dai looked appalled. "Have some respect."

She ignored that. "There's a vacancy, and I'm the most qualified person to fill it."

"You're hardly in the chain of command," Gurubai said.

She rolled her eyes. "The chain of command matters for real armies, not bandit camps squatting in the mountains hoping dirigibles won't see us when they fly overhead."

"Those men won't obey you," Gurubai said. "They hardly know you—"

For the first time Zhuden spoke. "We're with the girl."

Gurubai trailed off, staring at Zhuden in disbelief.

Rin suppressed a snicker.

"She's right," Zhuden said. "We're dying up here. We need to march while we've got fight left in us. And if you won't lead us, we're going with her."

"You don't control the entire army," Gurubai said. "You'll be fifteen hundred men at the most."

"Two thousand," Souji said.

Rin shot him a startled look.

Souji shrugged. "The Iron Wolves are going south, too. Been itching for that fight for a while."

"You said you didn't care about the Southern Coalition," Rin said.

"I said I didn't care about the rest of the Empire," Souji said. "This is different. Those are my people. And from what I've seen, you're the only one with balls enough to go after them instead of sitting here, waiting to die."

Rin could have shrieked with laughter. She looked around the table, chin out, daring anyone to object. Liu Dai shifted in his seat. Souji winked at her. Gurubai, utterly defeated, said nothing.

She could tell he knew what she had done. It was no secret. She'd admit it out loud if he asked. But he couldn't prove it, and nobody would want to believe him. The hearts of at least a third of his men had turned against him.

This wasn't news. This only made official whispers that had been circulating for a long, long time.

Zhuden nodded to her. "Your move, General Fang."

She liked the sound of those words so much she couldn't help but grin.

"Well, that's settled." She glanced around the table. "I'm taking the Third Division and the Iron Wolves to Rooster Province. We march at dawn."

CHAPTER 4

"I want fresh troops when we get to the Beehive," Rin said. "If we take the pace down to four-fifths our usual marching speed, we can still get there in twelve days. We'll take detours here and here to avoid known Mugenese outposts. It adds distance, but I'd prefer to keep the element of surprise as long as we can. It'll cut down their preparation time."

She spoke with more confidence than she felt. She thought her voice sounded inordinately high and squeaky, though she could barely hear it, her blood was pumping so hard in her ears. Now that she'd finally gotten what she wanted, her giddiness had died away, replaced by a frightful mix of exhaustion and nerves.

Night had fallen on their first day of marching out of Ruijin. They'd stopped to make camp in the forest. A circle of soldiers—Kitay, Zhuden, Souji, and a smattering of officers—sat clustered in Rin's tent, watching with rapt attention as she drew thick, inky lines across the maps before them.

Her hand kept shaking, scattering droplets across the parchment. It was so hard to write with her left hand. She felt as if she were taking an exam she hadn't studied for. She should have been relishing this moment, but she couldn't shake the feeling that she was a fraud.

You are *a fraud.* She had never led a proper campaign by herself before. Her brief stints as the commander of the Cike had always ended in disaster. She didn't know how to manage logistics on this scale. And worst of all, she was currently describing an attack strategy that she wasn't at all sure would work.

Altan's laughter echoed in her mind.

Little fool, he said. *Finally got yourself an army, and now you don't know what to do with it.*

She blinked and forced his specter to disappear.

"If all goes according to plan," she continued, "Leiyang will be ours by the next moon."

Leiyang was the biggest township in northern Rooster Province. She'd passed through there only once in her life, nearly five years ago when she'd made the long caravan trip north to start school at Sinegard. It was a central trading hub connected to dozens of smaller villages by two creeks and several wide roads so old they'd been paved in the days of the Red Emperor. Compared to any northern capital it was a shoddy, run-down market in the outskirts of nowhere, but back then Rin had found it the busiest market town she'd ever seen.

Kitay had dubbed the network around Leiyang the Beehive. Mugenese troops exercised some control over all villages in northern Rooster Province, but based on their troops' patrol and travel patterns, Leiyang was the central node.

Something important lay in that township. Kitay thought it was likely a high-ranking general who, after his homeland's demise, continued to wield regional authority. Or, as Rin feared, it was a weapons base that they didn't know about. Leiyang could be sitting on cans of yellow gas. They had no way of knowing.

That was the root of their problem. Rin's intelligence on Leiyang was terrible. She'd updated her maps with Souji's detailed descriptions of the surrounding terrain, but everything else he knew had been outdated for months. A handful of Iron Wolves were escaped survivors from Leiyang, but their reports of Mugenese troop presence varied wildly. They'd been the opposite of helpful.

Survivors almost always gave them bad information—either their terror made them exaggerate the threat, or they downplayed it in hopes they could entice a rescue force to help their village.

Rin had sent scouts ahead, but those scouts would have to be exceedingly cautious. Anything that tipped the Mugenese off to an impending ambush would spell disaster. That meant she could speculate as much as they liked, but she wouldn't know the full power of the fighting force at Leiyang until just before the battle began.

"How are you going to draw them out from behind the gates?" Zhuden asked. "We don't want to hit too close to civilians."

Well, that's obvious. Rin couldn't tell if he was being condescending or simply careful. It had suddenly become very hard not to read everything like a challenge to her authority.

"We'll give as much advance warning as we can without betraying our location. Souji has some local connections. But really we'll just have to adapt to contingencies," she added, knowing full well that was a bunch of babble that meant nothing.

She didn't have a better answer. Zhuden's question got to the critical strategic puzzle that, despite hours spent racking her brains with Kitay, she still hadn't cracked.

The problem was that the Mugenese troops near Leiyang were not clustered in one area, where a well-coordinated ambush could have herded them into a singular burning ground, but spread out over an entire village network.

Rin needed to figure out a way to draw the Mugenese out onto an open battlefield. In Khudla it had been easy to minimize civilian casualties—the majority of Mugenese troops had lived in camps separate from the village itself. But all the Iron Wolves she'd questioned had reported that the Mugenese at Leiyang had integrated fully into the township. They'd formed some strange occupational system of predatory symbiosis. That made distinguishing targets from innocents much, much harder.

"We can't make those calls now without more intelligence," Rin said. "Our priority for now is to get as close as we can to

Leiyang without any patrols seeing us coming. We don't want a citywide hostage situation." She glanced up. "Everyone clear?"

They nodded.

"Good," she said. "Zhuden, post some men to first watch."

"Yes, General." Zhuden stood up.

The other officers filed out behind him. But Souji remained cross-legged on the floor, leaning back against his outstretched arms. A single stalk of grain hung annoyingly out the side of his mouth like a judgmental, wagging finger.

Rin shot him a wary look. "Is something the matter?"

"Your plans are all wrong," he said.

"Excuse me?"

"Sorry, should have spoken up earlier. Just didn't want you to lose face."

She scowled. "If you're here just to whine—"

"No, listen." Souji straightened up, leaned forward, and tapped his finger at the little star that indicated Leiyang on the map. "For starters, you can't take your army through these back roads. They'll have sentries posted across every path, not just the main roads, and you *know* you don't have the numbers to survive a prepared defense."

"There's no other route except those back roads," Kitay said.

"Well, you're just not being very creative, then."

Irritation flickered across Kitay's face. "You can't drag supply carts through thick forest, there's no way—"

"Do you two just refuse to listen to anyone who's got advice to offer?" Souji spat the grain stalk out of his mouth. It landed on the map, smudging Rin's carefully drawn routes. "I'm just trying to help, you know."

"And we're Sinegard-trained strategists who know what we're doing," Rin snapped. "So if you haven't got anything more helpful to say than 'your plans are all wrong,' then—"

"You know that the Monkey Warlord wants you to fail, right?" Souji interrupted.

"Excuse me?"

"The Southern Coalition don't like you at all. Gurubai, Liu Dai, the whole cohort. They talk about you every time you're not in the room. Fuck, I'd just *gotten* there, and they were already trying to turn me against you. It's a boys' club, Princess, and you're the odd one out."

Rin kept her voice carefully neutral. "And what did they say about me?"

"That you're a little fool who thinks three years at Sinegard and a few months in the Militia can replace decades in the field," Souji said calmly. "That you wouldn't be worth keeping around if it weren't for your nice little party trick. And that you'll probably die at Leiyang because you're too stupid to know what you're up against, but then they'll at least be rid of one nuisance."

Rin couldn't stop the heat rising in her cheeks. "That's nothing new."

"Look, Speerly." Souji leaned forward. "I'm on your side. But Gurubai's right about some things. You *don't* know how to command, and you *are* inexperienced, especially in this kind of warfare. But I know how to fight these battles. And if my men are being dragged into them, then you're going to fucking listen."

"You're not giving me orders," Rin said.

"If you go in there according to those plans, then you'll die."

"Look, asshole—"

"Hold on." Kitay held up a hand. "Rin, just—listen to him for a second."

"But he's—"

"He's been here longer than we have. If he's got information, we need to hear it." Kitay nodded to Souji. "Go on."

"Thank you." Souji cleared his throat like a master about to deliver a lecture. "You're both going about all this wrong. You can't keep fighting like this is a war between two proper armies—open field combat, and all that. This isn't the same. This is about liberation, and liberation means small-scale tactics and deception."

"And those worked so well for you in Khudla," Rin muttered.

"Got overwhelmed at Khudla," Souji admitted. "Like I said.

We couldn't win on the battlefield. We didn't have the numbers, and we should have resorted to smaller tactics. You'd better learn from my mistakes."

"So what are you proposing?" Rin's voice had lost its edge. She was listening now.

"Go through the forest," Souji said. "I'll get your precious supply carts through. There are hidden pathways all over that area and I have men who can find them. Then establish contact with Leiyang's resistance leadership before you move in. Right now you don't have the numbers."

"Numbers?" Rin repeated. "I can—"

"You can burn a whole squadron down yourself, Speerly, I'm well aware. But you're only useful in your radius, and your radius by definition can't be too close to civilians. You need people to run interference. Keep the Mugenese off the very people you're trying to save. Right now you don't have the numbers for that, which is why I suspect you keep wincing every time you glance at your maps."

Souji, Rin realized reluctantly, was extraordinarily astute.

"And you've got a magic fix for that?" she asked.

"It's not magic. I've been to those villages. They've got underground resistance bands. Strong men, willing to fight. They just need someone to push them over the edge."

"You're talking a handful of peasants with pitchforks," Kitay said.

"I'm talking an extra hundred men wherever we go."

"Bullshit," Rin said.

"I'm from this region," Souji said. "I have contacts. I can win Leiyang for you, if you'll both just trust me. Can you manage that?"

He extended his hand toward her.

Rin and Kitay exchanged a doubtful glance.

"This isn't a trap," Souji said, exasperated. "Come on, you two. I'm just as eager to go home as you are."

Rin paused, then reached out to grasp his hand.

The tent flap swung open the moment their palms touched. A sentry stepped inside. "Mugenese patrol," he said breathlessly. "Two miles out."

"Everyone hide," Souji said. "There's tree cover for half a mile on both sides, have the men pack up and go."

"No—what?" Rin scrambled to her feet, fumbling to gather up the maps. "I'm the one giving orders here—"

He shot her an exasperated look. "So order them to hide."

"Fuck that," she said. "We fight."

The Mugenese had a single patrol group. They had an army. How was this a debate?

But before she could shout the order, Souji stuck his head out the tent flap, jammed two fingers in his mouth, and whistled thrice in succession so loudly Rin felt like knives had been driven through her ears.

The response astonished her. At once, the Iron Wolves got up and began packing their gear. In under two minutes they had rolled up their tents, bagged up their equipment, and disappeared completely from the campsite into the forest. They left no trace behind—their campfires were leveled, their litter cleaned. They'd even filled in the holes their tent pegs made in the dirt. No casual observer would ever guess this had once been a campsite.

Rin didn't know if she was furious or impressed.

"Still going to fight?" Souji inquired.

"You little shit."

"Better come with."

"Please, I've got a god—"

"And all it takes is one arrow to shut you up, Princess. No one's covering for you now. I'd follow along."

Cheeks flaming, Rin ordered Zhuden's men to clear their campsites and retreat into the trees.

They ran, pushing through branches that left thousands of tiny cuts in their exposed skin, before they stopped and hoisted themselves up into the trees. Rin had never felt so humiliated as she crouched, perched beside Souji, peeking through the leaves to track the incoming patrol.

Was Souji's plan to just wait the Mugenese out? He couldn't possibly intend to attack—it'd be suicide. This didn't check any of the prerequisites for an ambush they'd been hardwired for in Strategy class—they didn't have fixed artillery stations, they didn't have clear lines of communication or signal visibility between the ranks. By retreating into the forest they'd only scattered and disorganized their numbers, while Rin was now trapped in a fighting zone where her flames would easily grow out of control.

Several minutes later Rin saw the Mugenese patrol moving down the main road.

"We could have taken them in the clearing," she hissed at Souji. "Why—"

He clamped a hand over her mouth. *"Look."*

The patrol came thundering into clear view. Rin counted about twenty of them. They rode on sleek warhorses, no doubt fed with grain stolen from starving villagers, moving slowly as they examined the abandoned campsite.

"Come on," Souji muttered. "Move along."

No way, Rin thought. Her men were efficient, but not that efficient. Ten minutes wasn't enough to evacuate a campsite without leaving a single trace behind.

Sure enough, it took only a minute before the Mugenese captain shouted something and pointed at the ground. Rin didn't know what he'd seen—a footprint, a peg hole, a discarded belt—but it didn't matter. They'd been made.

"Now watch." Souji stuck his fingers into his mouth again and whistled, this time twice in succession.

The Iron Wolves loosed a round of arrows into the clearing.

They aimed true. Half the Mugenese patrollers dropped from the horses. The other half bolted and made to run, but another round of arrows hissed through the air, burrowing into throats, temples, mouths, and eyes. The last three patrollers raced farther down the road, only to be felled by a final group of archers stationed nearly a mile from where Rin hid.

"And that's the last of them." Souji dropped from the tree and extended a hand to help her down. "Was that so bad?"

"That was unnecessary." Rin batted Souji's hand away and climbed down herself. Her left arm buckled from the strain; she let go, dropped the last few inches, and nearly fell flat on her bum. Hastily she recovered. "We could have taken them head-on, we didn't have to hide—"

"How many troops do you think they had?" Souji inquired.

"Twenty. Thirty, maybe, I didn't—"

"And how many do you think we shot?"

"Well, all of them, but—"

"And how many casualties do we have?"

"None," she muttered.

"And do the Mugenese back in the Beehive know we're coming?"

"No."

"So there you go," he said smugly. "Tell me that was unnecessary."

She wanted to slap that look off his face. "*Hiding* was unnecessary. We could have just taken them—"

"And what, given them an extra day to muster defenses? The very first thing that Mugenese patrol teams do when they sense a fight coming is send back a designated survivor to report it."

She frowned. "I didn't know that."

"Course you didn't. You would have burned most of them where they stood, fine. But you can't outrun a horse. None of us have steeds faster than what they're riding. You slip up a *single time*, and you've given up all advantage of surprise."

"But that's absurd," she said. "We're not going to keep ourselves concealed all the way until we reach Leiyang."

"Fair enough. But we should *try* to keep our numbers concealed at least until we attack our next targets. Tiny strategic adjustments like this matter. Don't think about absolutes, think about the details. Every day, every *hour* that you can maintain an information asymmetry, you do it. It means the difference between two casualties and twenty."

"Got it," she said, chastened.

She wasn't too stubborn to admit when she'd been wrong. It stung to realize that she *had* been thinking about strategies in terms of absolutes. She'd gotten so used to it—the details had never seemed to matter much when her strategies boiled down to extermination by fire.

Cheeks burning, she brushed the leaves off her pants, and then uttered the words she knew Souji was waiting to hear. "You win, okay? You're right."

He grinned, vindicated. "I've been doing this for years, Princess. You may as well pay attention."

They made camp two miles south of where they'd seen the patrol, under tree cover so thick the leaves would dissipate the smoke from their campfires before it could furl higher into the air. Even so, Rin set strict limits—no more than one fire to every seven men, and all evidence would have to be tamped down and thoroughly concealed with leaves and dirt before they picked up again to march in the morning.

Dinner was measly, baked cornmeal wotou and unseasoned rice gruel. The Monkey Warlord hadn't let Rin take anything but the stalest provision sacks out of Ruijin, arguing that if she failed on this expedition then she at least shouldn't starve Ruijin at the same time. Rin hadn't pressed the point; she didn't want to push her luck.

But the Iron Wolves were eating suspiciously well. Rin didn't know where they'd found the ingredients, but the steam wafting from their bubbling cauldrons smelled *good*. Had they stolen extra rations from Ruijin? She wouldn't put it past Souji; he was enough of an asshole.

"If it's bothering you then just go ask them," Kitay said.

"That's stupid," Rin muttered. "I'm not going to make a fuss—"

But Souji was already walking toward them, carrying stacked bamboo steamers in both hands. His eyes alighted on their rations. His lip curled. "Looks appetizing."

Rin curled her fingers possessively around her wotou. "It's enough."

Souji sat down across from them and set the steamers on the ground. "You haven't learned to forage for yourselves?"

"Of course we can, there's just nothing edible on this stretch—"

"Really?" Souji lifted the steamer lids. "Look. Bamboo shoots. Freshly killed partridges. Cook all this up with a little salt and vinegar, and you have a three-course meal."

"But there's none of that around here," Kitay said.

"Right, we picked it up on the march. There was a bamboo grove right at the base of Ruijin, didn't you see it? Lots of baby saplings. Whenever you see something edible, you put it in your sack. First rule of march, no?"

The smell of partridge meat was making Rin salivate. She eyed the steamers with envy. "And how'd you catch the birds?"

"Simple. You can rig up a trap with next to nothing as long as you've got some cornmeal for bait. We can set some overnight and wake up to crackling partridge wings. I can teach you how."

Rin pointed to something yellow and mushy buried under the bamboo shoots. "What's that?"

"Bajiao bananas."

"Do they taste good?"

"You've never eaten these before?" Souji gave her an incredulous look. "They grow everywhere in these parts."

"We thought they might be poisonous," Kitay admitted. "They gave some men at Ruijin a bad stomachache, so we've stayed clear of them since."

"Ah, no, that's just when they're not ripe. If you can't tell from the color—darkish brown, you see?—you can peel it open and tell from the smell. If it's sour, put it back. None of your men knew about that?"

"None at our camp."

"Incredible," Souji said. "I suppose after a few centuries you start to forget the little things."

Rin pointed to a bowl of what looked like black, crispy, over-size beans. "What's that?"

"Bees," Souji said casually. "They're very tasty when you fry them up. You've just got to make sure you take all the stingers out."

She stared. "I can't tell if you're kidding or not."

"I'm not kidding." He picked one up and showed her the husk. "See? The legs are the best part. They soak up all the oil." He popped it into his mouth and chewed loudly. "Incredible. You want?"

"I'm good," she muttered.

"You're from the south. Thought you could eat anything."

"We never ate bugs in Tikany."

He laughed. "Tikany's hardly the poorest village in the south. Makes sense that you've never known famine."

She had to admit that was true. She'd gone hungry on plenty of nights, both in Tikany and at the Academy in Sinegard, but that was because of food withheld and not the sheer lack of it. Even after the Third Poppy War kicked off in earnest, when villagers across the Empire grew so desperate they resorted to eating wood bark, Rin had been able to rely on at least two square meals from army rations every day.

Of course. When things got bad, soldiers were fed first, and everyone else was left to die. Rin had been living so long on the extractive capabilities of the empire she fought for, she'd never learned to forage for herself.

"That wasn't an insult. Just being frank." Souji held the bowl of bees out toward her. "Want to try?"

They smelled terribly good. Rin's stomach let loose an embarrassingly loud growl.

"Eat up." Souji chuckled. "We've got rations to spare."

∞

They continued their march at dawn, trailing by the edge of the road, always ready to bolt back into the trees at the first signal from the scouts ahead. They quickened their pace slightly from the day before. Rin had wanted to make straight for the Beehive, but Souji had drawn a zigzag pattern on her map instead, creating a circuitous route that took them all around local power bases but avoided the center until the very end.

"But then they'll know we're coming," Rin said. "Isn't the whole point to keep the element of surprise until Leiyang?"

Souji shook his head. "No, they'll know we're out here in five days at most. We can't keep our approach a secret for that much longer, so we may as well get some good hits in when we can."

"Then what is the point of all these measures?"

"Think, Princess. They know we're coming. That's *all* they know. They don't know how many we are. We could be a band of ten. We could be an army of a million. They've got absolutely no clue what to be on the guard for, and the threat of the unknown hamstrings defense preparations. Preserve that."

Of course Rin had learned at Sinegard to strategize accounting for the enemy's state of mind. But she'd always thought of it as a matter of dominant strategies. What, given the circumstances, was their best option? And how should she prepare for their best option? The issues Souji obsessed over—fear, apprehension, anxiety, irrationality—were details she'd never much considered. But now, in this war of uncertainty and unbalanced forces, they seemed paramount.

So whenever the Southern Coalition encountered Mugenese soldiers, they either hid in the trees and watched them march past if they appeared not to have noticed anything, or pulled the same kind of lure tactic the Iron Wolves had used the first day. And whenever they came past occupied hamlets, they employed much the same sort of strategy—cautious baiting accompanied by strikes of limited force, just enough to achieve limited tactical objectives without ever escalating into a real battle.

Over eight days and numerous engagements, Rin witnessed the full range of Souji's favorite tactics. They revolved almost entirely around deception, and they were brilliant. The Iron Wolves were fond of waylaying small groups of Mugenese soldiers, always at night and never twice in the same spot. When the Mugenese returned with larger bands, the guerrillas were long gone. They feigned beggars, farmers, and village drunkards to draw Mugenese attacks. They deliberately created false campsites to agitate Mugenese patrols. Souji's favorite ploy was to send a group of Iron Wolves, all young women, out to fields near Mugenese encampments wearing the most brightly colored, provocative clothing that village women had access to. They were, without fail, assaulted. But girls with fire rockets and knives were harder to take down than the Mugenese soldiers' usual prey.

"You're fond of pretending to be weaklings," Rin observed. "Does that always work?"

"Almost every time. The Mugenese are terribly attracted to easy targets."

"And they never catch on?"

"Not as far as I've noticed. See, they're bullies. Weakness is what they want to see. They're so convinced that we're just base, cowardly animals, they won't stop to question it. They don't *want* to believe we can fight back, so they won't."

"But we're not really fighting back," Rin said. "We're only annoying them."

Souji knew that she wasn't thrilled with this tentative campaign—this sort of half fighting, of provoking from the shadows instead of facing the enemy head-on. It defied every strategic principle she'd ever been taught. She'd been taught to win, and to win conclusively to preempt a later counterattack. Souji, on the other hand, flirted with victory but never took the spoils. He left chess pieces open all over the board, like a dog might bury bones to savor later.

But Souji insisted she was still thinking about war the wrong way.

"You don't have a conventional army," he said. "You can't move into Leiyang and mow them down like you did when you fought for the Republic."

"Yes, I could," she said.

"You're good nine times out of ten, Princess. Then a stray arrow or javelin finds its way into your temple, and your luck's run out. Don't take chances. Err on the side of caution."

"But I hate this constant *running*—"

"It's not running. That's what you don't get. This is disruption. Think about how your calculations change if you're on the receiving end. You change your patrol pattern to keep up with the random attacks, but you can't anticipate when they'll happen. Your nerves get frayed. You can't rest or sleep because you're not sure what's coming next."

"So your plan is to annoy them to death," Kitay said.

"Bad morale is a big weapon," Souji said. "Don't underestimate it."

"I'm not," Rin said. "But it feels like we're just constantly retreating."

"The entire point is that *only you* have the ability to retreat. They don't; they're stuck in the places they've occupied because they can't give them up. Try to wrap your head around this, you two. Your default model of warfare won't work for you anymore. At Sinegard you're taught to lead large forces into major battles. But you don't have that anymore. What you *can* do is strike against isolated forces, multiple times, and delay their reinforcements. You have to deploy small operational units who have the latitude to make their own calls. And you want to delay head-on battles on the open field for as long as you possibly can."

"This is all bonkers." Kitay had the wide-eyed, slightly panicked look on his face he got when his mind was chewing frantically through new concepts. Rin could almost hear the whirring in his brain. "This cuts against everything the Classics ever said about warfare."

"Not really," Souji said. "What did Sunzi say was the fundamental theorem of war?"

"Subjugate the enemy without fighting," Kitay said automatically. "But that doesn't apply to—"

Souji cut him off. "And what does that mean?"

"It means you pacify an enemy with sheer, overwhelming superiority," Rin said impatiently. "If not in numbers, then in technology or position. You make him realize his inferiority so he surrenders without fighting. Saves your troops a battle, and keeps the battlefields clean. The only problem is that they *aren't* inferior on any plane. So that's not going to work."

"But that's not what Sunzi means." Souji looked frustratingly smug, like a teacher waiting for a very slow student to arrive at the right answer.

Kitay had lost his patience. "What, was half the text written in invisible ink?"

Souji raised his hands. "Look, I went to Sinegard, too. I know the way your minds work. But they trained you for conventional warfare, and this is not that."

"Then kindly explain what this is," Kitay said.

"You can't concentrate superior force all at once, so you need to do it in little parts. Mobile operations. Night movements. Deception, surprise, all that fun stuff—the stuff we've been doing— that's how you focus your optimal alignment, or whatever bogus word Sunzi calls it." Souji made a pincer motion with his hands. "You're like ants swarming an injured rat. You whittle it down with little bites. You never engage in a full-fledged battlefield encounter, you just fucking exhaust them.

"Sinegard's problem was that it was teaching you to fight an ancient enemy. They saw everything through the Red Emperor's eyes. But that method of warfare doesn't work anymore. It didn't even work against the Mugenese when you *had* the armies. And what's more, Sinegard assumed that the enemy would be a conquering force from the outside." Souji grinned. "They weren't in the business of teaching rebels."

∞

Despite her initial skepticism, Rin had to admit that Souji's tactics worked. And they *kept* working. The closer they got to Leiyang, the more supplies and intelligence they acquired, all without evidence that the Mugenese at Leiyang knew what was coming. Souji planned his attacks so that even Mugenese survivors wouldn't be able to report more than ten or twenty sighted troops at once; the full size of their army remained well concealed. And if Rin ever called the fire, she made sure she left no witnesses.

But their luck had to be running out. Souji's small-scale tactics worked for tiny targets—hamlets where the Mugenese guard numbered no more than fifty men. But Leiyang was one of the largest townships in the province. More and more reports corroborated the fact that their numbers were in the thousands.

You couldn't fool an army of thousands with skirts and firecrackers. Sooner or later, they'd have to stand face-to-face with their enemy and fight.

CHAPTER 5

On the twelfth day of their march, after an eternity of navigating winding, treacherous forest footpaths, they reached a vast plain filled with red stalks of sorghum. Against the otherwise overgrown wilderness, the sparse and dying trees that littered the roadside, those neatly cultivated fields stood out like a red flag of warning.

Armies only maintained fields once they'd settled down for permanent occupation. They'd reached the edge of the Beehive.

Rin's men wanted to move on Leiyang that night. They'd marched at a leisurely pace for the last two days; the forest routes didn't permit them to go any faster. They had energy, pent up and raging. They wanted blood.

Souji was the only holdout. "You've got to contact the local leadership first."

Rin humored him. "Fine. Where are they?"

"Well." Souji scratched his ear. "On the inside."

"Are you mad?"

"The civilians suffer the most from your little liberations," Souji said. "Or did you not count the casualties at Khudla?"

"Listen, we *freed* Khudla—"

"And burned a temple full of civilians to death," Souji said.

"Don't think I didn't know about that. We need to give them advance warning."

"That's too risky," Kitay said. "We don't know how many collaborators they have. If the wrong person sees you, they'll crack down on the civilians regardless."

"No one's going to report us," Souji said. "I know these people. Their loyalty runs thicker than blood."

Rin gave him a skeptical look. "You'd be willing to stake the lives of everyone in this army on that?"

"I'm staking the lives of everyone in that township on it," Souji said. "I've gotten you this far, Speerly. Trust me just a little longer."

So Rin found herself walking with Souji into the center of the Beehive, dressed in peasant rags, without her sword and without reinforcements. Souji had identified a lapse in the northern patrol, a thirty-second pocket of time between revolving guards that allowed them to sneak past the fields and over the city gates unnoticed.

What Rin saw inside Leiyang astonished her.

She'd never before encountered a Mugenese-occupied township where corpses weren't stacked in rotting, haphazard piles around every corner. Where the residents weren't utterly, uniformly, brutally crushed into submission.

But here in Leiyang, the Mugenese had embarked on something more like occupational state-building. And this, somehow, was scarier.

The civilians here were thin, haggard, clearly downtrodden, but alive—and not just alive, but *free*. They weren't locked up in holding pens, nor were they crouching inside their homes in fear. Civilians—visibly Nikara civilians—strode around the township so casually that if Rin didn't know better she wouldn't have guessed there was a Mugenese presence at all. As they snuck deeper into the township, Rin saw a band of men—laborers with farming implements that could easily be used as weapons—walking toward the fields without so much as a single armed guard. Closer to the town center, there were long queues looping around an unbelievable sight—a rationing station, where Mugenese troops doled out daily portions of barley grain to civilians waiting patiently with copper bowls.

She could barely form the question. "How—?"

"Collaboration," Souji said. "It's how most of us have been getting along. The Mugenese figured out pretty quickly that their original depopulation policy was only going to work if they were getting supplies from the island. Island's gone, and there's no point to clearing out space anymore. What's more, they need someone to do their cooking and cleaning."

So the soldiers without a home had formed a sick symbiosis with their intended victims. The Mugenese had merged with the Nikara into a society that, if not necessarily nonviolent, at least looked stable and sustainable.

Rin found evidence of wary coexistence everywhere she looked. She saw Mugenese soldiers eating at Nikara food stands. She saw Mugenese patrolmen escorting a group of Nikara farmers back through the city gates. No blades were drawn; no hands were bound. This looked routine. She even saw a Mugenese soldier fondly stroke the head of a Nikara child as they passed each other on the street.

Her stomach churned.

She didn't know what to do with this. She was so used to absolute destruction, a complete binary of the extremities of war, that she couldn't work her mind around this bizarre middle ground. How did it feel to live with a sword hanging over your head? How did it feel to look these men in the eyes, day by day, knowing full well what they were capable of?

Rin followed closely behind Souji as they moved through the streets, her eyes darting nervously about with every turn. No one had reported, or even seemed to care about, their presence. Occasionally someone narrowed their eyes at Souji in questioning recognition, but no one so much as breathed a word.

Souji didn't stop walking until they'd reached the far edge of the township, where he pointed to a small, thatched-roof hut half-hidden behind a cluster of trees. "The chief of Leiyang is a man named Lien Wen. His daughter-in-law came from the same village as my mother. He's expecting us."

Rin frowned. "How?"

"I told you." Souji shrugged. "I know these people."

A skinny, plain-faced girl about seven years old sat outside the door, hand-grinding sorghum grain in a small stone bowl. She scrambled to her feet when they approached and, without a word, gestured for them to follow her inside the hut.

Souji nudged Rin forward. "Go on."

For the home of a township chief, Lien Wen's was not particularly luxurious. The interior would barely have fit ten men standing shoulder to shoulder. A square tea table occupied the center, surrounded by three-legged stools. Rin squatted down on the nearest stool. The uneven, scratched-up legs wobbled every time she shifted position. That was oddly calming—this kind of poverty felt familiar.

"Weapons over there. Father's orders." The girl pointed at a cracked vase in the corner.

Rin's fingers twitched toward the knives hidden inside her shirt. "But—"

"Of course." Souji shot Rin a stern look. "Whatever Chief Lien asks."

Rin reluctantly dropped the blades into the vase.

The girl disappeared for several seconds, returned with a plate of coarse-grain steamed buns, and set it down on the tea table.

"Dinner," she said, then retreated to the corner.

The starchy grain smelled terribly good. Rin hadn't seen proper steamed buns in ages; in Ruijin, they'd long ago run out of yeast. She reached out for a bun, but Souji slapped her hand away.

"Don't," he muttered. "That's more than she eats in a week."

"Then why—"

"Leave it. They'll save it for later if you don't touch it, but if you touch it and put it down then they'll insist you take it with you when you leave."

Stomach growling, Rin returned her hand to her lap.

"I didn't think you'd come back."

A tall, broad-shouldered man filled the doorframe. Rin found his age impossible to place—his lined eyes and white whiskers could have made him as old as her grandfather, but he carried himself with his back straight and chin up, a warrior with decades of fight left in his body.

"Chief Lien." Souji stood up, cupped his hands, and bowed deeply at the waist. Rin hastily followed suit.

"Sit," Chief Lien grumbled. "This hut isn't big enough for all this commotion."

Rin and Souji returned to their stools. Chief Lien merely shoved his out of the way and sat down cross-legged on the dirt floor, which made Rin feel suddenly very childish, squatting as she was.

Chief Lien folded his arms across his chest. "So you're the ones who've been causing trouble up north."

"Guilty." Souji beamed. "Next up is—"

"Stop it," Chief Lien said. "I don't care what's next. Take your army, leave here, and don't come back."

Souji trailed off, looking hurt. Rin would have found that funny if she weren't also confused.

"They think our men are doing it," Chief Lien said. "They made the elders line up in the square the morning after the first patrolmen went missing and said they'd shoot them one by one until the culprits confessed. No one stepped forward, so they beat my mother within an inch of her life. That was over a week ago. She's not recovered. She'll be lucky if she makes it through tonight."

"We have a physician," Souji said. "We'll bring him to you, or we can just carry her out to our camps. We've got men in those fields, we can move on the crickets tonight—"

"No," Chief Lien said firmly. "You will turn around and disappear. We know how this story ends, and we can't suffer the consequences. Compliance is the only thing keeping us alive—"

"*Compliance?*" Souji had warned Rin to keep quiet and let him do the talking, but she couldn't help but interject. "That's your word for slavery? You like walking the streets with your head down, cringing when they approach you, licking their boots to win their goodwill?"

"Our township still has all our men," said Chief Lien.

"Then you have soldiers," Rin said. "And you should be fighting."

Chief Lien merely regarded her through his lined, tired eyes.

In the passing silence, Rin noticed for the first time a series of ropy scars etched across his arms. Others snaked up the side of his neck. Those weren't the kind of scars you got from a whip. Those were from knives.

His gaze made her feel so tiny.

Finally he asked, "Did you know that they take young girls with the darkest skin they can find and burn them alive?"

She flinched. "What?"

But then the explanation rose to her mind, slow and dreadful, just as Chief Lien spelled it out aloud. "The Mugenese tell stories about you. They know what happened to the longbow island. They know it was a dark-skinned girl with red eyes. And they know you're near."

Of course they know. They'd massacred the Speerlies twenty years ago; surely the myth of the dark-skinned, red-eyed race who called fire still circulated in their younger generations. And certainly they'd heard whispers in the south. The Mugenese troops who could understand Nikara would have picked up on whispered stories of the goddess incarnate, the reason why they could never go home. They would have tortured to discover the details. They would have learned very quickly who they needed to target.

But they couldn't find her, so they'd targeted anyone who might possibly look like her instead.

Guilt twisted in her stomach like a knife.

She heard the sudden noise of steel scraping against steel. She jumped and turned. The little girl, still sitting in the corner of the hut, had started fiddling with their weapons.

Chief Lien turned to look over his shoulder. "Don't touch that."

"She's all right," Souji said easily. "She ought to learn how to handle steel. You like that knife?"

"Yes," said the girl, testing the blade's balance on one finger.

"Keep it. You'll need it."

The girl peered up at them. "Are you soldiers?"

"Yes," Souji said.

"Then why don't you have uniforms?"

"Because we don't have any money." Souji gave her a toothy smile. "Would you like to sew us some uniforms?"

The girl ignored this question. "The Mugenese have uniforms."

"That's true."

"So do they have more money than you?"

"Not if we and your baba have anything to do with it." Souji turned back to Chief Lien. "Please, Chief. Just hear us out."

Chief Lien shook his head. "I won't risk the reprisals."

"There won't be reprisals—"

"How can you guarantee that?"

"Because everything they say about me is true," Rin interrupted. Little arcs of flame danced around her arms and shoulders, just enough to cast long shadows across her face. To make her look utterly inhuman.

She saw a faint look of surprise flicker across Chief Lien's face. She knew, despite the rumors, that until now he hadn't really believed what she was. She could understand that. It was hard to believe in the gods, to *truly* believe, until they stared you in the face.

She'd made believers of the Mugenese. She'd make him believe, too.

"They're killing those girls because they're afraid," she said. "They should be. I sank the longbow island. I can destroy everything around me in a fifty-yard radius. When we attack it won't be like the previous attempts. There will be no chance of defeat and no reprisals, because I cannot lose. I have a god. I only need you to bring the civilians out of range. We'll do the rest."

Chief Lien's jaw had lost its stubborn set. She'd won him over, she knew. She saw it in his eyes—for the first time, he was considering something other than compliance. He was thinking about how freedom might taste.

"You can ambush them at the northern border," he said at last. "Not many civilians live up there, and we can evacuate the ones who do. The reeds would be tall enough to conceal you—you could fit about five hundred men in those fields alone. They won't know you're here until you choose to reveal yourselves."

"Understood," Souji said. "Thank you."

"You'll only have a bit of time to get in position. They send troops with dogs and staves every few hours to track anyone who might be hiding in the fields."

"Combing their hair for lice," said the girl. "That's what they call it."

"We'll have to be clever lice, then," Souji said. Relief shone clear on his face. This wasn't a negotiation anymore; now it was just about logistics. "And do you know how many men they have?"

"About three thousand," Chief Lien said.

"That's very precise," Rin said. "How do you know?"

"They commission their grains from us. We know how much they eat."

"And you can calculate that by the *grain*?"

"It's simple multiplication," Chief Lien said. "We're not stupid."

Rin sat back, impressed. "All right. Three thousand, then."

"We can draw them two hundred yards out of the township if we split half our forces around and drive them into the fields," Souji said. "That's out of Rin's range—"

"No," said Chief Lien. "Four hundred."

"That might not be possible," Rin said.

"Make it possible," Chief Lien said. "You keep your fight away from this township."

"I understand," Rin said. Her voice turned hard. "You want your liberation without suffering the consequences."

Chief Lien stood up. The message was clear; this audience was over. "If you lose, they will come for us. And you know what they can do."

"Doesn't matter," Rin said. "We won't lose."

Chief Lien said nothing. His eyes followed them silently, judging, as they left the hut. In the corner, his daughter hummed and continued to scrape steel against steel.

"That went well," Rin muttered.

"Sure did." Souji was beaming.

"What are you so happy about? He's made this ten times harder than it had to be, and he hasn't given us anything in return—"

"That's not true. He gave us permission."

"Permission? Who the fuck needs *permission*—"

"You always need permission." Souji stopped walking. The grin slid off his face. "Every time you bring a fight to a village, you put every innocent civilian's life in danger. It's your obligation to warn them."

"Look, if every army behaved like that, then—"

"Listen. You're not fighting a campaign for this land, you're fighting for the people. And if you learn to trust them, they'll be your best weapons. They'll be your eyes and ears on the ground. They'll be natural extensions of your army. But you never, *ever* endanger them against their will. Do you understand?"

He glared at her until she nodded.

"Good," he said, and strode briskly toward the gate. Chastened, she followed.

Someone stood awaiting them in the shadows.

Rin pulled a flame into her hand, but Souji grabbed her elbow. "Don't. It's a friendly."

The man at the gate was, indeed, Nikara. He had to be—his clothes, ratty and faded, hung from his gaunt frame. None of the Mugenese soldiers were starving.

He was quite young—hardly more than a boy. He seemed terribly excited to see them. He took one look at Rin, and his entire face lit up. "Are you the Speerly?"

Something about him struck her as familiar—his thick eyebrows, his broad shoulders. He carried himself like a born leader, confident and resolute.

"You're Chief Lien's son," Rin said. "Aren't you?"

"Guilty," he said. "Lien Qinen. It's good to meet you."

"Come here, you bastard." Souji grasped Qinen's arm and pulled him into a tight embrace. "Does your father know you're here?"

"Father thinks I'm still hiding out in the woods." Qinen turned to Rin. "So *are* you the Speerly? You're smaller than I expected."

She bristled at that. "Oh, am I?"

He held out his hands. "No, no, I wasn't—I—wow." He blinked several times. "Sorry. I've just heard so much about you, I was expecting—I didn't know what to expect. It's good to meet you."

He wasn't being rude, Rin realized. He was *nervous*. Her expression softened. "Yes, I'm the Speerly. And you're here because—"

"I'm your ally." Qinen reached out quickly to shake her hand. His palms were slick with sweat. He gawked at her, mouth hanging slightly agape, as if he'd just watched her descend from the heavens on a staircase of clouds. Then he blinked and cleared his throat. "We're going to help you fight. I've got men prepared to come out for you, just say the word and we'll—"

"You'll do nothing," Souji said. "You know what your father demanded."

Qinen's face twisted in contempt. "My father's a coward."

"He's just trying to keep you alive," Souji said.

"Alive?" Qinen scowled. "He's sentenced us to a living hell. He thinks compliance means lenience, but he doesn't listen to reports from villages all around us. He doesn't know what they do to the women. Or he doesn't care." His fists tightened. "Thirty miles from here, a village tried to hide girls in nearby mines, and when the Mugenese found out, they sealed off the exits and let them suffocate over three days. When they finally let the villagers retrieve the corpses, they found the girls dead with their fingers cracked and bleeding from trying to claw their way out. But Father doesn't understand. He's been—I mean, since my brother died, he's . . ." His throat bobbed. "He's wrong. We aren't safe here; we'll never be. Let us fight beside you. If we die, then at least let us die like men."

This isn't about permission, Rin realized. Souji was wrong. Qinen was going to fight whether they agreed to let him or not. This was about validation. After everything Qinen had seen, he needed absolution for the guilt of remaining alive, and he could get that only by putting his life on the line. She knew that feeling.

"You and your friends aren't soldiers," Souji said quietly.

"We can be," Qinen said. "Did you think we'd just lie down and wait to be rescued? I'm glad to see you, brother, but we would have started this fight without you. You'll need us. We've been laying down our own preparations, we've already set your stage—"

"What?" Souji shot him a sharp glance. "What have you been doing?"

"Everything my father's been too scared to try." Qinen lifted his chin with pride. "We've taken down their patrol routes to the minute. They're all written down in a code they can't read. We've sent round signals so the villagers know exactly when to run or hide. We've made sure every household has a weapon. Knives made from stakes, or farming implements we've snuck out of the sheds one at a time. We're ready for this fight."

"If they found out they'd kill you," Souji said.

"We're braver than that," Qinen scoffed. "You saw my baby sister?"

"The girl in the hut?" Rin asked.

He nodded. "She's with us, too. The Mugenese have her working in the mess hall—that's where they force the children to work—so she slips a handful of water hemlock into a few bowls every time. It doesn't do much. Just induces some vomiting and diarrhea—but it weakens them, and no one ever suspects it's her."

Watching Qinen's face—his earnest, furious, desperate face—

Rin couldn't help but feel a mix of admiration and pity. His courage amazed her. These civilians were poking the dragon's nest, risking their lives every day, preparing for a rebellion that they must have known they wouldn't win.

What did they really think they could accomplish? They were farmers and children. Their little acts of resistance might infuriate the Mugenese, but wouldn't drive them away.

Maybe, Rin thought, under these circumstances, that kind of resistance—no matter how futile—was the only way to live.

"We can help you," Qinen insisted. "Just tell us where to be and when."

The ruthless side of her wanted to say yes. She could use Qinen. It was so easy to go through cannon fodder. Even the most inexperienced commander could buy seconds, even minutes, by throwing bodies at the enemy.

But she couldn't forget the look in Chief Lien's eyes.

She'd learned, now, what it meant to bring the war to the south.

She read the expression on Souji's face. *Don't you dare.*

And she knew that if she said the wrong thing now, then she'd lose the support of both Chief Lien and the Iron Wolves.

"Souji's right." She reached out to touch Qinen lightly on the arm. "This isn't your fight."

"The hell it isn't," Qinen snapped. "This is my home."

"I know." She tried to sound like she meant what she was saying. "And the best thing you can do is keep your countrymen safe when we attack."

Qinen looked crestfallen. "But that's nothing."

"You're wrong," said Souji. "That's everything."

Night had fallen by the time Rin and Souji rejoined the camp. They'd planned their attack for the following sunset. They had considered striking right then, under cover of darkness, and before any news had leaked of their arrival. But they'd decided to hold off until the next evening; Chief Lien needed time to orchestrate the villagers' evacuation, and the Southern Army needed time to scope out the terrain, to position their troops optimally within the fields. The general staff spent the next few hours huddled around maps, marking out lines of entry.

It was far past midnight when at last they disbanded to rest. When Rin returned to her tent, she found a slim scroll placed neatly at the top of her travel pack.

She reached out, paused, and then withdrew her hand. This wasn't right. Nobody at camp was receiving personal parcels. The Southern Coalition owned only one carrier pigeon, and it was trained to take a one-way message to Ankhiluun. Every instinct screamed that this was a trap. The scroll's exterior could be laced with venom—countless Nikara generals of old had tried that trick before.

She leaned over the scroll with a small flame bobbing in her palm, carefully illuminating its every angle. She couldn't see anything dangerous—no thin needles, no dark sheen on the parchment edge. Still, she used her teeth to pull her sleeve over her fingers before she picked the scroll up and unrolled it. Then she nearly dropped it.

The wax seal bore the dragon insignia of the House of Yin.

She exhaled slowly, trying to slow her racing heart. This had to be a joke—someone had pulled a deeply unfunny prank, and she would make sure they suffered for it.

The note inside was scrawled in a wobbly, childish font; the characters were so smudged and messy she had to squint to read it.

Hello, Rin,
They told me to write this in my own hand, but I don't see how it could have made a difference seeing as I could barely write when you left, so you wouldn't have recognized it anyway.

"This isn't funny," she muttered to herself.

But she knew this wasn't a joke. Nobody at camp could have done this. Nobody *knew*.

This is Kesegi, if you hadn't pieced that together. I've been in the New City prisons for a while and it was my fault, I got stupid and bragged to some people that you were my sister and I knew you, and then the talk trickled up to the guards so now here I am.

I'm sorry I did this to you. I really am.

Your friend says to tell you that this doesn't have to be difficult. He said to tell you I walk free if you'll come to the New City yourself, but if you bring an army then they'll behead me above the city gates. He says that this doesn't have to end in bloodshed, and that he only wants to speak. He says he doesn't want a war. He's prepared to grant clemency to every one of your allies. He only wants you.

Although to be honest—

The rest of the message had been scratched out with thick inky lines.

Rin snatched the scroll up and ran outside her tent.

She accosted the first sentry she saw. "Who delivered this?"

He gave her a blank stare. "Delivered what?"

She waved the scroll at him. "This was inside my travel pack. Did anyone deliver this to you?"

"N-No—"

"Did you see anyone going through my things?"

"No, but my watch has only just started, you'd have to ask Ginsen, he was here for three hours before that, and he should be—General, are you all right?"

Rin couldn't stop trembling.

Nezha knew where she was. Nezha knew where she *slept*.

"General?" the sentry asked again. "Is everything all right?"

She crumpled the scroll in her fist. "Get me Kitay."

"Shit." Kitay lowered the letter.

"I know," Rin said.

"Is this real?"

"What does that mean?"

"I mean, is there any chance this is a forgery? That this isn't really Kesegi?"

"I don't know," she admitted. "I've no idea."

She couldn't tell if that was really Kesegi's handwriting. Frankly, she wasn't even sure Kesegi knew how to read; her foster brother had rarely attended school. She couldn't tell if the letter sounded like him, either. Certainly she could imagine the words in his voice, could picture him sitting at a writing desk, wrists shackled, his thin face trembling as Nezha dictated the words to him one by one. But how could she know for sure? She'd barely spoken to Kesegi in years.

"And what if it's not?" Kitay asked.

"I don't think we should respond," Rin said in the calmest tone she could muster. "Either way."

She'd worked through the possibilities in the minutes it had taken Kitay to arrive. She'd weighed the cost of her foster brother's life, and she'd decided she could afford to lose him.

Kesegi wasn't a general, wasn't even a soldier. Nezha couldn't torture him for information. Kesegi knew nothing of importance about either the Southern Coalition or Rin. Everything he knew of Rin was the biography of a little girl that she'd killed long ago at Sinegard, a naive Tikany shopgirl who existed only in suppressed memories.

"Rin." Kitay put a hand on her arm. "Do you want to go after him?"

She hated how he was looking at her, eyes wide with pity, as if she were on the verge of tears. It made her feel so fragile.

But that's just what Nezha wants. She refused to let this shake her. Nezha had manipulated her with sentiment before. The Cike had died for her sentiment.

"The problem is not Kesegi," she said. "It's Nezha's troop placements. It's his fucking *reach*—I mean, he put a letter in my fucking *tent*, Kitay. We're just supposed to ignore that?"

"Rin, if you need to—"

"We need to discuss whether Nezha's forces are in the south." She had to keep talking; they had to move the conversation on to something else, because she was afraid of how her chest would feel if they didn't. "Which I don't think is possible—Venka says he's leading his father's troops in Tiger Province. But if they're in the south, they've hidden so well that not a *single* one of our scouts has seen any troops, dirigibles, or supply wagons."

"I don't think he's in the south," Kitay said. "I think he's just fucking with you. He's gathering information; he just wants to see how you'll respond."

"He won't get a response. We're not going to take the bait."

"We can discuss that."

"This isn't a discussion," she snapped. "This letter is a forgery. And Nezha's terms are absurd."

Her fingers clenched around the scroll. The remainder of the message had been written in Nezha's smooth, elegant calligraphy.

Hello, Rin,
It's about time we talked.
    You and I both know this war benefits no one. Our country has cracked apart. Our homeland has been ravaged, by war, by environmental catastrophe, by mindless evil. Nikan now faces her greatest test. And the Hesperians are watching us, waiting to see if we might stand strong or become another slave society for them to exploit.
    I understand why you hate them. I am not blind to their intentions, and I will not let them turn our Republic into their mining ground. I will not see this land ruled by foreign hands. I know you don't want that, either.
    Please, Rin. Come to reason. I need you at my side.

The terms he listed were simple and unacceptable. A truce, full-scale demobilization and disarmament, and Kesegi returned safely in exchange for Rin. The Southern Coalition would be allowed to walk free, or join the Republican Army if they wished.

Nezha hadn't specified what would happen to Rin. She suspected it involved hourly doses of laudanum and an operating table.

"I'm not crazy, right?" she asked. "This is clearly a trap?"

"I'm not sure," Kitay said. "I think there's a world where Nezha does want you alive. He's not stupid, he knows you'd be useful to him. He might try to talk you around—"

"The Hesperians are never going to let me walk free."

"If you take Nezha at face value, then it looks like he's trying to defy the Hesperians."

She snorted. "You really think he'd do that?"

"I don't know. The Yins . . . the House of Yin is far more comfortable working with foreigners than any Nikara leaders ever have been. It's the reason why they're rolling in silver. They might be fine with remaining stewards for the blue-eyed devils. But Nezha . . ."

"Nezha's a shaman."

"Yes."

"And you think the Hesperians know."

"I think *Nezha* knows that he cannot exist in a Hesperian-dominated world," Kitay said. "It's a world that labels him an abomination. Their vision of order demands his death and yours."

Was that what Nezha was trying to imply? That he'd changed his mind about shamans? That if she joined him at his side, he might break the alliance his father had forged?

"But I've had this argument with Nezha," she said. "And he thinks they're right. That we *are* abominations, and that we're better off dead. Only he can't die."

"So then we're back to square one. We have no idea what this letter implies. And we have no reason to trust Nezha."

Rin sighed. "So what's our move, then?"

"I think we start with deciding what to do about your brother."

"My foster brother," she corrected. "And I've told you, we're doing nothing."

"Why don't you even want to talk about this?"

"Because he's just my brother." She gave him a helpless look.

"And I am the last great hope of the south. How do you think history will judge me if I throw away its fate for one person?"

Kitay opened his mouth, paused, and closed it. Rin knew his mind was racing; he was trying to come up with a way to save Kesegi, a way to foil Nezha, or a justification why one life might be worth more than thousands.

They didn't exist. She knew that. She loved him for trying.

"Please," she said. "Please just let this go."

She was grateful he did not argue.

"Then we have a battle to win." He handed the scroll back to her. "And I think we can both agree that showing this to anyone else gets us nothing."

Rin understood his implication. The Southern Coalition could never know about this. Not Souji, not Zhuden, and certainly not Gurubai. The offer was admittedly attractive—even she found it tempting, might even have sacrificed herself for it if she weren't so sure that what lay at the other end were lies.

If this got out, the factional infighting would explode. The Monkey Warlord had taught her that much about southern politics. This had to remain her secret.

"Of course," she said.

She drew a ball of flame into her palm under the scroll. For a moment Nezha's words burned bright, searing red. The parchment edges blackened, crinkled, then curled in on themselves like the legs of a dying spider.

Rin spent the next few hours attempting to catch short bursts of fitful sleep. She didn't know why she tried; she could never sleep before battle. At last she gave up and passed the last hours until dawn pacing around the camp, watching for the sun to rise. She couldn't bear sitting still with her thoughts. She couldn't keep torturing herself with the possibilities—whether Kesegi was alive, whether Nezha was telling the truth, whether she should have responded to the letter rather than ignore it.

She needed a distraction. She needed this battle.

She felt good about their positions. They'd arranged their troops in a four-point formation. One squadron, the one she led, would spearhead the attack and tie the Mugenese soldiers down at the front near the sorghum fields, while two smaller squadrons would circle around the Mugenese flanks, hemming them inside a triangle to form a wedge between the village and the battlefield. Souji's Iron Wolves, the fourth squadron, would drive holes through the enemy lines in the back, preventing a rout toward the civilians' evacuation zone.

Preparations proceeded smoothly as the day wore on. Thanks to the Liens, they were operating with far more information than she'd ever been used to on the battlefield. She knew exactly where the Mugenese slept. When they ate. Where and when they patrolled. It was almost like a textbook case of an ambush, a test question on an exam she would have taken at Sinegard.

As the sun began its downward slope, Rin went over final instructions before she dispatched her squadron commanders to their spots. Their plans had come together with clockwork efficiency. They avoided the patrols they knew were coming. Their map directions lined up perfectly with the actual terrain. All squadron commanders fully understood their signals and timetables.

The only hiccup was their uniforms.

Chief Lien had requested they wear uniforms to distinguish themselves from civilians. Rin had protested that they didn't have any.

"Tough," Chief Lien said. "Find some, or your ambush is off."

They'd compromised at headbands—thin strips of cloth tied around their foreheads. But an hour before they were due to move out, the squadron leaders started reporting they didn't have enough excess cloth. Their soldiers were already marching in threadbare uniforms; they didn't have any spares to cut up. Zhuden asked Rin if they should start ripping strips from their trouser legs.

"Forget that," Rin grumbled. "Let's just send them out."

"You can't," Souji said. "You made a promise."

"It's idiotic! Who's going to care about uniforms at nighttime?"

"The Mugenese might care," Kitay said. "Killing their labor source doesn't work in a symbiotic relationship. It's a small measure, but it's the least you can do. It's the difference between ten lives and a thousand."

In the end they had their troops smear their faces with bright red mud from a nearby pond. It left crimson patches on their clothes wherever they touched, and it caked onto their skin in dry, rusty streaks that didn't rub off without water.

"We look stupid." Rin surveyed the ranks. "We look like children playing past our dinnertime."

"No, we look like a clay army." Souji dragged two fingers across his cheek, leaving a thick, clearly visible streak. "The Red Emperor's very finest, baked fresh from southern dirt."

Thirty minutes until sunset, Rin crouched low amid the sorghum stalks. The smell of oil hung heavy in the air—the two thousand men behind her held dripping torches, ready to light at her signal.

The Southern Coalition's soldiers had been trained to fight in the darkness as they had at Khudla. It hurt their visibility, yes, but the psychological advantage was significant. Troops under ambush in pitch-black night reacted with panic, confusion, and cowardice.

But tonight, Rin wanted the battlefield well lit. The Mugenese might fall back on the civilians in the chaotic dark. She needed to draw them out into the grain fields, which meant she needed to show them precisely where their enemy lay.

Are you ready, little warrior?

The Phoenix crooned in the back of her mind, eager, waiting. Rin let the old rage leak in, familiar and warming as a hearth fire, let it seep into her limbs while visions of destruction played in her head.

Oh, how she'd craved this fight.

I'm ready.

"Rin!"

She whipped around. Souji pushed his way through the sorghum stalks, red-faced and panting for breath.

Her stomach dropped. He wasn't supposed to be here. He was supposed to be on the eastern flank with his Iron Wolves, poised and ready to attack.

"What are you doing?" she hissed.

"Hold up." He doubled over, wheezing. "Don't give the signal. Something's wrong."

"What are you talking about? We're ready, it's time—"

"No. Look." He rummaged in his pockets, pulled out a spyglass, and tossed it toward her. "Look *carefully*."

She raised it to her eye at the township walls. She struggled to make anything out in the dark. "I don't see anything."

"Move to the west. Just over the fields."

Rin moved the lens. What she saw didn't make any sense.

Mugenese soldiers clustered around the township walls. More poured out with every passing second. They knew about the ambush. Something—or someone—had tipped them off.

But they weren't charging forward. Their blades weren't pointed outward. They weren't even arranging themselves into defensive formations of the kind Rin would have expected from an army under attack.

No—their weapons were pointed at the city gates. They weren't preventing the attackers from coming in, they were keeping the residents from coming out.

Then Rin understood their strategy.

They weren't going to fight a fair fight. They weren't planning to engage the Southern Coalition at all.

They'd simply taken all Leiyang hostage.

Rin grabbed the arm of the nearest field officer and hissed, "*Find Kitay.*"

He sprinted back toward the camp.

"Fuck." Rin slammed a fist against her knee. "Fuck—*how*?"

"I don't know." For the first time, the confident swagger was wiped from Souji's face. He looked terrified. "I've no idea, I don't know what we're going to do—"

What had given them away? They'd prepared this ambush with twice their usual caution. The patrols couldn't possibly have seen them; they'd worked around the guard schedule with clockwork precision. Had someone seen her and Souji leaving the township? That was possible, but then how would the Mugenese have known when the ambush was scheduled? And how did they know it would come from the north?

It didn't matter how. Even if there were spies within her ranks, she couldn't solve that now; she had a more pressing problem to deal with.

The Mugenese were holding Leiyang's civilians at knifepoint.

A small contingent of Mugenese soldiers started moving toward the ambush line. One of them waved a red flag. They wanted to negotiate.

Rin worked frantically through all the possible ways this could end, and couldn't come up with one where both the civilians and the Southern Army were safe. The Mugenese would have to secure a guarantee that Rin's troops would never come back.

They were going to demand a blood sacrifice. Most likely they'd massacre Rin's troops, one for every civilian kept alive.

Rin didn't know if she could pay that price.

"What's going on?"

Kitay, at last. Rin turned toward him, trying not to slip into a panicked babble as she started to explain what was happening, but the moment she twisted around she saw Souji's expression morph into horror as he lifted a finger, pointing, toward the village.

A second later, she heard an arrow shriek through the air.

The Mugenese flag-bearer dropped to the ground.

Instinctively she whipped her head around, searching the ranks for a raised bow, a twanging bowstring—who'd done it, which absolute *idiot* had—

"My gods," Souji murmured. His eyes were still fixed on the village.

Rin turned back around and thought she was hallucinating. What else explained that great column moving out of the township gates, a crowd nearly the size of an army?

She raised the spyglass back to her eye.

Qinen. It had to be. He'd mobilized his resistance band—no, from the looks of it, he'd mobilized the entire township. The column wasn't just the fighting men of Leiyang; they were the women, elders, and even some of the children. They held torches, plows, field hoes, kitchen knives, and clubs clearly made from legs torn from chairs.

They charged.

They knew their lives were the price of this battle. Rin's attack couldn't proceed so long as they were held hostage. They'd known the Mugenese would force her to choose.

They'd made this decision for her.

The Mugenese archers turned toward the township to commence the massacre. Their commander signaled an order.

Civilian bodies fell from the front of the column in a clean sweep. But the villagers kept marching over their dead, pressing inexorably forward like ants bursting forth. Another round of arrows. Another line of bodies. The villagers kept marching.

The Mugenese soldiers couldn't shoot quickly enough to keep them at bay. This was a clash of steel and bodies now, an utterly mismatched comedy of a melee. Federation soldiers cut the villagers down as quickly as they came. They knocked the weapons out of their hands, pierced them easily in their necks and chests because their victims had never been trained to parry.

The villagers kept marching.

The bodies piled up on the field. Rin watched, horrified, as a blade went clean through an old woman's shoulder. But the woman lifted her trembling hands and clenched the wrist of her attacker, held him still long enough for an arrow to find his forehead.

The villagers kept marching.

Souji's hand landed on her shoulder. His voice came out a strangled rasp. "What are you waiting for?"

She reached into the back of her mind, through the channel of Kitay's soul, to the god who lay patiently waiting.

Avenge this, she ordered.

Whatever you ask, said the Phoenix.

And Rin strode forward through the sorghum fields to rip the world open with fire. She killed indiscriminately. She turned them all to ash, civilians and enemies alike. Leiyang's civilians welcomed her flames with smiles.

This was their choice. Their sacrifice.

Her troops surged forth around her, blades glinting in the fiery night. They'd broken formation, but formation didn't matter anymore, only bodies, blood, and steel.

This is how we win the south, she thought as her surroundings dissolved into a blurry wave of heat. That made it easier to keep going. She couldn't see faces, couldn't see the pain. All she saw were shapes. *Not with our blades, but our bodies.*

They would take back the south with sheer numbers. The Mugenese and the Republic were strong, but the south was many. And if southerners were dirt like all the legends said, then they would crush their enemies with the overwhelming force of the earth until they could only dream of breathing. They would bury them with their bodies. They would drown them in their blood.

CHAPTER 6

After that, it was just cleanup.

Rin walked dazedly through the sorghum fields, razed now to a level sheet of dark gray ash. Smoke curled out of her clothes in lazy, indolent spirals. She hadn't touched opium since they'd set out on this march. But she was high now on a familiar euphoria, an exhilarating buzz that started in her fingertips and thrummed through her chest to her heart.

In Tikany, summer season was always overrun with ants. The vicious red creatures were driven into a frenzy by the dry heat, attacking whatever small children and animals crossed their paths. One bite alone raised a welt; a dozen could be fatal. The villagers retaliated with acid, using long poles to tip jars onto the anthills from a distance. Rin remembered how as a child she would crouch by the ground with empty jars in hand, squinting as destroyed civilizations frothed and burned under the sunlight.

She'd always lingered too long. She liked to listen to the acid hissing as it burrowed into the ants' deepest tunnels. Liked to see the ants pouring frantically out the top, fleeing straight into the pools of acid she'd laid carefully in a ring around the nest. Liked to watch their little legs wiggle as they frothed and dissolved.

She felt a similar kind of pleasure now, the sadistic glee of watching lives evaporate and knowing she'd done it. Of knowing she had that *power*.

What is wrong with me?

She felt the same bizarre, confused elation that'd come over her when she'd poisoned Ma Lien. This time she didn't push it away. She drank it in. Her power was derived from rage, and what she felt now was the other side of the coin—vengeance fulfilled.

Leiyang hadn't been completely lost. When Rin's soldiers searched the ruins for any civilians with breath left in their lungs, they found that the rate of survival was surprisingly high. The Mugenese attackers had been careless, acting from a frenzied panic rather than a calculated cruelty. They'd slammed steel haphazardly into any exposed flesh they saw instead of aiming for vital organs as they should have.

Leiyang the township was dead. Chief Lien's people couldn't live here any longer. Their numbers were too few; their homes and belongings were destroyed. They'd have to march south with Rin's army to seek new homes, would have to see their numbers cannibalized into whatever villages would take them.

But Leiyang's survivors were free. That, at least, was worth it.

Qinen, by some miracle, had made it out alive. Rin went to see him the moment she heard he was conscious.

The Southern Coalition's handful of physicians had set up a triage center in a butchery, one of the few structures in Leiyang's city center that hadn't burned to the ground. They'd sanitized the structurally intact interior to the best of their ability, but couldn't scourge the taint of burned pig intestines. By the end of the day the air was thick with the hot, tangy smell of blood, human and animal alike.

Rin found Qinen lying on a sheet outdoors, where the physicians had sent every patient not under immediate surgery. He looked awful. The burns that covered the right side of his body had twisted the skin on his face so badly that he could only speak in a hoarse, garbled whisper. His eyes were open but swollen, his right eye covered by a filmy white layer. Rin wasn't sure that he could see her until his face broke into an awful, painful smile.

"I'm sorry—" she started, but he reached out and seized her wrist with a force that surprised her.

"I told you," he rasped. "I told you we'd fight."

Qinen's band of resistance fighters hadn't been acting alone. Similar organizations had existed all throughout the Beehive. This Rin discovered when, one by one, the villages clustered around Leiyang began to liberate themselves with startling speed.

Without the central leadership at Leiyang, the remaining ranks of Mugenese soldiers were isolated, cut off from all communications, resources, or reinforcements. Villagers armed with knives and plows now stood a fighting chance. Reports began flooding in about the villagers all throughout Rooster Province rising up, taking up arms, and purging their villages of their former rulers.

After Rin sent squadrons of Zhuden's troops throughout the Beehive to speed up the process, the battle for the surrounding area took no more than two weeks. Some Mugenese troops put up a fight and went down in explosions of fire, yellow gas, steel, and blood. Others took their chances and surrendered, begging for exile or leniency, and were invariably executed by village committees.

When Rin toured the Beehive, she found herself witness to a wave of violence sweeping across the province.

In some hamlets, the civilians had already decapitated their Mugenese guards and strung their heads upside down along the town gates like a welcoming display of holiday lanterns. In other villages, Rin arrived while the executions were ongoing. These were drawn out over a period of days, a twisted parade whose centerpiece entertainment was an orgy of violence.

The sheer creativity astounded her. The liberated southerners marched the Mugenese naked in chains along the streets while onlookers reached out with knives to slice their flesh. They forced the Mugenese to kneel for hours on broken bricks with millstones hung around their necks. They buried the Mugenese alive, dismembered them, shot them, throttled them, and threw their bodies into dirty, rotting piles.

The victims were not limited to Mugenese troops. The victorious liberators' harshest punishments fell on the collaborators—the magistrates, merchants, and delegates who had succumbed to Federation rule. In one village three miles south of Leiyang, Rin stumbled upon a public ceremony where three men were tied to posts, naked and gagged with rags to muffle their screams. In the corner, two women held long knives over a barrel fire. The blades glowed a vicious orange.

Rin could guess this would end in castration.

She turned to Souji. "Do you know what those men did?"

"Sure," he said. "Traded girls."

"They—*what*?"

He spelled it out for her. "They struck a deal to stop the Mugenese from grabbing women off the street. Every day they'd take a few women—usually the poor ones, or the orphans, who had no one to fight for them—and deliver them to the Mugenese general headquarters. Then they'd go back at sunrise, retrieve the girls, clean them up best they could, and send them home. It kept the younger girls and the pregnant women safe, though I don't think the women they picked were too happy." He watched, unflinching, as a girl who couldn't have been more than fourteen ascended the stage and poured a vat of boiling oil over the men's heads. "They said it was for the good of the village. Guess not everyone agreed."

Loud sizzles mixed with the screams. Rin's stomach grumbled, tricked into thinking she'd smelled freshly cooked meat. She hugged her arms over her chest and looked away, suppressing the urge to vomit.

Souji chuckled. "What's wrong, Princess?"

"I just . . ." Rin wasn't sure how to articulate her unease, much less distinguish it from obvious hypocrisy. "Isn't this a bit much?"

"'A bit much'?" He scoffed. "Really? This from you?"

"It's different when . . ." She trailed off. How exactly was it different? What right did she have to judge? Why did she feel shame and disgust now, when the pain she regularly inflicted on the battlefield was a thousand times worse? "It's different when it's civilians doing it. It . . . it feels *wrong*."

"How did it feel when you called the Phoenix at Speer?"

She flinched. "What does that matter?"

"It was good, wasn't it?" His lip curled. "Oh, it was horrific, I'm sure, must have left a mental scar the size of a crater. But it was also the best thing you'd ever felt, wasn't it? It felt like you'd put the universe back in place. Like you were balancing the scales. Didn't it?"

He pointed to the men on the stage. They weren't screaming anymore. Only one was still twitching. "You don't know what these men have done. They might look like innocent Nikara faces, but you weren't here during occupation, and you don't know the pain they caused. The south doesn't burn its own unless there's a reason. You have no idea what these villagers are healing from. So don't take this from them."

His voice grew louder. "You don't fix hurts by pretending they never happened. You treat them like infected wounds. You dig deep with a burning knife and gouge out the rotten flesh and then, maybe, you have a chance to heal."

So when the south reclaimed itself in a sea of blood, Rin didn't stop it. She could only watch as the tide of peasant violence rose to a fever pitch that she wasn't sure she could control, even if she'd wanted to. Nobody would admit out loud how satisfying this was—the villagers had to pretend that this was a ritual of necessity and not of indulgence—but Rin saw the hungry gleams in their eyes as they drank in the screams.

This was catharsis. They needed to spill blood like they needed to breathe. Of course she understood that impulse; at night, alone with her pipe, she showed those bloody scenes over and over again to Altan so that her mind could find some semblance of peace while he could drink them hungrily in. The south needed retribution to keep going. How could she deprive them?

Only Kitay kept agitating to put an end to the riots. He could allow for the death penalty but he wanted order; he wanted public trials that weren't a sham and sentences more moderate than execution.

"Some of those people are innocent," he said. "Some of them were just trying to stay alive."

"Bullshit," Souji said. "They made their choice."

"Do you understand the choices they got?" Kitay pointed across the courtyard to where a man had been hanging upside down by his ankles for the past three days. "He served as one of their translators for seven months. Why? Because the Mugenese captured his wife and daughter and told him he could serve, or he could watch them be buried alive. Then they started torturing his daughter in front of him to drive home the point. What do you think he picked?"

Souji was utterly unmoved. "He helped them kill other Nikara."

"*Everyone* helped them kill other Nikara," Kitay insisted. "Ideological purity is well and fine, but some people were just trying to survive."

"You know, the Mugenese gave my sister a choice," Souji said. "Said she could be one of their double agents and rat on her fellow villagers, or they'd rape and kill her. You know what she picked?"

Kitay's cheeks flushed red. "I'm not saying—"

"Did you know the Mugenese liked to play games to fill their kill quota?" Souji inquired.

"I know," Kitay said. "At Golyn Niis—"

"I know what they did at Golyn Niis." Souji's voice was like steel. "Want to know what they did here? They'd drive mobs of villagers up to the roofs of the tallest buildings they could find. Then they'd tear down the stairs, set the bottom floors on fire, and stand back in a circle to watch while they screamed. *That's* what those collaborators had a hand in. Tell me we're supposed to forgive that."

"Kitay," Rin said quietly. "Drop it."

He didn't. "But they're not just targeting the Mugenese and their collaborators."

"Kitay, please—"

"They're targeting everyone who's ever been *remotely* suspected of collaboration," Kitay hissed. "This isn't justice, it's a killing frenzy, and whispers and pointed fingers are ending lives. You can't tell who's truly guilty and who's fallen on the bad side of their neighbors. It's not justice, it's chaos."

"So what?" Souji shrugged. "Hunt a rat, you're going to smash some dishes. This is a revolution. It's not a fucking tea party."

They marched in silent exhaustion on the road back to Leiyang. The thrill of victory had long since died off. Two weeks of screams and torture, no matter who the victims were, had left them all somewhat haggard and pale.

They were half a day's march out when a hooded rider appeared on the road. Rin's officers rushed forward, spears leveled, shouting for the rider to stop. The rider halted, raising their hands to indicate the lack of weapon.

"Get down!" Zhuden insisted. "Who are you?"

"Oh, for heaven's sake." Venka threw the hood off her face and dismounted from her horse. She strode forth, batting spear points away with one hand as if swatting at a cloud of gnats. "What the fuck, Rin? Call off these fools."

"Venka!" Rin darted forward and embraced Venka, but quickly let go; the stench was too much to bear. Venka smelled like a tannery on fire. "Great Tortoise, when's the last time you had a bath?"

"Cut me a fucking break," Venka said. "I've been fleeing for my life."

"You had time to put on fresh face paint," Kitay pointed out.

"Everyone was doing it in Sinegard. I had some left in my bag. Easier to access than soap, all right?"

Rin could only laugh. What else did they expect? Sring Venka was a prim, spoiled Sinegardian princess turned lethal soldier turned brittle survivor; of course she'd walk into a war zone with red paint on her lips simply because she felt like it.

"Anyway, it took you long enough to get back," Venka griped. "I've been pacing this patch of road since yesterday. They told me you were based in Leiyang."

"We were," Rin said. "Are. Left to do some cleaning up."

"What happened?" Kitay asked. "Thought you were just fine in the Republic."

Venka gave a dramatic sigh. "Broke my cover. It was the stupidest thing. There I was, an utterly invisible servant girl in a magistrate's household, and then the lady of the house started thinking I was trying to seduce her husband and dragged me out into the street."

"Were you—?" Kitay began.

Venka shot him a scathing look. "Of course not. It's not my fault that the stupid man couldn't keep his eyes off my ass."

Kitay looked flustered. "I was just going to ask if you were recognized."

"Oh. No, but it was a near thing. His wife had me fired, then she went around telling all the other households not to hire me. That brought a bit too much attention. So I looted the armory in the middle of the night, sweet-talked the stable boy into lending me a horse, and made my way down south." She recounted all this with such brazen flippancy she might have been chatting about Sinegard's latest fashions. "At Ruijin they said you'd gone south, so I followed the trail of bodies. Didn't take me long to track you down."

"We've, ah, split with Ruijin," Rin said.

"So I figured." Venka nodded to the waiting troops. "How'd you wrestle an army from Gurubai?"

"Created a vacancy." Rin glanced over her shoulder at her troops. Souji and the other officers were paused in the middle of the road, watching them curiously.

"She's an ally," Rin told them. "Carry on."

The column resumed its march toward Leiyang. Rin kept her

voice low as she spoke to Venka, glancing around to make sure Souji did not overhear.

"Listen, has Nezha started sending anyone south?"

Venka arched an eyebrow. "Not the last I heard. Why?"

"Are you sure?"

"Supposedly he's still cooped up in the palace. Rumor has it he's not doing so well, actually; he's been out of commission for a few weeks."

"What?" Rin asked sharply. Her heart was suddenly beating very quickly. "What does that mean?"

Kitay shot her a curious look. She ignored it. "Was he injured?" she asked.

"I don't think so," Venka said. "He hasn't been out on the field in weeks. Vaisra recalled him from Tiger Province last month. He's spent a lot of time with the Hesperians, negotiating with their delegates, and I think the prevailing rumor was that he's fallen ill. He looks weak, he's got shadows under his eyes, or so they say. It's hard to tell what's gossip and what's fact, since no one I knew had actually gotten a good look at him, but it seems serious."

Rin felt a stupid, instinctive stab of worry, the residue of concern. She quashed it. "You think he's going to die?"

"Not sure," Venka said. "They say he's got all the best Hesperian doctors working on him, though that might be doing more harm than good. I doubt he'll be leading troops out anytime soon."

Did that mean she was safe? Had Nezha just been fucking around with her? His illness did not negate the fact that he had spies in her camp, that he knew where she laid her head every night. But if Venka was right, and if Nezha and his father were indeed still preoccupied with the north, they might not have to worry about an impending ambush for the time being.

This reprieve might not last for long. But she'd take every extra day she had.

"What's the matter?" Venka asked. "You spooked about something?"

Rin exchanged a glance with Kitay. They'd come to an unspoken agreement—they wouldn't tell Venka about the letter. The fewer people who knew, the better.

"Nothing," Rin said. "Just—just wanted to make sure we're not getting blindsided."

"Trust me." Venka snorted. "I don't think he's even in a fit state to walk."

They rode for a few moments in silence. Rin could see the silhouette of Leiyang emerging from the horizon; from here on it was only flat roads.

"So what in the sixty-four gods has been happening here?" Venka asked after a while. "I passed a few villages on my way up here. They've all gone completely mad."

"Throes of victory," Rin said. "Growing pains."

"They're skinning people alive," Venka said.

"Because they traded little girls for food rations."

"Oh. Fair enough." Venka flicked an invisible speck of dust from her wrist. "I hope they castrated them, too."

Later that afternoon, as Rin headed to the fields to supervise basic training, she was accosted by a wizened old woman dragging two skinny girls along by their wrists.

"We heard you were taking girls," she said. "Will they do?"

Rin was so startled by her pushy irreverence that rather than directing the woman to the enlistment stand, she paused and looked. She was puzzled by what she saw. The girls were thin and scrawny, certainly no older than fifteen, and they cowered behind the old woman as if terrified of being seen. They couldn't possibly be volunteers—every other woman who had enlisted in the Southern Army had done so proudly and of her own volition.

"You're taking girls," the old woman prompted.

Rin hesitated. "Yes, but—"

"They're sisters. You can have them for two silvers."

Rin blinked. "Pardon?"

"One silver?" the woman suggested impatiently.

"I'm not paying you anything." Rin's brow furrowed. "That's not what—"

"They're good girls," said the woman. "Quick. Obedient. And neither are virgins—"

"*Virgins?*" Rin repeated. "What do you think we're doing here?"

The woman looked at her as if she were mad. "They said you were taking girls. For the army."

Then the pieces fell together. Rin's gut twisted. "We aren't hiring *prostitutes.*"

The woman was undaunted. "One silver."

"Get out of here," Rin snapped. "Or I'll have you thrown in jail."

The woman spat a gob of saliva at Rin's feet and stormed off, tugging the girls behind her.

"Hold it," Rin said. "Leave them."

The woman paused, looking for a moment like she might protest. So Rin let a stream of fire, ever so delicate, slip through her fingers and dance around her wrist. "I wasn't asking."

Hastily, the woman left without another word.

Rin turned to the girls. They had barely moved this whole time. Neither would meet her eyes. They stood still, arms hanging loose by their sides, heads lowered deferentially like house servants waiting for commands.

Rin had the oddest temptation to pinch their arms, check their muscles, turn up their chins, and open their mouths to see if their teeth were good. *What is wrong with me?*

She asked, for want of anything better to say, "Do you want to be soldiers?"

The older girl shot Rin a fleeting glance, then gave a dull shrug. The other didn't react at all; her eyes remained fixed on an empty patch of air before her.

Rin tried something else. "What are your names?"

"Pipaji," said the older girl.

The younger girl's eyes dropped to the ground.

"What's wrong with her?" Rin asked.

"She doesn't speak," snapped Pipaji. Rin saw a sudden flash of anger in her eyes—a sharp defensiveness, and she understood then that Pipaji had spent her entire life shielding her sister from other people.

"I understand," Rin said. "You speak for her. What's her name?"

The hostility eased somewhat from Pipaji's face. "Jiuto."

"Jiuto and Pipaji," Rin said. "Do you have a family name?"

Silence.

"Where are you from?"

Pipaji gave her a sullen look. "Not here."

"I see. They took your home, too, huh?"

Pipaji gave a listless shrug, as if she found this question incredibly stupid.

"Listen," Rin said. Her patience was running out. She wanted to be on the field with her troops, not coaxing words from sullen little girls. "I haven't got time for this. You're free of that woman, so you can do whatever you like. You can join this army if you want—"

"Do we get food?" Pipaji interrupted.

"Yes. Twice a day."

Pipaji considered this for a moment, then nodded. "Okay."

Her tone made it clear she had no further questions. Rin watched them both for a moment, then shrugged and pointed. "Good. Barracks are over there."

CHAPTER 7

Two weeks later they reached Tikany.

Rin had been prepared to fight for her hometown. But when her troops approached Tikany's earthen walls, the fields were quiet. The trenches lay empty; the gates hung wide open, with no sentries in sight. This wasn't the deceptive stillness of a waiting ambush but the listless silence of a place abandoned. Whatever Mugenese troops had once terrorized Tikany had already fled. Rin passed completely unobstructed through the northern gates into a place she hadn't seen since she'd left it nearly five years ago.

She didn't recognize it.

Not because she'd forgotten. As much as she'd once wanted to, she'd never erase the texture of this place from her mind—not the clouds of red dust that blew through the streets on windy days, covering everything with a fine sheen of crimson; not the abandoned shrines and temples around every corner, remnants of more superstitious days; not the rickety wooden buildings emerging from dirt like angry, resilient scars. She knew Tikany's streets like she knew the back of her hand; knew its alleys, hidden tunnels, and opium drop-off sites; knew the best hiding corners wherein to take refuge when Auntie Fang's temper bubbled over into violence.

But Tikany had changed. The whole place felt empty, hollowed, like someone had gouged its intestines out with a knife and devoured them, leaving behind a fragile, traumatized shell. Tikany had never been one of the Empire's great cities, but it had held life. It had been, like so many of the southern cities, a locus of small autonomy, carved defiantly into the hard soil.

The Federation had turned it into a city of the dead.

Most of the ramshackle buildings were gone, long since burned down or dismantled. The Mugenese had turned what was left into a spare military camp. The library, the outdoor opera stage, and schoolhouse—the only places in Tikany that had ever brought Rin any happiness—were skeletal structures that showed signs of deliberate deconstruction. Rin guessed the Mugenese had stripped down their walls for firewood.

In the pleasure district, the whorehouses alone remained standing.

"Take twelve troops—women, if possible—and scour every one of those buildings for survivors," Rin told the closest officer. "Hurry."

She knew by now what they would likely find. She knew she should have gone herself. She wasn't brave enough for it.

She kept walking. Closer to the township center, near the magistrate's hall and public ceremonies office, she found evidence of the public executions. Stage floorboards painted brown with months-old stains. Whips tossed onto careless piles under the spot where once, a lifetime ago, she'd read her Keju test score and realized she was going to Sinegard.

What she didn't see were corpses. In Golyn Niis, they'd been stacked up on every street corner. Tikany's streets were empty.

But that made sense. When your goal was occupation, you always cleaned up your corpses. Otherwise they stank.

"Great Tortoise." Souji whistled under his breath as he strode beside her, hands in his pockets, peering about the devastation like a child perusing a holiday market. "They really did a number on this place."

"Shut up," Rin said.

"What's the matter? Did they tear down your favorite tea-house?"

"I said *shut up*."

She hated the thought of crying in front of him, yet she could barely breathe for the weight crushing her chest. Her head felt terribly light; her temples throbbed. She dug her nails into her palm to ward off the tears.

She'd seen large-scale devastation like this only once before, and it had almost broken her. But this was worse than Golyn Niis, because at least in Golyn Niis, most everyone was *dead*. She would almost have rather seen corpses than the survivors she saw now, crawling out from whatever safe houses remained standing, blinking at her with the dazed confusion of animals who had spent too long living in the dark.

"Are they gone?" they asked her. "Are we freed?"

"You're freed," she said. "They're gone. Forever."

They registered these words with fearful, doubtful looks, as if they expected the Mugenese to return any moment and smite them for their temerity. Then they grew braver. More and more of them emerged from huts, shacks, and hiding holes, more than Rin had dared hope remained alive. Whispers arced through the ghost town, and gradually the survivors began to fill the square, crowding around the soldiers, homing in on Rin.

"Are you . . . ?" they asked.

"I am," she said. She let them touch her so that they knew she was real. She let them see her flames, spiraling high in delicate patterns, silently conveying the words she couldn't bring herself to say out loud.

It's me. I'm back. I'm sorry.

"They need to wash," Kitay said. "Almost everyone here's got a lice problem; we need to contain it before it spreads to our troops. And they need a good meal, we should get the rations in order—"

"Can you handle it?" she asked. Her voice rang oddly in her

ears when she spoke, as if coming from the other side of a thick wooden door. "I want—I need to keep walking."

He touched her arm. "Rin—"

"I'm all right," she said.

"You don't have to do this alone."

"But I do. You can't understand." She stepped away from him. Kitay knew every part of her soul, but he couldn't share this with her. This was about roots, about dirt. He wasn't from here; he couldn't know how it felt. "You—you take care of the survivors. Let me go. Please."

He squeezed her hand and nodded. "Just be careful."

Rin broke away from the crowd, disappeared down a side alley while no one was watching, and then walked alone across town to her old neighborhood.

She didn't bother going to the Fang residence. There was nothing for her there. She knew Uncle Fang was dead. She knew Auntie Fang and Kesegi had most likely died in Arlong. And aside from Kesegi, her memories of that house contained nothing but misery.

She went straight to Tutor Feyrik's house.

His quarters were empty. She couldn't find a single trace of him in any of the bare rooms; he might never have lived there at all. The books were gone, every last one. Even the bookshelves were missing. All that remained was a little stool, which she suspected the Mugenese had left alone because it was carved from stone and not wood.

She remembered that stool. She'd perched there so many nights as a child, listening to Tutor Feyrik talk about places she never thought she would see. She'd sat there the night before the exam, sobbing into her hands while he gently patted her shoulders and murmured that she'd be all right. *A girl like you? You'll always be all right.*

He might still be alive. He might have fled early, at the first warnings of danger; he might be in one of the refugee camps up north. If she tried hard enough, she could maintain the delusion that he was somewhere out there, safe and happy, simply out of her orbit. She tried to find comfort in that thought, but the uncertainty of not knowing, perhaps never knowing, only hurt more.

She tasted salt on her lips, and realized her face was wet with tears.

Abruptly, violently, she wiped them away.

Why do you need to find him? She heard the question in Altan's voice. *Why does it fucking matter?*

She'd hardly thought about Tutor Feyrik in years. She'd cut him out of her mind the same way she'd alienated herself from her sixteen years in Tikany, a snakeskin shed so she could reinvent herself from war orphan to student and soldier. She clung to his memory now out of some pathetic, cowardly nostalgia. He was only a relic—a reminder from an easier time when she was a little girl trying to memorize the Classics, and he was a kind teacher who'd shown her her only way out.

She was searching for a life she'd never have again. And Rin knew far too well by now that nostalgia could kill her.

"Find anything?" Kitay asked when she returned.

"No," she said. "There's nothing here."

Rin chose to make her headquarters in the Mugenese general's complex, partly because she felt like it was her right as liberator and partly because it was the safest place in the encampment. Before they moved in, she and Souji scoured each room, checking for any lurking assassins.

They encountered nothing but messy rooms still littered with dirty dishes, uniforms, and spare weapons. It was like the Mugenese had vanished into thin air, leaving all their belongings behind. Even the main office looked as if the general had simply stepped into the next room for a cup of tea.

Rin rooted through the general's desk, pulling out stacks of memos, maps, and letters. In one drawer she found sheaves of paper, all charcoal sketches of the same woman. This general had apparently considered himself an artist. The sketches weren't half bad—the general had rather painstakingly tried to capture his lover's eyes, to the neglect of other anatomical accuracies. The same Mugenese characters accompanied each sketch—*hudie*, meaning "butterfly" in Nikara; she'd forgotten its Mugenese pronunciation. It was likely not a proper name but an endearment.

He was lonely, she thought. How had he felt when he learned the fate of the longbow island? When he learned that no ships were ever sailing back across the Nariin Sea?

She found a note written on a folded sheet of paper wedged in between the last two sketches. The Mugenese script was not so different from Nikara—it borrowed heavily from Nikara characters, though their pronunciations were entirely different—but it took her several minutes of parsing through messy, scrawled ink to decipher what it said.

If it means I have a traitorous heart then yes, I wish our Emperor had not summoned you for duty, for he has ripped you from my arms.

The entirety of the eastern continent—no, the riches of this universe—means nothing to me in your absence.

I pray every day for the seas to bring your return.

Your butterfly.

It was an extract torn out of a longer letter. Rin couldn't find the rest.

She felt oddly guilty as she leafed through the general's things. Absurdly enough, she felt like an intruder. She'd spent so much time figuring out how to kill the Mugenese that the very idea that they could be people, with private lives and loves and hopes and dreams, made her feel vaguely nauseated.

"Look at those walls," Souji said.

Rin followed his gaze. The general had kept a detailed wall calendar, filled in neat, tiny handwriting. It was far more legible than the letter. She flipped to the very first page. "They arrived here just three months ago."

"That's just when they started keeping the calendar," Souji said. "Trust me, they've been in the south far longer than that."

His unspoken accusation lingered in the air between them. Three months ago she could have come south. She could have stopped this.

Rin had long since accepted that charge. She knew this was her fault. She could have taken the Empress's hand that day in Lusan, could have killed Vaisra's rebellion in the cradle and led her troops straight down south. But instead she'd played at revolution, and all that won her was a scar snaking across her back and an aching stump where her hand should have been.

She hated how nakedly transparent Vaisra's strategy had been from the start, and hated herself more for failing to see it. In retrospect it was so clear why the south had to burn, why Vaisra had withheld his aid even when the southern warlords came begging at his feet.

He could have easily stopped those massacres. He'd known the Hesperian fleet was coming to his aid; he could have dispatched half his army to answer the pleas of a dying nation. He'd deliberately crippled the south instead. He didn't have to grapple with the southern Warlords for political authority if he just let the Mugenese do his dirty work for him. And then, when the smoke cleared, when the Empire lay in fractured shambles, he would have marched in with the Republican Army and burned out the Mugenese with dirigibles and arquebuses. By then southern autonomy would have seemed laughable—whatever survivors remained would have fallen on their knees and worshipped him as their savior.

What if he had told you? Altan—Rin's hallucination of Altan— had asked her once. *What if he'd made you fully complicit? Would you have switched your allegiance?*

Rin didn't know. She had despised the southerners back then. She'd hated her own people, had hated them the moment she saw them in the camps. She'd hated their darkness, their flat-tongued rural accents and fearful, dull-eyed stares. It was so easy to mistake sheer terror for stupidity, and she'd been desperate to think of them as stupid because she knew *she* wasn't stupid, and she needed any reason to set herself apart.

Back then her self-loathing had run so deep that if Vaisra had simply told her every part of his plan, she might have taken his evil for brilliance and laughed. If he hadn't traded her away, she might never have left his side.

Anger coiled in her gut. She tore the calendar down from the wall and crushed it in her fingers.

"I was a fool for Vaisra," she said. "I shouldn't have counted on his virtue. But he didn't count on my survival."

Once they'd deemed the general's complex safe as a home base, Rin walked across town to the whorehouses. She didn't want to; she was hungry and exhausted, her eyes and throat felt sore from suppressed tears, and all she wanted to do was curl up in a corner with her pipe.

But she was General Fang the Speerly, and she owed this to the survivors.

Venka was already there. She'd begun the difficult work of marshaling the women from the whorehouses. Puddles and overturned buckets covered the cold stone floors where the women had showered, next to thick, dark piles of lice-ridden locks shorn from newly bald heads.

Venka stood now at the center of the square courtyard, hands clasped behind her back like a drill sergeant. The women clustered around her in a sullen circle, blankets clutched around their skinny shoulders, their eyes dull and unfocused.

"You have to eat," Venka said. "I'm not leaving you alone until I see you swallow."

"I can't." The girl in front of Venka could have been anywhere from thirteen to thirty—her skin was stretched so tight over her fragile, birdlike bones that Rin couldn't tell.

Venka grabbed the girl's shoulder with one hand; with the other, she held a steamed bun up so close to the girl's face that Rin thought she might start mashing it into her lips. "*Eat.*"

The girl pressed her mouth shut and squirmed in Venka's grasp, whimpering.

"What's wrong with you?" Venka shouted. "*Eat!* Take care of yourself!"

The girl wriggled free and backed away, eyes scrunched up in tears, shoulders hunched as if she expected a beating.

"Venka!" Rin hurried forward and pulled Venka back by the wrist. "What are you doing?"

"What the fuck do you think?" Venka's cheeks were chalk-pale with fury. "Everyone else has eaten, but this little bitch thinks she's too good for her food—"

One of the other women put an arm around the girl. "She's still in shock. Let her be."

"Shut up." Venka shot the girl a scathing glare. "Do you want to die?"

After a long pause, the girl gave a timid shake of her head.

"So *eat.*" Venka flung the bun at her. It bounced off her chest and landed on the dirt. "Right now you're the luckiest fucking girl in the world. You're alive. You have food. You're saved from the brink of starvation. All you have to do is put that bun in your fucking mouth."

The girl began to cry.

"Stop that," Venka ordered. "Don't be pathetic."

"You don't understand," choked the girl. "I don't—you can't—"

"I do understand," Venka said flatly. "Same thing happened to me at Golyn Niis."

The girl lifted her eyes. "Then you're a whore, too. And we should both be dead."

Venka drew her arm back and slapped the girl hard across the face.

"Venka, *stop*." Rin seized Venka's arm and pulled her out of the courtyard. Venka didn't resist; rather, she stumbled along willingly as if in a daze.

She wasn't angry, Rin realized. If anything, Venka seemed about to collapse.

This wasn't about the food.

Rin knew, deep down, that Venka hadn't turned her back on her home province and joined the Southern Coalition—a rebellion formed of people with skin several shades darker than hers—out of any real loyalty to their cause. She'd done it because of what had happened at Golyn Niis. Because the Dragon Warlord Yin Vaisra had knowingly let those atrocities at Golyn Niis happen, had let them happen across the entire south, and hadn't lifted a finger to stop them.

Venka had taken it upon herself to fight those battles. But as she and Rin had both discovered, the battles were easy. Destroying was easy. The hard part was the aftermath.

"Are you all right?" Rin asked quietly.

Venka's voice trembled. "I'm just trying to make this easier."

"I know," Rin said. "But not everyone is as strong as you."

"They'd better learn to be, or they'll be dead in a few weeks."

"They'll survive. The Mugenese are gone."

"Oh, you think it just ends like that?" Venka gave a brittle laugh. "You think it's all over? Once they're gone?"

"I didn't mean—"

"They're never gone. Do you understand? They still come for you in your sleep. Only this time they're dream-wraiths, not real, and there's no escape from them because they're living in your own mind."

"Venka, I'm sorry, I didn't—"

Venka continued like she hadn't heard. "Do you know that after Golyn Niis, the other two survivors from that pleasure house drank lye? Do you want to guess how many of these girls are going to hang themselves? They have no space to be weak, Rin. They don't have time to be *in shock*. That can't be an option. That's how they die."

"I understand that," Rin said. "But you can't take your shit out on them. You're here to protect. You're a soldier. Act like it."

Venka's eyes widened. For a moment Rin thought Venka might slap her, too. But the moment passed, and Venka's shoulders slumped, like all the fight had drained out of her at once.

"Fine. Put them under someone else's charge, then. I'm finished here." She pointed to the whorehouses. "And burn that place to the ground."

"We can't," Rin said. "They're some of the only walled structures still standing. Until we can rebuild some shelters—"

"Burn it," Venka snarled. "Or I'll get some oil and do it myself. Now, I'm not very good at arson. So you can set a controlled fire, or deal with an inferno. You pick."

A scout's arrival saved Rin the burden of a response.

"We found it," he reported. "Looks like there was only one."

Rin's stomach twisted. Not this. Not now. She wasn't ready; after the whorehouses, she just wanted to shrink into a ball somewhere and hide. "Where was it?"

"About half a mile south of the city border. It's muddy out there; you'll want to lace on some thicker boots. Lieutenant Chen told me to tell you he's already on the way. Shall I take you?"

Rin hesitated. "Venka . . ."

"Count me out. I don't want to see that." Venka turned on her heel and called over her shoulder as she stalked off, "I want the whorehouses in ashes by dawn, or I'll assume it's my job."

Rin wanted to chase after her. She wanted to pull Venka back by the wrist, hug her tight, and hold her close until they were able to sob, until their sobs subsided. But Venka would interpret that as pity, and Venka detested pity more than anything. She read pity as an insult—as confirmation that, after all this time, everyone still thought her fragile and broken, on the verge of falling apart. Rin couldn't do that to her.

She'd burn the whorehouses, she decided. The survivors could survive a few nights in the open air. She had fire enough to keep them warm.

"General?" the scout asked quietly.

Rin blinked. She'd been staring after Venka's retreating figure. "Give me a moment. I'll meet you at the east gate."

She returned to the general's complex to change her boots and ask around the barracks until someone lent her a spare shovel. Then she followed the scout to the killing fields.

The walk was shorter than she expected.

She knew the site from a quarter-mile off. She knew it from the smell, the rancid odor of decay under a thin sheen of dust; from the fat insects scurrying into the ground and the carrion birds that perched casually on white bone fragments sticking out of the ground. She knew it from the discolored and displaced soil, and the traces of hair and clothes strewn across the dirt where the Mugenese had hardly bothered to bury them.

She stopped ten feet before she reached the graves. She needed to breathe before she could bring herself to go any farther.

"Let someone else do this." Kitay put a hand on her shoulder. "You're allowed to go back."

"I'm not," she said. "And I can't. This has to be me."

It had to be her because this was her fault. She was obligated to look. She needed to afford the dead at least that modicum of respect.

She wanted to bury it all, to pile mounds of soil over this shallow grave, tamp it tightly against the ground with shovels, and then roll wagons over it to flatten this site so that it might fade back into the landscape until one day they could pretend it had never existed.

But they had to identify the bodies. So many southerners were currently trapped in that horrifying limbo of uncertainty with no way to know if their loved ones were dead, and that uncertainty could hurt more than grief. Once they found the bodies, at least they could mourn.

And then, because burial rituals were so important in the south, the bodies needed to be cleaned. In peacetime, funerals in Tikany were daylong affairs. Hordes of mourners—sometimes including hired professionals to inflate the ranks, if the deceased's family could afford it—moaned and wailed as they followed the coffin out of town to carefully prepared ancestral plots. The souls of the dead needed to be properly coaxed into their graves so they would rest instead of haunting the living; this demanded regular offerings of burned paper goods and incense to soothe them into the world beyond.

Rin had an idea of what the afterlife looked like now. She knew it was not some cute parallel ghost city where burned paper offerings might be translated into real treasures. But still, to leave a loved one's body to rot in the open was shameful.

She'd thrown away most of her Rooster heritage. She'd lost her dialect and her mannerisms; since her first year at school, she'd dressed and spoken like a Sinegardian elite. She didn't believe in southern superstition, and she wasn't going to start pretending now.

But death was sacred. Death demanded respect.

Kitay had taken on the gray-green pallor of someone about to vomit.

She reached for his shovel. "You don't need to stay if you can't. These aren't your people."

"We're bound." He pulled his shovel back from her grasp and gave her a wan, exhausted smile. "Your pain will always be mine."

Together they began to dig.

It wasn't difficult. The Mugenese had covered their handiwork with only a thin layer of soil, barely enough to conceal the tangled mass of limbs underneath. Whenever Rin had uncovered enough dirt to reveal the top layer of a corpse, she stopped and moved on, not wanting to break apart the already soft, decomposing bodies.

"In the north, we burn our dead," Kitay said after an hour. He reached up to wipe the sweat off his forehead, leaving behind a streak of mud. "It's cleaner."

"So we're vulgar," Rin said. "So what?"

She didn't have the energy to defend what they were doing. Earthen burial was the oldest of southern rituals. The Roosters were people of the earth, and their bodies and souls belonged in the ground—ancestral land that was marked, possessed, inhabited by generations stretching back as long as the history of the province. So what if that made them the Empire's mud-skinned refuse? The earth was permanent, unforgiving. The earth would rise up and swallow its invaders whole.

"They won't be able to recognize half these bodies," Kitay said. "They're too far decomposed, look—"

"They still have their clothes. Jewelry. Hair. Teeth. They'll find them."

They kept digging. No matter how many faces they uncovered, the shallow graves seemed to stretch on without end.

"Are you looking for someone?" Kitay asked after a while.

"No," Rin said.

She meant it. She had briefly considered searching for Tutor Feyrik. She'd tried to think of the distinct markers that might identify him. His height and build were too average. She could have searched for his beard, perhaps—but there were hundreds of old men in Tikany with beards just like his. His clothes had always been nondescript; perhaps he might have his lucky gambling dice in his front pocket, but Rin couldn't bear the thought of walking down the lines, ramming her hand down every bearded corpse's pocket to verify someone had already died.

She was never going to see Tutor Feyrik again. She already knew that.

Hours later, Rin at last called for a stop. They'd been digging for three hours. The sun drooped low in the sky; soon, it would be too dark to tell whether their shovel blades were hitting soil or flesh.

"Back to the village," she rasped. She desperately needed a drink of water. "We'll return tomorrow when the sun's come up—"

"Hold on," called a soldier farther down the path. "Something's moving over here."

At first Rin thought the slight movement she saw was a trick of light glinting against buried metal, or perhaps a lone vulture pecking at carrion. Then she drew closer and saw it was a hand—a scrawny hand forced through a gap in the pile of bodies, waving ever so faintly.

Her troops hastened to drag the corpses out of the way. Six bodies removed finally revealed the owner of the hand—a thin, coughing boy covered entirely in dried blood.

He was still conscious when they pulled him out of the grave. He blinked up at them, dazed. Then his eyes closed, and his head slumped to the side.

Rin sent a runner into the township for a physician. Meanwhile, they laid the boy out on the grass and wiped away the blood and dirt caked to his skin as best they could using water from their canteens. Rin watched the boy's chest throughout—it was bloody and discolored, caked over with dried blood and bruises, but still it rose and fell in a steady, determined rhythm.

When a physician arrived and cleaned the boy's torso with alcohol, they learned that the source of the blood wasn't deep—the wound was just a cut about two inches deep into his left shoulder. Enough to agonize but not to kill. The dirt had acted as a poultice, stemming a tide of blood that would have killed him otherwise.

"Hold him tight," said the physician. He uncorked a bottle of rice wine and tipped it over the wound.

The boy jerked awake, hissing in pain. His eyes fluttered open and locked on Rin's.

"You're okay," she said as she pinned his arms against the ground. "You're alive. Be brave."

His eyes bulged. A vein pulsed in his clenched jaw as he writhed under their hands, but never once did he scream.

He couldn't have survived out here for more than a few days.

The infection, and lack of water, would have killed him if it had been any longer than that. That meant the killing fields were fresh. The Mugenese had slaughtered them just days before the Southern Army arrived.

Rin tried to figure out what that meant.

Why would you mass-slaughter a town just before another army arrived?

To make Rin's victory shallow? To spit venom at an army they knew they couldn't beat? To leave one last, cruel message?

No. Gods, no, please, that could not be the truth.

But she couldn't think of any other rationale. Blood rushed to her temples as she watched the boy's eyes roll into the back of his head. She was afraid to stand; she thought she, too, might faint.

You did this, taunted the burial fields. *You made us kill them. We would have left this town alone unless you came, but you did, and so all this is your fault.*

Rin sent her soldiers back to the township ahead of her. She hung back, waiting for the sun to set. She wanted a few minutes of silence. She wanted to stand alone with the graves.

"There's nothing left alive here," Kitay said. "Let's go."

"You go," she said. "I'll be right behind you."

He paused in his steps. "Will this make you feel better?"

He didn't elaborate, but she knew what he meant. "Don't suggest that."

"But I'm right," he pressed. "It makes it easier."

She couldn't deny that. He knew what she couldn't admit out loud; he could read her mind like an open book.

"Please," she said. "Just let me have this. Please just go."

He knew better than to argue. He nodded, squeezed her hand, and left with the others.

Kitay was right. He knew what kind of absolution she sought from the killing fields. He knew that she needed to stay because if she seared the sight of what the Mugenese had done into her eyes, if she breathed the scent of half-rotted corpses, if she reminded herself why she had a reason to hate and keep hating, then it became easier to come to terms with what she had done to the longbow island.

It didn't matter how shrill the screams of dying Mugenese boys sounded in her dreams. They were still monsters, heartless things who deserved everything she had ever done and would ever do to them.

That had to be her truth, or she would shatter.

She didn't know how long she stood there. But when she finally moved to return to camp, the sun had disappeared entirely, and the uncovered graves had seared such a deep impression in her mind that every detail would remain forever. The arrangement of bones. How they curved and arched around one another. How they shone under the last rays of the dying sun.

You won't forget, assured Altan. *I won't let you.*

She pressed her eyes shut, took a deep breath, then turned back toward the village.

She made it two steps before she froze. Something gave her pause. She squinted at the trees. Yes—there it was, the flash of motion that had caught her eye the first time. Someone was running into the forest.

Rin dug her heels into the ground and gave chase.

"Hold it!"

She crashed through the trees, arms backlit with flame, casting hot light on the darkness all around her.

Then she stumbled to a halt. Her target had stopped—it wasn't a soldier or spy but a little girl, crouched at the bottom of a shallow ravine, arms wrapped around her legs and head ducked down while her lips moved like she was counting numbers.

Someone had taught her to do this. Someone had drilled her in it. Rin had been taught the very same lesson as a little girl—if they are chasing you, if you cannot outrun them, find somewhere to hide and count until they've gone away.

"Hey." She approached slowly, arms out, the fingers of her left hand splayed out in what she hoped was a nonthreatening gesture. "It's okay."

The girl shook her head and continued counting, eyes squeezed shut like if she couldn't see Rin, then she might disappear.

"I'm not Mugenese." Rin dragged her vowels out, trying to replicate an accent she'd long ago lost. "I'm a Rooster. One of you."

The girl's eyes opened. Slowly she lifted her head.

Rin stepped closer. "Are you alone?"

The girl shook her head.

"How many are you?"

"Three," whispered the girl.

Rin saw another pair of eyes in the darkness, wide and terrified. They ducked behind a tree as soon as they caught her looking back at them.

She quickly pulled a larger ring of fire into the air around her, just enough to illuminate the clearing. It revealed two emaciated little girls staring up at her with naked fascination. Their eyes looked huge on their hollow faces.

"What are you doing?" Footsteps crashed through the thicket. Rin spun around. A third figure—the girls' mother, or an older sister, she couldn't tell—dashed into the clearing and reached for the girls' wrists, dragging them away from Rin.

"Are you mad?" The woman shook the taller girl by the shoulders. "What were you thinking?"

"She was dressed in fire," said the girl.

"What?"

The girl hadn't stopped staring at Rin. "I wanted to look."

"You're in no danger," Rin said quickly. "I'm Nikara, I'm from Tikany. I'm a Rooster. I'm here to protect you."

But she already knew she didn't have to explain. The woman's eyes had widened in recognition, and she seemed to have realized, for the first time, that the flames lighting the clearing came not from a torch but from Rin's skin.

The woman spoke in a whisper. "You're the Speerly."

"Yes."

Her mouth worked for a few seconds before words came out. "Then are you—have they—"

"Yes," Rin said. "They're gone."

"Truly?"

"Yes. They're all dead. You're safe."

She saw no joy on the woman's face, only a stark, stunned disbelief. Upon a closer look the woman wasn't as old as Rin had thought. She was emaciated and terribly filthy, but beneath a thick layer of grime was the face of someone not so much older than herself.

"What are you doing in the forest?" Rin asked her.

"We ran," said the woman. "As soon as we heard the Mugenese were coming. I'd heard what they do to Nikara women. I wasn't going to—I mean, they weren't—"

"They're your sisters?"

"No," said the woman. "Just two girls who lived in my alley. I tried to get more to come with me. They wouldn't leave."

"You were wise to go," Rin said. "How have you survived all this time?"

The woman hesitated. Rin could read the lie assembling behind her eyes. The woman had an answer, she just wasn't sure if she should speak it.

The smallest girl piped up. "The lady in the hut."

The woman's face tightened, which meant the girl had told the truth.

"What lady?" Rin asked.

"She protects us," said the girl. "She knows things. She tells us when to hide and which roots we can eat and where to lay traps for birds. She said that as long as we obeyed her, then we would be safe."

"Then she should have taken you far away from this place," said Rin.

"She can't. She won't leave here."

Rin felt a sudden, scorching suspicion of who this lady was.

"And why can't she leave?" she asked.

"Shush," the woman told the girl, but the girl kept speaking.

"Because she says she lost her daughter in the Dragon King's palace, and she's waiting for her to come back."

Rin's mouth filled with the taste of blood. Her knees buckled. *What is she doing here?*

The woman put a tentative hand on Rin's elbow. "Are—are you all right?"

"She's here," Rin murmured. The words felt thick and coppery on her tongue. "Take me to her."

She had to go. She had no choice. She was a fly caught in a web; she was a hypnotized mouse crawling straight into a viper's jaws. She could not walk away now, not until she knew what Su Daji wanted.

CHAPTER 8

Rin followed the girls along a winding path deep into the heart of the forest. Moonlight did not penetrate the upper canopy; the trees seemed packed with threats that hissed, buzzed, and lurked hidden within the shadows. Rin kept a small flame burning in her hand to serve as a lamp, but the trees loomed so thick she was afraid to grow her fire any larger lest they catch ablaze.

She willed her racing heart to slow. She wasn't some scared little girl. She wasn't afraid of the dark.

But she couldn't quell her dread of what lay within.

"This way," said the woman.

Rin ducked beneath a cluster of leaves and pushed through the underbrush, wincing as thorny branches scraped at her knees.

What am I doing?

If Kitay were here, he'd call her an idiot. He'd suggest she set the whole forest on fire and be done with it, Trifecta be damned. Instead, Rin was walking straight into Daji's lair like dazed, entranced prey. Was stumbling right up to the woman who, for the better part of the last year, had spared no effort trying to torture, capture, or manipulate her.

But Daji didn't want to kill her. She hadn't ever before, and she didn't now. Rin was sure of that. If Daji had wanted Rin dead, she would have killed her at the base of the Red Cliffs. She would have pressed a shard of shrapnel deep into Rin's arteries and watched, smiling, as Rin bled out on the sand at her feet.

Rin had survived the Red Cliffs only because of Daji's design. The Vipress still needed something from her, and Rin had to at least find out what it was.

"We're here," said the woman.

Cautiously, Rin expanded her flame to illuminate their surroundings. They had stopped before a tiny hut constructed with tree branches, vines, and deer hides. The interior couldn't possibly fit more than two people.

The woman called toward the hut, "My lady, we've returned."

"I hear four pairs of footsteps." A feeble, trembling voice drifted from within. "What have you brought me?"

"A visitor," Rin said.

A short pause. "Come alone."

Rin dropped to her knees and crawled into the hut.

The former Empress of Nikan sat shrouded in darkness. Gone were her robes and jewelry. She was rank and filthy, wrapped in tattered clothes caked so thoroughly with dirt that Rin couldn't tell their original color. Her hair had lost its luster; the tantalizing gleam had disappeared from her eyes. She looked like she had aged twenty years in the span of months. This wasn't just the toll of war, wasn't the stress of scraping for survival while a nation fell apart. Something supernatural had gnawed at Daji's visage, had torn viciously at her beauty in a way time and hardship could not.

For a moment Rin stared in shock, wondering if she'd been wrong after all; if this was not the Vipress before her but just some old hag in the woods.

But then Daji locked her good eye onto Rin, and her cracked lips curved into an all-too-familiar smile. "Took you long enough."

Blood rushed to Rin's head, pounded in her ears. She glanced back to the entrance of the hut, outside of which the girls stood waiting.

"Leave us," she ordered.

The girls didn't budge. They looked to Daji, awaiting her command.

"Go," Daji told them. "Go back to the village. *Run.*"

They scattered.

The moment they were gone, Rin yanked a knife from her belt and jammed the edge at the soft flesh beneath Daji's chin. "Break the Seal."

Daji only laughed, white throat pulsing against the blade's tip. "You're not going to kill me."

"I swear to the gods—"

"You would have done it already." Daji batted at the knife the way a kitten might swat a fly. "Enough with the histrionics. You need me alive."

Rin held the knife firm. *"Break the Seal."*

Her vision pulsed red. She had to focus to keep her hand from slipping, from accidentally slicing skin. She had spent so many hours fantasizing about what she'd do if she ever found Daji at her mercy. If she could force Daji to remove the block on her mind, she'd never have to rely on Kitay again. She'd never again wake up in the middle of the night, mouth dry from nightmares, head swimming with visions of his death. She'd never have to see the evidence of how much she hurt him—the ghost-white pallor of his face, the crescent marks dug into his palm—every single time she called the fire.

"It's killing you, isn't it?" Daji tilted her head back, studying her with a lazy, amused smile. "Does he suffer?"

"Break the Seal. I won't ask again."

"What, the Sorqan Sira couldn't do it?"

"You know she couldn't," Rin snarled. "You're the one who put it on, it's *your* mark, and you're the only one who can take it off."

Daji shrugged. "Pity."

Rin pressed the blade harder into Daji's skin. How hard would she have to push to draw blood? Perhaps she shouldn't aim at the neck—it would be too easy to hit an artery, and then Daji would bleed out before she did anything useful. She moved the sharp, gleaming tip down to Daji's collarbone. "Perhaps some decorations will persuade. Which side do you favor?"

Daji feigned a yawn. "Torture won't help you."

"Don't think I won't do it."

"I know you won't. You're not Altan."

"Don't fucking test me." Rin sent a rivulet of fire arcing down the edge of the blade, just hot enough to singe. "I'm not living my whole life like a beast on a leash."

Daji watched her for a long moment. The glowing metal sizzled against her collarbone, burning dark marks into her flesh, yet Daji didn't even flinch. At last she lifted her hands in supplication. "I don't know how."

"You're lying."

"Dear child, I swear to you I can't."

"But you—" Rin couldn't stop her voice from catching. "Why not?"

"Oh, Runin." Daji gave her a pitying look. "Don't you think I've tried? You think I haven't been trying since you were born?"

She wasn't mocking Rin then. There wasn't a trace of condescension in her voice. This was an honest admission—that sorrow in her voice belied genuine vulnerability.

Rin wished so badly that Daji were mocking her.

"I'd do anything to break that Seal," Daji whispered. "I've been trying to break it for decades."

She didn't mean the Seal she'd put on Rin. She was speaking about her own.

Rin lowered the knife. Her flames receded. "Then why did you do it?"

"You were trying to kill me, darling."

"Not to me. To *them*."

"I didn't want to. But I thought that they were going to kill each other. And I didn't want to die." Daji met her eyes. "Surely you understand."

Rin understood.

She didn't know the full story—no one but Jiang and Daji knew the full story, and they'd both concealed it from her for reasons she might never know—but she knew enough. Once upon a time Daji had cursed the other two members of the Trifecta, the Dragon Emperor and the Gatekeeper, with a Seal that inhibited them all. And she hadn't been able to take it off. One fight, one mysterious fight two decades ago over reasons no one in the Empire understood, and the Trifecta had been reduced to nothing, because Daji *couldn't take it off.*

One will die, the Ketreyid girl Tseveri had said, just before the Trifecta tore her heart out of her chest. *One will rule, and one will sleep for eternity.*

In the end, Tseveri had gotten her revenge.

Rin sank back against her heels. All the fight had suddenly drained from her body. She should have been angry. She *wanted* to be angry, wanted to simply take Daji's head off in an unthinking rage. But all she could feel, looking at this old and desperate creature, was bitter, exhausted pity.

"I should kill you." The knife dropped from her hand. "Why can't I kill you?"

"Because you still need me," Daji said softly.

"Why did you come here?"

"To wait for you. Of course." Daji reached out and touched two fingers to Rin's cheek. Rin didn't flinch. The gesture wasn't cruel, wasn't condescending. It felt, bizarrely, like some attempt at comfort. "I meant what I said in Lusan. I wish you'd let me help you. There are so few of us left."

"But how did you—"

"How did I know you'd come to Tikany?" Daji sighed, chuckling. "Because you Speerlies are all the same. You're bound to your roots, they're what define you. You thought you could utterly reinvent yourself at Sinegard and kill the girl you used to be. But you can't help drifting back to the place you came from. Speerlies are like that. You belong to the tribe."

"My tribe is dead," Rin said. "This isn't my tribe."

"Oh, you know that's not true." Daji's mouth twisted into a pitying smile. "You are the south now. Rooster Province is part of your founding myth. You need it to be. You have nothing else left."

"This is insane," Kitay said.

"Well, we can't put her anywhere else," Rin said.

"So you're keeping her here?" Kitay flung his hands up, gesturing wildly around the general's office. "We *sleep* here!"

"So she'll sleep in another room—"

"You know that's not what I fucking meant. Are you going to tell Souji? Zhuden?"

"Obviously not, and neither should you—"

"Is this the anchor?" Daji asked from the doorway. Her eyes darted over Kitay, drinking in the sight of him as if he were some particularly juicy morsel of prey. "Are you sleeping with him?"

Kitay visibly flinched. Rin stared at Daji, momentarily too stunned to respond. "I—what?"

"You should try it sometime. The bond makes it something quite special." Daji stepped forward, lip curling as she continued to examine Kitay. "Ah, I remember you. From the Academy. Irjah's student. You're a smart boy."

Kitay's hand moved to his belt for his knife. "Take one step closer and I'll kill you."

"She's not our enemy," Rin said hastily. "She wants to help us—"

He barked out a laugh. "Have you gone mad?"

"She won't hurt us. If she wanted to hurt me she would have done it at the Red Cliffs. The balance of power has shifted now, she's got no reason to—"

"That bitch," Kitay said slowly, "is the reason why my father is dead."

Rin faltered.

"I am so sorry," Daji said. Oddly enough, she looked it—her

eyes were solemn, and the mocking curl had disappeared from her lips. "Minister Chen was a faithful servant. I wish the war had not taken him."

Kitay looked astonished that she had even dared to address him. "You are a monster."

"I spent three years living with the Ketreyids and I know infinitely more about the Pantheon than either of you do," Daji said. "I'm the only one who's ever fought a war against the Hesperians, or against Yin Vaisra, for that matter. You need me if you want any chance of surviving what's coming, so you'd best stop making threats, little boy. Is this the best intelligence you have?"

Daji turned abruptly toward Kitay's desk and started riffling through his carefully marked maps. Kitay moved to stop her, but Rin blocked his way.

"Just hear her out," she muttered.

"*Hear her out?* We're better off taking off her head!"

"Just *listen*," Rin insisted. "And if she's full of shit, we'll tell the villagers who she is and let them carry out their justice. You can take the first blow."

"I'd rather take it now."

Daji glanced up from the desk. "You're going to lose."

"Did anyone ask you?" Kitay snapped.

Daji tapped her fingernails against the maps. "It is so obvious how this will go. You might beat the Mugenese. You're not finished with this campaign yet, you know—you need to chase them south to prevent a regrouping. But you have momentum now. Train that little peasant army well, and you'll likely win. But the moment the Republic turns south, Vaisra will grind you into dust."

Daji's tone changed drastically as she spoke. The feeble, grandmotherly tremor disappeared, and her pitch deepened. Her words rang out clear, crisp, and assured. She sounded how she used to. She sounded like a ruler.

"We've been doing well enough on our own," Kitay said.

Daji snorted. "You barely survived on a single front. You didn't liberate Tikany, you occupied a graveyard. And you've no defenses against the Republic whatsoever. Did you think they'd forgotten you? Once you've cleaned the Federation out for them, they will strike, hard and fast, and you won't know what hit you."

"Our army is thousands strong and growing," Kitay said.

"Aren't you supposed to be the smart one? Against dirigibles and arquebuses, you'll need five times your current numbers." Daji arched an eyebrow. "Or you need shamans."

Kitay rolled his eyes. "We have a shaman."

"Little Runin is a single soldier with a limited battlefield range and a rather obvious vulnerability." Daji flicked her hand dismissively at Kitay. "And you can't hide out every battle, darling. Unless Rin unleashes a catastrophe on the scale of what she did to the Federation, then you are no match for Yin Vaisra and his army."

"I've buried a god," Rin said. "I can handle dirigibles."

Daji laughed. "I assure you, you cannot. You've never seen a full fleet of dirigibles in action. I have. Their combat craft are light and agile as birds. They may as well be calling gods of their own. You might call the fire, but they will bury you in missiles." She smacked her palm against the maps. "You are dreadfully outnumbered and overpowered and you need to take steps to correct that *now*."

Rin could see Kitay's expression morphing from indignant to curious. He understood Daji's logic—angry as he was, he was too smart to refuse the truth when he saw it. And he'd realized just as she had that Daji, unfortunately, had a point.

The question was what to do about it.

Rin knew her answer. She saw Daji watching her expectantly, waiting for her to voice her conclusion.

"We need more shamans," she said.

"Correct, dear. You need an army of them."

This statement was so absurd that for a moment Rin and Kitay could only gape at her. But at the same time Kitay was coming up with objections—and Rin knew he would only have objections, she could already tell from his expression—Rin was trying to imagine a world where this might succeed.

"That's what Altan wanted," Rin murmured. "Altan always wanted to release the Chuluu Korikh, he wanted an army of madmen—"

"Altan was an idiot," Daji said dismissively. "You can't bring back someone who's gone to the stone mountain. Their minds are shattered."

"Then how—"

"Come on, Runin. This is easy. You simply train new ones."

"But we don't have the time," Rin said lamely, because this, of all the possible objections, seemed the easiest to explain.

Daji shrugged. "Then how much time do you need?"

"This conversation isn't happening," Kitay said haplessly to the wall. "This isn't really happening."

"It took me years to recognize that the Pantheon existed," Rin said. "And we barely have weeks, we can't—"

"It would have taken you weeks if Jiang hadn't been so determined to drive the Phoenix from your mind," Daji said. "And half of your problem was eroding your preconceived notions of the world. Your mind didn't allow the possibility of shamanism. Those assumptions are broken now. The Nikara realize that this is a world where gods walk in men. They've seen you burn. They're already true believers." Daji reached out with a thin, pale finger and tapped Rin on the forehead. "And all you need to do is give them access."

"You want us to raise an army of people just like me." Rin knew she sounded idiotic, repeating a point that had been made clear over and over again, but she had to say it out loud for it to ring true.

She understood Kitay's incredulity. This solution was horrific. This was so inhumane, so atrociously irresponsible that in all the months she'd been on the run from the Hesperians, she had never once seriously considered it. It had crossed her mind, certainly, but she'd always dismissed it within seconds, because—

Because what?

Because it was dangerous? Every option on the table was dangerous. They'd opened the floodgates now; the entire country was at open war between three factions, one of which ruled the skies and possessed the power to reduce the terrain to ash in seconds, and if Rin didn't correct their power asymmetry somehow, *soon*, then she might as well deliver herself to Nezha in a coffin.

Because this was monstrous? But they were at the stage of war where every choice would be monstrous, and the only question now was which choice kept them alive.

"This is so simple, children," Daji said. "Bring religion back to this country. Show the Hesperians the truth about the gods."

She wasn't talking to Kitay anymore. Kitay might as well have not been in the room; neither of them had acknowledged a single one of his objections. Daji spoke directly to Rin, one shaman to another.

"Do you know what your problem is?" Daji asked. "You've been fighting this entire war on the defensive. You're still thinking like someone on the run. But it's time you started thinking like a ruler."

"You're not seriously considering this," Kitay said.

Daji was gone, banished to a corner room of the complex with a coterie of guards. This precaution was largely a bluff—Rin had no doubt Daji could take down an entire squadron if she wanted to—but the guards were equipped with signal horns. If anything happened, at least they could raise an alarm.

Rin remained in the office with Kitay. Her head felt dizzy, swimming with possibilities she'd never even considered. Several minutes passed in silence. Kitay had sunk into some kind of furious, speechless daze; Rin watched him warily, afraid he might explode.

"You're not even thinking about it?" she asked.

"You're joking," he said.

"Daji might be right. It would balance things out—"

"Are you shitting me? Seriously, Rin? She's manipulating you, that's what she *does*, and you're just eating shit straight out of her hand."

Rin supposed that was possible. Daji could be trying to orchestrate her ruin, and this would be the most sadistic way to do it. But she'd seen the look on Daji's face when she spoke about the Hesperians. She'd seen a glimpse of a girl not so much older than she was, a girl with more power than she knew what to do with, a girl who had just won her country back and was terrified it might be ripped away again.

"The stakes have changed," Rin said. "She's not the Empress anymore. She needs us just as much as we need her."

Kitay folded his arms over his chest. "I think you're entranced."

"What is that supposed to mean?"

"I mean that the Vipress has some weird effect on you—no, Rin, don't deny it, you know it's true. You don't behave rationally around her, you never do. You always overreact, do the opposite of what's prudent—"

"What? No, I don't—"

"What about at Lusan? The Red Cliffs? Twice now you've had the opportunity to kill her and you haven't. Why, Rin?"

"I would have! But she overpowered me—"

"Did she? Or did you let her?" Kitay's voice had gone furiously, dangerously quiet. Rin hated this; she would have preferred that he scream. "The Vipress makes you do shit that makes *no sense*, and I don't know if it's because she's still hypnotizing you, or if it's something else, but you've got to get your mind straight. You're thinking exactly what Daji wants you to think. She's seduced you, and I *know* you're not too stupid to realize that."

Rin blinked. Was he right? Had Daji left some taint of poison on her mind? Was she hypnotizing Rin through the Seal?

She stood silent for a moment, trying to think through this calmly. Objectively. Yes—if she was being honest with herself, Daji *did* have a strange, outsize effect on her psyche. When she was around the Vipress she found it hard to breathe. Her limbs shook, her flames seared, and she trembled from the desire to choke her, to *kill* her, or—

Or to be her.

That was it. Rin wanted what Daji had. She wanted her easy confidence, her calm authority. She wanted her power.

"You can't deny Daji's right about one thing," she said. "The southern front is a distraction. Our biggest problem now is how we're going to deal with Nezha."

Kitay sighed. "By creating an army of people like you?"

"Is that so wrong?" Rin was finding it harder and harder to come up with a good objection. Daji had presented the idea like a glittering gem and now she couldn't stop turning it over and over in her mind, ruminating on the possibilities.

Imagine an army of shamans, whispered a quiet voice in her mind. Altan's voice. *Imagine the sheer firepower. Imagine having the Cike back. Imagine getting a second chance.*

"We should at least talk this through," she said.

"No," Kitay said firmly. "We are ruling it out, now and forever."

"But why—"

"Because you can't *do* this to people," he snapped. "Ignore the realistic chances of global apocalypse for a moment—which I'm shocked you haven't considered, by the way. You know what it does to a person's mind. This isn't something you can inflict on anyone."

"I think I turned out all right."

"*All right* is not a term anyone would use to describe you."

"I'm functional," she said. "Which is all you need."

"Barely," he said, in the cruelest tone he could muster. "And you had training. But Jiang's gone, and the Sorqan Sira's dead. If you do this to anyone else, it's a death sentence."

"The Cike went through it," Rin pointed out.

"And you're willing to inflict the Cike's fate on anyone?"

Rin winced. There were, and only ever had been, two possible fates for the Cike—death or the Chuluu Korikh. Rin had heard this warning repeated countless times from the moment she joined the Bizarre Children, and she'd watched it play out, inevitably and brutally, over and over again. She'd seen Altan engulfed in flame. She'd seen Baji torn apart by bullets. She'd seen Suni and Feylen imprisoned in their own minds by demons that they couldn't exorcise. She'd almost succumbed to that fate herself.

Could she force it on someone else?

Yes. If that was their only hope against a fleet of dirigibles, then absolutely yes. For the future of the Nikara south, for the sake of their survival—yes.

"It's been done before," she said.

"But not by us. Never by us. We can't do this to other people." Kitay's voice trembled. "I won't be complicit in that."

She had to laugh. "This is the moral line you won't cross? Come on, Kitay."

"Do you not understand how that feels? Look at what happened to Nezha. You forced him to call his god and—"

"I never forced him to do shit," she snapped.

"Don't lie to yourself. You pushed him past his limits when you knew it was torture to him and look what that got you, a scar in your back the size of Mount Tianshan."

She recoiled. "Fuck you."

That was a low blow. Kitay knew that; he knew exactly where she hurt the most, and still he'd stabbed and twisted the blade.

He didn't apologize. Instead, he raised his voice. "If you'd put aside your wild dreams of conquest for a fucking second, if you'd stop getting drunk off the Vipress's very *presence*, you'd realize this is one of the worst things you could do to someone."

"Oh, like you'd fucking know."

"You think I don't know?" His eyes widened, incredulous. "Rin, I was at *Golyn Niis*, and the Phoenix ripping through my mind is still the cruelest torture I've ever felt."

That shut her up.

She wanted to kick herself for forgetting that she could call the fire only because he let her, because every day he let a vicious god claw through his mind into the material world. He'd borne it all in silence because he didn't want her to worry. He'd borne it so well that she'd stopped thinking about it entirely.

"I'm sorry," she said. She reached for his shoulder. "I'm sorry, I didn't think—"

"No, Rin." Kitay brushed her hand away. He wouldn't be appeased; he was finished talking. They weren't moving past this, at least not now. "You never do."

Rin walked through Tikany alone. Kitay had stormed off somewhere inside the general's complex, and she didn't bother trying to find him.

They had fought like this before. Not so frequently after the Battle of the Red Cliffs, but every few weeks the same argument bubbled up between them, a chasm they couldn't bridge. It always boiled down to the same fundamental impasse, with a hundred different manifestations. Kitay found her callous. Astonishingly careless with human life, he'd once put it. And she found him weak, too hesitant to take decisive action. She'd always been convinced that he didn't quite grasp the stakes at hand, that he clung still to some bizarre, pacifist hope of diplomacy. Yet somehow their fights always left her feeling guilty and strangely embarrassed, like a child who had acted out in the classroom.

Fuck this, she thought. Forget Kitay. Forget his morals. She needed to remind herself of the stakes.

Her troops had constructed a public kitchen in the town square. Soldiers doled out bowls of rice gruel and steamed shanyu to long lines of waiting civilians. Camp aides walked along the lines reminding the civilians not to eat too quickly; if their stomachs began to hurt, they should stop immediately. After prolonged periods of starvation, ruptured stomachs from overeating could prove fatal.

Rin cut the line and grabbed two bowls piled high with shanyu root, balancing one nimbly in the crook of her right elbow.

The tent complex in Tikany's northern quarter couldn't be

properly called an infirmary. It was more like an emergency tri-age center, constructed from the wreckage of what used to be the town hall. Cloth-covered bamboo mats had been laid out in neat lines outside the surgery room, through which harried-looking assistants ferried antiseptics and painkillers to peasants whose wounds had been festering for months.

Rin approached the nearest physician and asked for the boy from the killing fields.

"Over there in the corner," he told her. "See if you can get him to eat. He hasn't touched a thing."

The boy's torso was wrapped in bandages, and he looked just as pale and wan as when they'd found him in the graves. But he was sitting up, alert and conscious.

Rin sat down on the dirt beside him. "Hello."

He blinked owlishly at her.

"I'm Runin," she prompted. "Rin. I pulled you from the grave."

His voice was a breathy rasp. "I know who you are."

"And what's your name?" she asked softly.

"Zhen," he started, and then coughed. He pressed a hand against his chest and winced. "Zhen Dulin."

"Looks like you got lucky, Dulin."

He snorted at that.

She placed one bowl on the ground and held out the other. "Are you hungry?"

He shook his head.

"If you starve yourself to death, then you're just letting them win."

He shrugged.

She tried something else. "It's got salt."

"Bullshit," Dulin said.

She couldn't help but grin. Nobody south of Monkey Province had tasted salt in months. It was easy to take such a common con-diment for granted during peacetime, but after months of bland vegetables, salt became as valuable as gold.

"I'm not lying." She waved the bowl under his nose. "Try it."

Dulin hesitated, then nodded. She passed the bowl carefully into his trembling fingers.

He brought a spoonful of steamed shanyu to his mouth and nibbled at the edge. Then his eyes widened and he stopped bothering with the spoon, gulping the rest down like Rin might snatch it away from him at any moment.

"Take it slow," she cautioned. "There's plenty more. Stop if your stomach starts to cramp."

He didn't speak again until he'd nearly finished the bowl. He paused and sucked in a deep breath, eyelids fluttering. "I'd forgotten how salt tasted."

"Me too."

"You know how desperate we got?" He lowered the bowl. "We scraped the white deposits off tombstones and boiled it down because it resembled the taste. Tombs." His hands trembled. "My father's *tomb*."

"Don't think about that," Rin said quietly. "Just enjoy this."

She let him eat in silence for a while. At last he placed his empty bowl on the ground and sighed, both hands clutching his stomach. Then he twisted around to face her. "Why are you here?"

"I want you to tell me what happened," she said.

He seemed to shrink. "You mean at the—"

"Yes. Please. If you remember. As much as you can."

"Why?"

"Because I have to hear it."

He was silent for a long time, his gaze fixed on something far away.

"I thought I had died," he said at last. "When they struck me it hurt so much that everything turned black, and I thought that's what death was. I remember feeling glad that at least it was over. I didn't have to be scared anymore. But then I—"

He broke off. His entire body was shaking.

"You can stop," Rin said, suddenly ashamed. "I'm sorry, I shouldn't have made you."

But Dulin shook his head and kept going. "But then I woke

up in the field, and I saw the sun shining over me, and I realized I'd survived. But they were piling the bodies on top of me then, and I didn't want them to realize I was alive. So I lay still. They kept stacking the bodies, one after the other, until I could barely breathe. And then they packed on the dirt."

A pang of pain shot through Rin's palm, and she realized her fingernails had dug grooves into her skin. She forced them to relax before they drew blood.

"They never saw you?" she asked.

"They weren't looking. They're not thorough. They don't care. They just wanted it over with."

The unspoken implication, of course, was that Dulin might not have been the only one. Rather, it was more likely there *had* been other victims, injured but not dead, who toppled into an early grave and were slowly suffocated by dirt and the weight of bodies.

Rin exhaled slowly.

Somewhere in the back of her mind, Altan was appeased. This was her answer. This justified everything she'd done. This was the face of her enemy.

Kitay could spout on and on about ethics. She didn't care. She needed revenge. She wanted her army.

Dulin's shoulders started to heave. He was sobbing.

Rin reached out and patted him awkwardly on the shoulder. "Hey. You're all right—it's all right."

"It's not. I shouldn't be the only one, I should be dead—"

"Don't say that."

His face contorted. "But it shouldn't have been me."

"I used to hate myself for living, too," she said. "I didn't think it was fair that I'd survived. That others had died in my place."

"It's *not* fair," Dulin whispered. "I should be in the ground with them."

"And there will be days you'll wish you were." Rin didn't understand why she needed so urgently to comfort this boy, this stranger, only that she wished someone had told her the same thing months before. "It doesn't go away. It never will. But when it hurts, lean into it. It's so much harder to stay alive. That doesn't mean you don't deserve to live. It means you're brave."

Life returned to Tikany that night.

Rin had retreated early to the general's complex, intent on falling asleep the moment her face hit her mattress. But then a knock came at the door, and she opened it to find not the sentry or messenger she'd expected but a circle of women, eyes tilted sheepishly down, nudging one another as if daring someone else to be the first to speak.

"What is it?" Rin asked warily.

"Come with us," said the woman at the front.

Rin blinked at them, puzzled. "Where?"

The woman's face broke into a smile. "To dance."

Then Rin remembered that despite everything, this day had been a liberation, and liberations deserved to be celebrated.

So she followed them into the town center, where a crowd of hundreds had formed, holding bamboo torches and floating lanterns up against the moonless night. Drums beat incessantly, accompanying lilting flute melodies that seemed to come from everywhere, while firecrackers went off every few seconds like musical punctuation.

Dancers whirled in the center of the square. There were dozens of them, mostly young girls, all moving without choreography or order. None of this had been rehearsed. It couldn't possibly have been. Each dancer moved from memory, pulling together fragments of performances from earlier times, moving for the sheer joy of being alive and free.

It should have been an utter mess. It was the most beautiful thing Rin had ever seen.

The women entreated Rin to join. But she refused, preferring to sit down on an overturned barrel and watch. She'd never joined the dances when she'd lived here. Those dances were for rich girls, joyful girls, girls whose marriages were events to be celebrated and not feared. They weren't for war orphans. Rin had only ever watched. She wanted desperately to join them now, but she was afraid she wouldn't know how to move.

The drums sped up. The dancers became a hypnotic vision, ankles and arms moving faster and faster until they seemed a blur in the firelight, moving to a tempo that felt in tune with Rin's own pulse. She blinked, and for a moment she saw a different dance, heard a different song. She saw brown bodies dancing by the campfire, singing words that she'd heard a long time ago in a language that she couldn't speak but could almost remember.

She'd been seeing this vision since the first time she'd met the Phoenix. She knew this vision ended in death.

But this time the dancing bodies did not turn into skeletons, but instead remained furiously, resolutely, alive. *Here we are*, they said. *Watch us thrive. We've escaped the past, and we own the future.*

"Hey."

Rin blinked, and the vision disappeared. Souji stood before her, holding two mugs of millet wine. He held one out to her. "Mind if I sit?"

She shifted to make room for him. They clinked their mugs and drank. Rin sloshed the millet wine around her tongue, savoring the heady, sour tang.

"I'm surprised you haven't disappeared into an alley with one of them." Rin nodded to the dancers. Women seemed attracted to Souji like moths to a flame; Rin had seen him disappear into his tent with at least eight different companions since they'd left Ruijin.

"Still trying to pick," Souji said. "Where's your better half?"

"I'm not sure." She'd been scanning the crowd for Kitay since she arrived, but hadn't found him. "He might be asleep."

She didn't tell Souji that they'd fought. She and Kitay were a pair against the world; no one else should know about their rifts.

"He's missing out." Souji leaned back, watching the dancers with an amused, half-lidded expression. Rin could tell he was already quite drunk; his movements were slow and careless, and a cloud of sour fumes wafted toward her every time he spoke. "This is it, Princess. This is as good as it gets. Enjoy this while it lasts."

She gazed at the bonfire and tried to take Souji's advice, to lose herself in the music, the laughing, and the drums. But an uneasy darkness lingered in the pit of her stomach, a hard knot of fear that wouldn't dissipate no matter how hard she smiled.

She couldn't derive any joy from this.

Was this what liberation felt like? This couldn't be it. Freedom was supposed to feel like safety. She was supposed to feel like no one could ever harm her again.

No, it was more than that.

She wanted to go *back*. She couldn't remember a moment in the last two years that she had ever felt safe closing her eyes. If she chased that memory down, it would have last been when she was at the Academy, when the world seemed contained in books and exams, when war was a game mirroring something that might never come to pass.

And she knew she could never get that back again.

But she could get something close. Safety. Security. And that demanded total victory.

It didn't matter whether she wanted war. The Republic would bring war to her, would hunt her down until she was dead or it was. And the only way to be safe was to strike first.

Your life is not your own, Vaisra had once told her, and he had elaborated many times in the weeks that followed. You do not have a right to happiness when you hold this much power in your hands.

When you hear screaming, run toward it. His precise words. He'd only been trying to manipulate her; she knew that now. Still, the words rang true.

But where was the screaming now?

"What's wrong?" Souji asked.

She blinked and straightened up. "Hmm?"

"You look like someone's shat all over your ancestors' graves."

"I don't know, I just . . ." She struggled to name her discomfort. "This isn't right."

Souji snorted. "What, the dancing, or the music? Didn't know you were so picky."

"They're happy. Everyone's too happy." Her words spilled out faster and faster, spurred on by the millet wine burning in her gut. "They're dancing because they don't know what's coming, they can't see the entire world's about to end because this isn't the end of one war, it's the start, and—"

Souji's hand closed over hers. Rin glanced down, startled. His palm was rough and callused but warm; it felt surprisingly good. She didn't pull away.

"Learn to relax, Princess." His thumb stroked the top of her hand. "This life you've chosen, you won't get many moments like this again. But it's the nights like this that keep you alive. All you think about is who you're fighting against. But that?" He swung his mug toward the dancers. "That's what you're fighting for."

Several hours later Souji was so drunk that Rin didn't trust him to find the general's complex on his own. They walked up the dark, rocky path together, his arm draped heavily over her shoulders. Halfway up the hill his foot snagged on a rock and he pitched forward, looping his arm around her waist for balance.

The ploy was quite transparent. Rin rolled her eyes and extricated herself from his grasp. He fumbled for her breasts. She smacked his hand away. "Don't try that shit with me. I'll burn your balls off, I've done that before."

"Come on, Princess," he said. He wrapped his arm back around her shoulders, pulling her in close. His skin felt terribly hot.

Despite herself, Rin found herself curving into that heat.

"No one's here." His lips brushed her ear. "Why don't we have some fun?"

The embarrassing thing was that she *did* feel some interest, a faint, unfamiliar stirring in the pit of her stomach. She quashed it. *Don't be a fucking idiot.*

Souji didn't want her. Souji was the last man in the world to find her beautiful. He had his pick of willing conquests among the camp, all likely prettier and easier to deal with in the morning than Rin would be.

This wasn't about lust, this was about power. This was about possession. He wanted to dominate her just so that later he could crow that he had.

And Rin, admittedly, was tempted. Souji was undeniably handsome, and certainly experienced. He'd know what to do with their bodies even if she hadn't the faintest clue. He could show her how to do all the things she'd only heard of, had only imagined.

But she'd be stupid to go to bed with him. Once the word spread, no one would look at her the same way again. She'd been around soldiers long enough to know how this worked. The man got bragging rights. The woman, already likely the only female soldier in her squadron, became the camp whore.

"Let's get you back to your bed," she said.

"It'd be good for you." Souji didn't remove his arm from her shoulder. "You're too tense. All that pent-up anger. It'd do you good to let loose once in a while, Princess. Have some fun."

He caressed her collarbone. She shuddered. "Souji, *stop.*"

"What's the matter? Are you a virgin?"

He asked this so bluntly that for a moment all Rin could do was stare.

His eyebrows shot up. "No. Really, Princess?

She shoved his arm away. "It's none of your business."

But he'd found her weak spot. He knew it—he grinned, teeth glinting in the moonlight. "Is it true you have no womb?"

"*What?*"

"Heard a rumor around camp. Said you burned your womb out back at Sinegard. Doesn't surprise me. Smart, really. Pity about the Speerlies, though. Now you're the last. Do you ever regret it?"

She hissed through clenched teeth. "I've never regretted it."

"Pity." He put a hand on her stomach. "We could have made some nice brown babies. My brains, your abilities. Kings of the south."

That was enough. She jerked away from him, fist raised and knees crouched. "Touch me again and I'll kill you."

He just scoffed. His eyes roved up and down her body, as if evaluating how much force it would take to pin her to the ground.

Rin's breath caught in her throat.

What was wrong with her? She'd started and ended wars. She'd buried a god. She'd incinerated a country. There wasn't an entity on the planet that could face her in a fair fight and win. She was certain of her own strength; she'd sacrificed everything to make sure she never felt powerless again.

So why was she so afraid?

At last, he raised his hands in a gesture of surrender. "Just offering. No need to be like that."

"Get away from me." Her voice rang through the dark, louder than she'd intended. Someone might overhear. Perhaps that was what she should want—for someone, anyone, to come running. "*Now*, Souji."

"Are you always like this? Great Tortoise, that explains why—"

She cut him off. "Do you hear that?"

She thought she heard a faint whining drone—a sound like a faraway swarm of bees, growing louder and louder with every passing second.

Souji fell silent, brows furrowed. "What are you—"

"Shut up," Rin hissed. "Just listen."

Yes—the droning was distinct now. The noise wasn't just in her head. She wasn't panicking over nothing. This was real.

Souji's eyes widened. He'd heard it, too.

"Get down," he gasped, and lunged at her just before the first bombs exploded.

CHAPTER 9

They hit the ground together, Souji's elbows digging painfully into Rin's ribs. There was the briefest moment of silence, then an eerie ringing in her ears. She peered up from beneath Souji's splayed body, groaning, just as Tikany lit up in a flash of orange light.

Then the bombing resumed, a roll of thunder that just kept going.

Souji rolled off of Rin. She scrambled unsteadily to her feet.

Kitay. Her vision was half-gone, along with her balance; as she stumbled toward the general's complex she kept lurching to the side like a drunkard. *I have to find Kitay.*

A high, tortured keen sounded behind her. She turned around. By firelight she could just make out a young officer's face, one of Zhuden's men whose name she'd never learned. He lay on the ground several yards away. She stared at him for a moment, utterly confused. She and Souji had been alone in the street until now; all the other officers had remained at the bonfire, a good five minutes' walk from here.

Was it the blast? Could the force of the explosion have hurled him this far?

But the officer looked fine—his head, shoulders, and torso were all intact, unbloodied. Unburned, even. Why was he—

The black smudges cleared slowly from Rin's vision, and she saw what had at first been hidden by smoke and darkness. The officer's legs had been blown away from the upper thigh.

He was looking at her. Gods, he was still conscious. He lifted a trembling hand toward her. His mouth moved. No sound came out, at least none that she could hear, but she understood.

Please.

She reached for the knife at her belt, but her fingers fumbled clumsily against the sheath.

"I'll do it." Souji's voice rang as loud as a gong against her ears. He seemed to have sobered completely, his alcohol-drenched sluggishness evaporated by the same adrenaline pounding through her veins. He seemed far more in command of himself than she felt. With a brisk efficiency, he pulled the knife out of her hand and bent down to slit the officer's throat.

She stared, swaying on her feet.

We weren't ready.

She'd thought she had more time. When she'd destroyed Kesegi's message she'd known Nezha had her in his sights, but she'd thought she might have the chance to train her newly won Southern Army while the Republic finished their campaign in the north. She'd thought, after the Beehive fell, that they could take a moment to breathe.

She hadn't known Nezha was on their fucking doorstep.

Air cannons boomed continuously in harmony with the drone of dirigible engines. *A celestial orchestra*, Rin thought, dazed. The gods were playing a dirge to their demise.

She heard screaming from the town center. She knew that there was no mounted ground defense, no chance of fending the airships off. Her troops were flush with victory and drunk from revels. They'd only posted a skeleton guard at the township gates because they'd thought, for once, they were safe.

And the fucking *bonfires*—gods, the bonfires must have been like beacons, screaming out their location from the ground.

The shouts grew louder. Panicked, scattered crowds were flooding through the streets, away from the bonfires. A little girl ran screaming in Rin's direction, and Rin didn't have time to yell, *No, stop, get down*, before a blast rocked the air and flames shrouded the tiny body.

The same explosion knocked Rin off her feet. She rolled onto her back and moaned, her good hand pressed against her left ear. The bombing was so frequent that she could no longer hear any pause between drops, only an incessant rumble while fiery orange flares went off everywhere she looked.

She pushed her hand against the ground and forced herself to stand.

"We need to get out of here." Souji yanked her up by the wrist and dragged her toward the forest. Explosions went off so close that she felt the heat sear her face, but the dirigibles weren't firing over the forests.

They were only aiming at the campfires—at open, vulnerable civilians.

"Hold on," she said. "Kitay—"

Souji wouldn't let go of her arm. "We'll move farther into the trees. They haven't got visibility near the forest. We'll take the mountain routes, get as far as we can before—"

She struggled against his grip. "We have to get Kitay!"

"He'll make his own way out," Souji said. "But you'll be dead in seconds if you—"

"I'll manage." She didn't know how she'd fend off the dirigibles—they didn't seem to have weak points she could easily burn—but she might aim fire at the steering mechanisms, the ammunition basket, *something*. But she couldn't leave without Kitay.

Was he still in the general's complex, or had he gone to the center square? The complex up the hill was still untouched, hidden under the cover of darkness, but the square was now an inferno.

He couldn't be critically injured—if he were, she would feel it, and right now she didn't feel anything, which meant—

"Hold on." Souji's fingers tightened around her wrist. "It's stopped."

The sky had turned silent. The buzzing had died away.

They're landing, Rin realized. This was a ground assault. The dirigibles didn't want to eradicate all Tikany by air. They wanted prisoners.

But didn't they understand the dangers of a ground assault? They might have their arquebuses, but she had a *god*, and she would smite them down the moment they approached. They only bore a fighting chance against her if they hovered out of her range. They had to understand that sending down troops was suicide.

Unless—

Unless.

An icy chill crept through her veins.

She saw it now. The Hesperians didn't want her bombed. She was their favorite test subject; they didn't want her blown to pieces. They wanted her captured alive, delivered whole and writhing to the Gray Company's laboratories, so they'd brought the only person in the world who could face her in hand-to-hand combat and win.

Nezha, whose wounds stitched themselves back together as quickly as they opened.

Nezha, whose powers flowed from the sea.

"Run," she told Souji, just as another round of missiles tore them apart.

For a moment the world was silent.

All was darkness, and then colors began to return—only red at first, red everywhere she looked, and then muddled clumps of red and green. Rin didn't know how she managed to stand, only that one moment she was lying on the ground and the next she was staggering through the forest, lurching from tree to tree because her balance was broken and she couldn't stand up straight. She tasted blood on her lip, but she couldn't tell where she'd been hurt;

the pain was like a shroud, pulsing uniformly across her body with every step she took.

"Souji?"

No response. She wasn't sure if she'd gotten the sounds out— she couldn't hear her own voice, except for an odd muffle deep inside her skull.

"Souji?"

Still nothing.

She stumbled forward, rubbing at her eyes, trying to gain some better grasp on the world and her senses other than it hurt, it *hurt* . . .

A familiar smell suffused the air. Something nauseatingly, sickly sweet, something that made her stomach roil and her veins ache with longing.

The Republicans had set off opium bombs.

They knew her weakness. They intended to incapacitate her.

Rin took a deep breath and pulled a ball of flame into her hand. She had a higher opium tolerance than most, a gift of months and months of opium addiction and failed rehabilitation. All those nights spent high out of her mind, conversing with hallucinations of Altan, might buy her a few extra minutes before she was cut off from the Phoenix.

That meant she had to find Nezha *now*.

"Come on," she murmured. She sent the flame into the air above and around her. Nezha wouldn't be able to resist the flare; it'd function like a beacon. He was searching for her. He'd come.

"Where are you?" she shouted.

Lightning split the air in response. Then a sheet of rain abruptly hammered down so hard that Rin nearly fell.

This wasn't natural rain. The sky had been clear just a moment ago, there hadn't even been a whisper of clouds, and even if a storm had been brewing it couldn't have moved in so quickly, so coincidentally . . .

But since when could Nezha summon the *rain*?

In some awful way it made sense. Dragons controlled the rain, so said the myths. Even in Tikany, a place where religion had long been diminished to children's bedtime stories, the magistrates lit incense offerings to the dragon lords of the river during drought years to induce heavy showers.

But that meant Nezha's domain wasn't just the river but all the water around him. And if he could summon it, control it . . .

If this rain was his doing, he'd become so much more powerful than she'd feared.

"General?"

Rin turned. A band of troops had clustered around her. New recruits, she didn't recognize them—they'd survived, bless them; they were rallying toward her, even when they'd just seen their comrades ripped apart.

Their loyalty amazed her. But their deaths would accomplish nothing.

"Get away," she ordered.

They didn't move. The one in the front spoke. "We'll fight with you, General."

"Don't even try," she said. "He will kill you all."

She'd seen Nezha at the height of his abilities once before. He'd raised an entire lake to protect his fleet. If he'd perfected his skills since, then not a single one of them would survive for more than a few seconds.

This wasn't a war of men anymore. This was a war of gods. This had to end between her and Nezha, shaman to shaman.

All she could do before then was minimize the fallout.

"Go help the villagers," she told them. "Get them away from here, as many as you can. Seek cover under darkness and don't stop running until you're out of range of the rain. *Hurry.*"

They obeyed, leaving her alone in the storm. The rainfall was deafening. She couldn't see a single Republican soldier, Nikara or Hesperian, around her, which meant Nezha, too, had sent away his reinforcements.

He would have done it out of nobility. Typical. He was always the righteous ruler, the noble aristocrat. She could just imagine

Nezha giving the order in his arrogant, assured voice. *Leave her to me.*

Fire flickered around her body, winking in and out as sheets of rain kept crushing it away. The water was now coming down so hard it felt like repeated smacks from the flat side of a sword. She struggled to stand up straight. Her fingers trembled on the hilt of her blade.

Then at last she saw him, striding through rain that parted cleanly around him whenever he moved.

Pain arced through the knotted scar in her lower back. Memories stabbed her mind like daggers. A touch, a whisper, a kiss. She clenched her jaw tight to keep from trembling.

He looked older, though only several months had passed since she last saw him. Taller. He moved differently; his stride was more assertive, imbued with a new sense of authority. With Jinzha dead, Nezha was the crown prince of Arlong, the Young Marshal of his father's army, and the heir apparent to the Nikara Republic. Nezha was about to own the entire country, and only Rin stood in his way.

They regarded each other for a moment in a silence that seemed to stretch on for an eternity, the weight of their shared past hanging heavy between them. Rin felt a sudden pang of nostalgia, that complicated mix of longing and regret, and couldn't make it go away. She'd spent so long fighting by his side, she had to make herself remember how to hate him.

He stood close enough that she could see his grotesque smile, the tortured ripple that pulled at the scar lines drawn into the left half of his face. His cheeks and jaw, once angular perfection, were shattered porcelain. Cracked tiles. A map of the country falling apart.

Venka had claimed he was ill. He looked the furthest thing from ill—Rin couldn't detect a shred of weakness in the way he carried himself. He was primed for battle, lethal.

"Hello, Rin," he called. His voice seemed deeper, crueler. He sounded a near match to his father. "What happened to your hand?"

She opened her palm. Flame roared at his face. Dismissively he waved a hand, and a gust of rain extinguished the fire long before it reached him.

Fuck. Rin could feel her fingers going numb. She was running out of time.

"This doesn't have to be hard," he said. "Come quietly and no one else has to die."

She braced her heels against the dirt. "You're going home in a coffin."

He shrugged. The rain began to pound even harder, pummeling so vigorously that her knees buckled.

She gritted her teeth, fighting to stay upright.

She would not kneel to him.

She had to get past that rain; it was functioning too well as a shield. But the solution was so simple. She'd learned it long ago at Sinegard. Years later, the basic pattern of their fights remained the same. Nezha was stronger than she was. His limbs were longer. Then and now, she only stood a chance when she got in close, where his reach didn't matter.

She lunged. Nezha crouched, whipping his sword out. But she'd aimed lower than he'd anticipated. She wasn't going for his head—she wanted his center of gravity. He came down easier than she'd expected. She scrambled for control as they fell. She was so much lighter than he was, she'd only pin him down if she caught him at just the right angle—but he slashed upward, and she lost her balance as she ducked.

He landed heavily atop her. She thrashed. He jabbed his sword down, twice missing her face for mud.

She opened her mouth and spat fire.

It engulfed his face for one glorious moment. She saw skin crinkling and peeling back. She caught a glimpse of bone. Then a wall of water crashed over both of them, extinguishing her flame, leaving them both sputtering for breath.

She recovered first. She got her knee up in his solar plexus. He flailed backward. She wriggled out from under him and settled into a crouch.

The rain's stopped, she realized. The pressure was gone; the forest fell silent.

At the same time she felt a woozy tilt in her limbs, a heady rush in her temples.

So this was it. The opium had seeped too deep into her bloodstream. She didn't have the fire, and her only advantage was that he'd lost the water. This was now a matter of blades and fists and teeth.

She unsheathed her knife. They dueled for only a moment. It was no contest. He disarmed her first, and easily, sent her blade spinning far away into the dark.

No matter. She knew she couldn't match him with blades. The moment the hilt left her palm, she aimed a savage kick at Nezha's wrist.

It worked. He dropped his sword. Now they had only their fists. That was a relief. This was so much easier, more direct, more brutal. She clawed at his eyes. He slapped her hand away. She bit at his elbow. He shoved it at her mouth. Her head jerked back.

Blood stung her eyes and clouded her vision. She punched without looking. Nezha was doing the same. His blows came at her too fast for her to dodge or block but she gave as good as she got, landed just as many as he did, until she forgot she didn't have a right hand to punch with. She lashed out with her stump. He blocked it with his elbow. Awful, blinding pain ripped through the right half of her torso. For a moment she forgot how to breathe.

Nezha broke free of her grasp, jumped to his feet, and kicked down at her ribs. She curled into a ball, too winded to scream. He stomped on her stump. Her vision flashed white.

He kicked her in the side, again and again until she was lying on her back, too stunned to do anything but gasp like a fish out of water. He stumbled back, chest heaving. Then he dropped to his knees, straddled her chest, and pinned her arms down with his hands.

"I told you," he panted, "to come quietly."

She spat blood in his face.

He slammed his knuckles into her right eye. Her head thudded against the wet dirt. He wiped the back of his hand against his shirt, then drew it back to deliver a second punch to her left eye. She took the beating like a limp doll, without sound, without response. He punched her five, six, seven times. She lost count. She was dazed with pain and opium; the blows felt like raindrops.

But the fact that he was beating her meant something—the fact that she wasn't dead *meant something*. She should be dead right now. He should have just stabbed her in the heart or slashed her throat; it would have been easier. And Nezha wasn't sadistic, wasn't prone to torture over efficiency.

He's not aiming to kill, she realized. Nezha wanted her alive. He wanted to incapacitate. And right now, he just wanted to hurt.

That was the difference between them. *His loss.*

"You should have killed me at Arlong," she hissed.

The punches stopped.

Nezha reached down for her neck and began to squeeze.

She scrabbled frantically at his hands. Altan had taught her to escape chokeholds—hands were strong, single fingers weren't so much, so all you had to do was separate them. *One at a time.* She dug her fingers under his middle finger and detached it from the others, then pulled backward hard, harder—

He wasn't letting go.

Alternate means, then. She jammed her thumb toward his eyes. He twisted his face away. Her nails dug into his cheek instead, and she compensated by digging in so hard she drew blood. Three neat crimson streaks sliced down his right jaw.

His grip loosened, just the slightest bit, for a brief moment. That was all she needed.

She reached behind her, scrabbling to find his blade. She'd seen him drop it, it had to be within reach . . . but the first thing her fingers closed around was not the hilt but a stone, heavy and jagged, just about the size of her palm.

That would do.

She swung the stone up against Nezha's temple. It connected

with bone with a satisfying crunch. His grip loosened. She summoned every remaining ounce of her strength into her left arm and struck his head again. Blood gathered inside a gash by his right eye, as if hesitating, then started pouring out in thick rivulets.

He slumped to the side.

She wriggled out from beneath him. He toppled to the ground.

Was that it? Had she knocked him unconscious? Could this have been so easy? She leaned cautiously over him, hefting the rock in her hand for a third and final blow.

Then she paused, startled.

The blood flow had stopped. Nezha's skin was stitching itself together, pale skin growing back over red pulp as if time had simply reversed.

She watched in disbelief. Nezha could recover from blows with terrifying speed, she knew that, but the process had taken hours before. Now his body was erasing wounds in mere seconds.

She'd burned him earlier. Badly. There was no evidence of that, either.

What if she ripped his heart from his chest? Would a new one sprout? If she buried his sword between his ribs, would his heart grow around it?

Only one way to find out. She picked the sword up off the ground and knelt above him, straddling his torso with her knees.

Nezha made a soft moaning noise. His eyelids fluttered.

Rin raised her left hand high, blade pointed straight down. Her arm trembled; her fingers felt awkward around the hilt. But she couldn't miss, not from this angle. She had an immobile victim and a clear, open target; she couldn't possibly fuck this up.

One hard blow to the chest. That was all it would take. One blow, perhaps a twist for good measure, and all this would be over.

But she couldn't bring her arm down. Something stayed her hand. Her arm was like some foreign object, moving of its own will. She clenched her teeth and tried again. The blade remained suspended in the air.

She screamed in frustration, lunging forward over Nezha's

limp form, yet she still couldn't bring the blade anywhere near his flesh.

Nezha's eyes shot open just as a droning noise buzzed over their heads.

Rin glanced up. A dirigible approached, swooping low toward the clearing at a frightening speed. She dropped the sword and scrambled off Nezha's chest.

The dirigible landed only ten yards away. The basket had barely hit the ground before soldiers jumped out, shouting words that Rin couldn't understand.

She dove for the trees. For the next several moments she crawled desperately through the bushes, ignoring the thorns and branches scratching at her eyes, lacerating her skin. *Elbow, knee, elbow, knee.* She didn't dare look back. She just had to get away, quickly as she could. If they caught her now she was nothing; she had no sword, no fire, no army. If they caught her now, she was dead. Pain screamed for her to stop and fear propelled her forward.

She kept waiting for the shouts to catch up to her. For the cold steel at the back of her neck.

They never came.

At last, when her lungs burned red-hot and her heart felt like it would explode out of her chest, she stopped and peered behind her.

The dirigible rose slowly into the air. She watched, heart pounding, as it ascended above the trees. It teetered for a moment, as if unsure of where it was going, and then it veered sharply to the left and retreated.

They hadn't found her. They hadn't even tried.

Rin attempted to stand and failed. Her muscles wouldn't obey. She couldn't even sit up. The pummeling she'd just taken hit her all at once, a million different pains and bruises that kept her on the ground like firm hands pushing her down.

She lay curled on her side, helpless and immobile, shrieking in frustration. She'd squandered her chance. She wouldn't get it back. Nezha was gone, and she was alone in the mud, the dark, and the smoke.

CHAPTER 10

She awoke choking on mud. She'd rolled into it while unconscious, and it had caked over the lower half of her face. She
couldn't breathe and couldn't see; she clawed agitatedly at her
eyes, nose, and mouth, terrified a rocket had blown them off. The
mud came away in sharp, sticky tiles that left her skin raw and
stinging, and her panic subsided.

She lay still for a moment, breathing deep, and then rose
slowly to her feet.

She could stand without swaying. The opium high was fading. She knew this stage of the comedown—was familiar with
the numb dryness of her tongue and the faint, disorienting buzzing in her temples. She needed hours still before her mind fully
cleared, but at least she could walk.

Everything hurt. She didn't want to stop and take stock of her
wounds. She didn't want to know the full list of what was wrong
with her, not now. She could move all four limbs. She could see,
breathe, hear, and walk. That was good enough. The rest had to
wait.

She staggered back toward the village, wincing with every
step.

The sun was just starting to rise. The attack had occurred

just after midnight. That meant she'd been lying out there for five hours at least. That boded ill—if her army was still intact then their very *first* task would have been to search for her—their general, their Speerly.

But no one had come.

She knew they'd lost. That was a foregone conclusion; they'd never had a ground-based air defense to begin with. But how bad was the damage?

Silence met her in the town square. Small fires still crackled around every corner, smoldering inside bomb craters. A handful of soldiers moved through the streets, combing through the ruins and pulling bodies from the wreckage. So few of those bodies were moving. So few of those bodies were whole. Rin saw scattered parts wherever she looked: an arm here, a headless torso there, a pair of little feet on the dirt path right in front of her.

She couldn't even muster the strength to vomit. Still dazed, she focused on just breathing, on staying calm and figuring out what to do next.

Should they hide? Should she round up the survivors and send them fleeing to the nearest caves? Or were they temporarily safe, now that the dirigibles had gone? Kitay would know what to do—

Kitay.

Where was Kitay?

When she reached for the Phoenix, all she met was a wall of silence. She tried to suppress a rising wave of panic. If the back door wasn't working, then it only meant that Kitay was asleep or unconscious. It didn't mean he was gone. He *couldn't* be gone.

"Where is Kitay?"

She asked every person she saw. She shook exhausted soldiers and half-conscious survivors alike and screamed the question into their faces. But no one had any answers; they returned her pleas with stricken, glassy-eyed silence.

For hours she shouted his name around Tikany, limping through the lanes of wounded bodies, scanning the wreckage for any sign of his wiry, overgrown hair and his slender freckled limbs. When she found Venka, miraculously unhurt, they searched together, checking every street, alley, and dead end, even in the districts that had been far removed from the center of the bombing. They checked twice. Thrice.

He had to be here. He had to be fine. She had searched for him like this once before, in Golyn Niis, where his odds of survival had been far worse. Yet still he had answered then, and she hoped that he might again, that she would hear his thin voice carrying once more through the still air.

She knew he was alive. She knew he wasn't too badly wounded, not more than she was, because she would have felt it. *He has to be here.* She didn't dare consider the alternatives because the alternatives were too awful, because without Kitay she was just—

She was just—

Her whole body trembled.

Oh, gods.

"He's gone." Finally Venka said out loud what they both knew, wrapping her arms tight around Rin's waist as if she were afraid Rin might hurt herself if she moved. "They took him. He's not lost, he's gone."

Rin shook her head. "We have to keep looking—"

"We've walked twice through every square foot in a mile's radius," Venka said. "He's not here. We've got other things to worry about, Rin."

"But Kitay—we can't—"

"He might still be all right." Venka's voice was inordinately gentle; she was making a valiant effort to comfort. "There's no body."

Of course there was no body. If Kitay were dead then Rin wouldn't be standing—which left only one conclusion.

Nezha had taken him prisoner.

And what a valuable prisoner he was, a hostage worth his weight in gold. He was so smart, he was too fucking smart, and that made him vulnerable to anyone who had the faintest idea of who he was and what his mind could do. The Pirate Queen Moag had once locked Kitay in a safe house and assigned him to balance Ankhiluun's books. Yin Vaisra had made him a senior strategist.

What would Nezha use him for? How cruel would he be?

This was her fault. She should have killed him, she *couldn't* kill him, and now he had Kitay.

"Calm down." Venka gripped her by the shoulders. "You have to calm down, you're shaking. Let's get you to a physician—"

Rin jerked out of her grasp, more violently than she'd intended. "Don't touch me."

Venka recoiled, startled. Rin staggered away. She would have run off, but her left ankle screamed in protest every time she moved. She hobbled resolutely forward, trying to breathe, trying not to cry. It didn't matter where she was going, she just had to get away from these bodies—the smoke, the embers, the dying, and the dead.

Venka didn't follow.

Then Rin was halfway to the killing fields, alone on the dusty plain. No soldiers in sight, no spies or witnesses.

She tilted her head to the sky, shut her eyes, and reached for the fire.

Come on. Come on . . .

Of course the fire didn't come. She knew it wouldn't; she was trying only because she needed to confirm it, like the way one prodded the sore gap left by a wrenched tooth to examine the extent of the loss. When she groped for the void, tried to tilt backward into the Pantheon like she had done so many times before with ease, she came away with nothing.

Nothing but the Seal—always lurking, taunting, Altan's laughter echoing louder and louder to match her despair.

Kitay? She tried sending her thoughts out to him. That wasn't how the anchor bond worked; they couldn't communicate telepathically, they could only feel each other's pain. But regardless of distance, their souls were still linked—didn't that count for something?

Please. She threw her thoughts against the barrier in her mind, praying they might somehow reach him. *Please, I need you. Where are you?*

She was met with deafening silence.

She clutched her head, shaking, breathing in short and frantic bursts. Then came the sheer and utter terror as she realized what this meant.

She didn't have the fire.

She didn't have the fire.

Kitay was gone, truly gone, and without him she was vulnerable. Powerless. A girl who didn't have a fighting arm or the shamanic ability that justified her inability to wield a blade. Not a Speerly, not a soldier, not a goddess.

What army would follow her now?

Desperate, she gripped her knife and carved a shaky question mark into her upper thigh, deep enough to leave scars that might reappear as thin white lines on Kitay's skin. They'd communicated this way once before; it had to work again. She carved another mark. Then another. She sliced her thigh bloody. But Kitay never answered.

Tikany was shrouded in terrified silence when she returned from the fields. No one seemed to know what to do. Here and there Rin saw desultory efforts at rescue and reconstruction. A triage center was set up on the bonfire grounds, where the bombs had hit hardest, but Rin saw only two physicians and one assistant, hardly enough to deal with the lines of the wounded stretching around the square. Here and there she saw soldiers clearing away rubble or making futile attempts to create temporary shelters from the hollowed pits where once had stood buildings. But most of the survivors, civilians and soldiers both, just stood around looking dazed, as if they still couldn't quite believe what had just happened.

No one was giving orders.

Rin supposed *she* should have been the one giving the orders.

But she, too, walked about in a helpless fugue. She didn't know what to say. Every order, every action she could possibly take seemed utterly pointless. How could they come back from this?

She couldn't turn back time. She couldn't bring back the dead.

Don't be pathetic, Altan would have said. She could hear his voice loud and clear, as if he were standing right beside her. *Stop being such a little brat. So you lost. You're still alive. Pick up the pieces and figure out how to start over.*

She took a deep breath, squared her shoulders, and tried to at least act like she knew what she was doing.

Back to the basics. She had to know what assets she still had, and what she had lost. She needed to determine what her fighting capabilities were. She had to gather her officers.

She seized the arm of the first Iron Wolf she saw. "Where's Souji?"

She wouldn't have been surprised if he said he didn't know. Most of the Iron Wolves were milling about, looking just as confused and disoriented as the rest. But she wasn't prepared for the look of terror that came over his face.

He looked as if she'd just threatened to kill him.

He paused before he answered. "Ah, not here, ma'am—"

"I can see that," she snapped. "Find him for me. Tell him I want to see him. Right now."

The Iron Wolf seemed to be trying to decide something. He had a strange look in his eye that Rin couldn't quite read. Defiance? Mere disorientation? She opened her mouth to ask again, but he gave her a curt nod and headed off toward the wreckage.

She returned to the general's complex, one of the few buildings left intact thanks to its solid stone foundations. She sat behind the desk, pulled out a sheaf of planning documents from a drawer, and spread them on her desk. Then she started to think.

The opium was nearly gone from her bloodstream. Her mental clarity had returned. Her mind went back to the cool, logical plane where strategy existed outside the friction of war. It felt familiar, calming. She could do this. She'd been trained for this.

For a moment she forgot the trauma of what she'd just seen,

forgot the million hurts lacerating her body, and busied herself with next steps. She'd start with the tasks that she didn't need Souji for. First things first: She gathered a handful of reliable runners and ordered them to make assessments as quickly as possible. She took stock of how many men she had left based on triage reports and corpse counts. She wrote down a list of basic necessities the army would need to recover, find, or build within the next twenty-four hours—means of transportation, food stores, and shelter. She reread spy reports on the Republic's last known troop positions. That intelligence was clearly outdated, but it helped to know where the gaps in their knowledge were.

Then she tried to work out a way to destroy those damned dirigibles.

She could deal with arquebuses—they were more or less just faster, more lethal crossbows. But the fucking *airships* changed the landscape of battle, added an extra dimension on which she couldn't compete. She needed a way to bring them down.

She started by sketching out her best recollection of their build. She wished they'd managed to ground even one of those dirigibles for study, but memory would have to do for now. The images in her mind's eye were fuzzy; she had to focus through visions of smoke and thunder to recall where the cannons were positioned, how the passenger cradles were affixed to the balloons.

She knew one thing—the airships were frustratingly well-designed. They were heavily armored from below, with no visible chinks at which to aim, and they floated too high in the air for arrows or cannons to reach. The balloons that kept the dirigibles afloat made more promising targets. If she could puncture them she could send the whole ship crashing down. But they seemed to have been plated with some kind of light metal just strong enough to deflect arrowheads, and she'd never gotten a cannonball high enough to see what happened when they collided.

Rockets, then? Could they get the trajectory right? How much explosive force would those rockets need? And how would she organize those ground artillery forces?

She crumpled her diagram in frustration. These sorts of problems were Kitay's domain. He was her engineer, her problem solver. She devised grand schemes, but Kitay figured out the details. He would have cracked this already, would have already begun crafting together some idiotic invention that still somehow *worked*.

A pain that had nothing to do with her injuries stabbed at her chest and spread like blades splintering into daggers, gouging at her heart like grappling hooks. She gasped, then clenched her mouth with her hand.

Tears dripped down her fingers. She couldn't do this alone. Gods, she missed him so much.

Stop that, Altan admonished. *Stop being such a fucking baby.*

Kitay was gone. Bitching and moaning wouldn't change that. All she could do now was focus on getting him back.

She set her drawings aside. She wouldn't be able to solve this now. She had to think about basic survival, had to get what was left of the army through the night. For that she needed Souji, but he still hadn't appeared.

She frowned. *Why* hadn't he appeared? It had been over an hour. She hadn't seen him since the attack, but surely he wasn't dead or captured—she would have known by now. She stood up and strode to the door. She jumped, startled, when she saw the same Iron Wolf from earlier standing on the other side, hand raised as if he'd been about to knock. Souji was nowhere in sight.

"Where is he?" she demanded.

The Iron Wolf cleared his throat. "Souji requests that you meet him in his tent."

That immediately struck Rin as suspicious. Souji had made his quarters in the general's complex like the rest of the army leadership. What the hell was he doing in his tent? "Is he joking? I've been waiting for over an hour now, and he thinks he can just summon me?"

The Iron Wolf's expression remained studiedly blank. "That's all he said. I can take you if you like."

For a moment Rin considered refusing the summons. Who did Souji think he was? She outranked him. He wore the collar of authority around his neck. How dare he make her wait, how *dare*—

She bit her tongue before she said something rash.

Don't be an idiot. She couldn't afford a display of power now. Kitay was gone and the fire was gone. She had no leverage. This wasn't the time to bluff. For once, she'd have to be diplomatic.

"Fine," she said tightly, and followed the Iron Wolf out the door.

Souji wasn't waiting in his tent.

Rin stopped short at the entrance. "*You.*"

The Monkey Warlord rose from his seat. "Hello, Runin."

"What are you—" She inhaled sharply, then composed herself. "Get out."

"Why don't you sit down?" He gestured to the table. "We've much to discuss."

"Get out," she said again. Anger superseded her confusion. She didn't know why Gurubai was here, but she didn't care—she wanted him gone. He didn't deserve to be here. This wasn't his victory, his troops hadn't bled at Leiyang, and the very sight of him standing here in Rooster Province, where her people had died while he cowered in Ruijin, was almost too much to bear. If she still had the fire, she would have incinerated him where he stood.

"You should be glad we arrived when we did," he said. "My troops have been leading the rescue efforts, have you not noticed? Without us, hundreds more of you would be dead."

She barked out a laugh. "So that was your plan? Hide out in your mountains until I'd won your battles, follow us, and then claim our victory?"

Gurubai sighed. "I would hardly call this a victory."

The tent flaps parted before she could retort. Souji strode in, followed by three Iron Wolves and several of Zhuden's junior officers.

Rin looked at them in surprise. She'd been waiting for those officers just as long as she'd been waiting for Souji. Was this why no one had responded? Had they spent all this time together? Doing *what*?

"Oh, good," Souji said. "We're all here."

"Where the hell have you all been?" Rin demanded. "I've been sending for you since noon."

He sighed and shook his head. "Oh, Rin."

"What?" she demanded. "What's going on?"

None of Zhuden's officers would meet her eye.

Souji shot her an apologetic smile. His fingers played at the hilt of his sword. "You still haven't figured this out?"

Too late Rin realized she was alone.

Alone, and without her fire.

Her hand flew to her knife. Souji charged her. She unsheathed her blade, parried clumsily, and didn't last three seconds. He twisted her knife from her grip with a move used by novice swordsmen, then kicked it far out of her reach.

"Where's your fire?" he taunted.

She threw herself at his waist. Again, he overpowered her with ease. At the peak of her training she could have put up a good fight, could have scratched out his eyeballs or gotten a good, vicious grip on his crotch. But he was bigger and heavier, and he had both his hands. In two moves, he had her pinned to the ground.

"So it's true," he observed. "You've lost it."

She thrashed, shrieking.

"Shhh." Souji's fingers closed around her throat and squeezed. "Not so loud. Hurts my ears."

"What are you doing?" she gasped. "What the *fuck* are you—"

Gurubai raised his voice. "'He said to tell you I walk free if you'll come to the New City yourself.'"

He was reading from a scroll. Rin stared at him, bemused. Her mind was so fogged with panic it took her a moment to recognize those words. Where had she read those—

Oh.

Oh, no.

"'He says that this doesn't have to end in bloodshed,'" Gurubai continued, "'and that he only wants to speak. He says he doesn't want a war. He's prepared to grant clemency to every one of your allies. He only wants you.'" Gurubai set the scroll down. "Rather cold, I think, to sacrifice your only family."

"You snake," she hissed.

He had to have learned this from his spies—his fucking ubiquitous spies, eavesdropping on her wherever she went, even after they were leagues away from Ruijin. Who was it? The sentries? The guard outside her tent? Had he opened and copied the scroll before she'd ever seen it?

She thought she'd outplayed him, had finally gotten the upper hand. But he'd been playing the long game this entire time.

"When were you going to tell us there was a peace offer on the table?" Gurubai inquired. "Before or after you sacrificed us to an unnecessary war?"

"Nezha's a lying bastard," she choked. "He doesn't want to negotiate—"

"On the contrary," Gurubai said. "He seemed quite keen on our proposal. You see, *we* don't want to die. And we've no qualms about sacrificing you, particularly since you seemed so ready to do the same to us."

"Are you deluded? You need me—"

"We needed you in the south," Gurubai said. "We have the south. Now you're just a liability, and the only obstacle to a ceasefire with the Republic."

"If you think you're getting a truce, you're so stupid you deserve to die," she spat. "The Yins don't keep their word. I swear to the gods, if you deliver me then you're dead."

"And we're dead if we don't," Gurubai said. "We'll take our chances. Souji?"

Souji's grip tightened around her neck. "Sorry, Princess."

Rin writhed, just hard enough to force Souji to lean forward and use his weight to press her back against the dirt. That brought his wrist close enough to her mouth. She bared her teeth and bit down. She broke skin; she tasted copper and salt on her tongue. Souji shrieked. The pressure on her neck disappeared. Something slammed into the side of her head.

She fell back, temples ringing, blood dribbling onto her chin.

She saw two Soujis looming over her, and both looked so outraged that she couldn't help but laugh.

"You taste good," she said.

He responded with a slap to her face. Then another. The blows stung like lightning; head swimming, ears ringing, she could do nothing but lie still and absorb them like a corpse.

"Not so chatty now, are you?"

She gurgled something incomprehensible. He pulled his fist back, and that was the last thing she saw.

She was lying on the same floor when she awoke. Everything hurt. When she twitched, she felt the stretch of bruises along her back, bruises from blows she didn't remember taking. Souji had kept kicking long after she'd passed out.

Breathing was agony. She had to learn to take small, suffocatingly insufficient breaths, expanding her lungs just enough not to crack her likely broken ribs.

After a few seconds, her fear gave way to confusion.

She ought to be dead.

Why wasn't she dead yet?

"There you go." Souji's voice. She saw his boots standing several feet away. "I'm assuming we don't have to verify her identity."

Who was he talking to? Rin tried to crane her neck to see, but her puffy eyes limited her view, and she couldn't tilt her head up any farther than thirty degrees. She lay curled on her side; her field of vision was restricted to the dirt floor and the wall of the tent.

Footsteps sounded close to her head. Someone put the heel of their boot on her neck.

"The Young Marshal wants her alive," spoke an unfamiliar voice.

Rin stiffened. *The Young Marshal*. This man was Nezha's envoy.

"His orders were to take her alive if we can manage, and dead if she puts up a fight," said the envoy. "I say we preempt a resistance. I've seen what she can do when she's awake."

"We can keep her dosed," spoke another voice across the room. "We brought enough opium for the journey. That keeps her harmless."

"You're going to stake your lives on that?" Souji asked. "Go on, press a little harder. None of us will tattle."

Rin winced, bracing herself for the impact. But it never came—suddenly the boot lifted from her neck, and footsteps sounded away from her head. She heard the tent flaps rustle.

"You can't kill her."

Her eyes widened. *Daji?*

"Who's this hag?" Souji asked. "Someone toss her out."

There was a flurry of movement, a clash of steel, then a loud clatter as weapons dropped to the floor.

"Don't touch me," Daji said, very slowly, very calmly. "Now step away."

The tent fell silent.

"She's a chosen manifestation of the gods." Daji's voice grew louder as she crossed the tent toward Rin. "Her body is a bridge between this world and the Pantheon. If you hurt her, then her god will come flooding through in full force to our realm. Have you ever encountered the Phoenix? You will be ash before you can blink."

That's not true, Rin thought, befuddled. *That's not how it works*. If they hurt her now, without Kitay, the Phoenix could do nothing to help her.

But none of them knew that. No one objected. The men were utterly silent, hanging on Daji's every word.

Rin could imagine what was happening. She'd suffered the Vipress's hypnosis before. Daji's eyes induced paralysis—those bright, yellow serpent's eyes that enticed and beckoned; those pupils that engorged to become gates into dark and lovely visions of butterfly wings and wretched nostalgia. The Vipress made her prey desire. Yearn. Hurt.

When Souji at last spoke, his voice sounded different—dazed, hesitant. "Then what do we do?"

"There is a mountain in Snake Province," Daji said. "Not far from here. It will be quite a march, but—"

"We have a dirigible," said one of Nezha's envoys. He spoke eagerly, like he was trying to impress. If Rin weren't so terrified, she would have laughed. "We have the fuel. We could fly there in less than a day."

"Very good, officer," Daji cooed.

No one objected. Daji had these men well and truly trapped. *Good*, Rin thought. *Now gut them.*

But Daji didn't move.

"I've heard of this mountain," Souji said after a pause. "It's impossible to find."

"Only for those who don't know where they're going," Daji said. "But I have been there many times."

"And who are you?" Souji asked. The question didn't sound like a challenge. He sounded confused, rather, like a man who had just awoken from a deep slumber to find himself in unfamiliar forest. Souji was groping through the mist, trying desperately to catch hold of clarity.

Daji gave a low chuckle. "Only an old woman who has seen a fair bit of the world."

"But you don't . . ." Souji trailed off. His question dissipated into nothing. Rin wished she could see his face.

"The Young Marshal will want to see her first," said the first of Nezha's envoys, the one who had put his boot on Rin's neck. "He'll want to know that she—"

"Your Young Marshal will be content with your report," Daji said smoothly. "You are his loyal lieutenants. He'll trust your word. Wait any longer and you risk that she wakes."

"But we were tasked to—"

"Yin Nezha is weak and ailing," Daji said. "He cannot face the Speerly right now. What do you think he will do if she strikes? She will burn him in his bed, and you will be known as the men who brought this monster to his lair. Would you murder your own general?"

"But he said she'd lost the fire," said the soldier.

"And you trust this man?" Daji pressed. "You'll wager the Young Marshal's life on the words of a guerrilla commander?"

"No," the soldier murmured. "But we—"

"Don't think," Daji whispered. Her voice was like gossamer silk. "Why think? Don't trouble yourself with such thoughts. It's much easier to obey, remember? You only have to do as I say, and you'll be at peace."

Another meek silence descended over the room.

"Good," Daji cooed. "Good boys."

Rin couldn't see Daji's eyes, not from this angle, but even she felt drowsy, lured into the soft, comforting undulations of Daji's voice.

Daji bent over Rin and smoothed the hair away from her face. Her fingers lingered over Rin's exposed neck. "Now, you'll want to sedate her for the trip."

The trip.

This wasn't all just a ploy, then. They really were taking her to the Chuluu Korikh. The stone prison, the hell inside the mountain, the place where shamans who had gone mad were taken to be locked in stone, trapped forever, unable to call their gods and unable to die.

Gods, no. Not there.

Rin had been to the Chuluu Korikh once. The very thought of returning made her feel as if she were drowning.

She tried to lift her head. Tried to say something, to do anything. But Daji's whispers washed over her thoughts like a cool, cleansing stream.

"Don't think." Rin barely heard distinct words anymore, just music, just tinkling notes that soothed her mind like a lullaby.

"Give up, darling. Trust me, this is easier. This is so much easier."

PART II

CHAPTER 11

"Before humans lived on this earth, the god of water and the god of fire quarreled and split the sky apart," Riga said. "All that shiny blue ceramic cracked and fell to Earth, and the Earth in its greenery was exposed to the darkness like yolk inside a shattered egg. That's a nice image, isn't it?"

Daji moved cautiously toward him, fingers outstretched as if she were approaching a wild animal. She didn't know what to expect from him. Nothing Riga did was predictable anymore; these days she couldn't tell from second to second whether he was about to kiss her or hit her.

She would have been less surprised if he were shouting, slamming things and people against the walls because things had gone wrong, had been going wrong for weeks.

But Riga was reading. Everything they had built over the past few years, every rock of their castle, was falling apart around them, and he was standing by the window with a book of children's myths, flipping idly through its pages, fucking *reading out loud* like he thought she needed a bedtime story.

She kept her voice low so as not to startle him. "Riga, what's happening out there?"

He ignored her question. "You know, I think I've figured out where you get all that self-righteousness." He flipped the book around to show her the painted illustrations. "Nüwa mends the sky. You've heard this myth, haven't you? The men wreck the world, and the woman has to piece it back together. The goddess Nüwa patched up that rift they'd made in the sky, rock by rock, and the world was right again."

Daji stared at him, casting wildly about for something to say.

She never understood what he was talking about anymore. She didn't know when the changes had begun—perhaps after Lusan, or perhaps since the Hinterlands. It had started so gradually, like little dribbles of water that eventually burst forth through a dam, and now Riga had transformed into an utterly different person, a person who lashed out and hurt those around him and delighted in torturing her with riddles he knew she couldn't answer.

He used to only inflict his strength on others. Now the person whose fear he seemed to enjoy the most was hers.

Come back to me, she wanted to cry every time they spoke. Something had broken between them, some invisible wound. It had started with Tseveri's death and grown like gangrenous rot, and now it loomed behind every word they spoke, every order they gave.

One will die, one will rule, and one will sleep for eternity.

"You're rambling," she said.

He just laughed. "Isn't it obvious?" He nodded toward the window. "Our stories move in circles. The Classics predicted how this whole thing is going to go. Ziya and I are going to break the world. And you're going to mend it."

Daji could glimpse the burning shore from where she stood. She didn't need General Tsolin's powerful astrological scopes to see what was happening across the strait. A simple spyglass was enough.

Spots of orange lit up the night. If she didn't know better, she would have thought they were firecrackers.

She wondered, because she couldn't help it, if any of the children Shiro hadn't taken had at least made it off the island, if their parents had packed them away in boats and told them to row on, never looking back. But she knew better than to hope. The Mugenese were too thorough.

She knew that by morning, no one on that island would be left alive.

Riga's doomed us.

This was the end. She knew this like a fundamental truth, as certain as the Earth's rotation around the sun. They would suffer dearly for their sacrifice of Speerly blood. This kind of evil would not go unpunished—the gods would not allow it.

Everything they'd fought for, everything they'd built—gone up in smoke. All for some stupid, stupid gamble.

"Do you like what you see?" Riga approached her from behind and put his hands on her hips.

Did he find this erotic? He *would.*

She lowered the spyglass, trying to mask the frantic pounding of her heart. She turned around and attempted a smile. Riga liked her so much better when she smiled.

"Does Ziya know yet?" she asked.

"He'll be here soon enough," Riga said. "Didn't think he'd want to miss this."

"That's cruel."

He shrugged. "It'll be good for him. He's going too soft, we've got to whet that edge."

"And what happens when that edge turns against you?"

"He'd never." Riga squeezed her waist, chuckling. "He loves us."

The door burst open. Ziya stormed in, right on cue.

"What's happening?" he demanded. "They said Speer's under attack."

"Oh, Speer's been attacked." Riga gestured at the window. "This is just the aftermath."

"That's impossible." Ziya grabbed the spyglass out of Daji's hands. He tried to train it on the shore, but his hands trembled too badly to hold it still. "Where were Vaisra's ships?"

Riga, looking smug, didn't answer.

Daji put a hand on Ziya's arm. "You should—"

"*Where were Vaisra's ships?*" Ziya shouted. He was shaking, barely in control. Daji could see the faint silhouettes of inky creatures under his skin, straining to pour out from within him.

"Come on, Ziya." Riga sighed. "You know what we had to do."

Ziya's mouth worked soundlessly. Daji watched as his eyes darted between Riga's face and the window.

Poor Ziya. He'd always been so fond of Hanelai. There were moments when she'd feared he might try to marry that spirited little Speerly general of his. Riga wouldn't have allowed it, of course—he'd always been a stickler about Nikara purity, and he loathed Hanelai besides—but Ziya might have forced it anyway.

Misguided love. Jealous friends. She longed for the time when those were their biggest problems.

"I have to get to Speer," Ziya said. "I have to—I have to find her."

"Oh, come now. You know what you'll find." Riga gestured grandly at the burning shore. "You can see the island clearly enough from here. They're all dead, every single one of them. The crickets are nothing if not thorough. It's already over. Whatever fighting is happening now is just cleanup. Hanelai's dead, Ziya. I did tell you it was foolish to let her go."

Ziya looked as if Riga had taken a dagger and twisted it into his heart.

Riga clapped him on the back. "It's for the best."

"You didn't have the right," Ziya whispered.

Riga laughed a deep, cruel laugh. "Now is when you grow a spine?"

"Their blood is on you. You killed them."

"'*You killed them*,'" Riga imitated. "Don't speak to me about killing innocents. Who leveled the Scarigon Plateau? Who tore Tseveri's heart out of her chest?"

"Tseveri wasn't my fault—"

"Oh, it's never your fault," Riga sneered. "You just lose control and people *accidentally* end up dead, and then you wake up and start whining about the people who are bold enough to do what's necessary while fully conscious. Get a grip, brother. You murdered Tseveri. You let Hanelai go to her death. Why? Because you know what's necessary and what's at stake, and you know that in the grand scheme of things, those two little whores of yours were obstacles not worth mentioning. Think of what happened as a kindness. You know it probably was. You know the Speerlies would have botched self-rule the moment they got it, would have probably started butchering each other the moment we let them take charge. You know people like Hanelai were never particularly good at being free."

"I hate you," Ziya said. "I wish we were all dead."

Riga lifted a hand and casually backhanded him across the face. The crack echoed through the room.

"I freed you from your shackles." Riga advanced on the cringing Ziya, slowly unsheathing his sword. "I dragged both of you out of the occupied zone. I found the Hinterlanders, I took us to Mount Tianshan, and I brought you to the Pantheon. And you dare to defy me?"

The air thrummed, thick with something powerful, suffocating, and terrible.

Just bow, Daji wanted to cry at Ziya. *Bow and it'll be over.*

But she was mute, rooted in place by fear.

Ziya hadn't moved, either. The sight was bizarre, a grown man cowering like a child, but Daji knew what made him do it.

Fear was inscribed in Ziya's bones, just like it was in hers. Blow by blow, cut by cut—over the last decade, since they were children, Riga had made sure of it.

She realized that both of them were glaring at her. Demanding a response. But what was the question? What could she possibly do to fix this?

"Nothing?" Ziya demanded.

"She won't say anything," Riga scoffed. "Little Daji knows what's best for us."

"You're a coward," Ziya snarled at her. "You've always been."

"Oh, don't bully her—"

"Fuck you." Ziya slammed his staff against the floor. The sound made Daji jump.

Riga laughed. "You want to do this now?"

"Don't," Daji murmured, but the word came out in a terrified squeak. Neither of them heard.

Ziya flew at Riga. Riga opened his palm and immediately Ziya dropped to the ground, howling in pain.

Riga sighed theatrically. "You would lift your hand against me, brother?"

"You're not my brother," Ziya gasped.

A void opened in the air behind them. Shadowy beasts poured through, one after the other. Ziya pointed. They surged, but Riga sliced them down like paper animals, fast as they came.

"Please," Riga said. The smile never dropped from his face. "You can do better than that."

Ziya raised his staff high. Riga lifted his sword.

Somehow Daji found the strength to move. She flung herself into the space between them just before they rushed each other with enough force to split cracks in the stone floor, a force that shattered the world like it was an eggshell. Decades later she would wonder if she had known what she was doing back then, when she threw her hands against their chests and spoke the incantation she did. Had she known and accepted the consequences? Or had she done it by accident? Was everything that happened after a cruelty of chance?

All she knew in that moment was that all sound and motion stopped. Time hung still for an eternity. A strange venom, something she'd never summoned before, seeped through the air, rooted itself into all three of their minds, and unfurled to take a shape none of them had ever seen or experienced. Then Riga collapsed to the floor and Ziya reeled backward, and they both might have shouted, but the only thing Daji could hear past the blood thundering in her ears was the ghostly echo of Tseveri's cold, mirthless laughter.

CHAPTER 12

Private Memorandum on the Nikara Republic, formerly known as the Nikara Empire or the Empire of Nikan, to the Office of Foreign Affairs of the Republic of Hesperia.

Open trade in the Nikara territories continues to reveal assets justifying the Consortium's investment, and efforts to acquire these assets proceed smoothly as anticipated. The Consortium has secured the rights to several critical mining deposits with surprisingly little struggle (in truth, I imagine the Nikara are ignorant to the riches beneath their feet). Beyond tea and minerals, our agents have discovered a number of local goods that will find an eager market at home. Nikara porcelain has a shine and translucency that, quite honestly, bests our domestic wares. Nikara carved jade figurines will no doubt attract customers looking for novel interior decoration (see Box 3, attached). The local textile craftsmanship is impressive given their lack of automated looms—their artisans have developed particularly clever mechanisms to harness the power of water to spin cloth far faster than a single weaver could. (I expect our ladies will be parading the streets in silk robes and parasols before too long!)

∞

The Gray Company representatives of the Order of the Holy Maker have encountered more significant difficulties. Indigenous opposition to conversion proves thorny (see the attached letter from Sister Petra Ignatius of the Second Spire). This is not so much because of an existing religion that defies replacement—indeed, most of the natives seem to be quite indifferent to the question of religion—but because of the social discipline that religion entails. They find regular weekly worship a waste of time and resent being corralled to chapel. They are used to their squalid, superstitious ways and seem unable to accept the blinding proof of the Maker's eminence, even when laid out slowly before them in their own language. But our efforts will continue, surely if slowly; our duty to the Architect to bring order upon every corner of the world necessitates no less.

We find minimal risk that Nikara natives could mount a concentrated armed uprising. Our studies of the Empire have long indicated that their strategic culture is made pacifist and stagnant by an Empire with no inclination to territorial expansion. The Republic has never mounted a seafaring expedition to conquer another nation. Save for their conquest of the Isle of Speer, the Republic has only ever absorbed foreign aggression. Now that Yin Vaisra has finished quelling the remnants of Su Daji's regime in the north, we expect that over a five-year timeline our fears of domestic warfare can be put to rest.

The greatest threats now are the indigenous guerrilla movements in the south, whose bases are concentrated in Rooster and Monkey Provinces. Their perceived trump card is the Speerly Fang Runin, whose pyrotechnic displays have convinced them of a pagan shamanistic belief that rivals the Order of the Holy Maker. (Our liaisons in the Gray Company believe these shamanic abilities to be heretofore unseen manifestations of Chaos—see Addendum

1: Nikara Shamanism.) This threat should not terribly worry the Consortium. The numbers of shamans are few—aside from the Speerly and Yin Vaisra's heir, the Gray Company have identified no others on the continent. The southern rebels are still centuries behind even the old Federation of Mugen on every front, and they attempt to fight dirigibles with sticks and stones.

Their so-called gods will not save them. Sister Petra assures me that in addition to improved opium missiles, which we have confirmed negates shamanic ability, research efforts to devise countermeasures proceed smoothly, and that in several weeks we will have weapons even the Speerly cannot best. (See Addendum 2: Research Notes on Yin Nezha.) The south will fall when the Speerly falls. Absent some divine intervention, we shall promptly produce upon this barbarous nation every effect we could desire.

In the Name of the Divine Architect,
  Major General Josephus Belial Tarcquet

CHAPTER 13

When Rin awoke, her head was fuzzy, her mouth felt like it had been stuffed with silkworm cocoons, and a throbbing ache snaked from the scars in her back through every muscle in her lower body. She heard a roar so loud it seemed to envelop her, drowning out her thoughts, making her bones thrum with its reverberations.

Her gut dropped; the floor seemed to lurch. Was she *in a dirigible*?

Something cool and wet rubbed against her forehead. She forced her throbbing eyelids open. Daji's face came gradually into focus. She was wiping Rin's face with a washcloth.

"Finally," Daji said. "I was starting to worry."

Rin sat up and glanced around. Up close, the dirigible carriage was much larger than she'd always imagined. They sat alone in a room the size of a ship's cabin, which had to be one of many, for none of the Republican soldiers were in sight. "Get away from me."

"Oh, shush." Daji rolled her eyes as she continued scrubbing grime from Rin's cheeks. The washcloth had turned rust brown from dried blood. "I've just saved your life."

"I'm not going . . ." Rin struggled to make sense of her

thoughts, trying to remember why she was afraid. "The mountain. *The mountain.* I'm not going—"

"Eat." Daji pressed a hard, stale bun into her hand. "You need your strength. You won't survive immurement otherwise."

Rin stared helplessly at her. She didn't lift the bun; her fingers hardly had the strength to close around it. "Why are you doing this?"

"I am saving us both," Daji said. "Maybe your incipient southern empire, too, if you'll stop with the hysterics and *listen.*"

"The army—"

"Your army has abandoned you. Your loyal officers are in no position to help. You've been ousted by the Southern Coalition, and you can't call the fire." Daji smoothed Rin's hair back behind her ears. "I am guaranteeing us safe passage to the Chuluu Korikh."

"But *why*—"

"Because my strength now is not enough. We need an ally. A mutual friend, who to the best of my knowledge is currently whiling away eternity in a mountain."

Rin blinked. She understood Daji's words, but she didn't understand what she *meant*; it took a moment of thoughts churning sluggishly through her mind before the pieces fell together.

Then she balked.

She hadn't thought about Jiang for nearly a year. She hadn't let herself; the memories hurt too much. He'd been not just her teacher but her master. She'd trusted him; he'd promised to keep her safe. And then, the moment her world descended into war, he'd simply abandoned her. He'd left her to seal himself in a fucking rock.

"He won't come out," Rin said hoarsely. "He's too scared."

Daji's lip curled. "Is that what you think?"

"He wants to hide. He won't leave. He's—there's something wrong—"

"His Seal is eroding," Daji said fiercely. Her good eye glimmered. "I know. I've felt it, too. He's getting stronger—he's coming back to himself. I didn't know what I was doing when I Sealed the three of us, but I'd always suspected—hoped—I hadn't done it right. And I didn't. The Seal was a broken, imperfect thing, and now it's fading. Now I—*we*—get a second chance."

"Doesn't matter." Rin shook her head weakly. "He won't leave."

"Oh, he'll have to." Daji resumed dabbing at Rin's temples. "I need him."

"But *I* needed him," Rin said. She felt a sharp pang in her chest, a wrenching mix of frustration and despair that until now she'd been so good at suppressing. She wanted to kick something; she wanted to cry. How, after so much time, could old hurts sting so sharp?

"Perhaps you did." Daji gave Rin a pitying look. "But Ziya's not your anchor. He's mine."

The rest of the journey could have taken minutes or hours. Rin didn't know; she passed it in a painful daze, slipping in and out of consciousness as her body ached from its myriad contusions. Daji lapsed into silence, cautious of eavesdroppers. At last the engine roar slowed to a whine, then stopped. Rin jolted fully awake as the carriage thudded against the ground at an angle and screeched as it dragged several feet to a halt. Then Republican soldiers came into her compartment, loaded her bound form onto a wooden stretcher, and carried her out into the icy mountain air.

She didn't resist. Daji wanted her to play helpless.

She knew they had reached Snake Province. She recognized the shape of these mountains; she'd traveled this way before. But some part of her mind could not accept that they were really, truly, in the Kukhonin Mountains.

Less than a day had passed since Souji betrayed her in Tikany. They'd crossed half the country in the time since. But that couldn't be right—this journey should have taken weeks. Rin had seen dirigibles fly, she knew how fast they moved, but this was absurd. This took her ingrained conceptions of time, space, and distance, and ripped them to shreds.

Was this how the Hesperians regularly traveled? She tried to imagine spatiality from their perspective. What would society be like if one could traverse the continent in mere days? If she could wake up one morning in Sinegard, and go to bed in Arlong that evening?

No wonder they acted as if they owned the world. To them it must seem so small.

"Which way?" asked a soldier.

"Up," Daji said. "The entrance lies near the summit. There won't be space up there to land a craft. We'll have to climb."

Rin was strapped down so tightly to the stretcher she could barely lift her head. She couldn't see how much farther they had to march, but she suspected it would take hours. The only walking path to the entrance of the Chuluu Korikh grew treacherously narrow with altitude. There wouldn't have been space to land anything as large as a dirigible more than a third of the way up.

At least she didn't have to climb. As the soldiers hoisted her up the mountain, the rocking stretcher lulled her into a kind of half sleep. Her head felt light and fuzzy. She wasn't sure if they had sedated her, or if her body was breaking down from wounds sustained earlier. She passed the march in a barely conscious fugue, just dazed enough that the bruises from Souji's boot produced no more than a dull, nearly pleasant ache.

She didn't realize they'd reached the Chuluu Korikh until she heard the scrape of the stone door sliding open.

"We need a light," Daji said.

Rin heard a crackle as someone lit a torch.

Now, she thought. This was when Daji would turn on the soldiers, surely. She'd gotten what she wanted; she'd secured safe passage to the Chuluu Korikh, and now she only had to hypnotize them, lure them to the precipice, and push.

"Go on," Daji said. "There's nothing to fear here. Just statues."

The soldiers bore Rin into the looming dark. An immense pressure slammed over her, like an invisible hand clamped over her nose and mouth.

Rin gasped, arching her back against the stretcher. She gulped down huge mouthfuls of air, but it was thin and insufficient, and did nothing to stop the black spots creeping in at the edges of her vision. She could breathe so hard she ruptured her lungs and it still wouldn't be enough. The inside of the Chuluu Korikh was so *grounded*, so firmly material, a solid place with no possible crossover into the plane of spirit.

It felt worse than drowning.

Rin had barely tolerated the pressure the first time she'd come here with Altan. It was far worse now that she had lived and breathed for years with divinity just a glancing thought away. The Phoenix had become a part of her, a constant and reassuring presence in her mind. Even in Kitay's absence, she'd still felt the barest thread of a connection to her god, but now even that was gone. Now she felt as if the weight of the mountain might shatter her from inside.

The soldier at the front rapped his knuckles against her forehead. "Ah, shut up."

Rin hadn't even realized she was screaming.

Someone stuffed a rag in her mouth. That made the suffocation worse. Rational thought fled. She forgot that this was all a feint, all part of Daji's plan. How could Daji—*Su Daji*, who had lived with the voice of her god longer than Rin had been alive—withstand this? How could she walk calmly forward without screaming while Rin writhed, arrested in the last moment of drowning before death?

"All these were shamans?" The soldier bearing her legs whistled, a low sound that echoed through the mountain. "Great Tortoise. How long have they been here?"

"As long as this Empire has been alive," Daji said. "And they'll be here long after we're dead."

"They can't die?"

"No. Their bodies are no longer mortal. They have become open conduits to the gods, and so they are trapped here so they don't destroy the world."

"Fucking hell." The soldier clicked his tongue. "That's rough."

The soldiers halted and lowered Rin's stretcher to the floor. The one at her head leaned above her; his teeth gleamed yellow in the torchlight. "This is your stop, Speerly."

She stared past him at rows and rows of empty plinths, stretching farther into the mountain than Rin could see. Her mind was half-gone with fear. She flailed, helpless, as the soldiers unstrapped her from the stretcher and hauled her up toward the nearest pedestal.

Her eyes flashed to Daji, begging silently to no avail. *Why isn't she doing anything?* Hadn't this charade gone on long enough? Daji didn't need Rin immured. She only needed safe passage to the Chuluu Korikh. She had no use for the Republican soldiers anymore; she should have already disposed of them.

But Daji was just *standing* there, eyes lidded, face calm, watching as the soldiers positioned Rin on the center of the plinth.

A horrible thought crossed Rin's mind.

Daji hadn't just been bluffing.

Daji needed safe passage to the Chuluu Korikh. She needed Master Jiang. But nothing about her plan required Rin.

Oh, gods.

She had to get out of here. She wouldn't escape this—there was no way she could make it to the door and down the mountain ahead of them in her state, not with her legs bound so tightly. But she could get to the edge of the corridor. She could jump.

Anything was better than an eternity in the rock.

She stopped struggling and slouched against the soldiers' arms, pretending she'd fainted. It worked. Their grip loosened, just barely enough for her to wrench her torso free. She ducked beneath their hands and lunged toward the ledge. Her legs were tied so tightly she could only manage a lurching shuffle, but she was so close—it was only mere feet, she could evade them just two paces—

But then she reached the edge and saw the yawning abyss, and her limbs turned to lead.

Jump.

She couldn't.

It didn't matter that she knew eternity in the Chuluu Korikh was worse than death. She still couldn't do it. She didn't want to die.

"Come on." Strong arms wrapped around her midriff and dragged her back from the edge. "You're not getting off that easy."

The soldiers pulled her legs up so that between them they carried her like a sack of rice. Together, they flipped her up into a standing position and arranged her on the pedestal.

"Stop," Rin shrieked, but her words came muffled and meaningless behind her gag. "Stop, please don't—Daji! *Daji! Tell them!*"

Daji didn't meet her eyes.

"Make sure her feet are in the center," she said calmly, as if instructing servants on where to move a table. "Prop her up so that she's standing straight. The stone will do the rest."

Rin tried everything to escape—kicking, thrashing, writhing, and going limp. They didn't let go. They were too strong and she was too weak—famished, injured, dehydrated.

She had no more outs. She was trapped, and she couldn't even die.

"Now what?" one of them asked.

"Now the mountain does its work." Daji began to chant in Ketreyid, and the rocks came alive.

Rin watched the base of the pedestal in horror. At first its movement seemed a trick of the torchlight, but then she felt the icy touch of stone around her ankles as the plinth crept up and consumed her, solidifying into an immobile coat over the surface of her skin. She had no time to struggle; in seconds, it was up to her knees. The soldier holding her upright let go of her arms and sprang away when the rock reached her waist. Her upper body was now free but it made no difference; much as she flailed she couldn't break the stone's hold against her legs. Moments later it reached her chest, arrested her elbows where she'd bent them, and crept up her neck. She tilted her head up, desperate to get her nose away from the rock. It didn't matter. The stone crawled over her face. Closed over her eyes.

Then she saw nothing. Heard nothing. She did not feel the stone against her; it had become a part of her, a natural outer coating that rendered her completely still.

She couldn't move.

She couldn't *move*.

She strained against the rock but nothing budged even a fragment, and all that did was flood her nerves with such anxiety that she strained harder and harder while panic exploded inside her, intensifying second by second with no possible release.

She couldn't breathe. And at first she was at least grateful for that—without air, surely she'd soon lose consciousness, and then this torture would end. She could feel her lungs bursting, burning. Soon she'd black out. Soon it'd be over.

But nothing happened.

She was drowning, forever drowning, but *she couldn't die*.

She needed to scream and couldn't. She wanted so badly to writhe and flail that her heart almost burst out of her chest and even *that* would have been better because then she would at least be dead, but instead she hung still in a never-ending moment stretching on into a definite eternity.

The knowledge that this could and would continue, for days upon seasons upon years, was torture beyond belief.

I should have jumped, she thought. *I wish I were dead.*

The thought repeated in her mind over and over, the only salve against her new and terrifying reality.

I wish I were dead.

I wish I were dead.

I wish—

The mere thought of oblivion became a fantasy. She imagined she really had jumped, imagined the short, euphoric fall and the satisfying crunch of her bones against the bottom of the pit, followed by a blissful nothing. She repeated the sequence so many times in her mind that for brief seconds at a time she fooled herself into thinking she'd really done it.

She could not sustain her panic forever. Eventually it ebbed away, replaced by a dull, empty helplessness. Her body at last resigned itself to the truth—she would not escape. She would not die. She would remain standing here, half-dead and half-alive, conscious and thinking for eternity.

She had nothing now except for her own mind.

Once upon a time Jiang had taught her to meditate, to empty her mind for hours at a time while her body settled into the peaceful daze of an empty vessel. That was, no doubt, how he had survived in here all this time, why he had ever entered this place willingly. Rin wished she had that skill. But she had never once achieved that inner stillness. Her mind rebelled against boredom. Her thoughts had to wander.

She had nothing else to do but probe through memories for entertainment. She pored over them, picked them apart and stretched them out and relished them, prolonging every last detail. She remembered Tikany. Remembered those delicious warm afternoons she spent in Tutor Feyrik's room discussing every detail of the books he'd just lent her, stretching her arms to receive more. Remembered playing games with baby Kesegi in the yard, pretending to be every known beast in the Emperor's Menagerie, roaring and hissing just to get him to laugh. Remembered quiet, stolen minutes in the dark, brief interludes when she was all alone, free of the shop and of Auntie Fang, able to breathe without fear.

When Tikany failed to satisfy she turned her mind to Sinegard— that harsh, intimidating place that, paradoxically, now contained her happiest memories. She remembered studying in the cool basement chambers of the Academy library with Kitay, watching him pushing spindly fingers through his worried hairline as he riffled through scroll after scroll. Remembered sparring in the early mornings with Jiang in the Lore garden, parrying his blows with a blindfold tied around her head.

She got very good at exploring the crevices of her mind, excavating memories that she didn't know she still had. Memories she hadn't let herself acknowledge until now for fear they would break her.

She remembered the first time she'd ever laid eyes on Nezha, and then all the times thereafter.

It hurt to see him. It hurt *so much*.

They'd been so innocent once. It was agony to recall the face he wore just a year ago: pretty and cocky and unbearable at once, alternately grinning with delight or wearing the absurd snarl of an agitated puppy. But she was trapped here for an eternity. Those memories were the only things she had now, and the pain was the only way she'd feel anything ever again.

She retraced their entire history from the moment she met him first at Sinegard to the moment she felt his blade sliding into the muscles of her back. She remembered how childishly handsome he used to be, how she'd been both drawn to and repulsed by that haughty, sculpted face. She remembered how Sinegard had transformed him from a spoiled, petty princeling to a hardened soldier in training. She remembered the first time they'd sparred against each other and the first time they'd fought side by side in battle— how their animosity and partnership had both felt like such a natural fit, like slipping on a lost glove, like finding her other half.

She remembered how much taller than her he'd grown, how when they embraced, her head fit neatly under his chin. She remembered how dark his eyes had looked under the moonlight that night by the docks. Right when she thought he'd kiss her. Right before he'd pressed a blade into her back.

It hurt so much to riffle through those memories. It was humiliating to remember how readily she'd believed his lies. She felt like such a fool, for trusting him, for loving him, for thinking any of those thousands of tiny moments they'd shared during her brief time in Vaisra's army meant that he really, truly cared for her, when in truth Nezha had been manipulating her just like his father had.

She relived those interactions so many times that they began to lose all meaning. Their sting faded to a dull burn, and then nothing at all. She'd numbed herself to their significance. She'd grown bored of her own pain.

So she turned to the last thing that could still hurt her. She went looking for the Seal and found that it was still there, ready and waiting in the back of her mind, daring her to enter.

She wondered briefly why the Seal had not disappeared. It was the product of the goddess Nüwa's magic, and there was no connection to the gods in the Chuluu Korikh. But perhaps when Daji had brought the magic into the world, the connection severed, the same way venom lingered after the snake had died.

Rin was grateful for it. Here was at least a single distraction from her own mind. Something she could play with, flirt with. For prisoners in solitary confinement, a knife was better entertainment than nothing.

What happened if she touched it now? She might never come back. Here, with nothing from reality to distract her, she might end up trapped in a poison-soaked lie forever.

But she had nothing else. No reality to come back to, save her own stale memories.

She leaned forward and fell through the gate.

"Hello," said Altan. "How did we end up here?"

He was standing far too close. Only inches separated them.

"Stay back," she said. "Don't touch me."

"And I thought you wanted to see me." Ignoring her command he reached out, took her chin in his fingers, and tilted her head up. "What's happened to you, darling?"

"I've been betrayed."

"*I've been betrayed*," he mimicked. "Fuck that nonsense. You threw everything away. You had an army. You had Leiyang. You had the south in the palm of your hand and you fucked it all up, you mangy, dirt-skinned piece of shit—"

Why was she so afraid? She knew she had control. Altan was her imagination; Altan was *dead*. "Get back."

He only moved closer.

She felt a flash of panic. Where were his chains? Why wouldn't he obey?

He cast her a mocking smile. "You can't tell me what to do."

"You're not real. You only exist in my mind—"

"My darling, I *am* your mind. I'm you. I'm all you've got left. It's just you and me now, and I'm not going anywhere. You don't want peace. You want accountability. You want to know exactly what you've done and you don't want to forget it. So let's begin." His fingers tightened around her chin. "Admit what you did."

"I lost the south."

He smacked a palm against her temple. She knew the blow wasn't real, that everything she felt was a hallucination, but still it stung. She'd *let* it sting. This was her imagination, and she'd decided she deserved this punishment.

"You didn't just *lose* the south. You gave it away. You had Nezha at your mercy. You had your blade pressed to his skin. All you had to do was bring your arm down and you would have won. You could have killed him. Why didn't you?"

"I don't know."

"*I* know." Another ringing blow, this time to her left temple. Rin's head jerked to the side. Altan seized her throat and dug his fingernails into the skin around her larynx. The pain was excruciating. "Because you're pathetic. You need to be someone's dog. You need someone's boots to lick."

Rin's blood ran cold—not with self-induced misery, but with true, uncontrolled fear. She didn't know where this was going; she couldn't predict what her mind would do next. She wanted to stop. She should have left the Seal alone.

"You're weak," Altan spat. "You're a stupid, sentimental, sniveling brat who betrayed everyone around her because she couldn't get over her schoolyard *crush*. Did you think he loved you? Do you think he ever loved you?"

He drew his fist back again. A tremor rippled through the Seal. Altan's image wavered like a reflection on a lake dispelled by a stone. There came a second tremor. Altan disappeared. Then Rin understood this wasn't a hallucination—something was slamming into the stone inches from her face.

The third time, she felt it, a shake that started in her nose and vibrated through her entire body. Her teeth rattled.

Her teeth rattled.

Movement. Which meant—

A fourth tremor. The stone shattered. Rin spilled off the plinth and tumbled hard onto the stone floor. Pain shot up her knees; it felt wonderful. She spat the rag out of her mouth. The air inside the mountain, stale and dank as it was, tasted delicious. The suffocation she'd felt earlier was gone; compared to immurement, the open air tasted like the difference between mild humidity and being underwater. For a long time she knelt with her head hanging between her shoulders and just *breathed*, marveling at how it felt when air rushed in and out of her lungs.

She flexed her fingers. Touched her face, felt her fingers on her cheeks. The bliss of those sensations, of the sheer freedom of movement, made her want to cry.

"Great Tortoise," said a voice she hadn't heard in a lifetime. "Someone clearly never learned to meditate."

Rin's eyes took a moment to adjust to the torchlight. Two silhouettes stood over her. To the left, Daji. And on the right was Jiang, covered from head to toe with gray dust, smiling widely in greeting as if they'd seen each other only yesterday.

"You've got dirt in your hair." He reached down to unbind her legs. "My gods, it's everywhere. We're going to have to dunk you into a creek."

Rin recoiled from his touch. "Get away from me."

"You all right, kid?" His tone was so light. So casual.

She stared at him, amazed. He'd been gone for a year. It had felt like decades. How could he act as if everything were normal?

"Hello?" Jiang waved a hand in front of her face. "Are you just going to sit there?"

She found her voice. "You abandoned me."

His smile dropped. "Ah, child."

"You *left* me." His wounded expression only made her angrier.

It felt like a mockery. Jiang didn't get to skirt this conversation like he skirted everything, dodging responsibility by feigning madness so well that they all believed it. He'd never been as crazy as everyone thought. She wouldn't start falling for it now. "I needed you—Altan needed you—and all you did was, was—"

Jiang spoke so quietly she almost couldn't hear him. "I couldn't save Altan."

Her voice broke. "But you could have saved me."

He looked stricken. For once he had no quippy retort, no excuse or deflection.

She thought he might apologize.

But then he cocked his head to the side, mouth quirking back into a grin. "Why, and spoil all your fun?"

Once upon a time Jiang's humor had been irritating at worst, a welcome salve in an otherwise dreadful environment at best. Once upon a time he'd been the only person who regularly made her laugh.

Now she saw red.

She didn't think. She lashed out at him, fingers curling into a fist midway to his face. His hand flashed out of his sleeve. He caught her wrist, forced her arm away with more strength than she'd expected.

She always forgot how strong Jiang was. All that power, concealed inside a reedy, whimsical frame.

He held her fist suspended between them. "Will it make you feel better to hit me?"

"Yes."

"Will it really?"

She glared at him for a moment, breathing heavily. Then she let her hand go limp.

"You ran away," she said. It wasn't a fair accusation. She knew that. But there was a part of her that had never stopped being his student. The part that was terrified and needed, still needed, his protection.

"You left." She couldn't keep her voice from breaking. "You left me alone."

"Oh, Rin." His voice turned gentle. "Do you think this place was anything like a refuge?"

Rin didn't want to forgive. She wanted to stay angry. She'd been nursing this resentment for too long. She couldn't just let this go; she felt like she'd been cheated of something she was owed.

But the horror of immurement was too immediate. She had just escaped her stone prison. And nothing, *nothing*, could make her enter it again. She'd fling herself off the ledge first.

"Then why did you do it?" she asked.

"To protect you," he said. "To protect everyone around me. I'm sorry I couldn't think of a better way how."

She had no response to that. His words terrified her. If Jiang had seen this hell as the best of alternatives, then what had he been afraid of?

"I'm sorry, child." Jiang stretched out his hands in a conciliatory gesture. "I am so sorry."

She turned away and shook her head, hugging her arms to her chest. She couldn't forgive so easily. She needed time to let her anger burn down its wick. She couldn't meet his eyes; she was glad the firelight was too dim for him to see her tears.

"So what's changed?" she asked, wiping at her cheeks. "Your Seal has eroded. You're not afraid of what will come through?"

"Oh, I am terrified," Jiang said. "I have no idea what my freedom might cause. But suspending myself in time is no answer. This story must end, one way or another."

"This story will end." Daji had been watching their exchange in silence, her mouth twisted in an unreadable expression. Now, her cool voice sliced the air like a knife. "The way it was always meant to."

Jiang put his hand on Rin's shoulder. "Come, child. Let's see how the world has broken while I was gone."

Again, he offered her his hand. This time, she took it. Together they approached the open door, a circle of blinding light.

The sheer whiteness of the sun on snow was agony. But Rin relished the pain shooting through her eyes just as much as she delighted in the cold bite of wind on her face, stone and half-melted snow under her toes. She opened her mouth and took a deep breath of icy mountain air. In that moment, it was the loveliest thing she'd ever tasted.

"Be ready to march," said Daji. "I can't fly that airship. We'll have to go by foot until we can find some horses."

Rin glanced back at her and then blinked, startled.

The old hag from Tikany was gone. Entire decades had melted from Daji's face. The lines around her eyes had disappeared, the skin around her gouged eye was smooth and unscarred, and the eyeball somehow, miraculously, healed.

Jiang, too, was more vividly alive than she'd ever seen him. He didn't just look younger. That wasn't new—Jiang had always had an ageless quality about him, like he'd been ripped from a place out of time. But now he seemed *solid*. Powerful. He had a different look in his eyes—less whimsical, less placidly amused, and more focused than she'd ever seen him.

This man had fought in the Poppy Wars. This man had nearly ruled the empire.

"Something wrong?" he asked.

Rin shook her head, blinking. "Nothing. I just—um, where are Nezha's troops?"

Daji shrugged. "Dealt with them as soon as they got you in the mountain."

Rin was indignant. "And you couldn't have freed me a bit earlier?"

Daji cast her an icy smile. "I thought you should know how it felt."

They made shelter that night under a small alcove near the base of the mountain. Humming, Jiang set about constructing a fire. Daji disappeared into the trees and, twenty minutes later, returned with a string of dead rats, which she then proceeded to skin with a dagger.

Rin slumped back against a tree trunk, trying to keep her eyes open. The absurdity of this scene would have amazed her if she had the energy. She was sitting at a campfire with two of the most powerful figures in Nikara history, figures that to most people existed only in shadow puppet plays, watching as they prepared dinner. Anyone else would have been slack-jawed in awe.

But Rin was too exhausted to even think. The climb downhill hadn't been arduous, but the Chuluu Korikh had drained her; she felt like she'd barely survived tumbling down a waterfall. She had nearly drifted into sleep when Jiang poked her in the stomach with a stick.

She jumped. "What?"

He poked her again. "You're being very quiet."

She rubbed her side. "I just want to sit for a second. In peace. Can I do that?"

"Well, now you're just being rude."

She lifted a languid hand and whacked him on the shin.

He ignored that and sat down beside her. "We need to talk next moves."

She sighed. "Then talk."

"Now, Daji's only caught me up on a little bit." He rubbed his hands together and held them out over the flames. "It's been a very distressing day for me."

"Same," Rin muttered.

"But the way I understand it, you've gone and split the country in half."

"That wasn't my fault."

"Oh, I know. Yin Vaisra's always been a bloodthirsty little gremlin." Jiang winked at her. "So what shall we do now? Raze Arlong to the ground?"

She gaped at him for a moment, waiting for him to chuckle, before she realized he was being utterly serious. His gaze was earnest.

She had no idea what this new Jiang was capable of, but she had to take his words at face value.

"We can't do that," she said. "We have to infiltrate them first. They've—they've got someone."

"Who?"

Daji interjected from across the fire. "Her anchor."

"She has an anchor?" Jiang arched an eyebrow. "Since when? You might have told me."

"I only retrieved you from rock this afternoon," Daji said.

"But that seems *relevant*—"

"Kitay," Rin snapped. "Chen Kitay. He was in my class at Sinegard. Nezha took him from Tikany, and we need to get him back."

"I remember him." Jiang rubbed his chin. "Skinny kid? Big ears, hair like an overgrown forest? Too smart for his own good?"

"That's the one."

"Does the Republic know he's your anchor?" Daji asked.

"No." Aside from Chaghan, everyone who knew she had an anchor had died at Lake Boyang. "No one possibly could."

"And they don't have a reason to hurt him?" Daji pressed.

"Nezha wouldn't do that," Rin said. "They're friends."

"Friends don't send dirigible bombers after friends," said Jiang.

"The point is that Kitay is alive," Rin said, exasperated. "And the first thing we need to do is get him back."

Jiang and Daji exchanged a long, deliberating look.

"Please," Rin said. "I'll follow any plan you two want, but I need Kitay. Otherwise I'm useless."

"We'll get him back," Jiang assured her. "Is there any chance we can get you an army?"

Daji snorted.

Rin sighed again. "My troops betrayed me to the Republic, and their leader probably wants me dead."

"That's not great," Jiang said.

"No," Rin agreed.

"Then who owns the resistance army?"

"The Southern Coalition."

"Then that's who we'll deal with. Walk me through their politics."

If he wasn't going to let her sleep, Rin decided, then she might as well entertain him. "The Monkey Warlord Liu Gurubai controls the core of the army. Yang Souji commands the Iron Wolves. Ma Lien led the second-largest contingent, the bandit troops, before he died. Zhuden was his second-in-command. They were loyal to me for a bit, until . . . well. They thought they'd trade me for immunity."

"And who is the leadership now?"

"Gurubai, definitely. And Souji."

"I see." Jiang pondered this for a moment, then said in a cheerful tone, "You'll have to kill them all, of course."

"Sorry, what?"

He lounged back against the trunk, stretched out his legs, and propped one ankle over the other. "Strike as soon as you can after you rendezvous with the coalition. Get them in their sleep. Sometimes it's easier to take them out in battle, but that tends to leave a nasty public impression. Bad form, and all that."

Rin stared at him in disbelief. She didn't know what shocked her more—his suggestion, or the cavalier tone in which he said it. The Jiang she knew liked to blow bubbles in the creek with a reed for fun. This Jiang discussed murder as if relaying a recipe for porridge.

"What did you think would happen when you returned?" Daji asked.

"I don't know, I thought maybe—maybe they'd realize they need me." Rin hadn't thought that far. She had some half-formed notion that she might be able to talk her way into their good graces, now that they'd learned she was right about the Republic.

But now that she considered it, they were just as likely to shoot her on sight.

"You are so bad at this," Jiang said. "It's cute."

"You can't fight a war on multiple fronts." Daji slid a thin whittled branch through the skinned rats, then propped them over the crackling fire. "The moment you hear whispers of dissent in your own ranks, you flush it out. With all the force necessary."

"Is that what you did?" Rin asked.

"Oh, yes," Jiang said happily. "All the time. I handled the public murders, of course. Riga only had to utter the name, and I'd have the beasts rip them up from head to toe. The point was the spectacle, to dissuade anyone else from defection." He nodded at Daji. "And this one took care of everything we wanted to keep quiet. Good times."

"But they hated you," Rin said.

She knew little of the Trifecta's reign except from what Vaisra had told her, but she knew they'd been resented by almost everyone. The Trifecta had sustained political support through sheer violence. No one had loved them, but everyone had feared them. After Riga disappeared, the only reason why the Twelve Warlords never unseated Daji from the throne was because they hated one another just as much.

"Elites with entrenched interests will always hate you," Daji said. "That's inevitable. But the elites don't matter, the masses do. What you have to do is shroud yourself in myth. Your enemies' deaths become part of your legend. Eventually you become so far removed from reality that right and wrong don't apply to you. Your identity becomes part and parcel of the idea of the nation itself. They'll love you no matter what you do."

"I feel like you're underestimating the public," Rin asked.

"How do you mean?"

"I mean—nobody becomes a legend overnight. People aren't blind. I wouldn't worship an icon like that."

"Didn't you worship Altan?" Daji asked.

Jiang whistled through his teeth. "Low blow."

"Fuck you," Rin said.

Daji just smiled. "People are attracted to power, darling. They can't help themselves. Power seduces. Exert it, make a show of it, and they'll follow you."

"I can't just bully people into getting what I want," Rin said.

"Really?" Daji cocked her head. "How did you get command of Ma Lien's troops, then?"

"I let him die," Rin said.

"Rephrase," Daji said.

"All right. I killed him." That felt surprisingly good to say out loud. She said it again. "I killed him. And I don't feel bad about it. He was a shitty leader, he was squandering his troops, he humiliated me, and I needed him out of the way—"

"And that's not how you feel about the others?" Daji pressed.

Rin paused. How hard would it be to murder the entire southern leadership—Souji, Gurubai, and Liu Dai? She considered the details. What about their guards? Would she have to strike them all at once, in case they warned one another?

It scared her that this was no longer a question of whether to do it, but *how*.

"You can't lead by committee," Daji said. "The entire bloody history of this country is proof of that. You've seen the Warlord councils. You know they can't get anything done on their own. Do you know how the succession wars kicked off? One of the Red Emperor's favorite generals demanded that his rival give him a troupe of Hinterlander musicians captured in a raid on the borderlands. His rival sent him the musicians, but smashed all their instruments. The first general slaughtered the musicians in retaliation, and that kicked off nearly a century of warfare. That's how petty multifactional government becomes. Save yourself the headaches, child. Kill your rivals on sight."

"But that's not . . ." Rin paused, trying to tease out the exact nature of her objection. Why was it so hard to make the argument? "They don't deserve that. It'd be one thing if they were Republican officers, but they're fighting for the south. It's wrong to just—"

"Dear girl." Daji sighed heavily. "Stop pretending to care about ethics, it's embarrassing. At some point, you'll have to convince yourself that you're above right and wrong. Morality doesn't apply to you."

She turned the skewered rats over the fire, exposing their un-
cooked underbellies to the flames. "Get that in your head. You'll
have to get more decisive if you're ever going to lead. You're not
a little girl anymore, and you're not just a soldier, either. You're
in the running for the throne, and you've got a god on your side.
You want full command of that army? This *country*? You take it."

"And how," Rin said tiredly, "do you propose to do that?"

Daji and Jiang exchanged a look.

Rin couldn't read it, and she didn't like it. It was a look loaded
with decades of shared history, with secrets and allusions that she
couldn't begin to understand. Suddenly she felt like a little child
sitting between them—a peasant girl among legends, a mortal
among gods, woefully inexperienced and utterly out of place.

"Easily," Daji said at last. "We'll retrieve your anchor. And
then we'll go wake ours."

CHAPTER 14

The next morning they set off for the heart of enemy territory. They'd decided the Republican wartime headquarters was the most likely candidate for Kitay's location. Nezha and Vaisra had to be on the front lines, and if they were making use of Kitay as anyone in their position should, then he'd be right there with them.

The battlefront had moved far west in a very short period of time. They traversed through Snake Province and crossed over the northern tip of Dragon Province, and found the juncture of the Western Murui and Southern Murui in Hare Province, where they stole a raft and made a quick trip into Boar Province. Every passing mile where Rin did not find evidence of the Southern Coalition's resistance felt like another punch to the gut.

It meant Nezha had already pushed them this far across the country. It might mean they'd already been obliterated.

They tried their best to avoid civilians on their journey. That wasn't hard. This stretch of central Nikan was a war-stricken cesspool, much of which had lain straight in the paths of the destroyed Four Gorges Dam. The refugees who remained were scarce, and the few straggling souls they glimpsed tended to keep to themselves.

Rin stared at the banks as their raft floated through Boar Province, trying to imagine how this region would have looked barely a year ago. Whole villages, townships, and cities had thrived here once. Then the dam broke with no warning, and hundreds of thousands of villagers had either drowned or fled down south toward Arlong. When the survivors returned, they found their villages submerged still under floodwaters, ancestral lands that had housed generations lost to the river.

The region still hadn't recovered. The fields where once sorghum and barley crops grew lay under a sheet of water three inches thick, now rank from decomposing corpses. Occasionally, Rin glimpsed signs of life on the banks—either small camps of tents or tiny hamlets of no more than six or seven thatched huts. Never anything larger. These were subsistence hideaways, not long-term settlements.

It would take a long time for this region to sprout cities again. The destruction of the dam hadn't been the only source of devastation. The Murui was already a fickle river, prone to breaking its banks on unpredictably rainy years, and by destroying all vegetation cover, this great flood had destroyed the region's natural defenses. And before that, on their warpath inland, Mugenese soldiers had slashed and burned so many fields that they had ensured local starvation for years. Back in Ruijin, Rin had heard stories of children playing in the fields who had dug up explosives buried long ago, of children accidentally wiping out half their villages because they'd opened gas canisters in curiosity.

How many of those canisters still lurked hidden in the fields? Who was going to volunteer to find out?

Every day since the end of the Third Poppy War, Rin had learned that her victory on Speer mattered less and less. War hadn't ended when Emperor Ryohai perished on the longbow island. War hadn't ended when Vaisra's army defeated the Imperial Navy at the Red Cliffs.

She'd been so stupid to once think that if she ended the Federation then she'd ended the hurting. War didn't end, not so cleanly—it just kept building up in little hurts that piled on one another until they exploded afresh into raw new wounds.

Only when they reached the heart of Boar Province did they find evidence of recent fighting.

No—not fighting. *Destruction* was the better word. Rin saw the wreckage of thatched houses that still lay clumped near their foundations, instead of scattered in the patterns of older ruins. She saw scorch marks that hadn't yet been wiped away by wind and rain. Here and there, in ditches and along the stands, she saw bodies that hadn't fully decomposed—rotting flesh lumped over bones that hadn't yet been picked clean.

This proved the civil war wasn't over. Rin had been right—Vaisra hadn't rewarded the south for betraying her. He must have turned his dirigibles on the Southern Coalition the moment Rin and Daji left for the Chuluu Korikh. He'd chased them into Boar Province, and Boar Province must have put up a resistance. They had no reason to trust the Republic; their warlord had been unceremoniously decapitated at Arlong days after Daji's defeat. They must have rallied to the Southern Coalition's side.

From the looks of it, Vaisra had thrashed them for their impudence.

Rin whistled. "What happened here?"

They'd turned a corner of the river onto a bizarre shoreline; the area where trees should have stood was burned and flattened, like some flaming giant had come trampling through on a mindless rampage.

"Same thing that happened last time," Daji said. "They bring their bombers, and if they can't find their enemy they attack indiscriminately. They flatten the terrain to make it harder for the rebels to hide."

"But those aren't bombing marks," Rin said, still confused. "They're not all in crater patterns."

"No, that's the jelly," Jiang said.

"Jelly?"

"It's what they used last time. Something the Gray Company invented in their towers. It catches fire when it hits any living things—plants, animals, people. We never figured out how to put it out—water and smothering don't work. You have to wait for it to burn all the way through. And that takes a very long time."

The implications terrified Rin. This meant the Hesperians didn't just rule the skies; they also had flames that rivaled her own.

The destruction here was so much worse than the wreckage at Tikany. Boar Province must have fought so hard; that was the only thing that warranted retaliation on this scale. But they must have known they couldn't win. How did it feel when the heavens rained down a fire that wouldn't die? What was it like to fight the sky itself? She tried to imagine the moment when this forest turned into a chessboard of green, black, green, and black, when civilians running terrified through trees turned twitching and smoking into charcoal.

"The air campaigns are very clever, actually." Daji trailed her fingers idly through the water. "You drop bombs over dense areas with no built-in defenses, so they think they're entirely vulnerable. Then you fly your dirigibles over the widest possible area, so they know no one is safe no matter where they hide."

She wasn't speaking from conjecture, Rin realized. This was all from experience. Daji had fought this same war, decades before.

"You fly the airships at random schedules," Daji continued. "Sometimes at day and night, until the locals are terrified even of going outside, even though they're safer where their house won't collapse on them. Then you've robbed them of everything. Sleep, food, comfort, security. No one dares move in the open, so you've cut off communications and industry, too."

"Stop." Rin didn't want to hear any more. "I understand."

Daji ignored her. "You drive them into total collapse. Fear turns into despair, despair to panic, and then panic into utter submission. It's incredible, the power of psychological warfare. And all it takes is a couple of bombs."

"Then what did you do?" Rin asked.

Daji blinked slowly at her as if the answer were obvious. "We went to the Pantheon, darling."

"Things got a lot easier after that," Jiang said. "I used to snatch them out of the sky like mosquitoes. Riga and I made it a game. Record time was four crafts in five seconds."

He said this so casually that Rin couldn't help but stare. Immediately, like a gnat had buzzed into his ear, he shook his head quickly and looked away.

Whoever had emerged from the Chuluu Korikh was not the man she'd known at Sinegard. The Master Jiang at Sinegard had no recollection of the Second Poppy War. But this Jiang made constant offhand references about it and then backpedaled quickly, as if he were dipping his toes in an ocean of memory just to see if he'd like it, then cringing away because the water was too cold.

The memory lapses weren't the things about Jiang that bothered her. Ever since they'd left the Chuluu Korikh, she had been watching him, following his movements and vocal patterns to track the differences. He was refreshingly familiar and jarringly different all at once, often within the span of the same sentence. She couldn't predict the switches in the timbre of his voice, the sudden sharpness of his gaze. Sometimes he was affable, eccentric. And other times he carried himself like a man who had fought and won wars.

Rin knew his Seal was eroding. But what did it mean? Did it happen gradually, one regained memory at a time, until he collected everything that he'd lost? Or would it be erratic and unpredictable, like the way Jiang approached everything else?

What confused her even more were the times when Jiang slipped almost fully back into his former skin, when he acted so much like the teacher she'd once known that every day, for brief pockets of time, she almost forgot that anything had changed.

He would tease her about her hair, which was shorn so messily near her temples that she looked like she'd been raised in the wild. He would tease her about her stump ("Kitay's right, you should fix a blade on that"), about the Southern Coalition ("Losing a belt is one feat, losing an entire army is something else entirely"), about Altan ("You couldn't even mention him without blushing, you hopeless child"), about Nezha ("Well, there's no accounting for taste"). Those jokes would have prompted a slap if they'd come from anyone else, but when uttered in Jiang's detached, deadpan delivery, they somehow made her laugh.

During long, boring afternoons floating down empty stretches of river, he would tilt his head back at the clear sky and belt out bawdy, ribald songs whose lyrics made Daji snort and Rin blush. Occasionally, he'd even spar with her, teetering back and forth on the uneven raft, teaching her mental tricks to fix her balance, and jabbing her in the side with his staff until she corrected her form.

At those times Rin felt like a student again, eager and happy, learning from a master she adored. But inevitably, his smile always slipped, his shoulders tensed, and the laughter went out of his eyes, as if the ghost of who he had been had abruptly fled.

Only once, nearly three weeks into their journey, when Daji had fallen asleep during Jiang's watch rotation, did Rin work up the nerve to ask him about it.

"Get on with it," Jiang said promptly as soon as she opened her mouth.

"Um—sorry, what?"

"You've been eyeing me like a lovestruck village girl since we left the mountain," he said. "Go on. Proposition me."

She wanted to both laugh and hit him. A pang of nostalgia hit her stomach like a club, and her questions scattered on her tongue. She couldn't remember what she had wanted to ask him. She didn't even know where to start.

His expression softened. "Are you trying to see if I remember you? Because I do, you know. You're difficult to forget."

"I know you do, but . . ." She felt tongue-tied and bewildered, the way she'd often felt during the years she'd spent as Jiang's apprentice, groping at the truth about the gods before she even understood what she was looking for. She felt the absence of knowledge like a gap inside her. But she didn't know how to phrase her questions, couldn't trace the contours of what she lacked. "I suppose I wanted to know . . . well, the Seal, Daji said that—"

"You want to know what the Seal is doing to me." Jiang's voice took on a hard edge. "You're wondering if I am the same man who trained you. I am not."

Rin shuddered as memories rose unbidden to her mind: flashes of the vision the Sorqan Sira had once showed her, a nightmare of savaged corpses and manic laughter. "Then are you . . ."

"The Gatekeeper?" Jiang tilted his head. "Riga's right hand? The man who overthrew the Mugenese? No. I don't think I am him, either."

"I don't understand."

"How can I describe it?" He paused, tapping at his chin. "It's like seeing a warped reflection in a mirror. Sometimes we are the same and sometimes we are not; sometimes he moves with me, and sometimes he acts of his own volition. Sometimes I catch glimpses of his past, but it's like I'm watching from far away like a helpless observer, and that—"

He broke off, wincing, and pressed his fingers against his temples. Rin watched the headache pass; she'd witnessed these spasms before. They never lasted more than several seconds.

"And other times?" she prompted, after the lines around his eyes relaxed.

"Other times the memories are from my perspective, but it's like I'm experiencing them for the first time. For him, it's a memory. He already knows what happened. But for me, it's like watching a story unfold, but I don't know its ending. The only thing I do know, with absolute certainty, is that I did it. I see the bodies, and I know I'm responsible."

Rin tried to wrap her head around this, and failed. She couldn't see how one could live with two different sets of memories, belonging to two different personalities, and still remain sane.

"Does it hurt?" she asked.

"Knowing what I've done? Yes, it hurts. Unlike anything you could ever imagine."

Rin didn't have to imagine. She knew very well how it felt for a chasm of guilt to eat at her soul, to try to sleep when an abyss of vengeful souls whispered that she'd put them there, and for that she deserved to die.

But she had owned her memories. She knew what she'd done, and she'd come to terms with it. How did Jiang relate to his crimes? How could he take responsibility for them if he still couldn't identify with the person who had done them? And if he couldn't face his own past, couldn't even recognize it as *his*, was he doomed to remain a divided man, trapped in the schism of his psyche?

She phrased her next question carefully. She could tell she'd pushed him to the edge—he looked pale and skittish, ready to bolt if she said the wrong thing. She was reminded of her time at the Academy, when she'd had to mince and contort her words so that Jiang wouldn't mock them, skirt them, or simply pretend she hadn't spoken.

She understood now what he had been afraid of.

"Do you think . . ." She swallowed, shook her head, and started over. "Do you think you'll transform back to the person you were supposed to be? Before the Seal?"

"Is that who you want me to become?" he inquired.

"I think that's the man we need," she said. She blurted out her next words before her boldness receded. "But the Sorqan Sira said that man was a monster."

He didn't answer for a while. He sat back, watching the shore, trailing his fingers through the murky water. She couldn't tell what was going on behind those pale, pale eyes.

"The Sorqan Sira was right," he said at last.

Rin had thought—hoped, really—that when she came near enough to Kitay, she'd start sensing his presence, a warm familiarity that might gradually strengthen as she drew closer. She didn't think it would be so sudden. One morning she woke up shaking and gasping, nerves tingling like she'd been set on fire.

"What's wrong?" Daji asked sharply.

"Nothing, I'm . . ." Rin took several deep breaths, trying to pin down what had changed. She felt as if she'd been slowly drowning without realizing it until one day, abruptly, she broke for air. "I think we're close."

"It's your anchor." It wasn't a question; Jiang sounded certain. "How do you feel?"

"It's like—like I'm whole again." She struggled to articulate the feeling. It wasn't as if she could read Kitay's thoughts or sense his emotions. She still hadn't received any messages from him, not even scars in her skin. But she knew, as surely as she knew that the sun would set, that he was close. "It's as if—you know how when you're ill for a long time, you forget how it feels to be healthy? You get used to your head ringing, your ears being blocked, or your nose being stuffed—and you don't even notice you're not right anymore. Until you are."

She wasn't sure she'd made sense; the words sounded stupid tumbling out of her mouth. But Jiang and Daji only nodded.

Of course they understood. They were the only ones who could understand.

"Soon you'll start feeling his pain," Daji said. "If he's suffered any. That'll give us some clue about how he's been treated. And that feeling will get stronger and stronger the closer we get. Convenient, no? Our very own homing pigeon."

Their suspicions had been correct—Kitay was being held right on the Republican battlefront. The next morning, after long weeks on a road that seemed composed of never-ending bomb craters and ghost villages, the New City rose out of the horizon like a garish dash of color against a scorched background.

It made sense that the Republic would stake their base here, in one of the bloodiest cities in Nikara history. The New City, once named Arabak, had served as a military bastion since the campaigns of the Red Emperor. Originally it was a string of defensive forts over which warlords had fought for so long that the border between Boar and Hare Province was drawn in blood. The war machine required labor and talent, so over the years, civilians—physicians, farmers, craftsmen, and artisans—had moved with their families into the fortress complexes, which grew to accommodate the masses of people whose sole business was fighting.

Now, the New City was the frontier hub of the Republican Army and the air base of the Hesperian dirigible fleet. The Republican's senior military command was stationed behind those walls, and so was Kitay.

Rin, Jiang, and Daji had to get creative as they got closer to the city. They started traveling only at night, and even then in short, careful bursts, hiding in the forest undergrowth to avoid the dirigibles that circled the city in regular patrols, shining unnaturally strong lights at the ground below. They altered their appearances—Daji clipped her hair short above her ears, Rin started hiding her eyes behind messy shanks of hair, and Jiang dyed his white locks a rich brown with a mix of walnut hulls and ochre, ingredients that he found so easily that Rin had to assume he'd done it before. They agreed on a cover story in case they were stopped by sentries—they were a family of refugees, Rin their daughter, traveling from Snake Province to reunite with Daji's brother, a low-level bureaucrat in Dragon Province.

Rin found this last ploy ridiculous.

"No one's going to think I'm your daughter," she said.

"Why not?" Jiang asked.

"We look nothing alike! For one, your skin's infinitely paler than mine—"

"Ah, darling." He patted her on the head. "That's your fault. What did I tell you about staying out in the sun?"

Half a mile out from the gates they found crowds. Actual refugees, it turned out, had flocked to the New City in hordes. Those fortresses were the only thing within miles that guaranteed safety from the bombing campaigns.

"How are we going to get in?" Rin asked.

"The way you approach any other city," Daji said, as if this were obvious. "Right through the gates."

Rin cast a doubtful look at the lines snaking from the gates around the fortress walls. "They're not letting anyone in."

"I'm very persuasive," Daji said.

"You're not afraid they'll recognize you?"

Daji gave her a droll look. "Not if I instruct them to forget."

Surely it couldn't be so easy. Rin followed along, bewildered, as Daji led them straight to the gates, ignoring the cries of complaint from everyone else in the queue, and demanded so boldly to be let through that Rin was sure they were going to be shot.

But the soldiers only blinked, nodded, and parted.

"This never happened," Daji said as she passed. They nodded, eyes glazed. "You never saw me, and you have no idea what I look like."

She gestured for Jiang and Rin to follow. Astonished, Rin obeyed.

"Bothered?" Jiang asked.

"She just told them what to do," she muttered. "She just *told* them, without even—I mean, she wasn't even trying."

"Oh, yes." Jiang gave Daji a fond look. "We told you she's persuasive."

Persuasive didn't describe half of it. Rin knew about Daji's hypnosis. She'd been victim to it herself many times. But in the past, Daji's illusions had taken several long moments of careful coaxing. Never had Rin seen her utter such casual, dismissive commands with the full expectation that they would be obeyed.

Was it because Jiang was now freed from the Chuluu Korikh? Did Daji's powers amplify when her anchors grew stronger? And if so, then what would happen when they woke Riga?

Behind its walls, the New City felt like a punch to the face.

Rin had panicked the first time she'd ever left Tikany, when she'd woken up on the second morning of her journey to Sinegard and her caravan had traveled far enough that her surroundings felt truly foreign. It took her days to get used to the morphing landscape, the receding mountains, the terrifying reality that when she went to sleep at night on her cramped mat in the caravan wagon, Tikany's packed-earth walls no longer protected her.

She had traveled the Nikara Empire since then. She had been swept up in the overwhelming clamor of Sinegard, had walked the planks of the Floating City at Ankhiluun, had entered the Autumn Palace in lush, regal Lusan. She'd thought she understood the range of cities in the empire, spanning from the dusty poverty of Tikany to the winding disorder of Khurdalain's oceanside shacks to the sapphire-blue canals of Arlong.

But the New City was foreign on a different scale. The Hesperians had been here for only months—they could not possibly have dismantled and built over Nikara stone fortresses that had stood there for centuries. Yet its architectural skeleton seemed drastically altered—the old fortresses were augmented by a number of new installations that imposed a blockish sense of order, transforming the cityscape into a place of straight lines instead of the curved, winding alleys that Rin was used to.

Gone, too, were all Nikara-style decorations. She saw no lanterns, no wall banners, no sloping pagoda roofs or latticed windows, which would have appeared even in this sparsely utilitarian military city. Instead, everywhere she looked, she saw glass—clear glass on most windows, and colored patterns in the larger buildings, stained illustrations depicting scenes she did not recognize.

The effect was startling. Arabak, a city with more than a thousand years of history, seemed to have simply been erased.

This wasn't the first time Rin had seen Hesperian architecture. Khurdalain and Sinegard, too, had both been rebuilt by foreign occupation. But those were cities built first on Nikara roots, and later reclaimed by the Nikara. There, western architecture had been curious remnants of the past. The New City, on the other hand, felt as if a piece of Hesperia had simply been carved out and dropped whole into Nikan.

Rin found herself staring at things she had never dreamed could exist. On every street corner she saw blinking lights of every conceivable color powered not by flame, but by some energy source she couldn't see. She saw what looked like a monstrous black carriage mounted on steel tracks, chugging ponderously over the well-paved streets as thin trails of steam emitted from its head. Nothing pushed or pulled it—no laborers, no horses. She saw miniature dirigibles humming around the city, machines so perfectly small that she at first mistook them for loud birds. But their whine was unmistakable: a thinner, higher version of the airship engine whine she now associated with death.

No one controlled them. No one pulled their strings or even shouted out commands. The miniature airships seemed to have minds of their own; autonomously they dipped and swerved through the spaces between buildings, dodging deftly into windows to deliver letters and parcels.

Rin knew she couldn't keep gawking like this. The longer she stood here, eyes darting around at a million new and startling sights, the more she stood out. But she couldn't move. She felt dizzy, disoriented, like she had been plucked off the Earth and tossed adrift into an entirely different universe. She'd spent much of her life feeling like she didn't belong, but this was the first time she'd felt truly *foreign*.

Six months. Six months, and the Hesperians had transformed a riverside municipality into something like this.

How long would it take them to reconfigure the entire nation?

A whirring, apparently self-driving brass wagon across the street caught her eye, and she was so astonished that she didn't notice she was standing on two thin steel tracks. She didn't see the black horseless carriage sliding noiselessly in her direction until it was mere feet away, barreling straight toward her.

"*Move!*"

Jiang tackled her to the ground. The carriage zoomed past them both, chugging indifferently along its preordained route.

Heart pounding, Rin crawled to her feet.

"What is wrong with you?" Daji yanked her up by the wrist

and dragged her off the main road. They were attracting bystanders; Rin saw a Hesperian sentry eyeing them cautiously, arms cradling his arquebus. "Do you want to get caught?"

"I'm sorry." Rin followed her past a thicket of civilians into a narrow alley. She still felt terribly dizzy. She leaned against the cool, dark wall and took a breath. "It's just—this place, I didn't—"

To her surprise, Daji looked sympathetic. "I know. I feel it, too."

"I don't understand." Rin couldn't put her discomfort into words. She could barely breathe. "I don't know why—"

"I do," Daji said. "It's realizing that the future doesn't include you."

"Let's not dawdle." Jiang's tone was brusque, almost cold. Rin didn't recognize it at all. "We're wasting time. Where is Kitay?"

She shot him a puzzled glance. "How would I know?"

He looked impatient. "Surely you've sent a message."

"But there's no—" She faltered. "Oh. I see."

She glanced around the alley. It was thin and narrow, less a passageway and more a tight strip of space between two square buildings. "Can you cover me?"

Daji nodded. "Be quick."

They moved to guard either side of the alley. Rin sat down against a wall and pulled her knife out of her belt. She sent a probing question to the back of her mind, tentative, hopeful. *Are you there?*

To her surprise, a small flame flickered to life in her hand. She could have screamed in relief. She made a cage with her fingers over the blade, waiting until the tip glowed orange. She just needed to scar, not mutilate; a quick burn would be easier than drawing blood.

But Daji shook her head. "You have to press it in deep. You've got to bleed. Or he won't even feel it."

"Fine." Rin held the tip over the fleshy back of her lower left leg, but found that she couldn't stop her fingers from shaking.

"Would you like me to do it?" Daji asked.

"No—no, I'll do it." Rin clenched her teeth tight to make sure she wouldn't bite her tongue. She took a breath. Then she pushed the tip into her skin.

Her calf screamed. Every impulse told her to draw her hand away, but she kept the metal embedded inside her flesh.

She couldn't keep her fingers from shaking. The knife clattered to the ground.

She picked it up, embarrassed, unable to meet Daji's eyes.

Why was the pain so terrible now? She'd inflicted worse harms on herself before. She still had faint white burn scars on her arms from the candle wax she'd once dripped on herself to stay awake. Ridged, puckered marks covering her thighs where she'd once stabbed herself to escape her own hallucinations.

But those wounds were the product of fevered, desperate outbursts. She was sober right now, clear-minded and calm, and her full presence of mind made it so much harder to deliberately inflict pain.

She squeezed her eyes shut.

Get a grip, Altan said.

She thought of when a javelin had slammed her out of the sky over the Red Cliffs. Of when Daji had pinned her under a mast. Of when Kitay had smashed her hand apart, then pulled the mangled remnants through iron cuffs. Her body had been through so much worse than a shallow cut from a clean blade. This was a small pain. This was nothing.

She dug the metal under her skin. This time her hand held steady as she carved out a single character in clear, even strokes.

Where?

Minutes passed. Kitay didn't respond.

Rin glanced at her arm every several seconds, watching for pale scars that didn't emerge.

She tried not to panic. There were a million reasons why he

hadn't yet answered. He might be asleep. He might be drugged. He might have seen the message, but either lacked any means of responding, or couldn't because he was under surveillance. He needed time.

Meanwhile, they had nothing to do but wait.

Daji wanted to remain in hiding inside the alley, but Jiang suggested that they walk the length of the New City. This was purportedly to gather intelligence. He wanted to map out exit routes and mark down the guard post locations, so that if and when Kitay responded, they could smoothly get him out.

But Rin suspected that Jiang, like her, wanted to explore the New City simply out of sheer, sick fascination. To see how much had changed, to fully understand what the Hesperians were capable of.

"It's been decades," he told Daji when she objected. "We need to know what we're up against."

And so, scarves wrapped tight over their noses, they ventured back out onto the street.

The first thing Rin noticed was that the New City was *clean.*

She quickly discovered why. Ordinances printed on giant sheets of parchment were pasted all along the walls in Hesperian and Nikara characters. No urinating in the street. No dumping garbage from windows. No unlicensed sale of alcohol. No unleashed animals on the street. No fireworks, gambling, brawling, fighting, or shouting.

Rin had seen such ordinances before—Nikara magistrates often posted public notices like these in futile attempts to clean up their unruly cities. But here the ordinances were *followed.* The New City was far from pristine; it had all the crowded din of every large city. But that was a function of its swollen population, not their habits. The streets were dusty, but free from litter. The air smelled not of filth, excrement, or rotted trash, but of the normal stench of many tired humans crowded into one place.

"Look at that." Jiang paused by a metal plaque nailed to a streetlamp, engraved in alternating Nikara and Hesperian script.

The Four Cardinal Principles of Order
Propriety
Righteousness
Frugality
Modesty

Below that was a list of rules for the "Maintenance of Societal Order." *Do not spit. Queue politely in line to await your turn. Practice hygiene.* Under that last rule was another, indented list that clarified:

Practices that are unhygienic include:
Failure to wash hands before one cooks or eats.
Preparing raw meat with the same blade as vegetables.
Reusing cooking oil.

It went on for eight more lines.

"That's obnoxious." Rin had the sudden urge to rip it down, but the gleaming plaque looked so grand and official she was afraid one of the miniature dirigibles would start attacking her if she did.

"What's wrong with washing your hands?" Jiang asked. "Sounds fair to me."

"There's nothing *wrong*, it's just . . ." Rin trailed off, unsure how to phrase her discomfort. She felt like a little child being admonished to finish her rice. She didn't hate the idea of hygiene itself, but rather the presumption that the Nikara were so backward, so barbaric, that the Hesperians had to remind them in huge, clear text how not to behave like animals. "I mean, we know all this already."

"Do we?" Jiang chuckled. "Have you ever been to Sinegard?"

"There's nothing wrong with Sinegard." Rin didn't know why she was defending the old Nikara capital. She *knew* Sinegard was disgusting. The first time she'd traveled north, she'd been warned to eat nothing from dirt-cheap street vendors, since they produced their soy sauce from human hair and sewage. Yet now, for some reason, she felt territorial. Sinegard was the capital; Sinegard was a shining delight, and she would have far preferred its bustling din to this freak show of a city. "Let's just keep walking."

Her discomfort didn't ebb as they traveled farther into the New City. It worsened. Every time she turned a corner she saw something—new decorations, new technologies, new attire—that reinforced how *bizarre* this place was.

Even the background noise threw her off. She'd gotten used to the soundscape of her country; it was all she'd ever known. She knew its roadside shouts, its creaking wheels, its jabbering hagglers and crowded footsteps. She knew its language, had come to expect certain vowel-consonant combinations and vocal intonations. But the noises of the New City sounded on an entirely different register. From teahouses and street buskers she heard new strains of music, awful and discordant. She heard too many voices speaking Hesperian, or some accented attempt at Hesperian.

Nikara cities were loud, but their loudness was of a different type—local, discrete, irregular. The New City seemed run on an ever-present mechanical heartbeat, its thousand machines whirring, humming, and whining without end. Once Rin noticed it, she couldn't get it out of her head. She couldn't imagine living against this backdrop; it would drive her mad. How did anyone *sleep* in this city?

"Are you all right?" Jiang asked.

"What? Of course—"

"You're sweating."

Rin glanced down, and realized that the front of her tunic was soaked through.

What was wrong with her? She had never felt a panic like this before—this low, crescendoing distress of gradual suffocation. She felt like she'd been dropped blindfolded into a fairy realm. She did not want to be here. She wanted to run, back out past the walls and into the forests; anything to get away from this hopeless, confused alienation.

"This is how we felt last time." Daji's tone was uncharacteristically gentle. "They came in, rebuilt our cities, and transformed them according to their principles of order, and we almost couldn't bear it."

"But they have their own cities," Rin said. "What do they want here?"

"They want to erase us. It's their divine mandate. They want to make us better, to *improve* us, by turning us into a mirror of themselves. The Hesperians understand culture as a straight line." Daji dragged her finger through the air. "One starting point, and one destination. They are at the end of the line. They loved the Mugenese because they came close. But any culture or state that diverges is necessarily inferior. *We* are inferior, until we speak, dress, act, and worship just like them."

That terrified Rin.

Until now she had perceived the Hesperian threat in terms of hard power—through memories of airship fleets, smoking arquebuses, and exploding missiles. She'd seen them as an enemy on the battlefield.

She'd never considered that this alternate form of soft erasure might be far worse.

But what if the Nikara *wanted* this future? The New City was full of Nikara residents—they had to outnumber the Hesperians five to one—and they seemed completely fine with their new arrangement. Happy, even.

How had things changed so quickly? Once upon a time any Nikara on the continent would have run from the mere sight of the blue-eyed devils. They'd been primed for xenophobia by centuries of rumors and stereotypes, stories that Rin had half believed until she'd met the Hesperians in the flesh. *They eat their food raw. They steal orphan babies to cook them into stews. Their penises are three times larger than normal, and their women's openings are cavernous to accommodate.*

But the Nikara in the New City seemed to adore their new neighbors. They nodded, smiled, and saluted Hesperian soldiers as they passed. They sold Hesperian food from carts parked on street corners—rocklike brown pastries, hard yellow rounds that gave off pungent odors, and varieties of fish so stinkingly moist Rin was surprised they hadn't rotted. They—the upper class, at least—had begun to imitate Hesperian dress. Merchants, bureaucrats, and officers walked down the streets garbed in tight trousers, thick white socks pulled up to their knees, and strange coats that buttoned over their waists but draped in the back past their buttocks like duck tails.

They'd even started learning Hesperian. It sounded like bad Hesperian—a clipped, pidgin dialect that morphed the two languages and made them, oddly, mutually understandable. Foreign phrases peppered exchanges between merchants and customers, soldiers and civilians—*Good day. How much? Which ones? Thank you.*

But despite all their pretensions and efforts, they were not the Hesperians' equals. They couldn't be, by virtue of their race. This Rin noticed soon enough—it was clear from the ways the Nikara bowed and scraped, nodding obsequiously while the Hesperians ordered them about. This wasn't a surprise. This was the Hesperians' idea of a natural social order.

Sister Petra's words rose to her mind. *The Nikara are a particularly herdlike nation. You listen well, but independent thought is difficult for you. Your brains, which we know to be an indicator of your rational capacity, are by nature smaller.*

"Look," Jiang murmured. "They've started bringing their women."

Rin followed his gaze and saw a tall, wheat-haired woman stepping out of the horseless carriage, her waist enveloped in massive bunches of ruffled fabric. She stretched out a gloved hand. A

Nikara foot servant ran up to help her off, then stooped to pick up her bags.

Rin couldn't stop staring at the woman's skirts, which arced out from her waist in the unnatural shape of an overturned teacup. "Are they—"

"Wooden frame," Jiang said, anticipating her confusion. "Don't fret, it's still legs underneath. They think it's fashionable."

"*Why?*"

Jiang shrugged. "Beyond me."

Before now, Rin had never seen regular Hesperian civilians— Hesperians who were not soldiers, nor part of the Gray Company. Hesperians who purportedly had no official business in Nikan other than to keep their husbands company. Now they strolled the New City's streets as if they belonged.

She shuddered to think of what that meant. If the Hesperians were shipping in their wives, it meant they intended to stay.

A sudden sharp prickle stung her left shin. She dropped to her knee and tugged her pant leg up, hoping fervently that the pain would continue.

For a few seconds she felt nothing. Then came another stab of pain so sharp she felt as if a needle had pierced all the way through her flesh and emerged out the other side. She uttered a quiet moan of relief.

"What's wrong?" Daji asked sharply.

"It's Kitay," Rin whispered. "He's writing back, look—"

"Not here," Daji hissed. She yanked Rin up by the arm and pulled her down the street. Pain continued to lance up Rin's left leg, the agony intensifying by the second.

Kitay likely didn't have access to a sharp, clean blade. He was probably carving his flesh with a nail, a piece of scrap wood, or the jagged edge of a shattered vase. Perhaps he was using his own fingernails to carve out the long, jagged strokes that dragged in sharp twists down the length of her shin, creating scars she couldn't wait to see.

It didn't matter how badly it hurt. This felt *good*. Every stab was proof that Kitay was here, he'd heard her, and he was writing back.

At last they reached an empty street corner. Daji let go of Rin's arm. "What does it say?"

Rin rolled her pant leg up to the knee. Kitay had written four characters, engraved in pale white lines along her inner calf.

"Three, six," Rin said. "Northeast."

"Coordinates," Jiang guessed. "Has to be. The intersection of the third and sixth streets. That makes sense, this city's arranged like a grid."

"Then which one's the vertical coordinate?" Daji asked.

Rin thought for a moment. "How do you read wikki positions?"

"The board game?" Jiang thought for a moment. "Vertical first, then horizontal, origin point in the southwest. Does he—"

"Yes," Rin said. "He loves it." Kitay was wild about the strategy game. He'd always tried to get other students to play with him at Sinegard, but no one ever would. Losing to Kitay was too annoying; he kept lecturing you on all your strategic missteps as he cleaned your pieces off the board. "Third street north. Sixth street east."

None of them could place themselves in relation to the grid, so they had to first find the southwest corner of the city, then count the blocks as they moved northeast. It took them the better part of the hour. All the while Jiang complained under his breath, "Stupid directions, that boy; there are four sides of an intersection, he could be in any one of them, should have included a *description*."

But they didn't need one. When Rin turned the corner toward the sixth street, Kitay's location became obvious.

A massive building dominated the block in front of them. Unlike the other buildings, which were Hesperian scaffolds built over Nikara foundations, this had clearly been constructed from scratch. The red bricks gleamed. Stained-glass windows stretched along every wall, depicting various insignia—scrolls, scales, and ladders.

At the center was a symbol Rin knew too well: an intricate circle inscribed with the pattern of a timepiece, complicated gears interlocking in a symmetrical pattern. The symbol of the Gray Company. The Architect's perfect design.

Jiang whistled. "Well, that's not a prison."

"It's worse," Rin said. "That's a church."

CHAPTER 15

"This is easy enough," Jiang said. They stood huddled against the wall of a tea shop across the street, eyeing the church's thick double doors. "We'll just kill and impersonate one of those missionary fellows. Drag them into a corner, strip off their cassock—"

"You can't do that," Rin said. "You're Nikara. All the Gray Company are Hesperians."

"Hmm." Jiang rubbed his chin. "A devastatingly good point."

"Servant's entrance, then?" Daji suggested. "They've always got some Nikara on hand to sweep their floors, and I can talk them down until you've found Kitay."

"Too risky," Jiang said. "We don't know how many there are, and we need to buy more than five minutes to search."

"So I'll ask them what I need, then stick them with needles."

Jiang reached out to tuck a lock of hair behind her ear. "Darling, people pay you less attention when you don't leave a trail of bodies in your wake."

Daji rolled her eyes.

Rin glanced back toward the church. Then the solution struck her—it was so blindingly obvious, she almost laughed.

"We don't have to do any of that." She pointed to the line of

Nikara civilians stretching out the front of the building. As if on cue, the heavy double doors swung open, and a brother of the Gray Company stepped outside, hands stretched wide in welcome to the congregation. "We can just walk right in."

They shuffled into the church with their heads bowed, following obediently behind the rest of the crowd in a single-file line. Rin tensed as they passed the gray-cassocked priest standing at the doors, but all he did was place a hand on her shoulder and murmur low words of greeting as he welcomed her inside, just as he had every person in line before her. He never even glanced at her face.

The church interior was a single wide room with high beams, crammed with low benches arranged in neat double columns. Sunlight streaming through the stained glass windows cast colorful, oddly beautiful splotches onto the smooth wooden floor. At the front stood a podium on a raised platform where half a dozen gray-robed Hesperians stood waiting, watching imperiously as the Nikara took their seats.

Rin glanced about the room, trying to find doors that might lead to hidden chambers or passageways.

"There." Jiang nodded across to the other end of the hall, where Rin glimpsed a door tucked behind a curtain. A single priest stood in front of it; a circle of keys hung visibly from his belt.

"Wait here." Daji broke from the line and strode confidently across the room. The priest's eyes widened in confusion as she approached, but lost focus as Daji began to speak. Seconds later, the priest passed the keys into Daji's hands, opened the door, and then walked off in the other direction.

Daji turned over her shoulder and waved impatiently for Rin to join her.

"Go." She pushed the keys into Rin's palm. "These open the cell doors. You should be clear for an hour and a half, and then you can join the crowd as they leave."

"But aren't you—"

"We'll cover your exits from up here." Daji pushed Rin toward the door. "Be quick."

The Nikara had nearly finished filing into their seats; only a handful of people were still standing. Daji hurried back to Jiang's side, and together they sat down in the very back row.

Rin almost laughed at the absurdity. She'd come to the New City with two of the most powerful shamans in Nikara history, beings from myths and legends, and here they were paying obeisance to a false god.

A great screech echoed through the hall as the double doors swung closed, trapping them inside. Heart pounding, Rin slipped through the door and hastened down the stairs.

Behind the door lay a winding staircase that emptied out into a dark hallway. Rin pulled a small flame in her hand and held it before her like a torch. They were right—this whole basement had been converted into a prison, cells lining either side of the passageway. Rin shielded her face as she walked, glancing to either side to check for Kitay. She needn't have bothered. The prisoners were hardly alert. Most were slumped in the corners of their cells, either sleeping or staring into space. A few were moaning quietly, but none gave any indication they'd even noticed her.

How quaint, Rin thought. It made sense that the Hesperians would keep their sinners and believers under the same roof. The Gray Company liked their symmetry. The Divine Architect rallying against Chaos. Light against dark. Worshippers on the top, and sinners on the bottom, the unseen side of the ruthless, unsparing quest from barbarism toward a well-ordered civilization.

Kitay's cell was at the end of the next corridor. She knew right as she turned the corner. All she saw by her faint flame was the curve of his shoulder and the silhouette of his head, turned away from the bars. But she knew. Her whole body thrummed with longing anticipation, like a magnet straining for its opposite. She *knew*.

She broke into a run.

He was asleep when she reached his cell, curled up on a cot with his knees drawn up to his chest. He looked so small. His left pant leg was soaked through with blood.

Rin fumbled clumsily with the keys, trying several before she found the one that fit the lock. She yanked hard at the door. It scraped open with a loud metallic screech that echoed down the corridor.

Kitay gave a start and jerked to a sitting position, fists up as if ready to fight.

"It's me," she whispered.

He blinked blearily, as if unsure whether or not he was dreaming. "Oh, hello."

She rushed toward him.

They collided over his cot. He rose halfway to meet her, but she knocked him right back down, arms wrapped tightly around his skinny frame. She had to hold him, feel the weight of him, know that he was real and solid and there. The void in her chest, that aching sense of absence she'd felt since Tikany, finally melted away.

She felt like herself again. She felt whole.

"Took you long enough," he murmured into her shoulder.

"Could you tell I was coming?"

"Sensed you yesterday." He drew back, grinning. "I woke up, and it felt like I'd been doused with cold water. Never been happier."

He looked better than she'd feared. He was thin, of course, but he'd been painfully thin since Ruijin, and his cheekbones protruded no more than they already had. His arms and legs were unbound save for an iron cuff around his left ankle, attached to a chain with enough slack to give him free movement around the cell. He didn't look like he'd been tortured. There were no cuts, welts, or bruises on his pale skin. The only wounds he'd suffered recently were the gashes he'd opened in his shin.

His index finger was crusted over in dried blood. He'd done it with his nail.

She reached for his leg. "Are you—"

"It's fine. It's stopped bleeding, I'll clean it up later." Kitay stood up. "Who are you here with?"

"Two-thirds of the Trifecta."

He didn't miss a beat. "Which two?"

"The Vipress and the Gatekeeper."

"Of course. And when are we meeting the Dragon Emperor?"

"We'll discuss that later." She jangled the keys at him. "Let's get you out first. Padlocks?"

He shook his ankle at her, looking impressed. "How did you—"

"Daji is persuasive." She held a flame up to the lock and began flipping through the keys to find one that looked like it matched. "No more bone smashing for us."

He snorted. "Thank the gods."

She'd just found a silver key that looked about the right size when she heard the unmistakable screech of a door sliding open, followed by a faint patter of footsteps echoing through the corridor. She froze. Daji had promised her more than an hour; she'd been planning to hide out downstairs until whatever ritual was going on in the main chamber had ended. Had something gone wrong upstairs?

"Hide," Kitay hissed.

"Where?"

He pointed to his cot. Rin didn't see how that could possibly work—it was a flimsy, narrow structure, barely two feet wide, with crossed wooden legs that wouldn't conceal a rabbit.

"Get under this." Kitay tugged at his blanket. The cotton sheet was thin but solidly opaque; hanging off the edge of the bed, it was just long enough to stretch to the floor.

Rin crawled underneath the cot and shrank in on herself, fighting to make her breathing inaudible. She heard the lock click back into place as Kitay pushed the cell door shut.

She poked her head out from the blankets, confused. "Wait, why don't we just—"

"Shh," he whispered. "I said *hide*."

Footsteps grew louder and louder in the corridor, then stopped just outside the cell.

"Hello, Kitay."

Rin dug her nails into her palm, madly clenching her teeth in an attempt to keep quiet. She knew only one person who could speak with that precise mixture of confidence, condescension, and feigned camaraderie.

"Good evening." Kitay's tone was all light, cheery indifference. "Good timing. I've just taken my nap."

The door screeched open. Rin hardly dared to breathe.

If he made any moves toward the cot, she'd kill him. She held two advantages—the element of surprise and the fire. She wouldn't hesitate this time. First a torrent of flame to his face to startle and blind him, then four white-hot fingers in a claw around his neck. She'd rip out his artery before he even realized what was happening.

"How have you been?" Nezha was standing right above her. "Accommodations still adequate?"

"I'd like some new books," Kitay said. "And my reading lamps are running low."

"I'll see to that."

"Thank you," Kitay said stiffly. "And how is the lab rat life?"

"Don't be a prick, Kitay."

"My apologies," Kitay drawled. "You were just so quick to send Rin to the same fate, I'm always stunned by the irony."

"Listen, asshole—"

"Why do you let them do it?" Kitay asked. "I'm just curious. Certainly you don't *enjoy* getting hurt."

"It doesn't hurt," Nezha said quietly. "It's the only time it doesn't hurt."

There was a pause, which stretched into a longer, more awkward silence.

"I take it the council's still giving you grief?" Kitay finally asked.

She heard a shuffling noise. Nezha was sitting down. "They're madmen. All of them."

Kitay chuckled. "At least we agree about something."

Rin was astonished by how quickly they settled into amiable chitchat. No—*amiable* wasn't quite the right word; they sounded far from friendly. But they also didn't sound like a prisoner and his interrogator. They sounded like second-year students at Sinegard complaining about Jima's sentence-diagramming homework. They were old acquaintances taking their seats at a wikki board, resuming a game right where they'd left off.

But was this really so surprising? Nostalgia gnawed Rin's chest at the mere sound of Nezha's voice. She wanted this familiarity with him back, too. Never mind that thirty seconds ago she'd been ready to kill him. His voice, his very *presence*, made her heart ache—she wished desperately they could be caught in a stalemate, that for just one minute the wars surrounding them could be suspended, so that they might speak like friends again. Just once.

"Our northern allies won't commit further troops to Arabak until they get relief," Nezha said. "They think I'm rolling in silver, that I'm just withholding it—but damn it, Kitay, they don't understand. The coffers are empty."

"And where's the money gone?" Kitay asked.

He said it lightly, but he'd clearly meant to strike a nerve. Nezha's tone turned sharp. "Don't you dare accuse—"

"You're getting far too much aid from the Hesperians for your army to be so poorly outfitted. Someone's bleeding you dry. Come on, Nezha, we've been over this already. Get your house in order."

"You're making baseless accusations—"

"I'm just telling you what's right in front of you," Kitay said. "You know I'm right. You wouldn't keep coming here if you didn't think I could be useful."

"Say something useful, then." Nezha sounded so nasally petty then, so much like how he'd sounded their first year at Sinegard, that Rin almost laughed.

"I've been telling you things so obvious a child could see them," Kitay said. "Your generals are siphoning away funds meant for relief—probably squirreling them away to their summer palaces, so that's the first place you'll want to check. That's the problem with all that Hesperian silver. Your entire base has gotten corrupted. You might start with cutting down on the bribes."

"But you have to bribe them to keep them on your side," Nezha said, frustrated. "Otherwise they won't present a united front, and if we don't have a united front then the Hesperians just run roughshod over us like our government doesn't even exist."

"Poor Nezha," Kitay said. "They've tied your hands behind your back, haven't they?"

"This is all so fucking stupid. I need unified army command. I need freedom to put absolute priority on the southern front, and I want to divert forces from the north to deal with Rin without making all these compromises. I just don't know *why*—"

"I know why. You're not the grand marshal, you're the *Young Marshal*. That's your nickname, right? The generals and the Hesperians both think you're just a spoiled, stupid princeling who doesn't know what he's doing. They think you're just like Jinzha. And they wouldn't put you in charge of their dirigibles if you sank to your knees and begged."

Rin didn't know what surprised her most—Kitay's frankness, that Nezha hadn't yet punished him for it, or that anything Kitay was saying might be *true*.

None of this made sense. She had assumed Nezha was wallowing in power. That he had the entire dirigible fleet at his disposal. He'd seemed so dominant when he'd descended on Tikany, she'd thought he had the entire Republic at his back.

But this was her first indication that Nezha was not holding together as well as she'd thought. Here, alone in the basement with his old classmate and prisoner, perhaps the only person he could be honest with, Nezha just sounded scared.

"I'm guessing things haven't gotten better with Tarcquet, either," Kitay said.

"He's a patronizing fuck," Nezha snarled. "You know what he's blamed the last campaign on? Our lack of fighting spirit. He said that the Nikara inherently *don't have fighting spirit*."

"A rather bold claim given our history, I think."

Nezha didn't laugh. "There's nothing wrong with our troops. They're incredibly well trained, they're excellent on the field, but the problem is the restructuring and integrated forces—"

"The what now?"

"Another one of Tarcquet's ideas." Nezha spat the name like it was poison. "They want coordinated air and ground assault teams."

"Interesting," Kitay said. "I'd have thought they were too up their own asses for that."

"It's not real integration. It means they want us to lug their coal wagons for them wherever they decide to go. Means we're just their fucking mules—"

"There are worse roles to play on the battlefront."

"Not if we're ever going to earn their respect."

"I think we both know your chances of winning Hesperian respect sailed a long time ago," Kitay said lightly. "So who are you dropping bombs on next? Has Boar Province capitulated?"

A tinge of exasperation crept into Nezha's voice. "If you'd agree to help with planning, I could tell you."

Kitay sighed. "Alas, I'm not that desperate to leave this cell."

"No, you seem to like captivity."

"I like knowing that the words out of my mouth won't cause the deaths of people I've become quite fond of. It's this thing called ethics. You might try it sometime."

"No one has to die," Nezha said. "No one ever had to die. But Rin's suckered those fools into waging everything on an all-or-nothing outcome."

Rin flinched at the sound of her name from his mouth this time. He said it with such violence.

"Rin's not behind this," Kitay said cautiously. "Rin's dead."

"Bullshit. The whole country would be talking if she were gone."

"Oh, you think that your lovely airships managed to miss her?"

"She can't be dead," Nezha insisted. "She's just in hiding, she has to be. They never found a body, and the south wouldn't be fighting this hard if they knew she was gone. She's the only thing they're rallying around. Without her they have no hope. They would have surrendered."

Rin heard a rustle of clothing. Kitay might have been shrugging.

"I suppose you know better than me."

Another silence filled the cell. Rin lay utterly still, her heartbeat ringing so loudly she was amazed she had not been discovered.

"I didn't want this war," Nezha said at last. His voice sounded oddly brittle—defensive, even. Rin didn't know what to make of it. "I never did. Why couldn't she understand that?"

"Well, you did put a blade in her back."

"I didn't want things to be like this."

"Oh, gods, let's not go down this road again."

"We'd let her have the south if she'd just come to the table. Gods know we're grateful she got rid of the Mugenese for us. And she's a good soldier. The very best. We'd happily have her back on our side; we'd make her a general in a heartbeat—"

"You seem to have mistaken me for a dullard," Kitay said.

"It's a tragedy we're on different sides, Kitay. You know that. We would have been so good united, all three of us."

"We *were* united. And we *were* good. Your father had other plans."

"We can come back from this," Nezha insisted. "Yes, we've messed up—I've messed up, I'll admit that—but think about what the Republic could accomplish, if we really fought to make it work. You're too smart to ignore its potential—"

"You're still on about that shit? Please don't patronize me, Nezha."

"Help me," Nezha begged. "Together we could end this whole thing in weeks, regardless of whether Rin is dead or alive. You're the smartest person I've ever met. If you had access to our resources—"

"See, it's hard to take you seriously when you do things like drop bombs on innocent children."

"That ambush was a mistake—"

"Sleeping in past roll call is a mistake," Kitay snapped. "Neglecting to deliver my meals on time was a *mistake*. What you did was cold-hearted murder. And Rin and I know that if we join you, it'll happen again, because we and the south are utterly disposable to you. You and your father think we are tools to be traded or thrown away at your convenience, which is precisely what you did."

"I didn't have a choice—"

"You had a thousand choices. You drew the lines at Arlong. You started this war, and it's not my fault if you haven't got the balls to finish it. So tell Vaisra he might as well lop my head off, because then he could at least use it for decoration."

Nezha said nothing. Rin heard a rustle of cloth as he stood. He was leaving; his footsteps sounded hard and angry against the stone. She wished she could see his face. She hoped he might give some rejoinder, any kind of reaction, just so she would know if Kitay had rattled him or not. But she heard only the screech as he pushed the door shut behind him, and then the click of the lock.

"Sorry I didn't have time to warn you." Kitay pulled the blanket off the cot and helped Rin to her feet. "Just thought you should hear."

She passed him the keys. "How long has he been at it?"

"Every day since I got here. He was actually on pretty good behavior today; you didn't get to see him at his worst. He's tried a million different things to break me." Kitay bent over to unlock his shackles. "But he should have remembered he never figured out how. Not at Sinegard, and certainly not now."

Rin felt an aching burst of pride. She forgot sometimes how resilient Kitay could be. One would never have suspected it by looking at him—the archetypal reedy and anxious scholar—but he bore hardship with iron fortitude. Sinegard hadn't worn him down. Even Golyn Niis hadn't destroyed him. Nezha could never have broken him.

No, whispered the little voice in her head that sounded too much like Altan. *The only person capable of breaking him is you.*

"Behind you," Kitay said suddenly.

Rin twisted around, expecting a soldier. But it was just one of the Gray Company—a young man in a cassock, carrying a meal tray in his hands.

His mouth fell open when he saw her. His eyes flitted, confused, between her and Kitay, as if he was trying to determine the appropriate number of people for one cell. "You—"

Kitay twisted the key and jerked the cell door open.

Too late, the missionary turned to run. Rin dug her heels into the ground and chased him down. His legs were much longer than hers, and he might have gotten away, but he tripped over his cassock just as he reached the corner. He stumbled—only for a split second, but that was enough. Rin grabbed his arm, yanked him further off balance, and kicked at the backs of his knees. He fell. She called the fire into her palm. It came back so quickly, so naturally, a well-worn glove slipping over waiting fingers.

She jammed her clawed hand onto his throat. Soft flesh gave way to her burning nails like tofu parting under steel. Easy. It was done in seconds. He went without so much as a whimper; she'd chosen his throat because she didn't want him to scream.

She straightened up, exhaled, and wiped her hand on the wall. The magnitude of what she'd just done hadn't hit her; it had happened so quickly, it didn't even seem real. She hadn't decided to kill the missionary; she hadn't even thought about it. She'd simply needed to protect Kitay. The rest was an instinct.

She felt a sudden, bizarre urge to laugh.

She cocked her head, observing the crimson streaks shining wet and bright on marble. For some reason, it gave her a dizzying rush of delight, the same confusing ecstasy she'd felt when she poisoned Ma Lien.

It wasn't about the violence.

It was about the *power*.

It wasn't as good as killing Nezha, but it felt close. For a wild, untethered moment, she considered dragging her bloody finger along the wall and drawing him a flower.

No. No. Too indulgent. She didn't have time. The wave of vertigo passed. She came back to her senses; she was in control.

Focus.

"Come here," she called down the corridor. "Help me drag him into your cell. We'll put him on the cot, cover him with a blanket—it'll buy some time."

Kitay wandered out two steps from his cell, keeled over, and vomited.

Their escape from the church proceeded with astonishing ease. Rin and Kitay waited by the door to the dungeons, listening against the wood to an ongoing Hesperian sermon, until they heard the Nikara civilians standing up from their pews. Then they opened it a crack and slid out to join the press of moving bodies, invisible in the crowd. Jiang and Daji rejoined them as they spilled out of the doors, but none of them spoke until they'd walked for several minutes down to the other end of the street.

"You've gotten taller," Jiang told Kitay once they'd turned the corner. "Good to see you again."

Kitay stared at him for a moment, as if unsure how to respond. "So you're the Gatekeeper."

"That's me."

"And you've been hiding in Sinegard all this time."

"Lost my mind for a bit," Jiang said. "Just starting to get it back now."

"Makes sense," Kitay said weakly.

All considered, Rin thought, he was taking this rather well.

"Questions later." Daji tossed Kitay a brown tunic, which was far less conspicuous than the tattered rags he'd been wearing since Tikany. "Put this on and let's go."

They left the New City in a horse-drawn laundry wagon. Its original driver had carried a gate permit to take infirmary linens to the river for washing; Daji had charmed him into relinquishing the wagon and permit both. While Daji drove the wagon confidently through the streets, Rin, Kitay, and Jiang hid under piles of linen stacked so tall they could hardly breathe. Rin squirmed, hot and itchy, trying not to think about the brown stains surrounding her. She felt the wagon stop only once. Rin heard Daji answering a guardsman's questions in very convincing pidgin Hesperian, and then they passed through the gates.

Daji kept driving. She didn't let them emerge from the linen piles until over an hour later, when the New City was nothing but a tiny outline behind them, until the sound of dirigibles had faded away and the only noise around them was the constant hum of cicadas.

Rin was relieved when the New City faded out of her sight. If she could help it, she never wanted to set foot in that place again.

That night, over a meal of dried shanyu root and a stolen loaf of thick, chewy Hesperian bread, Daji and Jiang interrogated Kitay for every shred of information he'd gleaned about the Republic. He had no solid details on troop placements or campaign plans—Nezha had fed him only enough information to seek his advice without creating a liability—but the little he did know was tremendously useful.

"They're in endgame now, but it's taking longer than it needs to," Kitay said. "Vaisra turned on the Southern Coalition the moment they failed to produce your body, as you would have expected. But the Monkey Warlord—well, really it's probably Souji's work—rallied a surprisingly strong defense. They learned pretty quickly to create decent bomb shelters. Once he realized the airships weren't getting the job done, Vaisra sent in ground forces. The south have beaten a retreat back to the corner of Boar Province for now. They've holed up under the mountains and forced a standstill for weeks, hence why everyone's centered in Arabak."

"The New City," Rin amended.

He shook his head. "It's still Arabak. No one here calls it the New City but the Hesperians, or Nikara in Hesperian company."

"So the holdup is just a consequence of the terrain?" Daji

asked. "What about the Young Marshal? Word on the street is he's falling apart."

Rin shot her a surprised look. "Where'd you hear that?"

"A pair of old women were gossiping in the pew behind us," Daji said. "They said if Yin Jinzha were in charge then all the southern rebels would have been exterminated months ago."

"Jinzha?" Jiang frowned, digging his little finger into his ear. "The older Yin brat?"

"Yes," Daji said.

"I think I taught him at Sinegard. Utter asshole. Whatever happened to him?"

"He got plucky," Daji said. "I turned him to mincemeat and sent him back to Vaisra in a dumpling basket."

Jiang arched an eyebrow. "Darling, fucking *what*?"

"Nezha's exhausted." Kitay quickly returned to the subject. "It's not entirely his fault. His Hesperian advisers keep making insane demands that he can't accommodate, and the Republican cabinet are pulling him in twenty different directions so that he doesn't even know which way to shatter."

"I don't get it," Rin said. "You'd still think he'd be faring better with his advantages."

"It's not so simple. This remains a war on multiple fronts. The Republic's pretty much conquered the north—Jun's dead, by the way; they flayed him alive on a dais a few weeks ago—but there are still a few provinces holding out."

"Really?" Rin perked up. That was the first piece of good news she'd heard in a long time. "Any provinces that are armed?"

"Ox Province is putting up the best resistance for now, but they'll all be dead in a few weeks," Kitay said. "They've got no organization. They're split into three factions that aren't communicating—which was their advantage for a while, actually, because Nezha never knew what the individual battalions were going to do next. But that's not a sustainable defense strategy. Nezha just needs to take care of them one by one.

"And then there's Dog Province, which has always been so peripheral to the Empire that no one's thought to care much about them. But that's made them value their autonomy. And they're even less likely to bow to Vaisra now that the Hesperians want to go in and turn the whole region into coal mines."

"How many men do they have?" Daji asked.

"They haven't needed men yet. The Republic hasn't even sent a delegate to negotiate. For now, they're not on Nezha's map." Kitay sighed. "But once they are, they're finished. They're too sparsely populated; they won't have nearly enough troops to survive the first wave of attacks."

"Then we should join them!" Rin exclaimed. "That's perfect—we break our troops out past the blockade, send a sentry ahead and then rendezvous with the Dog Warlord—"

"It's a bad guest that shows up unannounced," Daji said.

"Not if a third guest is holding a knife to the host's throat," Rin said.

"This analogy has lost me," Jiang said.

"It's not the worst idea," Kitay said. "Nezha was convinced that Souji and Gurubai intended to send to Dog Province for help. So it's the predictable option, but it's also our only option left. We need allies where we can get them. Divided, we're carrion."

Rin frowned at him. Something sounded off about Kitay's tone, though she couldn't quite put her finger on it. He didn't sound as sharp and engaged as he usually did at strategy councils. Instead, the words came out in a flat monotone, as if he were half-heartedly reciting a memorized test answer.

What had happened to him in Arabak? He hadn't been physically tortured, but he'd been alone with Nezha for weeks. Had he turned against her? Was he only pretending to be their ally now? The possibility made her shudder.

But Kitay couldn't conceal a lie like that. Their souls were bound. She'd feel it. At least, she *hoped* she'd feel it.

Why, then, was he speaking like a man who had already lost?

"Dog Province, then. Interesting." Jiang turned to Daji. "What do you say? The route to their capital takes us close to the Tianshan range, and it'd be nice to have ground cover for at least part of it."

"Fine." Daji shrugged. "But I don't see why we need the Southern Coalition for that."

"It's thousands of warm bodies."

"Thousands we have to drag along through the mountains. What's more, they sold her out." Daji jerked her chin toward Rin. "They deserve to be left behind."

"That's the leadership's fault. The masses are malleable, you know that."

"It'll be messy."

"I've just escaped from the stone mountain. Let me stretch a little, dear. Get some exercise. It's good for the mind."

"Fair enough." Daji sighed. "Dog Province it is."

"I'm sorry." Kitay looked between them. "Did I miss something?"

Rin shared his confusion. The exchange between Daji and Jiang had passed so quickly that she'd barely followed what was happening. The two often spoke in a shorthand peppered with allusions to their shared past, a code that had made Rin feel constantly like an outsider on their journey to Arabak. It was a regular reminder that no matter how much power she wielded, the Trifecta had decades of history behind them that she knew only as stories. They'd seen so much more. Done so much more.

"It's decided," Daji said. "We'll go get your army and take them north. Agreed?"

Kitay looked baffled. "But—what about the blockade?"

Jiang stretched his arms over his head, yawning. "Oh, we'll break them out."

Kitay blinked at him. "But how are you going to do that?"

Daji chuckled. Jiang gave him a bemused look, as if surprised that Kitay had even asked.

"I'm the Gatekeeper," he said simply, as if that fact were answer enough.

The night was comfortably warm, so they doused the campfire after they'd eaten and slept on the wagon in shifts. Kitay volunteered to take first watch. Rin hadn't rested since sunrise—she was bone-tired, temples still throbbing from the sensory shock of the New City—but she put off sleep for several minutes so she could sit beside him. She wanted these few minutes with him alone.

"I'm glad you're here," she said. Shallow words and a shallow sentiment that didn't come close to expressing how she felt.

But Kitay just nodded. He understood.

She felt a spark of warmth from every point of contact between them—her hand lying against his, his arm curved around her waist, her head nestled between his chin and shoulder. She craved the feeling of his skin against hers. Every touch was a reassurance that he was real, he was alive, and he was *here*.

She shifted against him. "What's on your mind?"

"Nothing." He still spoke in that flat, wan tone. "I'm just tired."

"Don't lie to me." She wanted everything laid out in the open. She couldn't stand another moment of Kitay's strange resignation; she couldn't bear thinking there was a part of him that she didn't understand. "What's bothering you?"

He was silent for a long moment before he spoke. "It's just . . . I don't know, Rin. Arabak was—"

"It's awful."

"It's not necessarily awful, it's just strange. And I was there for so long, and now I'm out, I still can't stop thinking about the Hesperians."

"What about them?"

"I don't know, I just . . ." His fingers fidgeted in his lap; he was clearly struggling with how much he wanted to tell her. Nothing could have prepared her for what he said next. "Do you think they might just be *better* than us?"

"Kitay." She twisted around to stare at him. "What the *fuck* does that mean?"

"When Nezha first brought me into Arabak, he spent the first two days giving me a tour of the city," he said. "Showing me everything that they'd built in just a few weeks. Do you remember how insufferable he was when we first got to Arlong? Couldn't stop jabbering about this naval innovation and that. But this time, everything I saw really was a marvel. Everywhere I looked I saw things that I never dreamed could exist."

She folded her arms against her chest. "So what?"

"So how did they build them? How did they create objects that defy every known law of the natural world? Their knowledge of so many fields—mathematics, physics, mechanics, engineering— eclipses ours to a terrifying degree. Everything we're discovering at Yuelu Mountain, they must have known already for centuries." His fingers twisted in his lap. "Why? What do they have that we don't have?"

"I don't know," she said. "But it doesn't mean they're just naturally *better*, whatever the fuck that means—"

"But could it? Every member of the Gray Company I've met believes that they are just innately, biologically superior to us. And they don't say this to be cruel or condescending. They see it as fact. A scientific fact, as simple as the fact that the ocean is salty and that the sun rises every morning." His fingers wouldn't stop twisting. Rin had the sudden impulse to slap them. "They see human evolution as a ladder, and they're at its top, or at least as far as it can reach for now. And we—the Nikara—are clinging on to the lower rungs. Closer to animals than human."

"That's bullshit."

"Is it? They built dirigibles. Not only can they fly, they've been flying for *decades*, and here we are with only a rudimentary knowledge of seafaring because we bombed our own navies to bits in civil wars over nothing. Why?"

Dread twisted Rin's stomach. She didn't want to hear these words from Kitay's mouth. This felt worse than betrayal. This felt like discovering her best friend was an utter stranger.

She would be lying if she said she'd never asked these questions herself. Of course she had. She'd asked them during all those weeks she'd spent undergoing examinations in Sister Petra's cabin, putting her naked, helpless body at the Hesperian's disposal, letting her take measurements and write them down while explaining in a cold, matter-of-fact tone that Rin's brain was smaller, her stature was shorter, and her eyes saw less because of her race.

Of course she'd wondered, often, whether the Hesperians were right. But she hated how Kitay spoke as if he'd already decided they were.

"They could be horribly wrong about us," he said. "But they're right about almost everything else; they couldn't have built all that if they weren't. Look at a city they threw up in weeks. Compare that to the finest cities in the Empire. Can't you at least see where I'm coming from?"

Rin thought of the New City's spotless streets, its neat grid-like layout, and its quick, efficient modes of transportation. The Nikara had never built something like that. Even in Sinegard, the Red Emperor's capital and the crown jewel of the Empire, sewage had rushed freely down the streets like rainwater.

"Maybe it's their Maker." She tried to inject some levity into her voice. He was tired, she was tired; perhaps by morning, after they'd slept, this entire conversation would seem like a joke. "Maybe those prayers are working."

He didn't smile. "It's not their religion. Perhaps that's related— the Divine Architect is certainly more friendly to scientific research than any of our gods are. But I don't think they need deities at all. They have machines, and that's perhaps more powerful than anything they could summon. They rewrite the script of the world, just like you do. And they don't need to sacrifice their sanity to do it."

Rin had no rebuttal to that.

Jiang would have an answer. Jiang, who was so sure that the Pantheon lay at the center of the universe, had warned her once against treating the material world like a thing to be mechanized, dominated, and militarized. He'd believed firmly that the Hesperian and Mugenese societies had long ago forgotten their essential oneness with universal being, and were spiritually lost as a result.

But Rin had never been interested in cosmology or theology. She'd only been interested in the gods for what power they could give her, and she couldn't formulate what little she remembered of Jiang's ramblings into any sort of valid objection.

"So what?" she asked finally. "So what does that mean for us?"

She already knew Kitay's conclusion. She just wanted to hear him say it out loud, to see if he would dare. Because the logical conclusion was terrifying. If they were so deeply separated by race, if the Hesperians were innately more intelligent, more capable, and more powerful—then what was the point of resistance? Why shouldn't the world be theirs?

He hesitated. "Rin, I just think—"

"You think we should just surrender," she accused. "That we'd be better off under their rule."

"I don't," he said. "But I do think it might be inevitable."

"It's not inevitable. Nothing ever is." Rin pointed toward the wagon, where Jiang and Daji lay asleep. "They were children in the occupied north. They didn't have arquebuses or airships, and they expelled the Hesperians and united the Empire—"

"And they lost it just two decades later. Our odds aren't looking much better the second time around."

"We'll be stronger this time."

"You know that's not true, Rin. As a country, as a people, we're weaker than we've ever been. If we beat them, it will be due to a massive stroke of good fortune, and it will come at a great cost to human life. So don't blame me for wondering whether it's worth the struggle."

"Do you know what Sinegard was like for me?" she asked suddenly.

He frowned. "Why does that—"

"No, listen. Do you know what it was like to be the country idiot who everyone thought was barely literate because my tongue was flat, my skin was dark, and I didn't know that you're supposed to bow to the master at the end of every class?"

"I'm not saying—"

"I thought there was something inherently wrong with me," she said. "That I was just born uglier, weaker, and less intelligent than everyone around me. I thought that, because that's what everyone told me. And you're arguing that means I had no right to defy them."

"That's not what I meant."

"But it's analogous. If the Hesperians are so *innately better*, then the next rung on the ladder is pale-skinned northerners like you, and the Speerlies are sitting on the bottom." She was burning a handprint into the grass they were sitting on; smoke wafted around them. "And then, by your logic, it's fine that the Empire turned us into slaves. It's fine that they wiped us off the map, and that the official histories mention us only in footnotes. It's only natural."

"You know I'd never argue that," Kitay said.

"That's the implication of your logic," she said. "And I won't accept that. I can't."

"But that doesn't matter." He drew his knees up to his chest. He looked so small then, a much diminished version of the Kitay she'd always known. "Don't you get it? There is still no foreseeable path that leads to our victory. What do you think is going to happen after we get to Dog Province? You can hide from the airships for a little bit, but how the fuck are you going to defeat it?"

"Simple," she said. "We've got a plan."

He gave a shaky, helpless laugh. "Let's hear it, then."

"We've got a problem of power asymmetry now," she said.

"Which means we only win if this war occurs in three phases. The first is a strategic retreat. That's what is happening now, intentionally or not. Second is the long stalemate. Then, at last, the counteroffensive."

He sighed. "And how are you going to launch this counteroffensive? You have maybe a tenth of their ranged capabilities."

"That's fine. We have gods."

"You can't win this war with just a handful of shamans."

"I beat the Federation on my own, didn't I?"

"Well, barring *genocide*—"

"We can beat them with shamanism constrained to armed combatants on the battlefield," she insisted. "The same way we've been hunting down the Mugenese now."

"Maybe. But it's just you and Jiang and the Vipress, that's not nearly—"

"Enough?" She lifted her chin. "What if there were more?"

"Don't you dare open the Chuluu Korikh," Kitay said.

"No." She shuddered at the thought of that place. "We won't go back to that mountain. But Jiang and Daji want to march north. Up to Mount Tianshan."

"So I heard." He eyed her skeptically. "What's in Mount Tianshan?"

"Come on, Kitay. You can figure this out."

His gaze wandered over toward the Trifecta. She saw his eyes widen as the pieces clicked in his mind.

"You're crazy," he said.

"Probably."

His mouth worked for several seconds before he got the words out. "But—the stories—I mean, the Dragon Emperor's dead."

"The Dragon Emperor's sleeping," Rin said. "And he's been asleep for a very long time. But the Seal is eroding. Jiang's remembering who he was, what he once could do, which means Riga is about to wake up. And once he does, once we've reunited the Trifecta, then we'll show Hesperia what true divinity looks like."

CHAPTER 16

The battlefront under the Baolei Mountains was a conundrum.

The valleys were silent. Dirigibles weren't buzzing, swords weren't clashing, and the air wasn't thick with the acrid burn of fire powder. Rin neither saw nor heard any signs of active combat, at least not for the seven days it took for their party to reach the front lines.

Only when they drew closer did she realize why. The Southern Coalition was trapped. The Republic had pinned them against the mountainside behind a series of makeshift forts, each planted half a mile within the other, surrounded by lines of cannons and mounted arquebuses prepared to mow down any who tried to break out of the impasse. The forts were temporary constructions but they looked brick solid, supported by piles of sandbags, their stone walls impenetrable save for tiny slits just large enough for the firing end of an arquebus. Archery was certainly futile against those forts, and Rin suspected that rudimentary cannons of the type the Southern Coalition possessed would barely make a dent, either.

But the Republic also couldn't penetrate the mountainside. The ravines and caves along the southern Baolei range functioned as natural bomb shelters, which meant sustained dirigible attacks would only be a waste of ammunition. The underground terrain couldn't be mapped from the air, which gave the southerners a significant defensive advantage. This, Rin assumed, was the only reason the Republic hadn't yet mounted a ground assault.

The Southern Coalition didn't have the manpower to break out. The Republic didn't want to bleed the forces necessary to break in. For now, both sides remained holed up in their respective stations. But this standoff would end, as all sieges did, the moment the southerners finally ran out of food and water.

"Your old classmate is unfortunately very good at siege warfare," Daji said. They had spent the morning circling the blockade perimeter in the laundry wagon, searching for a way to sneak past Republican lines unnoticed. "He's got them fenced in at every critical juncture. No easy way to slip past those pillboxes unless we make a scene."

"I think a scene is exactly what we want," Rin said.

"No, that's what you want when you break *out*," Kitay pointed out. "But we've got to get inside and rally the forces first. We don't know what condition they're in. Making a scene puts a hard time limit on how long it takes the southerners to mobilize."

So the question remained: How did one sneak past the greatest assembly of military power ever seen on the continent?

"We could swim in," Kitay suggested after a pause. "I think I saw a stream a mile back."

"They'd shoot us in the water," Rin said.

"They're guarding the river flows leading out," Kitay pointed out. "They don't care so much about people sneaking in. We get some bamboo reeds, swim down in the bottom layers where it's muddy—best to do it when it's raining, too; that'll maximize our water cover."

He glanced around the wagon. Daji shrugged, silent.

"So we'll swim," Rin said, since it didn't appear anyone had a better plan. "What next?"

"You need to go through the old mining tunnels." Rin was

startled when Jiang spoke up. He'd been silent all morning, gazing placidly around the battlefront like he was touring a botanical garden. Now suddenly his gaze was focused, his voice firm and assured. "You won't be underground for long. Just until you emerge on the other side into the forests. It's not a perfect exit route— those tunnels aren't well lit, and quite a few people are probably going to fall down the pits and break their necks. But there's no other route that keeps you safe from the dirigibles."

Once again, his switch in demeanor was so abrupt that Rin couldn't help but stare. Jiang was acting like a seasoned general, casually spinning together pieces of a strategy like someone who'd planned ambushes like this a hundred times before. This wasn't him. This was a stranger.

"The real challenge is getting the southerners to follow you out," he continued. "You'll have to be discreet about it. If Souji tried selling you to Vaisra once, he might do so again. Is there anyone in the coalition you still trust?"

"Venka," Rin said immediately. "Qinen, too, probably, if he's still alive. We could try to swing Zhuden's officers, but they'll take convincing."

"Can Venka mobilize at least half the army?" Daji asked.

Rin considered that for a moment. She didn't know how much sway Venka held. Venka wasn't terribly popular among the southerners; she was by nature curt and abrasive, a pale-skinned northerner with a harsh Sinegardian accent who clearly didn't belong. But she could be charming when she wanted to be. She might have managed to talk her way out of any suspected ties to Rin. Or Souji might have had her killed long ago.

Rin decided to be optimistic. "Probably. We can get her to scare up a crowd, and once the battle's started, the rest should follow."

"I suppose we can't do better than that." Jiang pointed to Rin and Kitay. "You two go in first and find your people. Round up as many of them as you can within the next twenty-four hours, and tell them to press hard to the west-facing mines when we break through the front lines. If you have to break cover before then, just send up a flare and we'll break the front early."

"There are at least two thousand Republican troops on the front," Kitay said.

Jiang surveyed the forts for a moment, and then shook his head. "Oh, no. Double that, at least."

Kitay furrowed his brows. "Then how are you going to . . . ?"

"I said we'll break the front," Jiang said very calmly.

Kitay blinked at him, clearly at a loss for words.

"Just trust him," Rin muttered.

She thought back to memories of howling screeches, shapes of darkness furling out of nowhere. She thought of Tseveri's stricken face as Jiang's clawed fingers went into her rib cage.

She didn't trust this newly confident, capable Jiang. She had no idea who he was, or what he could do. But she feared him, which meant the Republic should, too.

"Fine." Kitay still looked baffled, but he didn't push the point. "What's your signal, then?"

Jiang just chuckled. "Oh, I think you'll know."

"You're shitting me," Venka said.

She looked terrible. She'd lost a startling amount of weight. She was wrung out, rangier, sharp cheekbones jutting beneath hollow, purple-ringed eyes.

She hadn't been easy to find. Rin and Kitay had climbed out of the river into what looked like a long-deserted army camp. The sentry posts nearest them were unmanned; the few sandbags visible were scattered uselessly across the dirt. Rin would have assumed the Southern Coalition had already fled, except that the charred logs near the mountainside were evidence of freshly doused campfires, and the latrine dugouts stank of fresh shit.

The entire army, it appeared, had gone underground.

Rin and Kitay had ventured into the tunnels, ambushed the first soldier they encountered, and demanded he lead them to

Venka. He sat tamely now in the corner of the dimly lit room, gagged with rope, eyes darting back and forth in equal parts terror and confusion.

"Hello to you, too." Kitay headed for a pile of maps lying on the floor and began to rummage through them. "Are these up to date? Mind if I take a look?"

"Do whatever you want," Venka said faintly. She didn't even glance at him. Her eyes, still wide in disbelief, were fixed on Rin. "I thought they carted you to that mountain. Souji kept crowing on and on about that, said you were stuck in stone for good."

"Some old friends broke me out," Rin said. "Looks like you've been doing far worse."

"Gods, Rin, it's been a nightmare." Venka pressed her palms against her temples. "I honestly don't know what Souji's plan is at this point. I was starting to think we'd be buried here."

"So Souji's in charge?" Rin asked.

"He and Gurubai together." Venka looked abashed. "You, ah, might hear about some things I said. I mean, after Tikany, they were out for me, too, and I—"

"I'm sure you said whatever you needed to to get them off your back," Rin said. "I don't care about that. Just fill us in on what's happened."

Venka nodded. "The Republic launched a second assault a few days after the first air raid. Souji led us in a retreat north—the idea was to get back to Ruijin—but the Republic kept pushing us eastward, so we got trapped up against these mountains instead. We're calling this the Anvil, because they keep slamming up against us and we've got nowhere to run. I'm sure they'll be making their final push any day now; they know we're nearly out of supplies."

"I'm shocked you made it to the mountains at all." Kitay looked up from the maps. "How on earth did you hold them off this long?"

"It's their artillery's fault," Venka said. "They keep shooting themselves in the feet. Literally. Nezha's got his army outfitted with new Hesperian technology, but they don't know how to use it, and I guess they moved out before they were properly trained, so half the time they try to hit us they blow themselves up in the process."

No wonder Nezha had sounded so rattled when complaining about force integration. Rin couldn't help but grin.

"Something funny?" Venka asked.

"Nothing," Rin said. "It's just—remember that night on the tower, how Nezha kept bragging about how Hesperian technology was going to win the Empire for us?"

"Yes, they've had growing pains," Venka said drily. "Unfortunately, a misfired cannonball hurts just as bad."

Kitay held up a map and tapped at an arrow snaking south. "Is this how you were going to get them out? A hard press by the southern border?"

"That's what Souji's planning," Venka said. "It seemed like our best bet. Nezha doesn't have his own men on that border; it's under the domain of the new Ox Warlord. Bai Lin. There are massive tungsten deposits on the Monkey Province side of the border, and Gurubai's offered to mine it for him if he'll carve us an escape corridor."

"That won't work," Kitay said.

Venka gave him an exasperated look. "We've been planning this for weeks."

"Sure, but I know Bai Lin. He used to come over to our estate in Sinegard to play wikki with my parents all the time. The man hasn't got a backbone—Father used to call him the Empire's greatest brownnoser. There's no way he'll risk pissing Vaisra off. He'll let Nezha decimate you and send laborers in to mine the tungsten himself."

"Fine." Venka jutted her chin out. "You come up with something better, then."

Kitay tapped a northern point on the blockade. "We have to go through the old mining tunnels. They'll bring us out onto the other side of the Baolei range."

"We've tried those tunnels," Venka said. "They're blocked up."

"Then we'll blow a hole through the entrance," Kitay said.

Venka looked doubtful. "You'd need a lot of firepower."

"Oh dear," Rin drawled. "I wonder how we'll manage that."

Venka snorted. "None of the cave tunnels here lead to the mines. We'd still have to get through the dead zone, which is at least a mile long. Nezha's got half his infantry stationed right outside. We're working with two-thirds the numbers we had at Tikany, and we don't have an air defense. This can't work."

"It'll work," Kitay said. "We've got allies."

"Who?" Venka perked up. "How many?"

"Two," Rin said.

"You assholes—"

"Rin brought the Trifecta," Kitay clarified.

Venka squinted at them. "What, like the shadow puppets?"

"The original Trifecta," Rin said. "Two of them, at least. The Empress. Master Jiang. They're the Vipress and the Gatekeeper."

"Are you telling me," Venka said slowly, "that Lore Master Jiang, the man who kept a *drug garden* at Sinegard, is going to single-handedly spring us out of this blockade?"

Kitay scratched his chin. "Pretty much, yeah."

"He's only the most powerful shaman in Nikan," Rin said. "I mean, so we think. Word's still out on the Dragon Emperor."

Venka looked like she didn't know whether to laugh or cry. A vein twitched beneath her left eye. "The last time I saw Jiang he was trying to snip my hair off with garden shears."

"He's about the same now," Rin said. "But he can summon beasts that can wipe out entire platoons in seconds, if history is anything to go by, so we've got a bit more to work with."

"I don't—I just—you know what? Fine. Sure. This might as well be happening." Venka dragged her palms down her face and groaned. "Fucking hell, Rin. I wish you'd gotten here just a few days earlier. You picked a dreadful time to show up."

"Why's that?" Rin asked.

"Vaisra's making his tour to inspect the troops tomorrow."

"Tour?" Kitay repeated. "Vaisra doesn't command?"

"No, Nezha's in command. Vaisra stays behind at Arlong, rules over his new kingdom, and plays nice with the Hesperians."

Of course, Rin thought. Why would she have expected otherwise? Vaisra had fought the civil war from his throne room in Arlong, sending Rin out like an obedient hunting dog while he sat back and reaped the rewards. Vaisra never dirtied his own hands. He just turned people into weapons and then disposed of them.

"He comes out to Arabak every three weeks," Venka said. "Then he flies out here to conduct a troop appraisal right before he leaves. A rallying ceremony of sorts—it's insufferable. We've figured out the schedule because they always start firing into the air when he's here."

"Why is that a problem?" Kitay asked. "That's good for us."

Venka wrinkled her nose. "How so? It means the entire front line will be fully armed and at attention, and that we'll have to deal with Vaisra's private guard on top of that."

"It also puts them on the defensive," Kitay said. "Because now they've got a target to protect."

"But you're not . . ." Venka glanced between them. "Oh. Oh, you're not fucking serious. *That's* your plan?"

Rin hadn't thought of targeting Vaisra until Kitay said it out loud. But it made perfect sense. If the Republic's most important figure was going to put himself on the front lines, then of course she should aim his way. At the very least, it would split the Republican Army's attention—if they were busy rallying around Vaisra, that drew troops away from the Southern Coalition's escape route.

"He's had it coming," she said. "Why not now?"

"I—sure." Venka was past the point of disbelief; now she simply looked resigned. "And you're *sure* Master Jiang can clear the dead zone?"

"We'll worry about breaking the front," she said. "You handle evacuation. How many people here will listen to you?"

"Probably a lot, if I tell them you're back," Venka said. "Souji and Gurubai haven't got much goodwill among the ranks right now."

"Good," Rin said. "Tell every officer you can find to drive north in a wedge formation when things start exploding at the border. When does Vaisra arrive?"

"Typically in the mornings. That's when they've had their parades the last two times he's visited."

"Crack of dawn?" Kitay asked.

"A little later. Twenty minutes, maybe?"

"Then we'll break to the mines twenty minutes after dawn." Rin turned to the gagged soldier in the corner. "Are you going to help us?"

He nodded frantically. She strode toward him and pulled the rope out of his mouth. He coughed to clear his throat.

"I have no idea what is going on," he said, eyes watering. "And I'm fairly sure that we're all about to die."

"That's fine," Rin said. "Just so long as you'll do as I say."

For the rest of the night Rin followed Venka through the caves and tunnels, whispering the same message to everyone who cared to listen. *The Speerly is back. She's brought allies. Pack your things and ready your arms. Spread the word. At dawn, we break.*

But when at last the hour came, the tunnels were depressingly quiet. Rin had seen this coming. The Southern Coalition was a threadbare army living on stretched rations. Exhaustion plagued the ranks; even those who fully believed in her didn't have the energy to lead the charge. They were suffering a collective action problem—everyone was hoping someone else would make the first move.

Rin was happy to do just that.

"Give them a kick in the ass if they won't mobilize," Jiang had told her. "Bring hell to their doorstep."

So twenty minutes after the sun rose, once faint notes of parade music began carrying over the still morning air from the Republican line, Rin walked out in front of the cave mouths, stretched her hand toward the sky, and called down a column of bright orange fire.

The flames formed a thick pillar stretching to the heavens. A beacon, an invitation. She stood with her eyes closed and arms outstretched, relishing the caress of hot air against her skin, basking in its deafening roar. A minute later, she saw through the heat shimmer a cluster of black dots—dirigibles rising to meet her.

Then the southerners burst out of their caves and tunnels like ants foaming from the dirt. They ran past her, half-packed satchels hanging from their shoulders, bare feet padding against the dirt.

Rin stood still at the center of the frenzied panic.

Time seemed to dilate for a moment. She knew she should join the fleeing crowd. She knew she had to rally them, to use her flame to corral their confused panic into a concentrated assault. In a moment, she would.

But right now, she wanted to enjoy this.

At last this war was back under her control. She'd chosen this battle. She'd determined its time and place. She spoke the word, and the world exploded into action.

This was chaos, but chaos was where she thrived. A world at peace, at stalemate, at cease-fire, had no use for her. She understood now what she needed to do to cling to power: submerge the world in chaos, and forge her authority from the broken pieces.

The Republican Army awaited them at the northern front.

The infantry stood behind several rows of cannons, mounted arquebuses, and archers—three types of artillery, a mix of Nikara and Hesperian technologies designed to rip flesh apart at a distance. Six dirigibles hovered in the sky above them like guardian deities.

Rin's heart sank as she scanned the horizon. Jiang was nowhere to be seen. He'd promised them safe passage. This was a death trap.

Where is he?

Her mouth filled with the taste of ash. This was her fault. Despite his clear mental volatility, she'd trusted him. She'd placed her life and the fate of the south in his hands with all the naivete of a pupil at Sinegard. And once again, he'd failed her.

"It's a suicide drive, then." Venka, to her great credit, did not sound the least bit afraid. She reached for her sword, as if that could do anything against the impending air assault. "I suppose this had to end sometime. It's been fun, kids."

"Hold on." Kitay pointed to the front line just as Jiang strode, seemingly out of nowhere, into the empty space between the two armies.

He wielded no weapon and carried no shield. He loped casually with slouched shoulders across the field, hands in his pockets, as if he had just stepped out his front door for a mild afternoon stroll. He didn't stop until he reached the very center of the line of dirigibles. Then he turned around to face them, head tilted sideways like a fascinated child.

Rin dug her nails into her palm.

She couldn't breathe.

This was it. She'd wagered the lives of everyone in the Southern Coalition on what happened next. The fate of the south hung on one man, one clearly unstable man, and Rin could not truthfully say whether she believed in Jiang or not.

The dirigibles dipped down slightly toward him, like predators stalking their prey. Miraculously, they had not yet begun to fire.

Did they intend to be merciful? Did they want to spare the Southern Coalition so that they could take them alive, to be tortured and interrogated later? Or were they so confused and amazed by this solitary, suicidal fool that they wanted to draw in closer for a better look?

Did they have any idea what he was?

Someone on the Republican front must have shouted an order, because the entire artillery swiveled their barrels around to aim at Jiang.

Something invisible pulsed through the air.

Jiang hadn't moved, but something about the world had shifted, had knocked its sounds and colors slightly off-kilter. The hairs stood up on Rin's arm. She felt intensely, deliciously light-headed. A strange, exhilarating energy thrummed just beneath her skin, an incredible sense of *potential*. She felt like a cotton ball suffused in oil, just waiting for the smallest spark to ignite.

Jiang raised one hand into the air. His fingers splayed out. The air around him shimmered and distorted. Then the sky exploded into shadow like an ink bottle shattered on parchment.

Rin saw the effects before the cause. Bodies fell. The entire archery line collapsed. The dirigible closest to Jiang careened to the side and struck its neighbor, sending both crashing to the ground in a ball of fire.

Only after the wave of smoke cleared did Rin see the source of the destruction—black, mist-like wraiths snaked through the air, shooting through bodies, weapons, and shields with uniform ease. At times they hung still and, ever so briefly, she could just barely make out their shapes—a lion, a dragon, a kirin—before they disappeared back into formless shadow. They followed no known laws of the physical world. Metal passed through them as if they were immaterial, but their fangs ripped through flesh just as easily as the sharpest of swords.

Jiang had called down every beast of the Emperor's Menagerie, and they were tearing through the material world like steel through paper.

The other four dirigibles never managed to fire. A fleet of black birdlike shadows ripped through the balloons that kept them afloat, puncturing the centers and flying out the other side in neat, straight lines. The balloons popped into nothing. The dirigible baskets plummeted with startling velocity, where Jiang's beasts continued wreaking havoc on the ground forces. The Republican soldiers struggled valiantly against the wraiths, swinging their blades desperately against the onslaught, but they might as well have been fighting the wind.

"Holy shit." Venka stood gaping, arms hanging by her side.

She should have been leading the charge toward the mines, but neither she nor any of the Southern Coalition had moved an inch. All that any of them seemed able to do was watch.

"Told you," Rin murmured. "He's a shaman."

"I didn't think shamans were *that* powerful."

Rin shot her an indignant look. "You've seen me call flame!"

Venka pointed to Jiang. He was still alone in the dead zone. He was so open, so vulnerable. But no bullets seemed able to pierce his skin, and every arrow aimed his way dropped harmlessly onto the ground long before it reached him. Everywhere he pointed, explosions followed.

"You," Venka said reverently, "cannot do *that*."

She was right. Rin felt a pang of jealousy as she watched Jiang conducting his wraiths like a musician, each sweep of his arm prompting another charge of shadowy havoc.

She'd thought she understood the limits of shamanic destruction. She'd leveled a field of bodies before. She'd leveled a *country*.

But what she'd done to the longbow island had been a singular episode of divine intervention. It could never—*should* never be repeated. In conventional combat, on a battlefield where discriminating between ally and enemy actually mattered, she couldn't compete with Jiang. She could burn a handful of soldiers at once, dozens if she had a clear, clustered target. But Jiang was blowing through entire squadrons with mere waves of his hand.

No wonder he'd acted so cavalier before. This wasn't a fight for him, this was child's play.

Rin wanted power like that.

She could see now how the Trifecta had become legend. This was how they had massacred the Ketreyids. This was how they had reunited a country, declared themselves its rulers, and yanked it back from both Hesperia and the Federation.

So how had they ever lost it?

At last the Southern Coalition came to their senses. Under Venka and Kitay's direction they began a frenzied drive toward the scattered blockade. Jiang's shadow wraiths parted to let them through unscathed. His control was astonishing—there must have been more than a hundred beasts on the field, each weaving autonomously through the mass of bodies, all distinguishing perfectly between southerners and Republicans.

Rin and Jiang alone remained behind the front lines.

This wasn't over. A second fleet of dirigibles was approaching fast from the east. Deafening booms split the sky. The air was suddenly thick with missiles. Rin threw herself to the ground, wincing as explosions thundered above her.

The Republican troops had realized their only viable strategy. They'd noticed Jiang's limits—his beasts might be able to knock missiles out of the air, but their numbers were constrained to a pack the size of a small field. He couldn't tear through the ground troops and defend against the dirigibles at the same time. He couldn't summon an unending horde.

Rin lifted her head just as three airships peeled away from the fleet and veered toward the mines. She understood their plan in an instant—they couldn't count on taking Jiang out, so they were going to take out the Southern Coalition instead.

They were going to fire on Kitay.

Oh, *fuck* no.

Your turn, Rin told the Phoenix. *Show them everything we've got.*

The god responded with glee.

Her world burst into orange. Rin had never called flames so great into battle before. She had always kept the fire reined in within a twenty-yard radius; any farther than that and she risked collateral damage to allies and civilians. But now she had clear targets across an empty field. Now she could send great roaring columns fifty yards high into the sky, could shroud the dirigible baskets in flame, could scorch the troops inside, could char the balloons until they imploded.

One by one the dirigibles dropped.

This felt deliriously good. It wasn't just the freedom of range, the permission to destroy without constraint. Everything felt so *easy*. She wasn't calling the flame, she *was* the flame; those great columns were natural extensions of her body, as simple to command as her fingers and toes. She felt the Phoenix's presence so closely she might have been in the world of spirit. She might have been on Speer.

This was Jiang's doing. He'd opened the gate to the void to let the beasts in, and now the gap between worlds had thinned just a little more. Such small shreds of reality separated them from a churning cosmos of infinite possibility, and that made the material world so very malleable. It made her feel divine.

She noticed one more dirigible flying in the opposite direction of the fleet. Its guns weren't firing. Its flight pattern seemed erratic—she couldn't tell if the dirigible had been damaged, or if something was wrong with the crew. It climbed several feet in altitude above the rest of the fleet, teetered for a moment, and then turned back in the direction of the New City.

Rin knew then exactly who was on that dirigible. Someone who badly needed protection. Someone who had to be extracted from the fracas, immediately.

"Master!" She shouted, pointing. Her flames couldn't reach that high, but perhaps his beasts could. "Bring down that ship!"

Jiang didn't answer. She wasn't even sure that he'd heard her. His pale eyes had gone entirely blank; he seemed trapped in the throes of his own symphony of ruin.

But then a small cluster of shadows peeled away from the rest, hurtled upward through the air, and fell on the balloon like a ravenous pack of wolves. Moments later the carriage started tumbling to the ground.

The crash shook the earth. Rin sprinted toward the wreckage.

Most of the crew had died on impact. She made short work of the survivors. Two Hesperian soldiers made staggering advances when they saw her coming. One had an arquebus, so she took him out first, shrouding his head and shoulders in a ball of flame before he had time to pull the trigger. The other soldier had a knife. But he'd been injured in the crash, and his movements were comically slow. Rin let him approach, twisted the hilt from his hand, and jammed the blade into his neck so hard the point came up through his eye.

Then she started digging through the debris.

Yin Vaisra was still alive. She found him pinned beneath part of the basket hull and the corpses of two of his guards, gasping hoarsely as he struggled to free himself. His eyes widened when he saw her. The twist of fear was visible for only an instant before his face resumed its habitual mask of calm, but Rin saw. She felt a vicious pulse of glee.

He reached for a knife lying by his waist. She wedged her toe beneath its hilt and flicked it out of his reach. She sat back and waited, expecting him to produce another weapon, but he seemed otherwise unarmed. All he could do was squirm.

Easy. This was so *easy*. She could kill him where he lay, could gut him with his own knife with no more ceremony than a butcher slaughtering a pig. But that would be so terribly unsatisfying. She wanted to milk this moment for all it was worth.

She braced herself under the carriage hull and pushed her legs against the ground. The hull was heavier than it looked. Those things seemed so elegant and lightweight in the air; now it took all her strength to shift it off Vaisra's legs.

At last, he struggled out from beneath the corpses. She dropped the hull.

"Get up," she ordered.

To her surprise, he obeyed.

Slowly he rose to his feet. It hurt him terribly to stand—she could tell from the stoop of his shoulders and the way he winced as his left leg shook beneath him. But he didn't make a sound of protest.

No, the first President of the Nikara Republic had too much dignity for that.

They stood face-to-face for a moment in silence. Rin looked

him up and down, etching every detail of him into her memory. She wanted to remember everything about this moment.

He really was the spitting image of Nezha—an older, crueler version, an unsettling premonition of everything Nezha was supposed to be. Small wonder she'd so eagerly cast him her loyalty. She'd been attracted to him; she could admit this to herself, now that it didn't matter. It couldn't humiliate her anymore. She could concede that not so long ago, she'd wanted to be commanded and owned by someone who looked like *Nezha*.

Gods, she'd been so stupid.

Every day since her escape from Arlong, she'd wondered what she would say to Vaisra if she ever saw him again. What she might do if he were ever at her mercy. She'd fantasized about this moment so many times, but now, as he stood weakened and vulnerable before her, she couldn't think of anything to say.

There was nothing more to be said. She sought no answers or explanations from him. She knew very well why he'd betrayed her. She knew he considered her less human than animal. She didn't need his acknowledgment or respect. She needed nothing from him at all.

She just needed him gone. Out of the equation; off the chessboard.

"You do realize they're going to destroy you," he said.

She lifted her chin. "Are those your last words?"

"Everything you do convinces them you should not exist." Blood trickled from his lips. He knew he was a dead man; all he could do now was try to rattle her. "Every time you call the fire, you remind the Gray Order why you cannot remain free. The only reason you stand here now is because you've been useful in the south. But they'll come for you soon, my dear. These are your final days. Enjoy them."

Rin didn't flinch.

If he thought he could unsettle her with words, he was wrong. Once, perhaps, he could manipulate her with coaxing, praise, and insults like she was clay in his hands. Once, she'd clung to everything he said because she was weak and drifting, flailing about for anything solid to hold on to. But nothing he said could shake her now.

She couldn't feel the revulsion she'd anticipated at the sight of him. She'd spent so long thinking of Vaisra as a monster. This man had traded everything for power—his southern allies, all three of his sons, and Rin herself. But she found she couldn't fault him for that. Like her, like the Trifecta, Vaisra had only been pursuing his vision for Nikan with a ruthless and single-minded determination. The only difference between them was that he'd lost.

"Do you know your biggest mistake?" she asked softly. "You should have gambled on me."

Before Vaisra could respond, she seized his chin and brought his mouth to hers. He tried to twist away. She gripped the back of his head and kept it pressed against her face. He struggled, but he was so weak. He bit desperately at her lips. The taste of blood filled her mouth, but she just pressed her lips harder against his.

Then she funneled flame into his mouth.

It wasn't enough simply to kill him. She had to humiliate and mutilate him. She had to force an inferno down his throat and char him from the inside, to feel his burned flesh sloughing away under her fingers. She wanted overkill. She had to reduce him to a pile of something unfixable, unrecognizable.

This couldn't undo the past. It couldn't bring Suni, Baji, or Ramsa back, couldn't erase all the tortures she'd suffered at his commands. Couldn't erase the scar on her back or restore her missing hand. But it felt good. The point of revenge wasn't to heal. The point was that the exhilaration, however temporary, drowned out the hurt.

He went limp against her. She let his body drop; he fell forward, chest curled over his knees, as if he were bowing to her.

She breathed deep, inhaling the smoky tang of his burning innards. She knew this ecstasy wouldn't last. It would fade away in minutes, and then she'd want more. She almost wished that he would come back to life so she could kill him again, and then again, that she might keep experiencing the thrill of glimpsing the wretched fear in his eyes before her flames extinguished their light.

She felt the same way now that she did every time she destroyed a Mugenese contingent. She knew revenge was a drug. She knew it couldn't sustain her forever. But right now, while she was riding the high, before her adrenaline crashed and the weight and horror of what she'd just done flooded back through the crevices of her mind, while she stood breathing hard over the blackened ashes of the man who had destroyed almost everything she loved, it felt better than anything in the world.

She didn't see the last dirigible swooping low through the smoke at Jiang until it was too late.

"*Watch out!*" she screamed, but the boom of cannons drowned out her voice.

Jiang dropped like a puppet with cut strings. His beasts vanished. The dirigible veered tentatively backward, as if trying to assess the damage before it took a second shot. She flung her head back and screamed fire. A single jet of flame ripped through the airship balloon. The carriage spiraled into the ground and exploded.

Rin sprinted through the raining wreckage to Jiang.

He lay still where he had fallen. She pressed her fingers into his neck. She felt a pulse, strong and insistent. Good. She patted her hand over his body, trying to check the extent of his wounds. But there was no blood—his clothes were dry.

They weren't safe yet. Arquebuses went off all around them; Jiang had not finished off the Republican artillery.

"Get him up." Daji materialized, seemingly from nowhere. Her eyes were wild and frantic; her hair and clothes singed black. She jammed her hands under Jiang's arms and hoisted him to a sitting position. "Hurry."

"What's wrong with him?" Rin asked. "He's not even—"

Daji shook her head just as the crack of arquebus fire echoed around them. They both ducked.

"Quickly!" Daji hissed.

Rin pulled one of Jiang's arms around her shoulder. Daji took the other. Together they staggered to their feet and ran for cover, Jiang lolling between them like a drunkard.

Somehow they made it unscathed to the Southern Coalition's rear guard. Venka and a line of defenders stood at the base of the mountains, firing back at the Republicans as the civilians clustered around the blocked tunnel entrances.

"Oh, thank fuck, there you are." Venka dropped her crossbow to help them hoist Jiang toward a wagon. "Is he hurt?"

"I can't tell." Rin helped Daji push Jiang's legs up over the cart. He didn't *look* wounded. In fact, he was still conscious. He pulled his knees up into a crouched sitting position, rocking back and forth, emitting bursts of low, nervous giggles.

Rin couldn't look at him. This was wrong, this was so wrong. Her gut wrenched with a mix of horror and shame; she wanted to vomit.

"Riga," Jiang whispered suddenly. He'd stopped giggling. He sat utterly still, eyes fixed at something Rin couldn't see.

Daji recoiled like she'd been slapped.

"Riga?" Rin repeated. "What—"

"He's here," Jiang said. His shoulders began to tremble.

"He's not here." The blood had drained from Daji's face. She looked terrified. "Ziya, listen to me—"

"He's going to kill me," Jiang whispered.

His eyes rolled up to the back of his head. He shuddered so hard his teeth clacked. Then he slumped to the side and lay still.

CHAPTER 17

The mining tunnels felt more like a tomb than an escape. After Rin blew open the entrances with flame and several well-placed barrels of fire powder, the Southern Coalition filed in a packed column of bodies through a passage wide enough to fit only three men walking side by side. It seemed to stretch on for miles. All around them was cold stone, stale air, and a looming black that seemed to constrict like a vise as they pressed farther into the belly of the deep.

They stumbled through the dark, groping at the tunnel walls and tapping the floor before them to check for sudden drop-offs. Rin hated this—she wanted to light every inch of her body aflame and become a human lantern—but she knew that in such packed quarters, fire would suffocate. Altan had showed her once, with a pigeon in a glass vase, how quickly flames could eat up all the breathable air. She remembered clearly the eager fascination in his eyes as he watched the pigeon's little neck pulse frantically, then go still.

So she walked at the head of the column, illuminating the way with a tiny flame flickering inside a cupped hand, while the back of the line followed in complete darkness.

An hour into their journey, the soldiers behind her began

begging that they stop. Everyone wanted to rest. They were exhausted; many of them were marching with undressed open wounds dripping blood into the dirt. The dirigibles couldn't reach them underground, they argued. Surely they would be safe for twenty minutes.

Rin refused. She and Jiang might have decimated the Republican front lines, but Nezha was certainly still alive, and she didn't trust him to give up. He would have called for reinforcements long ago. Ground troops might be preparing to enter the tunnels as they marched. Nezha could use explosives and poisonous gas to smoke them out like rats right now, and then the Southern Coalition would disappear with muffled screams beneath the earth, and the only evidence they had ever existed would be ossified bones revealed eons later as the mountains eroded.

She ordered that they continue until they emerged out the other side. To her pleasant surprise, the troops obeyed her without question. She had expected to hear at least a little pushback—she had only just rejoined their ranks, with no explanation or apology, before she thrust them into a war zone wreaked by gods.

But she had broken them out of the Anvil. She'd done what the Southern Coalition had failed to do for months. Right now, her word was divine command.

At last, after what felt like an eternity, they emerged into a marvelous accident of nature—a cavern whose ceiling split into a jagged crack in the darkness, revealing the sky above. Rin stopped walking and tilted her head up at the stars. After a day spent underground trying to convince her racing heart at every second that she wasn't being buried alive, she felt like she'd come up from drowning.

Had the night sky always shone so bright?

"We should rest here." Kitay pointed to a ridge in the opposite wall. Rin squinted and saw a staircase carved into the stone—a narrow, precipitous set of steps, likely built by miners who hadn't revisited these tunnels in years. "If anything starts coming through those tunnels, we've got a way out."

"All right." Rin suddenly felt a wave of exhaustion that until now had been kept at bay by adrenaline and fear. She was still afraid. But she couldn't push herself or the army any farther, or they'd collapse. "Just until dawn. We start moving the moment the sun comes up."

A collective moan of relief echoed through the tunnels when she gave the order. The southerners set down their packs, spread out through the cavern and its adjacent tunnels, and unfurled sleeping mats on the dirt. Rin wanted nothing more than to curl up in a corner and close her eyes.

But she was in charge now, and she had work to do.

She walked through the huddled masses of soldiers and civilians, taking stock of what kind of numbers she had left. She lit their torches and warmed them with her flame. She answered honestly every question they asked about where she'd been—she told them about the Chuluu Korikh, the Trifecta's return, and her break-in to Arabak.

She found, to her surprise, a great deal of new faces not from Monkey or Rooster Provinces, but from the north—mostly young and middle-aged men with the hardy physique of laborers.

"I don't understand," she told Venka. "Where'd they come from?"

"They're miners," Venka said. "The Hesperians set up tungsten mines all over the Daba range after they took over Arlong. They've got these drilling machines that blast through mountainside like you've never seen. But they still needed warm bodies to do the dangerous work—crawling into tunnels, loading the carts, testing the rock face. The northerners came down to work."

"I guess they didn't like it much," Rin said.

"What do you expect? No one flees a good job to join rebel bandits. From what I've heard, those mines were hell. The machines were death traps. Some of those men weren't allowed to see sunlight for days. They joined up the minute they saw us coming."

It took Rin nearly two hours to move through the tunnels. Everyone wanted to speak to her, to hear her voice, to touch her.

They didn't believe that she was back or that she was alive. They had to see her fire with their own eyes.

"I'm real," she assured them, over and over again. "I'm back. And I've got a plan."

Quickly their doubt and confusion turned to wonder, then gratitude, and then clear and adamant loyalty. The more Rin spoke to the troops, the more she understood how the past day had played out in their minds. They had been on the brink of extermination, trapped for weeks in tunnels without enough food or water, awaiting imminent death from bullets, incineration, or starvation. Then Rin had shown up, returned from the stone mountain with barely a scratch and two of the Trifecta in tow, and reversed their fortunes in a single chaotic morning.

To them, what had just happened was divine intervention.

They might have been skeptical of her before. They couldn't be skeptical now. She'd proven without a shadow of a doubt that Souji was wrong—that the Republic would never show them mercy, and that she was the south's best hope for survival. And Rin realized, as she walked through the crowds of awed, grateful faces, that this army was finally hers for good.

Jiang wasn't getting better.

He had recovered consciousness shortly after they reached the cavern, but he hadn't spoken an intelligible word since. He gave no indication that he saw Rin as she approached his sleeping mat, where he sat like a child with his knees drawn up into his chest. He seemed lost somewhere inside himself, somewhere troubled and terrifying, and although Rin could tell from the way his mouth twitched and his eyes darted back and forth that he was fighting to claw his way back, she had no idea how to reach him.

"Hello, Master," she said.

He acted as if he hadn't heard her. His fingers fidgeted mindlessly at the hem of his shirt. He'd turned ghastly pale, sapphire veins visible under his skin like watery calligraphy.

She knelt down beside him. "I suppose we should thank you."

She put her hand on his, hoping that physical contact might calm him. He yanked it away. Only then did he look directly at her. Rin saw fear in his eyes—not the momentary flinch of surprise, but a deep, bone-wrenching terror from which he couldn't break free.

"He's been like that for hours," Daji said. She was curled up against the wall several feet away, gnawing at a strip of dried pork. "You won't get any other response. Leave him alone, he'll be fine."

Rin couldn't believe how indifferent she sounded. "He doesn't look fine."

"He'll get over it. He's been like that before."

"I'm sure you'd know. You did that to him."

Rin knew she was being cruel. But she meant to hurt. She wanted her words to twist like daggers, because the pained expression they elicited on Daji's face was the only outlet for the confused dread she felt when she looked at Jiang.

"I am the only reason why he's alive at all," Daji said in a hard voice. "I did what I had to do to give him the only chance at peace he'd ever get."

Rin glanced back at Jiang, who was now hunched over, whispering nonsense into his curled fingers. "And that's peace?"

"Back then his mind was killing him," Daji said. "I silenced it."

"We've got a problem," Kitay announced, appearing around the cavern wall. "You need to do something about Souji and Gurubai."

Rin groaned. "Shit."

She hadn't seen a glimpse of Souji or Gurubai since the breakout began. They hadn't even crossed her mind. She'd been so caught up in the exhilaration of the escape, in the sole objective of rescuing the south, she'd completely forgotten that not all of them might welcome her back.

"They're making noises," Kitay continued. "Telling their troops they need to split off when we've found the exit. We fix this tonight, or we're facing a desertion or coup in the morning."

"The boy is right," Daji said. "You need to act now."

"But there's nothing to—oh." Rin's exhausted mind finally grasped what Daji was implying. "I see."

She stood.

"What?" Kitay's eyes darted back and forth between her and Daji. "We haven't—what are you—"

"Execution." Rin said. "Plain and simple. Do you know where they are?"

"Wait." Kitay blinked at her, stunned by this sudden escalation. "That doesn't mean—I mean, you just saved their lives—"

"Those two sold her to the Republic without a second thought," Daji drawled. "If you think they won't betray you again, then you're too stupid to live."

Kitay glared at Rin. "Was this her idea?"

"It's the only option you've got," Daji said.

"Is that how you ruled?" Kitay inquired. "Killing everyone who disagreed with you?"

"Of course," Daji said, unfazed. "You cannot lead effectively when you have dissidents with this much influence. Riga had many enemies. Ziya and I took care of them for him. That was how we kept the Nikara front united."

"That didn't last very long."

"*They* didn't last very long. I lasted twenty years." Daji arched an eyebrow. "And it wasn't by being lenient."

"We've done this before," Rin told Kitay. "Ma Lien—"

"Ma Lien was on his deathbed," Kitay snapped. "And that was different. We were operating from a point of weakness then, we didn't have any other choices—"

"We've got no other choices now," Rin said. "The ranks might obey me for the time being, but that loyalty isn't sustainable. Not where we're going. And Gurubai and Souji are too clever. They're intensely charismatic in a way that I'll never be, and given time and space they *will* find a way to oust me."

"That's not predetermined," Kitay said. "Mistakes aside, they're good leaders. You could work with them."

It was a weak argument, and Rin could tell that he knew it. They all knew that this night had to end in blood. Rin could not continue sharing power with a coalition that had defied, obstructed, and betrayed her at every turn. If she was going to lead the south, she had to do it by her own vision. Alone and unopposed.

Kitay stopped trying to argue. They both knew there was nothing he could say. They had only one option; he was too smart not to see it. He might hate her for this, but he would forgive her, as he always did. He'd always had to forgive her for necessity.

Daji calmly pulled her knife from its sheath and handed it hilt-first to Rin.

"I don't need that," Rin said.

"Blades are quieter," Daji said. "Fire agonizes. And you don't want their screams to disturb the sleeping."

Rin dealt with the Monkey Warlord first.

Gurubai had known she was coming. He was standing in the tunnels with his officers, the only people in the cavern who didn't appear to be asleep. They were quietly discussing something. They fell silent when they saw her approach, but they didn't move for their weapons.

"Leave us," Gurubai said.

His officers departed without another word. They kept their heads down as they filed past; none gave Rin so much as a parting glance.

"They're good soldiers," Gurubai told Rin. "You've no cause to hurt them."

"I know," she said. "I won't."

She meant it. Without Gurubai to lead them, none of his officers had any reason to betray her. She knew those men. They weren't ambitious power grabbers; they were capable, rational-minded soldiers. They cared about the south, and they knew now she was their best chance at survival.

Gurubai regarded her for a moment. "Will you burn me?"

"No." She drew the knife Daji had given her. "You deserve better."

Gurubai raised his arms in the air. He didn't reach for a weapon. He'd resigned himself to his fate, Rin realized. There was no fight left in him.

He had lost so thoroughly. He'd been cornered in the mountains and starved out by a boy general, and then his only salvation had been the Speerly he thought he'd sold to his enemy. If his gamble had worked, if Vaisra and the Republic had kept their word, then Gurubai would have become a national hero. The savior of the south.

But it hadn't, so he would die a disgraced traitor. So cruel were the whims of history.

"You are the worst thing to happen to this country," Gurubai said. His voice carried no anger or invective, just resignation. He wasn't trying to hurt her. He was delivering his final testimony. "These people deserve better than you."

"I'm exactly what they deserve," she said. "They don't want peace, they want revenge. I'm it."

"Revenge doesn't make a stable nation."

"Neither does cowardice," she said. "That's where you failed. You were only ever fighting to survive, Gurubai. I was fighting to win. And history doesn't favor stability, it favors initiative."

She pointed the blade at his heart and jerked her hand forward in one quick, smooth motion. His eyes bulged. She yanked the blade out and stepped back just before he crumpled, clutching at his chest.

She'd aimed badly. She'd known that as soon as she felt the blade make contact. Her left hand was clumsy and weak; she'd pierced not his heart but an inch below it. She had put him in excruciating pain, but his heart wouldn't stop beating until he bled out.

Gurubai writhed at her feet, but he didn't make a single sound. No screams, no whimpers. She respected that.

"You would have been a wonderful peacetime leader," she

said. He had been honest with her; she might as well afford him the same in return. "But we don't need peace right now. We need blood."

Footsteps sounded behind her. She swiveled around, then relaxed—it was just Kitay. He stepped forward and stood over Gurubai's silent, twitching form, mouth curling in distaste.

"I see you started without me," he said.

"I didn't think you wanted to come." Her voice felt detached from her body. Her hand shook as she watched Gurubai's blood pooling over the stone floor. Her entire *body* shook; she could hear her teeth clattering in her skull. She registered this physiological reaction with a bemused, distant curiosity.

What was wrong with her?

She'd felt this same nervous ecstasy when she killed Ma Lien. When she killed the priest in Arabak. All three times she'd killed not with fire, but with her own hand. She was capable of such cruelties, even without the Phoenix's power, and that both delighted and scared her.

Gurubai grabbed at Kitay's ankle, choking. Blood bubbled out of his mouth.

"Don't be cruel, Rin." Kitay took the knife from her hand, knelt over Gurubai, and traced the sharp tip along the artery in his neck. Blood sprayed the cavern wall. Gurubai gave a final, violent thrash, and then he stopped moving.

Rin caught Souji as he was trying to flee.

Someone in Gurubai's camp had warned him to run. They'd been too late. By the time Souji and his Iron Wolves made it to the cavern's western exit, Rin was already waiting in the tunnel.

She waved. "Going somewhere?"

Souji stumbled to a halt. His usual confident smirk was gone, replaced with the desperate, dangerous look of a cornered wolf.

"Get out of my way," he snarled.

Rin drew her index finger through the air. Casual streams of flame arced out the tip and danced along the tunnel walls.

"As you can see," she said, "I have my fire back."

Souji pulled out his sword. To Rin's surprise, the Iron Wolves didn't follow suit. They weren't crowded close behind Souji like loyal followers would be. No—if they were loyal, they would have already joined him in the charge.

Instead they hung back, waiting.

Rin read the looks in their eyes—identical expressions of calculating uncertainty—and took a wild gamble.

"Disarm him," she ordered.

They obeyed immediately.

Souji lunged at Rin. The Iron Wolves yanked him back. Two forced him to his knees. One wrenched the blade out of his hands and tossed it across the tunnel. The third jerked his head back so that he was forced to gaze up at Rin.

"What the fuck are you doing?" Souji screamed. "Let me go!"

None of the Iron Wolves spoke a word.

"Oh, Souji." Rin strode toward him and bent down to ruffle his hair. He snapped like a dog, but he couldn't reach her fingers. "What did you think was going to happen?"

Her heart pounded with giddy disbelief. This had gone wonderfully, ridiculously smoothly; she couldn't have imagined a better outcome.

She patted his head. "You can beg now, if you like."

He spat a gob of saliva onto her front. She slammed the toe of her boot into his stomach. He sagged to the side.

"Drop him," Rin ordered.

The Iron Wolves let Souji crumple to the ground. She kept kicking.

She didn't brutalize him like he had her. She kept her kicks confined to his gut, his thighs, and his groin. She didn't aim to crack his ribs or his kneecaps—no, she needed him able to stand in front of a crowd.

But it felt good to hear the little girlish gasps escape from his throat. It kept that nervous ecstasy pounding through her veins.

She couldn't believe she'd once, however briefly, considered sleeping with him. She thought about the weight of his arm around her waist, the heat of his breath against her ear. She kicked harder.

"You cunt," Souji gasped.

"I love the way you talk to me," she cooed.

He tried to hiss out another insult, but she slammed her foot into his mouth. Felt her toes split his lip against his teeth. She had never before mutilated an opponent with pure brute force. She'd done it plenty with fire, of course. But this was a different kind of satisfaction, like the pleasure she derived from hearing fabric rip.

Human bodies were so breakable, she marveled. So soft. Just meat on bones.

She restrained herself from kicking his skull in. She needed Souji's face intact. Broken, maybe, but recognizable.

She and Kitay had decided not to kill him now. His death had to be a public display, a spectacle to legitimize her authority and to transform her takeover from an open secret to a universally acknowledged fact.

Daji, who had done this sort of thing quite often, had emphasized the importance of performative execution.

Don't just let them fear, she'd said. *Let them know.*

"Tie him up," Rin told the Iron Wolves. She knew, with certainty, she could trust them. No one wanted to burn. "Guard him in shifts during the night. We'll finish this in the morning."

At dawn Rin stood at the center of the cavern, right beneath the single shaft of sunlight that pierced through the cracked stone ceiling. She was aware of how absurdly symbolic this looked—the way her skin shone like polished bronze, the way she was the brightest figure in the darkness. It didn't matter that the watching crowd knew this was orchestrated. This imagery would be seared into their minds forever.

Souji knelt beside her, hands bound behind his back. Dried blood crackled over every inch of his exposed skin.

"You may have asked where I've been these past months. Why I disappeared after the attack on Tikany." She pointed to Souji's bowed head. He didn't stir; he was only half-conscious. "This man ambushed me and sent me to the Chuluu Korikh to rot. He betrayed me to the Young Marshal. And he betrayed all of you."

The cavern was so silent that the only sound Rin heard in response was the echo of her own words.

The crowd was with her. She could see it in the grim set of their faces and the coldly furious glint in their eyes. Every person in this cavern wanted to see Souji die.

"This man trapped you in the Anvil. He tried to kill the only person who could save you. Why?" Rin aimed a hard kick at Souji's back. He lurched forward and gave a muffled moan. He couldn't speak up in his own defense; his mouth was stuffed with cloth. "Because he was jealous. Yang Souji couldn't stand to see a Speerly leading his men. He needed to take charge himself. He wanted to own the Southern Coalition."

She didn't know where her words were coming from, but they poured out with ridiculous ease. She felt like a stage actor, chanting lines from some classical play, each dramatic phrase delivered in a deep, powerful voice that sounded nothing like her own.

When had she learned to act like this? Deep down, a fragment of her was scared that any minute the facade would drop, that her voice would falter, and that they'd all see her for the terrified girl she was.

Play the part, she thought. That, too, was Daji's advice. *You only have to wear this skin long enough for it to become a piece of you.*

"The Southern Coalition is now finished," she declared.

Her words met with dead silence. No one reacted. They waited.

She raised her voice. "Yang Souji and the Monkey Warlord are proof of the failures of coalition politics. They nearly destroyed you with their infighting. They had no strategy. They betrayed me and led you astray. But I have returned. I am your liberation. And now I alone will make the decisions for this army. Does anyone object?"

Of course no one objected. She had them in the palm of her

hand. She was their Speerly, their savior, the only one who time after time had rescued them from certain death.

"Good." She pointed down to Souji. She knew no one would try to protect him. Not a single person had spoken up in his defense. They weren't watching to see whether she would kill him. They were watching to see how she would do it.

"This is what happens to those who defy me." She looked to one of the Iron Wolves. "Remove the gag."

The Iron Wolf stepped up and pulled the bunched-up rag from Souji's mouth. Souji lurched forward, gasping.

Rin pressed the point of her knife under his chin and forced his gaze up to the crowd. "Confess your sins."

Souji snarled and mumbled something incoherent.

Rin pushed the blade just a bit harder against Souji's flesh, watching with pleasure as his throat bobbed tensely against steel.

"All you have to do is confess," she said softly. "Then this all ends."

Kitay hadn't wanted her to force a confession. Kitay thought that Souji would rebel and lash out, that his dying words could only damage her. But Rin couldn't let Souji die with his dignity, because then her detractors might take solace in his memory.

She had to annihilate him. Rin knew that his betrayal hadn't been his decision alone—every person in this cavern was in some way complicit in his treachery. But she couldn't execute them all. Souji had to be the scapegoat. His body had to take on the burden of everyone's guilt. This leadership transition demanded public catharsis, and Souji was its sacrificial lamb.

She gave the knife another jab. Blood beaded on the tip. "*Confess.*"

"I didn't do anything," Souji said hoarsely.

"You sold me to Nezha," she said. "And you trapped them in this mountain to die."

That wasn't strictly true. Souji had only ever meant to protect the south. For all she knew, Souji had made the best strategic decisions possible given the Republic's overwhelming superiority.

Souji certainly thought he was the only reason why the Southern Coalition had survived as long as they had. Perhaps he was even right.

But logic didn't matter in this ritual. Fury and resentment did.

"Say it," she demanded. "You sold me. You betrayed them."

He turned to face her. "You belong in that mountain, you cunt."

She just laughed. She wouldn't lash out with flame, no matter how tempting that was. She had to maintain a facade of indifferent calm to exacerbate the difference between them—he the angry, snapping, cornered wolf and she the icy voice of unflappable authority.

"You sold me," she repeated steadily. "You betrayed them."

"You would have driven them to their deaths," Souji said. "I did what I had to do to save them from you."

"Then we'll let the people decide." Rin turned to the crowd. "Does anyone think this man saved you?"

Again, no one spoke up.

"Nezha told me he only wanted the Speerly." Souji raised his voice to address the crowd. His voice cracked with fear. "He promised that's all it would take, he *said*—"

Rin spoke over him. "Does anyone believe this man was stupid enough to make such a simple mistake?"

The implication was clear. She'd just accused Souji of collaboration. This was of course a lie, but she didn't need to show proof. She didn't even need to make a real argument. All she had to do was insinuate. These people would accept whatever narrative she gave them because they wanted to feed their anger. The judgment had concluded before the trial started.

"Show him." Rin pointed to Souji like a hunter indicating a target to a pack of dogs. "Show him what the south does to its traitors."

She stepped back. There followed a brief, anticipatory silence. Then the crowd surged forth, and Souji disappeared beneath a mass of bodies.

They didn't just beat him. They tore his flesh apart. He must have screamed, but Rin couldn't hear him. She couldn't see him, either; she caught only the faintest glimpses of blood shining through the crowd. It was incredible, really, how easily a mass of weakened, half-starved men and women could together wrench entire limbs from a torso. She saw pieces of Souji's uniform fly through the air. Beneath the feet of the crowd rolled what looked like an eyeball.

She didn't join in. She didn't have to.

"This is chaos." Kitay's face had turned a sickly gray. "This is dangerous."

"Not to us," Rin said.

This was violence, but it wasn't chaos. This anger was utterly controlled, fine-tuned, directed, a massive swell of power that only she could control.

And it wasn't just fueled by resentment toward Souji. In a sense, this massacre wasn't about Souji at all. This was about demonstrating a change in loyalty, a gruesome apology by anyone who had ever spoken against her before. This was a blood sacrifice to a new figurehead.

And if anyone still doubted her leadership, then the screaming would at least strike fear deep into their hearts. Anyone on the fringes now understood the cost of opposition. Through love or hate, adoration or fear, she would have them one way or another.

Daji, standing at the far end of the crowd, caught Rin's eye and smiled.

Rin's heart was pounding so hard she could barely hear.

She understood what Daji had meant now. She could achieve so much with a simple show of strength. All she had to do was become the symbolic embodiment of power and liberation, and she could kill a man by pointing. She could make these people do anything.

You've got a god on your side. You want this nation? You take it.

Gradually the frenzy ceased. The crowd dispersed from the

center of the cavern like a pack of wolves retreating when the meat was gone and the bones picked clean.

Souji was long dead. Not just dead—mutilated, his corpse so thoroughly desecrated that not a single part remained that looked recognizably human. The crowd had destroyed his body and in doing so demonstrated their rejection of everything he'd stood for—a wily mix of guerrilla resistance and clever politicking that, in different circumstances, might have succeeded. In different circumstances, Yang Souji might have liberated the south.

But so fell the whims of fate. Souji was dead, his officers were converted, and the takeover was complete.

CHAPTER 18

The soil inside the cavern was too stiff to dig a grave, so Rin and Kitay piled Gurubai's and Souji's remains together onto a messy pyramid in the center of the caverns, soaked them with oil, and stood back to watch them burn.

It took nearly half an hour for the corpses to disintegrate. Rin wanted to speed the process with her own flames, but Kitay wouldn't let her; he demanded they sit vigil before the pyre while the southerners marched on without them. Rin found this a colossal waste of time, but Kitay couldn't be dissuaded. He thought they owed this to their victims, that otherwise Rin would come off like a callous murderer instead of a proper leader.

Twenty minutes in, he clearly regretted it. His cheeks had gone ashen; he looked like he wanted to vomit.

"You know what I'll never get over?" he asked.

"What?" she asked.

"It smells so much like pork. It makes me hungry. I mean—I couldn't eat now if I tried to, but I can't stop my mouth from watering. Is that disgusting?"

"It's not disgusting," Rin said, privately relieved. "I thought it was just me."

But she *could* eat right now, even sitting before the corpses.

She hadn't eaten since the previous afternoon, and she was starving. She had a ration of dried shanyu roots in her pocket, but it felt wrong to chew on it while the air still crackled with the scent of roasted meat. Only when the corpses had shriveled into pitch-black lumps and the air smelled of charcoal instead of flesh did she feel comfortable enough to pull the rations out. She chewed slowly on the coin-shaped root slivers, working her tongue around the starchy chunks until her saliva softened them enough to swallow, while the last remains of Souji and Gurubai puttered into bones and ash.

Then she rose and joined her army in their march.

After they emerged out the other side of the mining tunnels, they continued along the forest with the mountain to their rear. She told the southerners they were moving north to rendezvous with the Dog Warlord and his rebels to form the last organized holdout against the Republic left in the Empire. They would fare better with their numbers combined. She wasn't lying. She did intend to seek the Dog Warlord's aid. If the rumors were true that he had swords and bodies, she'd be a fool to ignore them.

But she didn't tell anyone but Kitay about their plan to climb Mount Tianshan. She'd learned now that she always had to assume someone in her ranks was spying for the Republic. The Monkey Warlord's coup had proved that point. The last thing she wanted was for the Hesperians to raid Mount Tianshan before she reached it.

She also withheld the truth for a more fundamental reason. She needed her soldiers to believe that they mattered. That their blood and sweat were the only things that could turn the wheels of history. She intended to win this war with shamans, yes, but she couldn't keep her hold on the country without the people's hearts. For that she needed them to believe that they wrote the script of the universe. Not the gods.

The skies above were clear and silent. Nezha and his airships had held off for now, and perhaps indefinitely. Rin didn't know how long their grace period would last, but she wasn't going to sit and wait it out.

Her nerves were on edge as they moved along the foothills. Her troops were too exposed and vulnerable, and they moved at a frustratingly slow pace. It wasn't due to poor discipline. Her soldiers, already weakened by months under siege, were weighed down with wagons carrying weapons arsenals, medical equipment, and their scant remaining food supplies. And the relentless rain, which had started that afternoon as a drizzle and quickly turned into thick, heavy sheets, turned their roads into nothing but mud for miles.

"We won't make ten miles today at this rate," Kitay said. "We've got to offload."

So Rin gave the order to dump as many supplies as they could bear to lose. Food and medicine were invaluable, but almost everything else had to go. Everyone chose two changes of clothes and discarded the rest, largely light summer tunics that would offer no shelter from the mountain snow. They also got rid of many of their weapons and ammunition—they simply didn't have the men to keep lugging along the mounted crossbows, chests of fire powder, and spare armor that they'd dragged all this way from Ruijin.

Rin hated this. They all hated it. The sight of so much sheer waste was unbearable; it hurt to watch the weapons piled up in stacks ready to be burned just so that the Republic couldn't find and repurpose them.

"When the final battles commence, it won't come down to swords and halberds," Daji told Rin. "The fate of this nation depends on how quickly we get to Mount Tianshan. The rest is inconsequential."

Their marching rate sped up considerably after they had shed their supplies. But shortly thereafter, the rain shifted from a heavy shower into a violent and torrential downpour that showed no signs of ceasing throughout the afternoon. The mud became a nightmare. On parts of the road, they waded through black sludge up to their ankles. Their flimsy cotton and straw shoes couldn't keep it out; none of them were dressed for such a wet climate.

Rin's mind spiraled into panic as she considered the consequences. Mud like this wasn't just a nuisance, it was a serious threat to her army's health. Few of them had boots; likely they were all going to get infections. Then their toes would rot and fall off, and they'd have to sit down by the roadside to die because they couldn't keep walking. And if they escaped foot infections, they might still contract gangrene from wounds they'd sustained when the blockade broke, because there weren't near enough medical supplies to go around. Or they might simply starve, because she had no idea how they were going to forage at such high altitudes, or—

Her breath quickened. Her vision dimmed. She felt so dizzy she had to stop walking for a moment and breathe, her one good hand pressed against her pulsing chest.

The magnitude of this journey was starting to sink in. Now that the adrenaline of the morning had worn off, now that she wasn't reeling from a heady mixture of insane confidence and drunk exhilaration, she was beginning to understand the stakes of the path she'd charted for the southerners.

And it was very likely that they were all going to die.

Huge losses were inevitable. Their survival was uncertain. If they ventured on, they might write themselves out of history just as completely as if they had never existed.

But if they stayed where they were, they died. If they parleyed for surrender, they died. If they took their chances now against Nezha, three shamans and a weakened army against the combined military might of the Republic and the west, they died. But if they made it to Mount Tianshan, if they could wake the Dragon Emperor, then the playing field would become very, very different.

This could be the end of their story or the beginning of a glorious chapter. And Rin had no choice now but to drag them across the mountain range by her teeth.

∞

It was the weather, not the dirigibles, that quickly proved to be their greatest obstacle. They'd ascended the Baolei range in the middle of the late summer thaw, and that meant raging river torrents, roads slippery with mud, and rain showers that went on for days at a time. At several crossings the mud reached up to their waists, and they could proceed only after cutting down log strips of bamboo and building a makeshift bridge so that the supply wagons, at least, would not sink beneath the surface.

At night they sought shelter in caves if they could find them, for those offered a shield against the rain and ever-present threat of air raids. But, as Rin quickly discovered, they provided no protection against insects and vermin—bulging nests of spiders, little snakes huddled together in horrific, writhing balls, and sharp-toothed rats nearly the size of house cats. The route they'd chosen was so rarely traveled by humans that the pests seemed to have doubled their numbers to compensate. One evening Rin had just put a bedroll down when a scorpion the length of her hand skittered up to her, tail poised, stinger wafting back and forth in the air.

She froze, too scared to scream.

An arrow thudded into the dirt just inches before the scorpion. It skittered backward and vanished into a crack in the cave wall.

Venka lowered her bow. "You all right?"

"Yeah." Rin exhaled. Her head felt dizzyingly light. "Great fucking Tortoise."

"Burn some lavender and tung oil." Venka pulled a pouch out of her pocket and handed it to Rin. "Then rub the residue on your skin. They hate the smell."

Rin burned the mixture in her palm and rubbed it around her neck. "When did you figure that out?"

"The tunnels by the Anvil were crawling with those things," Venka said. "Didn't learn about it until after a couple soldiers woke up swollen and choking, and then we started sleeping in shifts and clearing out the walls with incense every evening. Sorry about that one. Someone should have warned you."

"Thanks regardless." Rin offered her hand to Venka. Venka scraped the residual ointment from Rin's skin and dabbed it around her collarbones. Then she set her mat next to Rin's, sat down, and pressed her palms against her temples.

"It's been a fucking week," she groaned.

Rin joined her on the bedroll. "Yeah."

For a moment they sat beside each other in silence, breathing slowly, watching the cracks in the wall for the scorpion's return. The cave was cramped and bone-achingly cold, so they pressed tight against each other, misty breaths intermingling in the icy air.

It felt good to have Venka back by her side. Funny how people changed, Rin thought. She would never have dreamed that Venka—Sring Venka, the pretty, pampered Sinegardian turned lean, ferocious warrior—would become such a source of comfort.

Once not so long ago they'd hated each other with the particular intensity only schoolgirls could summon. Rin used to grit her teeth every time she heard Venka's high, petulant voice, used to fantasize about gouging Venka's eyes out with her fingernails. They would have brawled like wildcats in the school courtyard if they hadn't been so afraid of expulsion.

None of that mattered anymore. They weren't stupid little girls anymore. They weren't students anymore. War had transformed them both into wholly unimaginable creatures, and their relationship had transformed with them. They had never commented on how it had happened. They didn't need to. Theirs was a bond forged from necessity, hurt, and a shared, intimate understanding of hell.

"Tell me the truth," Venka murmured. "Where the fuck are we going?"

"Dog Province," Rin yawned. She was already half-asleep; after a full day of climbing, her limbs felt heavier than lead. "Thought I made that clear."

"But that's just a fiction, isn't it?" Venka pressed. "The Dog Warlord's army isn't really there, is it?"

Rin paused, considering.

Telling Venka the truth was risky, yes. It was risky now to share secrets with anyone who didn't strictly need to know. But Venka was, startlingly, one of the most loyal people she knew. Venka had readily turned her back on her family to follow a group of southerners in revolt against her home province. She'd never once looked back. Venka could be rude and brittle, but she didn't have a capricious bone in her body. She was blunt and honest, often to the point of cruelty, and she demanded honesty in return.

"I'm not a fucking spy," Venka said, when Rin's silence dragged on for too long.

"I know," Rin said quickly. "It's just—you're right." Her eyes darted around the cave, making sure no one was listening. "I have no clue what's in Dog Province."

Venka raised her eyebrows. "Sorry?"

"That's the truth. I don't know if they have an army. They could be legion. Enough to push the Republic back. Or they could all have defected, or have died. My intelligence is based on Kitay's, and his is based on offhand comments Nezha made weeks ago."

"Then what's up north?" Venka demanded. "Where are you going? I don't care what you tell everyone else, Rin, but you have to tell *me*." She examined Rin's face for a moment. "You're going to wake the third, aren't you?"

Rin blinked, surprised. "How did you guess?"

"Isn't it obvious?" Venka asked. "You've dragged back Master Jiang and the Empress. The Gatekeeper and the Vipress. There's only one missing, and no one ever confirmed that he's dead. So where is he? Somewhere in the Baolei range, I'm assuming?"

"The Wudang Mountains," Rin answered automatically, disconcerted by Venka's matter-of-fact tone. "We have to get through Dog Province first. But how are—I mean, that's fine with you? You don't think that's insane?"

"I've seen stranger things in the past week," Venka said. "You wield fire like it's a sword. Jiang—I mean, Master *fucking* Jiang, the grand idiot of Sinegard, just ripped an entire fleet from the sky. I don't know what's insane anymore. I just hope you know what you're doing."

"I don't," Rin said. "I've no idea."

She was being honest. She didn't have the faintest clue what the Dragon Emperor could do. Daji and Jiang had been frustratingly cagey on the topic. Daji, when asked, gave only the vaguest descriptions—*he's powerful, he's legendary, he's like nothing you've ever seen*. Meanwhile, half the time Jiang acted as if he'd never heard the name Riga. The only thing Rin had to go on was that both of them seemed so very sure that the Dragon Emperor, once awakened, could flatten the Republic.

"All I know is that he scares Jiang," she told Venka. "And whatever scares *him* ought to terrify the world."

Their misery intensified in the following days, because at last they'd reached an altitude high enough that everything was paved with ice.

Rin was initially undaunted. She'd had some half-baked idea that she might be able to ease their journey with the sheer force of flame. It worked at first. She became a human torch. She melted the slippery roads until they were walkable sludge, boiled water to drink, lit campfires by pointing, and kept the train warm by walking among the ranks.

But after two days of this continuous flame, a numbing exhaustion set in, and she found it harder and harder to reach for a force that drained her and tortured Kitay.

"I'm sorry," she said every time she found him shaking atop a wagon, ghostly pale, fingers pressed into his temples so hard they left little grooves.

"I'm fine," he said every time.

But she knew he was lying. She couldn't keep pushing him like this; it would destroy them both. She started calling the fire only several hours a day, and then only to clear the roads ahead. The troops now had only their dwindling supply of torches to rely on for heat. Frostbite and hypothermia eroded their ranks. Soldiers stopped waking up after they'd gone to sleep.

Jiang, meanwhile, was deteriorating at a terrifying rate.

This march was killing him. There was no other way to describe it. He'd grown gaunt and pale, and he wasn't eating. He couldn't walk on his own anymore; they had to drag him along on a wagon. He hadn't regained his lucidity, either. Sometimes he was mercifully placid, affable, and easy to order about like a child. More often he turned in on himself, gripped by some terrible visions that the rest of them couldn't see, lashing out whenever anyone tried to help him. Then he became dangerous. Then the shadows started to creep.

Under Daji's advice they often kept him in a sedated state, plying him with laudanum tea until he sank back against the corners of the wagon in a stupor. It made Rin sick to see his eyes dulled and uncomprehending, drool leaking out the side of his mouth, but she couldn't think of any better options. They needed to keep him stable until they got to Mount Tianshan.

She didn't know what Jiang was capable of when unhinged.

But they couldn't sedate him constantly without doing permanent damage to his mind. He still needed regular stretches of sobriety, and these were so painful and humiliating that Rin couldn't bring herself to watch.

One night Jiang woke the camp with such tortured screaming that Rin dashed immediately out of the tent where she slept and rushed to his side.

"Master?" She clenched his hand. "What's wrong?"

His eyes flew open. He regarded her with his wide, pale eyes, and for a moment, he seemed almost calm.

"Hanelai?"

Rin reeled.

She'd heard that name before. Just once, just briefly, but she'd never forget it. She remembered kneeling on the freezing forest floor, her ankle throbbing, while Chaghan's aunt, the Sorqan Sira, gripped her face in her hands and spoke a name that made the surrounding Ketreyids bristle. *She looks like Hanelai.*

"Master . . ." She swallowed. "Who—"

"I know where we're going." Jiang's arm trembled violently. She tightened her grasp, but that only seemed to increase his agitation. "And I don't—we can't—*don't make me wake him.*"

"Do you mean Riga?" she asked cautiously. She wasn't prepared for the way he flinched at the name.

He gave her a look of sheer, abject terror. "He is evil incarnate."

"What are you talking about?" she demanded. "He's your anchor, why won't—"

"*Listen to me.*" Jiang reached out with his other hand and gripped her arm above the elbow. "I know what she wants to do. She's lying to you. You cannot go."

His nails dug painfully into her flesh. Rin squirmed, but Jiang's grip was like iron.

"You're hurting me," she said.

He didn't let go. He stared at her, eyes wild and intense like she had never seen them. Something was lost behind them. Something was broken, suppressed, desperately trying to claw its way out.

"You don't understand what you're about to do," Jiang said urgently. "Don't climb that mountain. Kill me first. Kill *her.*"

His grip tightened. Rin's eyes watered from the pain, but she didn't wrench her arm away; she was too afraid of startling him. "Master, please . . ."

"End this before it begins," he hissed.

Rin didn't know what to do or say. Where on earth was Daji? Only she knew how to keep Jiang calm; only she could whisper the right combination of words to stop his raving.

"What's on Mount Tianshan?" she asked. "Why are you afraid of Riga? Who is Hanelai?"

Jiang relaxed his fingers. His eyes widened just the slightest bit, and Rin thought she saw some fragment of rationality and recognition dawning on his face. He opened his mouth. But just when she thought he was on the verge of an answer, he threw his head back and laughed.

I should leave, Rin thought, suddenly terrified. She should never have approached him. She should have just left him to his screaming until it died away on its own. She should leave now, walk away, and when morning came, Jiang would be calm again and everything would be normal and they'd never speak of this again.

She knew he was trying to tell her something. There was a hidden truth here, something awful and terrible, but she didn't want to know. She just wanted to run away and cry.

"Altan," Jiang said suddenly.

Rin froze, crouched halfway between sitting down and standing up.

"I'm sorry." Jiang stared her in the eyes; he was addressing *her*. "I'm so sorry. I could have protected you. But they—"

"Stop." Rin shook her head. "Please, Master, stop—"

"You don't understand." Jiang reached out for her wrist. "They hurt me and they said they'd hurt you worse so I had to let you go, don't you understand—"

"*Shut up!*" Rin screamed.

Jiang recoiled as if she had hit him. His entire body started to shake so hard she was afraid he might actually shatter like a porcelain vase, but then, abruptly, he went still. He wasn't breathing; his chest did not rise or fall. For a long time he sat with his head bent and his eyes closed. When at last he opened them, they were a bright, terrible white.

"You should not be here."

Rin didn't know who was speaking through his mouth, but that wasn't Jiang.

Then he smiled, and it was the most horrible sight she'd ever seen.

"Don't you know better?" he asked. "He wants you all dead."

He rose and advanced toward her. She scrambled to her feet and took a single, trembling step backward. *Run*, whispered a small voice in her mind. *Run, you idiot.* But she couldn't move, couldn't take her eyes off his face. She was rooted in place, simultaneously terrified and fascinated.

"Riga's going to kill you when he finds you." He laughed again, a high and unnerving sound. "Because of Hanelai. Because of what Hanelai did. He'll kill you all."

He gripped her by the shoulders and shook her hard. Rin felt an icy chill as she realized for the first time that she wasn't safe here, *physically* was not safe, because she had no idea what Jiang could or would do to her.

Jiang leaned closer. He didn't have a weapon. But Rin knew he'd never needed one.

"You're all scum," he sneered. "And I should have just done what he fucking wanted."

Rin reached for the fire.

"Ziya, *stop!*"

Daji ran into the tent. Rin flinched back, heart pounding with relief. Jiang turned toward Daji, that horrible sneer still etched across his face. For a moment Rin thought that he would strike her, but Daji grabbed his arm before he could move and jammed a needle into his vein. He stood stock-still, swaying on his feet. His expression turned placid, and then he dropped to his knees.

"*You,*" he slurred. "You cunt. This is all your fault."

"Go to sleep," Daji said. "Just go to sleep."

Jiang said something else, but it was slurred and nonsensical. One arm scrabbled for the floor—Rin thought he was reaching for the needle, and tensed for a fight—but then he tilted forward and collapsed to the ground.

"Get away from here." Daji hustled Rin out of the tent into the cold night air. Rin stumbled along, too dazed to protest. Once they'd walked onto an icy ledge out of earshot of the main camp, Daji spun Rin around and shook her by the shoulders as if she were a disobedient child. "What were you thinking? Have you gone mad?"

"What was that?" Rin shrieked. She wiped frantically at her cheeks. Hot tears kept spilling down her face, but she couldn't make them stop. "*What is he?*"

Daji shook her head and pressed her hand against her chest. It took Rin a moment to realize she wasn't just posturing. Something was wrong.

"A flame," Daji whispered urgently. Her lips had turned a dark, shocking violet. "Please."

Rin lit a fire in her palm and held it out between them. "Here."

Daji hunched over the warmth. She stayed like that for a long time, eyes closed, fingers twitching over the fire. Slowly the color came back to her face.

"You know what that was," she said at last. "He's getting his mind back."

"But—" Rin swallowed, trying to wrap her mind around her racing questions, to configure them into an order that made sense. "But that's not him. He's not like that, surely he was never like *that*—"

"You didn't know the real Jiang. You knew a shade of a man. You knew a fake, an imitation. That's not Jiang, that never was."

"And *this* is?" Rin shrieked. "He was going to kill me!"

"He's adjusting." Daji didn't answer her question. "He's just . . . confused, is all—"

"*Confused?* Haven't you heard him? He's afraid. He's *terrified* of what's happening to him, and he doesn't want to become that person because he knows something—something you won't tell me. We can't do this to him." Rin's voice trembled. "We have to turn back."

"No." Daji violently shook her head. Her eyes glinted in the moonlight; with her disheveled hair and her hungry, desperate expression, she looked nearly as mad as Jiang. "There is no turning back. I've waited too long for this."

"I don't give a fuck what you want."

"You don't understand. I've had to watch him all these years, had to keep him confined to Sinegard knowing full well that I'd reduced him to a dithering idiot." Daji's voice trembled. "I took his mind from him. Now he has a chance to get it back. And I can't take that from him. Not even if he's happier like this."

"But you can't," Rin said. "He's so scared."

"It doesn't matter what this Jiang thinks. This Jiang isn't real. The *real* Jiang needs to come back." Daji looked like she was on the verge of tears. "I need him back."

Then Rin saw the tears glistening on Daji's cheeks. Daji, the Vipress, the former Empress of Nikan, was crying. The Vipress was fucking *crying*.

Rin was too upset for sympathy. No. No, Daji didn't get to do this, didn't get to stand here and whimper like she was innocent in the horrifying mental collapse they were witnessing, when Daji was the entire reason why Jiang was broken.

"Then you shouldn't have Sealed him," Rin said.

"You think I couldn't feel what I'd done?" Daji's eyes were red around the rims. "We are linked. You know what that's like. I felt his confusion. I felt how lost he was, I felt him probing at the corners of his mind for something he didn't know he'd lost, acutely so because I *knew* what he didn't have access to."

"Then why did you have to do it?" Rin asked miserably.

What was so terrible, so earth-wrenchingly terrible, that Daji would risk her own life and fracture Jiang's soul to stop it?

They quarreled, Daji had once told her.

Over what?

Daji just shook her head. Her pale neck bobbed. "Never ask me this."

"I have a right to know."

"You have a right to nothing," Daji said coldly. "They fought. I stopped them. That's all there is—"

"Bullshit." Rin's voice rose as the flame grew, stretching dangerously, threateningly close to Daji's skin. "There's more, there's something you're not telling me, *I deserve to know*—"

"Runin."

Daji's eyes glinted a snakelike yellow. Rin's limbs locked suddenly into place. She couldn't wrench her gaze from Daji's face. She understood immediately that this was a challenge—a battle of divine wills.

Do you dare?

Once Rin might have fought. She could have forced Daji into submission; she'd done it before. But she was so exhausted, stretched thin from day after day of pulling the Phoenix through Kitay's aching mind. She couldn't summon rage after what she'd just seen. She felt like a thin shard of frost, one touch from shattering apart.

Rin pulled her flame back into her hand.

Daji's pupils turned back to their normal, lovely black. Rin sagged, released from their grip.

"If I were you, I would stop worrying." Daji had stopped crying; the red around her eyes had faded away. Gone, too, was the fragile hitch in her voice, replaced by a cool, detached confidence. "Jiang's episodes will get worse. But he will not die. He cannot die—you can trust me on that. But the more you try to prod into his mind, try to retrieve whatever you think you've lost, the more you'll torture yourself. Let go of the man you remember. You're never going to get him back."

They returned together to Jiang's tent. Rin sat down next to where Jiang lay and watched him, her heart twisting with pity. He looked so miserable, even in dreamless, morphine-induced sleep. His features were pressed into a worried frown, his fingers clenching his blankets as if he were hanging on to the edge of a cliff.

This wasn't the last time she'd see him suffer like this, she realized. He was going to get worse and worse the closer they got to the mountain. He'd deteriorate until he finally snapped, and a victor emerged between the personalities battling in his mind.

Could she do this to him?

It would be easier if the Jiang who had been Sealed were truly derivative, if he were truly a pale shade of the other, genuine personality. But the Jiang she'd known at Sinegard was a full person in his own right, a person with wants and memories and desires.

That Jiang was so scared of who he used to be—who he was about to become. He'd found a refuge in his partitioned mind. How could she take that from him?

She tried to imagine how Jiang's Seal must have felt all those years he'd lived at Sinegard. What if she were blocked not only from the Pantheon but from her own memories? What if she were held captive behind a wall in her mind, screeching in silent anguish as a bumbling idiot took control of her limbs and tongue?

If she were him, of course she'd want to be free.

But what if someone could erase all memories of what she'd done?

No more guilt. No more nightmares. She wouldn't have flaring pockets in her memory like gaping wounds that hurt to touch. She wouldn't hear screams when she tried to sleep. She wouldn't see bodies burning every time she closed her eyes.

Maybe that was the coward's asylum. But she'd want it, too.

The next morning, Jiang had regained some degree of lucidity. Sleep, however forced, had helped—the shadows disappeared from under his eyes, and his face lost its rictus of dread, settling back into a placid calm.

"Hello, Master," she said when he awoke. "How are you feeling?"

He yawned. "I'm afraid I don't know what you mean."

She decided to push her luck. "You had a bad night."

"Did I?"

His amused indifference annoyed her. "You called me Altan."

"Oh, really?" He scratched the back of his head. "I'm sorry, that was terribly rude. I know you used to follow him around with those shining puppy eyes."

She brushed that off. *Shut up,* spoke a little voice in her mind. *Stop talking, walk away.* But she wasn't done. She wanted to push him, to see how much he remembered. "And you asked me to kill you."

She couldn't tell if his laugh sounded nervous, or if that was the way Jiang had always laughed—high, unsettling, and foolish.

"My goodness, Runin." He reached out to pat her on the shoulder. "Surely I taught you better than to fret over the little things."

Jiang's advice had been flippant. But as their altitude increased and the air grew thinner, Rin lost the mental energy to think about anything except the daily exigencies of the march. Her flames barely made the mountain pathways tolerable; the ice refroze almost as quickly as she melted it. At night, when the temperatures dropped dangerously low, the soldiers started sleeping only in one-hour shifts to prevent anyone from succumbing to the numb, beckoning dark.

At least the environment, not the Republic, formed the bulk of their problems. The first few days on the march Rin had kept her eyes trained on the pale gray sky, expecting dark shapes to materialize from the clouds any moment. But the fleet never came. Kitay floated a number of theories for why they weren't being pursued— the Hesperians were low on fuel, the misty mountain terrain made blind flying dangerous, or the fleet had been so badly damaged at the Anvil that the Hesperians wouldn't sanction sending out the remaining ships in pursuit of an enemy that could summon shadows from nothing.

"They've just seen what we can do," he told the officers, his tone so obviously full of artificial confidence. "They know it's suicide to come after us. They might be tracing where we are. But they won't risk an attack."

Rin hoped to the gods he was right.

Another week passed and the skies remained empty, but that didn't come close to putting her at ease. So what if Nezha chose to let them live for another day? He might change his mind tomorrow. He might cave under internal pressure for a quick victory. They couldn't be hard to pick out against the terrain—he might decide that following them through the mountains wasn't worth it, that the drain on fuel and resources was too great a cost to justify ferreting out whatever hotbed of shamanism he might find.

She was well aware that with every step she took, she moved under the threat of immediate extermination. The Republic was capable of inflicting mass death in seconds. They could end this at any time. But all she could do was forge ahead and hope that it would be far too late by the time Nezha realized he should have killed her long ago.

CHAPTER 19

Rin's journey by airship to the Chuluu Korikh had made the world seem so small. But their trek through the Baolei range felt infinite, and the mountains, which before now she had only ever known as little marks on a map, seemed to encompass a territory greater than the Empire itself. Exhausting weeks stretched into grueling, monotonous months and somehow, when the march had gone on for so long it seemed there had never been a time when they weren't climbing, the daily horrors they faced became routine.

They learned to scale tricky, narrow passages with rope and knives in lieu of ice picks. They learned to pour warm water over their genitals when they relieved themselves because otherwise the freezing temperatures would give them frostbite. They learned to drink boiled chili water constantly because that was the only thing that would keep them warm, which meant they spent half their nights crouching to relieve their diarrhea.

They learned how frightening snow blindness could be when their eyes grew red and itchy and their vision blinked out for hours at a time. They learned to focus on the dull gray of the paths beneath their feet instead of the snow that surrounded them. At noon, when the sun glinted so glaringly off the white peaks that it gave them headaches, they stopped and sat in their shaded tents until the brightness had dimmed.

They adapted in these ways and more. They had decided that if the best of Hesperian technology couldn't kill them, then the mountains certainly wouldn't, so they learned dozens of ways to stay alive in a terrain intent on burying them.

Jiang didn't recover, but his condition didn't become noticeably worse. Most days he sat obediently on the wagon, whittling sculptures of deformed animals out of half-frozen bark with a dull, worn knife because Rin and Daji didn't trust him with sharper objects.

His ramblings continued. They had spiraled past his usual nonsensical babbles. Every time Rin visited him, he launched into invectives involving people and events she had never heard of. Over and over, he addressed her as either Altan or Hanelai. Rarely did he call her by her name. Even more rarely did he look at her at all; more often he spoke to the snow, muttering with a hushed urgency, as if she were a chronicler present to record a history quickly slipping away from his grasp.

Daji remained tight-lipped when Rin pressed her about anything regarding the circumstances that led to Jiang's Seal. But, as if in exchange, she acquiesced to answering questions about Jiang's other utterances. Each night when they made camp, she sat with Rin and Kitay, recounting histories that Rin could never have found in the libraries of Sinegard. These discussions took the form of direct interrogations. Rin fired questions at Daji, one after the other, and Daji responded to everything that she could, often in great detail, as if by jabbering on about minor anecdotes, she could distract Rin from the important questions.

Rin knew what Daji was doing. She knew she was being deceived about *something*. But she took what she could get. Access to Daji was like an open scroll containing all the hidden secrets of Nikara history. She would be foolish not to play along.

"Why does Riga look so much like the House of Yin?" she asked.

"Because he's one of them," Daji said. "That should have been obvious. His father was Yin Zexu, the younger brother to the Dragon Warlord."

"Vaisra's brother?"

"No, Vaisra's uncle. The Dragon Warlord back then was Yin Vara. Vaisra's father."

So Nezha was Riga's nephew. Rin wondered if their power was passed through blood, like the Speerly affinity for the Phoenix. But the Yins had such different relationships to the Dragon. Riga was a true shaman, one who had been to the Pantheon and become imbued with a power freely given and freely received. Nezha was a slave to some perverted, corrupted thing, a creature that should never have existed in the material world.

"Zexu should have been the Warlord all along," Daji said. "He was a born leader. Decisive, ruthless, and capable. Vara was the eldest, but he was a child. Meek, terrified of confrontation. Always bowing to the men he feared, bending because he was so afraid to break. A few years into the occupation, the Hesperians decided they wanted to transport shipments of Mugenese opium into the harbor at the Red Cliffs. Vara agreed, and sent his younger brother out to guide the Hesperian cargo ships through the channel. Instead Zexu rigged the harbor with explosives and sank the Mugenese fleet."

"I like Zexu," Rin said.

"He was dead by the time I first heard his name," Daji said. "But Riga told me so much about him. He always admired his father. He was terribly hotheaded and impulsive. Never could stand an insult. You'd have gotten along splendidly, but only if you didn't kill each other first."

"I'm guessing the Hesperians had him shot," Rin said.

"They very much would have liked to," Daji said. "But open war hadn't broken out yet, and they didn't want to provoke it by killing a member of an elite family. Vara had Zexu exiled to the occupied zone in northern Horse Province instead. Sent his whole family away and cut him out of the lineage records. That's why you'll never find a portrait of him in the palace at Arlong. Riga was an orphan by the time we met. The Mugenese had worked his father to death in a labor camp, and the gods know what happened to his poor mother. When I first saw him, Riga was a pathetic thing, just skin and bones, scraping to tomorrow by stealing food out of trash heaps."

"So you met as children," Kitay said.

"We all grew up in the occupied north. Jiang and I might have been natives. Or children of refugees." Daji shrugged. "Now it's impossible to remember. We all lost our parents early on, before they could tell us what provinces we were from. Perhaps that's why we were so bent on unification. We were from nowhere, so we wanted to rule everywhere."

It felt bizarre to picture the Trifecta as young children. In Rin's mind, they had sprung fully formed into the world, powerful and godly. She'd rarely considered that there was a time when they were mere mortals just like she had once been. Young. Terrified. Weak.

They'd grown up during the bleakest period of Nikara history. Rin had known a country at relative peace before the third war, but the Trifecta had been born into misery. They'd grown up knowing nothing but oppression, humiliation, and suffering.

Small wonder they'd committed the atrocities they did. Small wonder they'd found them completely justified.

"How did you get out?" Rin asked.

"The Mugenese cared about grown soldiers, not children. No one noticed us. The hardest part, in fact, was getting me past the mistresses at the whorehouse." Some unrecognizable emotion flickered across Daji's face, a twist of her lip and a quirk of her eyebrow that quickly disappeared. "We didn't know where we were going, only that we wanted to get out. Once we crossed the border, we wandered for days on the steppe and nearly starved to death before the Ketreyids found us. They took us in. They trained us."

"And then you killed them," Rin said.

"Yes." Daji sighed. "That was unfortunate."

"They still hate you for it," Rin said, just to see how Daji might react. "They want you dead. You know that, right? They're just figuring out a way to get it done."

"Let them hate." Daji shrugged. "Back then our entire strategy was founded on crushing dissent. Wherever we could find it. In times like that, you couldn't let sleeping threats lie. I'm sorry Tseveri died. I know Jiang loved her. But I don't regret a thing."

Daji, it turned out, had done a terrible number of things worth regretting. Rin pried for details about all of them. She made her talk about the lies she had told. The rivals she had killed. The innocents she had sacrificed in the bloody calculus of strategy. Over talks that spanned days, and then weeks, Daji colored in a picture of a Trifecta who were so much more ruthless and capable than Rin had ever imagined.

But it wasn't enough. Daji always spoke only of the amusing stories, the minor details. She never spoke of the day she had Sealed her anchors. And unless prompted, she never spoke of Riga himself. She would answer any of Rin's questions about his past, but she only ever gave the barest, vaguest details about his abilities or his character.

"What was he like?" Rin asked.

"Glorious. Beautiful."

Rin made a noise of exasperation. "You're talking about a painting, not a man."

"There is no other way to describe him. He was magnificent. Everything you could want from a leader and more."

Rin found that deeply unsatisfying, but knew that line of questioning would only yield the same answers. "Then why did you put him to sleep?"

"You know why."

Rin tried to catch her off guard. "Then why are you afraid of him?"

Daji's voice retained its careful, icy calm. "I'm not afraid of him."

"That's bullshit. Both of you are."

"I am *not*—"

"Jiang is, at least. He screams Riga's name in his sleep. He flinches every time I mention him. And he seems convinced we're dragging him up the mountain to his death. Why?"

"We loved Riga," Daji said, unfazed. "And if we ever feared him, it was because he was great, and great rulers always inspire fear in the hearts of the weak."

Frustrated, Rin changed tack once again. "Who is Hanelai?"

For once, Daji looked startled. "Where did you hear that name?"

"Answer the question."

Daji arched an eyebrow, betraying nothing. "You first."

"The Sorqan Sira said once that I resembled Hanelai. Did you know her?"

Something shifted in Daji's expression. Rin couldn't quite read it—amusement? Relief? She seemed less on edge than she'd been just a moment ago, but Rin didn't know what had changed. "Hanelai doesn't matter to you. Hanelai's dead."

"Who was she?" Rin pressed. "A Speerly? Did you know her?"

"Yes," Daji said. "I knew her. And yes, she was a Speerly. A general, in fact. She fought alongside us in the Second Poppy War. She was an admirable woman. Very brave, and very stupid."

"Stupid? Why—"

"Because she defied Riga." Daji stood up, clearly finished. "Nobody defied Riga if they were smart."

The conversation stopped there. Rin tried many times again to broach the subject, but Daji refused to reveal anything more. She never spoke a word about what, precisely, Riga could do. Never a word about what Riga had done to Jiang, or the night that Jiang lost his mind, or how someone so supposedly great and powerful could possibly have missed the attack on Speer. Those gaps alone were enough for Rin to piece together the vaguest of theories, though she hated where it went.

She didn't want it to be true. The implications hurt too much.

She knew Daji was lying to her about something, but part of her didn't want to know. She wanted to just keep marching in a state of suspended disbelief, to keep assuming this war would be ended once they woke the Dragon Emperor. But the past kept prodding her mind like a tongue at an open sore, and the agony of not knowing, of being kept in the dark, grew too great to bear.

Finally, Rin decided to get her answers from Jiang instead.

That would be tricky. She'd have to get him alone. Daji was constantly at Jiang's side, day and night. They slept, marched, and ate together. In camp, they often sat with their heads pressed together, murmuring things that Rin could only guess at. Every time Rin attempted to speak to Jiang, Daji was present, hovering just within earshot.

She had to incapacitate Daji, if only for several hours.

"Can you get me a strong dose of laudanum?" she asked Kitay. "Discreetly?"

He gave her a concerned look. "Why?"

"Not for me," she said hastily. "For the Vipress."

Understanding dawned on his face. "You're playing a dangerous game there."

"I don't care," she said. "I have to know."

Daji proved shockingly easy to drug. She may have been vigilant as a hawk, but the demands of the march exhausted her just as much as they did everyone else. She still had to sleep. Rin only had to creep into Daji's tent and clamp a laudanum-soaked towel over her mouth for half a minute until her face went utterly slack. She snapped her fingers next to Daji's ears several times to check that she was fully unconscious. Daji didn't budge.

Then she shook Jiang awake.

He was trapped in another one of his nightmares. Sweat beaded on his temples as he twitched in his sleep, muttering invocations in a gibberish that sounded like a mixture of Mugini and Ketreyid.

Rin pinched his arm, then clamped a palm over his mouth. His eyes shot open.

"Don't scream," she said. "I just want to talk. Nod if you understand."

Miraculously, the fear withdrew from his face. To her great relief, he nodded.

He rose to a sitting position. His pale eyes moved about the tent and landed on Daji's limp form. His lips curled in amusement, as if he'd guessed exactly what Rin had done. "She's not dead, is she?"

"Only asleep." Rin stood up and gestured to the door. "Come on. Outside."

Obediently, he followed. Once they were out near the ledge, where the howling winds would drown out anything they said from eavesdroppers, she turned to Jiang and demanded, "Who is Hanelai?"

His face went slack.

"Who is Hanelai?" Rin repeated fiercely.

She knew from experience she might only get a minute or two of lucidity from him, so she needed to make the best use of that short window. She had spent that entire day with Kitay figuring out what to ask first. It was like trying to survey new territory in pitch darkness; there was simply too much they didn't know.

In the end, they had decided on Hanelai. Hanelai, aside from Altan, was the name Jiang called Rin most often whenever he forgot who she was. He uttered that name constantly, either in sleep or during his daily fitful hallucinations. She was a person he clearly associated with pain, fear, and dread. Hanelai linked the Trifecta with the Speerlies. Whatever Jiang was hiding from them, Hanelai was the key.

Her suspicions were right. Jiang shuddered at the word.

"Don't do this," he said.

"Do what?"

"Please don't make me remember." His eyes were like a child's, huge with fear.

He's not an innocent, Rin reminded herself. He was as much a monster as she and Daji were. He'd slaughtered the Sorqan Sira's daughter and half the Ketreyid clan with a smile on his face, even if he pretended not to remember.

"You don't get to forget," Rin said. "Whatever you did, you don't deserve to forget. Tell me about Hanelai."

"You don't understand." He shook his head frantically. "The more you press, the closer *he* comes, the other one—"

"He's going to come back regardless," she snapped. "You're just a front. You're an illusion you've constructed because you're too scared to face up to what you did. But you can't keep hiding, Master. If there's any shred of courage left in you, then you'll tell me. You owe that to me. You owe that to *her*."

She spat those last few words so forcefully that Jiang flinched.

She had been grasping at straws, throwing phrases out to see what stuck. She didn't know what Hanelai meant to Jiang. She hadn't known how he would react. But to her surprise, it seemed to work. Jiang didn't run away. He didn't shut down, the way he had so often before, when his eyes went glassy and his mind retreated back inside itself. He stared at her for a long time, looking not afraid, not confused, but *thoughtful*.

For the first time in a long time, he seemed like the man Rin had known at Sinegard.

"Hanelai." He drew the name out slowly, every syllable a sigh. "She was my mistake."

"What happened?" Rin asked. "Did you kill her?"

"I . . ." Jiang swallowed. The next words spilled out of him fast and quiet, as if he were spitting out a poison he'd been holding under his tongue. "I didn't want—that's not what I chose. Riga decided without me, and Daji didn't tell me until it was too late, but I tried to warn her—"

"Hold on," Rin said, overwhelmed. "Warn her about *what*?"

"I should have stopped Hanelai." He kept talking as if he hadn't heard. This wasn't a conversation anymore; he wasn't speaking to her, he was speaking to himself, unleashing a torrent of words like he was afraid if he didn't speak now then he'd never have the chance again. "She shouldn't have told him. She wanted help, but she was never going to get it, and I knew that. She should have left, if it hadn't been for the children—"

"Children?" Rin repeated. *What children?* What was Jiang talking about? This story had just become so much more complex and terrifying. Her mind spun, trying to fit together a narrative that made sense of it all, but everything it suggested horrified her. "Children like Altan? Like me?"

"Altan?" Jiang blinked. "No, no—poor boy, he never made it out—"

"Made it out of *where*?" Rin grasped Jiang by the collar, trying to catch the truth before it fled. "Jiang, who am I?"

But the moment had passed. Jiang stared down at her, his pale eyes vacant. The man who had the answers was gone.

"*Fuck!*" Rin screamed. Sparks flew out of her fist, singeing the front of Jiang's tunic.

He flinched back. "I'm sorry," he said in a small voice. "I can't—don't hurt me."

"Oh, for fuck's sake." She couldn't bear seeing him cower like this, a fully grown man acting like a child. She wanted to vomit from the shame.

She grabbed his arm and dragged him back toward his tent. He obeyed her instructions without a word, crawling meekly onto his blanket without even a glance at Daji's sprawled form.

Before Rin left she made him swallow a cup of laudanum tea. His sleep would be peaceful, dreamless. And tomorrow, if Jiang tried to tell anyone what had happened, she could easily pretend whatever he said was just his usual babbling nonsense.

"That's all he said?" Kitay asked for what felt like the hundredth time. "'If it hadn't been for the children'?"

"It's all I could get." Rin dragged one heavy foot before the other and pushed herself up the incline. They'd only been marching for an hour since sunrise, but she was already so exhausted she didn't know how she'd make it through the day. She hadn't been able to sleep, not with Jiang's words echoing over and over in her mind. They made no more sense now than they had when he'd first uttered them; her thousand unanswered questions had only sprouted a thousand more. "He didn't say whose, he didn't say where—"

"I mean, it's got to be the Speerly children," Kitay said. "Right? With Hanelai involved, there's no one else."

He'd said that already. They'd been running up against the same wall all morning, but that was the only conclusion they could deduce with any degree of certainty. Jiang had done something to Hanelai and the Speerly children, and he was still rotting with guilt over it.

But *what*?

"This is pointless," Kitay declared after a silence. "There are too many unknowns. We can't piece together a story through conjecture. We've no clue what happened twenty years ago."

"Unless we do that again," Rin said.

He shot her a sideways look. "*Are* you going to do that again?"

"Rin." Before Rin could respond, Venka pushed her way up to the front of the column, her face flushed red. This was rare. Typically Venka marched near the back of the line, overseeing the rear to keep an eye out for stragglers and deserters. "There's a problem."

Rin motioned for the troops to halt. "What's happened?"

"It's two girls." Venka had a strange expression on her face. "The soldiers are—ah, I mean, they're—"

"Have they touched them?" Rin asked sharply. She'd made her policy on sexual assault very clear. The first time two soldiers were caught cornering a young woman alone at midnight, she and Venka had castrated the soldiers and left them to bleed out in the dirt with their cocks shoved in their mouths. It hadn't happened again.

"It's not that," Venka said quickly. "But they've ganged up on them. They want punishment."

Rin furrowed her brow. "For what?"

Venka looked deeply uncomfortable. "For violating the bodies."

Hastily, Rin followed Venka down the column.

The first thing she saw when they broke through the gathered crowd was a corpse. She recognized the face of one of the Monkey Warlord's former officers. His body was splayed in the snow, arms and legs stretched wide as if he'd been prepared for a dissection. His midsection looked as if a bear had taken two large bites from his flesh—one around his chest, and one near his stomach.

Then Rin saw the girls, both kneeling with their hands tied behind their backs. Their hands were bloody. So were their mouths and chins.

Rin's stomach churned as she realized what had happened.

"They should burn," snarled a soldier—another one of Gurubai's men. He stood over the taller girl, one hand on his sword as if ready to behead her right then and there.

"Did they kill him?" Rin asked quickly.

"He was dead." The taller girl jerked her head up, eyes flashing with defiance. "He was already dead, he was sick, we didn't—"

"Shut up, you little whore." The soldier jammed his boot into the small of her back. The girl's mouth snapped shut and her eyes widened with pain, but she didn't whimper.

"Unbind them," Rin said.

The soldiers didn't move.

"What is this, a trial?" Rin raised her voice, trying to imbue it with that same ring that had come so easily in the cavern. "Justice is mine to deal, not yours. Unbind them and leave them be."

Sullenly they obeyed, then dispersed back to the marching column. Rin knelt down in front of the girls. She hadn't recognized them at first, but now she saw they were the girls she'd recruited at the Beehive—the pale, pretty waif and her shy, freckled sister. Their faces were gaunt and shrunken, but she recognized that hard, flinty look in their eyes.

"Pipaji?" At last their names came to mind. "Jiuto?"

They gave no indication that they had heard. Pipaji rubbed at Jiuto's arms, soothing her sister's whimpers with hushed whispers.

"You ate him," Rin said, because she wasn't sure what else to say. This was too bizarre, too unexpected. She didn't know what she was supposed to do next.

"I told you he was already dead." If Pipaji was scared, she did a remarkable job of hiding it. "He wasn't breathing when we found him."

Beside her, Jiuto sucked at her fingertips.

Rin stared at them, astonished. "You can't do that. That's not—I mean, that's a violation. That's disgusting."

"It's food." Pipaji gave her a very bored look—the sort of gaunt, indifferent stare that only starvation produced. *Go ahead*, said her eyes. *Kill me. I won't even feel it.*

Rin noticed then that the corpse was not so brutally savaged as it had first appeared. The bloodstained snow only made it seem that way. The girls had only made two neat incisions. One over the heart, and one over the liver. They'd gone straight for organs that would provide the most sustenance, which meant they'd harvested meat from bodies before. They were well practiced at this by now—this was just the first time they'd been caught.

But what was Rin supposed to do about it? Force them to starve? She couldn't tell them to subsist on rations. There wasn't enough of anything to go around. Rin had sufficient rations because of course she did; she was the general, the Speerly, the one person in this column who could not be allowed to go hungry. Meanwhile Pipaji and Jiuto were no one of importance, not even trained soldiers. They were expendable.

Could she punish these girls for wanting to survive?

"Take everything you want and put it in a bag," she said finally. She could barely believe the words coming out of her mouth, but in that instant, they seemed like the only appropriate things to say. "Wrap it in leaves so that the blood doesn't leak. Eat only when no one is looking. If they catch you again, they'll tear you apart, and I won't be able to help you. Do you understand?"

Pipaji's tongue darted out to lick the blood off the corner of her bottom lip.

"Do you understand?" Rin repeated.

"Whatever you say," Pipaji muttered. She gave Jiuto a nod. Without another word, they knelt back over the body and resumed deftly pulling the organs out of the carcass.

Pipaji and Jiuto were not the only ones who resorted to eating human flesh. They were just the first. The longer the march stretched on, the more it became apparent that their food supplies were not going to last. The army was subsisting on one ration of dried salted mayau and one cup of rice gruel a day. They foraged the best they could—some of the soldiers had even started swallowing tree bark to stifle their pangs of hunger—but at this altitude, vegetation was scarce and there was no wildlife in sight.

So Rin wasn't surprised when rumors circulated of corpses—usually victims of frostbite or starvation—divvied up and eaten raw, roasted, or parceled out for the road.

"Say nothing," Kitay advised her. "If you sanction it, you'll horrify them. If you denounce it, they'll resent you. But if you keep quiet, you get plausible deniability."

Rin couldn't see what other choice she had. She'd known this march would be hard, but their prospects looked bleaker with each passing day. Morale, which had been so blazingly strong at the start of their journey, began to wilt. Whispers of dissent and complaints about Rin riddled the column. *She doesn't know where she's going. Sinegard-trained, and she can't find her way through a damned mountain. She's led us up here to die.* Order collapsed along the column. Troops routinely ignored, or didn't hear, her commands. It took nearly an hour to rouse the camp into marching in the mornings. At first, the deserters numbered in handfuls, and then dozens.

Venka suggested sending search parties to chase them down,

but Rin couldn't see the point. What good would that do? The deserters had sentenced themselves to death—alone, they would freeze or starve in days. Their numbers made no difference to her ultimate victory or defeat.

All that mattered was Mount Tianshan. Their future was laid out in stark black and white now—either they woke Riga, or they died.

The days began blurring together. There was no difference between one instance of monotonous suffering and the next. Rin, fatigued beyond belief, started feeling a profound sense of detachment. She felt like an observer, not a participant, like she was watching a shadow puppet show about a beautiful and suicidal struggle, something that had already happened in the past and been enshrined in myth.

They weren't humans, they were stories; they were paintings winding their way across wall scrolls. The terrain transformed around them as they marched, became brighter, sharper, and lovelier, as if warping to match the mythic status of their journey. The snow gleamed a purer white. The mist grew thicker, and the mountains it shrouded seemed less solid, more blurred at the edges. The sky turned a paler shade of blue, not the cheery hue of a bright summer's day but the faded shade of water paint swept absently onto canvas with a thick rabbit-hair brush.

They saw crimson birds whose tails swept thrice the length of their bodies. They saw human faces etched into tree bark, not carved but organically grown—calm, beatific expressions that watched them go with no urgency or resentment. They saw pale white deer who stood utterly still when they approached, calm enough for Rin to run her hand over their soft ears. They tried hunting them for food, to no avail—the deer fled at the sight of steel. And Rin felt secretly relieved, because it didn't feel right to devour anything that beautiful.

Rin didn't know if they were hallucinations brought on by feverish fatigue. But if they were, then they were group hallucinations—shared visions of a lovely, mythical, incipient nation in becoming.

For it was wonderful to remember that this land could still be so breathtakingly beautiful, that there was more sewn into the heart of the Twelve Provinces than blood and steel and dirt. That centuries of warfare later, this country was still a canvas for the gods, that their celestial essence still seeped through the cracks between worlds.

Perhaps this was why the Hesperians so badly wanted to make Nikan their own. Rin could only picture their country by extrapolating from their abandoned colonial quarters, but she envisioned it as a dull place, gray and drab as the cloaks they wore, and maybe that was why they had to erect their garish cities of flashing lights and screaming noises: to deny the fact that their world was fundamentally without divinity.

Maybe that was what had driven the Federation, too. Why else would you murder children and hold a country hostage except for the promise of learning to speak to gods? The great empires of the waking world were driven so mad by what they had forgotten that they decided to slaughter the only people who could still dream.

That was what kept Rin going when her feet had gone so numb from the cold she could barely feel them as she dragged them through the snow, when her temples throbbed so badly from the glaring white that bright red flashes darted through her vision— the idea that survival was promised, victory was foreordained, because the truth of the universe was on their side. Because only the chaotic, incomprehensible Pantheon could explain the vast and eerie beauty of this land, which was something the Hesperians, with their obsessive, desperate clinging to order, could never understand.

So Rin marched because she knew that, at the end of their journey, divine salvation was waiting. She marched because every step brought her closer to the gods.

She marched until one morning Kitay abruptly stopped a few steps ahead of her. She tensed, heart already racing with dread, but when he turned around, she saw he was smiling.

He pointed, and she followed his gaze down the path to a single blue orchid pushing tentatively through the snow.

She exhaled and choked down the urge to cry.

Orchids couldn't grow at the altitudes at which they'd been marching. They could only grow in the lower elevations, in the valleys and foothills.

They'd crossed into Dog Province. They'd begun their descent. From here on out, they were marching down.

CHAPTER 20

Of all twelve provinces, Dog Province was the true wasteland of the Empire.

Rat Province was dirt poor, Monkey Province was an agriculturally barren backwater, and Boar Province was a lawless plain crawling with bandits. But Dog Province was remote, mountainous, and so sparsely populated that the yaks outnumbered the people—the only reason, perhaps, that it had not yet been invaded by the Republic.

When Rin and her troops descended the mountains over the border into the Scarigon Plateau, they saw no sign of human civilization.

She supposed it had been a foolish hope, that the Dog Warlord and his army might be waiting for them with open arms at the foothills of the Baolei Mountains. That rendezvous had always been an empty dream, a lie she'd told the southerners from the outset of the march to give them a reason to keep going. It had just been so long since they'd escaped from the Anvil that she'd started to believe it herself.

They might still find allies. Dog Province was a vast, open land, and they had only reached the southeastern edge of its border. Perhaps they might still find the nomadic herds of sheep and yaks that the Dog Province was known for. But Rin knew it would drive her mad to keep her eyes fixed on distant plains, hoping for silhouettes to appear on the horizon.

They could not assume aid would come. Their only option was to keep pushing forward to Mount Tianshan, alone.

The march across the plateau proceeded far more easily than their journey through the mountains. They were still exhausted; their numbers were still dwindling from starvation and disease. But now that the ground did not slip treacherously under their feet and the air couldn't bite hard enough to kill, they covered thrice the distance each day as they had on the Baolei range. Morale improved. The whispers of dissent grew quieter. And as the distant Tianshan range grew closer day by day, no longer a hazy line on the horizon but a distinct, ridged silhouette against the north sky, Rin began daring to hope that they might actually make it. That all their plans, all their talk of the Trifecta that up until now had seemed like a distant fantasy, might actually come to pass.

She just still hadn't figured out what she might do if they did.

"Rin." Kitay nudged her shoulder. "Look."

She'd been stumbling along in a daze, half-asleep from fatigue. "What?"

He tilted her chin up to stop her staring at the ground. He pointed. "Over there."

She didn't believe it when she saw it, but then a cheer went up through the column that confirmed everyone saw what she did—the outline of a village, clearly visible against the steppe. Thick clouds of smoke billowing up from rooftops of rounded huts that promised shelter, warmth, and a cooked dinner.

The column quickened its pace.

"Wait," Rin said. "We don't know if they're friendly."

Kitay shot her a wry look. Around them, the southerners marched with their hands on their weapons. "I don't think it matters much whether we're invited."

∞

"You're smaller than I thought you'd be," said the Dog Warlord, Quan Cholang.

Rin shrugged. "The last time a person said that to me, I had him torn apart by a mob."

She didn't elaborate. She was too busy chewing her way through the spread on the mat before her—tough, dry mutton; grainy steamed buns; sheep-stock gruel; and a cold, sour glass of yak's milk to wash it down. It was, by any standard, awful—Dog Province was often lampooned for its tough, tasteless food. But after months in the mountains, her tongue craved any flavors other than the dull sting of chili-boiled water.

She knew she was being rude. But as long as no one was actively trying to kill her, she was going to eat.

She sucked the last juicy mouthful of sheep marrow from bone, took a deep and satisfied breath, then wiped her hand on her pants.

"I don't recognize you at all," she said bluntly. "Leadership transition?"

She'd met the former Dog Warlord once before, just briefly, at the Empress's postwar summit in Lusan. He hadn't made much of an impression; she could only barely remember his features well enough to know that the man she dined with now was thinner, taller, and far younger. But she could also detect some family resemblances in his features—Cholang had the same long, narrow eyes and high forehead as the man Rin assumed had been his father.

Cholang sighed. "I told my father not to answer Vaisra's summons. He should have known better to assume the Dragon Warlord merely wanted to talk."

"Stupid of him," Kitay agreed. "Did Vaisra send back his head?"

"Vaisra would never be so compassionate." Cholang's voice hardened. "He sent me a series of scrolls threatening to skin my father alive and deliver to me his tanned hide if Dog Province didn't capitulate."

Kitay's tone was utterly neutral, without judgment. "So you let your father die."

"I know the kind of man my father was," Cholang said. "He would have fallen on his own blade rather than bow. Vaisra did send a parcel. I never opened it; I buried it."

His voice shook, just barely, as he finished speaking. *He's young*, Rin realized. Cholang carried himself like a general, and his men clearly treated him as such, but his voice betrayed a fragility that his sun-weathered skin and bushy beard couldn't hide.

He was just like them. Young, scared, without a clue about what he was doing, yet trying his best to pretend otherwise.

Kitay gestured around the camp. "I take it this is not the permanent capital?"

Cholang shook his head. "Gorulan is a lovely place. Temples carved into the mountainside, great statues the height of buildings everywhere you look. We abandoned it the moment they sent what I presume was my father's head back in a basket. Wasn't keen to get stabbed in my bed."

"Looks like you've been given a stay of execution for now," Rin said.

Cholang shot her a wry look. "Only because we've never figured largely on the Nikara chessboard before. No one quite knows what to do with us."

That was true. Dog Province had always been an outlier in Imperial politics. They were too distant from centers of power to feel the yoke of any regime, but none of the heartland emperors had ever tried very hard to exert more control, because the sparse, arid plateau held so very little worth controlling. The Dogs herded livestock for subsistence and they didn't trade. Their land wasn't worth cultivating; nothing but grass could take root in the thin, rocky soil.

"But you must know the Republic won't ignore you forever," Rin said.

"We're well aware." Cholang sighed. "It's about principle, I expect. Regime change requires total domination. Otherwise, if you've got cracks in your foundation even before you've begun to rule, that sets a poor precedent."

"It's not just that," Kitay said. "It's your minerals. Nezha told me the Hesperians were discussing it. They think there's coal, tungsten, and silver under this plateau. They're very excited about it—they've prepared all kinds of machines to drill beneath the earth's surface once they know it's safe to move in."

Cholang seemed unsurprised. "And I expect their definition of *safe* involves our complete removal."

"More or less," Kitay said.

"Then we're on the same page," Rin said eagerly. Perhaps too eagerly—she could hear the naked hunger in her own voice—but the Southern Army had marched for so long on only the smallest shreds of hope that she was desperate to solidify this alliance. "You need us. We need you. We'll take whatever hospitality you can offer—my soldiers are starved, but they're disciplined—and then we can take stock of how many forces we've got—"

Cholang held up a hand to cut her off. "You won't find your alliance here, Speerly."

She faltered. "But the Republic is your enemy."

"The Republic has enforced sanctions on the plateau since your march began." Cholang's voice bore no trace of hostility, only wary resignation. "We're barely holding out ourselves. And we have no defenses to mount. Our population has always been a fraction of those of other provinces, and we have no weapons other than bows and farming implements. Certainly no fire powder. I can offer you a good meal and a night's rest. But if you're looking for an army here, you won't find it."

Rin knew that. She'd noticed the obvious poverty in Cholang's camp. She could guess the extent of Dog Province's forces based on his paltry personal guard. She knew this was not a base from which she could mount a resistance—it was too bare, too open, too vulnerable to air raids. She knew there was no army here, and certainly not one that could defeat a horde of dirigibles.

But she hadn't come here for the army.

"This isn't about troop numbers," she said. "We just need a guide up the mountains."

Cholang's eyes narrowed. "Where are you trying to go?"

She nodded to the ridges in the distance.

His eyes widened. "Mount Tianshan?"

"There's something up there that will help us win," Rin said. "But you've got to escort us there."

He looked skeptical. "Are you planning on telling me what it is?"

Rin exchanged a glance with Kitay, who shook his head.

"It's best you don't know," she said truthfully. "Even my own officers don't know."

Cholang was quiet, examining her.

Rin understood his hesitation. He was a newly minted Warlord, saddled with his murdered father's legacy, trying to find some way to keep his people alive when all the options looked bleak. And here she was, the Republic's most wanted fugitive, asking him to defy caution to help her climb a distant mountain for a purpose he couldn't discern.

This proposal was ludicrous. But he had to know, after the death of his father, that this was the only choice he had. Defiance was ludicrous. *Hope* was ludicrous. And the longer Cholang sat in silence, brows furrowed, the surer Rin was that he'd realized this as well.

"They tell stories about that mountain," he said at last.

"What stories?" she asked.

"The mists up there are dense as walls," he said. "The paths don't act like paths should; they twist and loop back on themselves and send you walking in circles. If you lose your way, you'll never find it again. And no one who's ventured to the peak has come back alive."

"Three people have," Rin said. "And it's about to be four."

Cholang offered them hospitality in his settlement for the night. "It's not much of a shelter," he apologized. "This is a temporary outpost; it won't be very comfortable. And we haven't got the space to house everyone. But we can feed you, give you blankets, and send our physicians to tend to your wounded. My quarters are yours, if you want them."

At first Rin declined out of etiquette, insisting that her tent was enough. But then Cholang showed her and Kitay to his rounded hut, an impressively sturdy structure that could provide far better shelter against the howling night winds than the flimsy, tattered walls of her tent, and she immediately acquiesced.

"Take it," Cholang said. "I'll sleep under the stars tonight."

It had been so long since anyone had offered Rin such a simple kindness with no expectation of anything in return that it took her a moment to remember how to respond. "Thank you. Truly."

"Rest well, Speerly." He turned to leave. "We'll march for Tianshan at dawn."

A padded sleeping mat, at least two inches thick, occupied the center of the hut. Rin's back and shoulders ached just looking at it. After weeks sleeping curled on the cold, hard dirt, it seemed an unimaginable luxury.

"Nice digs," Kitay said, echoing her thoughts. "Do you want me to take the first watch?"

"No, you go ahead and sleep," she said. "I want to think."

She knew he was exhausted; she'd caught his eyes slipping closed more than once during their audience with Cholang. She sat cross-legged next to the mat, waited for Kitay to crawl under the covers, and then took his hand.

His fingers curled around hers. "Rin."

"Yeah?"

His voice sounded very small in the dark. "I hope we know what we're doing."

She took a deep breath, exhaled slowly, and squeezed his fingers. "Me too."

It was a meaningless, inadequate exchange, and didn't come close to expressing the worries that weighed on both their minds, nor the enormity of what was coming next. But she knew what he meant. She knew his confusion, his fear, and his deep, bone-rattling terror that none of their choices were good—that they were navigating a jungle of snakes carrying the weight of the south's future on their shoulders, and a single misstep would destroy it all.

They were going to wake Riga.

This, after many whispered debates, they'd decided. The calculation hadn't changed.

They weren't fools. They understood the risks, understood Jiang's cryptic warnings. They knew the Trifecta would not be so benevolent as Daji claimed—that whatever Riga was, when at last he awoke, might be more dangerous than Nezha or the Republic.

But the Trifecta were Nikara. Yin Riga, unlike his nephew, would never bow to the Hesperians. They might have committed atrocities, and they might do so again, but their regime at least was anathema to Hesperian encroachment.

To mount an armed resistance without them was suicide; to surrender to the Republic would lead them to a fate worse than death. The Trifecta had been monsters—and Rin knew with certainty that they would become so again—but she needed monsters on her side. What other choice did they have?

Necessity didn't make this any easier. Rin still felt, with every step they took toward Mount Tianshan, like a small animal walking into a trap. But they'd made their choice, and there was nothing they could do now but see it through and hope they came out alive.

She sat still in the darkness, holding Kitay's hand tight until finally his breaths settled into a slow, easy rhythm.

"Don't panic."

Rin jumped to her feet. Fire shrouded her body. She crouched, ready to spring. She'd have to fight with flame—her sword was lying on the other side of the sleeping mat, too far to reach.

Should have known better. Her thoughts raced. *Shouldn't have trusted Cholang so easily, should have known he'd sell us out—*

"Don't panic," the intruder said again, hands stretched out before him.

This time, his voice gave her pause. Rin recognized that voice. And she recognized the intruder's face, too, once he stepped forward and his features became visible in the dim firelight.

"Holy fuck." Despite herself, she burst out laughing. "It's *you*."

"Hello," said Chaghan. "Could I steal you for a chat?"

"How did you know I would be here?" Rin asked.

They walked through Cholang's camp unbothered. The sentries dipped their heads as they approached the perimeter and let them leave without question.

So Cholang must have known Chaghan was here. What's more, he must have permitted him entry into her hut without warning her.

Asshole, Rin thought.

"I've been tracking you since you left Arabak," Chaghan said. "I'm sorry for the surprise, by the way. I didn't want to announce my presence."

"How'd you convince Cholang to let you sneak through his camp?"

"The Hundred Clans have close ties to the frontier provinces," Chaghan said. "In the Red Emperor's time, Sinegard posted their poor bottom-ranked graduates out there to kill us."

"I take it that's not how things turned out."

"When you're alone on the front, waging unprovoked warfare is the last thing you want to do," Chaghan said. "We established strong trade relations a long time ago. We liked the Dog Province soldiers. We drew unofficial lines in the sand and agreed not to cross them, so long as they refrained from encroaching on our territory. It's worked so far."

Rin kept glancing sideways at him as they walked, amazed by how different he seemed. He was so much more *solid*. Before he'd been like a wraith, an ethereal spirit moving through the world like light passes through the air, present but never quite belonging. But now when he walked, he seemed as if he actually left footsteps.

"You're staring at me," he said.

"I'm curious," she said. "You look different."

"I feel different," he said. "When I leave the material plane now, there's no one on the other side pulling me back. I've had to learn to be my own anchor. It feels . . ."

She didn't ask what it was like to miss Qara, every second of every day. She didn't have to guess at the gaping pain, the clawing absence of that loss. She knew.

A thought struck her. "Then are you—"

"No. I'm dying," he said bluntly. He didn't seem bothered by this; he said it as casually as if informing her that he'd be going to market next week. "It gets harder every time—reaching the gods, I mean. I'm never going to be able to go as far out, or to stay as long, as I used to. Not if I want to wake up again. But I can't stand spending all my time in this realm, this horribly . . . *solid* place." He gestured about the steppe with disdain. "So I can't stop. And one day I'll go out too far. And I'm not going to come back."

"Chaghan." She stopped walking. She didn't know what to say. "I . . ."

"I'm not particularly worried," he said, and sounded like he meant it. "And I'd very much like to talk about something else."

She changed the subject. "So how did you get on back home?" The last time she'd seen Chaghan, he'd been racing north on a warhorse following his cousin Bekter's murderous coup. Back then, she'd feared he was riding to his death. But from the looks of it, he'd emerged from that power struggle unscathed, in charge, and with ample troops and resources.

"Well enough," said Chaghan. "Obviously, Bekter's not a problem anymore."

Rin was impressed, if not terribly surprised. "How did you manage that?"

"Murder and conspiracy. The usual means, of course."

"Of course. You lead the Ketreyids now, then?"

"Please, Rin." He shot her a thin-lipped smile. "I lead the Hundred Clans. For the first time in a century we are united, and I speak here on their behalf."

He nodded toward something in front of them. Rin glanced up. She had assumed they were only walking out of earshot of anyone in Cholang's settlement, but when she followed Chaghan's line of sight she saw campfires and lean silhouettes against the moonlight. They drew closer, and she made out dozens of cloth tents, resting horses, and sentries with bows at the ready. An army camp.

"You've brought a full contingent," she said.

"Of course," Chaghan said. "I wouldn't march against the Trifecta with anything less."

Rin stopped walking. The camaraderie between them vanished. She curled her palm into a fist, readying herself for a fight. "Chaghan—"

"I am here as a friend." He held his hands up to display that he had no weapon, though Rin knew that with Chaghan, it didn't matter. "But I know what you intend to do, and we desperately need to speak. Will you sit?"

"I want all your archers to leave their bows and quivers in a pile beside me," she said. "And I want you to swear on your mother's grave that I'll be back safe with the southerners before dawn."

"Rin, come on. It's me."

She held firm. "I'm not joking."

She'd last parted with Chaghan on friendly terms. She knew their interests, at least in regard to the Republic, were aligned. But she still didn't trust Chaghan, nor any of the Ketreyids, not to put an arrow in her forehead if they decided she was a threat. She'd dealt with Ketreyid justice before; she knew she'd only escaped because the Sorqan Sira had deemed her useful.

"As you wish." Chaghan signaled to his men, who reluctantly obeyed. "I swear on the grave of Kalagan of the Naimads that we won't harm you. Better?"

"Much." Rin sat and crossed her legs. "Go on."

"Thank you." Chaghan knelt down opposite her. He unrolled his satchel, pulled out a vial of cobalt-blue powder, and popped the cork off before offering it to her. "Lick your fingertip and dab it onto your tongue. Once should do. And get comfortable. It takes effect quickly, you remember—"

"Hold on." She didn't touch the vial. "Tell me what's going on before I hurl my spirit into the abyss with you. Which god are we visiting now?"

"Not the gods," he said. "The dead."

Her heart skipped a beat. "Altan? Did you find him?"

"No." A shadow of discomfort flitted across Chaghan's face. "He's not—I've never—no. But she is a Speerly. Most spirits dissolve into nothing when they pass. That's why it's hard to commune with the dead; they've already disappeared from the realm of conscious things. But your kind linger. They're bound by resentment and a god that feeds on it, which means often they can't let go. They're hungry ghosts."

Rin licked the tip of her index finger and poked it into the vial, swiveling it around until soft, downy powder coated her skin up to the first joint. "Are we speaking to Tearza?"

"No." Chaghan took the vial back and did the same. "Someone more recent. I don't believe you've met."

She glanced up. "Who?"

"Hanelai," Chaghan said bluntly.

Without hesitation Rin put her powder-covered finger in her mouth and sucked.

Immediately the Ketreyid campsite blurred and dissolved like paints swirled in water. Rin closed her eyes. She felt her spirit flying up, fleeing her heavy body, that clumsy sack of bones and organs and flesh, soaring toward the heavens like a bird freed from its cage.

"We'll wait here," Chaghan said. They floated together in a dark expanse—a plane not quite pitch-black, but rather shrouded in hazy twilight. "When I found out you were marching to Tianshan, I went searching. I needed to understand the risks. I know there's no one alive who could push you off the path you've chosen." He nodded toward a red ball of light in the void, a distant star that grew larger as it approached. "But she might."

The star became a pillar of flame and then a woman, drawn close before them, glowing red-hot like she was burning up from the inside.

Rin stared, speechless.

She knew this face. Knew that pointed chin, that straight jaw, and those hard, sullen eyes. She'd seen that face staring back at her from mirrors.

"Hello, Hanelai," Chaghan said. "This is the friend I've told you so much about."

Hanelai turned toward Rin, eyes roving imperiously over her like a queen surveying her subject. A curious feeling seized Rin's heart, some strange and unnameable longing. She'd felt it only once before, two years ago, when she'd held her fingers up against Altan's and marveled at how their dusky skin matched. She never thought she'd feel it again.

She suspected her relation to Hanelai. She'd suspected it for a long time. Now, staring at that face, she knew it was undeniable. She knew the word for it, a word she'd never used with anyone before. She dared not say it out loud.

Yet Hanelai showed no hint of recognition.

"You are the one traveling with Jiang Ziya?" she asked.

"Yes," Rin said. "And you're—"

Hanelai snarled. Her eyes glowed red. Her flames jumped and unfurled like an explosion suspended in time, deathly orange petals blooming outward at Rin.

"Don't be afraid," Chaghan said quickly. "The dead can't harm you. Those flames aren't real, they're only projections."

He was right. Hanelai frothed and snarled, screaming incoherently as fire shot out of every part of her body. But she never drew closer to Rin. Her flames bore no heat; though they curled and jumped, the twilight plane remained as neutrally cool as it had always been.

Still, she was terrifying. It took all Rin's willpower not to shrink away. "What's wrong with her?"

"She's dead," Chaghan said. "She's been dead for a long time.

And when souls don't fade back into the abyss, they need tethers, their lingering hatreds that keep them from passing. She's not a person anymore. She's rage."

"But I've seen Tearza before. Tearza wasn't—"

"Tearza had control," Chaghan said. "Her rage was tempered, because she chose the circumstances of her own death. Hanelai didn't."

Rin regarded Hanelai. Now her pulsing flames and twisted scowl didn't seem so frightening. They seemed wretched.

How long had Hanelai been drifting in her fury?

"You've nothing to be afraid of," Chaghan said. "She wants to talk to you, she just doesn't know how. If you speak to her, she'll answer. Go ahead."

Rin knew what she had to ask.

This was her chance, at last, to excavate the truth—the secret that had festered so long between her, Jiang, and Daji. She didn't want to know; she was afraid to know. It was like digging a knife into a poisoned wound to draw out the venom; the pain was daunting. But even if this secret destroyed her, she had to hear it. She had to climb that mountain with clear eyes.

She looked straight into Hanelai's furious, anguished face.

"What did he do to you?" she asked.

Hanelai howled.

Voices flew at Rin like an assault of arrows—not all of them Hanelai's, not all of them adult. Fragments of hundreds of grievances assaulted her like a mosaic of pain, cobbling together the details of a painting which, until now, she'd only glimpsed from a distance.

—*Riga*—

—*when they took our children*—

—*no other choice*—

—*would you have chosen?*—

—*it didn't matter, none of it mattered*—

—*they wanted the gods, they only ever wanted the gods, and we felt sorry for them because we could not imagine*—

—for our children—
—Riga—
—would have left us alone—
—just leave us alone, we never wanted—
—then Riga—
—Riga—
—Riga!—

"I understand," Rin said. She didn't, not fully, but she'd heard enough to piece together the outline and that was enough; she couldn't bear to hear more; she couldn't think of *Jiang* like that. "I understand, stop—"

But the voices did not stop, they only built, screams stacking upon screams at an unbearable volume.

—and Jiang didn't—
—Jiang never—
—he promised—
—when Riga—
—Ziya—
—he said he loved us—
He said he loved me.

"Stop it," Rin said. "I can't—"

"Can't?" Chaghan's voice cut through her mind like a shard of ice. "Or you don't want to know?"

The voices consolidated back into one.

"Traitor," Hanelai screeched, flying at Rin. "Stupid, imperialist, pathetic traitor—"

Her voice distorted into deep double timbre, which then split into a chorus. When Hanelai spoke, her mouth moved not only for herself but for a crowd of deceased. Rin could almost see them, a horde of Speerlies behind Hanelai, all spitting rage in her face.

"You hear our testimony and you refuse us, you defile the graves of your ancestors, you who escaped, you who carry our blood, how dare you call yourself a Speerly, *how dare you*—"

"Enough," Rin said. "Make her stop—"

"Listen to her," Chaghan said.

Fury surged in Rin. "I said *enough*."

Every time she'd used this drug before, Chaghan had guided her back from the world of spirit, dragging her bewildered, terrified soul into the land of the living. But Rin was done with wandering around like a lost child. Done with letting Chaghan manipulate her with wraiths and shadows.

The moment her soul hit her body, jolting her back into awareness like a swimmer breaking the surface, Rin clambered to her knees and seized him by the shoulders.

"What the hell was that?"

"You had to know," Chaghan said. "You weren't going to believe it from anyone else's mouth."

"So what, you were going to scare me off with a fucking ghost?"

"*Rin*. You're talking about reviving the man who murdered your race."

"The Mugenese murdered the Speerlies—"

"And Riga let them. Did you hear Hanelai? That's the full story. That's what the Vipress was never going to tell you. The Federation kidnapped Speerly children and demanded the secrets to shamanism as a ransom. Riga knew Hanelai was going to reveal everything to the Mugenese, he knew she cared more about those twenty children than the fate of the mainland, and he slaughtered her people for it. He thought the Speerlies were animals. Disposable. And you think he'll treat you any differently? Your ancestors would be disgusted. Altan wouldn't—"

"Don't," she said harshly. "Don't speak to me of Altan. You know very well what Altan would have done."

He opened his mouth to retort, saw the look on her face, and then closed it. He swallowed. "Rin, I'm just—"

"Riga is our best and only chance at winning this war," she said firmly.

"Perhaps. But what comes after that? Who rules the Empire then, you or them?"

"I don't know. Who cares?"

"You can't be this daft," he said, exasperated. "Surely you've considered this power struggle. It's not just about the enemy. It's about what the world looks like after. And if you intend to stay in charge, then you'd better start weighing your chances against the Trifecta combined. You think you can take them?"

"I don't know," she said again. "But I know one thing for certain. Without them, I have absolutely no chance against the Republic and the Hesperians. And they're the only opponents who matter right now."

"That's not true. Hesperian occupation will be difficult. But it is survivable—"

"Survivable to you," she scoffed, "only because you hide in a desert wasteland so dry and dead that no one would bother encroaching on your territory. Don't debate the stakes with me, Chaghan. You'll be just fine up north in your shithole no matter what happens."

"Watch how you speak to me," Chaghan said sharply.

Rin glared at him, incredulous. She remembered now why she had always resented him so, why she had always felt such an urge to smack the grim, all-knowing expression off his face. It was the sheer condescension. The way he always spoke as if he knew better, as if he were lecturing foolish children.

"I'm not the girl you met at Khurdalain anymore," she said. "I'm not the failed commander of the Cike. I know what I'm doing now. You're trying to protect your people. I understand that. But I'm trying to protect mine. I know what the Trifecta did to you, and I know you want your vengeance, but right now I need them. And you can't give me orders."

"Your obstinacy is going to destroy you."

She arched an eyebrow. "Is that a threat?"

"Don't start with that," he said, exasperated. "Rin, I came here as a friend."

She summoned a tiny spark of flame into her palm. "So did I."

"I'm not going to fight you. But you should know what you're getting into—"

"I know very well," she said loudly. "I know exactly what kind of man Jiang is, I know exactly what Daji is planning, and I *don't care*. Without Riga we have nothing. No army. No weapons. The dirigibles will bomb us out in seconds and that'll be it; this whole struggle will be over and we'll be nothing more than a blip in history. But the Trifecta give us a fighting chance. I'll deal with the fallout later. But I'm not crawling into oblivion with a whimper, and you should have known that before you came here. If you were this afraid of the Trifecta, then you should have tried to kill me. You shouldn't even have given me the choice."

She stood up. The Ketreyid archers swiveled to face her, alarmed, but she ignored them. She knew they wouldn't dare hurt her. "But you can't, can you? Because your hands are tied, too. Because you know that when the Hesperians are done with us, they'll come for you. You know about their Maker and how they look at the world. And you know their vision for the future of this continent does not include you. Your territories will shrink smaller and smaller, until the day the Hesperians decide they want you off the map, too. And you need me for that fight. The Sorqan Sira knew that. You're doomed without me."

She picked her knife off the floor. This audience was over. "I'm setting out for Mount Tianshan tomorrow. There's nothing you can do to stop me."

Chaghan regarded her with narrow, calculating eyes. "My men will be outside that mountain, ready to shoot at whatever emerges."

"Then aim well," she said. "So long as you're not aiming at me."

CHAPTER 21

Seven days later Rin stood with Jiang and Daji at the base of Mount Tianshan, preparing to make the final climb. Jiang carried a fawn slung over his shoulders, its skinny legs bound with rope. Rin tried not to look at its large, blinking eyes. There was power in a fleeing life, she knew. The incantation to break the eroding Seal required death.

The mountain loomed tall above them, deceptively pretty in its lush greenery and patches of clean snow, shrouded by its famous mists so thick she could barely see half a mile up the path. At twenty-five thousand feet, it was the tallest peak in the Empire, but the Heavenly Temple was only two-thirds of the way up the mountain. Still, it would take them the full day to climb, and they likely would not reach the temple until sunset.

"Well." Rin turned around to face Kitay. "See you tonight."

He wasn't coming with her. Despite his protests, they'd both agreed he would only be a liability on the mountain—he'd be safer in the valley, surrounded by Cholang's troops.

"Tonight," he agreed, leaning down to give her a tight, brief hug. His lips brushed against her ear. "Don't fuck this up."

"Can't promise anything." Rin gave him a wry chuckle. She had to laugh, to mask her apprehension with callous humor, otherwise she'd splinter from the fear. "It's only a day, dearest, don't miss me too much."

He didn't laugh.

"Come back down," he said, his expression suddenly grim. His fingers clenched tight around hers. "Listen, Rin. I don't care what else happens up there. But you come back to me."

The road up Mount Tianshan was a sacred path.

In all the myths, Tianshan was the site from which the gods descended. Where Lei Gong stood when he carved lightning into the sky with his staff. Where the Queen Mother of the West tended the peach tree of immortality that had sentenced the Moon Lady Chang'e to an eternity of torment. Where Sanshengmu, sister of the vengeful Erlang Shen, had fallen when the heavens banished her for loving a mortal.

It was clear why the gods would choose this place, where the rarefied air was cool and sweet, where the flowers that laced the road bloomed in colors so bright they did not seem real. The path, so rarely trodden it had nearly faded away, was silent as they walked. No one spoke. Save for their footsteps, Rin heard nothing—not the chirping of birds nor the hum of insects. Mount Tianshan, for all its natural loveliness, seemed devoid of any other life.

The dirigibles came at midday.

Rin thought she'd imagined the buzzing at first; it was so faint. She thought the droning was a fear-induced flashback, brought on by the nerves and pounding exhaustion.

But then Daji froze in her steps, and Rin realized she'd heard it, too.

Jiang glanced up at the sky and groaned. "Fucking hell."

Slowly the aircraft emerged from the thick white misty wall, one after another, black shapes half-hidden in clouds like lurking monsters.

Rin, Jiang, and Daji stood still below, exposed against the white snow, three targets laid bare before a firing squad.

How long had Nezha known where she was? Since she'd reached Dog Province? Since she'd begun the march? He must have tailed the southerners with reconnaissance crafts, lurking unseen beyond the horizon, tracing their movements across the Baolei range, waiting to see where they led him like a hunter following a baby deer to its herd. He must have realized they were marching west to seek salvation. And following his devastating loss at the Anvil, in desperate need of a victory to hand the Hesperians, he must have decided to wait to eliminate the resistance at its source.

"What are you waiting for?" Daji hissed. "Hit them."

Jiang shook his head. "They're not in range."

He was right. The airships crept hesitantly through the mist, patient predators watching to see where their prey scurried next. But they remained hovering at such a distance that they were only hazy shapes in the sky, where they knew Jiang's shades could not reach. They didn't approach. And they didn't fire.

Nezha knows, Rin thought. She was certain; that was the only explanation. Somehow, Nezha understood what she was attempting, or at least an approximation of it. He wasn't ready to murder the Trifecta just yet. He needed to find out, for the sake of his Hesperian overseers, what precisely lay in that chamber.

"Then hurry up," Daji said curtly, turning her gaze back to the path. "*Climb.*"

There was no other option but to follow.

Rin scrambled up the slippery rock, all reservations driven from her mind by sheer icy fear. Her questions about the Trifecta didn't matter now. Whatever Jiang had done, whatever he was hiding from her, whoever the children were—it didn't matter. Nezha lurked above her, ready to turn her bones to dust with a single order. She had one path to survival and that was Riga.

She could be about to wake a monster. She didn't care.

Farther up, the path was ensconced inside fog so thick that Rin could barely see or breathe. This was the famous mist of Mount Tianshan, the so-called impenetrable shroud of the Empress of the

Four Skies, cast down to keep mortals from discovering the doors to the heavens. The humidity was so dense she felt almost as if she were moving through water. She couldn't see even a foot in front of her; she had to scrabble along on all fours, listening desperately for the sound of Daji's footsteps.

She could still hear the dirigible fleet, but she couldn't see them at all now. The droning had become fainter, too, as if the fleet had first approached the mountain and then retreated backward.

Could they not see where they were going? That must be it—if the mist was hazardous to climbers, it must be doubly so for the aircraft. They must have fallen back to clearer skies, waiting until they figured out the precise location of their targets.

How long did that give them? Hours? Minutes?

She was finding it harder and harder to breathe. She had grown used to thin air on the march, but rarely had they ascended to such altitudes. Fatigue crept up her legs and arms and intensified to a screaming burn. Every step felt like torture. She slowed to a third of her initial speed, dragging her feet forward with every last ounce of energy she could squeeze from her muscles.

She couldn't stop. They'd initially agreed to camp halfway up the mountain if they tired too quickly, but with dirigibles following overhead, that was no longer an option.

One at a time, she told herself. One step. Then another. And then another, until at last, the steep path gave way to flat stone. She dropped to all fours, chest heaving, desperate for just a few seconds' reprieve.

"There," Daji whispered behind her.

Rin lifted her head, squinting through the fog, until the Heavenly Temple emerged through the mist—an imposing nine-story pagoda with red walls and slanted cobalt roofs, gleaming pristinely as if it had been built only yesterday.

The temple had no doors. A square hole was carved into the wall where one should have been, revealing nothing but darkness within. There was no barrier against the wind and the cold. Whatever lay inside needed no defenses—the interior pulsed with some dark, crackling power of its own. Rin could feel it in the air, growing thicker as she approached—a vague tension that made her skin prickle with unease.

Here, the boundary between the world of gods and the world of men blurred. This place was blessed. This place was cursed. She didn't know which.

The temple's dark entrance beckoned, inviting. Rin was seized by a sudden, heart-clenching impulse to flee.

"Well," Daji said behind her. "Go on."

Rin swallowed and stepped over the raised panel at the threshold, casting flames into the darkness to light her way. The room on the ground level wasn't warm. It wasn't cool, either. It was nothing at all, the absence of temperature, a place perfectly conditioned to leave her untouched. The air didn't stir. There was no dust. This was a space carved out of the boundaries of the natural world, a chamber outside of time.

Slowly her eyes adjusted to the dim interior.

The Heavenly Temple had no windows. The walls on all nine floors were solid stone. Even the ceiling, unlike ceilings in every pagoda Rin had ever seen, was closed off to the sky, blocking out all light except for the red glow in her palm.

Cautiously, she cast her flames higher and wider, trying to bring light to every corner of the room without setting anything ablaze. She made out the shapes of the sixty-four gods above her, statues perched on plinths exactly like those she'd always seen in the Pantheon. The flames distorted their shadows, made them loom large and menacing on the high stone walls.

Yes—the gods were undeniably present here. She didn't just feel them, she could *hear* them. Odd whispers arced around her, speaking fleeting words that disappeared just as she tried to catch them. She lingered under the plinth of the Phoenix. Its eyes gazed down at her—fond, mocking, daring. *Long time no see, little one.*

In the middle of the room stood an altar.

"Great Tortoise," Jiang said. "You really did a number on him."

The Dragon Emperor lay still on a bed of pure jade, hands

folded serenely over his chest. He didn't look like someone who had been comatose without food or water for two decades. He didn't look like a living person at all. He seemed a part of the temple, as still and permanent as stone. His chest did not rise or fall; Rin couldn't tell if he still breathed.

The Yin family resemblance was uncanny. His face was sculpted porcelain: strong brows, straight nose, a lovely arrangement of sharp angles. His long, raven-black hair draped elegantly over his shoulders. Rin felt dizzy as her eyes traced his noble sleeping features. She felt as if she were staring down at Nezha's corpse.

"Let's not draw this out," Daji said. "Ziya?"

Jiang moved fast. Before Rin could blink, he'd dropped the fawn onto the stone tiles and wedged a blade into its neck.

The fawn's mouth worked furiously, but no scream came out, only agonized gurgles and an astonishing tide of blood.

"Quickly now, before he's gone." Daji pulled Rin out of the way as Jiang dragged the fawn's writhing form against the base of the altar.

The fawn's choking went on for a torturously long time. Finally, its struggling dwindled to minute shudders as its blood seeped across the floor, running in straight, clean rivulets where the stone tiles met. All the while Daji knelt over it, one hand pressed against its flank, murmuring something under her breath.

A crackling noise filled the cave, a long, unceasing roll of thunder that grew louder and louder until it seemed the pagoda was about to explode. Rin felt power in the air. Too much power—it cloyed in her throat, choking her. She crouched back against the wall, suddenly terrified.

Daji spoke faster and faster, unintelligible words tumbling eagerly from her lips.

Jiang was utterly still. His face twisted in some strange and unfamiliar grimace; Rin couldn't tell if he was horrified or ecstatic.

Then shone a burst of white light, followed by a noise like a thunderclap. Rin didn't realize she'd been thrown off her feet until she felt her back slam against the far wall.

Stars exploded behind her eyelids. The pain was excruciating. She wanted to curl up into a ball and rock back and forth until it stopped, but fear dominated; fear made her crawl to her knees, coughing, squinting as she waited for her vision to return.

Jiang stood with his back against the opposite wall, unmoving, his expression blank. Daji was collapsed against the base of the altar. A thin trail of blood ran out from between her lips. Rin stumbled forth to help her up, but Daji shook her head and pointed to the altar, where, for the first time in over twenty years, Yin Riga rose.

The Dragon Emperor's eyes were pure, gleaming cobalt. They roved slowly about the room as he sat up, drinking in the sights of the pagoda.

Rin couldn't move. She couldn't even speak—all words seemed insufficient. Some force seemed to be clenching her jaw shut, some gravity that made the air in the temple thicker than rock.

"Can you hear me?" Daji, rising to her knees, pulled Riga's hands into her own. "Riga?"

He stared at her for a long time. Then he croaked, in a voice like scraping gravel, "Daji."

Jiang made a choking noise.

Riga's gaze flickered briefly toward him, then returned to Daji. "How long have I been gone?"

"Twenty years." Daji cleared her throat. "Do—do you know where you are?"

Riga sat silent for a moment, eyebrows furrowed.

"I've been drifting," he said. At least he sounded nothing like Nezha—his voice was hoarse from disuse, a rusted blade dragging against stone. "I don't know where. It was dark, and the gods were silent. And I couldn't get back. I couldn't find the way. And I kept wondering, who could possibly have . . ." His eyes refocused suddenly on Daji, as if he had just realized he was speaking out loud. "I remember now. We quarreled."

Daji's pale throat bobbed. "Yes."

"And you stopped it." His gaze lingered on Daji's face for a long while. Something passed between them that Rin did not understand—something full of remorse, longing, and resentment. Something dangerous.

Abruptly, Riga turned away.

"Ziya," he commanded. His voice grew smoother, louder, resounding off the pagoda walls.

Jiang's head jerked up. "Yes."

"You've come around, then?" Riga rose to his feet, shrugging off Daji's proffered arm. He was much taller than Nezha—if they'd been standing side by side, he would have made Nezha look like a child. "Have you gotten over that stupid girl? That's why we fought, wasn't it?"

Jiang's face was unreadable as stone. "It's good to see you again."

Riga turned toward Rin. "And what's this?"

Rin still couldn't speak. She tried to take a step backward, but to her horror she found herself frozen in place. Riga's gaze was like steel spikes nailing her feet to the ground, paralyzing her with seemingly no effort at all.

"How interesting." Riga tilted his head, eyes roving up and down her form as if surveying a pack animal at market. "I thought they killed them all."

Rin tried to draw her knife. Her arm wouldn't listen.

"Kneel," Riga said softly.

She obeyed instantly. His voice was like a physical force on its own, capable of bending her knees and forcing her gaze to the ground. It vibrated in her bones. It shook the very foundations of the pagoda.

Riga strode slowly toward her. "She's shorter than the others. Why is that?"

No one answered. He made a humming noise. "I suppose Hanelai was short. Does she follow orders?"

At last, Rin managed to spit out a word. "*Orders?*"

"Rin, be quiet," Daji said sharply.

Riga just laughed. "I'm impressed, Ziya. You really found another one to keep around, did you? You always did like your pets."

"I'm not his *pet*," Rin snarled.

"Oh, it talks."

Riga leaned down and gave her a wide, terrible smile. Then he reached out, seized her collar, and pulled her up into the air in one smooth, easy motion. Rin gasped as his thumbs dug painfully into her windpipe. She kicked out with her feet, but she was swinging entire inches off the ground, and all she could do was brush Riga's knees with her toes. All her flailing had no more effect than a child throwing a tantrum. Riga pulled her toward him until their eyes were level, their faces so close that she could feel the heat of his breath on her cheeks when he spoke.

"I've been asleep for a very long time, little Speerly," he whispered. "I'm not in the mood for contradiction."

"Oh, let her go," Daji said. "You're going to kill her like that."

Riga shot her a glare. "Did I give you permission to speak?"

"She's useful," Daji insisted. "She's strong, she helped us get here—"

"Really? That's pathetic. You used to get these things done on your own." Riga's lip curled in amusement. "What is it? Did Ziya fuck this one, too? I must say, his standards have dropped."

"It's nothing like that," Daji said quickly. "She's just a child, Riga, don't hurt her—"

"What's this, darling?" Riga gave a low chuckle. "Finally developing a conscience?"

Daji's voice became shrill. "Riga, listen to me, *let her go*."

Riga opened his fingers.

Rin dropped to the ground, clutching noiselessly at her throat. Riga's legs loomed above her. She cringed, bracing herself for a vicious kick, but he merely stepped over her as if she were a footstool.

He was headed for Daji.

"Riga—" Daji started, just before Riga drew his hand back

and slapped her across the face. Daji's head whipped to the side. She cried out and clutched her cheek.

"Shut up," Riga said, and slapped her again. Then again, and again, until a vivid crimson handprint bloomed on Daji's paper-white cheek. "*Shut up*, you fucking whore."

Rin watched them from where she lay, astonished.

For the longest time she had considered Daji—Su Daji, the Vipress, former Empress of Nikan—the most powerful being on earth. From the moment she'd met her, she'd feared her. She'd wanted terribly to *be* her.

But here Daji stood, shoulders hunched like she was trying to shrivel into nothing while Riga battered her like she was a dog. And she was just *taking* it.

"Did you think I'd forgotten?" Riga asked hoarsely. "You treacherous little bitch, did you think I don't know who put me here?"

He raised his hand high. Daji shrank against the wall and loosed a whimpering sob.

"Oh, don't be like that." He put his fingers under Daji's chin and forced her head up. He sighed. "You used to be so pretty when you cried. When did you stop being so pretty?"

Rin wanted to vomit.

Surely Daji wouldn't take this. Surely she would strike back. Surely Jiang would defend her.

But they only looked away—Daji at her hands, Jiang at the ground. They were both trembling. Then Rin realized that this was nothing new for them; this was a trained response to a terror they'd lived with for years. A terror so incapacitating that now, twenty years later, after half a lifetime of freedom from the man they'd hated, they still cowered meekly before him like whipped dogs.

Rin was astounded.

What had Riga done to them?

And if she brought him back down the mountain, what would he do to *her*?

Kill him, said the Phoenix. *Kill him now.*

Riga's back was turned to her. She could end this in seconds; all it took was a quick hop, lunge, and stab. She clasped the hilt of her knife, rose to her feet as silently as she could, and dug her heels into the ground. She could call on the Phoenix, but sometimes steel was faster than fire—

No. No. If she hurt the Trifecta, then she was alone. She'd come this far. He was her last, best hope; she couldn't throw this away.

She knew she'd woken a monster. But she'd known this from the start; she'd known she needed monsters on her side.

"I'm not your enemy," she said. "And I'm not your servant, either. I'm the last Speerly. And I came to seek your help."

Riga didn't turn around, but his hand dropped from Daji's chin. He stood very still, head cocked. Daji stumbled back, rubbing her jaw, staring at Rin with wide-eyed astonishment.

"I know what you did." Rin's words came out shaky and girlish; she couldn't help it. "I know everything. And I don't care. The past doesn't matter. Nikan is in danger *now*, and I need you."

Riga turned. His eyes were wide, his mouth half-open in an incredulous smile.

"You know?" He strode toward her, his steps low and menacing like a tiger approaching its prey. "What do you think you know?"

"Speer." Rin took a step back without thinking. Everything about him radiated danger; that grin on his face made her want to spin around and run. "I saw—I know—I know you gave it up. I know you let them."

"Is that what you think?" He bent toward her. "Then why don't you want to kill me, child?"

"Because I don't care," she breathed. "Because there's another enemy at our shores that's ten times worse than you, and I need you to destroy them. You made a necessary choice at Speer. I get it. I've traded lives, too."

Riga regarded her for a long moment in silence. Rin did her

best to meet his gaze, heart pounding so furiously she was afraid it might burst.

She couldn't read his expression. She had no idea what he was thinking. Something was off, something was wrong—she could tell from Daji's terrified expression—but she couldn't flee, she had to see this through.

Then Riga threw his head back and laughed. His cackle was a horrible thing, so like Nezha's, and so gleefully cruel. "You don't know shit."

"I don't *care*," Rin repeated desperately. "The Hesperians are *here*, Riga, they're right outside, you need to work with me—"

He lifted a hand. "Oh, shut up."

An invisible force slammed her forward into the ground. Her kneecaps screamed in agony. She hunched over on all fours, trying and failing to get up.

Riga knelt down before her and clasped her face in his hands. "Look at me."

Rin squeezed her eyes shut.

It didn't matter. Riga's fingertips dug so hard into her temples she thought he was about to shatter her skull in his hands. A cruel, cold presence forced its way into her mind, digging through her memories with callous disregard, wrenching out everything that made Rin go dry-mouthed in fright. Auntie Fang, twisting skin to form welts under her clothes where no one could see. Shiro, carelessly jamming needles into her veins with brutish force. Petra, tracing cold metal against her naked body, thin lips curling with amusement every time Rin flinched.

It went on for what seemed like an eternity. Rin wasn't aware she was screaming until her throat convulsed from the strain.

"Ah," Riga said. "Here we are."

The memories paused. She found herself bent over the floor, panting, drool dripping from her mouth.

"Look at me," Riga said again, and this time she wearily obeyed.

There was no fight left in her. She just wanted this over. If she just did what he said, would it be over?

"Is this what you wanted to see?" Riga inquired.

His face morphed into Altan's. He grinned.

And then, at last, Rin understood what Daji had meant when she said that Riga's power lay in fear.

He didn't just terrorize with brute force. He terrorized with pure, overwhelming *power*. He'd probed her memory for the one person she'd once thought so intimidatingly strong that she couldn't help but obey—no, *longed* to obey, because fear and love were really just opposite sides of the same coin.

She saw now what bound Jiang and Daji to Riga. It was the same reason she'd once been drawn to Altan. With Altan, it had always been so easy. She never had to think. He raged and she followed, blind and unquestioning, because marveling at his purpose was simpler than coming up with one of her own. He'd terrified her. She would have died for him.

"Altan Trengsin," Riga mused. "I remember the name. Hanelai's nephew, wasn't he, Ziya? Pride of the island?"

New images invaded her mind.

She saw waves crashing against a jagged shore. She saw a boy wading through the shallows. He was very young, no more than four or five. He stood alone on the beach, trident in his hand, his dark eyes narrowed in concentration as he watched the waves. His inky-black hair fell in soft curls around sun-bronzed cheeks, and his face was tight with a mature, intense focus that belonged to someone much older. Slowly, without glancing away from the water, he lifted the trident over his shoulder in a practiced stance Rin had seen many times before.

She realized with a jolt that she was looking at Altan.

"Come," said a voice—Riga's voice from her mouth, for this was Riga's memory, and she was experiencing something Riga had already done from within his body.

Twenty years ago, Yin Riga approached Altan Trengsin and said, "Come now. Your aunt is waiting."

Riga extended his hand. And Altan, without question or hesitation, took it.

She heard Riga's laughter ringing in her mind. *Now do you see?*

Rin stumbled back, horrified, but she was still caught in the vision, forced to watch as long as Riga wanted her to, and she couldn't bring herself back to her senses. She couldn't bring herself back to her body, couldn't return to Mount Tianshan—could only keep watching as Riga led Altan to a boat waiting down the shore, a boat flying Federation colors.

Other children were waiting on the decks. Dozens of them. And standing among them, one man—a thin, spindly man whose hands moved across the children's shoulders, whose narrow eyes danced with curious glee as he observed them the same way he had once observed Rin, whose narrow, sharp-chinned face had hovered above her in the worst moments of her life and haunted her nightmares even now.

Shiro.

Twenty years ago, Dr. Eyimchi Shiro took Altan's hand and guided him on board.

Then it all fit together; the final, horrible piece of the puzzle fell into place. The Federation had not kidnapped Speer's children. It was the Trifecta. It had been Riga all along; Riga who delivered the children to the Federation; Riga who forced Hanelai's hand when she dissented, and then watched her island go up in smoke when she made the wrong choice.

"You're right." Riga removed his hands from Rin's temples, leaving her gasping on her knees. "I make hard choices. I do whatever I must. But I do not work with Speerlies. I tried with Hanelai. That bitch tried to defect. Your kind don't serve, they only cause trouble. And you'll be no different."

Rin's head throbbed. She heaved for breath, glaring at the floor until her vision stopped spinning, trying to buy a few seconds.

She'd been so terribly wrong. There was no appeasing Riga. She couldn't beg an alliance from someone who didn't think her human.

This wasn't about humiliation.

This was about survival.

Then the calculus became starkly clear.

She'd hoped so desperately for a different outcome. She'd climbed that mountain willing to do almost anything for the Trifecta. She'd known they had done awful things. She would have overlooked those things, if only she could borrow their power. If it meant victory against the Republic, she would have forgiven the Trifecta for almost anything.

But not this.

She lifted her head. "Thank you."

Riga's mouth twisted into a sneer. "What for, little girl?"

"For making this easy." She closed her eyes, focusing through her pain onto a singular point of rage. Then she turned her palm out.

The burst of flame lasted for only two seconds, just long enough to singe Riga's clothes before it died away.

The Phoenix hadn't disappeared. Rin could still feel her link to the god, clearer than ever in the Heavenly Temple. But the Phoenix was suppressed, screeching, struggling against an enemy that Rin could not perceive.

Somewhere on the spiritual plane, the gods were at war.

Hand-to-hand combat, then.

Rin drew her sword. Riga pulled his blade from atop the altar just before she charged at him, parrying with a force that sent shock waves ripping through her arm.

He was unexpectedly slow. Bizarrely clumsy. He made the right moves, but always a split second behind, as if he were still remembering how to channel thoughts into actions. After twenty years asleep, Riga had yet to acclimate to his physical body, and only that disadvantage was keeping Rin alive.

It wasn't enough. Her swordplay was awful. She never practiced with her left hand. She had no balance. Slow as he was, she only barely managed to keep pace, and in seconds he put her on the defensive. She couldn't even think about striking back; she was so focused on avoiding his blade.

Riga raised his sword overhead. She jerked her blade up just in time to meet a blow meant to cleave her in two. Her shoulder buckled from the impact. She tensed, anticipating a side strike, but Riga did not lift his blade from hers. He pressed down, harder and harder, until the crossed steel was inches from Rin's face.

"Kneel," he said.

Rin's knees shook.

"I will be merciful," he said. "I will permit you to serve. You need only kneel."

Her arm gave out. He sliced down. She dove to the left, barely avoiding his blade, as her own sword dropped from her numb fingers to the floor. Riga scraped his foot over the hilt and kicked it to the other side of the room.

"Ziya." He glanced over his shoulder. "Get rid of that."

Jiang was still standing where he'd frozen when Riga stepped off the altar. At the sound of his name, he lifted his head, brows furrowed in confusion.

"Master," Rin breathed. "Please . . ."

Jiang moved slowly toward the sword, bent over to pick it up, then hesitated. His eyes landed on Rin and he frowned, squinting as if he was trying to remember where he had seen her before.

"Come now, Ziya." Riga sounded bored. "Don't dawdle."

Jiang blinked, then lifted the sword off the ground.

Rin hastened to her feet, hand scrabbling for her knife only to remember that she was reaching with phantom fingers, that her right hand *wasn't there*.

She lunged at Riga's legs. If she could just knock him off balance, get him on the ground—

He saw her coming. He stepped aside and swept his knee up high into her sternum. Something cracked in her rib cage. She dropped to the floor, unable to even gasp.

"Had enough?" He bent down, seized her collar, and dragged her up to face him. Then he slammed a fist into her stomach.

The blow sent her careening back until she hit the wall. Her head cracked against stone. Stars exploded behind her eyes. She slid bonelessly to the ground, choking. She couldn't breathe. Couldn't move. Couldn't perceive anything but pulsing, white-hot flashes of pain.

She had no weapon, no shield, and no fire.

For the first time, it sank in that she might not leave this temple alive.

"I hate to do this." Riga tapped his blade to the side of her neck, as if practicing his swing before he took it. "Killing off the last of you. It's so final. But you Speerlies never gave me a choice. You always had to be so very *troublesome.*"

He drew his sword back. Rin squeezed her eyes shut and waited for the blade to land.

It never did.

She heard a splintering crack. She opened her eyes. Jiang stood between her and Riga. His staff was in splinters, and crimson stained both his torso and Riga's blade. Jiang twisted around. Their eyes met.

"Run," he whispered.

Riga swung his sword again. Something black whistled through the air, and Riga's blade skidded across the ground.

"I forgot," Riga sneered. "You always had a soft spot for Speerlies."

He aimed a savage kick at the wound in Jiang's side. Jiang doubled over. In the corner, Daji gasped and clutched her stomach, her faced pinched with pain.

Rin hesitated, torn between Jiang and the door.

"He can't kill me," Jiang hissed. "*Run.*"

She staggered to her feet. The door was ten feet away. That was nothing. Her legs hurt so much, everything hurt so much, but she bit down the pain and forced herself to keep moving. Five feet—

A bang exploded behind her. She tripped and fell.

"*Run,*" Jiang repeated, though his voice sounded strained. Rin smelled blood. She wanted to look back but knew she couldn't, knew she had to keep moving. Three feet. She was so close.

"Call them," Jiang shouted. "End this."

Rin knew precisely what he meant.

Outside, she stumbled into the fog.

She refused to feel guilt for this. This was her only option; this was what Jiang wanted. He'd made his choice, and now she made hers. She turned an open palm to the sky.

I unleash you.

This time the Phoenix came. The Dragon was distracted, struggling against the Gatekeeper, and so her god was free. The fire surged through her arm and up into the mist, a shining beacon against a backdrop of gray.

The Phoenix shrieked, delighted. In that moment Rin felt its divine presence closer, more intimately than she ever had, a synchronicity that surpassed what she had once felt on Speer. Here where the boundary between man and god was blurred, their wills overlapped until they were not separate beings, one channeled through the other, but a single entity, ripping through the fabric of the world to rewrite history.

Fire pierced the dense mist, spiraling into a pillar so tall and bright that Rin thought it must be visible to the entire world. The clouds that shrouded Mount Tianshan shriveled away, exposing the pagoda against the bare face of stone.

Nezha must have seen. Rin was counting on it. He'd been following her all this way, and now she'd delivered to him everything he and the Hesperians wanted—all the world's most powerful shamans clustered in one place, open targets trapped atop the mountain.

Here's your chance, Nezha. Now take it.

One by one, the airships appeared from behind the clouds, blurry black shapes that homed in on her unmistakable beacon. They had been hovering, waiting, searching for a target. Now they had it.

They flew into a semicircular formation, surrounding the pagoda from every angle. Rin couldn't see Nezha from this distance, but she imagined he was riding in the center of the fleet, eyes trained on her. She raised her hand and waved.

"Hello there," she murmured. "You're welcome."

Then she extinguished her flames and ran, just as every dirigible in the sky turned its cannons toward the mountain and fired.

Booms split the sky. They didn't fade. They rolled on like endless thunder, growing louder and louder until Rin couldn't hear her own thoughts. She couldn't tell if she'd been knocked off the ground; she moved her legs but couldn't feel anything below her knees except deep reverberations in her bones. She moved like she was floating, buoyed by a numbing shock that muted all pain.

Something pulsed in the air. Not a noise, but a *sensation*—she could feel it, thick like congealed porridge, a crackling stillness that by now was all too familiar.

She hazarded a glance behind her. Beasts poured out of the pagoda—not the malformed, shadowy entities that Rin had seen Jiang summon before, but solid creatures, infinite in number, color, size, and shape, as if Jiang had really opened the gates to the Emperor's Menagerie and let every single one of those clawed, fanged, winged, and screeching creatures into the mortal world.

They shifted endlessly between forms. Rin watched as a phoenix became a kirin became a lion became some winged *thing* that shot toward the dirigible fleet like an arrow, accompanied by the screeching cacophony of its brothers and sisters.

The Hesperians fired back. The rumbling grew so loud that the mountain itself seemed to shake.

Good, Rin thought. *Hit them with everything you have.*

Let this be the ultimate test. Let this prove that even the most legendary shamans in Nikara history could not stand up to the machines of the Divine Architect.

Can you see this, Sister Petra? Is this vindicating?

She wanted to stand still and watch, to marvel at destruction that for once was not her own doing. She wanted to see, the same way little children ripped down birds' nests with glee, just how great a scar the two self-proclaimed great powers on this earth could rip into the fabric of the world.

A missile exploded overhead. Rin flung herself forward just as a boulder crashed into the dirt behind her. Shards of debris, still red-hot from impact, splattered the backs of her legs.

Get a fucking grip, said Altan's voice as she clambered upright, heart slamming against her ribs. *And get the fuck off this mountain.*

She needed a quicker way down. The missiles hadn't hit her yet, but they inevitably would; when dirigibles fired en masse they were not discriminate.

She paused, considering the fleet.

The airships weren't going to land. That would be stupid. But they had to get in close. They couldn't aim properly at the pagoda from too far away; they had to dip down to get a good shot at the Trifecta.

Which gave Rin a single, obvious way out.

She exhaled sharply. *Ah, fuck.*

She saw only one dirigible in jumping range, and she wasn't sure she'd be able to make that leap. In top fighting condition, she'd have taken it with confidence. But she was exhausted. Every part of her body was battered and hurting. Her legs felt weighed down with anchors, and her lungs burned for breath.

The closest dirigible was veering upward. If it scaled too high she'd never catch it—she couldn't jump at that trajectory.

No more time to think. It was now or never. She crouched low, pushed her feet against the dirt, and summoned every last ounce of her strength as she took a running leap off the cliff.

Her fingers just snagged an iron rod at the bottom of the carriage. The dirigible tilted dangerously to one side, jerked down by her sudden weight. Rin curled her fingers tighter as her other wrist flailed uselessly in the air. The dirigible readjusted its balance. Its pilot must have known she was there—he swerved back and forth, trying to shake her off. The thin metal rod dug into her flesh, nearly slicing through her joints. She screamed in pain.

Something—one of Jiang's beasts, a misfired missile, or flying debris; Rin couldn't see—struck the opposite side of the carriage.

The dirigible lurched, flipping her upward. She strained to maintain her grip. They weren't anywhere near solid ground yet—if she let go now she'd fall to her death.

She made the mistake of looking down. The chasm loomed. Her heart skipped a beat, and she squeezed her eyes shut.

The dirigible kept rising. She felt it turn away from the mountain, retreating to safer skies. The lurching had stopped.

The pilot had figured out who she was. He wanted to take her alive.

No. Oh, no no no . . .

Something shrieked above her head. Rin glanced up. Something had punctured the side of the dirigible—the balloon deflated as air escaped the hole with a deafening whistle.

The dirigible's movements grew erratic, dipping toward the mountain one moment and twisting away the next. Rin fought to keep a hold but her fingers were slick with sweat; her thumb slipped off the iron bar, numb, and then it was just four fingers between her and the chasm.

The pilot had lost all control. The dirigible was starting to nosedive.

But—thank the gods—it was careening *toward* the mountain.

Rin eyed the craggy surface, fighting to stay calm. She had to jump as soon as she was close enough, just before the airship crushed her in its wreckage.

The rock face loomed closer and closer.

She took a deep breath.

Three, two, one. She exhaled and let go.

Am I dead?

The world was black. Her body was on fire, and she could not see.

But death would not hurt so much. Death was easy; she'd come close so many times now that she knew dying was like falling backward into a black pit of comforting nothingness. Death made the pain go away. But hers only intensified.

Ah, Rin. Altan's voice rang in her temples—amused, teasing. *Ever the surprise.*

For once she did not recoil from his presence. She was grateful for the company. She needed him to filter through the horror.

Something wrong?

"I'm the only one now," she said. "They . . . they're not . . . I'm the only one."

It's nice to be the only one.

"But I wanted allies."

He just laughed. *Shouldn't you know better by now?*

And he was right—she should have known better than to put her fate in the hands of people more powerful than she. She should have learned, many times over, that everyone she pledged her faith to would inevitably use and abuse her.

But she'd *wanted* to follow the Trifecta. She wanted someone else to fight her battles for her, because she was so, so exhausted. She wanted Jiang back, and she wanted to believe Daji was the woman she hoped she'd be. She'd wanted to believe she could foist this war onto someone else. And she'd always clung far too hard to her illusions.

Forget those assholes, Altan said. *We can do this on our own.*

She snorted, tasting blood. "Yeah."

After a long time, the explosions stopped. By then, Rin's vision was fully restored. At first she'd seen only blotches of color—great patches of red against the white sky, flaring with every boom. Then her vision clarified, differentiated between billows of smoke and the fires that created them.

She lay flat on her back, head tilted to the sky, and laughed.

She'd done it.

She'd fucking done it.

In one blow, she'd rid herself of the Trifecta and the Hesperian fleet. Two of the greatest forces the Empire had ever seen—gone, wiped off the face of the earth with no monument but ash. The entire balance of the world had just changed. She saw the forces reversing in her mind.

For so long she'd been fighting a mad, hopeless, desperate war. And now it looked so very, very winnable.

Ever so faintly in the back of her mind, though muted and strained by the spiritual back door that ran through Kitay's mind, she heard the Phoenix laughing, too—the low, harsh cackle of a deity who had finally gotten everything it had wanted.

"Fuck you all," she whispered at the coiling smoke that dissipated up into the reforming mist. She made a rude gesture with her hand. "That's for Speer."

She would have seen something if anyone in the Heavenly Temple were still alive. She would have seen movement. As she stared, the mountain mist played tricks on her eyes, kept making her believe she'd caught the faintest glimpse of a silhouette stumbling out of the pagoda. But whenever she looked closer, all she saw was smoke.

It took a few moments for her rational mind to start working again.

Basics first. First she had to get off this mountain. Then she had to get medical care. Her open wounds weren't deep, and most of them had stopped bleeding, but a million other things—exposure, cracked ribs, bruised organs—might kill her if she didn't move fast.

But moving was agony. Her knees buckled with every step. Her ribs shrieked in protest every time she breathed. She clenched her teeth and willed herself to trudge forward. She couldn't manage more than a pathetic lurch with every step. The pain in her legs intensified—something, somewhere, was broken. It didn't matter. Kitay was waiting for her below. She just had to get back to Kitay.

Silent wreckage littered the base of Mount Tianshan. Not just the debris of ruined dirigibles—Nezha's bombers had also decimated Cholang's troops. She saw fragments of ground cannons mixed in with airship shells. Craters formed horribly clean hemispheres in the dirt.

She stood a moment in the silence, breathing in the ash. Nothing moved. She was the only survivor in sight.

Then she heard it—a distorted hum, the sloping whine of a dying engine. She spun around. Looked up.

In the moonlight she saw only its black silhouette—small but growing, flying straight toward her. It wouldn't make it. Whatever kept it alight was ruined—she saw smoke trailing out the back in thick, billowing clouds.

But it was still firing.

Fuck.

Rin dropped to the ground.

The bullets scattered pointlessly across scorched ground. The pilot wasn't aiming, he just needed to destroy something, anything, before his life spiraled out of his hands. The dirigible loosed one last round of cannons, then careened into the side of the mountain and exploded in a ball of fire.

She stood up, unscathed.

"You missed me!" she screamed at the mountainside, at the spot where plumes furled up from the last dirigible's wreckage. "*You fucking missed!*"

Of course no one answered. Her voice, thin and reedy, faded without echo into the frigid air.

But she screamed it again, and then again, and then again. It felt so good to say that she'd survived, that she'd fucking finally come out on top, that she didn't even care that she was screaming to corpses.

PART III

CHAPTER 22

ARLONG, NINE YEARS PRIOR

"Nezha." Yin Vaisra beckoned with one finger. "Come here."

Delighted, Nezha ran to his side. He'd been in the middle of a grueling Classics lesson, but his tutor had bowed and left the room as soon as his father appeared in the doorway.

"How go your studies?" Vaisra asked. "Are you working hard?"

Nezha swallowed his instinct to babble, instead mulling carefully over his response. Vaisra had never asked him questions like this before; he'd never displayed much interest in any of his children except Jinzha. Nezha didn't want his father to think him a braggart or a fool.

"Tutor Chau says I'm progressing well," he said cautiously. "I've mastered the fundamentals of Old Nikara grammar, and I can now recite one hundred and twenty-two poems from the Jin dynasty. Next week we'll—"

"Good." Vaisra sounded neither particularly interested nor pleased. He turned. "Walk with me."

Somewhat crestfallen, Nezha followed his father out of the eastern wing into the main reception hall. He wasn't quite sure where they were going. The palace of Arlong was a grand, chilly place consisting mostly of empty air and long, high-ceilinged hallways draped with tapestries depicting the history of the Dragon Province dating back to the fall of the Red Emperor's dynasty.

Vaisra paused before a detailed portrait of Yin Vara, the former Dragon Warlord before the Second Poppy War. Nezha had always hated this tapestry. He'd never known his grandfather, but Vara's stern, gaunt visage made him feel small and insignificant every time he passed beneath.

"Have you ever wanted to rule, Nezha?" Vaisra asked.

Nezha frowned, confused. "Why would I?"

Ruling had never been in his stars. Jinzha, the firstborn son, stood to inherit the title of Dragon Warlord and all the responsibilities that came with it. Nezha was only the second son. He was destined to become a soldier, his brother's most loyal general.

"You've never considered it?"

Nezha felt vaguely as if he were failing a test, but he didn't know what else to say. "It's not my place."

"No, I suppose not." Vaisra was silent for a moment. Then he asked, "Would you like to hear a story?"

A *story*? Nezha hesitated, unsure of how to respond. Vaisra never told him stories. But although Nezha had no idea how to converse with his father, he couldn't bear to let this opportunity pass.

"Yes," he said carefully. "I would."

Vaisra glanced down at him. "Do you know why we don't let you go to those grottoes?"

Nezha perked up. "Because of the monsters?"

Would this be a monster story? He hoped it would be. He felt a flicker of excitement. His childhood nurses knew that his favorite tales were about the myriad beasts rumored to lurk in the grottoes—the dragons, the cannibal crabs, the fish-women who made you love them and then drowned you once you got too close.

"Monsters?" Vaisra chuckled. Nezha had never heard his father chuckle before. "Do you like the grotto stories?"

Nezha nodded. "Very much."

Vaisra put a hand on his shoulder.

Nezha suppressed a flinch. He wasn't afraid of his father's touch—Vaisra had never been violent toward him. But Vaisra had never caressed him like this, either. Hugs, kisses, reassuring touches—those belonged to Nezha's mother, Lady Saikhara, who nearly suffocated her children with affection.

Nezha had always thought of his father as a statue—remote, foreboding, and untouchable. Vaisra seemed to him less like a man than a god, the perfect ideal of everything he'd been raised to become. Every word Yin Vaisra articulated was direct and concise, every action efficient and deliberate. Never did he show his children affection beyond the odd somber nod of approval. Never did he tell fairy tales.

So what was going on?

For the first time Nezha noticed that his father's eyes looked somewhat glassy, that his speech seemed much slower than usual. And his breath . . . a pungent, sour smell wafted into Nezha's face every time Vaisra spoke. Nezha had smelled that odor twice before—once in the servants' quarters, when he'd been wandering around past bedtime where he shouldn't have been, and once in Jinzha's room.

He squirmed under Vaisra's hand, suddenly uncomfortable. He didn't want a story anymore. He wanted to get back to his lesson.

"I'll tell you a grotto story," Vaisra said. "You know Arlong rose as a southern power in the decades of warfare after the Red Emperor's death. But in the last years of the Red Emperor's reign, after he abandoned Dragon Province to build a new capital at Sinegard, Arlong was regarded as a cursed place. These islands lay inside a valley of death, of crashing waves and flooding riverbanks. No ships that sailed past the Red Cliffs survived. Everything smashed to death against those rocks."

Nezha kept utterly still as he listened. He had never heard this story before. He wasn't sure that he liked it.

"Finally," Vaisra continued, "a man named Yu, learned in shamanic arts, called down the Dragon Lord of the Western River and begged his help to control the rivers. Overnight, Arlong transformed. The waters turned calm. The flooding ceased. Arlong's people built canals and rice paddies between the islands. In a few short years, Dragon Province became the jewel of the Nikara Empire, a land of beauty and plenty." Vaisra paused. "Only Yu continued to suffer."

Vaisra seemed caught in a reverie, speaking not to Nezha but at the tapestries, as if he were reciting dynastic lineage into the silent hall.

"Um." Nezha swallowed. "Why—"

"Nature can't be altered," Vaisra said. "Only held at bay. Always, the waters of Arlong threatened to break their leash and drown the new city in their fury. Yu was forced to spend his life in a state of shamanic hallucination, always calling upon the Dragon, always hearing its whispers in his ears. After several dozen years of this, Yu wanted desperately to end his life. And when the god's takeover was complete, when he could no longer die, he wanted to ensconce himself in the Chuluu Korikh. But he knew that if he sought peace, someone had to take up his mantle. Yu could not be that cruel, nor that selfish. So what happened?"

Nezha didn't know. But he could put this together like the pieces of a logic puzzle, like the kind that his tutors were always training him to solve for the Keju exam.

Father said this was a grotto story. And grotto stories were about monsters.

"Yu transformed," Nezha said. "He became the monster."

"Not a monster, Nezha." Vaisra stroked a lock of hair behind Nezha's ear. "A savior. He made the ultimate sacrifice for Arlong. But Arlong forgot him almost immediately. They saw his horrifying new form, his winding coils and sharp scales, and they received him with not gratitude but fear. Even his own wife did not recognize him. She took one look at him and screamed. Her brothers threw rocks at him and drove him out of the village, back into the grotto where he had spent decades praying to protect them. He . . ."

Vaisra's voice trailed away.

Nezha glanced up. "Father?"

Vaisra was gazing silently at the tapestries. Confused, Nezha followed his eyes. None of these tapestries contained the story he'd just heard. They were all dynastic portraits, an endless row of finely embroidered likenesses of Nezha's long-dead predecessors.

What was Father trying to tell him?

What sacrifices had the House of Yin made for Arlong?

"Your tutors told me you wanted to visit the grottoes," Vaisra said suddenly.

Nezha stiffened. Was that what this was about? Was he in trouble? Yes, he'd asked, many more times than he should have. He'd begged and whined, pledging to keep to the shallows or even the opposite riverbank if only they'd let him get near enough to catch a glimpse inside the cave mouths.

"I apologize, Father," he said. "I won't ask again—I was just curious—"

"About what?"

"I thought—I mean, I'd heard about treasures, and I thought . . ." Nezha trailed off. His cheeks flamed. His words sounded stupid and childish as he uttered them. Silently he swore never to disobey his father's word again.

But Vaisra didn't chide him. He just gazed at Nezha for a very long time, his expression inscrutable. At last, he patted Nezha again on the shoulder.

"Don't go to those grottoes, Nezha." He sounded very tired then. "Don't take on the burden of an entire nation. It's too heavy. And you aren't strong enough."

CHAPTER 23

"If I counted right, the explosions on Mount Tianshan destroyed almost two-thirds of the Hesperian fleet in Nikan," Kitay said. "That's . . . that's a lot."

"Just two-thirds?" Cholang asked. "Not all?"

"Nezha didn't send the entire fleet west," Kitay said. "The last I heard, the Consortium had lent him forty-eight aircraft. We brought down six at the Anvil. I saw about thirty at the mountain. And we know that two escaped back west."

"With any luck, Nezha wasn't on them," Venka muttered.

Rin rubbed at her aching eyes, too exhausted to laugh. The four of them—herself, Cholang, Kitay, and Venka—stood around the table in Cholang's hut. They were all wan and twitchy with fatigue, yet their conference felt suffused with an urgent, burning energy. A quiet, astonished confidence; a taste of hope that none of them had felt for months.

This was the difference between fleeing for their lives and planning an assault. They all understood the magnitude of what might be in reach. It was madness. It was thrilling.

"How quickly do you think the Hesperians will send replacements?" Rin asked.

"I'm not sure," Kitay said. "They're probably vacillating. When

I was in Arabak, I kept hearing rumors that the Consortium was reconsidering their investments. The longer Nezha took to solidify the south, the touchier they got about military aid. The Consortium's a tricky entity—they need a unanimous vote from all member countries to commit troops in any foreign location. And their constituents are getting less comfortable losing lives—and the costs of airships, which are considerable—to a power they can't understand."

"So they're cowards," Cholang said. "Paper tigers. They came in ready to win our wars for us, but the moment they get scared, they're all going to back off?"

"It won't end this easily," Rin said. "They've had designs on this continent for too long. We won't scare them away with mere threats. We have to make it real." She swallowed and lifted her chin. "If we want to finish this for good, we'll have to occupy Arlong."

No one laughed.

It was amazing how that simple sentence, which a week ago would have just sounded like a cruel joke, now seemed completely feasible. Defeating the Republic wasn't a daydream anymore. It was a question of time frame.

Rin had survived the long march with only the barest fragments of an army. The numbers Kitay had collected were depressing. Half the soldiers who had left the Anvil were now dead or missing. The casualty rate for civilians reached two-thirds.

But Rin still commanded the survivors. And right now, she held the biggest military advantage she'd possessed since this war began.

The Hesperians were rattled. Nezha had just suffered a defeat of epic proportions. Instead of bombing her to pieces under open skies, he'd followed Rin to Mount Tianshan and lost most of his fleet. This disaster fell on his shoulders, and the Consortium surely knew it. For once, the southerners had a fighting chance at defeating the Republic. But to capitalize on their momentum, they had to move out as quickly as they could.

"We should attack on two fronts." Rin made a pincer move-ment with her hand. "A double-pronged strategy from the north and south, like the one the Mugenese tried during the Third Poppy War."

"Didn't work so well for them," Venka said.

"Save for me, it would have," Rin said. "They had the right idea—they forced the Empire to split reinforcements along two vulnerable fronts. What's more, Nezha knows he's running low on manpower. He'll throw everything he has at us if we're concen-trated in a single front. I don't want to take that gamble. I'd rather bleed him dry."

"Then we hit him from the northwest and the northeast." Seamlessly, Kitay picked up Rin's thoughts and spun them out loud into an articulable plan. "We send a first column through Ram, Rat, and Tiger Provinces. Then the main force will strike in the heartland, right when he's spread his forces thin trying to maintain territory that he's just gotten his hands on. If we act fast, we could have this wrapped up within six months."

"Hold on," said Cholang. "You'll accomplish all this with what army?"

"Well," Kitay said, "yours."

"I lost eighty soldiers at Mount Tianshan," Cholang said. "I'm not about to send more to their deaths."

"You'll die if you stay here," Rin said. "Did you think Nezha would leave you alone now that you've cast your lot? You're al-ready dead men walking. It's a question of when and how."

"You might buy a few extra months while he's occupied with us," Kitay added. "But if the Republic can finish us off, then you certainly have no chance. Ask yourself if it's worth several more months living in tents on the plains."

Cholang said nothing.

"You won't think of a rejoinder," Venka informed him. "He's thought about five arguments ahead."

Cholang scowled. "Go on, then."

"The northeastern front will obviously be a feint—it doesn't determine the endgame—but we still gain a hard material advantage from striking there early," Kitay said. "It's got bases of wartime industry—armories, shipyards, all that good stuff. So even if Nezha doesn't take us seriously up north, it's a win either way." He nodded to Venka. "You go with Cholang. Take a couple hundred men from the Southern Army; you pick."

"Not that I'm refusing this assignment," Venka said, "but suppose you've miscalculated, and we head straight into a bloodbath?"

"That won't happen," Kitay assured her. "Nezha doesn't have a loyal local base in the north. They've only recently bowed to the Republic, and the civilians couldn't care less who wins this fight. They've lost their Empress, they've lost Jun Loran, and they're rankling under Arlong's rule just as much as we are. They don't have an ideological stake in this."

"They're the north, though," Venka said. "Part of their ideology is hating you lot. They won't bow to peasants."

"Then it's a good thing we're sending Sring Venka," Kitay said. "You porcelain-faced Sinegardian princess, you."

Venka snickered. "Fine."

"But what are you doing on the southeastern front?" Cholang asked. "We'd be leaving you with shards of an army."

"That's fine," Rin said. "We've got shamans."

"What shamans?" Cholang asked. "You're the only one left."

"I don't have to be."

It was as if she'd placed a lit fuse on the center of the table. The room fell silent. Kitay stiffened. Venka and Cholang stared at her, openmouthed.

Rin refused to let that faze her. She wouldn't get defensive; that would only justify their incredulity. She had been wondering how to introduce this proposal since she descended from the mountain. And then it became obvious—to make madness seem normal, she merely had to discuss it as if it were common sense. She just had to distort their idea of *normal*.

"Su Daji had the right idea," she continued calmly. "The only way we have a chance against the Hesperians is to match their Maker with our own gods. The Trifecta could have managed it. They might even have seized the Empire by now, if I'd let Riga have his way. But they were despots. Over time, they would have done more harm than good."

Now for the crucial leap of logic. "But if we haven't got them, we need our own shamans. We've got hundreds of soldiers who would be willing to do it. We just need to train them. We've set a campaign schedule of six months. I can get recruits in fighting form in two weeks."

She looked around the table, waiting for someone to object.

Everything hinged on what happened next. Rin was testing the boundaries of her authority in the aftermath of a tectonic shift in power. This felt so different from the first time she'd vaulted herself into leadership, mere months ago when she'd addressed Ma Lien's men with a dry mouth and quivering knees. Back then she'd been scared, grasping for straws, and disguising her utter lack of a strategy with feigned bravado.

Now she knew exactly what she needed to do. She just needed to force everyone onto the same page. She had a vision for the future—something horrifying, something grand. Could she speak it into reality?

"But back when . . ." Venka opened her mouth, closed it, then opened it again. "Rin, I'm just—you told me once that—"

"I understand the risks," Rin said. "Back then I didn't think they were worth it. But you saw what happened on that mountain. It's clear now that they are. The Hesperians still have at least fourteen airships, and that gives them an advantage we can't counter. Not without more of—well, *me*."

There was another silence.

Then Cholang shook his head and sighed. "Look. If any of my men want to volunteer, I won't stop them."

"Thank you," Rin said.

Good enough—that was as much of an endorsement as she was

going to get. So long as Cholang didn't try to stop her, she didn't care how uncomfortable he looked.

She glanced to her right. "Kitay?"

She needed to hear him speak before she could continue. She wasn't waiting for his permission—she'd never needed his permission for anything—but she wanted to hear his confirmation. She wanted someone else, someone whose mind worked far faster than hers ever would, to assess the forces at play and the lives at stake and say, *Yes, these calculations are valid. This sacrifice is necessary. You aren't mad. The world is.*

For a long time Kitay stood still, staring at the table, fingers tapping erratically against the wooden surface. Then he looked up at her. No, he looked right through her. His mind was already somewhere else. He was already thinking past this conversation. "No more than several—"

"We won't need more than a handful," she assured him. "Three at most—just enough that we can spread an attack around multiple planes."

"One for every cardinal direction," he murmured. "Because the impact is exponential if . . ."

"Right," she said. "I get a lot done. I'm not enough. But even one other shaman throws off defense formations like we couldn't dream."

"Fucking hell," Venka said. "How long have you been thinking about this?"

Rin didn't miss a beat. "Since Tikany."

She still hadn't fully won them over. She saw doubt lingering in their eyes—they might not have raised objections, but they still didn't like it.

She felt a pulse of frustration. How could she make them *see*? They had long surpassed wars of steel and bodies clashing on mortal fields. War happened on the divine plane now—her gods versus the Hesperians' Maker. What she'd seen on Mount Tianshan was a vision of the future, of how this would inevitably end.

They couldn't flinch away from that future. They had to fight the kind of war that moved mountains.

"The west does not conceive of this war as a material struggle," she said. "This is about contesting interpretations of divinity. They imagine that because they obey the Divine Architect, they can crush us like ants. We've just proven them wrong. We'll do it again."

She leaned forward, pressing her palm against the table. "We have one chance right now—probably the only chance we'll ever get—to seize this country back. The Republic is reeling, but they're going to recover. We've got to hit them hard before then. And when we do, it can't be a half-hearted assault. We need *overkill*. We need to scare Nezha's allies so badly that they'll scuttle back to their hemisphere and never dare to come back here again."

No one objected. She knew they wouldn't. The objections didn't exist.

"What's your plan for when they lose control?" Kitay asked quietly.

He'd said *when*. Not *if*. This wasn't a hypothetical. They'd moved into the realm of logistics now, which meant she'd already won.

"They won't," she said. The next words she spoke felt like reopened scars, familiar and painful, words that bore the weight of all the guilt that she'd tried so long to suppress. Words belonging to a legacy that now, she knew, she had no choice but to face. "Because we'll be Cike. And the first rule of the Cike is that we cull."

The world looked different when Rin walked out of Cholang's hut.

She saw the same haphazard army camp that she'd encountered walking in. She passed the same flimsy fires flickering under harsh steppe winds; the same clusters of underweight soldiers and civilians with too little to eat, drink, or wear; the same thin, worn, and hungry eyes.

But Rin didn't see weakness here.

She saw an army rebuilding. A nation in the making. Gods, it excited her. Did they understand what they were about to become?

"Look," Kitay said. "They're telling myths about you already."

Rin followed his gaze. A handful of younger soldiers had erected a stage in the center of the camp by pushing two tables together. A white sheet stretched taut between two poles, behind which a small lamp burned, throwing distorted silhouettes onto the blank canvas.

She paused to watch.

The sight of the canvas brought back memories so sweet they hurt: four days of summer among the hot, sticky crowds of Sinegard; the cool relief of the marble flooring in Kitay's family's estate; five-course banquet meals of rich foods she'd never tasted before and hadn't touched since. This puppet show wasn't a fraction as professional as the performance she'd seen during the Summer Festival in Sinegard, which had involved puppets that moved so smoothly, their rods and strings so invisible that Rin almost believed there were little creatures dancing on the other side. These puppeteers were quite visible behind the stage, wearing shabby, hastily stitched props on their hands that vaguely resembled people.

Rin didn't realize that the formless blue figure in front was Nezha until the play began.

"I am the Young Marshal!" The puppeteer adopted the nasal, reedy voice of a petulant child. "My father said we were supposed to win this war!"

"You've led our fleet to disaster!" The other actor spoke in guttural, broken Nikara, signifying a Hesperian soldier. "You idiot boy! Why would you fire on the Trifecta?"

"I didn't know they could fire *back*!"

The following scenes were equally bad, line after line of crude, stupid humor. But in the aftermath of Tianshan, crude humor was what the southerners wanted. They reveled in Nezha's humiliation. It made their impending fight seem winnable.

"Come on." Kitay resumed walking. "It's just more of the same."

"What else are they saying?" Rin asked.

"Who cares?"

"I don't care what they say about Nezha. What are they saying about me?"

"Ah."

He knew what she was really asking. *What do they know?*

"No one knows you turned on the Trifecta," he said after a pause. "They know you went to Mount Tianshan to seek help, and that the shamans inside sacrificed themselves to save us from the dirigible fleet. That's all they know."

"So they think the Trifecta died heroes."

"Wouldn't you assume the same?" Kitay raised an eyebrow at her. "Are you going to correct them?"

She considered that for a moment, and found herself in the curious position of determining a nation's historical narrative.

Did she let the Trifecta's legacy survive?

She could ruin them. She *ought* to ruin them, for what they had done to her.

But the hero narrative was halfway true. One of the Trifecta had died for honor. One, at least, deserved to be remembered as a good man. And that made a lovely myth—the shamans of a previous era of Nikara greatness had given up their lives to ensure a dawn of a new one.

Rin had ended the Trifecta. She could afford them dignity in death, if that was what she chose. She loved that she had the power to choose.

"No," she decided. "Let them linger on in legend."

She could be generous to the Trifecta's ghosts. They could become legends—legends were all they would ever be. For all of Riga, Jiang, and Daji's dreams of glory, their story had ended in the Heavenly Temple. She could allow them to occupy this little prelude in history. She had the far more delightful task of shaping the future. And when she was finished, no one would even remember the Trifecta's names.

Rin had another audience that night before she slept.

She set out alone to meet Chaghan in his camp. The Ketreyids were packing up. Their campfires were stamped out and the evidence buried; their yurts and blankets were rolled up and lashed onto their horses.

"You're not sticking around?" she asked.

"I did what I came here to do." Chaghan didn't ask her what had happened on the mountain. He clearly already knew; he'd greeted her with an impressed grin and a shake of his head. "Well done, Speerly. That was clever."

"Thank you," she said, pleased in spite of herself. Chaghan had never paid her a compliment before. For nearly the entirety of their relationship, since the day they'd first met at Khurdalain, he had treated her like some wayward child incapable of rational decisions.

Now, for the first time, he acted as if he truly respected her.

"Do you think they're dead?" she asked him. "I mean, there's no chance they—"

"Absolutely," he said. "They were powerful, but their anchor bond kept them in command of their own bodies, which means they were always mortal. They've passed on. I've felt it. And good riddance."

She nodded, relieved. "It's what you're owed. For Tseveri."

His lip curled. "Let's not pretend you did that for a blood debt."

"It was a blood debt," she said. "Just not yours. And now you must know what I have to do next."

He exhaled slowly. "I can guess."

"You're not going to try to stop me?"

"You confuse me with my aunt, Rin."

"The Sorqan Sira would have killed me on the spot."

"Oh, she would have assassinated you long ago." Chaghan ran his hand gently across the length of his horse's neck. Rin realized that she knew the creature—it was the same black warhorse that Chaghan had ridden out of the forests by Lake Boyang the last time she'd seen him. He adjusted his saddle as he spoke, tightening every knot with practiced care. "The Sorqan Sira was petrified of the resurgence of Nikara shamanism. She thought it would spell the end of the world."

"And you don't?"

"The world is already ending. You see, the Hundred Clans know that time moves in a circle. There are never any new stories, just old ones told again and again as this universe moves through its cycles of civilization and crumbles into despair. We are on the brink of an age of chaos again, and there's nothing we can do to stop it. I just prefer to back certain horses in the race."

"But you're going to watch the rest from a safe distance," Rin said.

She was being facetious. She knew better than to ask Chaghan to stay and help. She wasn't that selfish—the Nikara had exploited Chaghan's people enough.

If she had to be honest, she would have liked Chaghan to come south with her. She'd never been able to stand him before, but the sight of him brought back memories of the Cike. Of Suni, Baji, Ramsa, and Qara. Of Altan. Of all the Bizarre Children, they were the only ones left, both tasked independently with bringing order to their fracturing nations. Chaghan, somehow, had already succeeded. Rin desperately wished he might lend her his power.

But she'd taken so much from him already. She couldn't demand more.

"With you, I've learned it's best to keep a safe distance from the fallout." Chaghan yanked tight the last knot and patted the horse behind its ears. "Good luck, Speerly. You're mad as they come, but you're not quite as mad as Trengsin."

"I'll take that as a compliment."

"It's the only reason I think you might win."

"Thank you," Rin said, surprised. "For everything."

He acknowledged that with a thin-lipped smile. "There's one last thing before you go. I didn't just want to say goodbye. We need to talk about Nezha."

She tensed. "Yes?"

The horse, as if sensing her unease, whinnied in agitation and stamped its front hooves against the dirt. Chaghan hastily handed its reins off to the nearest rider.

"Sit down," he told her.

She obeyed. Her heart was pounding very hard. "What do you know?"

He sat cross-legged across from her. "I started looking into the Yins after I heard what happened at the Red Cliffs. It was difficult to parse truth from legend—the House of Yin is shrouded in rumors, and they're good at protecting their secrets. But I think I've gotten a better idea of what happened to Nezha. Why he is the way he is." He tilted his head at her. "What do you know about where Nezha derived his abilities?"

"He told me a story once," she said. "It's . . . it's odd. It's not how I thought shamanism worked."

"How so?" Chaghan pressed.

Why did it suddenly feel like her head was swimming? Rin pressed her nails into her palm, trying to slow down her breathing. It shouldn't be this hard to talk about Nezha. She'd been discussing how to kill him with Kitay for months now.

But Chaghan's question brought back memories of Arlong, of rare moments of vulnerability and harsh words she regretted. They made her feel. And she didn't want to feel.

She forced her voice to keep level. "When we need our gods, we call them. But Nezha never sought the dragon. He told me he encountered one when he was young, but when he spoke about it, he made it sound . . . real."

"All gods are real."

"Real on *this* plane," she clarified. "In the material world. He said that when he was a child, he wandered into an underwater grotto and met a dragon, which killed his brother and claimed him—whatever that means. He made it sound like his god walks this earth."

"I see." Chaghan rubbed his chin. "Yes. That's what I thought."

"But—that's—can they *do* that?"

"It's not inconceivable. There are pockets of this world where the boundary between our world and the world of spirit is thinner." Chaghan pressed his palms together to demonstrate. "Mount

Tianshan is one. The Speerly Temple is another. The Nine Curves Grotto is a third. That cave is the source of all Nezha's power.

"The Yins have been linked to the Dragon for a long time. The waters of Arlong are old, and those cliffs are powerful with their history of the dead. Magic flows smoothly through those waters. Have you ever wondered how Arlong is so rich, so lush, even when its surrounding provinces are barren? A divine power has protected the region for centuries."

"But how—"

"You've been to the Dead Island. You see how nothing grows there. Have you ever wondered why?"

"I thought—I mean, wasn't that just Mugenese chemical warfare? Didn't they just poison it?"

Chaghan shook his head. "That's not all. The Phoenix's aura pulses through the island, just like water pulses through Arlong."

"So then the Dragon . . ."

"The Dragon. If you can call it that." Chaghan made a disgusted face. "More like a poor enchanted creature that might have once been a lobster, starfish, or dolphin. It must have swum in the web of the true Dragon's magic and unwittingly become a physical manifestation of the ocean, whose desire is to—"

"To destroy?"

"No. The Phoenix's impulse is to destroy. The ocean wishes to drown, to possess. The treasures of all great civilizations have inevitably fallen into its dark depths, and the Dragon yearns to possess them all. It likes to collect beautiful things."

The way he said it made Rin cringe. "And it's collecting Nezha."

"That's a nice euphemism for it. But the word is too tame. The Dragon doesn't just want to *collect* Nezha like he's some priceless vase or painting. It wants to own him, body and soul."

Bile rose up in Rin's throat as she recalled the way Nezha had shuddered when he spoke of the Dragon.

What did I do to him?

For the first time, she felt a twinge of guilt for pushing Nezha to the edge, for calling him a coward for refusing to invoke the power that might have saved them.

Back then she'd thought Nezha was just acting spoiled and selfish. She'd never understood how he could loathe his gifts so much when they were so clearly useful. She'd hated him for calling them both abominations.

She'd never taken a moment to consider that unlike her, he hadn't chosen his pain as tribute. He couldn't derive satisfaction from it like she could, because for him, it wasn't the necessary price of a way out. For him, it was only torture.

"He's drawn to that creature," Chaghan said. "And he's drawn to that place. He's physically anchored. It is the source of all his power."

Rin took a deep breath. *Focus on what matters.* "That doesn't tell me how to kill him."

"But it tells you where to strike," Chaghan said. "If you want to end Nezha, you'll have to go to the source."

She understood. "I have to take Arlong."

"You must *destroy* Arlong," he agreed. "Otherwise the water will keep healing him. It'll keep protecting him. And you should know by now that when you leave your enemies alive, wars don't end."

CHAPTER 24

The next morning, Rin stepped out of Cholang's hut to discover a crowd of people so vast she couldn't see where it ended.

Kitay had sent out a call summoning volunteers the night before, specifying soldiers older than fifteen but younger than twenty-five. Rin wanted recruits around her age. She needed their rage to be all-consuming and untempered; she needed soldiers who would throw their souls into the void without the cautious timidity she'd grown to associate with men twice and thrice her age.

But it was clear no one had heeded the age limit. The people in the crowd ranged from civilians over sixty to children as young as seven.

Rin stood before the crowd and let herself imagine, just for a moment, what might happen if she made shamans of them all. It wasn't a true option, just an awful, indulgent fantasy. She pictured deserts shifting like whirlpools. Oceans towering like mountains. She saw the whole world turned upside down, frothing with primordial chaos, and it tickled her something awful to know that if she wanted to make that happen, she could.

You would have been so proud, Altan. This is what you always wanted.

"The parameters were fifteen to twenty-five," she told the crowd. "When I come back I don't want to see anyone who doesn't qualify."

She turned and walked back into the hut.

"What now?" Kitay asked, amused. "A written exam?"

"Make them wait," she said. "We'll see who really wants it."

She let them sit for hours. As the day stretched on, more and more trickled away, disabused by the blinding sun and relentless wind. Most of them—the ones that Rin suspected had volunteered out of a temporary, unsustainable bravado—left within the first hour. She was glad to see them go. She was also relieved when the youngest volunteers finally stood and left, either on their own or dragged along by their mothers.

But that still left a crowd of nearly fifty. Still far too many.

Late in the afternoon, after the sun had cut its scorching arc through the sky, Rin came back out to address them.

"Dig a blade under the nail of your fourth finger from the tip to the bed," she commanded. It was a good test of pain tolerance. She'd learned from Altan that that sort of wound healed easily and wasn't prone to infection, but it *hurt*. "If you want this, show me your blood."

Murmurs of hesitation rippled through the crowd. For a moment no one moved, as if they were all trying to decide whether or not she was joking.

"I'm not joking," Rin said. "I have knives if you need them."

Eight volunteers dug their knives into their nail beds as she'd asked. Dark red droplets splattered the dirt. Two screamed; the other six suppressed their cries with clenched jaws.

Rin dismissed everyone else and brought the silent six into the hut.

She recognized only two of them. There was Dulin—the boy she'd found buried alive in Tikany. She was glad to see he had survived the march. Then, to her surprise, there was Pipaji.

"Where's your sister?" Rin asked.

"She's fine," Pipaji said, and didn't elaborate.

Rin regarded her for a moment, then shrugged and surveyed the others. "Did any of you make the march with your families?"

Two of them, both boy soldiers with the faintest hint of whiskers, nodded.

"Do you love them?"

They nodded again.

"If you do this you'll never see them again," Rin said. It wasn't quite the truth, but she had to test their resolve. "It's too dangerous. Your power will be volatile, and I don't have the experience to help you rein it in around civilians, which means you'll only be permitted to spend time around other people in this squadron. Think carefully."

After a long, uneasy silence, both boys stood up and left. Four remained.

"Understand the sacrifice you're making," Rin told them. She felt by now she was belaboring the point. But she owed it to them to reiterate this warning as many times as she could. She didn't need all four shamans. She needed troops who wouldn't lose their nerve halfway through training or scare the others off. "I'm asking you to gamble with your sanity. If you go into the void you'll find monsters on the other side. And you might not be strong enough to claw your way back. My masters died before they could teach me everything they knew. I'll only be a halfway decent guide."

No one said a word. Were they too terrified to speak, or did they just not care?

"You could lose control of your body and mind," she said. "And if that happens, I'll have to kill you."

Again, no reaction.

Dulin raised his hand.

She nodded to him. "Yes?"

"Will we be able to do what you do?" he asked.

"Not so well," she said. "And not so easily. I'm used to it. It will be painful for you."

"How painful?"

"It will be the worst thing you've ever known." She had to be honest; she could not ensnare them in something they didn't understand. "If you fail, then you will lose your mind forever. If you succeed, you'll still never have your mind to yourself again. You'll live on the precipice of insanity. You'll be constantly afraid. Drinking laudanum might become the only way you can get a good night's sleep. You might kill innocent people around you because you don't know what you're doing. You might kill yourself."

Her words were met with blank stares. Rin waited, fully prepared for all of them to stand up and leave.

"General?" Again Dulin raised his hand. "With all due respect, could we stop fucking around and get started?"

So Rin set about the task of creating shamans.

They spent the first evening sitting in a circle on the floor of the hut, resembling village schoolchildren about to learn to write their first characters. First Rin asked for their names. Lianhua was a willowy, wide-eyed girl from Dog Province who bore a series of terrible scars on both arms, her collarbones, and down her back as far as Rin could see. She did not explain them, and nobody was bold enough to ask.

Rin wasn't sure about her. She seemed so terribly frail—she even spoke in a tremulous, barely audible whisper. But Rin knew very well by now that delicate veneers could conceal steel. Either Lianhua would prove her worth, or she'd break down in two days and stop wasting her time.

Merchi, a tall and rangy man a few years older than Rin, was the only experienced soldier among their ranks. He'd been serving in the Fourth Division of the Imperial Militia when the Mugenese invaded; he'd been part of the liberation force on the eastern coast after the longbow island fell, and he'd witnessed the aftermath of Golyn Niis. He'd first seen combat at the Battle of Sinegard.

"I was in the city when you burned half of it down," he told

Rin. "They were whispering about a Speerly then. Never thought I'd be here now."

The one thing that bound them all was unspeakable horror. They had all seen the worst the world had to offer, and they had all come out of the experience alive.

That was important. If you didn't have an anchor, you needed something to help you return from the world of spirit—something thoroughly mortal and human. Altan had his hatred. Rin had her vengeance. And these four recruits had the ferocious, undaunted will to survive under impossible odds.

"What happens now?" Pipaji asked once introductions were finished.

"Now I'm going to give you religion," Rin said.

She and Kitay had struggled all day to come up with a way to introduce the Pantheon to novices. At Sinegard, it had taken Rin nearly an entire year to prepare her mind to process the gods. Under Jiang's instruction she'd solved riddles, meditated for hours, and read dozens of texts on theology and philosophy, all so that she could accept that her presumptions about the natural world were founded on illusions.

Her recruits didn't have that luxury. They'd have to claw their way into heaven.

The necessary, fundamental change lay in their paradigms of the natural world. The Hesperians and the majority of the Nikara both saw the universe as cleanly divided between body and mind. They saw the material world as something separate, immutable, and permanent. But calling the gods required the basic understanding that the world was fluid—that existence itself was fluid—and that the waking world was nothing more than a script that could be written if they could find the right brush, a pattern they could weave in completely different colors if they just knew how to work the loom.

The hardest part of Rin's training had been belief. But it was so easy to believe when the evidence of supernatural power was right in front of you.

"We trust that the sun will rise every morning even if we don't know what moves it," Kitay had said. "So just show them the sun."

Rin opened her palm toward the recruits. A little string of fire danced between her fingers, weaving in and out like a carp among reeds.

"What am I doing right now?" she asked.

She didn't expect any of them to know the answer, but she needed to be clear on their preconceptions.

"Magic," Dulin said.

"Not helpful. 'Magic' is a word for effects with causes we can't explain. How am I causing this?"

They exchanged hesitant glances.

"You called the gods for help?" Pipaji ventured.

Rin closed her fist. "And what are the gods?"

More hesitation. Rin sensed a budding annoyance among the recruits. She decided to skip over the next line of questioning. All she'd ever wanted from Jiang were direct answers, but he'd withheld them from her for months. She didn't need to repeat that frustration. "The first thing you must accept is that the gods exist. They are real and tangible, as present and visible as any of us are. Perhaps even more so. Can you believe that?"

"Of course," Dulin said.

The others nodded in agreement.

"Good. The gods reside in a plane beyond this one. You can think of it as the heavens. Our task as shamans is to call them down to affect the matter around us. We act as the conduit—the gateway to divine power."

"What kind of place is the heavens?" Pipaji asked.

Rin paused, wondering how best to explain. How had Jiang once described it? "The only place that's real. The place where nothing is decided. The place you visit when you dream."

This met with puzzled stares. Rin realized she wasn't getting anywhere. She decided to start over, trying to think of the right words to explain concepts that by now were as familiar to her as breathing.

"You've got to stop thinking of our world as the one true domain," she said. "This world isn't permanent. It does not objectively exist, whatever that means. The great sage Zhuangzi once said that he didn't know whether he dreamed of transforming into a butterfly at night, or whether he was always living in a butterfly's dream. This world is a butterfly's dream. This world is the gods' dream. And when we dream of the gods, that just means we've woken up. Does that make sense?"

The recruits looked bewildered.

"Not in the least," Merchi said.

Fair enough. Rin could hear how much her own words sounded like gibberish, even though she also fully believed them to be true.

Small wonder she'd once thought Jiang mad. How on earth did you explain the cosmos while appearing sane?

She tried a different approach. "Don't overthink it. Just conceive of it like this. Our world is a puppet show, and the things we think of as objectively material are only shadows. Everything is constantly changing, constantly in flux. And the gods lurk behind the scenes, wielding the puppets."

"But you want us to seize the puppets," Pipaji said.

"Right!" Rin said. "Good. That's all shamanism is. It's recasting reality."

"Then why would they let us?" Pipaji asked. "If I were a god I wouldn't want to just lend someone my power."

"The gods don't care about things like that. They don't think like people; they're not selfish actors. They're . . . they're *instincts*. They have a single, focusing drive. In the Pantheon, they're kept in balance by all the rest. But when you open the gate, you let them inflict their will on the world."

"What is the will of your god?" Pipaji asked.

"To burn," Rin said easily. "To devour and cleanse. But every god is different. The Monkey God wants chaos. The Dragon wants to possess."

"And how many gods are there?" Pipaji pressed.

"Sixty-four," Rin said. "Sixty-four gods of the Pantheon, all opposing forces that make up this world."

"Opposing forces," Pipaji repeated slowly. "So they are all different instincts. And they all want different things."

"Yes! Excellent."

"So then how do we choose?" Pipaji asked. "Or do they choose us? Did the god of fire choose you because you're a Speerly, or—"

"Hold on," Merchi interrupted. "Can we bring this down from the level of abstraction? The gods, the Pantheon—great, fine, whatever. How do we call them?"

"One thing at a time," Rin told him. "We've just got to get through basic theory—"

"The drugs are the key, right?" Merchi asked. "That's what I've heard."

"We'll get there. The drugs give you access, yes, but first you have to understand what you're accessing—"

"So the drugs give you abilities?" Merchi interrupted again. "Which drugs? Laughing mushrooms? Poppy seeds?"

"That's not—we're not—no. Have you even been listening?" Rin had the sudden urge to smack him on the temple, like Jiang used to whenever he thought she was getting too impatient. She was starting to understand, now, what an insufferable student she must have been. "The drugs don't bestow abilities. They don't do anything except allow you to see the world as it really is. The gods bear the power. They *are* the power. All we can do is let them through."

"Why don't you ever need to take drugs?" Pipaji asked.

That caught Rin off guard. "How do you know that?"

"I was watching you during the march," Pipaji said. "You had a fire in your hand from day to night, but you always seemed so lucid. You can't have been swallowing poppy seeds the entire time. You would have walked straight off the side of the mountain."

The other recruits giggled nervously. But Pipaji stared expectantly at Rin with an intensity that made her uncomfortable.

"I'm past that point," Rin said.

Pipaji looked unconvinced. "Sounds like you're at the point where we need to be."

"Absolutely not. You don't want that. You never want that."

"But *why*—"

"Because then the god is always in your head," Rin snapped. "They're always screaming at you, trying to get you to bend to their will. Trying to *erase* you. Then there's no escape. Your body isn't mortal anymore, so you can't die, but you can't take back control, so the only way to keep the world safe from you is to lock you up in a stone mountain with the other hundreds of shamans who have made that mistake." Rin gazed around the room, staring levelly into each of their eyes in turn. "And I'll put a fist through your hearts before it comes to that. It's kinder that way."

They stopped giggling.

Late that evening, after several more hours of describing precisely how it felt to enter the Pantheon, Rin gave her recruits their first doses of poppy seeds.

Nothing much happened. All of them became stupidly, giddily high. They rolled around on the floor, tracing patterns through the air with their fingers and droning on and on about inane profundities that made Rin want to put her eyes out with her thumb. Lianhua was overcome with a fit of high-pitched giggles every time someone spoke a word in her direction. Merchi kept stroking the ground and murmuring about how soft it was. Pipaji and Dulin sat absolutely still, eyes pressed shut with something Rin hoped might be concentration, until Dulin began to snore.

Then they all came down and vomited.

"It didn't work," Pipaji groaned, rubbing at her bloodshot eyes.

"It's because you weren't trying to see," Rin said. She hadn't expected any of them to succeed on the first try, but she had been hoping for *something*. The faintest hint of a divine encounter. Not just four hours of idiocy.

"There's nothing *to* see," Merchi complained. "Whenever I

tried to tilt back, or whatever you said it felt like, all I saw was darkness."

"That's because you wouldn't concentrate."

"I was trying."

"Well, you weren't trying hard enough," Rin said testily. Supervising a group of tripping idiots was hardly fun when she was the only sober person in the room. "You might have at least *thought* about the Pantheon, instead of trying to do unspeakable things to a mound of dirt."

"I thought plenty about it," Merchi snapped. "You might have given us clearer instructions than *get high and summon a god.*"

Rin knew he was right. The fault lay with her teaching. She just didn't know how to explain things more clearly than she had. She wished she still had Chaghan with her, who knew the cosmos and its mysteries so well that he could easily break it into concepts they could understand. She wished she had Daji or even the Sorqan Sira, who could implant a vision in their minds that would shatter their conceptions of real or not real. She needed some way to break the logic in their brains like Jiang had done to her, but she had no idea how to replicate his yearlong syllabus, much less condense it down to two weeks.

She stretched her arms over her head. She'd been sitting in a hunched position for hours, and her shoulders felt terribly sore.

"Head back to your tents and go to sleep," she told them. "We'll try again in the morning."

"Maybe this was a stupid idea," she admitted to Kitay after the third night of getting her recruits high with no results. "Their minds are like rocks. I can't get anything in, and they think everything I say is stupid."

He rubbed her shoulder in sympathy. "Look at it from their perspective. You thought everything was stupid when you first pledged Lore. You thought Jiang was clearly off his rocker."

"But that was because I didn't know what the fuck we were doing!"

"You must have had some idea."

He had a point. Back in her second year, she hadn't known Jiang's true identity, but she had known he could do things that he shouldn't be able to. She'd seen him call shadows without moving. She'd felt the wind blow and the water stir at his command. She'd known he had power, and she'd been so hungry to acquire that power, she hadn't cared what sort of mental hurdles he made her jump. And it had still taken her nearly a year.

But most of that year had been taken up by Jiang's endless series of precautions to prevent her from becoming precisely what she ultimately became. Rin didn't need to bother with safety or long-term stability. She just needed troops from whom she could squeeze, at maximum, several months' utility.

"Take your mind off it for a bit," Kitay suggested. "No point bashing your head against the wall. Come see what I've been working on."

She followed him out of the tent. Kitay had set up an outdoor work station a ten-minute walk from the camp, which consisted of tools strewn across the ground, diagrams held down with rocks to keep them from flying away in the relentless plateau winds, and one massive structure covered with a heavy canvas tarp. He reached up and pulled the tarp away with both hands, revealing a dirigible flipped on its side and split in two, its inner workings on display like a gutted animal's intestines.

"You're not the only one leveling out the power asymmetry," he said.

Rin moved in closer to inspect the airship engine's interior, running her fingers over the hull's outer lining. It wasn't made of any material she could recognize—not wood, not bamboo, and certainly not heavy metal. The power mechanisms appeared even more foreign, a complicated, interlocking set of gears and screws that brought to mind Sister Petra's round, fist-size clock, that perfectly intricate machine that the Hesperians believed to be irrefutable proof that the world was designed by some grand architect.

"It's the only craft that remained relatively intact," Kitay said.

"The rest were burned, shattered wreckage. But this one must have only lost power when it was fairly close to the ground. Its gears are all still working."

"Hold on," Rin said sharply. She'd thought Kitay had only been studying how they worked, not how to operate them. "You're telling me we can *fly* this?"

"Maybe. I'm still a few days from attempting a test flight. But yes, once we get the basket fitted together, I theoretically should be able to get it up . . ."

"Tiger's tits." Rin's pulse quickened just thinking about what this could mean. All kinds of tactical maneuvers opened up if they had a working dirigible. They still couldn't go toe-to-toe with the Hesperian fleet in the open air—they'd simply be outnumbered— but they could use air travel for so many other purposes. "This solves so much. Bulk transportation. Quick supply movements. River crossings—"

"Not so fast." Kitay tapped a winding copper cylinder at the center of the intestinal mess. "I've finally figured out its fuel source. It burns coal, but very inefficiently. These things are built with material that is as lightweight as possible, but they're still awfully heavy. They can't remain afloat for more than a day, and they can't carry enough coal to lengthen their journey otherwise they'll sink."

"I see," she said, disappointed.

So that partly solved the central mystery of why Nezha had used the fleet with such restraint during the march over the Baolei Mountains. Dirigibles were a decent quick show of force. But they did not give the Hesperians full reign over the sky. They still depended on ground support for fuel.

"It's still better than nothing," Kitay said. "I'll try to have it flying within the next week."

"You're incredible," Rin murmured. Kitay had always been so wonderfully clever—really, she should have stopped feeling surprised by his inventions after he'd found a way to make her *fly*—but learning to work a dirigible was an achievement on an entirely different scale. This was alien technology, technology supposedly centuries ahead of Nikara achievements, and somehow he'd pieced together its workings in mere days. "Did you figure this out just by looking at it?"

"I took apart the pieces that seemed removable, and spent a long time staring at the pieces that didn't." He pushed his fingers through his bangs, surveying the engine. "The basic principles were easy enough. There's still a lot I don't know."

"But then—then how." She blinked at the complex metal gears. They looked dauntingly sophisticated. She wouldn't have known where to start. "I mean, how did you figure out the science?"

"I didn't." He shrugged. "I can't. I don't know what half these things are or what they do. They're a mystery to me and will remain so until I'm versed in the fundamentals of this technology, which I won't be until I've studied in their Gray Towers."

"But if you didn't even have the fundamentals, then how—"

"I didn't need them, see? It doesn't matter. We're not building any dirigibles of our own, we just have to learn how to fly this one. I've only got to poke around until I re-create the original working circumstances."

She froze. "What did you say?"

"I said, I've only got to poke around until—" He broke off and gave her an odd look. "You all right?"

"Yes," she said, dazed. Kitay's words echoed in her mind like ringing gongs. *The original working circumstances.*

Great Tortoise, was it that easy?

"Fuck," she said. "Kitay, I've got it."

At last, Rin dragged her recruits to the Pantheon by force.

It was such a simple solution. Why hadn't she seen it before? She should have started here, by re-creating the original working circumstances of her own encounter with divinity.

She had first called the Phoenix a full year before Jiang took her to the Pantheon. She hadn't known what she was doing. All she remembered was that she'd beaten Nezha in a combat ring, had pummeled him within an inch of his life because he had slapped her and she couldn't *bear* the indignation, and then she'd rushed out of the building into the cool air outside because she couldn't contain the wave of power surging inside her.

She hadn't summoned fire that day. But she *had* touched the Pantheon. And that was the catalyst for everything that had happened thereafter—once she'd met the gods, it ripped a hole in her world that nothing but repeated encounters with divinity could fill.

What had driven her to the gods before she ever knew their names?

Anger. Burning, resentful anger.

And fear.

"What's the worst thing that's ever happened to you?" Rin asked her recruits.

As usual, they responded with puzzled hesitation.

"You don't . . ." Pipaji hesitated. "You don't actually want us to *say*, do—"

"I do," Rin said. "Tell me. Describe the very worst thing you've ever been through. Something you never want to happen again."

Pipaji flinched. "I'm not fucking—"

"I know it's hard to relive," Rin said. "But pain is the quickest way to the Pantheon. Find your scars. Drag a knife through them. Push yourself. What memory just surfaced in your mind?"

Two high spots of color rose up in Pipaji's face. She began blinking very rapidly.

"Fine. Take a moment to think about it." Rin turned to Dulin. "How long did you spend in that burial pit?"

He balked. "I . . ."

"Two days? Three? You looked close to decomposing when we found you."

Dulin's voice was strangled. "I don't want to think about that."

"You *have* to," Rin insisted. "This is the only way this works. Let's try a different question. What do you see when you see the face of the Mugenese?"

"Easy," Merchi said. "I see a fucking bug."

"Good," Rin said, though she knew that was bravado, not the corrosive resentment she needed from them. "And what would you do to them if you could? How would you crush them?"

When this elicited awkward stares, she hardened her voice. "Don't act so shocked. You're here to learn to kill, that's why you signed up. Not for self-defense, and not out of nobility. Every one of you wants blood. *What would you do to them?*"

"I want them helpless like I was," Pipaji burst out. "I want to stand over their faces and spit venom into their eyes. I want them to wither at my touch."

"Why?"

"Because they touched me," Pipaji said. "And it made me want to die."

"Good." Rin held the bowl of poppy seeds out toward her. "Now let's try this again."

Pipaji succeeded first.

The last few times Pipaji had gotten high she'd rocked back and forth on the ground, giggling to herself at jokes that only she could hear. But this time she sat perfectly still for several minutes before suddenly falling backward like a puppet with cut strings. Her eyes remained open but were terrifyingly white; her pupils had rolled entirely into the back of her head.

"Help!" Lianhua gripped Pipaji's shoulders. "Help, I think she's—"

But Pipaji's hand shot up into the air, fingers splayed outward in a firm and unquestionable gesture. *Stop.*

"Let her lie," Rin said sharply. "Don't touch her."

Pipaji's fingers curled like claws against the ground, digging long grooves into the dirt. Low, guttural moans emitted from her throat.

"She's in pain," Merchi insisted. He scooped her up from the floor and pulled her into his lap, patting her cheeks frantically. "Hey. *Hey.* Can you hear me?"

Pipaji's lips moved very quickly, uttering a stream of syllables that formed no language Rin could recognize. The tips of her fingers had turned a rotted purple beneath the dirt. When her eyes fluttered open, all Rin saw beneath her lashes were dark pools, black all the way through.

Finally. Rin felt a pulse of fierce, vicious pride, accompanied by the faintest pang of fear. What kind of deity had Pipaji called back from across the void? Was it stronger than she was?

Merchi's voice faltered. "Pipaji?"

Pipaji lifted a trembling hand to his face. "I . . ."

Her face spasmed and stretched into a wide smile with tortured eyes, like something inside her, something that didn't understand human expressions, was wearing her skin like a mask.

"Get back," Rin whispered.

The other recruits had already retreated to the opposite end of the hut. Merchi looked down, and his face went slack with confusion. Black streaks covered his arms everywhere his skin had touched Pipaji's.

Pipaji blinked and sat up, peering around as if she'd just awoken from a deeply absorbing dream. Her eyes were still the same unsettling obsidian. "Where are we?"

"Merchi, *get back*," Rin shouted.

Merchi pushed Pipaji away. She collapsed into a pile on the floor, limbs shaking. He shrank away, wiping furiously at his forearms as if he could rub his skin clean. But the black didn't stop spreading. It looked as if every vein in Merchi's body had risen to the surface of his skin, thickening like creeks transforming into rivers.

I have to help him, Rin thought. *I did this, this is my fault—*

But she couldn't bring herself to move. She didn't know what she would do if she could.

Merchi's eyes bulged wide. He opened his mouth to retch, then toppled sideways, writhing.

Pipaji shuffled backward, fingers clenched over her mouth. Sharp, hiccuping breaths escaped from behind her fingers.

"Oh, gods," she whispered, over and over. "Oh, *gods*. What did I do?"

Dulin and Lianhua were backed up against the opposite wall. Lianhua kept eyeing the door, as if considering bolting away. Pipaji's whimpers rose to a screaming wail. She crawled over to Merchi and shook his shoulders, trying to revive him, but all she did was dig craters into desiccated flesh wherever her fingers met his skin.

Finally Rin came to her senses.

"Get in the corner," she ordered Pipaji. "Sit on your hands. Touch no one."

To her great relief, Pipaji obeyed. Rin turned her attention to Merchi. His thrashing had subsided to a faint twitching, and black and purple blotches now covered every visible inch of skin, under which his veins bulged like they had crystallized into stone.

She had no idea what Cholang's physicians could possibly do for him, but she owed it to him to try.

"Someone help me lift him," she ordered. But neither Dulin nor Lianhua moved; they were frozen with shock.

She'd have to drag Merchi out herself, then. He was too tall for her to hoist up onto her shoulder; her only choice was to drag him by a leg. She bent and grasped his shin, careful not to brush against his exposed skin. Her shoulder throbbed from his weight as she pulled, but her adrenaline kicked in, counteracting the pain, and somehow she found the energy to drag him out of the hut and toward the infirmary.

"Hang in there," she told him. "Just breathe. We'll fix this."

She might as well have been talking to a rock. When she glanced back moments later to check how he was doing, his eyes had gone glassy, and his flesh had deteriorated so much he looked like a three-day-old corpse. He didn't respond when she shook him. His pulse was gone. She didn't know when he'd stopped breathing.

She kept limping forward. But she knew, long before she reached the infirmary, that she didn't need a physician now but a gravedigger.

∞

Pipaji was gone when Rin returned to the hut.

"Where is she?" she demanded.

Dulin and Lianhua were sitting shell-shocked against the wall where she'd left them. They'd clearly been crying; Dulin's eyes were bloodshot and unfocused, while Lianhua sat trembling with her fists balled up against her eyes.

"She ran," Dulin said. "Said she couldn't be here anymore."

"And you *let* her?" Rin wanted to slap him, just to wipe that dull, dazed expression off his face. "Do you know where she went?"

"I think up toward the hill, maybe, she said—"

Rin set out at a run.

Pipaji was thankfully easy to track; her slender footprints were stamped fresh in the snow. Rin caught up to her at a ledge twenty feet up the hill. She was doubled over, coughing, exhausted by the sprint.

"Where do you think you're going?" Rin called.

Pipaji didn't respond. She straightened up and faced the ledge, stretching out one slim ankle as if testing out the empty space before she hurtled forward.

"Pipaji, get away from there." Rin measured the distance between them, calculating. If she took a running leap she might seize Pipaji by the legs before she jumped, but only if Pipaji hesitated. The girl looked ready to spring—any sudden movements could startle her off the edge.

"You're confused." Rin kept her tone low and gentle, hand stretched out as if approaching a wild animal. "You're overwhelmed, I understand, but this is normal . . ."

"It's horrible." Pipaji didn't turn around. "This is—I didn't—I can't . . ."

She was dawdling. She wasn't sure yet whether she wanted to die. *Good.*

Her fingers, Rin noticed, were no longer purple. She'd wrested some control back over herself. That made her safe to touch.

Rin lunged forward and tackled her by the waist. They landed sprawled together in the snow. Rin clambered up, jerked the un-resisting Pipaji back from the ledge by her shirt, then pinned her down with a knee against her stomach so that she couldn't flee.

"Are you going to jump?" Rin asked.

Pipaji's narrow chest heaved. "No."

"Then get up." Rin stood and extended Pipaji her hand.

But Pipaji remained on the ground, shoulders shaking violently, her face contorted again into sobs.

"Stop crying. Look at me." Rin leaned down and grabbed Pipaji by the chin. She didn't know what compelled her to do it. She'd never acted like this before. But Vaisra had done this to her once, and it had worked to command her attention, if only by shocking the fear into the back of her mind. "Do you want to quit?"

Pipaji stared mutely at her, tears streaking her face. She seemed stunned into silence.

"Because you can quit," Rin said. "I'll let you go right now, if that's what you want. No one's forcing you to be a shaman. You don't ever have to go to the Pantheon again. You can quit this army, too, if you'd prefer. You can go back to your sister and find somewhere to live in Dog Province. Is that what you want?"

"But I don't . . ." Pipaji's sobs subsided. She looked bewildered. "I don't know. I don't know what I . . ."

"I know," Rin said. "I know you don't want to quit. Because that felt good, didn't it? When you brought down the god? That rush of power was the best thing you've ever felt and you know it. How good is it to realize what you can *do*? Unfortunate that your first victim was an ally, but imagine laying your hands on enemy troops. Imagine felling armies with just a single *touch*."

"She told me . . ." Pipaji took a deep, rattling breath. "The god-dess, I mean . . . she told me I'll never be afraid again."

"That's power," Rin said. "And you're not giving that up. I know you. You're *me*."

Pipaji stared, not quite at Rin, but at the blank space behind her. She seemed lost in her own mind.

Rin sat down beside Pipaji so that they were side by side, looking out over the ledge together. "What did you see when you swallowed the seeds?"

Pipaji bit her lip and glanced away.

"Tell me."

"I can't, it's . . ."

"Look at me." Rin lifted her shirt. Her upper torso was wrapped tight in bandages, ribs still cracked from where Riga had kicked her. But Altan's black handprint, etched just as clearly as the day he'd left it, was visible just below her sternum. Rin let Pipaji stare long enough to understand its shape, and then twisted to the side to show her the raised, bumpy ridges where Nezha had once slid a blade in her lower back.

Pipaji's face went white at the sight. "How . . . ?"

"I received both these scars from men I thought I loved," Rin said. "One is dead now. One will be. I understand how humiliation feels. Keep your secrets if you want. But there's nothing you can say that will make me think any less of you."

Pipaji stared for a long time at Altan's handprint. When she spoke at last, it was in such a low whisper that Rin had to lean in close to hear her over the wind.

"We were in the whorehouse when they came. They started marching up the stairs, and I told Jiuto to hide. She—" Pipaji's voice caught. She took a shaky breath, then continued. "She didn't have time to get out the door, so she hid under the blankets. I piled them on her. Piles and piles of winter coats. And I told her not to move, not to make a single sound, no matter what happened, no matter what she heard. Then they came in, and they found me, and they—they—" Pipaji swallowed. "And Jiuto didn't move."

"You protected her," Rin said gently.

"No." Pipaji gave her head a violent shake. "I didn't. Because—because after they'd gone, I opened the cabinet. And I took the blankets off. And Jiuto wasn't moving." Her face crumpled. "She hadn't moved. She was suffocating, she couldn't fucking *breathe* under there, and still she hadn't moved because that's what I told her. I thought I'd killed her. And I didn't, because she started breathing again, but I'm the reason why . . ."

She gave a little wail and pressed her face into her hands. She didn't continue. She didn't need to; Rin could piece the rest of this story together herself.

That explained why Jiuto followed her sister everywhere. Why Pipaji had never left her alone until now. Why Jiuto didn't— *couldn't*—speak. Why she responded to everyone who spoke to her with a dead, haunted stare.

Rin wanted to put an arm around Pipaji's shaking shoulders, hold her tight, and tell her she had nothing to be ashamed of and nothing to repent for. That she'd survived, and survival was enough. She wanted to tell her to go to her sister and run far away from this place and to never think about the Pantheon again. She wanted to tell Pipaji it was over.

Instead, she said in the hardest voice she could imagine, "Stop crying."

Pipaji lifted her head, startled.

"You're living in a country at war," Rin said. "Did you think you're special? You think you're the only one who's suffered? Look around. At least you're *alive*. There are thousands of others who weren't nearly as lucky. And there are thousands more who will meet the same fate if you can't accept the power you could have."

She heard a steely, ruthless timbre in her own voice that she had never used before. It was a stranger's voice. But she knew exactly where it came from, for everything she said was an echo of things Vaisra had once told her, the only true gift he'd ever given her.

When you hear screaming, run toward it.

"Everything you just told me? That's your key to the gods. Hold that in your mind and never forget the way you're feeling right now. That's what gives you power. And that's what is going to keep you human."

Rin seized Pipaji's fingers. They were slender fingers, dirty and scarred. Nothing like how a pretty young girl's fingers were supposed to look. They were fingers that had broken bodies. Fingers just like hers.

"You have the power to poison anyone you touch," she said. "You can make sure no one ever suffers like you and your sister again. *Use it*."

The other breakthroughs came much faster after Pipaji's success. Two days later, Lianhua gave a little whimper and slumped over on her side. At first Rin was afraid she'd overdosed and fainted, but then she noticed that the scars across Lianhua's arms and collarbones were disappearing—smooth new skin knitted over areas that had previously been cruelly crosshatched by a blade.

"What did you see?" Rin asked when Lianhua awoke.

"A beautiful woman," Lianhua murmured. "She held a lotus flower in one hand, and a set of reed pipes in the other. She smiled at me and said she could fix me."

"Do you think she could help you fix others?" Rin asked.

"I think so," Lianhua said. "She put something in my hands. It was white and hot, and I saw it shining through my fingers, like—like I was holding the sun itself."

Great Tortoise. Rin's heart leaped at the implications. *We can use this*.

When Lianhua managed to call her goddess while retaining consciousness, Rin had her test her abilities on a succession of injured animals—squirrels with shattered legs, birds with broken wings, and rabbits burned half to death. Lianhua had the good sense not to ask where the animals were coming from. When she restored all the creatures to full health without any apparent side effects, Rin let Lianhua experiment on her own body.

"It's these two ribs that are giving me trouble," she said, lifting her shirt up. "Do you need the bandages off, too?"

"I don't think so." Lianhua trailed her fingers over the linen strips so lightly they tickled. Then Rin felt a searing heat at an intensity straddling the line between relief and torment. Seconds later, the pain in her ribs was gone. For the first time since ascending Mount Tianshan, she could breathe without wincing.

"Great Tortoise." Rin marveled as she twisted her upper body back and forth. "*Thank you.*"

"Do you . . ." Lianhua's fingers hovered in the air over Rin's right arm, as if awaiting permission. She was staring at the stump. "Um, do you want me to try?"

The question caught Rin by surprise. She hadn't even considered trying to restore her lost hand. She blinked, not answering, caught between saying the obvious *yes, please, try it now,* and the fear of letting herself hope.

"I don't know if I can," Lianhua said quickly. "And I mean—if you don't want to—"

"No—no, sorry," Rin said hastily. "Of course I want to. Yes. Go ahead."

Lianhua peeled the sleeve back from over her stump and rested her cool fingers where Rin's wrist ended in a smooth mound. Several minutes passed. Lianhua sat still, her eyes squeezed tight in concentration, but Rin felt nothing—no heat, no prickle—except a phantom tingle where her hand ought to be. Minutes trickled by, but the tingle, if it was ever real, never intensified into anything else.

"Stop it," she said at last. She couldn't do this anymore. "That's enough."

Lianhua seemed to shrink in apology. "I guess, um, there are limits. But maybe I can try again, if . . ."

"Don't worry." Rin yanked the sleeve back over her wrist, hoping that Lianhua didn't notice the catch in her voice. Why did her chest feel so tight? She'd known it wouldn't work; it'd been stupid to imagine. "It's fine. There are some things you can't fix."

In terms of sheer spectacle, Dulin trumped all of them. One week later, after so many failed attempts that Rin considered putting him out of his misery, he took an extra dose of poppy seeds with a look of stubborn determination on his face and promptly summoned the Great Tortoise.

In every myth Rin had ever been told, the Tortoise was a patient, protective, and benevolent creature. It was the dark guardian of the earth, representing longevity and cool, fertile soil. Villagers in Tikany wore jade pendants etched like tortoiseshells to bring good luck and stability. In Sinegard, great stone tortoises were often planted in front of tombs to safeguard the spirits of the dead.

Dulin evoked none of that. He opened a sinkhole in the ground.

It happened without warning. One moment the dirt was steady beneath their feet, and the next a circle with a diameter of about five feet appeared inside the hut, dropping down to pitch-black, uncertain depths. By some miracle none of them fell inside; shrieking, Pipaji and Lianhua scrambled away from the edge.

The sinkhole ended right at Dulin's feet. It had stopped growing, but the soil and rocks at the edges were still crumbling into the hole, echoing into nowhere.

Rin spoke slowly, trying not to startle Dulin in case he accidentally buried them all. "Very good. Now do you think you might be able to close that thing back up?"

He looked dazed, gaping at the sinkhole as if trying to convince himself that not only did it exist, he was in fact the one who had created it. "I don't know."

He was trembling. Lightly, she placed a hand on his shoulder. "What are you feeling?"

"It's—it's *hungry*." Dulin sounded confused. "I think—it wants more."

"More what?"

"More . . . exposure. It wants to see the sunlight." His voice caught. Rin could guess which memory he'd invoked when he reached the Pantheon. She knew he was remembering how it felt to be buried alive. "It wants to be free."

"Fair enough," Rin said. "But perhaps try that when you're a good distance away from the rest of us."

Dulin swallowed hard, then nodded. The pit stopped rumbling.

"General Fang?" Pipaji called from across the sinkhole. "I think we need a bigger hut."

The next day Rin and her recruits set out before sunrise to trek out into the desert plateau, where nothing they summoned could hurt anyone at Cholang's settlement.

"How far out are you going?" Kitay asked.

"Five miles," she said.

"Not far enough. Go at least ten."

"I'll be out of your range!"

"Eight, then," he said. "But get them as far away from here as you can. There's no point wiping us out before Nezha does it for us."

So Rin slung a satchel stuffed with four days' worth of provisions and enough drugs to kill an elephant over her back, then led her recruits out toward the vast expanse of the Scarigon Plateau. They marched for the better part of the morning, and didn't stop until the sun climbed high into the cloudless, intensely blue sky, baking the air into a scorching heat that even the winds couldn't dissipate.

"Here is good," Rin decided. Flat, arid steppe extended in every direction as far as her eye could see. They were nowhere near any trees, boulders, or hills that could serve as shelter, but that would be all right; they'd packed canvas for two tents, and the skies didn't promise any precipitation for several days at least.

She pulled her satchel off and let it drop on the ground. "Everyone have a drink of water, then we'll get to work."

Pipaji was already suckling greedily from her canteen. She hiccuped and wiped her mouth with the back of her hand. "What exactly are we doing?"

Rin grinned. "Stand back."

They took a few steps backward, watching her warily.

"Farther."

She waited until they were at least twenty paces away. Then she stretched a hand into the sky and called down the fire.

It rippled through her like a bolt of lightning. It was delicious. She pulled forth more, reveling in the wanton release of power, the reckless indulgence that brought echoes of the sheer ecstasy she'd experienced on Mount Tianshan.

She saw their faces, wide-eyed with admiration and delight, and she laughed.

She lingered in the column of heat for just a few more delectable seconds, and then pulled the flames back into her body.

"Your turn," she said.

For the next few hours Rin supervised as Pipaji and Lianhua pitted their skills against each other. Pipaji would kneel down and press her hands against the dirt. Seconds later all kinds of creatures— worms, snakes, long-legged steppe rats, burrowing birds—would bubble up to the surface, writhing and screeching, clawing desperately at the black veins that shot through their bulging forms.

"Stop," Rin would say, and Lianhua would hastily begin the process of reversal, healing the creatures one by one until the rot had faded away.

The limits to Lianhua's skills quickly became obvious. She could make superficial wounds disappear in under a minute, and she could heal broken bones and internal hemorrhaging if given a little more time, but she seemed only able to reverse injuries that were not life-threatening. Most of Pipaji's targets were close to death within seconds, and even Lianhua's best efforts could not bring them back.

Pipaji's limits were less clear. At first Rin had thought she required skin-to-skin contact with her victims, but then it became clear her poison could seep through dirt, reaching organisms up to several feet away.

"Try the pond water," Rin suggested. A horrible, exciting thought had just occurred to her, but she didn't want to voice it aloud until she had confirmation. "See if that speeds up dissemination."

"We need that water to drink," Dulin protested. "The next pond's a mile away."

"So fill up your canteens now, and then we'll move our camp to the other pond once Pipaji's finished," Rin said.

They obeyed. Once all the canteens were full, Pipaji crouched over the pond, frowning in concentration as she dipped her fingertips into the water. Nothing happened. Rin was hoping to see black streaks shooting through the pond, but the water remained a murky greenish-brown. Then fish began floating belly-up to the surface, bloated and discolored.

"Gross," Dulin said. "I guess we're catching dinner somewhere else."

Rin didn't comment. She was clenching her fist so hard her knuckles had turned white.

This was it. This was how she beat Nezha.

Nezha couldn't be killed because the Dragon was always protecting him, stitching his wounds back together seconds after they opened. But Chaghan had told her that the source of his power was the river running through the grottoes of Arlong.

What if she attacked the river itself?

"Can I stop?" Pipaji asked. Fish, toads, tadpoles, and insects were still bubbling up dead in the water around her. "This feels, um, excessive."

"Fine," Rin murmured. "Stop."

Pipaji stood up, looking disgusted, and quickly wiped her fingers on her trousers.

Rin couldn't stop staring at the pond. The water was pitch-black now, an inkwell of corpses.

Nezha had never met Pipaji before. He would have no idea who she was or what she could do. All he would see was a thin, pretty girl with long-lashed doe's eyes, looking utterly out of place on the battlefield, right before she turned his veins to sludge.

∞

Next Rin focused her attentions on Dulin. He had a penchant for sinkholes—by the first day, he could easily summon one on command of any shape or size within a diameter of ten feet. But the sinkholes had to open up right next to where he stood; his feet had to be at the edge of the crevice.

This posed a problem. Certainly the sinkholes had great potential for tactical disruption, but only if Dulin was standing directly in the line of fire.

"Can you do anything more with the earth?" Rin asked him. "If you can move it down, can you move it up? Sideways? Vibrate in place?"

She wasn't sure what she had in mind. She had some vague picture of great pillars of dirt thrashing through the air like vipers. Or perhaps earthquakes—those could disorient and scatter defensive lines without excessive civilian casualties.

"I'll try." He lowered his chin, brows furrowed in concentration.

Rin felt tremors under her feet, so faint at first that she was unsure whether she was imagining them. They grew stronger. The thought that perhaps she should get back briefly crossed her mind before she went flying.

Her back slammed against the ground. Her head followed with a snap. She stared at the sky, mouth open like a fish, trying to breathe. She couldn't feel her fingertips. Or her toes.

She heard screaming. Dulin's and Lianhua's faces appeared above her. Pipaji was shouting something, but her voice was muffled and muted. Rin felt Lianhua's hands moving under her shirt, pushing up to rest on her ribs, and then a wonderful, scorching heat spread through her torso and head until Dulin's shouting sharpened into intelligible words.

"Are you all right?"

"Fine," she gasped. "I'm fine."

When Lianhua took her hands away, Rin curled onto her side

and laughed. She couldn't help herself; it spilled out of her like a waterfall, urgent and exhilarating.

Lianhua looked deeply concerned. "General, are you . . . ?"

"We're going to win," Rin said hoarsely. She couldn't understand why she was the only one laughing. Why weren't they laughing? Why weren't they beside themselves with delight? "Oh, my gods. Holy fucking shit. This is it. We're going to *win*."

They spent the last two days fine-tuning their response times, limitations, and necessary dosages. They determined how long it took after ingesting seeds for their highs to kick in—twenty minutes for Pipaji and Lianhua, ten for Dulin. They learned how long they were useful on their high—no more than an hour for any of them—and how long it took for them to come down from their useless, drooling state.

Their skills remained an imperfect art—they couldn't possibly achieve in two weeks the military efficiency of the original Cike. But they'd become sufficiently accustomed to reaching for their gods that they could replicate their results on the battlefield. That was as good as they were going to get.

Rin told them to return to the base camp without her. She wanted to journey out a bit farther before she turned back. They didn't ask where she was going, and she didn't tell them.

Alone, she walked until she found a secluded area at the base of a hill, in full view of the distant Mount Tianshan.

She picked up the largest rocks she could find and arranged them in a circular pile facing the setting sun. It was a shabby memorial, but it would stay in place. Barely anyone visited this mountain. In time, the wind, snow, and storms would eradicate every trace of these rocks, but for now, this was good enough.

Jiang didn't deserve much. But he deserved *something*.

She'd seen the look on his face before she escaped the temple. He knew full well what he'd done. In that moment he was complete and aware, reconciled with his past, and fully in control. And he'd chosen to save her.

"Thank you," she said. Her voice sounded reedy and insufficient against the chilly, dense air. Her chest felt very tight.

She'd loved him like a father once.

He'd taught her everything he'd known. He'd led her to the Pantheon. Then he'd abandoned her, returned to her, betrayed her, and saved her.

He'd let so many others die—he'd let *her people* die—but he had saved her.

What the fuck was she supposed to do with a legacy like that?

Hot tears welled up in her eyes. Irritated, she wiped them away. She wasn't here to cry. Jiang didn't deserve her tears. This wasn't about grief, this was about paying respects.

"Goodbye," she muttered.

She didn't know what else to say.

No, that wasn't true. Something else weighed on her mind, something she couldn't leave unsaid. She'd never dared to say it to his face when he was alive, though she'd thought it many times. She couldn't keep silent now. She kicked at the rocks and swallowed again, but the lump in her throat wouldn't go away. She cleared her throat, tears streaming down her cheeks.

"You were always such a fucking coward."

"We're marching out," she told Kitay when she returned. She bustled around the hut, flinging things into her travel bag—two shirts, a pair of trousers, knives, pouches of poppy seeds. She'd been walking for six hours straight, but somehow felt bursting with energy. "I'll tell Cholang to have his men ready to march in the morning. Is the dirigible ready to go?"

"Sure, but—hold on, slow down, Rin." Kitay looked concerned. "So soon? Really?"

"It has to be now," Rin said. She couldn't stay in Cholang's settlement, the capital of bum-fuck nowhere in the Scarigon Plateau, any longer. Her mind spun with possibilities for the campaign ahead. Never before had the cards lain so clearly in her favor. The Republic had one shaman in Nezha against Rin's four, and their best defense mechanism was opium bombs, which incapacitated troops on both sides without discrimination.

Of course Rin's recruits could have used another week of training. Of course it would have been ideal if they'd had time to fine-tune their abilities, to learn consistently to force the gods back out of their minds when the voices became too loud. But Rin also knew that every day they waited to move out east was another day Nezha had to prepare.

Nezha was licking his wounds now. She had to acquire as much territory as possible before he was ready to strike back. Armies were marching one way or another, and she wanted to be the first.

"For once, time's on our side," she said. "We won't get this chance again."

"You're sure they're ready?"

She shrugged. "About as ready as I was."

He sighed. "I'm sure you know that thought gives me no comfort at all."

CHAPTER 25

Rin's first major metropolitan target in Republican territory was Jinzhou—the Golden City, the opulent pearl of the Nikara mideast. After three weeks' march it rose out of the treetops, all high walls and thin, reaching pagodas. Its blue, dragon-emblazoned flags streamed from atop sentry towers like a glaring invitation to attack.

Jinzhou's other, less savory moniker was the Whore. It sat square on the intersection of three provinces and, thanks to its proximity to thriving mulberry farms that provided wagonfuls of silkworm cocoons and some of the largest coal deposits in the Empire, could afford to pay taxes to all three. In return, Jinzhou had received thrice the military aid throughout the Poppy Wars. Not once in recent history had it been sacked; it had only ever been passed from ruler to ruler, trading compliance and riches for protection.

Rin intended to end that streak.

The military strategist Sunzi once wrote that it was best to take enemy cities intact. Prolonged, destructive campaigns benefited no one. Jinzhou, which offered a potential taxation base and was positioned well against multiple transport routes, would have served better as a sustained resource base than as a ruined city left in the Southern Army's wake.

Once again, Rin rejected Sunzi's advice.

In the south she'd been fighting to claim territory back from the Federation. That was a war of liberation. But now her army was homeless, fighting in territory where they'd never lived, and they could never return to their home provinces in peace while the Republic was still angling for control. The problem with trying to hold on to territory was that she would bleed troops expending them to maintain conquered areas. That was the same reason why Nezha was bound to lose—he'd been forced to split his troops across both the northern and southern fronts.

The upshot of all this was that Jinzhou was expendable.

Rin didn't care about preserving it. She didn't want Jinzhou's economy, she wanted to cut Nezha off from its riches.

What I can't have, he can't have.

Jinzhou was a flagrant display of power. Jinzhou was a message.

As her troops approached the city's thick stone gates, Rin didn't feel the same nervous flutter she always had before a fight. She wasn't anxious about the outcome, because this was not a contest of strategy, numbers, or timing. This wasn't a battle of chance.

This time the victor was guaranteed. She had seen what her shamans could do and knew, no matter how good the city's defenses, they had nothing that could defy an army that could move the earth itself.

Jinzhou's fate was already a foregone conclusion. Rin was just curious to see how badly they could break it.

But first, they had to settle the question of battlefield etiquette. Prudence prevailed, because Kitay prevailed. Rin couldn't feed and clothe her army if she didn't amass resources as they went, and those were harder to obtain from burned, sacked cities.

"I know you want a fight out of this," Kitay said. "But if you start tearing walls down without giving them the chance to surrender, then you're just being stupid."

"Negotiations give them time to prepare defenses," she objected.

He rolled his eyes at that. "What defenses could they possibly mount against you?"

The first messenger they sent returned almost immediately. "No surrender," he reported. "They, ah, laughed in my face."

"That's it, then." Rin stood up. "We'll head out in five. Someone get Dulin and Pipaji—"

"Hold on," Kitay said. "We haven't given them fair warning."

"Fair warning? We just offered them surrender!"

"They think you're a scruffy peasant army with rusty swords and no artillery to speak of." Kitay gave her a stern look. "They don't know what they're sentencing themselves to. And you're not being fair."

"Sunzi said—"

"I think we both agree Sunzi's playbook stopped being relevant a long time ago. And when Sunzi wrote about preserving information asymmetries so that your enemy would underestimate you, he was talking about troop numbers and supplies. Not earth-shattering, godlike powers." Kitay smoothed a piece of parchment over the table. He didn't even wait for her response before he began penning another missive. "We give them another chance."

She made a noise of protest. "What, you're just going to reveal our new weapons before they've even seen their first battle?"

"I'm a bit concerned that you're referring to people as weapons. And no, Rin, I'm only telling them that they ought to consider the many innocent lives at risk. I won't include details." Kitay scribbled for a bit longer, glanced up, and reached toward his forehead to tug at a hank of hair. "This confirms one thing, though. Nezha's not in the city."

Rin frowned. "How do you figure?"

They'd decided there was perhaps a fifty-fifty chance that Nezha would remain at the front to defend Jinzhou in person. On one hand, Jinzhou was such a massive treasure trove it was hard to imagine the Republic would relinquish it so easily—the coal stockpiles alone could have kept the airships flying indefinitely. On the other hand, every report they received indicated that Nezha had fled east as far as he could. And Jinzhou, though rich, did not have the strongest defense structures—it was a city founded on trade, and trading cities were designed to invite the outside world in, not to keep it out. This would have been a stupid place for Nezha to make his last stand.

"We know he's not here because the magistrate would have invoked his name if he was," Kitay said. "Or he would have shown up to negotiate himself. The whole country knows what he can do now. They know he'd be a better deterrent than anything else they could muster."

"He could be trying to ambush us," Rin said.

"Maybe. But Nezha sticks even harder to Sunzi's principles than you do. Don't push where there's already resistance; don't bleed troops where you're already at a disadvantage." Kitay shook his head. "I suppose we can't be certain. But if I were Nezha, I wouldn't try to kill you here. Not enough water access. No, I think he's going to give you this one."

"How romantic," she sneered. "Then let's make him regret it."

They camped outside Jinzhou's walls for a while, passing the spyglass back and forth as they waited for their delegation to return. Minutes passed, then hours. After a while Rin got bored and went back inside her tent, where her recruits sat in a circle on the floor, waiting for the summons.

"They're not going to surrender," she told them. "Everyone ready?"

Lianhua chewed her bottom lip. Dulin was shaking; he kept rubbing his elbows as if he were freezing. They looked so much like nervous Sinegard students about to take an exam that Rin couldn't help but feel a small flicker of amusement. Only Pipaji looked completely and utterly calm, sitting back against the wall with her arms crossed as if she were a patron at a teahouse waiting to be served.

"Remember, it's different when there are bodies," Rin said. They'd discussed many times by now how everything changed in the heat of battle, how the safe predictability of practice in no way resembled actual warfare, but she wanted to drill it into their skulls again. She wanted it to be the last thing on their minds before they saw combat. "The blood will startle you. And it gets much harder when you hear the screams. The gods get excited. They're like wild dogs sniffing for fear—once they get a whiff of chaos, they'll try much harder to take over."

"We've all seen bodies," Pipaji said.

"It's different when you're the one who broke them," Rin said. Dulin blanched.

"I'm not trying to scare you," Rin said quickly. "I just want you on guard. But you can do this. You've practiced this, you know what to expect, and you'll stay in control. What do you do if you feel the god taking over?"

They chanted in unison like schoolchildren. "Chew the nuggets."

Each of them carried enough opium for a fatal overdose in their pockets. They knew precisely how much to swallow to knock themselves unconscious.

"And what do you do if your comrades are out of control?"

Pipaji flexed her fingers. "Deal with them before they deal with us."

"Good girl," Rin said.

The door swung open. All of them jumped.

It was a scout. "Jinzhou's sent word, General. No surrender."

"More's their loss." Rin motioned for them to stand. "Let's go show them what you can do."

At Sinegard, Strategy Master Irjah had once taught Rin's second-year class how to play an ancient game called shaqqi. He'd made them play plenty of common strategy games before—wikki for foresight and decisiveness, mahjong for diplomacy and exploiting information asymmetry. But shaqqi wasn't a game Rin had ever

encountered before. Its list of basic rules went on for three book-
lets, and that didn't include the many supplemental scrolls that
dictated standard opening maneuvers.

Kitay was the only one in the class who had even played shaqqi,
so Master Irjah chose him to help demonstrate. They spent the
first twenty minutes drawing random tiles determining their share
of pieces representing troops, equipment, weaponry, and terrain
allocations. When all the pieces were finally on the map, Master Irjah and Kitay had sat opposite each other with their eyes
trained on the board. Neither of them spoke. The rest of the class
watched, increasingly bored and irritated as the face-off stretched
on for nearly an hour.

At long last, Kitay had sighed, tipped his emperor piece over
with one finger, and shook his head.

"What's going on?" Nezha had demanded. "You didn't even
play."

But they had played. Rin had only realized that near the last five
minutes of the game. The entire match had taken place through
silent mental calculations, both sides considering the balance of
power created by their randomly assigned lots. Kitay had eventually come to the conclusion that he couldn't possibly win.

"Warfare rarely works this way," Irjah had lectured as he
scooped up the pieces. "In real battle, the fog of war—*friction*,
that is—overrides everything else. Even the best-laid plans fall victim to accident and chance. Only idiots think warfare is a simple
matter of clever stratagems."

"Then what's the point of this game?" Venka had complained.

"That asymmetries do matter," Irjah said. "Underdogs can often find a way out, but not always. Particularly not if the side with
the upper hand has anticipated, as well as is possible given the
information at hand, everything that *could* go wrong. Because
then it becomes an issue of winning in the most elegant, confident
way possible. You learn to close off every possible exit. You fore-
see all the ways they could try to upset your advantage, and you
must do it all ahead of time. On the flip side, sometimes you have

no possible path to victory. Sometimes engaging in battle means suicide. It's important to know when. That's the purpose of this game. The gameplay doesn't matter half so much as the thinking exercise."

"But what if the players don't agree who has the advantage?" Nezha had asked. "If no one surrenders?"

"Then you play it out until someone does," Irjah said. "But then it's doubly embarrassing for the loser, who should have conceded from the outset. The point is to train your mind to see all the strategic possibilities at once so that you learn when you can't win."

Shaqqi, it turned out, had been the only strategy game that Rin never managed to grasp. They played many times in class throughout the year, but never could she bring herself to surrender. She'd played the role of the underdog since she could remember. It seemed so ludicrous to ever give up, to simply acknowledge defeat as if the future might not offer some chance, however slim, to reverse her fortunes. She'd been relying on those slim chances for her entire life.

But now, standing with her army outside Jinzhou's city gates, she was on the other side of the table. Now she possessed the overwhelming advantage, and her puzzle was how one should leverage three people who could rewrite reality in a conventional battle without killing everyone around them.

Victory was already assured. Right now she only had to worry about the loose ends.

This was the sort of puzzle that Altan had been constantly trying to solve when he'd commanded the Cike. How did you win a game of chess when your pieces were the most freakishly powerful things on the board, and the opponent was only equipped with pawns? When the objective is no longer victory, but victory with the lowest casualty rates possible?

Rin and Kitay had agreed early on that the battle hinged on Dulin. Lianhua's involvement was out of the question—they would keep her busy in the infirmary for days on end after the battle concluded, but she had no place on the battlefield. Pipaji was more lethal in close quarters, but Dulin had the wider range of impact. He could set off earthquakes and sinkholes in a ten-yard radius around him, whereas Pipaji had to enter deep into the fray to inflict her poison. That posed too great a risk—Rin needed Pipaji out of harm's way until she reached Arlong.

But Rin was quite sure she could shatter Jinzhou's resistance with Dulin alone.

"You get two major hits," Rin told him. "Both right at the start of the fighting. Our opening salvos. They'll think the first was a freak act of nature, or some very powerful conventional weapon. After the second, they'll know we have a shaman. Beyond that point, our forces will have mixed too much for you to get in a discriminate hit."

"I don't have to be in the melee, though," Dulin said. "I mean, couldn't I just target the city?"

"And then what?" Kitay asked sharply. "You'll massacre all the innocent civilians inside?"

Dulin's cheeks colored. The thought had clearly never even crossed his mind. "I hadn't—"

"I know you haven't thought it through," Kitay said. "But you've got to put your head back on straight. Just because you can alter the world on a ridiculous scale doesn't mean the normal calculations no longer apply. If anything, you must now be doubly careful. Do you understand?"

"Yes, sir." Dulin looked duly chastened. "Where do you want your sinkholes, then?"

"Jinzhou's got six walls," Kitay said. "Take your pick."

One hour later, a squadron of fewer than fifty soldiers charged out from the forest toward Jinzhou's western gate. Rin and Kitay waited in the trees with the rest of their army, watching through spyglasses as their troops rushed the high stone walls.

This first assault was a decoy. Jinzhou's leadership had to understand what Rin could do. After the Battle of the Red Cliffs, her abilities were no longer a frightful rumor but a well-known fact. So if Jinzhou's magistrate had rebuffed her offer of lenience for surrender, then he had to be very confident in his defenses against her fire. Rin wasn't stupid enough to enter the fray until she knew what Jinzhou had up its sleeve.

It had been so easy to design a dummy probe. Shamanic fire was the simplest weapon to simulate. It only took seconds for fifty soldiers wielding torches, gunpowder, and oil-soaked flags to create a scorching wave of flame that, when caught by the wind, towered close to the heights that Rin could summon herself.

Jinzhou's defenders responded seconds later. First came the standard volley of arrows. Then followed a thicker round of missiles—bombs that did not burst into balls of flame, but rather leaked a slow, greenish smoke as they hit the ground.

"Opium bombs," Kitay observed. "Is that all they had?"

He looked disappointed. Rin, too, couldn't help a fleeting sense of dismay. Jinzhou had refused negotiations with such confidence that Rin had seriously wondered, even hoped, that they could display some secret, innovative defense to back it up.

But instead, they'd merely signed their own death warrants.

The decoy squadron was breaking up. They were allowed to fall back—they'd only been charged with drawing out the artillery, not breaking Jinzhou's defenses. The wave of fire disintegrated into dozens of individual torches, snuffed out as fleeing soldiers dropped them on the dirt.

The retreat looked messy, but those troops would be fine. They'd gone in prepared with cloth masks soaked in water. It wouldn't keep the opium out for long, but it bought them sufficient time to scatter and retreat.

Rin turned to Dulin. He held his spyglass very still to his face. His right hand was curled in a fist, beating out an erratic pattern against his knee.

Battle nerves, Rin thought. *Adorable.* And she wished, just briefly, she were not so accustomed to war so that she could still feel that lurching, electrifying thrill of sheer nervous distress.

"Your turn," she told him. "Let's go."

They broke out of the trees to meet with a hail of arrows. Jinzhou's defenders hadn't been foolish enough to imagine the probe constituted Rin's entire attack. They'd fortified all six of their walls with artillerymen, and more rushed toward the eastern wall when Rin's troops began pouring out the forest.

The southerners locked shields over their heads as they surged toward the gates in a clustered formation. Rin's arm shook as arrow after arrow slammed into the inch of wood separating iron from skin. Then it went numb. She gritted her teeth and pushed forward, eyes locked on the great stone walls ahead. In training, she'd determined that Dulin could open a sinkhole from a distance of ten yards. Ninety yards to go.

A boom echoed ahead to her left. Blood and bone splattered the air; bodies hit the ground. Rin kept moving, stepping over the gore. Seventy yards.

"Holy shit," Dulin whispered. "Holy shit, I can't . . ."

"Shut up and move," Rin said.

Fifty yards. Something shrieked overhead. They both ducked but kept running. The missile exploded behind them, accompanied by screams. Ten yards.

Rin halted. "Close enough for you?"

Troops locked their shields in a protective shell over Dulin as he stood still, eyes tightly shut. Rin watched his twitching face, waiting.

The seconds that followed felt like an eternity.

He's too scared. She was suddenly anxious. *He can't focus, it's too much* . . . The missiles and arrows landing around them suddenly seemed so close. They'd been wildly fortunate, really, to have lasted so long without being hit. But now they were open, unmoving targets, and one of those volleys had to land eventually . . .

Then the ground shook, rippling in a way that soil was not supposed to move. The stone walls vibrated, which looked so absurd that Rin thought surely she must be the one shaking and not that massive structure, but then dust and pebbles poured down the walls in trickles that turned to torrents.

The wall came down.

It didn't collapse. Didn't implode. There was no messy, cascading collision of faults in stone shattering in a chain reaction, then crumbling under its own weight, the way a broken wall was *supposed* to fall. Instead, the ground beneath opened into a gaping maw. And the wall simply *disappeared*, taking the artillery line with it, exposing the city inside like a layer of flesh peeled away from pulsing organs.

The air was still. The firing had stopped.

Dulin sank dazed to his knees.

"Well done," Rin told him.

He looked like he was about to vomit.

He'll be fine, she thought. *Break a few more cities, and it'll feel routine.* She didn't have time to play wet nurse now; she had a city to conquer. She raised her left arm in the air in a signal to charge, and the Southern Army burst over the rubble through the missing wall.

Squadrons split off to the north and south to drive through Jinzhou's defenses, while Rin alone took the center quadrant. She heard panicked shouting as she approached. As flames licked up her shoulders, she heard her targets screaming for reinforcements—high-pitched voices called over and over again for opium bombs—but it was too late. Far too late. They'd directed their opium missiles to the western wall, and by the time they brought them anywhere near her this battle would be finished.

All Jinzhou's soldiers had now were their conventional weapons, and those were so miserably insufficient. Their sword hilts burned white-hot in their hands. Everything they hurled at her—arrows, spears, javelins—turned to ash in midair. No one could come within a ten-foot distance of her, for she was ensconced inside a searing, impenetrable column of flame.

They tumbled before her like sticks.

She tilted her head back, opened her mouth, and let fire rip forth through her throat.

Gods, this release felt good. She hadn't realized how much she missed this. She'd reached such a delirious thrill on Mount Tianshan and then on the training grounds on the plateau, when she'd let the flames roar unrestrained through her body. Every waking moment since then had felt muted and muzzled. But now she got what she wanted—mindless, careless, untrammeled destruction.

But something felt off. A niggling sensation chewed at her gut, a guilty compunction that only grew as the screams intensified and the bodies around her crumpled, blackened, and folded in on themselves.

She felt no rage. This had nothing to do with vengeance. These troops hadn't done anything to her. She had no reason to hate them. This didn't feel righteous, this just felt *cruel*.

Her flames sagged, then shrank back inside her.

What was wrong with her? It was usually so easy to sink into that rhapsodic space where rage met purpose. She'd never had to struggle to find anger before; she carried it around with her like a warm coal, forever burning.

She'd turned her fire on her fellow Nikara before. She'd done it easily at the Red Cliffs; she'd set entire ships aflame without thinking twice. But this was the first time she'd ever burned an enemy that hadn't attacked her first.

This wasn't self-defense or vengeance. This was plain, simple aggression.

But they chose this, she reminded herself. *We gave them two chances to surrender, and they refused. They knew what I am. They dug their graves.*

She reached deep into a dark pit inside her, and her column of fire burst forth anew, blazing this time with a wicked kind of energy.

She wielded now a different fire; a fiercer, hungrier fire; one that wanted to burn not as a reaction to fear and pain, but with a rage that sprang from *power*. The fury of being disrespected, of being defied.

This fire felt hotter. Darker.

Rin realized with a shudder that she rather liked this feeling.

She was as close to invincible as humans could get, and Jinzhou was about to fall into her lap.

Never grow cocky, Irjah had been so fond of repeating. *True warfare never goes according to plan.*

Oh, but it did, when the powers at play were this unbalanced, for even the inevitability of chance could not undo the infinite disparity between gods and men. She watched the battle unfold, mapping perfectly onto the chessboard in her mind's eye. Pieces toppled with the push of a finger, all because she'd willed them to. Cities shattered.

It took her a long moment to notice that the clang of steel had long since died down, that no one was shooting at her, that no one was charging forward. Only when she called the flames away did she see the white flags, now blackened at the edges, waving from every door of every building. The city had surrendered to the Southern Army long ago. The only one still fighting was her.

The battle had ended barely an hour after it had begun. Rin accepted Jinzhou's surrender, and her soldiers switched from the frenzied rush of battle to the somber business of occupation. Yet even as order was restored to the city, the ground continued to shake, rocked by a series of faraway booms that reverberated so strongly that Rin's teeth shook in her skull.

Dulin had lost control.

But she had expected this. This was the worst, and likeliest, outcome. She'd prepared for it. If Dulin couldn't summon the awareness to calm his mind with opium, she'd force it into him.

She turned on her heel and dashed back through the charred city toward the open wall. Her flames flickered and disappeared—

she was too panicked to focus on rage now—but no one bothered attacking her. Civilians and soldiers on both sides were all fleeing the shuddering city, dodging and weaving as great chunks of stone tore from the sides of buildings and smashed into the dirt.

The booms grew louder. Great crevices started ripping through the earth like gaping wounds left by some invisible beast. Rin saw two men in front of her disappear, screaming, as the ground opened up beneath them. For the first time on this campaign, a dagger of fear broke through her calm. The Great Tortoise had gotten a taste of freedom. It wanted more. If this continued, Dulin would put the entire city into the earth.

But miraculously, the ground seemed calmer the closer Rin got to the eastern wall. She realized the tremors were spreading out in a circular pattern, and the damage rippled out inversely, gaining destruction rather than fading at larger diameters. But the epicenter—the ground under Dulin's feet—was calm.

Of course. The Great Tortoise wanted liberation. It wanted to see the sky. It might bury everything in its vicinity, but it would not bury its mortal host.

Dulin was bent over where she'd left him, hands clutching at his head as he screamed. Rin spied Pipaji crouched several yards away, half kneeling like she couldn't decide whether or not to spring at him. Her eyes widened when she saw Rin. "Should I—"

"Not yet." Rin pushed her out of the way. "Get back."

Dulin's thrashing meant that he was still fighting. The Great Tortoise hadn't yet won; she could still bring him back. She fleetingly considered trying to shout him down, the way Altan had done for Suni so many times.

But Jinzhou was crumbling. She didn't have the time.

She ran forward, lowered her head, and tackled him at the waist.

He hit the ground with no resistance. Rin had forgotten how weak he really was, a spindly adolescent who'd been chronically malnourished over many months. He flailed beneath her, but to no avail; she held him still using only her knees.

The rumbling grew louder. She heard another ear-splitting

crash from within the city boundaries. Another building had just gone down. She fumbled hastily in her back pocket for the opium pouch, ripped it open with her teeth, and shook its contents out onto the dirt.

Dulin arched his back, twisting beneath her. Dreadful gargling sounds escaped his throat. His eyes flitted back and forth, alternating brown and shiny black every time he blinked.

"Hold still," she hissed.

His eyes fixed on hers. She felt a flutter of fear as something ancient and alien bore into her soul. Dulin's features contorted in an expression of absolute terror, and he began rasping out guttural words in no language she could recognize.

Rin snatched the nuggets off the dirt and shoved them all in his mouth.

His eyes bulged. She lurched forward and clamped her hand tight over his mouth, clenching his jaw shut as best she could. Dulin struggled but Rin squeezed harder, pressing her stump against his neck for leverage, until at last she saw his throat bob. Several minutes later, once the opium had seeped into his bloodstream, the earth at last fell silent.

Rin let go of Dulin's jaw and reached under his neck to feel for his pulse. Faint, but insistent. His chest was still rising and falling. Good—she hadn't choked him to death.

"Get Lianhua," she called to a cowering Pipaji. Foam bubbled out the sides of Dulin's clammy lips, and Rin wondered vaguely how quickly opium poisoning could kill a person. "Be quick."

As Jinzhou was falling, its city magistrate had realized that defeat likely meant death, so he'd fled out the back gates concealed under pig carcasses in a livestock cart. He left his pregnant wife and three children behind, barricaded in the inner chamber of their mansion, where several hours later they were found suffocated under collapsed rubble.

Rin learned all this as her troops took swift, efficient command of the city.

"Everyone we've interrogated confirms he's heading east," said Commander Miragha. She was a brutally efficient young woman, one of Cholang's subordinates from Dog Province, and she'd rapidly become one of Rin's most capable officers. "He's got allies in the next province over. What do you want to do?"

"Pursue him," Rin ordered. "Pursue anyone who's fled the city, and don't let up until you've dragged them back into the jails. I don't want anyone outside Jinzhou to know what happened here today."

Of all Souji's lessons, the one that had struck the hardest was that in campaigns of resistance, information asymmetry mattered more than anything. The playing field had leveled somewhat now, but Rin still didn't want Nezha to know her army had new shamans until Dulin and Pipaji became impossible to conceal. She knew she couldn't keep this secret for long, but there was no point giving Nezha extra time to prepare.

"Kill or capture?" Miragha pressed.

Rin paused, considering.

That question had bearing on the larger issue of how to handle Jinzhou's occupation. Most civil wars, like Vaisra's campaign, were fought by redefining territorial borders. Enemy land was hard to maintain, so grafting onto local power structures had historically been the easiest way to seamlessly take control of a city without breakdown of civil functions. If Rin had wanted Jinzhou to resume normal functions, then she'd try to keep as many fleeing officials alive as she could. But she was focused on obtaining resources, not territory—she didn't have the troops to station in every city that stood between her and Arlong.

Of course, that wasn't a strategy for sustained long-term rule. But Rin wasn't concerned with long-term rule right now. She wanted Nezha dead, the Republic collapsed, the south freed, and the Hesperians banished. She didn't care much what happened to the Nikara heartland in the interim.

This region would likely fall into a temporary chaos while local powers either reestablished themselves or became victim to opportunistic coups. Small-scale wars were bound to break out. Bandits would run rampant.

She had to bracket all that as a problem for later. It couldn't be hard to reassert control after she'd defeated the Republic. She'd be the only alternative left. Who could possibly challenge her?

"Capture them if you can," she told Miragha. "But no need to go out of your way."

For the rest of the afternoon, Rin's troops plundered Jinzhou for its riches.

They did it as politely as possible, with minimal brutality. Rin gave strict orders for her soldiers to leave the terrified civilians and their households alone. Even accounting for the buildings shattered by Dulin's earthquake, Jinzhou wallowed in so much wealth that the destruction had barely made a dent; the warehouses, granaries, and shops that remained standing still burst with enough goods to sustain the army for weeks. Rin's troops loaded their wagons with sacks of rice, grain, salt, and dried meat; restocked their stores of bandages and tinctures; and replaced their rusty, broken-down carts with new vehicles with wheels and axles that glinted silver in the sunlight.

By far their best discovery was bolts and bolts of cotton linen and silk stacked up in massive piles inside a textile warehouse. Now they could make bandages. Now they could repair their shoes, which were in such tatters after the march over Baolei that many of Rin's soldiers had fought the battle of Jinzhou barefoot. And now, for the first time in its short history, the Southern Army would have a uniform.

Up until now they'd been fighting in the same rags they'd worn out of the Southern Province. In battle they distinguished themselves with streaks of mud like Souji had suggested back when they'd broken the Beehive, or by putting on anything that wasn't blue and hoping they weren't killed by friendly fire. But now Rin had cloth, dyes, and a terrified guild of skilled Jinzhou seamstresses who were eager to comply with her every request.

The seamstresses asked her to pick a color. She chose brown, largely because brown dyes were the cheapest, made with tannins easily found in tree bark, shells, and acorn cups. But brown was also fitting. The Southern Army's first uniforms had been dirt from a riverbed. When the Snail Goddess Nüwa had created the first humans, she had lovingly crafted the aristocracy from the finest red clay, lost patience, and hastily shaped the rest from mud. At Sinegard, they'd called her a mud-skinned commoner so often the insult felt now like a familiar call to arms.

Let them think of us as dirt, Rin thought. She *was* dirt. Her army was dirt. But dirt was common, ubiquitous, patient, and necessary. The soil gave life to the country. And the earth always reclaimed what it was owed.

"Great Tortoise," Kitay said. "You'd think this was a Warlord's palace."

They stood in the main council room of Jinzhou's city hall, a vast chamber with high ceilings, elaborately carved stone walls, and ten-foot-long calligraphic tapestries hanging at every corner. Long shelves gilded each wall, displaying an array of antique vases, swords, medals, and armor dating back as far as the Red Emperor. Miraculously, it had all survived the earthquakes.

Rin felt deliciously guilty as she perused the room and its treasures. She felt like a naughty child rummaging through her parents' wardrobe. She couldn't shake the sense that she shouldn't be in here, that none of this belonged to her.

It does, she reminded herself. *You conquered them. You razed this place. You won.*

They'd sell it all, of course. They'd come here to find treasures they could turn to silver through Moag's trading routes. As she ran her fingers over a silk fan, Rin fleetingly imagined herself wielding it, dressed in ornate silks of the kind Daji used to wear, carried through adoring crowds on a gilded palanquin.

She pushed the image away. Empresses carried fans. Generals carried swords.

"Look," Kitay said. "Someone certainly thought highly of themselves."

The magistrate's chair at the end of the room was laughably ornate, a throne better fit for an emperor than a city official.

"I wonder how he made it through any meetings," Rin said. The chair was nailed to a raised dais about half a foot off the floor. "You'd have to crane your neck just to look at anyone."

Kitay snorted. "Perhaps he was just very short."

Curious, Rin climbed up and settled into the chair. Contrary to expectations, the seat had actually been built for someone much taller than her. Her feet swung childishly from the edge, nowhere close to scraping the floor. Still, she couldn't help feeling a small thrill of excitement as she looked out over the gilded chamber and the long council table at whose head she sat. She imagined the seats filled with people: soldiers, advisers, and city officials all listening attentively to her bidding.

Was this how it felt, day by day, to rule? Was this how Nezha felt seated within Arlong's cerulean halls, halfway across the country?

She knew very well how total, dominating power tasted. But as she sat on the conquered throne, gazing down at the empty seats below, she understood for the first time the delicious authority that went with it. This was not a taste she had inherited from Altan, because Altan had only ever concerned himself with destructive retribution. Altan had never dreamed of seizing a throne.

But Rin could burn, *was* burning, much more brightly than Altan ever had.

Small wonder Nezha had chosen his Republic over her. She'd have done the same in a heartbeat.

Enjoy your Republic, she thought, fingers curling against the cold armrest. *Enjoy it while it lasts, Young Marshal. Take a good look at your splendor, and remember well how it feels. Because I am coming to burn it all down beneath you.*

CHAPTER 26

In the *Principles of War*, the strategist Sunzi wrote at length about a concept he named *shi*, which from Old Nikara translated vaguely into "energy," "influence," or "strategic advantage." *Shi* was water rushing so quickly downstream it could dislodge stones from riverbeds. *Shi* was the devastation of boulders tumbling down a steep mountain slope. *Shi* dictated that energy, when present, accumulated and amplified itself.

Rin's victory at Jinzhou was the push that sent the first rock rolling.

Things became so easy after that. Nezha didn't have the troops to defend his outlying territories, so he rapidly retreated southeast, back behind the Qinling and Daba Mountains that served as Arlong's natural defenses. Assaulted on two fronts, he made the only strategic decision he could—to center his defenses in Dragon Province, leaving the rest of the Republic to fend for itself.

On their way through Ram Province, Rin's troops came across nothing but scorched fields and abandoned villages—evidence of civilians ordered to pack their things overnight and retreat into the mountains or back behind Republican lines. Anything the refugees couldn't take, they had left out in the sun to spoil.

On many occasions, the Southern Army stumbled upon piles and piles of animal carcasses, flies buzzing over split-open pigs whose meat might have been good just two or three days ago.

There was a classic principle of Nikara warfare: when facing enemy invasion, clear the countryside and erect high walls. When things looked dire, Nikara leaders destroyed rural settlements and moved food, people, and supplies behind walled cities to prevent them from becoming enemy assets. What couldn't be moved was burned, poisoned, or buried. It was the oldest practice of Nikara military tradition, and amplified the suffering of innocents. Someone wants to conquer you, someone else wants to prevent you from turning into an asset, and you get fucked from both sides.

From the Mugenese, such extravagant waste would have been an act of spiteful defiance. But from Nezha, who had provinces to rule and subjects to protect, this was the ultimate sign of weakness. It meant his Hesperian allies were abandoning him. It meant he knew he couldn't stop the southerners from marching on Dragon Province; he could only try to slow them down.

But the Southern Army had *shi*. It could not be slowed. Rin's troops were running high on victory. They had sharper swords now, better armor, and more food than they could eat. They were fighting with more skill and energy than they ever had before. They carved through the countryside like a knife through tofu. More often than not, villages surrendered without their having to lift a finger; some villagers even readily enlisted, happy for the chance at steady coin and two square meals a day.

The reversal of fortunes was astonishing. Months ago, Rin had led a desperate march into mountains, had gambled the lives of thousands on the barest chance of survival. Now she marched on the offensive, and Nezha had lost almost everything that made her fear him. He was a boy king, limping by with the support of a recalcitrant ally that, judging from the quiet skies, had strongly reconsidered its commitments. Meanwhile, Rin had an army swelling in confidence, experience, and supplies. Above all, she had shamans.

And they were performing marvelously. After Dulin's near breakdown at Jinzhou, Rin hadn't expected them to last so long. She'd thought she might get a few weeks' use from them at most before they inevitably died in battle or she had to kill them. She'd been particularly concerned about Lianhua, who regularly sank into daylong catatonic trances after her shifts on triage duty. This frightened Pipaji so much that she soon grew terrified of calling her own god, and had to be coaxed into participating in the next few battles.

But all three were getting more stable over time. Aside from a brief episode when Dulin was struck in the shoulder by an arrow and accidentally prompted an earthquake that split the battle-field with a ten-foot ravine, he never lost control again. Lianhua's trances decreased to once a week, and then ceased completely. Pipaji managed to overcome her nerves; three weeks after Jinzhou, she infiltrated a village posing as a refugee and took out its entire defensive line that night by slipping through their ranks, brushing her fingers against every patch of exposed skin.

They all learned to cope in their own ways. Dulin started meditating at night, sitting cross-legged on the dirt for hours on end. Lianhua sang to herself while she worked to keep herself grounded, going through a wide array of folk ballads and ditties in an impressively lovely soprano. Pipaji began disappearing from camp every evening shortly after dinner, and rarely came back until after dusk.

One night Rin, slightly worried, followed her out of camp. She was relieved to discover that all Pipaji did was stand still in the forest, surrounded by trees with no other human beings in sight, and breathe.

"You're not very good at hiding," Pipaji said after a while.

Rin stepped into the clearing. "I didn't want to disturb you."

"It's all right." Pipaji looked somewhat embarrassed. "I don't ever stay out here for very long. I just like to go where it's quiet. Where there's nobody I can hurt. It's, um, relaxing."

Rin felt an odd twinge in her chest. "That's prudent."

"You can stay if you want."

Rin lifted her eyebrows, somewhat touched. "Thank you."

For a moment they stood side by side, listening to the katydids shriek. It was, Rin agreed, oddly relaxing.

"You don't get to go back to normal," Pipaji said abruptly.

"Hmm?"

"I noticed your eyes. They're always red. Our eyes go back to normal. Yours don't. Why?"

"Because I'm too far gone," Rin said. She was only partly lying. "I can't shut it out anymore."

"Then what brings you back?" Pipaji demanded. "Why haven't you lost it like—like the rest of them?"

Rin considered telling her about the anchor bond. But what was the point? That option would never be possible for Pipaji—revealing it would only be cruel. And the fewer people who knew about Kitay, the better.

She liked Pipaji, but she wasn't going to trust the girl with her life.

"I've struck a deal with my god," she said after a pause. "And it's learned to stay put."

"You didn't tell us about that."

"Because it's the least likely outcome," Rin said. "You knew how this would end. There's no point giving you hope."

Her words came out flat and cold. She couldn't think of anything reassuring to say, and she suspected Pipaji didn't want to hear it. All her recruits had known this could only end two ways for them: death, or the Chuluu Korikh. She'd warned them many times over; she'd made sure they understood that volunteering was a death sentence.

"I'm not going to survive this war," Pipaji said after a long silence.

"You don't know that," Rin said.

Pipaji shook her head. "I'm not strong enough. You'll kill me. You'll need to kill me."

Rin gave her a pitying look. What good would lying do?

"Do you want me to say I'm sorry?"

"No." Pipaji snorted. "We knew what we signed up for."

And that was all it took to assuage Rin's conscience. She hadn't done anything wrong if they'd chosen this themselves. Dulin, Lianhua, and Pipaji were still here because they'd decided it was worth it. They'd foreseen and accepted their deaths. She'd offered them weapons, the only weapons strong enough to alter their miserable world, and they'd taken them. These were the choices war produced.

Several weeks later they occupied a small port town on the Western Murui at the border between Ram and Hare province, and made camp as they awaited an old friend.

"Well, look at you." Chiang Moag, Pirate Queen of Ankhiluun, stepped off the gangplank and strode down the pier with a broad smile on her face. "Look what you've made of yourself."

"Hello, Moag," Rin said. They regarded each other for a moment. Then, because Moag hadn't yet tried to stick a knife in her back, Rin waved down the twenty hidden archers who had been waiting to put an arrow through her head.

"Cute," Moag said when she saw them disperse.

"Learned that from you," Rin said. "I'm never quite sure what side you're on."

Moag snorted. "Oh, let's call this what it is. The Republic is done for. That pretty little boy they've got on Arlong's throne couldn't manage even a village without his father's help. I know where to throw in my lot."

She sounded convincing, but Rin knew better than to take her words at face value. Moag was, and always would be, a liability. True, she'd granted Rin safe haven in Ankhiluun after her escape from Arlong, but she hadn't lifted a finger to help since Rin left for the south. This entire war Moag had remained hidden in Ankhiluun, bolstering her fleets against an anticipated Hesperian attack. Moag was hedging her bets, waiting to see if she'd be better off resisting the Republic or playing by its rules.

Momentum was on Rin's side right now. But should anything go wrong, Moag was just as likely to sell her out to Arlong. She'd done it before.

For now, Rin was willing to swallow that risk. She needed ammunition—all the fire powder, cannons, and missiles that she hadn't been able to loot. Mobile warfare tactics worked well enough on underdefended cities from which Nezha's troops had been hastily recalled. But she needed proper artillery to breach the dragon's lair.

"It's nice to see you in charge." Moag clapped a broad hand on Rin's shoulder. "What did I tell you? You were never meant to serve, much less beneath snakes like Vaisra. Women like us have no business putting our services for sale."

Rin laughed. "It's good to see you."

She meant it. She'd always respected the Pirate Queen's blunt, naked self-interest. Moag had risen from an escort to the ruler of Nikan's only free city through ruthless, brilliant pragmatism, and though Rin knew very well this meant Moag was loyal to no one, she still admired her for it.

"What do you have for me?" she asked.

"See for yourself." Moag stuck two fingers in her mouth and whistled to her crew. "Some old toys, some new ones. I think you'll like them."

Over the next hour, Moag's crew and Rin's troops together unloaded dozens of crates onto the riverbank. Moag unlocked one and kicked open the hatch, revealing coffins stacked in neat rows of four.

"Does this trick really work?" Rin asked.

"It does if you claim they're plague victims." Moag motioned to one of her crew. He pulled the nearest coffin out of the crate, jammed a crowbar under the lid, and pushed down until the lid popped open. A thick pile of fire powder glinted in the sunlight, fine and shiny. Rin had the absurd impulse to bathe in it.

"It's an old smuggler's trick," Moag said. "Shockingly effective. Everyone's prudent, but no one wants to die."

"Smart," Rin said, impressed.

"Save the coffins," Moag suggested. "They're good for fire-wood."

For the rest of the afternoon they traded coffins crammed with swords, shields, missiles, and fire powder for the riches Rin's troops had accumulated throughout Ram Province. All this happened outside on the riverbank. Rin didn't want to let Moag near her camp—the less intelligence Moag gleaned about her forces the better—and Moag didn't want to wander too far from her ships. The riverbank was a buffer that assuaged their mutual distrust.

Moag was thorough. She inspected every item in every trunk of jewelry, rubbing the larger pieces between her fingers to determine their value before nodding her permission for her soldiers to lug it back on board.

Rin watched the two lines walking in parallel, trading. There was a lovely symbolism to it. All the treasures of one bloated city, in exchange for enough cold steel and fire powder to bring down the rest.

"Now, then." Moag stood back as the final crate was unloaded from her skimmers. "There's the issue of payment."

Rin balked. "What are you talking about?"

Moag showed her the figures she'd been marking in a ledger. "I've just unloaded twice as much weaponry as this pays for."

"By what standards?" Rin asked. "Those prices are made up. Your whole pricing system is shot; we're the only ones buying right now. You'd hardly be able to cut a deal in Arlong."

"True," Moag said. "But city magistrates are always buying. And I'm sure there are plenty of local platoons looking to improve their defenses now that they all know what's coming their way."

"If you try that shit," Rin said very calmly, "I will kill you."

There followed a long pause. Rin couldn't read Moag's expression. Was she afraid? Furious? Deliberating whether to strike first?

Rin's eyes darted around the beach, mapping out the possible fallout. Her first move would be to incinerate Moag where she stood, but she had to hedge against the Black Lilies, any one of whom could take her out with a well-aimed poisonous hairpin. If she expanded her radius she could take the Lilies out, too, but they were intermingled with southern troops, almost certainly on purpose. If she killed Moag, then she'd have to suffer at least a dozen casualties.

Her fingers curled into a fist. She could absorb those losses; no one would fault her for it. But she had to strike first.

Then Moag burst out laughing, a full-throated, booming laugh that startled Rin.

"Tiger's tits." Moag clapped a hand on her shoulder, grinning. "When did you grow such a massive pair of balls?"

Rin, wildly relieved, forced her grimace into a smile.

"But I will be coming to collect," Moag continued. "Not immediately," she amended quickly, noticing Rin's scowl. "I want to see you succeed, little Speerly. I won't get in your way. But you'd best start thinking about how to scrounge up some profits from your empire."

"Profits?" Rin wrinkled her nose. "I'm not running a business here—"

"Correct. You're about to run a nation." A familiar look of patronizing pity crossed Moag's face, the look she'd always put on when she thought Rin was being particularly naive. "And nations need silver, girlie. War is costly. You've got to pay your soldiers somehow. Then you've got to pay back the masses whose homelands you've just wrecked. Where are they supposed to live? What are they going to eat? You need lumber to rebuild village settlements. You need grain to ward off the famine you're facing down, since I guarantee your crop yields this year will be shit. No one plows when there's a war going on. They're too busy being, you know, refugees."

"I . . ." Rin didn't know what to say. She had to admit those were real problems, problems she had to deal with eventually, but they seemed so far off that she'd never given them any thought. Those seemed like good problems to have, because by the time they became relevant, it would mean that she'd won. But what was the point of daydreaming about an empire when Nezha still ruled the southeast? "I haven't—"

"Ah, don't look so scared." Moag gave her shoulder a condescending pat. "You'll be sitting on a throne of riches soon enough. That's what I'm trying to tell you. The Consortium wants to be here for a reason. All those silks? Porcelains? Tungsten deposits? Antique vases? They want that shit, and they'll pay good money for it."

"But they're not going to trade with us," Rin said. "Are they? I mean, if we win, won't they just blockade us?"

"They will, on paper, refuse to trade with the Nikara Empire." Moag spread her hands in a magnanimous gesture. "But I've got ships aplenty, and I know a million ways to disguise the trade channels so it's not coming directly from you. You can always find a way to make a sale when there's demand. I'll take a cut, of course."

Rin was still confused. "But if it's Nikara goods they're buying, won't they know—"

"Of course they'll know," Moag said. She shook her head, casting again that pitying smile. "Everyone knows. But that's the business of statecraft. Nations rise and fall, but appetites remain the same. Trust me, Speerly—you'll be carting in Hesperian grain weeks after you boot them from your shores, so long as you're willing to send back some of Arlong's treasures in return. The world runs on trade. Send an envoy when you're ready to start."

The battles got harder as the Southern Army moved farther east. Rin had expected this. She was essentially knocking on Nezha's door now; they were only several months' march from Arlong. Now well-trained Republican troops occupied every major city in their path. Now Rin regularly encountered artillery formations armed with opium missiles, which forced her to get more and more creative with how and when she deployed shamans. In half her battles she didn't send in Pipaji or Dulin at all, relying instead on conventional military means to break the opposition. More often than not she was the only shaman in action, since she had a higher opium tolerance than the rest; she could withstand close to twenty minutes of smoke, during which she could do incalculable damage before she was forced to retreat.

The fighting turned vicious. The defenders weren't so quick to surrender anymore; more often they fought to the death, taking as many southerners with them as they could. Her casualty rates, once in the dozens, climbed to triple digits.

But Rin was also blessed by the fact that Nezha's troops were so fucking *slow*. They weren't mobile in the least. They were stationary defenders—they stuck behind city walls and protected them as best they could, but never did they attempt the roving strikes that might have put the Southern Army in real trouble.

"It's likely because they're weighed down by tons of Hesperian equipment," Kitay guessed. "Mounted arquebuses, multiple fire cannons, all that heavy stuff. They haven't got the transportation support to take it on the road, so they're always tethered to one place."

That turned Nezha's troops into sitting targets and offset the technology imbalance somewhat—Nezha's troops were committed to their trenches with their heavy machinery, while Rin's squadrons were quick and agile, always on the offensive. They were fighting like a turtle and a wolf—one retreating into its evershrinking shell, while the other paced its boundaries, waiting for the slightest weakness to strike.

That suited Rin just fine. After all, she, Kitay, and Nezha had all been taught since their first year at Sinegard that it was always, *always* better to be on the offensive.

Despite the increased resistance, week by week they continued to gain ground, while Nezha's territory crumbled.

Rin knew Nezha's losses weren't entirely his fault. He had inherited a Republic fractured and riddled with resentment toward his father, as well as a massive, unwieldy army that was tired of fighting a civil war they'd been promised would end quickly. His

inner circle was getting smaller and smaller, reduced now to a
Hesperian attaché who did little more than make snide comments
about how Nezha was on his way to losing a country, and a handful of Vaisra's old advisers who resented that he wasn't his father.
She heard rumors that since Mount Tianshan, he'd already had to
quash two attempted coups, and although he'd swiftly jailed the
perpetrators, his dissenters had only increased.

Most importantly, he was losing the support of the countryside.

Most of the Nikara elite—aristocrats, provincial officials, and
city bureaucrats—remained loyal to Arlong. But the villagers had
no entrenched interests in the Republic. They hadn't benefited fi-
nancially from Nezha's new trade policies, and now that they'd
tasted life under Hesperian occupation, they threw their support
behind the only other alternative.

The upshot of this was that as Rin moved south, she stumbled
into a remarkable intelligence network. In the countryside, everyone was tangentially connected to everyone else. Market gossip
became a hub for crucial information. It didn't matter that none
of her new sources were privy to high-level conversations, or that
none of them had ever seen a map of troop placements. They saw
its evidence with their own eyes.

Three columns crossed this river two nights ago, they told her.

We saw wagons of fire powder moving east this morning.

*They are building temporary bridges across the river at these
two junctions.*

Much of this ground-level, eyewitness intelligence was useless. The villagers weren't trained spies, they didn't draw accurate
maps, and they often embellished their stories for dramatic effect.
But the sheer volume of information made up for it; once Rin had
reports from at least three different sources, she and Kitay could
piece them together into a mostly accurate composite image of
where Nezha had arranged his defenses, and where he intended to
strike next.

And that, again, confirmed what Rin had believed since the

start of her campaign—that Nikan's southerners were weak but many, and that united, they could topple empires.

"Nezha can't be doing this on purpose," Kitay said one evening after yet another city in Hare Province had tumbled into southern hands with barely so much as a whimper. "It's like he's not even trying."

Rin yawned. "Maybe it's the best he can do."

He shot her a wary look. "Don't get cocky."

"Yeah, yeah." She knew she couldn't really take credit for their victory. They both knew that their ongoing streak of wins was in large part because Nezha simply had not committed as many troops or resources as they had.

But *why*?

They had to assume at this point that Nezha's dominant strategy was to hole up in Arlong and concentrate his defenses there. But surely he knew better than to put all his eggs in one basket. Arlong was blessed with a bevy of natural defenses, but defaulting to a siege mentality this early screamed of either desperation or insanity.

"He must be confident about something," Kitay mused. "Otherwise the only possible explanation for all this is that he's gone batshit crazy. He's got to have something up his sleeve."

Rin frowned. "More dirigibles, you think?" But that didn't seem likely. If Nezha had increased Hesperian aid, he would have subjected them to air raids already, while they were still on open, distant terrain, instead of near his prized capital. "Is he wagering everything on the Dragon? Some new military technology that's more lethal than shamanism?"

"Or some military technology that can counteract shamanism," Kitay said.

Rin shot him a sharp look. He'd said it too quickly—it wasn't a guess. "Do you know something?"

"I, ah, I'm not sure."

"Did Nezha say something?" she demanded. "In the New City, when Petra was—I mean—did he—"

"He didn't know." Kitay tugged uncomfortably at a lock of hair. "Petra never told him anything. He went through her—her tests. The Hesperians lent him weapons. That was the deal they offered him, and he took it. They didn't think he had the right to know what they were researching."

"He could have been lying."

"Maybe. But I've seen Nezha lying. That wasn't it. That was just despair."

"But there's nothing Petra could invent," Rin insisted. "They've got nothing. Their theology is wrong. Their Maker doesn't exist. If they had some anti-shamanic tool, they would have used it to protect their fleet, but they didn't. All they have is conventional weapons—fire powder and opium—and we know how to counteract those. Right?"

Kitay looked unconvinced. "As far as we know."

She crossed her arms, frustrated. "Pick a side, Kitay. You just said there's no proof—"

"There's no proof either way. I'm just floating the possibility, because we have to consider it. You know that unless Nezha has something like this up his sleeve, his strategy so far has been utterly irrational. And we can't proceed assuming the worst of him."

"Then what? You want to divert from Arlong?"

Kitay mulled that over for a moment. "No. I don't think we change our overall strategy. We keep gaining ground. We keep bolstering our resources. Based on the information we have, we take Arlong on schedule. But I'm saying we need to be cautious."

"We're always cautious."

He gave her a tired look. "You know what I mean."

They left it at that. There was nothing else to discuss; without further proof, there was nothing they could do.

Privately, Rin thought Kitay was being paranoid.

What if Nezha didn't have some secret weapon? What if Nezha was just destined to lose? She couldn't shake the feeling that maybe, just maybe, the end to this story was a foregone conclusion. After all, the last several months had made it clear that she couldn't be defeated. Battle by battle, victory by victory, she became more and more convinced of the fact that she'd been chosen by fate to rule the Empire. What else explained her streak of incredible, implausible victories and escapes? She had survived Speer. Golyn Niis. Shiro's laboratory. She'd taken an army through the long march. She'd emerged victorious from Mount Tianshan. She'd outwitted and outlasted the Mugenese, the Trifecta, and Vaisra. And now she was about to conquer Nezha.

Of course, she couldn't leave everything to the fates. She couldn't stop meticulously preparing for every battle just because she hadn't yet lost a single one. Nikara history was crammed with fools who imagined themselves kings. When their luck bled out, they died like anyone else.

That was why she never voiced this feeling out loud to Kitay. She knew what he would say. *Come on, Rin. You're losing your grip on reality. The gods don't choose their champions. That's not how this works.*

And while she understood that in the rational part of her mind, she still knew *something* had changed when she'd come back down from Mount Tianshan, when she'd survived an explosion that killed the greatest figures in Nikara history and nearly wiped out the Hesperian fleet. The tides of history had shifted. She had never before believed in fate, but this she came to know with more and more certainty as each day passed: the script of the world was now wholly, inalterably colored by a brilliant crimson streak.

Rin's favorite part by far of the southeastern campaign was the Southern Army's slow acquisition and mastery of Hesperian military technology. She made a game of it—the standing rule was double portions of dinner to the squadron that returned from active engagement with the largest haul of functioning Hesperian equipment.

Most of the pieces they retrieved were minor improvements on equipment they already had—more accurate compasses, sturdier splints for the physicians, more durable axles for their wagons. Often they found contraptions they had no idea what to do with— little lamps without wicks that they didn't know how to light, ticking orbs that resembled clocks but whose arms corresponded to inexplicable letters and numbers, and whirring mini-dirigibles that Rin assumed were messenger crafts, which she couldn't fly. She felt stupid, turning the devices over and over in her fingers, unable to find the controls to make them start. Kitay fared slightly better—he finally determined that the lamps were activated with a series of taps—but even he grew frustrated with machines that seemed to run purely on magic.

Three miles out from Bobai, a recently abandoned Republican holdout, they found under a thin layer of soil a hastily buried crate of functioning arquebuses.

"Fuck me," Kitay murmured when they pried the lid off the crate. "These are almost brand-new."

Rin lifted an arquebus from the top of the pile and weighed it in her hand. She'd never held one before; she hadn't dared. The steel was icy cool to the touch. It was heavier than she imagined— she found a new respect for Hesperian soldiers who lugged these running into battle.

She glanced at Kitay, whose jaw hung open as he knelt down to examine the weapons. She knew what he was thinking.

These changed everything.

They'd made it this far with minimal ranged capabilities. There were only several dozen archers in the Southern Army, and their ranks weren't growing. It took weeks for a novice soldier to learn to properly fire an arrow, and months if not years for them to fire with decent accuracy. Archery required tremendous arm strength, particularly if arrows were meant to pierce armor.

The next best thing they had to arrows were fire lances, a recent Republican invention Kitay had heard about during his stay in the New City, then reverse engineered. Those were tubes made of sixteen layers of thin wrapped paper, a little longer than two feet, stuffed with willow charcoal, sulfur, saltpeter, and shards of iron. The lances could shoot flames nearly ten feet when lit, but they still required a ready fire source to activate, and they back-fired easily, often exploding in the hands of their wielders.

But arquebuses required less arm strength than bows, and they were more reliable than fire lances. How long would it take to train troops to shoot? Weeks? Days, perhaps, if they devoted their time to nothing else? If she could get just twenty to thirty soldiers who were halfway proficient with the arquebus, that would open up a host of new strategies they'd only dreamed of.

"Think you can figure out how to use these?" she asked Kitay.

He chuckled, brushing his fingers over the metal tubes. "Give me until sunset."

Kitay took only the afternoon before he called her over into a clearing, empty except for the dozen dissembled arquebuses scattered around the grass. Pale little notches dotted the trunks of every tree in sight.

"It's actually quite simple." He pointed at various parts of the arquebus as he spoke. "I thought I was going to have to interrogate some Hesperian prisoners, but the design really revealed its own function. Very clever invention. It's basically a cannon in miniature—you set off some fire powder inside the barrel, and the force of the explosion sends the lead ball ricocheting out."

"How does the firing mechanism work?" Rin asked. "Do they have to light a spark every time?"

This seemed inconvenient to her, as well as implausible; the Hesperians seemed to fire at will without fumbling for flint.

"No, they don't," said Kitay. "They've done something clever with the match. It's already a burning fuse—you can light it before you're out on the field. Then when you're ready to shoot, you squeeze this lever here, and it brings the match down into the powder. Click, boom." He reached for an intact arquebus. "Here, I've loaded that one. Want to give it a try?"

She waved her stump at him. "Not sure if I can."

"I'll aim for you." He stood behind her and wrapped his arms around her torso, pointing the barrel at a thick tree across the clearing. "Ready when you are."

She curled her fingers around metal latch. "I just squeeze this?"

"Yup. Make sure you plant your feet, there'll be a kickback against your shoulder. Remember, it's a miniature cannon explosion. And give it a hard yank, it's quite resistant—prevents accidental firing."

She bent her knees as he demonstrated, took a deep breath, and pulled the trigger.

A bang split the clearing. The gun jerked backward at her chest and she flinched, but Kitay's firm grip kept it from slamming into her ribs. Smoke poured out of the muzzle. She turned her head away, coughing.

"That's one disadvantage," Kitay said after the smoke had cleared. "Takes a while to see whether you've actually hit anything."

Rin strode toward a tree on the opposite end of the clearing, where smoke unfurled into the air like little dragons. The pellet had struck true, burrowing deep into the center of the trunk. She stuck her finger into the groove. It sank into wood up to her third knuckle, until she couldn't dig her finger in any farther, and even then she couldn't feel the pellet.

"Holy fucking shit," she said.

"I know," Kitay said. "I've tried firing on armor, too. We've seen what they do to flesh, but these things penetrate *steel*."

"Fuck. How long does that take to reload?"

"It's taking me about half a minute now," he said. "It'll be faster with training."

So that meant three, perhaps four, shots per minute. That was nothing near what an archer like Venka could manage in the same time span, but the arquebus's superior lethality more than compensated.

"How many of your shots end up anywhere close to the target?" she asked.

He gave a sheepish shrug. "Eh. One in six hit the trunk. That should improve."

"And how many of those bullets did we find?"

"Three boxes. About two hundred bullets in each."

She frowned. "Kitay."

He sighed. "I know. We're going to run out."

She took a moment to do the math in her head. Thirty soldiers on arquebuses firing at an ambitious rate of three shots per minute would run out of ammunition in less than—

"Six to seven minutes," said Kitay. "We're out in six to seven minutes."

"I was getting there."

"Course you were, I just figured I'd speed things up. Yes, that is the problem." He rubbed his chin. "There were armories in that town we passed through last week. We could make some casts, melt some scrap metal down . . ."

"What scrap metal?" Rin asked. They were short on swords as it was, and they both knew it was folly to trade swords for bullets when most of their troops were far better in close-range combat.

"Then we've got to obtain it somehow," Kitay said. "Or steal ammunition. But that'll be tough—they've been pretty good about guarding their weapons so far, and those arquebuses were a rare find—"

"Hold on." An idea had just struck her. "Master Irjah gave us a puzzle like this once. Almost *exactly* like this."

"What are you talking about?"

"Don't you remember? What do you do when you need your enemy's ammunition?" She nudged his elbow. "Come on."

He shook his head. "Rin, that worked for *arrows*."

"So what? Same principle."

"Steel pellets are different," he insisted. "They distort upon impact; you can't just collect them and shove them right back into the barrel."

"So we'll melt them down," she countered. "Why is this so implausible? The Hesperians love firing on things. It'll be easy enough to bait them, we just need to give them any reason to shoot. And we're about to hit a tributary, which means—"

"It won't work," he interrupted. "Come on. They've got better spyglasses than we do. Straw targets will be too obvious, they'll know they're decoys."

"That's easy," she said. "We'll just use the real thing."

And so, three days later, they found themselves fastening corpses to the mast and railings of an opium skimmer. The key, Rin learned, was a combination of nails and twine. Ropes would have been ideal, but they were too visible to the naked eye. Nails she could pound through bare flesh, and easily conceal the protrusions under layers of clothing. Anyone who stared long enough through a spyglass could see these were clearly corpses, but Rin hoped the Republican artillerymen would be too trigger-happy for that to matter.

When they'd populated the upper deck with enough corpses to make it look manned, they sent it floating down the river with a sole helmsman whose job was to keep it from crashing onto the bank. They'd chosen a wide, fast-moving stretch of water, with a current quick enough to pull the skimmer out of Republican range before anyone tried to board it.

"Gross." Rin wiped her hand on her tunic as she watched the skimmer drift out of view. "This smell isn't coming out for days, is it?"

"Just as well," Kitay said. "We still have to cut the bullets out."

When at last they neared the southern border of Hare Province, they found a messenger waiting with a letter from Venka. She and Cholang had been sending regular updates throughout the campaign. They'd swept through the north easily enough, as predicted. They hadn't had much to do; Nezha seemed to have pulled his troops in from the east and north alike, concentrating them in a last stand in Dragon Province. So far Venka's missives had involved happy updates of townships captured, shipments of historical artifacts she'd looted in magistrates' estates, and the occasional crate of armor from Tiger Province's famed blacksmiths.

As both divisions of the Southern Army moved closer to the center, Venka's correspondence had come back faster and faster. Now Venka and Cholang were merely a week's ride away—close enough to converge on Arlong in a joint attack.

"This is from six days ago." The messenger handed Rin the scroll. "She wants a quick response."

"Understood," Rin said. "Wait outside."

The messenger gave a curt nod and left the command tent. Rin checked that he was out of hearing range, then ripped the scroll open with her teeth.

> Change of plans. Don't move yet on Arlong—my scouts say he's taking forces north to meet us between the mountains. Rendezvous at Dragab? Please confirm as soon you can; we'd rather not walk alone into a massacre.

"Dragab?" Rin asked. "Where's that?"

"Little outpost south of Xuzhou." Kitay had been reading over her shoulder. "And Xuzhou is, I assume, where the Republic intends to meet us."

"But that's . . ." Rin trailed off, trying to work through her mental map of Southern and Republican troop placements. This didn't track. All this time they had assumed Nezha would keep his forces in Arlong city proper, where the Red Cliffs and canals offered him the clearest advantage. "Why would he push north?"

"I can guess three reasons," Kitay said. "One, Xuzhou's situated over a narrow mountain channel, which restricts the fighting terrain to the opposite cliffsides and the wide ravine beneath. Two, it's monsoon season, and the water locks into the pass when the rains get heavy. And three, it's on our only route to Arlong."

"That's not true," she said. "We could cut around it, there are forest passes—"

"Yes, with roads so bumpy we won't be able to move any of our heavy artillery, and then we'll still have to scale down mountain faces that leave us wide open for their archers. Nezha knows we're coming through for him. He intends to choke us off in the mountains, where your shamans can't strike with discrimination, which forces the battle into a conventional bloodbath."

"So this isn't some last, desperate feint," Rin said. "It's an invitation."

Then why on earth should the Southern Army accept?

Even as the question rose to her lips, the answer became obvious. They should take Xuzhou as their next battleground, purely because it wasn't Arlong.

Nezha's power amplified the closer he was to sources of water. Under the Red Cliffs, where the Murui filtered into canals that surrounded every inch of Arlong, he'd be nearly unstoppable. He'd be right on top of the Dragon's grotto. Xuzhou was their last, and best, chance to fight him while separating him from his god.

Rin saw the grim press of Kitay's mouth, and knew that he'd realized the same. Xuzhou might be Nezha's dominant strategy, but it was theirs, too.

He nodded to the scroll. "Shall we give him what he wants?"

Rin hated that phrasing. This choice was frustrating. Unanticipated. She didn't like meeting their opponent on a terrain of his choosing, under the least favorable strategic conditions possible.

And yet, deep in her gut, she felt a hot coil of excitement.

Until now, this had not been a true war, only a series of skirmishes against cowards in retreat. Every win so far had meant nothing except as instrumental fuel for this moment, when at last they'd meet true resistance. This was the final test. Rin wanted to go up against Nezha's best-prepared strategy and see who came out on top.

"Why not?" she said at last. "Nezha's finally putting his pieces on the board. So let's play."

She stepped outside the tent to summon the messenger. He extended his hand, expecting a written reply, but she shook her head. "I'll be brief. Tell Venka to route to Dragab quick as she can. We'll be waiting."

CHAPTER 27

"I see you found some seamstresses." Venka's eyes roved over the Southern Army's neat brown uniforms as she dismounted from her horse to clasp Rin's hand in greeting. "Do I get one?"

"Of course," Rin said. "It's waiting in the tent."

"General's stripe and everything?"

"Is this your way of asking for a promotion?" Kitay asked.

"I've just handed you the north," said Venka. "That's half a fucking country, mind you. I think the title General Sring is a little overdue, don't you?"

"Honestly," said Rin, "I thought you'd just take the title for yourself."

"Honestly," said Venka, "I did."

They grinned at each other.

Venka and Cholang's troops filed into the southern camp at Dragab, falling eagerly on the prepared meals by the campfires. They'd emerged from their northern expedition with close to their original numbers—an impressive achievement, given that the Dog Province's militia had historically only waged battle against underequipped raiders from the Hinterlands. They also came bearing gifts—wagon upon wagon of spare armor, swords, and shields carted down from the forges in Tiger Province.

After Venka and Cholang had eaten, they joined Rin and Kitay on the floor of the command tent with a map spread between them to piece together their joint intelligence.

"It's an odd play." Venka marked Republican columns in blue ink along the eastern end of the Xuzhou ravine. "I really don't know why he's not just committing all his defenses to Arlong, especially if he can control the fucking river."

"Agreed," Kitay said. "But we think that's the point. He wants to take the Phoenix out of the equation."

"Why, just because we'll be fighting in close quarters?" Cholang asked.

"And because of the rain," Rin said. "He can call the rain, can make it fall as hard or as thick as he likes. Bit hard to sustain a flame when the sky keeps putting it out."

They all regarded the map for a few seconds in silence.

The battle for Xuzhou had become a game of warring tactics, a puzzle that Rin had to admit was highly entertaining. It felt like the sort of exam question she might receive from Master Irjah. Xuzhou was the field of engagement. The limiting conditions were known: The rain disadvantaged them both by damping down fire and fire powder alike. Nezha had superior numbers, better artillery capabilities, and fresher troops due to a shorter march. Nezha had the rain. But Rin had shamans Nezha didn't know about, and she could get to Xuzhou first.

Given the circumstances, piece together a winning strategy.

After a moment, Venka sighed. "What's this coming down to, then? Pure attrition? Are we just going to slug it out in the mud?"

None of them wanted that. No good commander ever left an outcome to the chances that sheer, mindless friction produced. The brunt of the fighting might very well come down to swords, spears, and shields, but they had to find some gambit, some hidden advantage that Nezha hadn't thought of.

Suddenly Kitay began to chuckle.

"What?" Rin asked. She didn't follow; she didn't know what

he'd seen that she hadn't. But that didn't matter. Kitay had solved it, and that was all she needed.

"This is very smart," he said. "You've got to give Nezha credit, really. He's reduced the number of factors at play until the only vectors that matter are the ones where he holds the advantage. He's swept almost all the chess players off the board."

"But?" Rin pressed.

"But he's forgotten one thing." He tapped his forehead. "I've always thrashed him at chess."

Xuzhou was a city of tombs. The Red Emperor had designed it to be an imperial graveyard, the final resting place for his most beloved generals, advisers, wives, and concubines. He'd commissioned the most skilled sculptors, architects, and gardeners across his territories to build grand monuments to his regime, and over the decades, what had begun as a single cemetery sprawled into a memorial the size of a city. Xuzhou became a place with the sole economy of death—its inhabitants were artisans employed to sweep the tombs, light incense, play ritual concerts to tame vengeful ghosts, and craft intricate mansions, clothes, and furniture out of paper to be burned as offerings so that the deceased might receive them in the afterlife. Even after the Red Emperor's regime collapsed, the caretakers remained employed, their salaries paid by one ruler or another out of reverence to the dead.

"Can you imagine such an old civilization built all this?" Kitay ran his hands across remarkably well-preserved limestone as they walked through the central cemetery, staking out vantage points for their artillery units. "They didn't have anything like modern tools. I mean, they barely even had *math*."

"Then how'd they manage it?" Venka asked.

"Sheer human labor. When you can't figure something out, you just throw bodies at it." Kitay pointed to the far end of the graveyard, where a forty-foot sculpture of the Red Emperor loomed over the ravine. "There are bones in that statue. Actually, there are probably bones in all these statues. The Red Emperor believed that human souls kept buildings structurally sound forever, so when the laborers were done chiseling his face into stone, he had them bound up and hurled into the hollow centers."

Rin shuddered. "I thought he wasn't religious."

"He wasn't a shaman. Still superstitious as fuck." Kitay gestured to the monuments surrounding them. "Imagine you're living in a land of beasts and Speerlies. Why wouldn't you believe in spells?"

Rin craned her head up at the Red Emperor. His face had been weathered by time, but had retained its structural integrity well enough that she could still make out his features. He looked the same way he did on all the replicas she'd ever seen of his official portrait—a severe, humorless man whose expression displayed no kindness. Rin supposed he'd had to be cruel. A man who intended to stitch the disparate, warring factions of Nikan into a united empire had to have a ruthless, iron will. He couldn't bend or break. He couldn't compromise; he had to mold the world to his vision.

His first wife stood at the opposite end of the graveyard. The Winter Empress was famously beautiful and famously sad. She'd been born with such impossible, heavenly beauty that the Red Emperor had kidnapped her as a mere child and deposited her in his court. There, her constant weeping only heightened her beauty because it made her eyebrows arch and her lips purse in such an enticing manner that the Red Emperor would watch as she cried, fascinated and aroused.

According to the stories, she looked so beautiful when she was in pain that no one realized she was wasting away from a heart disease until one day she collapsed in the garden, fingers clawing futilely at her snow-white chest. In the old stories, that counted as romance.

But Rin recognized the stone face across the graveyard. And that wasn't, *couldn't* be, the Winter Empress.

"That's Tearza," she murmured, amazed.

"The Speerly queen?" Venka wrinkled her nose. "What are you talking about?"

Rin pointed. "Look around her neck. See that necklace? That's a Speerly necklace."

She'd seen that crescent moon pendant before in her dreams. She'd seen it hanging on Altan's neck. She knew she couldn't have imagined it; those visions were branded into her mind.

Why would the Red Emperor cast Tearza as his Empress?

Was it true, then, that they'd been lovers?

But all the tales said he'd tried to kill her. He'd sent assassins after her since the moment they met. He'd tried many times on the battlefield to take her head. He had been so afraid of her that he ensconced himself in an island hideout surrounded by water. When she'd died, he'd made her island his colony and her people his slaves.

Yet, Rin supposed, lovers could still inflict that kind of violence on each other. Hadn't Riga loved Daji? Hadn't Jiang loved Tseveri?

Hadn't Nezha once loved her?

"If that's Mai'rinnen Tearza," Kitay said, "that's a history no one's ever written."

"Only because the Red Emperor wrote her out of history," Rin said. "Wrote her out so cleanly that no one even recognized her face."

She had to respect the man. When you conquered as totally and completely as he had, you could alter the course of everything. You could determine the stories that people told about you for generations.

When they sing about me, she decided, *Nezha won't warrant even a mention.*

Under her direction, the Southern Army finished preparing the city for Nezha's arrival. They hid cannons behind every statue. They dug trenches and tunnels. They placed their sandbags around their forts. They staked out target points for Dulin, identifying weak points in the stone that could bring entire structures down on the Republican Army.

Then they hunkered down to wait.

Rainfall started that evening and continued steadily through the night, fat droplets hammering down in unrelenting sheets that turned the ground beneath their feet to such slippery mud that they had to prop their carts up on boulders so their wheels wouldn't get stuck overnight. Rin hoped the heavy downpour might drain the clouds empty by morning, but the pattering only intensified as the hours drew on. At dawn, the gray shroud over Xuzhou showed no sign of thinning.

Rin tried to snatch a bit of sleep, but the rain battering against her tent made it impossible. She gave up and waited out the night sitting outside, keeping watch over the graveyard beneath Tearza's statue.

Nezha had been right to attack in monsoon season. Her fire would do very little today aside from keeping her warm. She'd tested it throughout the night, sending arcs of flame across the night sky. They all fizzled away in seconds. She could still incinerate anyone within her immediate proximity, but that didn't help in a ranged battle. Cannons and arquebuses wouldn't be half as effective in this weather; the fuses would take forever to light. Both sides had been largely reduced to brutal, primitive, and familiar weapons—swords, arrows, and spears.

The winner today would be determined by sheer tactical proficiency. And Rin, despite herself, couldn't wait to see what Nezha had come up with.

The sun crept higher in the sky. Rin's troops were awake, armed, and ready, but there was still no word from the sentries. They waited another hour in tense anticipation. Then, suddenly, the rain intensified from a loud patter to a violent roar.

It might have been an accident of nature, but Rin doubted it. The timing was too abrupt. Someone was hauling that rain down from the heavens.

"He's here." She stood up and waved to her officers. "Ready the columns."

Seconds later, her sentries caught on to what she already knew, and a series of horns resounded across the tombstones.

The Republican Army appeared at the other end of the ravine, fanning out beneath the Red Emperor's feet.

Rin scanned the front lines with her spyglass until she spotted Nezha marching at the fore. He was dressed in a strange hybrid fashion; his chest was clad in the familiar blue cloth and lamellar plating of the Dragon Army, but his arms and legs were wrapped in some armor made of overlapping metal plates. It looked obstructively heavy. His shoulders, usually so arrogantly squared, seemed to sag.

"What's that around his wrists?" Kitay asked.

Rin squinted into her spyglass. She could just barely make out golden circlets around both of Nezha's wrists. They served no function she could discern—they didn't seem a part of his armor, and she couldn't imagine how they might be used as weapons.

She shifted the spyglass down. Another pair of golden circlets was visible over his boots. "Did he have those in Arabak?"

"Not that I remember," Kitay said. "But I remember seeing these odd scars once, right around—"

"He's seen us," Rin said abruptly.

Nezha had taken out a spyglass, too. He was looking right back at them.

She was struck by the symmetry of the scene. They could have been a painting—two opposing factions lined under statues that may as well have been their patron gods. Tearza and the Red Emperor, Speerly against conqueror, the newest participants in a centuries-old conflict that had never died, but had only continued to reverberate through history.

Until now. Until one of them ended it, for better or for worse.

Nezha raised a hand.

Rin tensed. Blood roared in her ears; the familiar, addictive rush of adrenaline thrummed through her body.

So this was how it began. No pleasantries, no obligatory attempt at negotiation; just battle. Nezha brought his hand down and his troops began charging down the ravine, feet thundering against the mud.

Rin turned to Commander Miragha. "Send in the turtles."

Throughout Nikara history, the traditional way to deal with arrow fire had been sending in shielded front lines to absorb the blow. Dozens of guaranteed fatalities bought time for melee combatants to breach the enemy lines. But Rin didn't have the dozens of warm bodies to spare.

Enter the turtles. These were one of Kitay's recent inventions. Inspired by the thickly armored turtle boats in the Republican Fleet, he'd designed small cart-mounted vehicles that could survive heavy fire of almost any kind. He hadn't had the time nor resources to construct anything sophisticated, so he'd cobbled the turtles together from wooden tables, water-soaked cotton quilts, and scavenged plates of Hesperian armor that, combined, kept out most flying projectiles.

One by one they rolled out from behind the tombstones into the ravine. As if on cue, Nezha's archers launched their opening volleys, and arrows dotted the surfaces of the turtles until they looked like roving hedgehogs.

"They look so stupid," Rin muttered.

"Shut up," Kitay said. "They're working."

Republican missiles landed two lucky hits, launching turtles into the air like spinning balls of fire. Undaunted, the other armored vehicles barreled forward. A symphony of whistling sounds filled the air as the Southern Army returned the Republic's fire. This was largely for show—most of their projectiles skidded ineffectively off the Republic's metal shields—but the volleys forced the Republican artillery to duck, creating a reprieve for the advancing turtles. Venka's contingent, stationed with long-distance crossbows on a protruding ledge near the middle of the ravine, landed the most hits, picking off Nezha's cannon operators with well-placed bolts.

Over the din of the rain, Rin could just barely make out a distinct, low rumble echoing across the ravine. She bent low, placed her hand to the shuddering ground, and smiled.

Dulin was right on time.

They'd determined during training that he couldn't summon earthquakes outside a ten-yard radius, which meant he couldn't meaningfully affect fighting conditions inside the ravine unless they threw him into the melee. Rin couldn't keep him there for long. The turtles weren't invincible—half had been reduced to smoldering wrecks, obliterated by a concentrated round of missiles.

But Dulin didn't need to last the entire battle. He only needed to take out the Republic's upper-level artillery stations. He was so close now, even as his marked turtle vehicle stuttered to a halt, barraged by bolts and arrows.

Come on.

The cliffs began to vibrate. Rin tilted her spyglass up at the artillery stations. Stones slid like powder off the cliffside, cascading over one line of crossbows. The ledge shifted and collapsed, sending Republican troops tumbling dozens of feet into the ravine.

Nearly there, just finish it . . .

A rocket exploded right in front of Dulin's turtle, flipping the vehicle backward into the air.

Rin let out a wordless screech.

Kitay seized her arm. "It's fine, he's fine, look—"

He was right. The cliffs were still quaking, the artillery stations buried in rubble beneath. Dulin was still alive, still channeling the Tortoise. Three armored vehicles clustered protectively around the wreck of Dulin's turtle, shielding it from the next barrage of bullets. Through her spyglass, Rin saw Dulin climb out from beneath the overturned craft and limp toward the nearest turtle. Soldiers popped out of the hatch to drag him into the armored belly. Then the cart reversed course and started retreating back behind Rin's waiting infantry.

Nezha's troops didn't pursue him. Like everyone else, Nezha was preoccupied with the melee inside the ravine, which—as predicted—had now turned into an utter clusterfuck. No one could aim properly under the rain. Arrows forced off course by the weather buried themselves uselessly in the dirt or ricocheted off the ravine walls. Occasionally someone managed to keep a flame alight long enough to light a fuse, but the battlefield was now too muddled to land a clear hit. Cannonballs, mortar shells, and fire rockets hurtled haphazardly into allies and enemies alike. The silver lining was that Nezha's wheeled arquebuses had become useless, bogged down in thick mud, their range limited only to the midsection of the ravine.

The remaining four turtles continued their advance toward him, followed by a press of the Southern Army's infantry. They wouldn't get far. Nezha's front line was armed with halberds, extended straight outward in an impaling welcome.

But the turtles weren't intended to breach the lines. They only needed to get close enough to toss their pipe bombs. Each squadron had set out with a lit coal shielded inside an iron tin. Ten feet from Nezha's front lines, they lit the bomb fuses and tossed them out the carts' top hatches.

Several seconds passed. Rin tensed. Then Nezha's front lines blew apart like ripped paper, and Rin's infantry surged through.

The battle had now turned into a conventional bloodbath. Swords, halberds, and shields clashed in a frenetic crush of bodies. It should have been a massacre—Nezha's troops were better trained and better armed—but the rain and mud had made it impossible for anyone to see, which allowed Rin's peasant infantry to last much longer than they should have.

But they didn't need to last forever. Just long enough.

Rin felt a sudden, bizarre sense of detachment as she watched the carnage playing out from the far side of the ravine. *None of this seems real.* Yes, she knew the costs were real—she knew that below her feet, real bodies were bleeding and breaking as a consequence of orders she'd given, that real lives were being snuffed out in the rain while she waited out the timetable of her plan.

But the adrenaline, that mad rush of energy that accompanied the irrepressible fear of death, was missing. Here she stood, watching from an angle so safe that Kitay was standing right next to her. None of those missiles could reach her. None of those swords could touch her. Her only true opponent was Nezha, and he hadn't entered the fray, either. Like her, he waited from his vantage point, calmly observing the chaos playing out below.

This wasn't really a fight. This wasn't one of those bare-knuckled, bruising scuffles they'd been so fond of at school. This battle was, at its core, a contest of their ideas. Nezha had gambled on the environment—the rain and ravine. Rin had placed her hopes on wild, distracting gambits.

They'd learn soon who had placed the better bet.

An arrow thudded into the ground ten feet away. Rin glanced down, jerked from her reverie. The arrow shaft was wrapped with red ribbon—Venka's signal: *Your turn.*

Kitay noticed it, too.

"Turtle's ready behind the third column," he said, lowering his spyglass. "Quickly, before he notices."

Rin sprinted down into the ravine. A last turtle cart awaited her near the front lines, already manned by waiting troops. They grasped her by the arms and hauled her into the center of the cart, where she crouched down, arms folded over her knees. Two soldiers set off at a run, pushing the cart downhill until it gained momentum.

Rin braced herself in the cramped, dark interior, jolting from side to side as the cart careened over bumpy terrain. She heard loud thuds as arrows assailed the sides of the cart. The tip of a spear slammed through the wall in front of her, wedged between a chink in the armor plating.

She hugged her knees tighter. *Almost there.*

Everything up until now—Dulin's avalanches, the initial charge of turtle carts, the pipe bombs, and the infantry rush—had been a distraction. Rin knew she couldn't win a battle of attrition against Nezha's ranks; she'd just put up the front of trying.

Nezha had chosen this graveyard, in this weather, to neutralize the Phoenix. The bloodbath happening below only mattered because the rain kept Rin from igniting everyone in a blue uniform.

But what did you do when nature presented your greatest disadvantage?

How did you shut out nature itself?

The turtle cart jerked to a halt. Rin peeked out through the top hatch. When she squinted, she could just make out thin black ropes stretched taut over the top of the ravine, and a massive tarp meant for a battleship slowly unfurling from one side of the cliffs to the other.

Her troops, who knew to watch for the tarp's unfolding, were already retreating, shields locked behind them. The Republican soldiers seemed confused. Some half-heartedly gave chase, and some fell back, as if sensing some impending disaster.

Within seconds, the tarp reached the other end of the pass, secured from both sides by Venka's squadrons. Rain hammered hard against the canvas, but nothing penetrated the pass. Suddenly the middle patch of the ravine was gloriously, miraculously dry.

Rin climbed out of the turtle and reached into her mind for the waiting god. *Your turn.*

The Phoenix surged forth, warm and familiar. *Finally.*

She flung her arms up. Flames burst into the pass, a crescent arc roaring outward at Nezha's forces.

His front lines charred instantly. She advanced unobstructed, picking her way over bodies sizzling black under glowing armor. Her flames shimmered around her, forming a shield of unimaginable heat. Arrows disintegrated in the air before they reached her. Nezha's mounted arquebuses and cannons glowed bright, twisting and crumpling beyond use. The Southern Army advanced behind her, bowstrings taut, cannons loaded, fire lances aimed forward and ready to launch.

She only had minutes. She kept her fire concentrated low inside the ravine, but at this heat, the tarp would burn from sheer proximity, which meant she had to end this fast.

She could make out Nezha's figure through the wall of orange—alone and unguarded, shouting orders to his men as they fled. He had not retreated ahead of his troops; he was waiting until the last of his ranks reached safe ground. He'd refused to abandon his army.

Always so noble. Always so stupid.

She had him. She'd won this game of ideas, she had him in sight and in range, and this time she would not falter.

"*Nezha!*" she screamed.

She wanted to see his face.

He turned around. They stood close enough now that she could make out every detail on his lovely, wretched, cracked-porcelain face. His expression twisted as he met her eyes—not in fear, but in a wary, exhausted sorrow.

Did he realize he was about to die?

In her daydreams, whenever she'd fantasized about the moment that she would truly, finally kill him, he had always burned. But he stood just out of range of the tarp, so iron and steel would have to do. And if his body still kept stitching itself together, then she would take him apart piece by piece and burn them down to ash until not even the Dragon could put him back together.

She nodded to her waiting army, signaled with a hand. "Fire."

She pulled her flames back inside her and knelt. A great rip echoed through the ravine as projectiles of every type surged over her head.

Nezha raised his arms. The air rippled around him, then appeared to coalesce. Time diluted; arrows, missiles, and cannonballs hung arrested in midair, unable to budge forward. It took Rin a moment to realize that the projectiles had been trapped inside a barrier—a wall of clear water.

Again, she slashed a hand through the air. "Fire!"

Another volley of arrows shrieked over the ravine, but she knew before she even gave the command that it would make no difference. Nezha's shield held firm. Her troops shot another round, then another, but everything they hurled at Nezha was swallowed into the barrier.

Fuck. Rin wanted to scream. *We're just dumping weapons into the river.*

She'd known he could control the rain. She'd watched him do it at Tikany—had felt it pummeling against her like a thousand fists as he called it down harder and harder. But she hadn't known he could manipulate it at such a massive scale, that he could pull all the water out of the sky to construct barriers more impenetrable than steel.

She hadn't imagined his link to his god might now rival her own.

Nezha used to fear the Dragon more than he feared his enemies. He used to call his god only when forced to with his back against the wall, and every time he'd done so, it had looked like torture.

But now, he and the water moved like one.

This means nothing, she thought. Nezha could erect all the shields he wanted. She'd simply evaporate them.

"Get back," she ordered her troops. Once they'd retreated ten yards she pulled another parabola of flame into the ravine and brought its heat to the highest possible intensity, sinking deeper and deeper into the Phoenix's reverie until her world turned red. Heat baked the air. Above, the tarp sizzled and dissipated to ash.

Rin pushed the parabola forward. Two walls met at the center of the pass—blue and red, Phoenix and Dragon. Any normal body of water should have long since dissipated. This divine heat could have evaporated a lake.

Still the barrier held firm.

Burn, Rin prayed frantically. *What are you doing, burn—*

The Phoenix stunned her with a reply. *The Dragon is too strong. We can't.*

Her flames shrank back into her body. Rin glared at Nezha through the water. He grinned back, smug. His army had completed their retreat. Her troops could still pursue them overland, but how would they get past Nezha?

Then it all struck Rin with devastating clarity.

Nezha had never intended to make a stand at Xuzhou. Sending his men to the ravine had been a ploy, an opportunity to find out the extent of Rin's new capabilities, both shamanic and conventional, with minimal loss of his own forces. He hadn't come to fight, he'd come to embarrass her.

He'd pitted his god against hers. And he'd *won*.

Nezha lowered his arms. The barrier crashed down, splashing hard against the rocks. The clouds resumed their heavy downpour. Rin spat out a mouthful of water, face burning.

Nezha gave her a small, taunting wave.

He was alone, but Rin knew better than to pursue. She knew the threat on his mind, could predict exactly what he would do if her troops surged forward.

Just try. See what the rain does then.

Though it felt like ripping her heart out to say it, she turned back to the Southern Army and gave the only order she could. "Fall back."

They hesitated, their eyes darting confusedly to the clearly vulnerable Nezha.

"*Fall back*," she snapped.

This time they obeyed. Sparks of humiliated rage poured off her shoulders as she followed them in retreat, steaming the water from her armor in a thick, choking mist. *Fuck.*

She'd had him.

She'd *had* him.

She hadn't felt this sort of petty rage, this sheer *indignation*, since Sinegard. This wasn't about troops, this was about pride. In that moment they were schoolchildren again, pummeling each other in the ring, and he'd just laughed in her face.

CHAPTER 28

"What just happened?" Cholang demanded. "What *was* that?"

"He's got a god." Rin paced back and forth before the general staff, cheeks flushed with humiliation. They were supposed to be celebrating. She'd promised them resounding victory, not this embarrassing stalemate. "The Dragon of Arlong, the ruler of the seas. I've never seen him pull rain into a shield like that. He must have gotten stronger. Must have—must have practiced."

She kept her voice low so it wouldn't carry. Outside the tent, the Southern Army waited in baffled suspense, their disappointment tinged with a mounting fear.

She knew whispers about Nezha were spreading throughout the troops. *The gods favor the Young Marshal,* they said. *The Republic called down the heavens, and they've granted them a power to rival our own.*

"Then why are we just sitting around?" Venka asked. "We were thrashing them, we should have given chase—"

"If we give chase, we'll drown," Rin snapped.

Xuzhou lay only miles north of the Western Murui. Any follow-up strike would be futile. Nezha had certainly positioned himself along the riverbanks, and as soon as their troops at-

tempted a crossing he'd wrap the rapids around them like a fist
and drag them to the Murui's muddy depths.

Rin remembered vividly how it felt to drown. But this time
Nezha wouldn't save her. This time, he might pull her to the bottom of the river himself, holding her still as she thrashed until her
lungs collapsed.

I can't beat him.

She had to face that stark, immutable fact. The Phoenix had
made that abundantly clear. Right now she could not engage
Nezha one-on-one and win. It didn't matter how many soldiers
she had; it didn't matter that she now controlled twice as much
territory as he did. If they met again on the battlefield, he could
easily kill her in a thousand different ways, because in the end, the
sea and its dark, swallowing depths would always conquer fire.

And she knew Nezha would only get stronger the closer she
marched to Arlong. He'd created a shield thick enough to ward
off bullets with mere rainwater. It terrified her to imagine what he
might do in a river so vast it looked like an ocean.

Days ago, she'd held every strategic advantage. How had her
momentum vanished so abruptly?

If the entire leadership weren't watching her, she would have
screamed.

"There's no way around this," Kitay said quietly. "We've got to
heed Chaghan's advice. Back to the original plan."

Rin met his eyes. Silent understanding sparked between them,
and instantly the pieces of the obvious, inevitable strategy fell into
place.

It terrified her. But they had no other choice. They had only
one path forward, and now it was a matter of working through
the logistics.

"We'll have to stick to land routes as long as we can," she said.

"Right," he said. "Get over the river. Head straight down the
mountains to the capital."

"And when we've reached the Red Cliffs—"

"We'll find the grotto. Kill it at the source."

Yes. This was it. She'd been stupid to think that she might win this campaign without touching Arlong, when that was the locus of power all along.

Nezha fell if Arlong fell. Nezha died if the Dragon died. Nothing short of that would do.

"I don't understand." Venka glanced between them. "What are we trying to do?"

"We're going to the Nine Curves Grotto," Rin breathed. "And we're going to kill a dragon."

Rin ordered everyone out of the tent but Kitay.

They both knew, without saying it out loud, that what came next had to be delicately and discreetly planned. There were many roads to Arlong, but only one route that got her army there intact. Altan had once taught her that amateurs obsessed over strategy, and professionals obsessed over logistics. The logistics involved now meant the difference between dozens of casualties and thousands, and they could not be leaked.

Rin waited until the footsteps outside the tent had faded into silence to speak. "You know what we've got to do."

Kitay nodded. "You want a decoy."

"I'm thinking several. All pursuing separate crossings, with no knowledge of the other crossings, just the rendezvous point."

That was the only way this could work. Nezha controlled the entire river, which meant he had every advantage except one. He didn't know where or how Rin would cross it.

Meanwhile, Rin's problem was how to move a large column over the river at a point that Nezha wouldn't anticipate. She wasn't working with a fast, tiny strike force anymore; she couldn't pull off the kind of surprise ambushes she used to.

Moreover, she had to assume Nezha had spies within her ranks. Perhaps not in her inner circle, but certainly from the officer ranks down. That was inevitable in war—she had to plan every operation with the assumption that something would be leaked. The question was whether she could limit how much they knew. If she could trust Cholang and Venka, then she could break up a plan into pieces to give her generals limited, but sufficient, information.

"We split this army into seven parts," she said. "Nezha could get lucky with a random pick if we split into just two or three. Seven makes guessing much harder."

"The consequence, of course, is that you send at least a seventh of your army to certain death," said Kitay.

She paused, then nodded. They'd have to stomach that. They had to accept that they wouldn't only lose troops—they'd lose good officers, too, because a clear imbalance in power distribution would appear all too suspicious.

There was no way around it. They had to absorb the risk, and hope that the other six squadrons made it across to rendezvous outside Arlong.

"Let's assume the worst," Kitay continued. "Assume Nezha realizes we've got to set up decoys, and he splits his forces accordingly. Suppose you end up with only three squadrons at the rendezvous. How do you distribute those along Arlong's forces?"

"We don't have to conquer Arlong," Rin said. "We just have to poison the grotto. And you don't need six squadrons for that, you just need one."

"Fine." He nodded grimly. "So let's figure out how to get the one."

For the next three hours they hashed out an itinerary over the most detailed maps they could find. One squadron, led by Venka, would cross over the Sage's Ford. That was where Nezha would expect them to go—it was the shallowest crossing, the one that didn't involve bridge-building equipment. But the obviousness of that strategy, combined with the fact that Rin was visibly absent, should be enough to deter Nezha from striking hardest at Venka. They would dispatch three other squadrons to wide bridges, and one to a narrow ford crossing, and one to a stretch along the Murui where there was no crossing at all.

During the long march, Kitay had come up with an ingenious

design for a self-supporting bridge that could be assembled in minutes from portable wooden crossbeams. They hadn't used it in the mountains for want of lumber, but now they had plenty. If the bridge didn't exist, they'd build it.

"And where do we cross?" Kitay asked.

"Anywhere." Rin nudged the pieces. "Does it matter? It's a one-in-seven chance no matter where we go."

He shook his head. "One in seven is too high. There must be some way to reduce it to zero."

"There's not." She understood his urge for perfectionism, knew he'd be anxious unless he resolved every last variable, but she also knew better than to underestimate Nezha a second time. They could make their chances pretty good by avoiding the bulk of the Republican defense line, assuming their intelligence was accurate, but otherwise one in seven would have to be good enough.

"We'll take the narrow bridge at Nüwa's Waist," she decided. "Our squadron won't have to move any heavy artillery, so the width constraints won't matter."

"Then how do you want to cross?" he asked.

"What are you talking about? There's a bridge."

"But suppose they blow up the bridge in advance," he said. "Or suppose they've got soldiers stationed all around it. How do we get around that?"

These questions were rhetorical, Rin realized. Kitay leaned back, watching her with a familiar, anticipatory grin.

"You are not sending me up in a kite," she said.

He beamed. "I'm thinking something bigger."

"No," she said immediately. "You've never gotten that thing up in the air. And I'm not dying in a Hesperian death trap."

His grin widened. "Come on, Rin. Trust me. I gave you wings once."

"Yes, and that's how I got this scar!"

He reached over and patted her on the shoulder. "Then it's a good thing you've never cared much about looking pretty."

∞

Six squadrons dispersed the next morning to designated crossing points spread out over a ten-mile radius. Most had a good chance of making it across. Kitay had sent crews out to decoy crossing points the night before to chop haphazardly at nearby bamboo groves. Bamboo made good material for temporary bridges or fording walkways. Nezha's scouts would see the cut forests and, hopefully, anticipate bridge crossings that would never happen.

Rin, Dulin, and Pipaji, accompanied by just enough troops to drag the dirigible along in three carts, headed straight south.

Five miles from their camp outside Xuzhou was a shallow stretch of river called Nüwa's Waist, named for the way it curved sharply to the east. The bridge had indeed been dismantled, but the water there was only about knee-deep. Despite the swollen, monsoon-drenched rapids, well-prepared troops with flotation bags could wade across without being swept away.

It was a boring plan. Good enough not to arouse suspicion, but also not optimal. They weren't going to take it.

They detached from a decoy crew at Nüwa's Waist and continued marching two miles farther south, where the river was wider and faster. Earlier that morning, Kitay had dismantled his dirigible and loaded the parts into three wagons. They spent two hours on the riverbanks reconstructing it according to his careful instructions. Rin felt every second ticking by like an internal clock as they worked, nervously watching the opposite bank for Republican troops. But Kitay took his sweet time, fiddling with every bolt and yanking at every rope until he was satisfied.

"All right." He stood back, dusting the oil off his hands. "Safe enough. Everyone in."

The shamans stood back, staring at the basket with considerable hesitation.

"There's no way that thing actually flies," Dulin muttered.

"Of course they fly," Pipaji said. "You've seen them fly."

"I've seen the *good* ones fly," Dulin pointed out. "That thing's a fucking mess."

Rin had to admit Kitay's repairs did not give her much confidence. The airship's original balloon had ripped badly in the explosion at Tianshan. He'd patched it up with cowhide so that, fully inflated, it looked like a hideous, half-flayed animal.

"Hurry up," Kitay said, annoyed.

Rin swallowed her doubts and stepped into the basket. "Come on, kids. It's a short trip."

They didn't need a smooth, seamless flight. They just needed to get up in the air. If they crashed, at least they'd crash on the other side.

Reluctantly, Pipaji and Dulin followed. Kitay took a seat in the steering chamber and yanked at several levers. The engine roared to life, then maintained a deafening, ground-shaking hum. From a distance, the engine noise had always sounded like bees. Up close, Rin didn't hear the drone so much as she *felt* it, vibrating through every bone in her body.

Kitay twisted around, waved his hands over his head, and mouthed, *Hold on.*

The balloon inflated with a whoosh above their heads. The carriage tilted hard to the right, lurched off the ground, then wobbled in the air as Kitay worked frantically to stabilize their flight. Rin clutched the handrail and tried not to vomit.

"We're fine!" Kitay shouted over the engine.

"Guys?" Pipaji pointed over the side of the carriage. "We've got company."

Something shot past her head as she spoke. The rope by her arm snapped, ends frayed by an invisible arrow. Pipaji flinched back, shrieking.

"Get down," Rin ordered. That was redundant—everyone had already dropped to the carriage floor, arms over their heads as bullets whizzed above them.

Rin crawled to the far edge of the basket and pressed her eye against a slit in the carriage. She saw a mass of blue uniforms racing toward the riverbanks, arquebuses pointed to the sky.

Fuck. Nezha must have deployed troops along every stretch of the river once he'd realized the Southern Army had split into parts. And their aircraft was now visible from miles off, a clear target hanging plump in the air.

Another round of fire rocked the basket. Someone screamed in pain. Rin glanced over her shoulder to see one of her soldiers clutching his leg, his foot a bloody mess below the ankle.

"Use the cannons!" Kitay shouted, wrestling at the levers. He was managing to steer, but badly—the dirigible veered sharply east, wrenching them closer to both the opposite shore and the ambush. "They're loaded!"

"I don't know how!" Rin screamed back. But she ducked down beside him and fumbled at the cannons regardless. *Ingenious*, she thought, dazed. The handles let her swerve the gun mouths nearly 360 degrees, aiming at anything except herself.

Squinting, she aimed one cannon as best she could toward the ground platoon and funneled a stream of fire into the barrel.

The blowback flung her against the wall of the carriage. She scrambled to her knees, clambered forth, and grabbed the handle of the second cannon. Same process. This time she knew to drop down before the blowback could hit her. She couldn't see the fallout, not from where she was crouched, but the ensuing crash and screams promised good results.

The carriage lurched to the left. Rin careened into Kitay's side.

"The balloon," Kitay gasped. He'd given up with the levers. "They've pierced it, we're falling—"

She opened her mouth to respond just as they tilted again, veering hard in the other direction.

"Get out," Kitay said sharply.

She understood. Together they scrambled out of the steering chamber into the main carriage. They had no hope of flying this thing anymore; they just had to hold steady until they got near enough to the ground. Closer, *closer*—

Rin jumped from the basket, landing knees bent, hoping to distribute the impact across her body. It didn't work. Pain shocked through both her ankles, so intense that she doubled over for several seconds, screaming wordlessly, before she caught a grip on herself. "Kitay—"

"Right here." He clambered to his knees, coughing. Scorch marks streaked through his wiry hair. He pointed at something behind her. "Take care of—"

Rin reached out with her palm. Fire exploded out, arced around them in a parabola, and pushed forth twenty, then thirty yards. Rin forced as much fury as she could into that inferno, made it wickedly, devastatingly hot. If anyone in the Republican ambush had survived the airship cannons, they were ashes now.

"Enough." Kitay put a hand on her arm. "That's enough."

Rin called the flame back in.

Pipaji and Dulin climbed out of the basket, coughing. Pipaji moved with a limp, hopping along with her arm slung over Dulin's shoulder, but neither looked seriously wounded. A handful of soldiers filtered out of the dirigible behind them,

Rin loosed a sigh of relief. They hadn't been too high up before they'd crashed. This could have been so much worse.

"General?" Pipaji pointed at the wreck behind her. "There— there's someone . . ."

Only one of the soldiers hadn't made it out. He lay pinned under the side of the engine. He was still conscious—he groaned, face twisting in anguish. His legs were a ruin under the mass of warped steel.

Rin recognized him. He was one of Qinen's friends, one of the young, stubble-chinned men who had unhesitatingly followed her all the way from Leiyang to Mount Tianshan.

Ashamed, she realized she couldn't remember his name.

Together the soldiers strained against the side of the carriage, but nobody could move it. And what was the point? It had crushed more than half of the soldier's body. Rin could see fragments of his hip bone littered across the scorched earth. They couldn't possibly get him to Lianhua in time. There was no recovery from this.

"Please," said the soldier.

"I understand," Rin said, and knelt down to slit his throat.

Once she would have hesitated; now she didn't even blink. His agony was so obvious, and death so necessary. She jerked her knife through his jugular, waited several seconds for the blood to run its course, then pulled the soldier's eyes shut.

She stood up. Dulin's eyes were huge. Pipaji had a hand clamped over her mouth.

"Let's go," Rin said curtly. "Time to kill a dragon."

CHAPTER 29

From the wreckage of the dirigible, it was a quick three-mile march through the mountainside to the edge of the cliffs that sealed in Arlong like an oyster shell. When at last they pushed through the wall of thick forest, the great, wide Murui river lay on their horizon, stretching on without end as if it were the ocean. Before them lay Arlong's famous Red Cliffs, glinting in the noon sun like freshly spilled blood.

Rin halted at the ledge, searching the opposite wall until she found a string of characters, carved at a slant into the rock face so that they were only visible when the light caught them just so.

Nothing lasts.

Those were the famous words, written in near-indecipherable Old Nikara, carved into the Red Cliffs by the last minister loyal to the Red Emperor just before his enemies stormed the capital and hung his flayed body above the palace doors.

Nothing lasts. The world does not exist. Nezha and Kitay had come up with those conflicting translations. They were both wrong, and they were both right. Their translations were two sides of the same truth—that the universe was a waking dream, a fragile and mutable thing, a blur of colors shaped by the unpredictable whims of divinity.

The last time Rin had been here, a year that felt like a lifetime ago, she'd been blinded by loyalty and love. She'd been soaring between these cliffs on wings borne by fire, fighting on Yin Vaisra's behalf for a Republic founded on a lie. She'd been fighting to save Nezha's life.

Past the narrow channel, she could just barely make out the silhouette of the capital city. She fished her spyglass from her pocket and examined the city perimeter for a moment, until she glimpsed movement near each of its gates—her squadrons, moving in like chess pieces falling neatly into formation. From what she could see, at least four of the decoys had made it past the Murui. Venka's column, to her relief, was among them—as Rin watched, they marched steadily down the slopes from the northeast. She saw no sign of the last two squadrons, but she couldn't worry about that now. In minutes, the ground invasion of Arlong would commence.

That part of the assault was just noise. The four columns encircling Arlong were armed with the flashiest projectiles in their arsenal—double-mounted missiles, massive short-range cannons, and repurposed firecrackers stuffed with shrapnel. These were meant to capture Nezha's attention, to fool him into thinking the overground assault was a more significant effort than it was. Rin knew, based purely on the numbers, that she couldn't win a sustained ground battle, nor a protracted siege. Not when Nezha had been laying his defenses for weeks; not when all the Republic's last tricks and weapons lay hidden behind those walls.

But they didn't have to win, they only had to make a racket.

"Good luck," Kitay said. He would stay behind atop the Red Cliffs—close enough to witness everything through his spyglass, but far enough that he'd remain well out of harm's way. He squeezed her wrist. "Don't do anything stupid."

"Stay safe," Rin responded.

She forced her voice to remain casual. Brusque. No time to get emotional now. They already knew this might fail; they'd said their goodbyes last night.

Kitay gave her a mocking salute. "Give Nezha my regards."

A round of cannon fire punctuated his words from across the channel. Venka's smoke signals flared bright against the gray sky. The final invasion had begun. While Arlong erupted in explosions, Rin and her shamans descended the cliffside to finish things once and for all.

Rin had been worried that the grotto might be difficult to find. All she had to go on were fragments remembered from one of the most painful conversations she'd ever had, echoing through her mind in Nezha's low, tortured voice. *There's a grotto about a mile out from the entrance to this channel, this underwater crystal cave.*

But once she was down in the shadow of the Red Cliffs, wading through the same shallows where Nezha and his siblings had played so long ago, she realized the path to the Dragon was obvious. Only one side of the channel was lined with cave mouths. And if she wanted to find the Dragon's lair, all she had to do was follow the jewels.

They lay embedded in the river floor, glinting and sparkling underneath the gentle waves. The treasures piled up higher the closer they drew to the caves—jade-studded goblets, gilded breastplates, sapphire necklaces, and golden circlets, littered against a dazzling array of silver ingots. Small wonder Nezha and his brother had once ventured foolhardily into the grotto. It wouldn't have mattered how many times they'd been warned to stay away. What small child could resist this allure?

Rin could sense she was close. She could feel the power emanating from the grotto; the air felt thick with energy, laced with a constant, inaudible crackle, so very similar to the atmosphere she'd felt on Mount Tianshan.

The boundary between the mortals and the divine here was extraordinarily thin.

Rin paused for a moment, struck with the oddest sense that she'd been here before.

Right outside the grotto's entrance, the jewels gave way to

bones. They were startlingly pretty, lighting up the water with their own faintly green luminescence. This was no product of rot and erosion. Someone—*something*—had constructed this pathway, had lovingly peeled the flesh off its collected corpses and arranged the bones in a neat, glowing invitation.

"Great Tortoise," Dulin muttered. "Let's just blow this whole place out of the water."

Rin shook her head. "We're too far out."

They hadn't even seen the Dragon. They needed to draw much closer—if they lit their missiles now, they'd only alert Nezha's sentries. "Hold your fire until we see it move."

She strode boldly forward, trying to ignore the ridged bones beneath her boots. She opened her palm as she passed into the dark interior, but her flames only illuminated a few feet into the cave. The darkness beyond seemed to swallow it whole. Rin traced her fingers along the ridges in the wall for something to guide her, then yanked her hand back when she realized what they were. Her stomach churned.

The walls were lined with faces—beautiful, symmetrical faces of every size and shape; of grown men and little girls; faces without hair, without eyes, and without expression. Rot had not touched the pristine, bloodless skin. These heads hung in a space carved outside of time, now and forever.

Rin shuddered.

The ocean likes to keep its treasures. The ocean doesn't destroy. The ocean collects.

Once upon a time, Nezha had walked hand-in-hand with his little brother toward this grotto. He'd ignored the countless warnings because Mingzha had begged so hard, and because Nezha could refuse Mingzha nothing. He hadn't known the danger, and no one had stopped him. Of course no one had stopped him—because Vaisra had let him go, had deliberately sent him in, because he'd known that one day, he'd need the monster that Nezha would become.

Rin realized now why the grotto felt so familiar. This wasn't like Mount Tianshan at all. The Heavenly Temple was a place of lightness, clarity, and air. This place bore a heavier history. This place was tainted with a mortal stain, was suffused with pain and sorrow, was a testament to what happened when mortals dared to wrestle with the gods.

She'd felt divinity like this only once before, an eternity ago, on the worst day of her life.

Right then, she could have been standing in the temple on Speer.

"General!"

A burst of shouts echoed from the cave mouth. Rin spun around. Her soldiers pointed across the river, where a small, sleek sampan flew over the water toward them. That speed couldn't be achieved with sails or paddle wheels.

Nezha was on that boat.

"Now," Rin ordered Dulin.

He knelt and pressed his hands against the grotto floor. Vibrations rolled under Rin's feet, echoing down the cave's unfathomable depths. Dust and water streamed from the cave roof, coating them all in dirt.

But the rumbling did not crescendo to an earth-shattering quake. The grotto's interior did not collapse.

"What are you doing?" Rin hissed. "Bury that thing."

A vein protruded from Dulin's temple. "I can't."

The sampan was already halfway across the river; it'd reach them in seconds. *Conventional means, then.* Rin nodded to her troops.

"Fire."

They obliged, hefting their rocket lances. They aimed; she sent a flame snaking out to light the fuses. Eight lances tipped with powerful explosives flew screeching into the cave mouth. She couldn't see how far they went, but a moment later, she heard a muffled boom and, beneath that, a low, rumbling groan that sounded almost human.

Then the river surged, and Nezha was upon them.

∞

Rin crouched, bracing for his opening strike. It didn't come.

Nezha stepped off the side of the sampan, moving as casually as if he'd just arrived for teatime. He'd come alone. His feet didn't sink when they touched the water, but trod flatly over the river's surface as if it were marble.

He didn't pull a shield around him as he drew closer. He didn't need to. He was confident here in his domain, protected by endless water on all sides. He could ward off any attack she might attempt without trying.

She knew very well she remained standing only because he was curious.

"Hello, Rin," he said. "What do you think you're doing here?"

"Why don't you ask yourself?" She nodded toward Arlong. "City's burning."

"I noticed. So why aren't you there?"

"Thought they could manage without me."

Her eyes flitted toward Pipaji, who stood hunched inconspicuously behind Dulin. Her eyes were closed, lips moving silently as she sank into a trance. A small black cloud formed around her ankles, gave a tentative pulse, then began to stretch toward Nezha like tendrils of smoke unfurling underwater.

Good girl. Rin just needed to buy her several seconds of time.

"Tell me," Nezha said. "What did you think you'd do, once you found the grotto?"

"I'd think of something," Rin said. "I always do."

Nezha hadn't even glanced at Pipaji. His eyes were locked on Rin's. He approached slowly, fingers stroking the hilt of his sword. *He's gloating*, Rin realized. He thought he'd blown her plan wide open. He thought he'd won.

He shouldn't be so careless.

The inky tendrils reached the water under Nezha's feet.

Rin sucked in a sharp breath.

Nezha flinched and stumbled backward. The poison followed

him, racing up his legs and under his clothes. Black lines emerged from beneath his collars and sleeves. Where they touched his golden circlets, they hissed.

Pipaji made an inhuman growling noise. Her eyes shone dark violet, and her mouth was twisted into a cruel sneer that Rin had never seen on her face.

"Shatter," she whispered.

But Nezha didn't fall. He was clearly in great pain—he convulsed where he stood, the lines of poison writhing around his body like a horde of black snakes. But his skin didn't wither; his limbs didn't rot and corrode. Pipaji's victims usually succumbed in seconds. But something under his skin repelled the dark streaks, repairing their corrosion.

Pipaji glanced down at her fingertips, puzzled, as if checking that they were still black.

Nezha stopped writhing. He straightened up, rubbing at his neck. The black had already faded from his skin.

"Ah, Rin." He sighed theatrically. "That would have worked, too. But you showed your hand too early."

He made a fist and brought it down in a savage slash. A column of water rose behind Pipaji and smashed her into the river. Pipaji, sputtering, tried to rise to her feet. But the water rose and fell, slamming her again and again to her knees.

Pipaji shrieked. The black in her fingers stretched up through her arms. More indigo clouds blossomed underwater, racing toward Nezha like sea creatures. Nezha made a cupping motion. The water beneath Pipaji's feet shot up, flinging her several feet back. This time she lay still. The dark streaks disappeared.

"That's the best you could come up with?" Nezha sneered. "You came after me with a *little girl*?"

Rin couldn't speak. Panic fogged her mind. There was nothing she could say, nothing she could do—even the Phoenix was terrified, reluctant to lend its flames, already anticipating a losing battle.

Nezha stretched his fingers toward Pipaji. Rin thought the girl had died—part of her *hoped* she'd just died—but Pipaji was alive and conscious, and she screamed as a mass of water lifted her up, encircled her waist, then crept up her shoulders.

"Stop!" she shrilled. "Stop, please, mercy—"

The river closed over her face. Her screams cut to nothing. Nezha raised his arm to the sky. Pipaji hung high over the river, suspended inside a towering column of water. She thrashed wildly, trying to swim her way out, but the water just bulged to accommodate her flailing. Dulin drew his sword and hacked wildly at the pillar like one might a tree, but Nezha twisted his fingers, and the water wrenched Dulin's blade from his grasp.

Pipaji's mouth contorted in desperation. Rin could read her lips. *Help me.*

Without another thought, Rin pulled fire into her hand and lunged.

Nezha flicked his wrist. A wave rose before her and crashed, knocking her flat on her back. Nezha sighed and shook his head.

"That's all?"

Horror squeezed her chest as she rose. So easy. This was *so easy* for him.

"Now you." Nezha directed a fist at the charging Dulin.

Dulin never stood a chance. Rin didn't see what Nezha did. She was still clambering to her feet, blinking water from her eyes. All she felt was a hard tug, like a temporary current, then a crash of water. When she finally straightened up, Dulin was gone.

"Here's the thing about the ocean." Nezha turned back toward Pipaji. "If you swim down deep enough, the pressure can kill you."

Ever so casually, he squeezed his fist. Pipaji's eyes bulged. Nezha made a throwing motion. The water pillar flung Pipaji to the side like a rag doll. She landed facedown, limp, in the shallows. She floated, but did not stir.

Rin rolled onto her side and sent a jet of fire roaring at Nezha's face. He waved a hand. Water shot up to diffuse the flames. But that bought Rin a few precious seconds, which she used to regain her footing, crouch, and leap.

She had to get him on the ground. Ranged attacks wouldn't work; his shields were too strong. Once again, her only hope was a blow at close quarters. For the briefest moment, as she barreled into his side, the gods didn't matter—it was only the two of them, mortal and human, rolling and twisting in the river. He kneed her in the thigh. She groped around his face, trying to gouge out his eyes. His hands found a grip around her neck and squeezed.

Water crashed over them and forced them down, holding them beneath the surface. Rin kicked and choked to no avail. Nezha's fingers tightened on her neck, thumbs crushing her larynx.

Help me. Rin cast her thoughts wildly toward the Phoenix. *Help me.*

She heard the god's reply like a muted, distant echo. *The Dragon is too strong. We cannot—*

She clung at their connection. *Yanked* at it. *I don't care.*

Heat surged through her veins. She forced her mouth onto Nezha's. Flames erupted underwater, and the river exploded around them. Nezha's grip broke loose. She saw bubbles roiling over his skin, searing pink marks across his face.

Rin broke the surface, gasping. The world seemed swathed in black fog. She sucked in several hoarse, deep breaths. Her vision cleared, and from the corner of her eye she saw Nezha standing up.

She crouched, flames sparking around her, ready for a second round.

But Nezha wasn't looking at her. He struggled upright, his clothes ripped and burned beneath his armor, his face shining red with quickly disappearing blisters. His eyes, wide with horror, were fixed on something behind her.

She turned.

Deep within the grotto, something moved.

Nezha gave a low moan of terror. "Rin, what have you *done*?"

She had no response. She was rooted to the floor with sheer terror, unable to do anything but watch in fascinated horror as the Dragon of Arlong emerged from its lair.

It moved slowly, ponderously. She struggled to take in its shape; it was so massive she couldn't grasp its outline, only the scale of it. When it reared its head, it cast them all—Rin, Nezha, and her troops—in its mountainous shadow.

Dragons in Nikara myth were elegant creatures, wise, sophisticated lords of rivers and rain. But the Dragon was nothing like the sleek cerulean serpents that hung in paintings around the palace in Arlong. It looked vaguely like a snake, thick and undulating, its dark, bulbous body ending in a ridged, bumpy head. It was the underbelly of the ocean come alive.

The Dragon collects pretty things. Was it because the sea absorbed anything it touched? Because it was so vast and so unfathomably dark that it sought whatever ornament it could find to give it shape?

The Dragon tilted its massive head and roared—a sound felt rather than heard, a vibration that seemed capable of shattering the world.

"Hold your ground," Rin told her troops, trying her best to keep her voice level. She wasn't scared. *She wasn't scared*—if she acknowledged she was scared, then she'd go to pieces. "Stay calm, aim for its eyes—"

The Dragon surged. To the troops' great credit, they never faltered. They held their weapons high and useless until the very end.

It was over in seconds. There was a flash of movement, a split second of screams, and then a rapid retreat. Rin didn't see its jaws move. All she saw were discarded weapons, red streaks spreading over the surface, and scraps of armor floating on the bobbing waves.

The Dragon reared back, its head cocked to the side, examining its remaining prey.

Nezha swept his arms up. The river surged into a barrier between him and the Dragon, a blue wall stretching nearly twenty feet into the sky. The Dragon moved like a flicking whip. Something huge and dark crashed through the water. The barrier dissolved, ripped through like a flimsy sheet of paper.

Let me, urged the Phoenix. Its voice rang louder in her mind than she'd ever heard it, momentarily drowning her own thoughts. *Give me control.*

Rin hesitated. An objection half formed. *Kitay—*

The boy will be no barrier, said the Phoenix. *If you will it.*

Rin's eyes flickered toward the Dragon. What choice did she have?

I will it.

The Phoenix took full rein. Flames poured from her eyes, nose, and mouth. The world exploded into red; she could perceive nothing else. She couldn't tell if Nezha was safe, or if he'd been burned alive by their mere proximity. She couldn't have stopped it if he was. She had no agency now, no control—she was not calling the fire; she was merely its conduit—a ragged, unresisting gate through which it roared into the material realm.

The Phoenix, racing free, howled.

She reeled, overwhelmed by the double vision of the spiritual plane layered onto the material world. She saw pulsing divine energies, vermilion red against cerulean blue. The river bubbled and steamed. Scalded fish bobbed to the surface. Something flashed in her mind, then the river and grottoes disappeared from her sight.

All she could see now was a vast black plain, and two forces darting and dueling within it.

She couldn't feel Kitay. In that moment, he seemed so distant that they might not have been anchored at all.

Hello again, little bird. The Dragon's voice was a rumbling groan, deep, yawning, and suffocating. It sounded how drowning felt. *You are persistent.*

The Phoenix lunged. The Dragon reared back.

Rin struggled to make sense of the colliding gods. She couldn't follow their duel; this battle was happening on planes far too complex for her mind to process. She could see only hints of it; great explosions of sound and color in unimaginable shades and registers as forces of fire and water tangled, two forces strong enough to bring down the world, each balanced only by the other.

How can you win? she thought frantically. The gods were not personalities; they were fundamental forces of creation, constituent elements of existence itself. What did it mean for one to conquer another?

Over the din, she thought she heard Nezha screaming.

Then the heat inside her crescendoed, burning so white-hot she was afraid she'd evaporated. The Phoenix seemed to have gained the upper hand—bursts of crimson dominated the spirit plane now, and Rin could vaguely make out a great funnel of fire surrounding the Dragon's dark form.

Had they done it? Had they *won*? Surely nothing, no man or god, could survive that onslaught. But when it was over—when her flames died away, when the material world reappeared in her vision, when her body became hers and she staggered and tripped in the shallow water, struggling to breathe, she saw that she was still in the great beast's shadow.

Her fire had done nothing to the Dragon at all.

The Phoenix was silent. Rin felt the god recede from her mind, a spot of heat fleeing like a dying star, growing colder and more distant until it was gone.

Then she was alone. Helpless.

The Dragon cocked its head, as if to ask, *What now?*

Rin tried to stand and failed. Her legs were logs in the water; they would not obey. She scooted back, numb fingers fighting to keep hold of her sword. But it was such a tiny, fragile thing. What scrap of metal could even scratch that creature?

The Dragon drew itself to its full height, darkening the entire river with its shadow. When it surged forth, all she could do was close her eyes.

She felt the impact later, an earth-shaking crash that left her ears ringing. But she wasn't dead. She wasn't even hurt. She opened her eyes, confused, then glanced up. A great shield of water stood above her. Beside her stood Nezha, hands stretched to the sky.

His mouth was moving. Several seconds passed before his shouts became audible through her ringing ears.

"—you fucking *idiot*—what were you—"

"I thought I could kill it," she murmured, still dazed. "I thought . . . I really thought—"

"Do you know what you've done?"

He nodded toward the city. Rin followed his gaze. Then she understood that the only reason that either of them was still alive was because the Dragon was preoccupied with a far greater prize.

Massive waves rose ponderously from the river and surged, unnaturally high and unnaturally slowly, down the channel. The gray clouds darkened, thickening within seconds into an impending storm. From this distance, Arlong looked so flimsy. A tiny sand castle, so fragile, so *temporary*, in the shadow of the risen depths.

"Help me up," Rin whispered. "I almost did it, I can try again—"

"You can't. You're too weak." Nezha spoke without inflection or spite. It wasn't an insult, it was simple fact. As he watched the dark form moving beneath the surface toward the city, his scarred face set in resolve. He dropped the water barrier—it was hardly necessary now—and began striding toward the Dragon.

Rin reached instinctively for his hand, then drew back, confused by herself. "What are you—"

"Keep down," he said. "And when you get the chance, run."

She was too stunned to do anything but nod. She couldn't get past how bizarre this was; how they had suddenly stopped trying to kill each other; how they were, of all things, fighting again on the same side. She couldn't fathom why Nezha had saved her. Nor could she understand the way her heart twisted as she watched him walk forth, arms spread and vulnerable, offering himself to the beast.

She remembered that stance. She remembered watching a long time ago as Altan walked toward a frothing Suni, unafraid and unarmed, speaking calmly as if chatting with an old friend. As if the god in Suni's mind, strange and capricious, would not dare to break his neck.

Nezha wasn't trying to fight the Dragon. He was trying to tame it.

"Mingzha." He shouted the word over and over, waving his arms to get the Dragon's attention.

It took Rin a moment to remember what that meant—Yin Mingzha, Nezha's little brother, the fourth heir to the House of Yin, and the first of Vaisra's sons to die.

The Dragon paused, then rose up out of the water, its head cocked back toward Nezha.

"Do you remember?" Nezha shouted. "You ate Mingzha. You were so hungry, you didn't keep him for your cave. But you wanted me. You've always wanted me, haven't you?"

Astonishingly, the Dragon lowered its head, dipping low until its eyes were level with Nezha's. Nezha reached out as if to stroke its nose. The Dragon did not stir. Rin clamped her hand over her mouth, terrified beyond words.

He looked so *small*.

"I'll go," Nezha said. "We'll go into that grotto. You don't have to be alone anymore. But you have to stop. Leave this city alone."

The Dragon remained very still. Then, ever so slowly, the waters began to recede.

The Dragon made a slight motion toward Nezha that seemed bizarrely affectionate. Rin stared, mouth agape, as Nezha pressed his hand against the Dragon's side.

I'll go.

With that one gesture, he'd prevented hundreds of thousands of deaths. He'd tamed a god that she'd woken, he'd prevented a massacre that would have been her fault, and he'd thrown her this victory.

"Nezha," she whispered, "what the *fuck*?"

Too late, she heard a faint and distinctive drone.

The aircraft emerged over the side of the cliff and dove, fast and low, straight over the grotto. It was much smaller than the bomber dirigibles that had pursued Rin through the mountains; its cockpit seemed large enough for only one person. Stranger still was its underbelly—extending from the bottom of its basket where its cannon should have been was a long, glinting wire that branched into several curved points like a reaching claw.

Rin glanced to Nezha. He stood stock-still, eyes wide in horror. But the Hesperians were his allies. What did he have to fear?

She pulled fire into her hand, deliberating whether to attack. Before, she wouldn't have hesitated. But if the dirigible had come to fight the Dragon . . .

The dirigible veered sharply toward her. *That answers that.* She aimed her palm at the cockpit. But before she could pull her fire forth, a thin line of lightning, lovely and absurd, arced through the blue sky. A second later, she saw a blinding white light. Then nothing.

She wasn't hurt. She felt no pain. She was still standing; she could hear and move and feel. Though her vision blurred for a moment, it returned after several blinks. But something had shifted about the world. It seemed, somehow, stripped of its life and luster—its colors were drained, blues and greens muted into shades of gray, and its sounds reduced to sandpapery scratches.

The Phoenix went quiet.

No—the Phoenix *disappeared.*

Rin strained in her mind, flailing desperately through the void to pull the god through Kitay's mind into hers, but she grasped at nothing. There was no void. There was no gate. The Pantheon was not drifting beyond her reach, it simply *wasn't there.*

Then she screamed.

She was in the Chuluu Korikh again. She was drowning in air, sealed and suffocating, imprisoned this time not in stone but in her own heavy, mortal body, pounding helplessly against the walls of her own mind, and that was such unbearable torture that she barely registered the lightning still coursing through her body, making her teeth chatter and singeing her hair.

You are nothing but an agent of Chaos. Sister Petra's voice rose unbidden to her mind—that cold, clinical voice speaking with assured confidence that until today had never seemed justified. *You*

*are not shamans, you are the miserable and corrupted. And I will
find a way to contain you.*

She'd found it.

Child. Rin heard the Phoenix's voice. Impossible. And yet the
fire returned; a warm heat surged over her body, cradling her,
protecting her.

The lightning now landed on Nezha.

He stood with his back to her, arms splayed out like he was
being crucified, twitching and jerking as crackling brightness ricocheted across his body. Sparks arced back and forth from his
golden circlets, which seemed to amplify the electricity before it
burrowed deep into his flesh.

The bolts thickened, doubled, and intensified. Harsh, ragged
sobs escaped Nezha's throat. The Dragon, too, seemed racked with
pain. It was performing the oddest dance, head jerking and body
writhing, flailing back and forth through the air in a way that
would have been funny if it weren't so horrific.

Rin's mouth filled with bile.

Focus, child, the Phoenix urged. *Strike now.*

Rin's glance darted between the Dragon and the dirigible.

She knew she had one chance to attack—but which target?
Nezha had saved her from the dirigible; the dirigible was saving
her from the Dragon. Who was her enemy now?

She raised her left hand. The dirigible darted backward several
yards, as if sensing her intentions. She opened her palm and aimed
a thick stream of flame at its balloon, forcing it faster and higher,
hoping desperately that she had the range.

A ripping noise shattered the sky. The dirigible balloon glowed
orange for an instant, burst, then vanished. The basket hurtled
toward the cliffs; the lightning disappeared.

Nezha crumpled.

Rin's first instinct was to rush toward him. She took two steps,
then caught herself, utterly bewildered. Why would she help him?
Because he'd just saved her? But that was his mistake, not hers—
she shouldn't bother, she should just let him die—

Shouldn't she?

The water turned icy cold around her knees. She felt a wave of exhausted dread.

But the Dragon did not attack. Incredibly, it seemed frightened into submission. It turned its head toward the grotto and slithered back into the dark. Suddenly the air was not so heavy. The gray clouds disappeared, and sunlight was again visible against the glinting waves. Gravity took hold over the river once again, and the suspended waters dropped with a resounding crash.

I must get to shore.

The thought ran like a mantra several times through Rin's mind before it finally registered into action. Swaying and stumbling like a drunkard, she made her way to the riverbank. She felt detached, distant, as if someone else were clumsily controlling her body while her mind raced with questions.

What had just happened? What had Nezha just done? Was that a surrender?

Had she *won*?

But none of her dreams of victory had looked anything like this.

She heard a faint, pitiful gurgle. She turned. Pipaji lay farther down the sands, curled into a fetal position. Her face was barely above water; Rin didn't know how she hadn't drowned. But her narrow shoulders rose and fell, and her fingers scratched tiny, desperate patterns in the mud as she whimpered.

Rin hastened to her side.

"Oh, gods." She propped Pipaji up in her arms and slammed her fist against the girl's narrow back, trying to force the water from her lungs. "Pipaji? Can you hear me?"

Water dribbled from Pipaji's mouth—just a little trickle at first, and then her shoulders heaved and a stinking torrent of river water and bile spewed from her mouth. Pipaji gagged and slumped weakly against Rin's chest, breathing in shallow, desperate hitches.

"Hold on." Rin slung Pipaji's right arm around her shoulder

and pulled her to her feet. The positioning was awkward, but Pipaji was so thin and light that Rin found it surprisingly easy to drag them both forward, one step at a time. "Just hold on, you're going to be fine, we'll just get you to Lianhua."

They'd made it ten steps up the shore when Rin heard a vicious fit of coughing. She twisted her head over her shoulder. Nezha was doubled over on his knees in the shallows, shoulders heaving.

She halted.

He was only several yards away. He was so close she could make out every detail on his face—his chalk-white pallor, his red-rimmed eyes, the faded scars on porcelain-pale skin. She couldn't remember the last time they'd stood so close without trying to kill each other.

For a moment, they merely looked at each other, taking stock of one another, staring as if they were strangers.

Rin's gaze dropped to the golden circlets around his wrists. Her stomach twisted as she realized what they were. Not jewelry. Conductors. They hadn't attracted the lightning by accident. They'd been *designed* for it.

Then it dawned on her, what Nezha must have gone through in the year since she'd left Arlong. After Rin escaped, Petra had needed a shaman upon whom to experiment.

After the Cike were killed, that left only one in the Republic.

The skin around his wrists and ankles was badly discolored, mottled shades of bruised purple and angry red. The sight made her chest tighten. She'd seen Nezha's body stitch itself together from wounds that should have killed instantly. She'd seen his skin smooth itself over from burns that had turned it black. She'd thought the Dragon's powers could heal anything. But they couldn't heal this.

Rin had once been so absolutely sure the Pantheon constituted the whole of creation. That there was no higher power, and that the Hesperian religion, their Divine Architect, was nothing more than a convenient story.

Now she wasn't so sure.

Slowly, miserably, Nezha stood and wiped the back of his mouth with his hand. It came away bloody. "Is she alive?"

Rin was so bewildered that his words didn't process. Nezha nodded at Pipaji and repeated the question. "Is she alive?"

"I—I don't know," Rin said, startled into a response. "She—I'll try."

"I didn't want to . . ." Nezha coughed again. His chin glistened red. "It wasn't her fault."

Rin opened her mouth to respond, but nothing came out.

The problem wasn't that she had nothing to say. It was that she had too much, and she didn't know where to begin, because everything that came to mind seemed so utterly inadequate.

"You should have killed me," she said at last.

He gave her a long look. She couldn't read his face; what she thought she saw confused her. "But I never wanted you dead."

"Then *why*?"

Those two words weren't enough. Nothing she could think to say was enough. The gulf between them was too vast now, and the thousand questions on her mind all seemed too shallow, too frivolous to have the slightest chance of bridging it.

"Duty," he said. "You couldn't understand."

She had nothing to say to that.

He watched her in silence, his sword dangling uselessly at his side. His face spasmed, as if he, too, was struggling with thoughts he could never say out loud.

It would be so easy to kill him. He could barely stand. His god had just fled, shuddering from some greater power that she hadn't even known existed. If she'd carved him open right then, the wounds likely wouldn't heal.

But she couldn't make the flame come. That required rage, and she couldn't even summon the faintest memory of anger. She couldn't curse, or shout, or do any of the million things she'd imagined she might do if she had the chance to confront him like this.

How many chances, asked Altan, *are you going to throw away?*

At least one more, she thought, and ignored his jeering laughter.

If she could remember how to hate Nezha, she would have killed him. But instead, she turned her back and let him make his retreat while she made hers.

CHAPTER 30

Pipaji was dying.

Her condition deteriorated rapidly in the half hour it took for Rin to drag her toward her main forces in the city and flag down soldiers to find and fetch Lianhua. By the time Rin had her laid out on a dry tarp on the beach, her pulse had grown so faint that Rin almost thought she'd already died, until she lifted Pipaji's eyelids and saw her twitching eyeballs flickering dangerously between brown and black.

She'd tried giving the girl opium. She always kept a packet in her back pocket, and she'd started carrying double ever since she began sending the shamans into battle. It didn't work. Pipaji obediently inhaled the smoke, but her whimpering didn't stop, and the purple veins protruding grotesquely from her skin only grew thicker.

The god was taking control.

Great Tortoise. Rin stared down at Pipaji's white face, trying not to panic. Shamans who lost their minds to the gods couldn't be killed. They were trapped inside bodies turned divine, sentenced to live until the world stopped turning.

Rin couldn't sentence Pipaji to that.

But that meant she had to kill her, while her eyes were still flickering back to brown, while she still clung to a shred of mortality.

Rin reached a shaking hand toward Pipaji's throat.

"I have opium!" Lianhua shouted as she rushed down the beach. She halted over Pipaji, panting. "Do you—"

"I've tried it," Rin said. "Didn't work. She's losing it, she's on the edge—the pain's not helping, she's hurt on the inside, Nezha did something to her and I can't see but I think there's bleeding on the inside and I need you to—*don't touch*."

Lianhua, now kneeling over Pipaji, jerked her hands back.

"Touch her over her clothes," Rin said. "And watch the sand. Be careful. She's not in control."

Lianhua nodded. To her great credit she didn't seem afraid, just focused. She exhaled, closed her eyes, and spread her fingers over Pipaji's torso. A soft glow illuminated Pipaji's drenched uniform.

Pipaji's eyelids fluttered. Rin held her breath.

Maybe this wasn't the end. Maybe the pain was the only problem; maybe she'd come back to them.

"Pipaji? *Pipaji!*"

Rin glanced up and cursed under her breath. The little sister—Jiuto—was racing down the beach, screaming.

Who had let her out here? Rin could have throttled someone.

"Get back." As Jiuto approached, Rin whipped out an arm to bar her from her sister. Jiuto was tiny, but she was scared and hysterical; she wriggled ferociously from Rin's grasp and dropped to her knees beside her sister.

"Don't—" Rin shouted.

But Jiuto had already pushed Lianhua aside. She flung herself over her sister, sobbing. "Pipaji!"

Just as Rin and Lianhua reached to drag Jiuto away, Pipaji lifted her head. "Don't."

Her eyes shot open. They were their normal, lovely brown.

Rin hesitated, left hand clutching the neck of Jiuto's shirt.

"It's okay." Pipaji reached her arms up, stroking her sister's hair. "Jiuto, calm down. I'm okay."

Jiuto's sobs instantly subsided to frightened hiccups. Pipaji rubbed her hand in circles against her sister's back, whispering a stream of comfort into her ear.

Rin shot Lianhua a glance. "Is she—"

Lianhua sat frozen, hands outstretched. "I'm not sure. I fixed the rib, but the rest—I mean, there's something . . ."

Pipaji met Rin's gaze over Jiuto's shoulder. Her face was pinched in discomfort. "They're so loud."

Rin's heart sank. "Who's being loud?"

"They're screaming," Pipaji murmured. Her eyes darkened. "They're so . . . oh."

"Focus on us," Rin said urgently. "On your sister—"

"I can't." Pipaji's hands, still wrapped around Jiuto's shoulders, started to twitch. They curved into claws, scratching at the air. "She's *in* there, she's . . ."

"Get her away," Rin ordered Lianhua.

Lianhua understood immediately. She wrapped her arms around Jiuto's waist and pulled. Jiuto struggled, wailing, but Lianhua didn't let go. She dragged Jiuto away from the beach and up toward the forest, until finally Jiuto's wails faded into the distance.

"Stay with me," Rin told Pipaji. "Pipaji, *listen to my voice*—"

Pipaji didn't respond.

Rin didn't know what to do. She wanted to wrap her arms around Pipaji and comfort her, but she was afraid to touch. A great purple cloud blossomed around Pipaji's collarbones, stretching up to her neck, turning her entire visage a bright, smooth violet. Pipaji's back arched. She choked wordlessly, struggling against some invisible force.

Rin skirted backward, suddenly terrified.

Pipaji turned her head toward Rin. The movement looked horrifically unnatural, as if her limbs were being yanked this way and that by unseen puppet strings.

"Please," she said. Her eyes flickered the faintest brown. "While I'm here."

Rin held her gaze, stricken.

Death or the Chuluu Korikh. Five simple, devastating words. Rin had known them from the start. There were only two possible fates for the Cike: death or immurement. A commander made sure it was the first. *A commander culls.*

"I need you to focus." Rin spoke with a calm she did not feel. She could not relinquish her responsibility; she had to do this. At this point, it was a mercy. "You still have to fight it. You can't poison me."

"I won't," Pipaji whispered.

"Thank you." Rin reached out, cupped the side of Pipaji's head with her left hand, pressed one knee against Pipaji's shoulder for leverage, and wrenched.

The crack was louder than she'd expected. Rin shook out her fingers, focusing on the pain so she wouldn't have to look at Pipaji's glassy eyes. She'd never broken a neck before. She'd been taught the method in theory; she'd practiced plenty of times on dummies at Sinegard. But until now, she hadn't realized how much force it really took to make a spine snap.

Then it was over.

Rin entered the city on foot. No one announced her presence; no musicians or dancers followed in her wake. Barely anyone noticed her; the city was too consumed with its own collapse. In her exhaustion, all she perceived was a great flurry of movement; of burned and bloody bodies carried into the city on stretchers; of crowds streaming out of Arlong's gates dragging along sacks spilling with clothing, heirlooms, and silver; of bodies packed in teetering hordes atop the remnants of Arlong's fleet, escaping in the few ships that hadn't been sunk in the Dragon's wrath.

Vaguely she understood that she had won.

Arlong was destroyed. The Hesperians had fled. Nezha and his government had made a hasty retreat out the channel. Rin learned these facts over the next hour, had them repeated to her over and over again by ecstatic officers, but she was drifting about in a fugue state, so tired and confused that she thought they were joking.

For how could this be called a victory?

She knew what victory felt like. Victory was when she scoured enemy troops from the field with a divine blaze, and her men rallied around her, screaming as they took back what was rightfully theirs. Victory felt deserved. *Just.*

But this felt like cheating—like her opponent had tripped and she'd been declared the winner by accident, which made this outcome a slippery, precarious thing, a victory that could be torn away at any time for any reason.

"I don't understand," she kept saying to Kitay. "What happened?"

"It's over," he told her. "The city's ours."

"But how?"

He responded patiently, the same way he had all afternoon. "The Dragon destroyed the city. And then you banished the Dragon."

"But I didn't do that." She gazed out at the flooded canals. "I didn't do anything."

All she'd done was poke a beast she couldn't handle. All she'd done was lie flat on her ass, scared out of her wits, while Nezha and a Hesperian pilot fought a battle of lightning that she didn't understand. She'd meddled in forces she couldn't control. She'd nearly sunk the entire city, nearly drowned every person in this valley, all because she'd thought she could wake the Dragon and win.

"Maybe he's seen what they're like," Kitay guessed, after she'd told him all that transpired in the river. It made absolutely no sense that Nezha would have just given up, had just retreated when he could have killed Rin and stopped the Dragon in one fell swoop. "The Hesperians, I mean. And maybe he doesn't want to let go of the only forces that can stop them."

"Seems like a belated realization," Rin muttered.

"Maybe it was self-preservation. Maybe things were getting worse."

"Maybe," she said, unconvinced. "What do you think he'll do now?"

"I don't know. But we've got a more pressing issue at hand." Kitay nodded to the palace gates. "We just deposed the ruler of half this country. Now you've got to present yourself as his replacement."

There were troops to address. Speeches to make. A city to occupy, and a country to claim.

Rin shuddered with exhaustion. She didn't feel like a ruler; she barely felt like the victor. She couldn't think of anything she wanted less right now than to face a crowd and pretend.

"Tomorrow," she said. "Give me today. There's something I have to do."

In Tikany there was a little graveyard hidden deep in the forest, concealed so well behind thickets of poplar trees and bamboo groves that the men never found it by accident. But every woman in Tikany knew its location. They'd visited it with their mothers, their mothers-in-law, their grandmothers, or their sisters. Or they'd made the trip alone, pale-faced and crying while they hugged their wretched loads to their chests.

It was the graveyard of babies. Infant girls smothered in ash at birth because their fathers only wanted sons. Little boys who'd died too early and left their mothers grief-stricken and terrified of being replaced by younger, more fertile wives. The messy products of miscarriages and late-term abortions.

Arlong, Rin assumed, had an equivalent. Every city needed a place to hide the shameful deaths of its children.

Venka knew where it was. "Half a mile past the evacuation cliffs," she said. "Turn north when you can see the channel. There's a footpath in the grass. Takes a while to see it, but once you've got it in sight, it'll take you all the way."

"Will you come with me?" Rin asked.

"You're fucking kidding me," Venka said. "I'm never going back there again."

So at sunset, Rin wrapped the jar containing Pipaji's ashes inside several layers of linen, shoved it in a bag, and set out for the cliffs with a shovel strapped to her back.

Venka was right—once she knew what she was looking for, the hidden path was clear as day. Nothing marked the graves, but the tall grass grew in curious whorls, twisting and spiraling as if avoiding the once-loved bones in the soil beneath.

Rin surveyed the clearing. How many bodies had been buried here, over how many decades? How far did she have to walk until her fingers wouldn't lodge into tiny bones when she pushed them into the dirt?

Her fingers kept trembling. She glanced around, made sure that she was alone, then sat down and pulled a pipe out of her pocket. She didn't take enough opium to knock herself unconscious—just enough to get her hand steady so she could firmly grip the shovel.

"It's not easy, is it?"

She saw Altan in the corner of her gaze, following her down the rows of unmarked graves. His shape lingered only if she looked elsewhere; if she focused where she thought he stood, he disappeared.

"They were like children," she said. "I didn't—I didn't want . . ."

"You never want to hurt them." Altan sounded gentler than she'd ever heard him—gentler than she'd ever permitted his memory to be. "But you have to. You have to put them through hell, because that's the only way anyone else will survive."

"I would have spared them if I could have."

For once, he didn't jeer. He just sounded sad. "Me too."

Finally she found a spot where the soil looked undisturbed and the grass grew straight. She put the linen-wrapped jar on the ground, clenched the shovel tight, and began to dig while Altan watched silently from the shade. Several long minutes trickled by. Despite the evening chill, sweat beaded on the back of her neck.

The ground was rocky and stiff, and the shovel kept wobbling out of her grasp. Eventually she found a perilous equilibrium, using her hand to guide the shovel and her foot to wedge it farther into the ground.

"I think I understand you now," she said after a long silence.

"Oh?" Altan cocked his head. "What do you understand?"

"Why you pushed me so hard. Why you hurt me. I wasn't a person to you, I was a weapon, and you needed me to work."

"You can still love your weapons," Altan said. "You can beat them into shape and then watch them destroy themselves and know that it was all fully necessary, but that doesn't mean you can't love them, too."

She didn't need to dig quite so long or so hard—nobody was ever going to come disturb these graves—but something about the difficult, repetitive motion soothed her, even as the ache in her shoulder grew worse and worse. It felt like penance.

At last, when the hole stretched so deep that the dying sunlight couldn't hit the bottom, when the soil went from brown and rocky to a soft and sludgy clay, she stopped and carefully lowered Pipaji's ashes into the grave.

She wished she could have buried Dulin, too. But she'd scoured the channel for hours, and she hadn't even been able to find a shred of his uniform.

"Does it ever get easier?" she asked.

"What? Sending people to their deaths?" Altan sighed. "You wish. It'll never stop hurting. They'll think that you don't care. That you're a ruthless monster in single-minded pursuit of victory. But you do care. You love your shamans like your own family, and a knife twists in your heart every time you watch one of them die. But you have to do it. You've got to make the choices no one else can. It's death or the Chuluu Korikh. Commanders cull."

"I didn't want it to be me," she said. "I'm not strong enough."

"No."

"It should have been you."

"It should have been me," he agreed. "But you're the one who got out. So see this through to the end, kid. That's the least you owe to the dead."

Kitay stood waiting for her at the bottom of the cliffs, holding a bundle of incense sticks in one hand and a jug of sorghum wine in the other.

"What's all this?" she asked.

"Qingmingjie," he said. "We have to keep vigil."

Qingmingjie. The Tomb-Sweeping Festival. The night when the hungry ghosts of the restless dead walked the world of the living and demanded their due. She'd seen others celebrating it in Tikany, but she'd never participated in the rituals herself. She'd never had anyone to mourn.

"That's not for two weeks," she said.

"That's not the point. We have to keep vigil."

"Do we have to?"

"Thousands of people died to win you this war. It wasn't just your shamans. It was soldiers whose names you never even learned. You're going to honor them. You're going to keep vigil."

She was so tired she almost simply walked away.

What did ritual matter? The dead couldn't hurt her. She wanted to be finished with them; she'd done enough penance today.

But then she saw the look on Kitay's face and knew she could not refuse him this. She followed him quietly down to the valley.

The field of corpses was so quiet at night that she might never have known a battle had been fought on these grounds. Mere hours ago it was a site of shouting, of detonations, of clashing steel and smoke. And now the show was over, the puppet strings were cut, and everyone lay in silent repose.

"It's so odd," she murmured. "I wasn't even here."

She hadn't commanded this battle. She hadn't witnessed how it had played out, didn't know which side breached first, didn't know how it would have gone if the Dragon had not raised the Murui. She'd been occupied with an entirely different fight, too busy in the realm of gods and lightning to remember that a conventional battle was even happening, until its aftermath was laid out before her eyes.

"What now?" she asked.

"I'm not sure." Kitay lifted the incense sticks half-heartedly, as if he'd just realized what an inconsequential gesture this was. They couldn't begin to count the bodies in the valley. All the incense in the world could not repay this sacrifice.

"In Tikany we burn paper," she said. "Paper money. Paper houses. Sometimes paper wives, if they were young men who died before they were married." She broke off. She didn't have a point. She was babbling, afraid of the silence.

"I don't think it's the paper that's important," Kitay said. "I think we just need to . . ."

His voice trailed away. His eyes widened, focused on something just over her shoulder. Too late she heard it as well, the crunch of footsteps over burned grass and bone.

When she turned, she saw only one silhouette against the dark.

Nezha had come alone. Unarmed.

He always looked so different in the moonlight. His skin shone paler, his features looked softer, resembling less the harsh visage of his father and more the lovely fragility of his mother. He looked younger. He looked like the boy she'd known at school.

Rin wondered briefly if he'd come back to die.

Kitay broke the silence. "We brought wine."

Nezha held out a hand. Kitay passed him the bottle as he approached. Nezha didn't bother to sniff for poison; he just tossed back a mouthful and swallowed hard.

That gesture confirmed the spell—the suspension of reality all three of them wanted. The unwritten rules hung in the air, reinforced by every passing moment that blood wasn't spilled. No one would lift a weapon. No one would fight or flee. Just this night, just this moment, they had entered a liminal space where their past and their future did not matter, where they could be the children they used to be.

Nezha held out a bundle of incense. "Do you have a light?"

Somehow they found themselves sitting in a silent triangle, shrouded in thick, scented smoke. The wine bottle lay between them, empty. Nezha had drunk almost all of it, Kitay the rest. Kitay had been the first to reach out with his fingers, and then all three of them were holding hands, Nezha and Rin on either side of Kitay, and it felt and looked absolutely, terribly wrong and still Rin never wanted to let go.

Was this how Daji, Jiang, and Riga had once felt? What were they like at the height of their empire? Did they love one another so fiercely, so desperately?

They must have. No matter how much they despised one another later, so much that they'd precipitated their own deaths, they must have loved one another once.

She tilted her face up at the low crimson moon. The dead were supposed to talk to the living on Qingmingjie. They were supposed to come through the moon like it was a door, transfixed by the fragrance of incense and the sound of firecrackers. But when she gazed out over the battlefield, all she saw were corpses.

She wondered what she would say if she could reach her dead.

She would tell Pipaji and Dulin that they had done well.

She would tell Suni, Baji, and Ramsa that she was sorry.

She would tell Altan that he was right.

She would tell Master Jiang thank you.

And she would promise them all that she would make their sacrifice worth it. Because that was what the dead were for her—necessary sacrifices, chess pieces lost to advance her position, tradeoffs that, if she were given the chance, she would make all over again.

She didn't know how long they sat there. It could have been minutes. It could have been hours. It felt like a moment carved out of time, a refuge from the inexorable progress of history.

"I wish things had been different," Nezha said.

Rin and Kitay both tensed. He was breaking the rules. They

couldn't maintain this fragile fantasy, this indulgence of nostalgia, if he broke the rules.

"They could have been different." Kitay's voice was hard. "But you had to go and be a fucking prick."

"Your Republic is dead," Rin said. "And if we see you tomorrow, then so are you."

No one had anything to say after that.

There would be no truce or negotiation tonight. Tonight was a borrowed grace, innocent of the future. They sat in miserable and desperate silence, wishing and regretting while the bloody moon traced its ponderous path across the sky. When the sun came up, Rin and Kitay got up, shook the ache from their bones, and trudged back toward the city. Nezha walked in the other direction. They didn't care to watch where he went.

They marched back to Arlong, eyes fixed forward on the half-drowned city whose ruins shone in the glimmering light of dawn.

They'd won their war. Now they had a country to rule.

CHAPTER 31

Arlong had fallen immediately upon Nezha's retreat. That morn-ing, the Southern Army swept through the city streets just as the Hesperians and the Republic finished their final evacuations. They found a confused, uneven city—half its districts were still populated with Nikara civilians with nowhere else to go, and the other half had become hollow ghost towns. The barracks and residential complexes that once housed Hesperian soldiers had been abandoned. Inside the wrecked shipyards, large hangars that must have been used to house dirigibles now stood empty, their floors littered with spare tools and leftover parts.

"I'll permit plunder to a reasonable extent," Rin told her of-ficers. "Take whatever you want. But be civilized—no brawling over spoils, and keep to the affluent neighborhoods. Leave the poorest districts alone. Target the Hesperian quarters first—they won't have been able to take everything. Weapons, trinkets, and clothes are fair game. But food supplies come back to the palace for central redistribution."

"How should we deal with armed resistance?" asked Com-mander Miragha.

"Avoid bloodshed if possible," Kitay said. "Capture over

kill—we want their intelligence. Bring all soldiers to the dungeons and keep the Hesperians and Republican soldiers apart."

The Republican soldiers who hadn't managed to escape on the ships were desperately trying to pass themselves off as civilians. The streets were strewn with discarded uniforms; an hour into the occupation, Rin received a report of an entire squadron of naked men begging for secondhand civilian clothes so that they might disguise their identities. She laughed for a good five minutes, then ordered the men to be rounded up in chains and made to stand naked on the dais outside the palace for the rest of the day.

"Good for morale," she told Kitay when he protested.

"It's excessive," he said.

"It's exactly the right amount of public humiliation. A secret underground resistance might have credibility with the civilians." She pointed at the shivering men. "*They* certainly won't."

He didn't have a rebuttal.

While her troops continued their takeover of the streets, Rin made her way to the Red Cliffs to watch the last of the evacuation ships hurrying out of the narrow channel.

She remembered the day, nearly a year ago now, when she first saw the Hesperian fleet arrive on Nikara shores. How relieved she'd been then. How grateful. The white sails had represented hope and survival. Divine intervention.

But they hadn't come until the Republic had nearly bled itself out. They could have ended the whole civil war in minutes from the very beginning. They could have saved the entire country months of starvation and bloodshed. But they'd waited out the unnecessary tragedy until the very end, when they could simply step in and call themselves the heroes.

They were nowhere near so pompous in their departure.

"Bloody cowards," Venka said. "You're just going to let them go?"

"Dunno," Rin said. "Could be fun to sink all those ships in the harbor."

Kitay sighed. "Rin."

"I'm serious," she said.

"Occupying a city is one thing," he said. "Setting civilians on fire is quite another."

"But it'd be so funny." She was only half joking. She felt a thrill of dark, vindictive glee as she watched the mangled, escaping fleet. If she wanted to, she could turn every ship in that channel to ash. She had that power.

"Please, Rin." Kitay shot her a wary look. "Don't be an idiot. Right now the Hesperians are retreating because they're exhausted, they've expended everything on a war on a continent that they don't care for. They gambled on the wrong faction and lost. Right now, they're just licking their wounds. But if you send flames after *fleeing women and children*, they really just might reconsider."

"Spoilsport," said Venka.

Rin sighed. "I so hate when you're right."

So she let the ships sail undisturbed out of the harbor. She'd let the Hesperians think, for now, that her new regime bore them no ill will. That her priorities lay within Nikan's boundaries. She'd let them think they were safe.

And then, when they'd been lulled into complacency, when they'd become convinced that perhaps those dirty, stupid, inferior Nikara didn't pose such a great threat after all—that was when she would strike.

Rin's next task was to occupy the palace.

The place was in shambles. The grand painted doors had been left hanging ajar, hallways strewn with shattered vases that had fallen out of hastily packed wagons. The vast hall in the palace center had been stripped of almost all its furnishings; only the wall tapestries remained, too heavy and unwieldy to pull down and carry away.

The Yin family portrait hung at the far end of the chamber. Rin stood beneath it for a moment, gazing at the faces of the family that had imagined they might rule the Empire.

Whoever had woven this had rendered the Yins with impressive accuracy. Standing together, their similarities were even more pronounced. They all had the same high cheekbones, arched eyebrows, and sculpted, angular jaws. None of them smiled—not even the children, who gazed over the empty hall with identically haughty, contemptuous expressions.

At first Rin mistook Jinzha for Nezha, but then realized that the youths standing to their father's right must be the firstborn twins—Jinzha and Muzha. Nezha was by himself, somber and forlorn, to his father's left. This tapestry must have been completed years ago—he was represented here as a small child, barely rising to his father's waist. To the far right stood Lady Yin Saikhara, cradling a baby in her arms. That had to be Mingzha—Nezha's dead baby brother, the one lost to the Dragon.

What a beautiful family, destroyed in only the span of a year. Jinzha was captured and ground into dumpling stuffing at Lake Boyang. The charred remnants of Vaisra's body lay indistinguishable from the burned wreckage of his fleet. Muzha had reportedly drowned in the Dragon's attack on Arlong. And Nezha was broken and defeated, a slave to his Hesperian masters.

Rin wished, with a pulse of vicious hatred, she could have ended the lineage herself.

But the Lady Saikhara had escaped her justice. She'd flung herself off the highest tower of the palace when she saw the banners of southern troops marching into the city. Her fragile bones smashed like porcelain against the execution grounds outside the palace, and she joined a long tradition of noblewomen who had died along with their dynasties.

Rin learned from reports that Arlong's residents had come to hate Saikhara in the final days. It was no great secret that the House of Yin had profited greatly from the civil war, even as it impoverished entire populations just on its border. Nezha's sister, Muzha, had become rich acting as the go-between for Hesperian traders and the powerful merchant cronies that crowded the Republican court.

When Lady Saikhara had come back from her grand publicity tour in Hesperia, it had been revealed that she and Muzha had dumped huge swaths of Nikara goods into waiting Hesperian markets while everyone else was hoarding food and buying in a panic from rapidly inflating markets.

Popular opinion had called for Nezha to sanction his mother and sister, but he did nothing except remove them from his cabinet. So Nezha's moniker had gone from the Young Marshal to the Filial Fool, while his mother was titled the Whore of the West. In the past week, the streets had been calling so loudly for her punishment that if the Southern Army hadn't stormed Arlong's gates then she might very well have been torn apart by the mobs regardless.

"You'd think she would have gotten out with the Hesperians," Kitay said as they stood on the second-floor balcony, watching as servants scrubbed Saikhara's blood from the steps. Her body lay several feet away, wrapped unceremoniously in a spare canvas sheet. Rin planned to weigh it down with rocks and toss it into the harbor for the fish. "I thought they loved her."

"I think they left her behind," Rin said. "I think they had to save their own skins."

They would have done it. The Hesperians, facing an overwhelming tide of public hatred, wouldn't have dared trying to ferret the despised Saikhara out of the city.

It didn't matter that Lady Saikhara spoke fluent Hesperian, that she worshipped their Maker, or that she'd been masquerading as a Hesperian woman for half her life. In the end she was still Nikara, still one of the inferior race, and the Hesperians only looked out for their own.

The adjacent hallways were crammed with riches that put those in Jinzhou to shame. Rin had walked through those corridors a dozen times before, always on her way to Vaisra's office, though she'd never dared to pause and peruse. Back then, their mere proximity had filled her with awe; those artifacts were shining evidence of a historical elite that she had, somehow, been invited to join.

Walking through the hallways felt very different now that she knew everything displayed on the walls belonged to her.

"Look." Kitay stopped before a very old, very shiny helmet. "It says this belonged to the Red Emperor."

"There's no way."

"Read the placard."

The helmet did look old enough. Rin could see little jade stones embedded into the forehead. She reached into the case, plucked the helmet out, and tried it on. It was uncomfortably cold, obstructively heavy. Quickly she pulled it off. "I don't know how anyone managed to fight wearing this."

"It's ceremonial, probably," Kitay said. "I doubt he actually wore it into battle. This place is loaded with his stuff—look, there's his breastplate, and that's his old tea set."

His fingers hovered over the relics, as if he was too awed to touch them. But Rin, glancing about the hall, was struck with a deep sense of pity. The Red Emperor was the greatest man in Nikara history, a man so famous that every child in the Empire knew his name by the time they could speak. The myths about him could and did fill up entire bookshelves. He'd united the country for the very first time; he'd brought fire and bloodshed on a scale the land had never witnessed before; and he'd built cities that remained intellectual, cultural, and commercial centers of the Empire.

And now, a millennium later, all that remained were his helmet, his breastplate, and a tea set.

His dynasty had not even survived a generation. Upon his death his sons had immediately fallen upon each other, and after the centuries of bloodshed that followed, the Empire was split under a provincial system that the Red Emperor had not designed nor intended. His bloodline was lost, his heirs extinguished within the first twenty years of the civil war they started. If his line persisted, no one recognized it.

He was king for a day. For a brief moment, he stood in the center of the universe. And for what?

He should have married Tearza, Rin thought. He was a fool to make the shamans his enemies. He should have leashed them to his regime. He should have put a Speerly on the throne, and then his Empire would have lasted for an eternity. By now their heirs would have conquered the world.

"This one has your name on it," Kitay called from farther down the hall.

"What?"

"Look." He pointed. It was the sword—the twin of the one she'd lost in the water during the battle at the Red Cliffs, the second one crafted from Altan's melted-down trident.

They'd kept it as a trophy. *Speerly mineral*, read the placard, *last wielded by Fang Runin.*

Rin drew the sword out of its case and blew the dust off the blade. She'd thought it had sunk to the bottom of the river forever.

Her placard was so small. There were no further details, no reports of her exploits, just her name and the weapon's make. She snorted. That was just like Vaisra. If he'd had his way, then she would only ever have remained a footnote in history.

When they build museums to my regime, Vaisra, I won't even give you a plaque.

Nearly half the artifacts were missing from their cases. They looked recently pilfered, likely by Republican leadership; dust hadn't had time to settle in the outlines they left behind. Rin couldn't tell by reading the plaques why some had been stolen and some were left behind; the missing items were valuables of all types from all eras, and appeared to have been packed away at random.

One empty case stood on a prominent display—a shelf protruding from the wall, rimmed with golden edges to draw the viewer's attention.

Rin picked up the plaque.

Imperial Seal of the Red Emperor.

She nearly dropped it. *Incredible.* She'd learned about this seal at school. When the Red Emperor died, he'd declared that his seal could only pass, along with the mandate of heaven, to the next rightful ruler of the Empire. It was promptly stolen the morning after his funeral. In the centuries after, the seal changed hands between princes, generals, clever concubines, and assassins, followed wherever it went by a trail of blood. Three hundred years later it finally dropped off the historical record, though provincial Warlords still claimed occasionally to have it locked in their private vaults.

So the House of Yin had kept it all along.

Of course Nezha had taken it with him. Rin found that hilarious. He'd lost the country, but he'd taken the ruler's mandate.

Keep it, asshole, she thought. Nezha could have the seal, and every other shiny piece of junk his staff had loaded into their wagons. It didn't matter that those treasures were hallmarks of Nikara history. That history didn't matter to Rin. It was a record of slavery, oppression, misrule, and corruption. She wanted no heirlooms of her predecessors. She did not carry their legacy. She intended to build something new.

Vaisra's throne remained at the end of the hall, too heavy to be carted away.

Rin felt very small as she approached it. It was much grander than the throne she'd sat on at Jinzhou. This was a proper emperor's throne—a high-backed, ornamented chair on a multi-stair dais. An intricate map of the Empire was inked in black ridges across the entire marble floor. Sitting atop that throne, one surveyed the world.

Kitay nodded at the seat. "Gonna give it a try?"

"No," Rin said. "That's not for me."

She knew as she stood in this dark, cold palace that she could never make this place hers. She'd never feel comfortable here; this place was haunted by the ghosts of the House of Yin. And that was just as well. The seat at Arlong had never ruled the entire Empire. It was the home of traitors and imposters, pretenders to the throne doomed to fail. She would not be the latest imposter to rule from the Dragon Province.

This was only a temporary base from which she would solidify her hold on the rest of the country.

The palace interior suddenly felt icy cold. *We have so much work to do,* Rin thought. The task before her seemed so monumental it did not quite seem real. She'd ripped the world apart, had inflicted one great tear that stretched from Mount Tianshan to the Nine Curves Grotto. And now she had to stitch it back together.

Had to restore order in the provinces. Had to clear the corpses off the streets. Had to put food on people's tables. Had to return this country, which had fallen apart in every way conceivable, to normal.

Oh, *gods.* She swayed on her feet, suddenly dizzy. *Where do we even start?*

A knock sounded against the great hall's heavy doors, echoing through the vast, dark space.

Rin blinked, struck from her reverie. "Come in."

A young officer stepped through the doors. He was one of Cholang's staff. Rin could remember his face—she'd seen it before in the command tent—but not his name. "Commander Miragha sent me to tell you we've found it."

"Where?" Rin asked sharply.

"The far end of the Hesperian quarters. We have it surrounded, but haven't moved in yet. No one's going in or out. They're waiting on your orders."

"Good." Rin had to pause for a moment before she could move. She couldn't tell if the woozy rush in her limbs was a product of excitement or fatigue. When she took a step, it felt as if she were floating through air. "I'll go now."

She shrugged off Kitay's concerned glance as she followed the officer out of the palace. They'd already concluded this debate. He knew what she intended. They agreed on what was necessary.

There was no room to hesitate. It was time for a reckoning.

The last time Rin had been near Arlong's Hesperian quarter, she'd killed a man by burning off his testicles. Her clearest memories of this place were seeped in fear and panic—were of frantically dragging a body to a sampan, paddling out toward the harbor, and weighing the corpse down with rocks before anyone saw her and shot her full of bullets.

But then, all her memories involving the Hesperians were laced with fear. Even though they'd first come to Arlong as Vaisra's allies, and even though for half a year they'd nominally fought on the same side, Rin could only associate the Hesperians with alien superiority: forceful, groping hands; steel instruments; and cold indifference.

Sister Petra's laboratory occupied a square one-story building opposite the barracks. Rin's troops surrounded the perimeter, armed and waiting. Commander Miragha saluted Rin as she approached.

"It's locked from the inside," she reported. "Someone's definitely in there."

"Have you communicated with them?" Rin asked.

"We shouted for them to come out, but they didn't respond. Heard a bit of banging about—whoever is in there, they're bracing for a fight."

Rin knew most of the missionaries had already fled the city. She'd seen their slate-gray cloaks on the first boats out of the harbor, easily identified even from across the channel. The Gray Company were revered like royalty in the west; the remaining Hesperian troops would have personally escorted them out of the city.

That meant whoever was barricaded in the laboratory had remained there on purpose.

Outside the door, four of Miragha's men stood ready around an iron-plated, wheeled battering ram the size of a small tent.

"That looks like overkill," Rin said.

"We only bring our best," Miragha said. "Ready whenever you are."

"Hold on." Rin scanned the soldiers until she found one holding a halberd. "Give me that."

She wrapped a discarded Hesperian flag around the blade,

knotted it tightly, and set the tip ablaze. She handed it back to the soldier. "You go in first. Let her think you're me."

He looked alarmed. "But—General, then—"

"You'll be fine," Rin said sternly. The arc of lightning, whatever it was, had not done lasting physical damage to her or Nezha. Against someone who wasn't a shaman, it ought to have no effect at all. "Just prepare for a shock."

She was impressed when he did not argue. He held the flaming halberd firm and gave her a curt, obedient nod.

"Do it," Rin told Miragha.

Miragha gave the order. Her soldiers dragged the battering ram back several yards, then pushed it running against the door.

The wooden door smashed inward upon impact. The soldier with the halberd burst through, waving the torch about the dim interior, but nothing happened. The room was empty. When Rin walked inside, all she saw were toppled chairs and bare tables— and a trap door in the corner.

She pointed. "Down there."

The soldier with the halberd descended first, Rin following several steps behind. The makeshift torch seemed a plausible imitation; its flame flickered and curved like something alive, casting distorted shadows against the wall.

Lightning immediately arced through the dark. The soldier yelped and dropped the halberd. In the brief, bright flash, Rin glimpsed a silhouette across the room—a crouched figure behind something the shape of a mounted cannon. That was enough. Flames burst from her palm and roared across the room. She heard a high mechanical whine, then saw an explosion of sparks, ricocheting across the room like a thunderstorm concentrated inside a jar.

The cannon-like device exploded. The lightning disappeared. When the smoke cleared, Rin's flames, dancing steadily around her arms and shoulders as a makeshift lamp, illuminated a mass of scattered metallic parts and a limp form curled up in the corner.

Too easy, Rin thought as she crossed the room. If a soldier had designed this ambush, they wouldn't have been so trigger-happy with the lightning. They would have known they would only get one chance; they would have waited until they'd established a clear line of fire at Rin.

But Sister Petra Ignatius was a scholar, not a soldier.

Rin pushed at Petra's ribs with her foot, shoving her over onto her back. "If you wanted an audience, you could have just asked."

Petra cringed under her boot. A thin trickle of blood ran down the left side of her face where shrapnel had sliced her temple, and bright red burn marks scorched her hands and neck, but she looked otherwise unharmed. Her eyes were open. She was conscious. She could talk.

Rin turned to the stairs, where Miragha waited with her troops. "Leave us."

Miragha hesitated. "You sure?"

"She's unarmed," Rin said. "Post two troops to guard the exits and dispatch the rest back to the city center."

"Yes, General." Miragha followed her men back up through the trap door. The single column of sunlight winked out as they lowered the door closed behind them.

Then Rin and Petra were alone in the dim, fire-lit basement.

"Was that all you had?" Rin dragged a chair out from Petra's work table and sat down. "An amateur's ambush?"

Petra moaned softly as she drew herself to a sitting position.

"What is this?" Rin demanded. She snatched one of the machine's broken fragments from the ground. The metal was spun in a tight coil, cold to the touch. "What does this do?"

Petra responded with wary silence. She tilted her head back against the wall, her stone-gray eyes roving up and down Rin's form as if sizing up a wild animal.

Fine, thought Rin. Then she'd just have to resort to torture. She'd never done that before—she'd only ever watched Altan extract information with well-placed, sadistic bursts of flame—but the basic principles seemed simple enough. She knew how to hurt.

Then, absurdly, Petra began to laugh.

"As if you'd ever understand." She raised an arm to wipe the blood from her eyes. "What, did you imagine you might devise a countermeasure? The theory behind my machines is centuries beyond your grasp. I could show you every component, every draft of my designs, and you still wouldn't understand. You don't have the *brains*."

She rose to her feet. Rin tensed, prepared to strike. But Petra only stumbled to the chair opposite her and sat down, hands folded primly in her lap in some sick imitation of a teacher lecturing a student.

"It terrifies you, doesn't it?" she sneered. "That your gods are nothing?"

Burn her, said the Phoenix. *Make her scream.*

Rin pushed away the impulse. She had this one chance to get information. She'd get her revenge later.

She held the metal coil out again and repeated the question. "What does this do?"

"Didn't you feel it?" Petra's bloody lips split in a grin. For the first time since Rin had met her, she saw a manic glint in the Gray Sister's eyes, a crack in her inhumanly calm facade. "It silences your god. It *nullifies*."

"That's not possible," Rin objected, despite herself. "The gods are fundamental forces; they made this world, they can't just be cut off by some piece of metal, that's not—"

"Listen to you," Petra crooned. "Clinging to your pagan babble, even now. Your gods are nothing but a delusion. A chaotic rot in your brains that has plagued your country for centuries. But I've found the cure. I fixed that boy, and I'll fix you, too."

She was gloating now. She didn't mind explaining—she *wanted* to explain, because even now, she wanted to wave her superiority in Rin's face. Torture wouldn't be necessary, Rin realized. Petra was going to tell her everything she wanted, because she knew she was about to die, and gloating was all that she had left.

"The principle was quite simple. In Hesperia, we have shock therapies for souls who have lost their grip on reality. The electricity calms their madness. It banishes Chaos from their brains. And once I realized that your shamanism was just madness of the extreme sort, the solution was so easy. Chaos was worming through your minds into the material world. So all I had to do was *shut it off*."

She leaned forward. Blood had dripped again into her left eye, but she just blinked without wiping it away. "How does it feel? To know that your gods are nothing before the Divine Architect? We tamed the Dragon. We tamed your so-called Phoenix. Without your shamans, your army is an untrained, backward mass of idiot peasants that will never, *ever*—"

"Conquer Arlong?" Rin interrupted. She shouldn't have burst out; she should have just let Petra keep talking, but she couldn't stand the *fucking condescension*. "The Republic's finished. Your people fled the harbor the first chance they got. You've lost."

Petra barked out a laugh. "And you think you've *won*? The Gray Company's network spans the world. We have eyes on every continent. And those pieces of trash"—she kicked at a bent shard of metal at her feet—"were only prototypes. When I understood what made Yin Nezha bleed, I sent my notes to the Gray Towers. They'll have perfected my designs by now. The next time you encounter one will be the last.

"The Architect works in mysterious ways. Sometimes he moves slowly. Sometimes he makes sacrifices." Petra took a rattling breath, coughed, then sighed. "But the world marches inevitably, inexorably toward order. This is his intent. The Gray Company is greater than you could ever imagine, and we now have the weapons to burn Chaos out of the world. You kill me and you accomplish nothing. Your world as you know it will end."

Rin remained silent.

Petra meant to provoke. She wanted Rin to lose control, to explode and rage, all to prove her point that in the end, Speerlies were no better than animals. During those weeks on the northern expedition, Petra had always maintained such a cool placidity when she made Rin moan and thrash and howl, the condescending control of a woman who believed she was superior in every way.

But this time Rin was in control. She would not squander it.

She had meant to burn Petra alive. When Miragha's messenger arrived in the palace, Rin had seen an immediate, fantastical vision of Petra screaming and writhing on the floor, begging for mercy as flames corroded her pale white flesh.

But all that now seemed so trite, so easy. Petra deserved no mundane death. Mere bodily torture wouldn't satisfy. Rin had just been struck by a far better idea, something so deliciously cruel that part of her was astonished, amazed by her own creativity.

"I'm not going to kill you," she said with as much calm as she could muster. "You don't deserve that."

For the first time, fear flickered across Petra's face.

"Get up," Rin ordered. "Get on the table."

Petra remained in her chair, body tensing as if trying to decide whether to run or resist.

"*Get on the table.*" Rin let the flames around her shoulders jump higher, resembling wings for an instant before they flared out toward Petra. "Or I will char every part of your body. I'll do it slowly, and I'll start with your throat so I don't have to hear you scream."

Trembling, Petra stood up, climbed onto the examination table, and lay down.

Rin reached over the side of the table for the straps. Her left hand fumbled with the buckles, but she managed to loop them through the metal rings on the sides of the table and yank them tight. Petra lay still all the while. Rin could see the veins protruding from her jaw where she clenched it tight, trying to conceal her fear. But when Rin pulled the straps around Petra's waist, pinning her arms to her sides, a keening whimper escaped the sister's throat.

"Calm down." Rin gave her cheek a patronizing pat. Somehow, that felt better than a slap. "It'll be over soon."

A year ago Petra had strapped her naked to a table and lectured her on the inferiority of her mind, the shortcomings of her body, and the genetically determined backwardness of her race. In the months since then, she'd likely done the same to Nezha. She'd probably stood where Rin stood now, watching impassively as lightning arced through his body, taking meticulous notes while her subject contorted in pain. She'd probably lectured him, too, on why this was the Divine Architect's intention. Why these humiliations and violations were necessary for the slow, holy march toward civilization and order.

Now it was Rin's turn to proselytize.

"Remember that time you drew my blood?" She smoothed Petra's hair back with her fingers. "You filled entire jars with it. You didn't need that much; you told me so yourself. You just wanted to punish me. You were angry because you wanted proof of Chaos, but I couldn't show you the gods."

A pungent smell filled the air. Rin glanced down and saw a damp spot spreading through Petra's robes. She'd soiled herself.

"Don't be scared." Rin reached into her back pocket and withdrew a sachet of poppy seeds. "I'm giving you what you want. I'm going to show you the gods."

She pulled the sachet open with her teeth, tipped it into her palm, and clamped it over Petra's mouth.

A soldier might have been able to resist—might have held their breath, bit Rin's palm hard enough to draw blood, or concealed the seeds under their tongue and spat them out the moment they broke free. But Petra didn't know how to struggle. The Gray Company were untouchable in Hesperia; she'd never had the need. She wriggled pathetically under Rin's grasp, but couldn't break free; Rin jammed her stump over her nose, restricting her air flow, until at last she had no choice but to open her mouth and gasp.

Rin saw her throat bob. Then, several long minutes later, she saw her eyes flutter closed as the drug seeped through her bloodstream.

"Good girl." She removed her palm—empty, good—and wiped it against her pant leg. "Now we wait."

She wasn't sure this would work. Petra could not even conceive of the Pantheon's existence, much less how to get there. And Rin was not Chaghan; she could not flit back and forth between planes, dragging souls along like a shepherd.

But she could call upon the gods, and hers was the god of vengeance.

She dragged a chair next to the table, sat down, and closed her eyes.

The Phoenix answered immediately. It sounded amused. *Really, little one?*

Bring her to me, Rin thought. *And take us to your brethren.*

The Phoenix cackled. *Whatever you wish.*

Darkness rushed in around her. The workroom faded away. She felt herself hurtling into the void, spiraling through the bridge in her mind like an arrow shot straight into the heavens.

"Where are we?" Petra's presence lashed out, panicked. "What is this?"

Rin could sense her fear like a tidal wave, an ongoing flood of horrified, uprooted alienation. This was the same emotion Rin had felt in the New City dialed to the extreme: the jarring realization that the world was not what she thought it was, that everything she believed, everything she had faith in, was wrong.

Petra wasn't just scared, she was falling apart.

"It's divinity," Rin told her gleefully. "Look around."

Suddenly the Pantheon was visible, a circle of plinths surrounding them like spectators around a stage. They crept closer, cruel and curious, one and sixty-three entities entranced by the presence of a soul that refused to acknowledge their presence.

"These are the forces that make up our world," said Rin. "They have no intent. They have no agenda, and they do not tend toward order. They want nothing more than to be what they are. And they don't care."

Petra uttered something low and fearful, some repetitive chant in a language that sounded almost like Hesperian but not quite.

A curse? A prayer? Whatever it was, the Pantheon did not care, because the Pantheon, unlike the Maker, was real.

"Take me back," pleaded Petra. She'd lost all dignity; she'd lost all faith. Without her Maker she was stripped to a lost and terrified core, flailing wildly for something to cling to. "Take me—"

The gods pressed in.

Sound did not quite exist in the plane of spirit. What Rin perceived as words were transmitted thoughts, all equal in volume despite distance or intensity. She knew this in abstract. She knew that here, one could not really scream.

But the sheer intensity of Petra's desperation came close.

"Bring me back down," Rin told the Phoenix. "I'm finished here."

She landed back in her body with a jolt. She opened her eyes.

Sister Petra lay still on the table. Her eyes were wide open. Her pupils darted fretfully about, tracking nothing. Rin watched her for a long while, wondering if she might find her way back to her body, but the only movement she made was the occasional tremor in her shoulders. A choked murmur escaped her throat.

Rin prodded Petra's shoulder. "What was that?"

Drool trickled from the side of her mouth. Petra gurgled something incomprehensible, then fell silent.

"Congratulations." Rin patted her head. "You've finally found religion."

CHAPTER 32

Safely ensconced in a heavily guarded house behind the barracks, Rin slept better that night than any night she could remember in years. She didn't need laudanum to knock herself unconscious. She didn't wake up multiple times in the night, sweaty and shivering, straining to hear a dirigible attack she'd only imagined. She didn't see Altan, didn't see the Cike, didn't see Speer. The moment she lay down she slid into a deep, dreamless sleep, and didn't awake until warm rays of sunlight crept over her face.

She was twenty-one years old and it was the first night she could remember that she could close her eyes without fearing for her life.

In the morning she stood up, combed the tangles out of her hair with her fingers, and stared at herself in front of the mirror. She worked at the muscles in her face until she looked composed. Assured. Ready. Leaders couldn't display doubt. When she walked out that door, she was their general.

And then what? asked Altan's voice. *Their Empress? Their President? Their Queen?* Rin didn't know. She and Kitay had never discussed what kind of regime they might replace the Republic with. This whole time, they had—rather naively, she now realized—assumed that once they won, life in the Empire could go back to normal.

But there was no normal. In the span of a year they had smashed apart everything that was *normal*. Now there were no Warlords, no Empresses, and no Presidents. Just a great, big, beautiful, and shattered country, held together by common awe of a single god.

She was just General Fang for now, she decided. She didn't have a kingdom to rule yet. Not until the Hesperians had been decisively defeated.

She walked out of the house. Five guards stood waiting outside her door, ready to escort her across the city. When they reached the palace, she had to stop and remind herself that she wasn't dreaming. Ever since the start of the campaign from Ruijin, she'd spent so long thinking about what would happen if she were in charge that it seemed unreal that she was truly standing here, about to seize the levers of power.

Never mind that she had been in here only yesterday, pulling artifacts off the walls like she owned the place—because she *did* own the place. Yesterday was about a takeover, about eradicating the last traces of Republican authority. Today was the first day of the rest of Nikara history.

"You good?" Kitay asked.

"Yeah," she breathed. "Just—trying not to forget this."

She stepped over the threshold. Blood rushed to her head. She felt buoyant, weightless. The scales of everything had shifted. The decrees she wrote in that palace would ripple across the country. The rules she conceived would become law.

Overnight, she had become as close to a god as a mortal could be.

I've reached behind the canvas, she thought. *And now I hold the brush.*

Rin ran her administration not from the grand, empty great hall—that room was too cavernous, too intimidating—but from Vaisra's smaller war office, which was furnished with only a single spare table and several uncomfortable hard-backed chairs. She couldn't have sat on the palace throne—it was too grand, too dauntingly official. She wasn't ready to play the role of Empress yet. But she felt comfortable in this cramped, undecorated chamber. She'd fought campaigns from this room before; it felt like the most natural thing in the world to do so again. Sitting at this table with Kitay to her right and Venka to her left, she didn't feel like such an imposter. This was just a much nicer version of her tent.

This is not right, said a small voice in the back of her mind. *This is insane.*

But what in the past two years had not been insane? She had leveled a country. She'd destroyed the Trifecta. She'd commanded an army. She'd become, for all intents and purposes, a living god.

If she could do that, why could she not run a country?

The first thing on their agenda that morning was deciding what to do about Nezha. Rin's scouts reported that he'd fled the country along with his closest officers and advisers, all packed into every last merchant skimmer and fishing dinghy that the Republic could scrounge together.

"Where have they gone?" Rin asked. "Ankhiluun? Moag won't put him up."

Kitay lowered the last page of the dispatch. "A little farther east."

"Not the longbow island," she said. "The air there is still poison."

He gave her an odd look. "Rin, he's on Speer."

She couldn't stop herself; she flinched.

So Nezha had taken refuge on the Dead Island.

It made sense. He couldn't go all the way to Hesperia; that was as good as a surrender. But he must have known that he wasn't safe anywhere on the mainland. If he wanted to stay alive, he needed to put an ocean between them.

"That's cute," she said with as much calm as she could manage. She saw them both watching her; she couldn't let them think she was rattled. Nezha had certainly chosen Speer to aggravate her. She could just hear the taunts in his voice. *You might have everything, but I have your home. I have the last piece of territory that you don't control.*

And she did feel a flicker of irritation, a sharp jolt of humiliation in her back where once he'd twisted a blade. But that was all she felt—annoyance. No fear, no panic. Escaping to Speer was an annoying move, but it was also the ultimate sign of weakness. Nezha had no cards left. He'd lost his capital and his fleet. He ruled a Republic in name only, and he'd been relegated to a cursed, desiccated island where nothing lived and where hardly anything grew. All he could do was taunt.

Moreover, according to dispatches, he'd lost the faith of his allies. The Hesperians didn't listen to him anymore. The Consortium had chosen to cut their losses.

"He's not received any reinforcements since Arlong fell," Venka read. "And the Hesperians stripped his authority to command ground troops. He's only got Nikara infantry at his disposal now, and a third of those numbers deserted after Arlong." She glanced up from the report. "Incredible. You think the Consortium's finished?"

"Perhaps for now—" Kitay began, at the same moment that Rin said, "Absolutely not."

"They've withdrawn all their forces," Kitay said.

"They'll come back," Rin said.

"Perhaps in a few months," Kitay said. "But I think they've suffered more losses than they—"

"Doesn't matter," Rin said. "They'll be back as soon as they possibly can. Could be days, could be weeks. But they're going to hit back, hard, and we've got to be prepared. I told you what Petra said. They don't merely think we're just—just obstacles to trade. We're not inconveniences to them. They think we're an existential threat. And they won't stop until we're dust."

She looked around the table. "We're not done fighting. You all understand this, don't you? They didn't request an armistice. They haven't sent diplomats. We don't have a peace, we've only got a reprieve, and we don't know how long it'll last. We can't just sit around and wait for it. We've got to strike first."

If Rin had her way, the rest of the day would have been occupied with military remobilization. She wanted to open the ranks for enlistment. She wanted to set up training camps in the fields to plunder Arlong for Hesperian military technology and get her troops learning how to use it.

But her first priority had to be civil reconstruction. For armies were fueled by cities, and the city was on the verge of falling apart.

They upturned Arlong in a flurry of restoration. Work teams deployed to the beaches to run rescue operations on the settlements the Dragon had flooded. Triage centers opened across the city to treat civilians who had been injured in the battle and subsequent occupation. Lines formed before the public kitchens and stretched around the canals, intimidating crowds composed of thousands upon thousands of people whom she was now responsible for feeding.

Governance required a wholly different set of skills from commanding an army, very few of which Rin possessed. She didn't know the first thing about civil administration, yet suddenly a million mundane tasks demanded her immediate attention. Relocation for civilians whose homes were underwater. Law enforcement against looting and pillaging. Finding caretakers for children whose parents were dead or missing. It was going to be a gargantuan task just to restore the city to a minimal level of functionality, and its difficulty was compounded by the fact that the public officers normally responsible for keeping the city running were either dead, imprisoned, or had fled with Nezha to Speer.

Rin was astonished they got anything done. She certainly couldn't have gotten through that first morning without Kitay, who seemed undaunted by the impossibility of their mission, who calmly summoned staff and designated responsibilities like he knew exactly where everything was and what needed to be done.

Still, that morning did not quite seem real. It felt like a dream. It was *absurd*, the fact that the three of them were running a city. Her mind kept ricocheting between the wildly arrogant conviction that this was fine, they were managing, and doing a better job of it than any of Arlong's corrupt leadership ever had; and the crippling fear that they weren't qualified for this at all because they were just *soldiers*, just kids who hadn't even graduated from Sinegard, and so wholly unprepared for the task of ruling that the city was going to collapse around them any minute. Despite Kitay's astounding competency, their problems only kept stacking up. The moment they resolved one issue, they received reports of a dozen more. It felt as if they were trying to plug a dam with their fingertips while water kept bursting forth around them. If they strayed off focus for even one minute, Rin feared, they'd drown.

By midmorning she wanted to curl up and cry, *I don't want this, I can't do this*; wanted to hand off her responsibilities to an adult.

But you waged this war, Altan reminded her. *You wanted to be in charge. And now you are. Don't fuck it up.*

But every time she got her thoughts back in order, she remembered that it wasn't just Arlong at stake—it was the country.

And Arlong's problems paled in comparison to what was going on across Nikan. The Republic had been holding together worse than she'd thought. Grain deficiencies plagued every province. The livestock trade was nearly nonexistent; it had been wrecked by the Mugenese invasion, and the following civil war had afforded it no space to recover. Fish, a staple in the southeast, was in short supply since Daji had poisoned the rivers a year ago. Rates of infectious diseases were skyrocketing. Almost every part of the country was suffering epidemics of typhus, malaria, dysentery, and—in a remote village in Rat Province—unprecedented cases of leprosy. These diseases affected rural populations on a cyclical schedule, but the tumult of war had uprooted entire communities and forced masses of people—many of whom had never been in contact with one another before—into smaller, cramped spaces. Infections had exploded as a result. Hesperian medicine had helped, to some extent. That wasn't available anymore.

Then there were the normal by-products of war. Mass displacement. Rampant banditry. Trade routes were no longer safe; entire economies had ceased to function. The normal flow of goods, that crucial circulation that kept the Empire running, had broken down and would require months, if not years, to restore.

Rin wouldn't have known about half of these issues if she hadn't learned about them from Nezha's private papers—a stack of neat, startlingly comprehensive accounts of every plea for government assistance over the last six months, kept fastidiously in elegant, oddly feminine handwriting. Despite herself, Rin found them immensely helpful. She spent hours poring over the scrolls, marking down his reflections and suggested solutions. They displayed the thoughts of someone trained for statesmanship since he could read. A distressing number of his proposals were better than anything she or Kitay could have thought of.

"I can't believe he left all this behind," she said. "They're not that heavy. He could have done a lot more harm by taking them with him. You think they're sabotage?"

Kitay looked unconvinced. "Maybe."

No, they both knew that wasn't true. The notes were too detailed, too clearly compiled over months of difficult rule, to be staged overnight. And too many of Nezha's warnings— the importance of dam reconstruction, of vigilant canal traffic management—had turned out to be salient.

"Or," Kitay ventured, "he's trying to help you out. Or at least, he's trying to keep the city's disasters to a minimum."

Rin hated that explanation. She didn't want to credit Nezha with that generosity. It painted a different picture of Nezha—not as the vicious, opportunistic bootlicker to the Hesperians that she'd been rallying against this entire campaign, but as a leader genuinely trying his best. It made her think of the tired boy in the cell. The frightened boy in the river.

It made it so much harder to fixate on planning his death.

"It doesn't matter," she said curtly. "Nezha couldn't hold on to his city, let alone a country. These are our problems now. Pass me that page."

They were deep into the afternoon before they broke for a mid-day meal, and only then because Kitay's stomach began rumbling so loudly the distraction became unbearable. Rin had been so absorbed in Nezha's documents, she'd forgotten she was hungry until a junior officer set plates of steamed scallion buns, boiled fish with chilis, and braised cabbage before them. Then she was ravenous.

"Hold on," Kitay said, just as Rin reached for a bun. "Who cooked this?"

"Palace staff," said the officer who'd brought it in.

"They're still working the kitchens?" Venka asked.

"You said to keep all palace staff in their positions if they wished to defect," said the officer. "We're quite sure the food is safe. We had guards watching when they prepared it."

Rin stared at the array of dishes, amazed. It hadn't really hit her, not until then, that she ruled Nikan. *She ruled Nikan*, which meant all the privileges along with the responsibilities. She had an entire palace staff waiting on her. She'd never have to cook her own meals again.

But Kitay didn't look quite as delighted. Just as she lifted a morsel of fish to her mouth, he slapped the chopsticks from her hand. "Don't eat that."

"But he said—"

"I don't care what he said." He dropped his voice so the officer couldn't overhear. "You don't know who cooked this. You don't know how it got here. And we certainly didn't request lunch, which means either this kitchen staff had a remarkably quick change of heart, or someone had a vested interested in feeding us."

"General?" The officer shifted from foot to foot. "Is there something you—"

"Bring us an animal," Kitay told him.

"Sir?"

"A dog, ideally, or a cat. The first pet you can find should do. Be quick."

The officer returned twenty-five minutes later with a small, fluffy white creature with perky ears, head drooping under the weight of an ornate collar of gold and jade. This breed, Rin thought, must have been very popular with Nikara aristocracy; it resembled very much the pups she'd once seen at Kitay's estate.

Kitay seemed to have noticed this, too; he winced as the officers set the dog on the floor.

"The servants said this used to belong to the Lady Saikhara," said the guard. "They call it Binbin."

"Good gods," Venka muttered. "Don't tell us its name."

It was over quickly. The dog set eagerly at the boiled fish, but it had barely swallowed two bites before it stepped back and began to whine piteously.

Kitay started forward, but Rin held him back. "It could bite."

They remained in their seats, watching as the dog slumped to the floor, sides heaving. Its stubby front paws scrabbled at its bloated stomach, as if trying to scratch out some parasite gnawing at its innards. Gradually its movements grew weak, then listless. It whimpered once and fell silent. It seemed to take an eternity for it to stop twitching.

Rin felt a violent wave of nausea. She was no longer remotely hungry.

"Arrest the kitchen staff," Kitay ordered calmly. "Detain them in separate rooms and keep them isolated until we've time to interrogate them."

"Yes, sir."

The officer left. The door slammed shut. Kitay turned to Venka. "It could've been—"

"I know," Venka said curtly. "I'm on it."

She stood up, plucked her bow off the table, and left the room—

presumably to see whether the officer would carry out his orders or flee.

She and Kitay sat in stunned silence. Kitay's temporary calm had evaporated—he was staring at the dishes, blinking very rapidly, mouth half-open as if unsure what to say. Rin, too, felt lost in a fog of panic. The betrayal had been so sudden, so unexpected, her overriding thought was fury at her sheer *stupidity*, for accepting food from the kitchens without even stopping to think.

Someone was trying to kill her. Someone was trying to kill her in the most obvious way possible, and they'd almost succeeded.

She realized then that she could never feel safe in her own office again.

The door creaked open.

Rin jumped. "What is it?"

It was a messenger. He hesitated, taking in their distressed faces, and then tentatively lifted a scroll in Rin's direction. "There's, ah, a missive."

"From who?" Kitay asked.

"It's sealed with the House of—"

"Bring it here," Rin said curtly. "Then get out."

The moment the door swung closed, she ripped the scroll open with her teeth. She didn't know why her heart was hammering so loudly, why she still felt a surge of fearful anticipation even though Nezha had *lost*, had fled, had retreated so far out into the ocean that he couldn't possibly threaten her here.

Calm down, she told herself. *This is nothing. He has nothing. Just a formality from a defeated foe.*

Hello, Rin. Hope you're enjoying the palace. Did you take my old rooms?

You'll have realized by now, I think, that this country is in deep shit. Let me guess, Kitay's been going through agricultural reports all morning. He's probably losing his mind over the inconsistencies. Here's a hint—the smarter magistrates always underreport their crop yields to get more subsidies. Or they might really just be starving. Hard to know, huh?

"That patronizing shit," Rin muttered.

"Hold on." Kitay was already on the second page. He skimmed the bottom, blinked, and then handed it to her. "Keep reading."

The kitchen staff are good, but you'll find that several are quite loyal to my family. I hope you didn't eat the lunch.

Rin's mouth went dry. He couldn't know that. How did he know that?

Don't punish them all. It'll either be the head cook, Hairui, or his assistant. The others don't have a backbone. I mean, knowing you, you've probably had them all thrown in prison. But at least let Minmin and Little Xing back in the kitchens. They make excellent steamed buns. And you like those, don't you?

She lowered the letter. She suddenly found it hard to breathe; the walls seemed to constrict around her, the air deprived of oxygen.

Someone's spying on us.

"Nezha's not on Speer," she said. "He's *here*."

"He can't be," Kitay said. "Our scouts saw him leaving—"

"That means nothing. He could have snuck back. He controls the fucking water, Kitay, you don't think he could have traveled up the river in one night? He's *watching us*—"

"There's no place for him to go," Kitay said. "That'd be suicide. Come on, Rin—what, do you think he's crouched in a shack somewhere in the city? Peeking out at you from behind corners?"

"He knows about the granaries." Her pitch shot up several octaves. "He knows about the fucking *cooks*! Pray tell, Kitay, how the *fuck* would he know that unless he—"

"Because it's the easiest guess in the world," Kitay said. "And he knows about the granaries because those were the same problems that he's been dealing with for months. Up until we arrived, feeding this country was *his* problem. He doesn't have eyes over your shoulder, he's just trying to rattle you. Don't let him win."

Rin shot him an incredulous look. "I think you're giving quite a lot of credit to his capabilities for conjecture."

"And I think you're massively overestimating how much Nezha wants to die," Kitay said. "He's not hiding in the city. That's certain suicide. He's got scouts, yes, but we're in his fucking capital—of course people are going to report to him."

"Then he'll *know*—"

"So he'll know. We've just got to operate assuming Nezha has a good idea of what we're planning. That's inevitable with regimes in power—you can't keep your operations secret for long, there are too many people involved. In the end, it won't matter. We've got too many advantages. You just can't squander them by freaking the fuck out."

She forced herself to take several deep, shaky breaths. Gradually, her pulse slowed. The darkness creeping at the edges of her vision faded away. She squeezed her eyes shut, trying to organize her thoughts, trying to take stock of the problem.

She knew she had enemies in Arlong. She'd known that from the start. She'd had no choice but to ask many of the former administrative personnel to stay on in their roles, simply because she had no qualified staff who could fill their positions. She didn't know how to run a country, so she'd had to employ Republicans who did. They'd all nominally defected to her regime, of course, but how many of them were secretly plotting against her? How many was Nezha still in correspondence with? How many tiny traps had he left in his wake?

Her breathing quickened. The panic returned; her vision ebbed black. She felt a low, creeping dread, a prickling under her skin as if a million ants were crawling over her body.

It didn't go away. It persisted throughout the afternoon, even after they'd interrogated the kitchen staff and executed the cook in charge. It intensified into a flurry of symptoms: a debilitating fatigue; a throbbing headache that developed as her eyes grew strained, darting around for shadows where they didn't exist.

The palace didn't seem such an empty playground anymore. It seemed a house of infinite darkness, crowded with thousands of enemies that she couldn't see or anticipate.

"I know," Kitay said, every time she voiced her fears. "I'm scared, too. But that's ruling, Rin. There's always someone who doesn't want you on the throne. But we've just got to keep going. We can't let go of the reins. There's no one else."

The days stretched on. Slowly, incredibly, the business of city administration stopped feeling like a fever dream and started feeling more like a familiar duty as they fell into a routine—they woke an hour before sunrise, sifted through intelligence reports during the early hours of the morning, spent the afternoon checking in on reconstruction projects they'd set underway, and put out fires as they arose throughout the day.

They hadn't brought Arlong back to normal. Not even close. Most of the civilian population was still displaced, camping out in makeshift shacks on the same grounds where once Vaisra had corralled all the southern refugees. Food shortages were a persistent problem. The communal kitchens always ran out of food long before everyone in the line was served. There simply weren't enough rations, and Rin didn't have a clue where they could extract more on short notice. Their best hope was to wait for Moag's missives and hope she could convert boatloads of Nikara antiques into smuggled Hesperian grain.

But somehow, as days turned into weeks, their hold on the city seemed to stabilize. The civil administration, comprising southern soldiers with no experience and Republican officials who had to be guarded at all times, became semifunctional and self-sustaining. Some semblance of order had been restored to the city. Fights and riots no longer broke out on the streets. All Republican soldiers who hadn't fled had either stopped trying to cause trouble or had been caught and locked in prison. Arlong had not quite welcomed the south with open arms, but it seemed to have reluctantly accepted its new government.

Those seemed like tentative signs of progress. Or that was, at least, the lie Rin and Kitay told themselves, to avoid facing the crushing pressure of the fact that they were children, unprepared and unqualified, juggling a towering edifice that could collapse at any minute.

Rin, Kitay, and Venka always holed up in the war room long past sunset. As the moon crept across the sky, they went from slouching at the table to sitting on the floor to lying by the hearth, swigging at bottles of sorghum wine recovered from Vaisra's private cellars, all pretense of work forgotten.

All three of them had started drinking religiously. It felt like a compulsion; by the end of the day, alcohol seemed as necessary as eating or drinking water. It was the only thing that took the edge off the debilitating stress that pounded their temples. In those hours, they lurched to the opposite of anxiety. They became temporary, private megalomaniacs. They fantasized about everything they would change about the Empire once they'd gotten it into their order. The future was full of sandcastles, flimsy prospects to be destroyed and rebuilt at will.

"We'll ban child marriage," Rin declared. "We'll make matchmaking illegal until all parties are at least sixteen. We'll make education mandatory. And we'll need an officers' school, obviously—"

"You're going to reinstate Sinegard?" Venka asked.

"Not at Sinegard," Kitay said. "That place has too much history. We'll build a new school, somewhere down south. And we'll revamp the whole curriculum—more emphasis on Strategy and Linguistics, less focus on Combat . . ."

"You can't get rid of Combat," Venka said.

"We can get rid of Combat the way Jun taught it," Rin said.

"Martial arts don't belong on the battlefield, they belong on an opera stage. We have to teach a curriculum geared for modern warfare. Artillery—arquebuses, cannons, the whole gamut."

"I want a dirigible division," Venka said.

"We'll get you one," Kitay vowed.

"I want a dozen. All equipped with state-of-the-art cannons."

"Whatever you like."

As the night drew on, their ideas always went from bold to wishful to simply absurd. Kitay wanted to issue a standardized set of abacuses because pea-size beads, apparently, made better clacking noises. Venka wanted to ban intricate, heavy hair ornaments required by women of aristocracy on the grounds that they strained the neck, as well as the black, double-flapped headwear favored by northern bureaucrats on the grounds that they were ugly.

Those last few proposals were trivial, so obviously not worth their time. But it still thrilled them, tossing out ideas as if they had the power to speak them into being. And then remembering that they *did*, they fucking did, because they owned this country now and everyone had to do what they said.

"I want free tuition at all the scholars' academies," Rin said.

"I want the punishment for forced sexual intercourse to be castration," Venka said.

"I want multiple copies made of every ancient text in the archives that will be disseminated to each of the top universities to prevent knowledge decay," Kitay said.

And they could have it all. Because fuck it—they were in charge now; absurd as it was, they sat on the throne at Arlong, and what they said was *law*.

"I am the force of creation," Rin murmured as she stared at the ceiling and watched it spin. Vaisra's sorghum wine burned sweet and sour on her tongue; she wanted to swig more of it, just to feel her insides blaze. "I am the end and the beginning. The world is a painting and I hold the brush. I am a god."

∞

But morning always came and, along with the stabbing headaches of the previous night's indulgences, returned the exhaustion, exasperation, and mounting despair that came with trying to repair a country that had spent the majority of its history at war.

Every bit of progress they made in Arlong, it seemed, was constantly being undone by bad news from the rest of the country. Bandit attacks were rampant. Epidemics were getting worse. Power vacuums had sprung up throughout the southeastern provinces Rin's army had conquered, and since she didn't have enough troops to deploy nationwide to cement her regime, a dozen pockets of local rebellion were forming that she'd later have to put down.

The biggest emergency was food. They were arguing about food in the war room. Dwindling grain was the subject of every missive they received from outlying cities, was the cause of almost every riot Rin's troops had to quell. Until now Arlong had been fed by regular shipments of Hesperian supplies, and now those were gone.

Even Kitay couldn't find a solution. No amount of juggling resources, diplomacy, or clever reorganization could mask the fact that the grain stores simply were not there.

Moag, who had been Rin's best option, sent back a brief letter quashing their hopes.

No can do, little Speerly, she wrote. *Can't get you that much grain in such a short time frame. And Arlong's treasures aren't trading for much on the market right now. First of all, they're hard to get past the embargo when they're so obviously Nikara; second, Yin family artifacts have gone down quite a bit in value. I'm sure you can see why. Keep looking, I'm sure you'll find something they want.*

The perverse upside to the impending famine was that enlistment numbers shot up, since army recruits were the only ones guaranteed to receive two full rations a day. But then, of course, once this became widespread knowledge, fights and protests started breaking out around the barracks over this perceived injustice.

This, Rin thought, was a dreadfully apt metaphor for her frustrations with the city. For why *shouldn't* the army receive priority? The strength of their defenses was critical, now more than ever— why couldn't anyone else see that?

Every endless meeting, every redundant conversation they had about how to feed the city felt much more frustrating because Rin couldn't shake the feeling that this was all a mere distraction. That she was wasting her time trying to restore a broken country back to functionality, when what clearly should have been prioritized was driving her victory home.

She was so close to the end, she could nearly taste it.

One more campaign. One more battle. Then she'd be the only one left, sitting on her throne in the south, set up to remake this broken country to her liking.

But this wasn't about her personal ambitions. This was about the threat, the ever-looming threat that no one else seemed to realize was so much more frightening than famine.

The Hesperians were coming back.

Why wouldn't they? And why wouldn't they strike *now*, when they knew Rin's incipient regime was on such shaky ground? If Rin led the Hesperians, she would call for additional airships and launch a counterstrike as soon as she could, before the Nikara could rebuild their army.

Rin didn't have artillery forces capable of taking down dirigibles. She had only half of her original numbers, now that Cholang and his troops had retreated home to Dog Province. She had no other offensive shamans; the Trifecta were gone, Dulin and Pipaji were dead. She didn't have anything but fire with which to stop the west, and she didn't know if she alone was enough.

In her dreams she saw the dirigibles again, a buzzing horde that blotted out the sky, more than she could count. They descended in full force on Nikara shores, circling the air above her. She saw the faces of their pilots: uniformly pale, demonic blue eyes laughing at her as they trained their cannons in her direction.

And before she could lift her arms to the sky, they opened fire. The world erupted in scattered dirt and orange flame, and for all her bravado, all she could do was kneel on the ground, wrap her arms around her head, and hope that death came quickly.

"Rin." Kitay shook her by the shoulders. "*Wake up.*"

She tasted blood in her mouth. Had she bitten her tongue? She turned to the side, spat, and winced at the crimson splatter on her sheets.

"What?" she asked, suddenly afraid. "Was there—"

"Nothing's happened," he said. He pulled down his lip. Angry scars dotted the inside of his mouth. "But you're hurting me."

"Gods." She felt a twist of guilt. "I'm sorry."

"It's fine." Kitay rubbed at his cheek and yawned. "Just—try to go back to sleep."

It struck her then how incredibly tired he looked, how shrunken and diminished, so wholly different from the confident, authoritative persona he acquired during the daytime.

That scared her. It seemed like physical evidence that everything was, after all, a farce. That they were pretenders to the throne, playing at competency, while their victory slipped from their fingers.

The Empire was fracturing. Their people were starving. The Hesperians were going to return, and they had nothing with which to stop them.

She reached for his fingers. "Kitay."

He squeezed her hand in his. He looked so young. He looked so scared. "I know."

Worst of all, the letters did not stop.

They were relentless. Nezha, apparently, was trying to wage psychological warfare through a sheer barrage of scrolls. They appeared outside her quarters. They found their way into her intelligence reports. They kept showing up with her meals. Rin had changed the kitchen staff so many times that the quality of food was now decidedly poor, but each day at noon a scroll invariably appeared tucked underneath her porridge bowl.

One morning a letter showed up on her pillow, and Rin immediately launched a manhunt in an attempt to find the messenger. But a thorough search of the entire barracks revealed no leads. Eventually she stopped trying to root out suspected couriers—that would have required replacing nearly her entire staff—and started venting by ripping up and burning Nezha's scrolls instead.

But only after she read them. She always had to read them first. She really should have just burned them without looking—she knew that reading them just meant she was playing into his game. But she couldn't help it. She had to know what he knew.

She could never quite pin down their tone. Sometimes they were mocking and patronizing—he knew she had no aptitude for governance, and he was clearly relishing this fact. But sometimes they were genuinely helpful.

Lao Ho's a good man to supervise regional taxation if you haven't thrown him in prison yet. And tell Kitay that as much as he wants to reorganize the labeling system for the old annals in the library, we've kept them that way for a reason. The first numerals stand for relative importance, not scroll size. Don't let him get confused.

He alternated constantly between writing taunts and delivering pieces of accurate, important information. Rin couldn't grasp what was going on in his mind. Was he just playing games? If so, it was working—the taunts redoubled her frustrations, made her furious that their mistakes were so visible they were obvious all the way across the strait; the pieces of advice were even more torturous, because she never knew whether to take them at face value, and spent so much time second-guessing his tips, trying to discover his underlying motives, that she got less done than if she'd never read them at all.

He always ended his letters with the same offer. *Come to the negotiating table. The Hesperians always produce grain at a surplus—they've got machines doing the planting for them. They have food aid to spare. Just make a few concessions and you've got it.*

It never sounded the slightest bit more attractive. The more missives she received, the more condescending they became.

Keep your grain, she wanted to write back. *I'd rather choke than let you feed me. I'd rather starve to death than take anything from your hands.*

But she bit down the impulse. If she sent Nezha any response, then he'd know she'd been reading his letters.

But he must have known anyways. Every missive was terrifyingly omniscient. He identified so clearly the same issues they were struggling with that he might have been standing over their shoulders in the war room. She knew he was trying to make her paranoid, but it *worked*. She didn't feel safe in her own room anymore. She couldn't get any rest—she and Kitay had to start sleeping in shifts again, guarding each other in the same bed, otherwise she was too overcome with anxiety to even close her eyes. She could hardly focus anywhere she went; her eyes were too busy darting about, watching for spies or assassins. She started spending each day holed up in the war room because it was the only place where she felt safe, with the only window three floors up, and its single door guarded by a dozen handpicked soldiers.

"You need to stop reading those," Venka said.

Rin was staring at the latest missive, glaring at the characters until they felt seared into her eyelids, as if she could decipher Nezha's intent if she stared at them long enough.

"Put that down, Rin. He's just fucking with you."

"No, he's not." Rin pointed. "Look. He knows we tried getting contraband grain from Moag. He *knows*—"

"Of course he knows," Venka said. "That's an obvious guess; what else are we going to try? You're only letting him win when you read those. He's just messing with you because he's exiled on an island in bum-fuck nowhere and can't do anything except squeal for attention—"

"*Squeal for attention.*" Rin lowered the scroll. "That's an interesting phrase."

There was an awkward silence. Kitay glanced up from a stack of trade reports, brows lifted.

Venka blinked. "Sorry?"

For a moment Rin just stared at her, expression blank, while her mind spun to catch up to the conclusion she'd just formed.

No cards left to play. She'd just read those words in Nezha's handwriting—they'd caught her eye because it had been such a specific phrasing. *I'm sure you think I'm just squealing for attention, but take a look at the ledgers and you'll know I'm right.* It hadn't been in any of Nezha's previous letters; she would have remembered it. And Venka hadn't yet read the one she was holding in her hand, unless—

Unless.

The room seemed to dim. Rin narrowed her eyes. "How did you know that Nezha was going to make a stand at Xuzhou?"

Venka's throat pulsed. "What do you mean?"

"Answer the question."

"We intercepted their messengers, I told you—"

"You're very good at that," Rin said.

She saw the muscles in Venka's face working, as if she couldn't decide whether to smile and accept the compliment. She looked scared. Did that mean she was lying? It had to—what other reason did she have to be afraid?

"Answer this." Rin stood up. "How do you think Nezha knew we were trying to reach the Trifecta?"

Venka's mouth worked soundlessly for a moment. "I don't understand."

"I think you do." Rin took a step toward her. Her ears were ringing. Her voice dropped low. "Do you know how many people knew about that plan? Five. Me, Kitay, Master Jiang, the Vipress, and you."

Venka stepped back. "I don't know what—"

"Rin," Kitay interrupted. "Don't do this. Let's talk—"

Rin ignored him. "I have another question." She wouldn't give Venka a chance to collect her thoughts, to spin together a cover. She wanted to launch all her suspicions at once, to build a mounting case from every angle until Venka cracked from the pressure. "Why didn't you tell us Nezha was going to bomb Tikany?"

Venka shot her an incredulous look. "How the fuck would I have known about that?"

"You made us think that we were safe once we'd taken the Beehive," Rin said. "You told me Nezha was nowhere close to launching a southern strike. You said he was ill."

"Because he *was*!" Venka's voice rose several octaves in pitch. "Everyone was gossiping about it, I wouldn't make that up—"

Kitay grasped Rin's elbow. "That's *enough*—"

Rin shook her arm from his grasp. "And yet two weeks later he was in Tikany, miraculously cured. Answer this, Venka: Why did they leave you alive in the Anvil? The Southern Army was under siege for months, but you came out just fine. Why?"

Venka's cheeks went a pale, furious white. "This is bullshit."

"Answer the question."

"You think I'm a spy? *Me?*"

"Why did you leave Arlong that night?" Rin pressed.

Venka threw her hands up. "*What* night?"

"In Arlong. The night we escaped. We all had reasons to go, we were all running for our lives, except you. No one was coming after you. So why did you leave?"

"Are you fucking kidding me?" Venka snapped. "I left for *you*."

"And why would you do that?" Rin pressed. This was all so obvious now; the pieces fit so well. Venka's sudden change of heart, the implausibility of her motivations—the contradictions were so glaring, she was amazed she hadn't seen it before. "You never liked me. You *hated* me at Sinegard; you thought I was dirt-skinned trash. You think all the south are dirt-skinned trash. What changed your mind?"

"This is fucking unbelievable," Venka spat.

"No, what's unbelievable is a Sinegardian aristocrat deciding to throw her lot in with southern rebels. How long has it been? Were you reporting to Nezha from the start?"

Kitay slammed a fist against the desk. "Rin, shut the fuck up."

Rin was so startled by his vehemence that, despite herself, she fell silent.

"You're exhausted." Kitay grabbed the scroll from her hand and began ferociously ripping it to tiny, then tinier shreds. "You're not reading these anymore. You're giving Nezha exactly what he wants—"

"Or it could be I've just found his mole," Rin said.

"Don't be ridiculous," he snapped.

"You read that scroll, Kitay, you saw those words—"

"It's a fucking turn of phrase—" Venka started.

"It's a turn of phrase that only *you* used." Rin jabbed a finger at her. "Because you wrote these, didn't you? You've been drafting them all this time, laughing at us, watching us sweat—"

"You're fucking crazy," Venka said.

"Oh, I'm sure that's what you want me to think," Rin snarled. "You and Nezha both—"

Something shifted suddenly in Venka's face. "Get down."

Then she flung herself at Rin, arms reaching for her waist as if to pin her to the ground.

Rin hadn't processed what she'd heard. She saw Venka advancing and her vision went red, locked into the fight response that had so far kept her alive, and instead of twisting and ducking to the ground, she grabbed Venka by the shoulders and brought her knee up against her thigh instead.

Afterward, she'd torture herself wondering whether it was her fault. She'd run through the list of all the things she should have done. Should have realized Venka's last words were a warning, not a threat. Should have noticed Venka was unarmed, and that her hands weren't going for Rin's head and neck, the way they would have if Venka truly meant to hurt her. Should have seen that Venka's face was contorted in fear, not anger.

Should have understood that Venka was trying to save her life.

But in that moment, she was so convinced that Venka was the traitor, that Venka was *attacking* her, that she didn't notice the crossbow bolt in Venka's neck until they'd both collapsed to the floor. Until after she'd already burned ridges into Venka's shoulders. Until she realized that Venka was twitching, but she wasn't getting up.

Too late, she noticed the figure in the window.

Another bolt shrieked through the air. Rin watched its path, helpless and terrified, but it missed Kitay by a yard. He dove under the table; the bolt buried its head in the doorframe.

Rin flung her palm at the window. Flames roared; the glass exploded. Through the blaze, she saw the dark-clothed figure tumbling through the air.

She wriggled out from under Venka's body and ran toward the window. The assassin lay in a crumpled heap three floors below. He wasn't stirring. Rin didn't care. She pointed down, and a stream of flame shot toward the ground, licking hungrily around the corpse.

She thickened the flame, made it burn as hot as she was capable, until she couldn't see the body anymore, just thick, roiling waves of orange under shimmering air. She didn't want to preserve the assassin's body. She knew who had sent him: either Nezha or the Gray Company or the two acting in tandem. There was no mystery to solve here; she'd learn nothing from interrogation. It might have been prudent to try, but in that moment, all she wanted was to watch something burn.

CHAPTER 33

The next morning the Southern Army departed for Tikany.

Rin couldn't rule from Dragon Province. That should have been evident from the start—it wasn't her hometown, she didn't know the city's inner workings, and she had no local supporters. In Arlong, she was a foreign upstart working against centuries of anti-southern discrimination. Venka's death was just the final straw—proof that if Rin wanted to cement her rule, she had to do it from home.

A small crowd of civilians gathered in the valley to watch as the columns marched past. Rin couldn't tell from their grim expressions if they were sending the Southern Army off with respect, if they were simply glad to see their backs, or if they were scared she was carrying off all their food.

She'd left behind a minimal force—just three hundred troops, the most she was willing to spare—to maintain occupation of the city. They'd likely fail. Arlong might collapse under the strain of its myriad resource shortages; its civilians might emigrate en masse, or they might overthrow the southern troops in internal revolt. It didn't matter. Arlong was no great loss. One day the city would be well and properly hers, purged of dissenters, stripped of its treasures, and transformed into a tame, obedient resource hub for her regime.

But first, she had to reclaim the south.

Rin kept her mind trained on Tikany, on going home, and tried not to think about how much their departure stank of failure.

She and Kitay spent much of the journey in silence. There was little to talk about. By the fourth day, they'd exhausted all discussion of what resources they had, what troop numbers they were now working with, what kind of foundation they'd have to build in Tikany to train a fighting force capable of taking on the west. Anything else at this point lapsed into useless conjecture.

They couldn't talk about Venka. They'd tried, but no words came out when they opened their mouths, nothing but a heavy, reproachful silence. Kitay thought Venka's death exonerated her. Rin was still convinced Venka might have been the informant, but any number of alternatives were possible. Venka was not the only one with access to the information Nezha kept hinting at. Some junior officer could easily have been passing intelligence to the Republic throughout their march. The scrolls had stopped appearing since Venka's death, but that might have simply been because they'd left Arlong. Venka remained an open question, a traitor and ally both at once, which was the only way Rin could bear to remember her.

She didn't want to know the truth. She didn't want to even wonder. She simply couldn't think about Venka for too long because then her chest throbbed from a twisting, invisible knife, and her lungs seized like she was being held underwater. Venka's confused, reproachful face kept resurfacing in her mind, but if she let it linger, then she started to drown, and the only way to make those feelings stop was to burn instead.

It was much easier to focus on the rage. Through all her confused grief, the one thought that burned clear was that this fight was not over. Hesperia wanted her dead; Hesperia was coming for her.

She no longer dreamed of Nezha's death. That grudge seemed so petty now, and the thought of his broken body brought her no satisfaction. She'd had the chance to break him, and she hadn't taken it.

No, Nezha wasn't the enemy, just one of its many puppets. Rin had realized now that her war wasn't civil, it was global. And if she wanted peace—true, lasting peace—then she had to bring down the west.

Two weeks out, the road to Tikany became a mosaic of human suffering.

Rin didn't know what she'd expected when she passed into the south. Perhaps not the joyful shouts of the liberated—she wasn't that naive. She knew she'd assumed responsibility for a broken country, wrecked in every way by years of constant warfare. She knew mass displacement, crop failure, famine, and banditry were problems that she'd have to deal with eventually, but she'd slotted them to the back of her mind, deprioritized against the far more urgent problem of the impending Hesperian attack.

They were far harder to ignore when they stared her in the face.

The Southern Army had just crossed over the border to Rooster Province when supplicants began coming out to meet them on the roadside. It seemed word had spread through the village networks about Rin's return, and as the marching column wound into the southern heartland, large crowds started appearing on every stretch of the road.

But Rin found no welcome parties on her journey. Instead she was witness to the consequences of her civil war.

Her first encounter with starvation shocked her. She had seen bodies in almost every state of destruction—burned, dismembered, dissected, bloated. But she had never in her life witnessed famine this severe. The bodies that approached her wagon—*living* bodies, she realized in shock—were stretched and distorted, more like a child's confused sketch of human anatomy than any human bodies she'd ever encountered. Their hands and feet were swollen like grapefruits, bloated extremities hanging implausibly from stick-thin limbs. Many of them appeared unable to walk; instead they crawled and rolled toward Rin's wagon in a slow, horrific advance that made Rin burn with shame.

"Stop," she ordered the driver.

Warily he regarded the approaching crowd. "General . . ."

"I said *stop*."

He reined the horses to a halt. Rin climbed out of the wagon.

The starving civilians began to cluster toward her. She felt a momentary thrill of fear—there were so many of them, and their faces were so unnaturally hollow, so caked with dirt that they looked like monsters—but quickly pushed it away. These weren't monsters, these were her people. They'd suffered because of her war. They needed her help.

"Here," she said, pulling a piece of hard jerky from her pocket.

In retrospect she should have realized how stupid it was to offer food to a horde of starving people when clearly she didn't have enough to go around.

She wasn't thinking. She'd seen miserable, gnawing hunger, and she'd wanted to alleviate it. She didn't expect that they'd begin stampeding, pulling one another to the ground, bare feet crushing frail limbs as they surged forth. In an instant, dozens of hands reached toward her, and she was so startled she dropped the jerky and stumbled back.

They fell on the food like sharks.

Terrified, and ashamed by her terror, Rin clambered back on the wagon.

Without asking, the driver urged the horses forward. The wagon lurched into a speedy pace. The starving bodies did not follow.

Heart pounding, Rin hugged her knees to her chest and swallowed down the urge to vomit.

She felt Kitay's eyes on her. She couldn't bear to meet them. But he was merciful, and said nothing. When they stopped for dinner that night, the food tasted like ashes.

∞

The roadside parties became a daily sight as they drew closer to Tikany. It didn't matter that the wagons never stopped, never distributed rations to pleading hands because their own supplies were running so short. They had just enough bags of grain and rice to keep the army alive for three more months; they could spare nothing out of charity. The soldiers learned to march with their eyes trained forward as if they hadn't seen and hadn't heard. But still the crowds persisted, arms stretched out, murmuring pleas in breathy whispers because they didn't have the energy to shout.

The children were the hardest to look at because their bodies were the most distorted. Their bellies were so swollen they looked pregnant, while every other part of them had shriveled to the width of reeds. Their heads bobbled on their thin necks like wooden toys Rin used to see at market. The only other parts of them that did not shrink were their eyes. Their beseeching, sorrowful eyes protruded from shrunken skulls, as if, with their limbs whittled away, they had been reduced to those desperate gazes.

Gradually, through interview after interview with those starving civilians who could still muster the energy to talk, Rin and Kitay learned the full picture of how bad famine had grown in the south.

It wasn't just a lean year. There simply wasn't any food at all. Fresh meat had been the first to disappear, then spices and salts. The grain lasted several months, and then the starving villagers had turned to any sort of nutrients at all—chaff, tree bark, insects, carrion, roots, and wild grasses. Some had resorted to scooping the green scum off pond surfaces for the protein in algae. Some were cultivating plankton in vats of their own urine.

The worst part was that she couldn't chalk this up to enemy cruelty. Those grotesque bodies weren't the product of torture. The famine wasn't the fault of Federation troops—they had slashed and burned on their march south, but not at the scale necessary to cause starvation this bad. This hadn't been caused by the Republicans or the Hesperians. This was just the shitty, shitty result of ongoing civil war, of what happened when the whole country was upended in lost labor and mass migration because nowhere was safe.

Everyone was just trying their best to stay alive, which meant no one planted crops. Six months later, no one had a shred to eat.

And Rin had nothing to give them.

She could tell from their resentful glares that they knew she was holding resources back. She made herself look away. It wasn't hard to steel her gaze against misery; it didn't take any special emotional fortitude. All it took was repeated, hopeless exposure.

She'd witnessed this kind of desperation before. She remembered sailing slowly up the Murui River to Lusan on Vaisra's warship, the *Seagrim*, observing from the railings as crowds of displaced refugees stood on soggy banks where their flooded villages once lay, watching the Dragon Warlord—the rich, powerful, affluent Dragon Warlord—sail by without tossing them so much as a silver. She'd been astounded by Vaisra's callousness back then.

Yet Nezha had defended it. *Silver won't help them,* he'd told her. *There's nothing they can buy with it. The best thing we can do for those refugees is to keep our eyes on Lusan and kill the woman who brokered the war that put them there.*

Back then that logic had seemed so cold and distant, so clinical compared to the real evidence of suffering before her face.

But now, as Rin occupied the position Vaisra once held, she understood his reasoning. Deep-seated problems couldn't be fixed with temporary solutions. She couldn't let every skeletal child distract her when the final cause of their suffering was so obvious, was still lurking out there.

She consoled herself and her troops by reminding them that wouldn't go on for much longer. She'd fix this, soon; she'd fix everything soon. She reminded herself of that every time she saw another hollow, bony face, which was the only way she could face the dying southerners and not empty out everything in their supply wagons on the spot.

They only had to hold on for a little longer.

This became a mantra, the only thing capable of strengthening her resolve. Only a little longer, and she'd finish this war. She'd subdue the west. And then they'd have all the sacks of golden, glorious grain they wanted. They'd have so much to eat they would fucking choke.

"Rin." Kitay nudged her shoulder.

She stirred. "Hmm?"

It was midday but she'd fallen asleep, lulled by the rhythmic bouncing of the wagon. They'd been marching for four weeks, now into the final stretch, and the bleak monotony, silent hours, and restricted diet had her eyes fluttering shut whenever she wasn't on watch duty.

"Look." He pointed. "Out there."

She sat up, rubbed her eyes, and squinted.

Rows and rows of scarlet emerged on the horizon. She thought it a trick of the light at first, but then they drew closer and it became apparent that the brilliant red sheen that covered the fields was not a reflection of the setting sun but a rich hue that came from the blossoms themselves.

Poppy flowers were blooming all around Tikany.

Her mouth fell open. "What the—"

"Shit," Kitay said. "Holy shit."

She jumped out of the wagon and began to sprint.

She reached the fields in minutes. The flowers stood taller than any flowers she'd ever seen; they nearly came up to her waist. She took a flower in her hand, closed her eyes, inhaled deeply.

A heady thrill flooded her senses.

She still had this. Nothing else mattered. Venka's betrayal, her enemies in Arlong, the violence dissolving the country—none of that mattered. Everything else could crumble and she still had this, because *this* Moag could trade. Moag had told her, months ago, that this was exactly the kind of liquid gold she needed to acquire Hesperian resources.

These fields were worth ten times as much as all the treasures in Arlong. These fields were going to save her country.

She sank to her knees, pressed a palm to her forehead, and laughed.

"I don't understand." Kitay joined her by her side. "Who . . ."

"They listened," she murmured. "They knew."

She seized him by the hand and led him toward the flat, humble outline of the village on the horizon.

A crowd was forming near the gates. They'd seen her coming; they'd come out to welcome her.

"I'm here," she told them. And then, because they could not have possibly heard her from this distance, she sent a flare into the air: a massive, undulating phoenix, wings unfolding slowly against the shimmering blue sky, to prove that she was back.

Tikany, against all odds, had survived. Despite the famine and firebombs, many of its residents had stayed, largely because there was nowhere else for them to go. Over months it had become the center of its own beehive as residents from smaller, decimated villages came with their homes and livelihoods loaded up on carts to settle in one of the lean-to shacks that now formed the bulk of the township. Famine had not hit Tikany as hard as it had other parts of the Empire—during their occupation, the Mugenese had stockpiled an astonishing amount of rice, which Tikany's survivors had judiciously rationed out over the months.

Rin learned from the de facto village leadership that the decision to plant opium had been made in the wake of Nezha's firebombing. Grain did not grow well in Rooster Province, but opium flowers did, and poppy in these quantities, in a country where everyone needed respite from pain, was worth its weight in gold.

They'd known she'd come back. They'd known she would need leverage. Tikany, the least likely of places, had kept its faith, had invested its future in Rin's victory.

Now she stood facing the assembled villagers in the town square, the several thousand thin faces who had handed her the keys to the final stage of her war, and she loved them so much that she could cry.

"This war is ours to win," she said.

She gazed over the sea of faces, gauging their reaction. Her throat felt dry. She coughed, but a lump remained, sitting heavy on her prepared words.

"The Young Marshal has fled, of all places, to the Dead Island," she said. "He knows he isn't safe anywhere on Nikara soil. The Consortium have lost their faith in the Republic, and they are inches from pulling away entirely. All we need is to make our final drive. We just—we just need to last a little longer."

She swallowed involuntarily, then coughed. Her words floated, awkward and hesitant, over dry air.

She was nervous. Why was she so nervous? This was nothing new; she had rallied gathered ranks before. She'd screamed invectives against Vaisra and the Republic while thousands cheered. She'd whipped a crowd up to such frenzy once that they'd torn a man apart, and the words had come so easily then.

But the air in Tikany felt different, not charged with the exhilarating thrill of battle, of *hate*, but dead with exhaustion.

She blinked. This couldn't be right. She was in her hometown, speaking to troops who had followed her to hell and back and villagers who had turned the fields scarlet for her. For *her*. They thought her divine. They adored her. She'd razed the Mugenese for them; she'd conquered Arlong for them.

But then why did she feel like a fraud?

She coughed again. Tried to inject some force into her words. "This war—"

Someone in the crowd shouted over her. "I thought we won the war."

She broke off, stunned.

No one had ever interrupted her before.

Her eyes roved over the square. She couldn't find the source of the voice. It could have belonged to any one of these faces; they all looked equally unsympathetic, equally resentful.

They looked like they *agreed*.

She felt a hot burst of impatience. Did they not understand the threat? Hadn't they been here when Nezha dropped a hundred tons of explosives on unarmed, celebrating civilians?

"There is no armistice," she said. "The Hesperians are still trying to kill me. They watch from the skies, waiting to see us fail, hoping for an opportunity to take us down in one fell swoop. What happens next is the great test of the Nikara nation. If we seize this chance, then we seize our future. The Hesperians are weak, they're unprepared, and they're reeling from what we did at Arlong. I just need you behind me for this final stretch—"

"Fuck the Hesperians!" Another shout, a different voice. "Feed us first!"

A good leader, Rin knew, did not respond to the crowd. A leader was above hecklers—answering shouted questions only granted them legitimacy they did not deserve.

She cast about for the sentence where she'd left off, trying to resume her train of thought. "This opium will fuel—"

She never finished her sentence. A din erupted from the back of the crowd. At first she thought it was another bout of heckling, but then she heard the clang of steel, and then a second round of shouting that escalated and spread.

"Get down." Kitay grasped her wrist to pull her down from the stage. She resisted just for a moment, bewildered as she faced the crowd, but they weren't paying attention to her anymore. They'd all turned toward the source of the commotion, which rippled out like ink dropped in water, an unfurling cloud of chaos that dragged in everyone in the vicinity.

He yanked harder. "You need to get out of here."

"Hold on." Her palm was hot, ready to funnel flame, though she had no clue what she meant to do. Who did she aim at? The crowd? Her own *people*? "I can—"

"There's nothing you can do." He hustled her away from the riot. People were screaming now. Rin glanced over her shoulder and saw weapons flashing through the air, bodies falling, spear shafts and sword hilts smashing against unprotected flesh. "Not now."

"What the fuck is wrong with them?" Rin demanded.

They'd retreated to the general's headquarters, where she'd be safe and out of sight, out of earshot while her troops finished re-imposing order in the square. Her shock had worn off. Now she was simply pissed, *furious* that her own people would act like such a brainless, petulant mob.

"They're exhausted," Kitay said quietly. "They're hungry. They thought this war was over, and that you'd come home to bring them the spoils. They didn't think you were going to drag them into another one."

"Why does everyone think this war is over?" Rin's fingers clawed in frustration. "Am I the only one with eyes?"

Was this how mothers felt when their children threw tantrums? The sheer fucking *ingratitude*. She had walked through hell and back for them, and they had the nerve to stand there, to *complain* and demand things that she couldn't spare.

"The Hesperians were right," she snapped. "They're fucking sheep. All of them."

No wonder Petra thought the Nikara were inferior. Rin saw it now. No wonder the Trifecta had ruled like they did, with abundant blood and ruthless iron. How else did you stoke the masses, except through fear?

How could the Nikara be so shortsighted? Their stomachs weren't the only things at stake. They were on the edge of something so much greater than a full dinner if they'd just *think*, if they'd just rally for one more push. But they didn't understand. How could she make them understand?

"They're not sheep. They're ordinary people, Rin, and they're tired of suffering. They just want this to be over."

"So do I! I'm offering them that chance! What do they want us to do?" she demanded. "Hang up our swords, throw down our shields, and wait for them to kill us in our beds? Tell me, Kitay, are they honestly *so stupid* they think the Hesperians will just turn around and leave us alone?"

"Try to understand," he said gently. "It's hard to prioritize the enemy that you can't see."

She scoffed. "If that's how they feel, then they don't deserve to live."

She shouldn't have said that. She knew as soon as the words left her mouth that she was wrong. She'd spoken not in anger, but from panic, from icy, gut-twisting fear.

Everything was falling apart.

Tikany was supposed to be the bastion of her resistance, the base from which she launched her final assault on the west. Symbolically, geographically, Tikany and its people were *hers*. She'd been raised on this dirt. She'd returned and liberated her hometown. She'd defended them first from the Mugenese, and then from the Republic. Now, when she most needed their support, they wanted to fucking riot.

Either they fear you, or they love you, Daji had told her. *But the one thing you can't stomach is for them to disrespect you. Then you've got nothing. Then you've lost.*

No. No. She pressed her palm against her temple, trying to slow her breathing. This was only a setback; she hadn't lost yet. She tried to remind herself of the assets she still held—she had Moag; she had the opium fields; she had a massive reserve of troops from across the Empire, even if they still needed training. She had the financial resources of the entire country; she just needed to extract them. And she had a *god*, for fuck's sake, the most powerful god left in the Nikara Empire.

So why did she feel like she was on the verge of defeat?

Her troops were starving, her support base hated her, her ranks were plagued with spies she could not see, and Nezha was taunting her at every turn, twisting his knife where it hurt the most. Her regime, that frail edifice they'd built at Arlong, was crumbling in every corner and she didn't have enough strength to hold it all together.

"General?"

She whipped around. "What?"

The aide looked terrified. His mouth worked several times, but no sound came out.

"Spit it out," Rin snapped.

His wide eyes blinked. His throat bobbed. When at last he spoke, his voice was such a timid croak that Rin made him repeat himself twice before she finally heard him.

"It's the fields, General. They're burning."

It took Rin several long seconds to register that she was not dreaming, that the red clouds in the distance, glowing so brightly against the moonless sky they seemed surreal, were not an illusion.

The opium fields were on fire.

The blaze grew as she watched, expanding outward at a terrifying rate. In seconds it could encompass the entirety of the fields. And all Rin could do was stand there, eyes wide, struggling to comprehend what she saw before her—the destruction of her only trump card.

Dimly she heard Kitay issuing orders, calling for evacuation from the shacks nearest the fields. From the corners of her eyes she saw a flurry of movement around her as troops sprang into action, forming lines from the wells to pass buckets of water to the fields.

She couldn't move. Her feet felt rooted, trapped in place. And even if she could—what could she possibly do? One more bucket of water wouldn't help. All the fucking buckets in Tikany wouldn't help. The blaze had ripped through more than half the fields now; the water did little more than sizzle into steam that unfurled, joining the great clouds of smoke that now billowed over the horizon.

She couldn't call her god to stop this. The Phoenix could only start fires. It couldn't put them out.

She knew these fields hadn't caught fire by accident. No, accidental wildfires spread outward from a single source, but this fire had several—at least three initial points of burn whose ranges gradually converged as the fire spread wider and wider.

Nezha had done this, too.

This was sabotage, and the perpetrators were long gone, disappeared into the dark.

You led them here, said Altan's voice. *You brought them in your caravan because you couldn't root out the spies, and you showed them exactly where they needed to strike.*

The wave of despair hit so wrenchingly deep that it almost felt funny. Because of course, of fucking *course*, at the end of the line, when everything whittled down to a single hope, she'd lose that, too. This wasn't a surprise, this was just the culmination of a series of failures that had begun the moment she occupied Arlong, and then spiraled when she hadn't noticed; a sudden, unpredicted reversal of the rolling ball of fortune that had won her the south.

She couldn't stop this. She couldn't fix this.

All she could do was watch. And some sick, desperate part of her wanted to watch, found some perverse glee in staring as the flowers withered and crumpled into ash, because she wanted to see how far the hopelessness would go, and because the destruction felt good—the wanton erasure of life and hope felt *good*, even if the hope going up in smoke was her own.

"You have to talk to the Republic," Kitay said.

They were alone, just the two of them inside the office, all their aides and guards banished out of earshot. Everyone was clamoring for answers; they wanted orders and assurances, and Rin had nothing to give them. The burned fields were the final blow. Now Rin had no plan, no recourse, and nothing to offer her men. She and Kitay had to solve this, and they could not leave the room until they did.

But to her disbelief, the first suggestion he made was surrender.

The way he said it made it sound like a foregone conclusion. As if he knew this to be true, had known months ago, and was only now bothering to let her in on it.

"No," she said. "Never."

"Rin, come on—"

"This is what they want."

"Of course it's what they want! Nezha's offering food aid. He's been offering that from the start. We have to take it."

"Are you working with them?" she demanded.

He recoiled. "No—what are you—"

"I knew it. I fucking *knew it.*" That explained everything— why he'd bogged her down with mindless, exhausting tasks at Arlong, why he'd kept detracting from the military front, why he'd kept willfully ignoring the clear threat of Nezha's constant letters. "First Venka, now you? Is that what this is?"

"Rin, that's—"

"Don't call me crazy."

"You *are* being crazy," he snapped. "You're acting like a maniac. Shut up for a moment and face the fucking facts." She opened her mouth to retort but he shouted over her, hand splayed in front of her face as if she were a misbehaving child. "We're dealing with famine—not something cyclical, not something we can weather out, but the worst famine in recent history. There's no grain left in the entire fucking country because Daji poisoned half the south, the entire heartland was too busy fleeing for their lives to till the fields, our rivers are flooded, and we've had an unnaturally cold and dry winter that's shortened the growing season for crops, which has made things doubly difficult for anyone who even tried planting."

His breathing grew shaky as he spoke; his words spilled out at such a frantic rate that she could barely understand him. "No irrigation or flood control projects. No one's been maintaining or supervising the granaries, so if any existed, they've been plundered empty by now. We've got no leverage, no backup options, no money, nothing—"

"So we fight for it," she said. "We *beat* them, and then we take what we want—"

"That's insane."

"Insane? Insane is giving them what they want. We can't stop here, we can't just let everything go, we can't let them win—"

"*Shut up!*" he shouted. "Can you even hear yourself?"

"Can *you?* You want to give up!"

"It's not what I want," he said. "It's the only option that we have. People are starving. *Our* people. Those corpses on the roadside? Pretty soon that's going to be the entire country, unless you learn to swallow your pride."

She almost screamed.

This wasn't how it was supposed to work.

She'd won. She'd fucking won, she'd razed Nezha's city, she'd obliterated her enemies, she'd conquered the Nikara south, she'd *won*, so why, *why* were they talking like they'd already been defeated?

Suddenly her rage dissipated. She couldn't be furious with Kitay; yelling at him wouldn't change the facts.

"They can't do this to me," she said dully. "I was supposed to win."

"You *did* win," he said sadly. "This entire country is yours. Just please don't throw it away with your pride."

"But we were going to rebuild this world," she said. The words sounded plaintive as she said them, a childish fantasy, but that was how she felt, that was what she really believed—because otherwise, what the fuck was this all for? "We were going to be free. We were going to *make* them free—"

"And you can still do that," he insisted. "Look at what we've done. Where we are. We've built an entire nation, Rin. We don't have to let it collapse."

"But they're going to come after us—"

"I promise you they won't." He took her face in his hands. "Look at me. Nezha's defeated. There's no fight left in him. What he wants is what we all want, which is to stop killing our own people.

"We're about to have the world we fought for. Can't you see it? It's so close, it's just over the horizon. We'll have an independent south, we'll have a world free from war, and all you have to do is *say the word.*"

But that wasn't the world she'd fought for, Rin thought. The world she'd fought for was one where she, and only she, was in charge.

"We told them they were free," she said miserably. "We won. We *won*. And you want us to go back to the foreigners and bow."

"Cooperation isn't bowing."

She scoffed. "It's close enough."

"It's a long march to liberation," he said. "And it's not so easy as burning our enemies. We won our war, Rin. We were the righteous river of blood. But ideological purity is a battle cry, it's not the stable foundation for a unified country. A nation means nothing if it can't provide for the people in it. You have to act for their sake. Sometimes you've got to bend the knee, Rin. Sometimes, at least, you've got to pretend."

No, that's where he was wrong. Rin *could not bow*. Tearza bowed. Hanelai bowed. And look what that got them: quick, brutal deaths and complete erasure from a history that should have been theirs to write. Their fault was that they were *weak*, they trusted the men they loved, and they didn't have the guts to do what was necessary.

Tearza should have killed the Red Emperor. Hanelai should have murdered Jiang when she'd had the chance. But they couldn't hurt the people they loved.

But Rin could kill anything.

She could unshackle this country. She could succeed where everyone else had failed, because she alone was willing to pay the price.

She'd thought Kitay understood the necessary sacrifice, too. She'd thought that he, if anyone, knew what victory required.

But if she was wrong—if he was too weak to see this revolution through—then she'd have to do it alone.

"Rin?"

She blinked at him. "What?"

"Tell me you see it, too." He squeezed her shoulders. "Please, Rin. Tell me you get it."

He sounded so desperate.

She looked into his eyes, and she couldn't recognize the person she saw there.

This was not Kitay. This was someone weak, gullible, and corrupted.

She'd lost him. When had he become her enemy? She hadn't seen it happening, yet now it was obvious. He might have been turned against her at Arabak. He might have been planning his eventual betrayal ever since they'd left Arlong. He might have been working against her this entire time, holding her back, stopping her from burning as brightly as she could. He might have been on Nezha's side all along.

The only thing she knew for certain was that Kitay was no longer hers. And if she couldn't win him back, then she'd have to do the rest of this by herself.

"Please, Rin," he urged. "*Please.*"

She hesitated, carefully weighing her words before she answered.

She had to be clever about this. She couldn't let him know that she'd seen through him.

What was a plausible lie? She couldn't simply agree. He'd know she was faking it; she'd never conceded a point so easily.

She had to feign vulnerability. She had to make him believe this was a hard choice for her—that she'd broken, just like he wanted her to.

"I'm just . . ." She let her voice tremble. She widened her eyes, so that Kitay would think she was terrified rather than capricious. Kitay would believe that. Kitay had always wanted to see the best in people, damn him, and that meant he would fucking fall for anything. "I'm scared I can't come back from this."

He pulled her close against him. She managed not to flinch against his embrace.

"You can come back. I'll bring you back. We're in this together, we're linked . . ."

She started to cry. That, she didn't have to fake.

"All right," she whispered. "All right."

"Thank you."

He squeezed her tight. She returned his embrace, pressing her head against his chest while her mind raced, wondering where she went from here.

If she couldn't count on her people and she couldn't count on Kitay, then she'd have to finish things herself. She had the only ally she needed—a god that could bury countries. And if Kitay tried to deny her that, then she'd just have to break him.

She knew she could do it. She'd always known she could, since the day they knelt before the Sorqan Sira and melded their souls together. She could have erased him then. She almost had; she was just that much stronger. She'd held herself back because she loved him.

And she still loved him. She'd never stop. But that didn't matter.

You've abandoned me, she thought as he wept with relief into her shoulder. *You thought you could fool me, but I know your soul. And if you're not with me, you'll burn, too.*

CHAPTER 34

Nezha would meet them alone in three weeks on Speer. No guards, no delegates, no troops lying in wait, and no Hesperians. Rin and Kitay would represent Nikan, and Nezha would speak for the Republic and the Consortium both. If Rin caught even a glimpse of anyone else on the island, the cease-fire was off.

Those were the terms she demanded in the first and only response to Nezha's letters. She was stunned when he and the Consortium agreed without question.

But then, the Hesperians could not understand the power that lay in the sands of the Dead Island. They thought Nikara superstitions were the products of feeble, uncivilized minds, that her command of fire was nothing more than an outburst of Chaos. They couldn't know that Speer was suffused with history and blood, with the power of thousands of vengeful deceased who haunted its every corner.

There are places in the world where the boundaries between the gods and mortals are thin, Chaghan had once told her. Where reality blurs, where the gods very nearly materialize.

The Speerlies had made their home in such a place, right on the edge of mortality and madness, and the Phoenix had both punished and blessed them in turn.

The Dead Island's legacy ran through Rin's blood. Now it called her home to finish what she'd started, to see her revenge through to the end. When she returned to that island, she'd be in the Phoenix's holy domain, one step closer to divinity.

She'd destroyed a nation from that island once before. She wouldn't hesitate to do it again.

They crossed the channel in a small fisherman's dinghy. Rin sat with her knees pulled up to her chest, shivering against the ocean breeze while Kitay fussed with the sails. Neither of them spoke. There was nothing more to be said. Everything had been spilled the night the fields in Tikany burned, and now what lay between them was a quiet, exhausted resignation. There was no point in commiseration or reassurance. Rin knew what happened next and Kitay thought he did; now there was only the wait.

When the Dead Island emerged on the horizon, a gray, ashy mound that at first seemed indistinguishable from the mist, Kitay reached over and rubbed his thumb over her wrist.

"It'll be all right," he murmured. "We'll fix this."

She gave him a tight smile, twisted around to face the island, and said nothing.

Nezha was waiting on the beach when their vessel approached the shallows. He didn't appear to be armed, but that didn't matter. Neither of them was far from their army. Rin had troops waiting in ships off the coast of Snake Province, spyglasses trained on the horizon for the first sign of her beacon. She could only assume that Nezha's reinforcements were doing the same.

No, she was counting on it.

"Scared?" she inquired as she stepped onto the sand.

He gave her a hollow smile. "You know I can't die."

"We're trying to broker a peace here." Kitay dropped an anchor off the side of the dinghy, then followed Rin onto the shore. "Let's not start off with death threats, shall we?"

"Fair enough." Nezha gestured farther up the beach, where

Rin saw he'd prepared three chairs and a square tea table covered in ink, brushes, and blank parchment. "After you."

They crossed the length of the beach in silence.

Rin couldn't help but take quick, furtive glances at Nezha as she walked beside him.

He looked wrecked. He still carried himself like a general. His shoulders never slumped; his voice never wavered. Yet every part of him seemed diminished, stretched thin and whittled down. His scarred mouth, once twisted on one side into a jeering grin, now seemed trapped in a painful rictus.

She'd expected him to jeer at her, to gloat over their capitulation, but he didn't seem at all like he was enjoying this. He looked exhausted. He looked like someone waiting to die.

They pulled their chairs out and sat. Rin nearly laughed when the first thing Nezha did was politely, meticulously pour each of them a full, steaming cup of tea. It lent such an air of ceremony, of *normalcy*, to negotiations made possible by an ocean of blood.

Neither she nor Kitay touched their cups. Nezha drained his in a single swallow.

"Well, then." He reached for an ink brush and held it lightly over the parchment. "Where shall we start?"

"Tell us their final terms," Rin said.

Nezha faltered for a moment. He'd expected more of a dance. "You mean—"

"Lay it all out," she said. "List every last thing it'll take to get the Hesperians off our back. We're not here to bandy words. Just tell us how much it'll cost."

"As you wish." He cleared his throat. He had no papers to consult; he knew by heart what the Hesperians wanted. "The Consortium is willing to withdraw their forces, commit to a signed armistice, and provide enough shipments of grain, dried meat, and starches to tide the entire country over to the next harvest."

"Great Tortoise," Kitay breathed. "Thank—"

Rin spoke over him. "And in return?"

"First, full amnesty for all soldiers and leadership involved with the Republic," Nezha said. "That benefits you, too. You need people to keep the country running. Let them go back home with their safety guaranteed, and they'll work for you. I'll vouch for that. Second, the Consortium wants designated treaty ports—at least one in each province that borders the ocean. Third, they'd like their missionary privileges back. The Gray Order conduct proselytization with immunity, and anyone who lays a finger on them gets extradited to Hesperia for punishment."

"And what about me?" she pressed.

He held out his arms. Golden circlets gleamed bright around pale skin rubbed painfully raw. Up close, it was clear they were fitted perfectly to the width of his wrists. She didn't know how he ever took them off, or even if he could. "You'll put these on. You'll never call the Phoenix again. You'll never pass on your knowledge of how shamanism works in any form to anyone alive, and you'll cooperate with hunting down everyone in Nikan who is even suspected to know about the Pantheon. You can walk free in the south—even rule it, if you like—so long as you make yourself available."

"Available in what ways?" Kitay asked.

Nezha swallowed. "In the same ways I was."

A heavy silence descended on the table. Nezha wouldn't meet their eyes. But neither did his gaze drop—he stared straight forward, shoulders still squared, meeting their pity with silent defiance as they stared at his circlets.

"Why?" Rin asked at last. She couldn't keep her voice from breaking. The sight of the circlets was suddenly too much to bear. She wanted to rip them off his wrists, to cover them with his sleeves—anything to make them disappear. "Nezha, why the *fuck*—"

"Because they had all the power," he said quietly. "Because they still do."

She shook her head, astonished. "Have you no pride?"

"It's not about pride." He withdrew his arms. "It's about sacrifice. I chose the Hesperians because I recognize that they aren't just decades but *centuries* ahead of us in every way that matters, and if they decide to work with us, we could use their knowledge to make life better for millions of people. Despite the cost."

"The costs are where we differ," she said coldly.

"You've only seen one side of them, Rin. You've seen them at their very worst, but you also stand for everything they can't abide. But what if you didn't? I know they are condescending, I know they don't think we're human, I know—" His throat pulsed. He coughed. "I know the depths of their cruelty. But they were willing to cooperate with me. They're getting this close to respecting me. And if I just had *that*—"

"What's it going to take?" Kitay asked abruptly. "For them to respect you?"

Nezha didn't hesitate. "Your deaths."

There was no malice in his voice. That wasn't a threat, just a simple statement of fact. Nezha had not been able to deliver Rin's corpse, despite having ample opportunity to kill her, and for that he'd given up a nation.

Kitay gave a slight nod, as if he'd fully expected that answer. "And what's it going to take for them to respect *us*?"

"They'll never respect you," Nezha said tonelessly. "They will never see you as anything more than subhuman. They will work warily with you because they're afraid of you, but you'll always have to stay on edge. You'll always have to grovel to get what you want. My father's Republic was the only regime they would ever have willingly supported, and they still wouldn't ever have really trusted me unless I delivered your heads."

Rin snorted. "So there's the impasse."

"Come on. You know that's not what I'm here for." He pressed his fingers against his temples. "You won, Rin. Fair and square. I'm not angling for the throne. I'm just trying to make this less painful for everyone involved."

"You seem so certain that I'll be an awful ruler."

"It's not an insult. I just think you have no interest in ruling at all. You don't care about statecraft. You're not an administrator, you're a soldier."

"I'm a general," she corrected.

"You're a general who's conclusively wiped everyone else off the map," he said. "You won, all right? You beat me. But your role—that role, at least, is over. You've got no wars left to fight."

"You know that's not true."

"It *can* be true," he insisted. "This isn't what Hesperia wants. This war continues if you bring it to them. But if you work with them, if you let them believe you're not a threat, they won't treat you like one. If you make concessions, if you stay in their good graces—"

"That's bullshit," she snapped. "I've heard that logic before. Su Daji initiated the Third Poppy War because she thought losing half the country was better than losing it all. And what happened then, Nezha? How'd you get that scar on your face? How'd we get to Golyn Niis?"

"What you're doing," Nezha said quietly, "will be worse than a thousand Golyn Niises."

"Not if we win."

He gave her a wary look. "This is a peace negotiation."

"It's not," she said softly. "You know it's not."

His eyes narrowed. "Rin—"

She pushed her chair back and stood up. Enough of these pretensions. She hadn't come to sign a peace treaty, and neither had he.

"Where is the fleet?" she asked.

He tensed. "I don't know what you mean."

"Call them out." She let flames roll down her shoulders. "That's what I came for. Not this charade."

Kitay stood up. "Rin, what are you doing?"

She ignored him. "Call them out, Nezha. I know they're hiding. I won't ask again."

Nezha's expression went slack. He exchanged a bewildered glance with Kitay, and the sheer patronization of that gesture made her flames jump twice as high.

"Fine," she said. "I'll do it myself."

Then she turned toward the ocean and unleashed a brilliant flare into the sky.

A fleet of dirigibles immediately emerged over the horizon.

I was right. She felt a hot wave of satisfaction. The Hesperians hadn't been bold enough to conceal their airships on Speer—smart of them, for she would have decimated them otherwise—but they'd kept them waiting all along the coast of Snake Province.

So much for Nezha's cease-fire. This confirmed everything she'd suspected. The Hesperians weren't interested in peace, and neither was she. Both just wanted to finish this. They'd come for an ambush, and she'd just called their bluff.

Nezha stood up. "Rin, they're not—"

"Liar," she snarled. "They're *right there.*"

"They're backup," he said. "In case—"

"In case what?" she demanded. "In case you couldn't get the job done? You wanted to end this, so let's end this. Let's answer this question once and for all. Let's pit their god against mine. Let's see which one is real."

Her beacon surged higher, a pillar so searingly bright it cast an orange hue over the entire shore. The fleet surged forth. They were already halfway across the channel; they'd be over Speer in seconds.

Rin watched the horizon and waited.

She and Kitay had determined her maximum radius a long time ago. Since they had been anchored, it had always been fifty yards in any direction. She could never push farther without Kitay collapsing, without losing access to the Phoenix.

But now she was on Speer. Everything changed on Speer.

When the first of the airships drew close enough that she could see its cannons, she swept it out of the sky. The cannons never fired; it plummeted straight into the ocean like a rock.

The rest of the fleet advanced, undaunted.

Keep coming, she thought, exhilarated. *I'll smite you all.*

This was it. This was the moment she rewrote history. The Hesperian fleet would crowd the sky like storm clouds, and she'd destroy it in minutes. This would be more than a crushing victory. It would be a display of force—an undeniable, irrefutable display of divine authority.

Then the Hesperians she permitted to survive would flee, this time for good. They would never return to the eastern hemisphere. They would never dare threaten her people. And when she demanded gold and grain, they wouldn't dare say no.

This was what Speer had always been capable of, what Queen Mai'rinnen Tearza had been too afraid to do. The last Speerly queen let her homeland become an island of slaves because she thought unleashing the Phoenix might burn down the world. She could have had everything, but she didn't have the *will*.

Rin would not make that same mistake.

"I didn't want this." Dimly, over the roar of the flames, she heard Kitay pleading to Nezha. "That's not what she—"

"Stop her," Nezha said.

"I can't."

Nezha stood, pushing his chair to the ground. Rin grinned. When he lunged, she was ready. She'd seen the bulge under his shirt where he'd concealed a knife. She knew that when he had the initiative, he favored a right-handed strike to the upper torso. She twisted to the side. His blade met empty air. When he tried tackling her, she mirrored his momentum and rolled with him to the ground.

Subduing him was so easy.

It should have been a struggle. Nezha had all the advantages in hand-to-hand combat—he was just taller and heavier, his limbs were longer, and every time they'd ever brawled, unless she pulled a gimmick, he'd always managed to pin her through sheer brute force.

But something was wrong.

That formidable skill wasn't there. Strength, speed—both gone. His strikes were stiff and sluggish. She couldn't see proof of any wounds, yet he winced with every motion, as if invisible knives were digging into his flesh.

And he wasn't calling the Dragon.

Why wasn't he calling the Dragon?

If Nezha had demanded more of her focus she would have noticed the way his golden circlets rang eerily every time he moved, darkening the skin around his wrists and ankles. But her mind was not on Nezha. He was just an obstacle, a great, blockish object that she needed out of the way. In that moment, Nezha was an afterthought.

Her mind was on the sky; her focus was on the fleet.

Was this how Jiang had always felt on the battlefield, when he'd felled columns with little more than a thought? The difference in scale was inconceivable. This wasn't fighting. There was no struggle involved in this, no effort. She was simply writing reality. She was *painting*. She pointed, and balloons incinerated. She clenched her fist, and carriages exploded.

Her vision lurched, sharpened, *expanded*. When she'd sunk the Federation she'd been underground, alone inside a stone temple, and yet when she'd awakened the dormant volcano it had felt like she was floating right above the archipelago, keenly aware of the million sleeping souls beneath her, flaring like match heads, only to go suddenly, irreversibly dark.

Now, again, she saw the material world—such a flimsy thing, so fragile and temporary—through the eyes of a god. She saw the airships in such close detail she could have been standing under them. She saw the smooth texture of the airship balloons. Time dilated as she watched the fire ignite around them, ripping through whatever gas filled their interiors that was so *delicious* to the flame—

"Rin, *stop!*" She saw Nezha's mouth moving seconds before she realized he was yelling. He wasn't even really fighting anymore—he certainly couldn't be trying, because his blows hardly landed, and his parries were sluggish.

She jerked her knee into his side, clamped her left hand against his shoulder, and pushed him hard to the ground.

His head slammed against the corner of the table. He slumped sideways, mouth agape. He didn't get up.

She turned back to the fleet.

The beach faded from her sight. She saw what the fire saw— not bodies or ships but simply *shapes*, all equal, all simply kindling for the pyres of her worship. And she knew the Phoenix was pleased because its screeching laughter grew louder and louder, its presence intensifying until their minds felt as if they were one, as, from one end of the horizon to the other, she methodically wrecked the fleet—

Until it went silent.

The shock sent her reeling.

The sky seemed very blue and bright; the airships so far away. She was just a girl again, without fire. The Phoenix was gone, and when she reached to find it she met only a mute, indifferent wall.

She whirled on Kitay. "What have you—"

He was barely managing to stand, clutching the table for support. His face had turned a deathly gray. Sweat dripped from his temples, and his knees buckled so hard she was sure he was about to collapse.

"You can't," he whispered.

"Kitay—"

"Not without my help. Not without my permission. That was our deal."

She gaped at him, astonished. He'd cut her off. The *traitor*, he'd fucking *cut her off*.

Kitay was her back door, her bridge, her single channel to the Phoenix. Since the moment they'd been anchored he'd always kept it open, had let her abuse his mind to funnel as much fire as she desired. He'd never closed it off. She'd almost forgotten that he *could*.

"I didn't think I could, either," he said. "I thought I couldn't deny you anything. But I can, I always could, I'd just never really tried."

"Kitay . . ."

"Stop this," he ordered. A spasm rippled through his body and he lurched forward, wincing, but caught himself on the edge of the table before he fell. "Or you'll never call the fire again."

No. No, this wasn't how this ended. She hadn't come this far to be thwarted by Kitay's idiotic scruples. He didn't get to withhold her power like a condescending parent, dangling her toys just out of reach.

She saw the defiance in his eyes, and her heart shattered.

You, too?

She didn't attack first. If Kitay hadn't taken the first blow, she might not have had the will to strike him. Despite his betrayal he was still *Kitay*—her best friend, her anchor, the person she loved most in the world and the one person she'd sworn to always protect.

But he did take the blow.

He lunged forward, fists aimed at her face, and once he did, it was like a glass pane had shattered. Then there was nothing holding her back, no sentiment, no pangs of guilt when she redirected her fury toward him.

She'd never fought Kitay before.

She realized this as they wrestled to the ground—a dim, floating observation that was really quite amazing, for almost everyone in her class at Sinegard had fought everyone else at some point. She'd sparred against Venka and Nezha plenty of times. Her first year, she'd tried so hard to kill Nezha that she'd nearly succeeded.

But she'd never once touched Kitay. Not even in practice. The few times they were paired against each other they found excuses to seek different partners, because neither of them could stand the thought of trying to hurt the other, not even for pretend.

She hadn't realized how strong he was. Kitay in her mind was a scholar, a strategist. Kitay hadn't seen combat since Vaisra's northern expedition. He always waited out battles from a distance, kept safe by an entire squadron.

She'd forgotten that he, too, had been trained as a soldier. And he'd been very, very good at it.

Kitay was not as strong as Nezha, nor as fast as her. But he struck with crisp, deadly precision. His attacks landed with maximal force concentrated to the thinnest point of impact—the knife edge of his hand, the point of his knuckle, the protruding cap of his knee. He chose his targets carefully. He knew her body better than anyone; he knew the spots where she hurt the most—her amputated wrist, the scars along her back, her twice-cracked ribs. And he attacked them with brutal precision.

She was losing. She was getting exhausted, slowed by the accumulated hurts of a dozen direct blows. He'd maintained the offensive from the start. She was flailing to even parry; she wouldn't last another minute.

"Give up," he panted. "Give up, Rin, it's over."

"Fuck you," she snarled, and flung her right fist toward his eye.

In her fury she forgot that fist did not exist, that she would not meet the sharp bones of his face with curled knuckles but the stump of her wrist, sore and vulnerable and protected only by a thin, irritated layer of skin.

The pain was white-hot, debilitating. She howled.

Kitay staggered back, out of her range, and picked Nezha's knife up from the ground.

She flinched back, arms flung up instinctively to protect her chest. But he hadn't pointed the blade at her.

Fuck.

She lunged and caught his wrist just as he plunged the blade toward his chest. She wasn't strong enough; the tip burrowed under his skin and slid down, slicing a gash across his ribs. They struggled against each other, her pulling with all her might while he pushed the knife against himself, the sharp blade trembling just an inch from his chest.

She wasn't going to win.

She couldn't overpower him. He was stronger. He had both his hands.

But she didn't have to physically defeat him—she only needed to break his will. And she knew one unspoken fact for a certainty, one truth that had underlined their bond since the day she'd met him.

Her will was so much stronger than his. It always had been.

She acted. He followed. Like two hands on a sword's blade, she determined the direction and he provided the force; she was the visionary, and he was her willing executioner. He'd always enforced what she wanted. He would not defy her now.

She focused all her thoughts toward the Phoenix, railing against the fragile barrier of Kitay's mind.

I know you're there, she prayed to the silence. *I know you're with me.*

"Give up," Kitay said. But sweat was dripping down his forehead; his teeth were clenched with strain. "You can't."

Rin shut her eyes and redoubled her efforts, grasping around the void until she found a tiny filament, the barest hint of divine presence. That was enough.

Break him, she told the Phoenix.

She heard a shattering sound in her mind, a porcelain cup dashed against stone.

She saw a flash of red. The beach disappeared.

They were alone in the plane of spirit, standing on opposite sides of a great circle, both of them naked and fully revealed. It was all there, laid out between them. All their shared fury, vindictiveness, bloodlust, and guilt. Her cruelty. His complicity. Her desperation. His regret.

She saw him across the circle and knew that if she wanted to subdue him, all she had to do was think it. She'd nearly done it before—the instant they were anchored, in the first moments after she'd reestablished her bond with the Phoenix, she'd nearly erased him. She could rip the god's power through his mind like he was nothing more than a flimsy net.

He knew it, too. She felt his resignation, his wretched surrender.

Surrender, not agreement. They were enemies now—and she could bend his will, but she'd never again have his heart.

Yet something—sentiment, heartbreak—compelled her to try.

"Kitay, please—"

"Don't," he said. "Just—go ahead. But don't."

His body went limp. The spirit world disappeared. Rin came to her senses just as Kitay slumped to the ground, falling heavily against her arms. Then, somehow, she was kneeling above him with her hand on his neck, her thumb resting against the bulge of his throat.

Their eyes met. She felt a shock of horror.

She recognized the way he was looking at her. It was how she'd once looked at Altan. It was the way she'd seen Daji look at Riga—that look of wretched, desperate, and reproachful loyalty.

It said, *Do it.*

Take what you want, it said. *I'll hate you for it. But I'll love you forever. I can't help but love you.*

Ruin me, ruin us, and I'll let you.

She almost took that for permission.

But if she did, if she broke through his soul and took everything she wanted . . .

She'd never stop. There would be no limits to her power. She'd never stop using him, ripping his mind open and setting it on fire every hour and minute and second, because she would always need the fire. If she did this then her war would extend across the world and her enemies would multiply—there would always be someone else, someone like Petra trying to banish her god and crush her nation, or someone like Nezha trying to foment rebellion from within.

And unless she killed every single one of them, she would never be safe and her revolution would never succeed, and so she'd have to keep going until she reduced the rest of the world to ashes, until she was the last one standing.

Until she was alone.

Was that peace? Was that liberation?

She could see her victories. She could see the burned wreckage of Hesperian shores. She could see herself at the center of a conflagration that consumed the world, scorched it, cleansed it, ate away its rotted foundations—

But she couldn't see where it ended.

She couldn't see where the pain stopped—not for the world, and not for Kitay.

"You're hurting me," he whispered.

It was like being doused in ice water. Repulsed, she gave a sharp sob and jerked her hand away from his neck.

The humming above crescendoed to a deafening roar.

Too late, Rin glanced up. Lightning enveloped her body, a dozen painless arcs of light a thousand times brighter than the sun. The Phoenix went silent. So did the rage; so did the crimson visions of a world on fire. The lightning vanished her divinity, and all that it left behind was utter horror at what she'd nearly done.

Kitay moaned, touched two fingers to his temple, and went limp. Rin clutched him against her chest and rocked back and forth, dazed.

"Rin," croaked Nezha.

She twisted around. He was sitting up. Blood dribbled down the side of his head, and his eyes were bleary, unfocused. He stared at the electricity dancing across Rin's body, mouth agape. He rose slowly, but she knew he wasn't going to attack. He was the furthest thing from a threat at that moment—he just looked like a young boy, scared and confused, utterly at a loss for what to do.

There's nothing he can do, Rin realized. Neither Nezha nor Kitay could determine what happened next. They weren't strong enough.

This choice had to be hers.

She saw it in a flash of utter clarity. She knew what she had to do. The only path, the only way forward.

And what a familiar path it was. It was so obvious now. The world was a dream of the gods, and the gods dreamed in sequences, in symmetry, in patterns. History repeated itself, and she was only the latest iteration of the same scene in a tapestry that had been spun long before her birth.

So many others had stood on this precipice before her.

Mai'rinnen Tearza, the Speerly queen who chose to die rather than bind herself to a king she hated.

Altan Trengsin, the boy who burned too bright, who became his own funeral pyre.

Jiang Ziya, the Dragon Emperor's blade, the monster, the murderer, her mentor, her savior.

Hanelai, who fled to her death before she knelt.

They'd wielded unprecedented power, unimaginable and unmatchable power capable of rewriting the script of history. And they'd written themselves out.

Now here they were again: three people—children, really; too young and inexperienced for the roles they'd inherited—holding the fate of Nikan in their hands. And Rin was poised to acquire the empire Riga had wanted, if only she could be just as cruel.

But what kind of emperor would Riga have been? And how much worse would she be?

Oh, but history moved in such vicious circles.

She could see the future and its shape was already drawn, predetermined by patterns that had been set in motion before she was born—patterns of cruelty and dehumanization and oppression and trauma that had pulled her right back into the place where the Trifecta had once stood. And if she did this, if she broke Kitay like Riga would have broken Jiang, she would only re-create those patterns—because there *would* be resistance, there would be blood, and the only way she could eliminate that possibility was by burning down the world.

Yet a single decision could escape the current, could push history off its course.

It's a long march to liberation, Kitay had said.

Sometimes you've got to bend the knee.

Sometimes, at least, you've got to pretend.

She finally understood what that meant.

She knew what she had to do next. It wasn't about surrender. It was about the long game. It was about survival.

She stood up, reached for Nezha's hand, and curled his fingers around the handle of the knife.

He stiffened. "What are you—"

"Get their respect," she said. "Tell them you killed me. Tell them everything they want to hear. Say whatever you need to to get them to trust you."

"Rin—"

"It's the only way forward."

He understood what she meant him to do. His eyes widened in alarm, and he tried to wrench his hand away, but she clenched his fingers tight.

"Nezha—"

"You can't do this for me," he said. "I won't let you."

"It's not for you. It's not a favor. It's the cruelest thing I could do."

She meant it.

Dying was easy. Living was so much harder—that was the most important lesson Altan had ever taught her.

She glanced down at Kitay.

He was awake, his face set in resolve. He gave her a grim nod.

That was all she had to see. That was permission.

She couldn't release him. Neither of them knew how. But she knew, as clearly as if he'd said it out loud, that he intended to follow her to the end. Their fates were tied, weighed down by the same culpability.

"Come, now." She linked her fingers around Nezha's. Closed both his hands around the cold, cold hilt as lightning arced around them, between them. Brought the blade round to the front. "Properly this time."

"Rin." Nezha looked so scared. It was a funny thing, how fear made him look so much younger, how it rounded his eyes and erased the cruel grimace of his sneer so that he looked, just for an instant, like the boy she'd first met at Sinegard. "Rin, don't—"

"Fix this," she ordered.

Nezha's fingers went slack in hers. She tightened her grip; she had enough resolve for the both of them. As the dirigibles descended toward Speer, she brought Nezha's hand up to her chest and plunged the blade into her heart.

EPILOGUE

She was so small.

Nezha couldn't register the choking gurgles in her throat, the glassy panic in her eyes, or the warmth of her blood as it spilled down his hands. He couldn't, or he would shatter. As Rin bled out over the sand, the only thought running through his mind was that she was so small, so light, so fragile in his arms.

Then the twitching stopped, and she was gone.

Kitay lay still beside him. He knew Kitay was gone, too—that Kitay had died a bloodless death the moment he plunged the blade into Rin's heart, because Rin and Kitay were bonded in a way that he could never understand, and there was no world where Rin died and Kitay remained alive. Because Kitay—the third party, the in-between, the weight that tipped the scale—had chosen to follow Rin into the afterlife and to leave Nezha behind. Alone.

Alone, and shouldering the immense burden of their legacy.

He couldn't move. He could hardly breathe. As he stared down at the tiny body in his arms—so limp and lifeless, so utterly unlike the vicious human hurricane he knew as Fang Runin—all he could do was tremble.

You bitch, he thought. *You fucking bitch.*

He realized dimly that he ought to be glad she was dead. He should have been fucking *delighted*. And rationally, intellectually, he was. Rin was a monster, a murderer, a destroyer of worlds. Nothing but blood and ashes ever trailed in her wake. The world was a better, safer, and more peaceful place without her in it. He believed that. He had to believe that.

And yet.

And yet, when he looked at that broken body, all he wanted to do was howl.

Why? He wanted to scream at her. He wanted to shake her, throttle her, until she answered. *Rin, what the* fuck?

But he knew why.

He knew exactly what choice she'd made and what she'd intended. And that made everything—hating her, loving her, *surviving* her—so much harder.

Fix this.

He tilted his head back. His knees shook from a wave of exhaustion washing over his limbs, and he took a deep, rattling breath as he contemplated the monumental task before him.

Fix this? *Fix this?* What did he have left to work with? She'd broken *everything*.

But theirs had always been a broken country. It had never been unified, not truly; it had only ever been held tightly together by steel and blood, a facade of internal unity, while factions always threatened to split from within. Rin had forced those tensions to the surface, and then to their breaking point. She'd forced the Nikara to confront the greatest lie it had ever told about itself—that there had ever been a united Nikara Empire at all.

And yet, she'd laid a foundation for him. She'd burned away all that was rotten and corrupt. He didn't have to reform the Warlord system because she'd destroyed it for him. He didn't have to face backlash from the crumpling system of feudal aristocracy, because she'd already wrecked it. She'd wiped clear the maps of the past. She'd hurled the pieces off the board.

She was a goddess. She was a monster. She'd nearly destroyed this country.

And then she'd given it one last, gasping chance to live.

He knew she hadn't done this for him. No, she'd done him no great mercy. She'd known that his future—the future she'd just assigned him—was full of horrors. They both knew that Nikan's only path forward was through Hesperia—through a cruel, supercilious, exploitative entity that would certainly try to remold and reshape them, until the only vestiges of Nikara culture that remained lay buried in the past.

But Nikan had survived occupation before. If Nezha played his cards right—if he bent where he needed to, if he lashed back at just the right time—then they might survive occupation again.

He didn't know how he'd weather what came next, but he had to try.

He owed it to her to try.

Nezha lowered Rin's body to the ground, stood up, squared his shoulders, and awaited the coming of the fleet.

DRAMATIS PERSONAE

THE SOUTHERN COALITION AND ITS ALLIES

Fang Runin: a war orphan from Rooster Province, former commander of the Cike, the last living Speerly

Chen Kitay: the son of the former Imperial defense minister, heir to the House of Chen, Rin's anchor

Sring Venka: an archer from Sinegard, daughter of the former Imperial finance minister

Liu Gurubai: the Monkey Warlord, a brilliant politician

Ma Lien: bandit chief, member of the southern leadership

Liu Dai: member of the southern leadership, Gurubai's longtime ally

Yang Souji: resistance leader from Rooster Province, commands the Iron Wolves

Quan Cholang: the young, newly appointed Dog Warlord

Chiang Moag: Pirate Queen of Ankhiluun, aka the Stone Bitch and the Lying Widow

THE HOUSE OF YIN

Yin Vaisra: the Dragon Warlord and leader of the Nikara Republic

Yin Saikhara: the Lady of Arlong and the wife of Yin Vaisra

*Yin Jinzha: the oldest son of the Dragon Warlord and the grand marshal of the Republican Army, killed by Su Daji

Yin Muzha: Jinzha's twin sister, Vaisra's only daughter

Yin Nezha: the second son of the Dragon Warlord

*Yin Mingzha: the third son of the Dragon Warlord, killed by the Dragon of Arlong as a child

THE TRIFECTA

Su Daji: formerly the Empress of Nikan, aka the Vipress, calls on the Snail Goddess of Creation Nüwa

Jiang Ziya: the Gatekeeper, calls on the beasts of the Emperor's Menagerie

Yin Riga: the Dragon Emperor, presumed dead since the end of the Second Poppy War

THE HESPERIANS

General Josephus Tarcquet: the leader of the Hesperian troops in Nikan

Sister Petra Ignatius: a representative of the Gray Company (the Hesperian religious order) in Nikan, one of the most brilliant religious scholars of her generation

THE CIKE

*__Altan Trengsin:__ a Speerly, formerly the commander of the Cike
*__Ramsa:__ a former prisoner at Baghra, munitions expert
*__Baji:__ a shaman who calls on the Boar God
*__Suni:__ a shaman who calls on the Monkey God
Chaghan Suren: a shaman of the Naimad clan and the twin brother of Qara
*__Qara Suren:__ a sharpshooter, speaker to birds, and the twin sister of Chaghan
*__Aratsha:__ a shaman who calls on a river god

*Deceased

ACKNOWLEDGMENTS

Four years, three books, and countless memories. We started this journey when I was nineteen and now, at twenty-three, I can't quite believe that we actually did it. Rin's story, and this chapter of my publishing career, are finished. I've got a lot of people to thank for getting me here.

I'm so grateful to the team at Harper Voyager who've done such a fantastic job publishing these books—David Pomerico, Natasha Bardon, Mireya Chiriboga, Jack Renninson, Pamela Jaffee, and Angela Craft. Jung Shan Ink keeps dazzling me with the loveliest illustrations a writer could ask for. Hannah Bowman, the best and sharpest agent in the business, had faith in what this trilogy could be from the start, even when I didn't. Havis Dawson, Joanne Fallert, and the rest of the team at Liza Dawson Associates have continued to bring my books to the rest of the world. Thank you all for seeing me through to the end.

To all my teachers, mentors, and professors: Jeanne Cavelos, Kij Johnson, Ken Liu, Fonda Lee, Mary Robinette Kowal, Adam Mortara, Howard Spendelow, Carol Benedict, John McNeill, James Millward, Hans van de Ven, Heather Inwood, and Aaron Timmons—thank you for guiding me to become a person who can, in the way I think, write, and treat others, be a little bit more like you.

To friends and family who helped me feel like a real human being and encouraged me to keep writing until the very last page: Mom, Dad, James, Grace, Jack-Jack, Tiffany, Ben, Christine, Chris, Coco, Farah, Josh, Linden, and Pablo—thank you for your constant love and support.

To the Marshfam and beyond: Joani, Martin, Kobi, Kevin, Nancy, Katie, Aksha, Sarah, Julius, Taylor, Noam, Ben, Rhea, and David—thank you for lighting up my life, and for giving me two years in England full of laughter, home-cooked creations, and board games.

To Magdalene College, Cambridge, and University College, Oxford: thank you for being such magical places to write, and places I was lucky to call home.

To the Vaults & Garden Café: more characters were killed under your roof than you will ever know. Thanks for the scones.

And to Bennett, who's been on this ride from the start: I can't wait to see where we go next, together.